The Search for the SilvaGryphie

~Ellendrii~

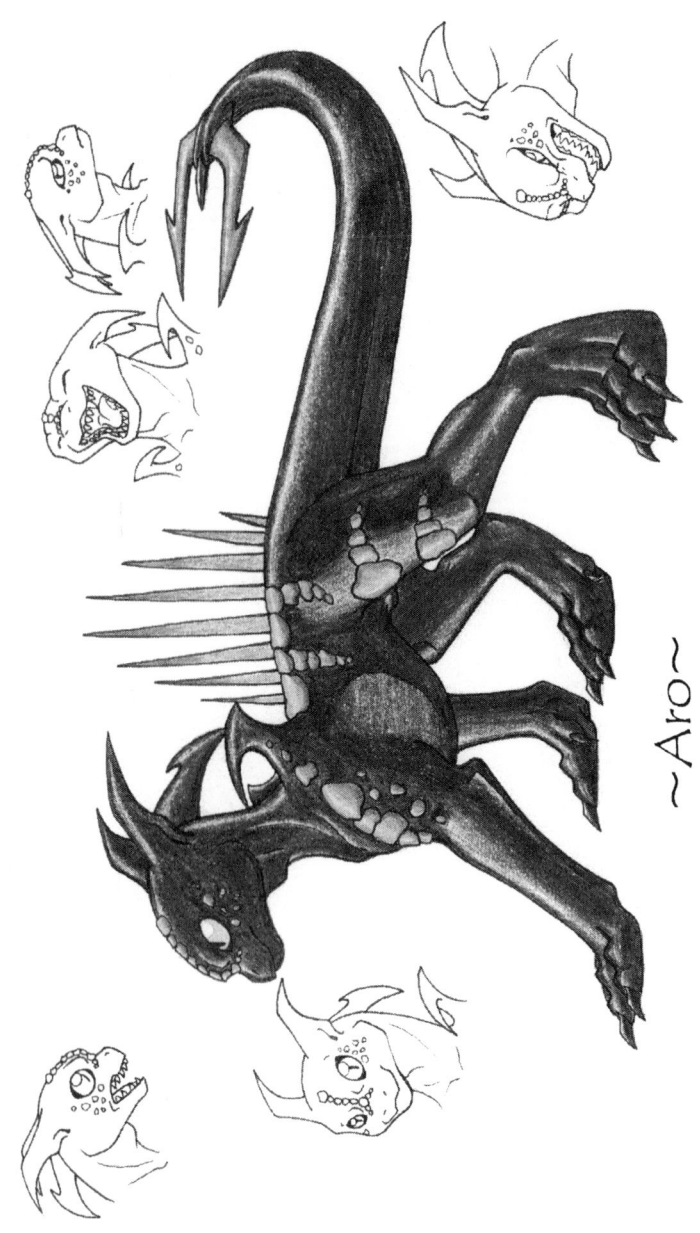

~Aro~

4

~Sierra~

~Reo~

~Lord Scerniss~

The Search for the SilvaGryphie

A novel by Lara Ryan

First Printing: 2016

ISBN 978-1-326-77517-9

Explore more at www.gryphiesaga.co.uk

This book is dedicated again to my amazing parents who support me in all that I do. Also to my friends for being there and encouraging me and for those who have enjoyed the first book, "Danger in the Darkness" so much. Thank you all!
Please enjoy the second part of the Gryphie Saga!

Prologue

It had been many, many seasons since the battle for Shernaron between the Gryphies and the Lizariaouses. The latter, lead by the evil Zephirak, had waged war on the Gryphie territory of Shernaron in order to gain control of it and enslave the Gryphies who lived there. The Forest Gryphies and those from the nearby Metal Mountains had bravely fought to keep their freedom and had won in the end.

Now peace reigned between Shernaron and the Lizariaous territory of Dyarkroeen. The two species had formed a friendship and now lived in harmony since the winning of the war, the death of Zephirak and the new leadership of Mordred, his once second in command who hadn't approved of Zephirak's greed. Mordred ruled over the Lizariaouses fairly and all were happy.

Leida and Diabloss had had a son, Ellendrii. He was an adventurous and outgoing teenaged Gryphie, always ready to explore and learn things and not one to back down from a challenge. He enjoyed listening to his mother tell him stories of her bravery in the war. Leida flew with Diabloss and his squadron of Gryphies to protect the Forest and all around it. She had become good friends with Tranzoss from Diabloss' squadron. Leida and Diabloss led the squad as equals.

Mordred and his mate Schaarl were the proud parents of three kids; two girls and a boy. Now that there was no threat of war, they felt it was safe to raise their own family.

Shernaron, the larger territory consists of the Forest, High Mountains and all in between and extends as far as the coast. Also included is the realm of the Sky Gryphies, though they are rarely seen and the Dark Plains, where no one ever ventures. It is the mysterious realm of the Deamon Gryphies and incredibly dangerous to go there. No one is ever bold enough to explore there and it is rarely spoken about. The Deamon Gryphies also keep to themselves and nearly nothing is known about them aside from the fact that they are very dangerous.

Past the neutral Outlands area between, lies the territory of Dyarkroeen. It is mostly barren and rocky, few trees grow there. Even though it is smaller, it still extends for many, many miles and is littered with caves and rocky cliffs and outcrops.

Due to there being peace between the Gryphies and Lizariaouses now, both species regularly venture into the other's territory to strengthen friendships and learn from each other. They do however still live in their own territories. Both have found that they prefer living in their own territory as opposed to the others'.

Days are called "Sun Cycles", nights "Moon Cycles", a "Lunar" is a month and "Seasons" measure years – four seasons to a year. Nightmares are referred to as "Moonmares".

Chapter 1
Back to the Forest

The sun was shining brightly in Shernaron; it was a lovely sun cycle. A red and black Lizariaous male trotted through the trees. It was Jadariol. He was on his way to see Lunara.

In the time since the war for Shernaron, Mystik the healer had taught Lunara as much as she knew about herbs and medicines. Lunara had pretty much moved in with her as they would stay up late at moon cycle talking and teaching. Mystik knew her time was short now. She wanted to pass on her important knowledge to Lunara so she could pass on into the next realm knowing that she had done at least some good.

She had in fact done a lot of good. The reason the Gryphies had done so well for themselves regarding illness and injury had been mostly down to Mystik. However, her mind and heart were clouded until the sun cycle she died by what, in her mind, had been the mistake of saving Mettalika, which only aided the friction between the Gryphies and the Lizariaouses and the war that ensued. Mystik never forgave herself for saving Mettalika, even though it had essentially been the right thing to do.

But she did not die sad or alone. When the sun cycle came, Lunara and her other friends stood by her. She lay on her bed of soft grass at the back of the huge old tree she lived in; the largest tree in the Forest. Leida, Diabloss, Tranzoss, Lunara, Jadariol and as many as could fit into the tree crowded around to say their last goodbyes. Mystik was very old; bearing in mind Gryphies outlive most species on our own planet. Their life spans are more akin to those of tortoises. They spend many seasons as teenagers and young adults before reaching full maturity.

Mystik slowly looked at those gathered from her position on the bed of soft grass and she smiled.

"Thank you all, thank you for visiting me on my last sun cycle and letting me see all your faces for the final time before I soar in the light of Forever." Her eyes were moist and the thinning fur on her face lined with wrinkles of age and wisdom.

The gold rings in her ears and her bracelets were tarnished and dull with age, matching her golden eyes.

"Lunara, come forward." She smiled at her apprentice and Lunara stepped forward from the others and crouched down to be level with the old Gryphie.

"Lunara, you have truly done me proud with all that you have learned...." she paused; speaking was a little trouble.

"I want you to have these...." she paused again and slowly removed her leather necklaces. There were three in all. One held a small scented gourd. It smelled of spices and smells that brought back a satisfying memory of nostalgia to one's nose. The second necklace held a tiny purple bead. It was smooth and strangely reassuring to the touch. The third held a shining turquoise crystal. As Mystik removed it, its dull glow faded to nothing. When Lunara put the necklace on, the crystal shone brightly, illuminating the faces of both herself and Mystik with its light. She donned the other necklaces too.

"You are now a fully fledged healer. I know you will do justice to what I have taught you and I trust you will not make the terrible mistake I did. Use your senses, instincts and your inner self and trust in yourself. Do me proud, my dear." Mystik reached forward, cupped Lunara's face with her hands and rested their foreheads together, closing her eyes, tears sparkling on her cheeks in the light of the crystal.

"I shall, Mystik" replied Lunara, closing her eyes, her own cheeks wet with tears as she laid her ears back and suppressed a choked sob. They stayed like that for a while, silently saying goodbye before Mystik's hands couldn't hold on any more and she rested them back on the grass. Lunara sat up and rested a hand on Mystik's.

"Please don't be sad, my dear. I will live on in your heart through all the happy memories you have of me. And I will always be watching over you, to guide you from the other realm." Mystik smiled at Lunara who nodded and sobbed. Then Mystik looked at the others.

"Thank you for sharing your lives with me, my friends. I will be watching over you too, from the light of Forever."

"We will never forget you, Mystik. Thank you for helping, for healing and for being there with your wisdom." Leida spoke softly. Several of the others sniffed back tears.

Mystik nodded, then, smiling she looked to Lunara, gave her hand a last squeeze and rested her head down on the grass. She closed her eyes and took a final satisfied, deep breath before sleeping forever more.

The gathered Gryphies sat in silence, a few sobs getting louder now that Mystik was gone. Slowly they filed out one by one leaving only Leida, Diabloss, Jadariol and Lunara.

Leida put a hand on Lunara's shoulder.

"It will be ok" she said.

"No it won't" replied Lunara, "How can I do all the things Mystik did?? I know she's taught me well but how can I carry on her legacy? She was so wise and ancient and me? I'm barely past my kitten seasons." She sighed sadly.

"You are an adult now. Fully fledged, like Mystik said. A young adult, with her whole life ahead of her to learn and grow and become ancient and wise like Mystik was. You will learn." Leida smiled.

"We must prepare the funeral pyre to see her into the next realm" said Diabloss and headed out. Leida followed, leaving Lunara and Jadariol to prepare Mystik for her funeral. As soon as the others had left though, Lunara burst into tears, hugging Jadariol tightly and sobbing on his shoulder. Jadariol awkwardly patted her back. Even though he had learned a lot from the Gryphies about sympathy, he had a very weak grasp on the concept.

"Umm...there, there" he managed to mumble. Lunara hadn't really heard him so his awkwardness was overlooked. She still clung to him, sobbing hopelessly. He let her calm down before continuing.

"Shall we prepare her? It would be the respectful thing to do..." Preparing the deceased for a funeral was also a foreign concept to him.

Lunara sat back and nodded, wiping her eyes. She smelled the little gourd and it brought back happy memories with Mystik; it was reassuring and she pulled herself together enough to gather the required herbs from the shelves carved into the walls of the tree to prepare Mystik for her funeral.

Soon, Mystik had carefully been wrapped up in thick brown grass with her body sprinkled with herbs. A funeral procession of Gryphies took her up to the high cliffs overlooking the bay. She was carried by Diabloss, Leida, Jadariol and Lunara and carefully placed on the large flat funeral rock. The rock had been covered in grasses and leaves so that the large bundle containing Mystik had a soft resting place. Diabloss spoke.

"We stand together before our friend on this sun cycle as she rests forever more.

Let her body drift away and may her soul spread its wings to the sky to soar.

We will always remember, she lives in our hearts, our voices lift to sing,

Dear Mystik as we say goodbye, the light of Forever sets free your soul to take wing.

Fly high, as our voices cry, we bid you goodbye, TAKE TO THE SKY!"

With that, Diabloss, Leida, Lunara and Tranzoss flamed the bundle with all their might as the rest of the funeral gathering roared out loud and proud to the ocean. They believed the next realm was beyond that ocean. Since no one had ever even attempted to cross it because it extended beyond as far as they could see, they figured there must be something mystical and magical the other side. Blue flames leaped up high, Mystik's bundle catching alight and the scent of the herbs billowing all around the gathering. Jadariol roared too, he was soon joined by Diabloss, Leida, Lunara and Tranzoss as the bundle had been lit. Each Gryphie roared with the strength of the love they had for the old ancient Mystik. For all the times she had helped them. For all the times she had healed them. For all the advice she gave them. For always having a friendly face and a tree to gather in. For all the love they had in their hearts.

Since then, Lunara had done Mystik proud. She was perfectly capable of doing a lot of the things Mystik had taught her but the initial death of the old one had terrified her. She had always been there to watch over Lunara, so that had given Lunara confidence not to mess things up. After she had gone, it meant that Lunara was on her own in the teachings.

Jadariol knew some of the techniques as well because Mystik had taught him too, knowing that the Lizariaouses needed a healer as well but he had never quite got the hang of a few things and struggled more, especially when it came to picking herbs. His clawed paws were much clumsier than the hand-like front paws of a Gryphie. Lunara had known Mystik was old and wouldn't be around much longer but the idea still scared her more than she cared to admit.

This had happened three seasons ago, back in the season where the leaves fell. Since then, Lunara had developed more confidence in her craft and didn't worry so much. Jadariol was on his way to fetch some herbs from her. After gathering their own herbs had proved rather difficult, Lunara had told him that the Lizariaouses could take some of hers instead. Lizariaouses didn't need healing that much. They usually put up with their injuries, but sometimes herbs were needed to keep wounds sterilized.

Jadariol reached the huge old tree that was now Lunara's home. Since there was peace now, several Gryphies he was friendly with waved to him on his way, including some of Lunara's kittenhood friends.

"Lunara! Lunara? Are you in there?" he trotted up to the entrance of the tree and peered in. He could hear something in the back, sounded like things falling off shelves and someone grumbling.

"Lunara?" he stepped in and followed the sounds. Lunara was at the back of the tree in the area she used to sleep, where the bed of soft grass was.

"Oh, Jaddy!" Lunara flashed him a smile before nearly tripping up and dropping the items she was carrying. "I'll be with you in a minute. I was trying to organise the medicines in this room. I've already done the ones in the main part of the tree. Mystik kept supplies and things here. It was more of a stock....woops....stockpile really..." She went to pick up the gourd she'd dropped but Jadariol grabbed it for her and put it on a nearby shelf. He admired the fact that Gryphies were

21

quadrabipedal, able to walk on both all fours like a Lizariaous but also two legs, which made carrying things easier. However, they always seemed to try to carry too many things at once and he often felt the ability was wasted on them.

"All these things are really old. Most of them aren't any good anymore. I left it this long because I felt bad about throwing them away since they were hers but I guess she wouldn't mind." Lunara set the things on a shelf, examining them and throwing one to one side.

Jadariol assumed this one was no good anymore.

"Well duh, she wouldn't keep around things that didn't work" he said, shrugging and sitting down. He took off the little carry bag he was wearing and set it in front of him ready for her to put the herbs in.

"How are you this sun cycle anyway? I haven't seen you for a while" Lunara had placed the herbs for Jadariol to one side and was now gathering them up and putting them in his bag. She trailed a bit of a scattering of some of them as she carried them to the bag. Jadariol smirked and rolled his eyes. Carrying too much and wasting an ability!

"I've been ok.....actually I met someone." Jadariol's cheeks went a bit pink.

"Oooh! Who's the lucky Lizariaous?" grinned Lunara, sitting facing him.

"Her name is Lexaron. We met some lunars ago and got chatting. She'd heard about me and how Zephirak tried to manipulate me. I'm kinda famous in Dyarkroeen, not in a very good way though. More in a "they take pity on me" kinda way. I don't like it much. Anyway she wanted to get to know me; we've found we had a lot in common. So we've been walking together. I guess it's been taking my time up, sorry I haven't been visiting so much." He looked sheepish. Lunara was his best friend. After the war, they had spent a lot of time together and she was important to him but at the same time, Lexaron was new in his life and they had a lot to do and talk about. He still felt guilty though.

"No, it's fine! I'm happy you've found someone. You deserve someone nice." Lunara was genuinely happy for him and hugged him in joy.

22

"What does she look like?" she asked.

"She's deep blue.....like the vast water. And she has these pretty yellow scales that shine like the sun....." Jadariol trailed off. This was not the classic talk of a Lizariaous; clearly the Gryphie attitude and romance had rubbed off on him! Most Lizariaouses would simply say she was dark blue with yellow scales. Lunara giggled at this.

"Well I hope it works out. Why don't you bring her over sometime? I'd love to meet her!"

"Sure, I've told her about you and how kind you were to me even when I kept pushing you away. If not for our friendship, I think Zephirak would have won." Jadariol looked at her seriously.

"I don't know; he was very strong and manipulative."

"Yes, but if I hadn't met you, I wouldn't have had any second thoughts about the things I did. I wouldn't have feared for your life when he attacked. I may even have been over there ruling the place with him by now." Jadariol shuddered at this thought.

"Well you're not. It all worked out and everyone is at peace now. I'm only sad Mystik still had regrets even until she passed. I tried to convince her it wasn't her fault and she wasn't to know. Leida had tried to convince her too but nothing really worked. She blamed herself till the end and even now it bothers me. I just hope she was happy in her heart when she passed over." Lunara wiped an eye.

"I'm sure she was happy. Her friends were around her. Everyone makes mistakes. I still regret being so stupid and naive believing Zephirak like that. I was a dumb little kid and I looked up to him like a blind idiot. Now I think about it, I think I was actually scared of him; that was the reason I was so in awe of him. He terrified me. And I thought if someone could be THAT terrifying, then they must be awesome and to be looked up to and respected." He shook his head at his past self and put a paw on her shoulder to comfort her.

"Anyway, enough of the past, let's look to the future and enjoy what we have. It's NEVER been like this before. Gryphies and Lizariaouses living in harmony? Never. Not in all our seasons of existence. So that's something good that came about because of Zephirak and because of what Mystik did saving Mettalika as well. And I think that's something great! Everything seems to happen for a reason even the bad things and in the end if bad stuff happens; it doesn't matter because good might come of it." Lunara looked at him, taken back by his little speech. She could hardly believe that it was a Lizariaous that had said these things and she smiled warmly at him.

"You're right. No more tears and sadness! Even in the seasons since the war we've learned so much from each other. And our compassion and good nature is wearing off on the other Lizariaouses and that's no bad thing. Also your bravery as a species is rubbing off on us. I think what we lacked was the ability to challenge. We only ever backed down and defended. We never challenged what we wanted to change, to make that change. We were too caught up in trying to remain amiable. Sometimes you need to stand up and roar instead of backing down and closing your wings around yourself in a bubble of defence. We can now take on the good points of the other species and become more rounded ourselves. So yes, you're right; Zephirak did do some good after all!"

"Yeah! Haha if Zephirak could see what has become and how we all are now, he'd be jumping in his death cave!" Jadariol grinned. Lizariaouses believe that when they die, the dead live in dark places known as death caves. Instead of soaring to the sky, they, being ground creatures, go deep into the earth and their next realm is buried, thus they bury their dead. When they can be bothered to. Obviously a dead Lizariaous who isn't buried decays into the ground anyway, so it is believed that those who aren't helped there by burial will make their way there anyway and so often they just aren't buried but simply left.

"He certainly wouldn't be happy" Lunara smirked.

"Well, I should probably get back to Dyarkroeen with these herbs. Actually my father, Karnoss has an infected leg. So that's another reason I needed a lot of the herbs. I still have some supplies but it's not enough to treat such a large area."

"Why did you leave it so long?" asked Lunara, concerned.

"He never told me about it. I live in my own cave now, obviously, because I'm meant to be the healer, though I have a couple who help me out sometimes and I'm trying to teach the whole pack basic sterilization skills but it's a bit like hitting my head on a rock at times for all the listening they do. Anyway he didn't want to bother me and he felt like a wuss admitting he had a problem so he was hoping it would go away on its own. He wasn't even washing it though so of course it got worse. My father is an idiot." Jadariol rolled his eyes and snorted.

"He's not, he just doesn't know any better" said Lunara.

"Or refuses to know any better" muttered Jadariol.

Just then a light blue Gryphie entered the tree. He brushed right past Jadariol, all but ignoring him and bounding up to Lunara in a bit of a panic.

"Lunara! Len's gone and got his foot caught in a pokey bush again. Can I use the grabbing claws? I have to pull the thorns out of his foot the silly idiot."

"Again? That's the third time this lunar! Does he never watch where he's going?" Lunara grunted and gave the Gryphie the tiny grabbing claws. We would call them tweezers and they were fashioned from the dextrous claws of a Furmine.

"Apparently not; I think he has a problem with his eyes too." Suddenly the Gryphie noticed Jadariol. He frowned slightly.

"Hiryasis." Jadariol grinned cockily, showing off his sharp teeth. Lunara's kittenhood best friend Hiryasis hadn't changed much since they were young but of course his pale blue coat had darkened as he'd grown. Not too dark. Now he was just light blue instead of pastel. Hiry had never liked Jadariol, feeling that the Lizariaous was somewhat of a wedge between him and Lunara. Not that Jadariol ever had the sort of feelings for her that Hiry had. Hiry wanted to make her his mate but so far had been too nervous to say anything. He was still jealous of Jadariol and the time he'd spent with Lunara and Mystik. Gryphies and Lizariaouses didn't and couldn't interbreed anyway but Hiry still loathed Jadariol. He just tried not to show it so as Lunara wouldn't notice. She knew though. She also knew Hiry liked her but said nothing. She wanted him to be the big male and approach her himself. He had nothing against other Lizariaouses, only Jadariol. And he utterly hated how Lunara called him "Jaddy". In fact, Jadariol only relented to her using the name on him in the end because he knew Hiryasis didn't like it. In Hiry's mind, "Jaddy" was a far too affectionate name for someone like Jadariol. Even though Jadariol had been used and lead astray and was good now, Hiry had still seen him kill a Gryphie in the war when he was a kid and would never like or trust him. Jadariol's Lizariaous side showed when Hiry was around because part of him enjoyed winding Hiry up simply because the Gryphie was making a fuss over nothing. His jealousy was unfounded since Jadariol did not share the same feelings for Lunara that Hiry had.

"Jadariol." Hiryasis narrowed his eyes at the Lizariaous just slightly, so only Jadariol could see and Lunara wouldn't notice.

"Come on guys, play nice or I'll have to ask you to leave my tree. There is only peace here." Lunara stepped between them.

"I need to get back to Len anyway" Hiryasis said shortly, passing Jadariol and flicking his tail in the way known universally as rather disrespectful.

"And *I* need to get back to my business in Dyarkroeen" smirked Jadariol, getting up and heading out after Hiryasis. Lunara watched them leave.

"Well just play nice!" she called after them.

"We will" they replied in unison and then scowled at each other.

Lunara shook her head smiling. The two species still had a lot to learn to get along. Outside, Hiryasis was quite further ahead than Jadariol. He was walking faster in the hopes that the Lizariaous wouldn't catch up to him and annoy him. But Jadariol was enjoying the other's aggravation and he quickly caught up to him.

"So...how are things going with you?" he smirked, quirking an eyeridge at Hiry.

"As if you care" spat Hiry.

"Aww don't be like that! Why would I ask if I didn't care?" Jadariol feigned hurt. He actually liked the Gryphies a lot, he didn't mind Hiry that much either any more but he did get a kick out of Hiry's attitude.

"I'm not talking to you!" Hiry held his head high and carried on.

"Seems we're going in the same direction though, so I guess we don't have a choice." Jadariol grinned, annoyingly.

"Still doesn't mean I have to talk to you!" Hiry tried to cup his wings around his body and block out Jadariol.

"Well fine." Jadariol replied and they walked along in silence for a while. Then Jadariol started rattling his needles in an annoying manner.

"Would you stop that!" snapped Hiry, stopping suddenly and causing Jadariol to almost bump into him.

"Stop what?" smirked Jadariol.

"Arghh!! That's it, I'm flying!" Hiryasis bounded up the nearest tree and took flight upon reaching the top.

"Spoilsport" yelled Jadariol after him. Even though he didn't mind Hiry, he still loved to wind him up, it was just so easy! Jadariol shook his head and smiled, carrying on. As he walked, he spied Leida's kitten, Ellendrii. Not so much a kitten though, more a teenage Gryphie in our age scale. Ellendrii appeared to be foraging for something. Jadariol didn't know him very well as he had spent most of his time with Lunara and Leida was busy these sun cycles with Diabloss and her own activities.

Ellendrii had finished flight school and was well on his way to doing whatever it was Gryphies chose to do after they graduate. For Ellendrii it was more flying. He loved flying; he spent most of his time in the air. He was always challenging his peers to races in the air and he usually beat them. No one had the speed and skill Ellendrii had obtained through endless practising. It was his passion. At the moment though he was rather frustrated. He was looking for the leg of a forest deer he'd accidentally dropped on his way back to the tree he shared with his parents. It wasn't like him to drop things but he had been trying a new technique for entering the thicker trees and it hadn't gone so well. If he hadn't been carrying anything it would have been fine but unfortunately the leg had snagged on a branch and he'd lost hold of it. He hadn't calculated the extra space needed to carry his cargo through as well.

"Grik! Where is it!" he demanded to no one in particular. Ellendrii was light blue all over with a purple muzzle and belly. He had five long spikes along his spine, longer than his mother's spikes and a similar shaped grey tailspade to his mother only without the yellow flashes on it. His mane was similar to Leida's too, only dark brown instead of tan. He had three wing fingers, the light blue on each finger darkening towards the end. The backs of his wings were dark blue and he had light green eyes.

"Looking for this?" Jadariol stepped up with the deer leg in his mouth. He dropped it before Ellendrii.

"Thanks!" Ellendrii replied gratefully and picked it up.

"It's kinda meagre," remarked Jadariol. "Where's the rest of it?"

"I shared it with my friend Aro. This is what's left and I'm going to keep it for a late moon cycle snack," explained Ellendrii.

Jadariol nodded in understanding. "Well, see ya," he said and carried on.

Ellendrii headed back to his parents' tree. It was later in the sun cycle and he wanted to get a good moon cycle's rest so he could get up early and practise more flying tricks. When he reached the tree, his parents still weren't back from their patrolling. There wasn't much to patrol now the war was over but they were still a little leery about things and felt it best to make sure everyone was still behaving. So far there had been less and less incidents the more time passed. At first a few Lizariaouses who had still supported Zephirak had tried to sneak in and take young and weaker Gryphies in an effort to try and resurrect Zephirak's plans for the territories. This had quickly been stopped without casualties. Well, without Gryphie casualties. Mordred had been pretty harsh on the guilty Lizariaouses. They had been punished severely for even daring to carry out more of the late Zephirak's wishes. Apparently Zephirak had told a few of his closest followers that if he died in the war, they needed to continue his work. Not that it would probably have meant a full scale invasion again but it would mean Gryphies would be picked off one by one and their numbers lessened even more.

However there weren't many of these close followers of Zephirak in the end who actually would dare to do such things and so it was put a stop to pretty quickly.

Once things had settled down, Leida and Diabloss decided to raise a family and so Ellendrii was born.

Right now Ellendrii was sat at the very top of their tree. He liked it best up there and he always slept on the highest branches so he had a good view of everything. The trees in this world have much thicker branches than the ones we know, so they hold a large Gryphie easily. Also the branches stay larger even towards the top of the tree. They are not large enough to hold a fully grown Gryphie for long periods though so it's usually the younger Gryphies that can actually sleep or sit on them for long periods at a time. Ellendrii had never really thought about when he would be too big to sleep on these branches. All he thought about was flying. As a result he didn't have many friends. Most of the other young Gryphies got bored of him yakking on about flying all the time as they saw flying only as a useful ability but didn't plan to make anything of it other than using it to get around. He did race with other adrenalin junky Gryphies, flying even as far as the High Mountains but they soon got bored of him winning all the time and out manoeuvring them. After all, it was no fun if the same Gryphie wins constantly and out flies everyone else. So friendship with other Gryphies was a rare thing with Ellendrii. He didn't let it get him down though. He had a friend anyway. But it wasn't a Gryphie. It was a Lizariaous, about the same age as Ellendrii. Mordred's son. Mordred and Schaarl had three kids; two girls and a boy; Aro. Since their parents were friends, it made sense that the youngsters got to know each other too. Aro's sisters, Zixiniss and Scit (which was pronounced Skit) had no interest in hanging around with a male Gryphie, or their brother Aro. Like young human females at a certain age, they found boys to be "icky" and "boring" and not only that but they had no interest whatsoever in Aro's passion, which was exploring and adventuring and which they considered to be even more boring and pointless. But Aro and Ellendrii grew close and soon became best friends. Ellendrii liked Aro because he was not jealous of Ellendrii's speed and prowess like the other Gryphies were. Aro liked Ellendrii because he was always looking to explore and adventure and Aro loved adventuring.

So Ellendrii was happy with what he had and his friend Aro. But he yearned for more as far as flying went. He just couldn't seem to find it.

A while later, Leida returned to the tree.

"Hey Mum," Ellendrii greeted her. "Have a good sun cycle?"

"Yes it was ok. We flew out as far as the valleys to see how things are going there. Everything seems pretty good. To be honest I don't know why we continue to patrol but you never know when trouble might start and it's better to catch it before it gets too bad. We did see some Gryphies from the valleys tormenting a Grypher though. Even though Gryphers aren't as evolved as us, they still have feelings and they never bother to hurt us, so we mustn't do such things to them." Gryphers are a lower sub specie of Gryphie. They range mostly in the Forest and are usually pretty shy. They cannot talk but they are not considered meal creatures. They can fly but don't very often. Gryphies from the valleys are just Forest Gryphies who live in the valley areas.

"Now I'm pretty tired. I don't know how you stay in the air flying all sun cycle and not get tired." Leida lay down on the branch she was on and sighed.

"Cos I'm younger," grinned Ellendrii and sat beside her.

"I'm not old!" snapped Leida but she did it with a sense of humour. Ellendrii giggled.

They watched the setting sun together and soon Diabloss returned as well.

"Another good sun cycle, not much to report thankfully. Apart from those Gryphies in the valley, everything else looks good." Diabloss settled down with the meal he'd caught, sharing it with Leida. Ellendrii was old enough to catch his own food so his parents rarely shared their food with him anymore. He never complained.

"I've no doubt you're getting up early again to go out flying?" Diabloss asked Ellendrii. He knew the answer.

"Of course! Flying early means the sky is clearer and less busy with other Gryphies around. I want to go cloud dodging again." Ellendrii would make his own obstacle courses to weave in and out of; clouds! Since they changed shape and never remained the same, it gave him a good course to practise on. He would weave and dodge the clouds as he flew. He had grown strong wing muscles through doing this and other sky based activities. Another reason why the other Gryphies got annoyed with him; he had more stamina. Much more.

Diabloss shook his head and smiled. "I don't know why you don't join my squad. You would do so well in it. Able to stay in the sky for long periods at a time, able to fly long distances without tiring, you would be the perfect sentry."

"Yeah and it's boring. Who wants to fly around keeping watch? I want to race and fly competitively. I don't want to just fly and watch, that's a waste of the skills I've been working so hard on. I'm sure it's a good squad but I have different plans." Ellendrii was confident with what he wanted to do.

"And I respect that. It was only a suggestion."

"I know, Dad and I'm happy you want to help. But I have bigger plans for my life than that."

Diabloss smiled at him. He was glad they had raised a kitten who was confident with his life and trained his skills well. They wouldn't have wanted him to be lazy after all. Joining the squad had only been a suggestion.

Ellendrii ate his supper and then headed up to the uppermost branches of the tree to sleep. Diabloss and Leida slept in their usual sleeping place; the hollow of the tree high up and just below where they had sat to eat.

As he normally did, Ellendrii sat and looked out over the forest. The moon was bright and full and illuminated his fur as it shone down. He sighed. He was happy but he yearned for more. He just didn't know where to find it just yet. He had tackled and overcome pretty much every type of competitive

31

flying there was to do in the Forest and around. He looked up at the sky and tried to count the stars. There were too many though. He soon lost count and started to feel sleepy, in a similar way that counting sheep would make us feel sleepy. He sighed and headed down to his branch. There was a smaller hollow where the branch met the main trunk of the tree and he slept in there when the colder weather came. Now though it was warm, it was summer. Not too far into it either. It would get warmer.

Sitting on his branch, Ellendrii thought about what to do when the sun rose. He would go cloud dodging. It was always a good way to start the sun cycle. Then he would get something to eat. He was in top form and very healthy due to how active he was.

He yawned and settled down. The light of the moon shone down a little through the leaves as they moved in the gentle breeze. The trees in the Forest were evergreen so they were always covered with leaves. They helped keep out the chill in the winter and shaded the inhabitants from the heat of the summer. In the winter, Gryphies slept further down the trees and in the hollows in the trunks. But in the summer they liked to sleep out on the branches and enjoy the warm moon cycles.

Ellendrii found it hard to get comfortable this moon cycle though. He was bothered by what he wanted to do. Life was becoming boring and he needed a new perspective. But what? Surely he could go further with his flying. He lay on his back and stared up at the leaves. He was deep in thought. He hoped that thinking so deeply would also make him sleepy. But it only kept him up longer. He flicked his tail and watched it, for lack of anything else to do. Now he wanted to go to sleep. If he didn't, he might not wake up at early sun and miss the quiet skies. He grumbled quietly and shifted around a little. Then he lay on his tummy with his legs dangling down either side of the branch. He looked down. The ground far below stared back up at him. He sighed again. He listened. He could hear other Gryphies in the Forest sleeping and a couple of young Gryphies passed by down below, heading who knows where. Sometimes they had gatherings in deeper parts of the Forest that they met at and messed around, much like human teenagers. Ellendrii had never been interested in hanging around at these evening gatherings, mostly because he had no friends. But also because it meant going to bed late and not getting up early with the sun. He liked to get up when the sun rose and in the summer season this was very early.

He closed his eyes, ears twitching. Time to settle down. He was determined to go to sleep now. He kept his eyes shut in the hopes it would mean they wouldn't open again until sunrise. He didn't normally have such trouble falling asleep but his mind was so full of thoughts right now that he couldn't help himself. He tried to clear his mind. Sunrise would be the time for thoughts! It seemed to be working though because he felt himself getting sleepy now. He had after all, thought a lot about his situation. Maybe there was nothing more to think of until sunrise. He sighed again and slowly drifted off to sleep as the moon watched on through the leaves.

Chapter 2
An Impossible Idea

The sun rose bright and early and Ellendrii was ready for it! He was cloud dodging before his parents were even awake.

He soared and wheeled in the sky, which was a pretty pink and orange sunrise, laughing and roaring with happiness. Flying made him feel really free.

Faster and faster he flew, dodging in and out of the clouds, dispersing them as he went and whipping up the sky. Turning round and round in endless loop the loops and cartwheels, spiralling through the clouds, shaping and forming them into different formations. Faster than the other Gryphies, with swifter reflexes he was an expert at this. He didn't care in which direction he went or how far he flew from the Forest, he was just having fun and training himself.

Soon he ended up near the coast. The sea sparkled in the early morning sun, the pink of the sky turning into a pale blue, nearly the same colour as Ellendrii's fur. He blended in very well. Swooping down, his claws touched the surface of the water as he flew down low, causing a glittering spray to be whipped up as he moved. He flew up in a curved arc and back into the clouds again, dodging some more, spinning through them with the sun shining on his wings. His healthy fur was polished to a sheen and he was a sight to behold as he practised what he loved.

Soon he felt hungry. It was time for breakfast and what better to eat than a sea vulture, since he was near the coast. He spied some congregating around a cliff face and dived for them. The angry birds screeched at him and started dive-bombing him for being near their nests. Ellendrii didn't care. The birds were too small in comparison to him to bother about them hurting him. He targeted one of the nasty screaming creatures and went for it, folding his wings against his body to give him a torpedo shape and make him faster as he chased after it. He was soon on its tail. It was heading towards the cliff again and he hoped to catch it before it got too close. Although he could swerve and miss the cliff, he didn't want to get too close because of his size; it would be harder for him to swerve than it would be for the bird.

He spread his wings out and hovered as the cliff neared. The bird had wisely decided to return to the cliff. Ellendrii smirked and began flapping his wings in huge sweeping motions, blowing some of the birds off the cliff and into the air. Then he went after another one.

A Gryphie who wanted an easy meal would land on the cliff face and simply raid the nests for chicks and eggs. The birds couldn't stop them doing this; the most they could do is peck and dive on the Gryphie. They were wary of getting too close because of the Gryphie's sheer size anyway. But Ellendrii wanted a challenge. He didn't want to do things the easy way.

So he was after another target bird. This one wasn't so smart as to land on the cliff and it tried flying out to sea. Big mistake. Ellendrii dived at it, catching it in his claws and killing it before taking it to the top of the cliff to eat it.

He looked out to sea. Catching the sea vulture had really worked up an appetite! The sun was fully risen now and the sky was blue. There weren't many clouds. Ellendrii looked up and examined the sky, looking for any clouds that might be lingering. He could see very few. He looked up higher and saw a sort of pale mist way up high, higher than he had ever flown. He knew such a mist sometimes formed around the peaks of the High Mountains. It was a strange sort of mist, it seemed to be made up of clouds, some larger than others. Ellendrii squinted and stared, trying to make sense of whatever it was. He had never noticed it before. After all, who bothers to look up when they can already fly higher than a bird? And when they do look up from the ground, they never bother to look higher than the clouds because the clouds are the place where they fly.

As he was contemplating all this, a Lizariaous bounded up to him. It was Aro. He was jet black with turquoise scales along three quarters of his back, his upper forelegs and his upper hind legs. The scales on his hind legs and back formed a pattern of two stripes. He also had the same scales travelling down the front of his face and under his eyes. His crest was a half arrow shape, as were the two points on his tail blade. He had sharp, forward facing shoulder spikes and golden yellow eyes. He had eight needles running the length of his spine.

"I knew I'd find you here!" he yelled, reaching Ellendrii and plonking himself down next to the Gryphie.

"It's nice to watch the sun rise," said Ellendrii quietly. Aro's arrival had completely crashed his train of thought.

"Cloud dodging?"

"Yup. There were some good ones this morning, though a lot of them dispersed when the sun rose." Ellendrii finished his meal quickly. Aro was known for trying to scrounge food.

"So what do you do when there's no clouds?" asked Aro.

"I don't cloud dodge, of course. There tend to be less clouds in the warm seasons but in the cold seasons they aren't as well formed. They are more misty and there's no point trying to dodge something like that. There are no shapes."

Aro was a sturdy young Lizariaous. His favourite pastime of course was adventuring with Ellendrii. He often got frustrated because he couldn't fly. It meant Ellendrii could cover much more ground than he could and get to places he couldn't. But Ellendrii valued his friendship so he tended not to fly as much when Aro was around. Give and take. Aro found his sisters to be boring but he liked watching his father as he oversaw the happenings in Dyarkroeen. His sisters hung out with their mother more. Mordred was very busy most of the time however, and Aro often got bored so he would head over to Shernaron and hang around with Ellendrii. He was nosy and rarely took anything seriously. He hadn't chosen his life goals yet; he only wanted to explore and play. Ellendrii was a little younger but the more mature of the two. Aro was able to choose whatever he wanted as a life goal. Digging and building, protecting, hunting. That was really as far as the Lizariaous way of life extended. Soldiers were now protectors, upholding what little laws they had in Dyarkroeen and making sure there weren't any more rebellion groups of Zephirak followers. Aro seemed to think he could hang around with Ellendrii the rest of his life and just go adventuring.

36

He and Ellendrii looked up at the sky now. Aro wished even more that he could fly. Ellendrii had tried carrying him once. But Aro was too heavy and they'd both crashed into a tree. Aro had found it exhilarating and wanted to go again. Ellendrii wasn't so sure. He'd nearly got poked on Aro's poisonous needles twice. Aro was hard to carry with those on his back. But he couldn't ride on the back of Ellendrii either because it impeded his wing movements. So he'd ended up asking Aro to shoot all his needles and then he tried to carry him. Aro was rather good at being persuasive, or rather, nagging. He didn't do it very often though and Ellendrii was usually happy to go along with whatever he wanted since he never asked that much, but the flying thing had been rather unwise and they never attempted it again.

"Have you eaten?" asked Ellendrii. Aro nodded.

"Ages ago. I caught a cave cat in a nearby cavern. They seem to congregate in there because it's the biggest in the territory. I think it belonged to Zephirak. My parents tried living in it but it creeped them out too much so they moved back to our cave. Things happened there, Ellendrii, horrible creepy things that we don't speak of." Aro shuddered. Ellendrii knew of the war but he didn't know much about the Lizariaous side of it, only what his mother had told him of what Zephirak did to her. He wasn't interested in what didn't concern him though. His mind drifted back to the sky. Aro didn't think much about the war or Zephirak either, even though his parents had told him a little about it.

"So, what are we gunna do this sun cycle?" he asked in excitement.

"Hmm, not sure..." Ellendrii trailed off, still staring up at the sky.

"What about that weird cave the other side of the Forest? Before it goes into the valley? You know, the one that smells weird..." Aro suggested.

Ellendrii put his ears back and sighed. What did he have to lose after all? And he could think more along the way.

"Sure, let's go!" He got up and headed away from the cliff edge, Aro excitedly in tow.

"Great! It's been bothering me for ages that cave," he remarked.

"I don't think it's a cave. We don't have any caves here as far as I'm aware," said Ellendrii. "I think it's just a load of deep bushes that something might have been using as a killing spot or something like that."

"Well, we'll find out," grinned Aro. Ellendrii followed his friend back into the Forest. Walking took so much longer than flying but he didn't mind so long as he had company. Aro chatted away about various goings on in Dyarkroeen and Ellendrii told him how his training was going, although Aro knew most of this. Ellendrii really didn't have much more training to do that he could see. The journey to the odd cave passed quickly with the two of them chatting together.

The smell hit them before the actual cave could be seen.

"Ew, it's horrible," winced Ellendrii, holding his nose. "It doesn't smell like anything I've smelled before. It doesn't smell like something dead, it smells like something's still alive and rotting away. Blegh!"

Among the leaves the entrance could be spied, Aro pushed the bushes back with a paw. They weren't close to the swamp, where smells like this usually resided. Aro screwed up his snout but he didn't seem as badly affected by the smell as Ellendrii was. Probably because of the amount of rotting meat that Lizariaouses have around. Sometimes they try to save meat in the back of a cave for eating later. Also their constitutions are sturdier than a Gryphie; it takes a lot to make a Lizariaous sick from eating bad meat.

Aro headed in first. It was dark and damp and generally unpleasant. Ellendrii yelped a little when he stood in something squishy.

"Aro, why do you get us looking in these places?" he asked with a groan.

"Aww c'mon, you wanted to look in here too!" replied Aro defiantly.

"Well yeah but I didn't think it would stink this much!" Ellendrii coughed.

"I wish I could see better. We need glowbugs." Aro had laid his needles flat along his back because the cave was low but he still had a bit of trouble with it and soon they were nearly crawling. Suddenly Aro tripped up.

"Ouch.....OUCH!!!" Ellendrii had bumped into him with a thud. It was just too dark to see anything. Also the cave appeared to have turned into some sort of tunnel. It was going too far back and was too low to be a cave. They picked themselves up and decided not to carry on without proper equipment; glowbugs. And they could only get glowbugs at moon time. There was no light at the other end of the tunnel; it was just too long and too dark. And they couldn't turn around either so they had to go out backwards, which was also difficult.

Once they were out, Ellendrii sat down.

"My fur's all muddy. You really do choose the weirdest and most difficult places for us to explore, Aro."

"Sorry, but it's too mysterious to just not bother with. What's causing that smell?" Aro looked back at the mouth of the cave or tunnel or whatever it was and sniffed slightly, then wrinkled his nose up.

"Damp I'd say. It's very wet in there. And because it's dark and the sun doesn't get to it to dry it, then any moisture just lingers and gets worse. We'll have to get some glowbugs this moon cycle and come back to it when the sun rises." Ellendrii said, pondering.

"Why when the sun rises? Why not this moon cycle? After all, it's so dark in there that it shouldn't matter when we go in. We can't see any more when the sun is about than we can when the moon is out." Aro had a point.

"Ok, we'll come back to this later, when the moon is out then. And with glowbugs. I'll have to find something to put them in though. That will be tricky. Normally we just spread tree sap or natural syrup on the trees and they come to eat it."

"Why not put it on a stick or something? They'll probably gather round it and come with us."

"I doubt they'll want to go in that dark, wet tunnel. I'll go to Lunara and ask if she's got anything we can put them in. That way they won't escape and suddenly leave us when we're in the middle of that weird smelling tunnel."

"Good idea!" Aro was rolling around on the ground and wiping off the mud from the tunnel. Lizariaouses didn't groom themselves; they either left the dirt or rubbed it off. Gryphies however, preferred to wash it off in fresh water. Ellendrii got up.

"Where are you going?" asked Aro.

"To wash off this grime of course. There is a river in the valley and since we're near it, I may as well use it." Ellendrii started walking, Aro joined him.

"I wonder where it leads, if it *is* a tunnel," he pondered.

"I bet it'll just be an annoying dead end or something," sighed Ellendrii.

"Hey what's got into you? You're usually more upbeat than this." Aro stopped him.

"I...I just dunno what to do with my life. There must be more to flying than what I know already. It's my passion and yet I feel I've reached the end of the path with it. It's getting me down. Sorry." Ellendrii sighed. Aro patted him on the shoulder.

"We'll find something you can do with your wings! Maybe you can join a flying squad?"

"Dad already suggested that. I don't want to do that. I want to do competitive flying."

Aro thought about this. He didn't know much about flying really, or Gryphie life choices. Everything was pretty much set out for most Lizariaouses.

"How about some sort of long distance thing? Maybe go on a journey or something and discover other places?" Aro wasn't good at suggestions.

"I suppose I could try flying higher, maybe exploring where no other Gryphie has been, I can already fly higher than most of the others because I've practised. Most Gryphies are strong flyers but to fly that high you have to be an even stronger flier, which I am. I spend most of my time in the air after all, well other than when I'm with you of course."

"Going on awesome adventures on the ground" grinned Aro. Ellendrii laughed.

"Yes! There are lots of neat places to explore down here." Though nothing beats the sky he thought afterwards, privately to himself, so as not to upset Aro. He really did enjoy hanging with his friend but it was still small stuff compared to the sky and flying.

They carried on to the river and Ellendrii waded in, washing off the grime from the tunnel.

"You won't be able to do that this moon cycle" observed Aro, sitting at the water's edge and watching him. Ellendrii shrugged.

"Then I'll have to put up with the grime until the sun rises and I can fly to water and clean it off. This is a much nicer place to bathe than the water by the cliffs. That's salty and leaves a nasty crust on one's fur. I don't mind waiting so long as it doesn't smell too bad. It shouldn't do once we're out of that weird tunnel, right Aro?" Ellendrii looked at him for confirmation but Aro really didn't know how to answer. It could smell or it might not.

"I'm sure it'll be fine" muttered Aro. "Not like that time we went exploring that bog and we got stuck in it and the smell didn't come out for sun cycles afterwards!"

"More like lunars" murmured Ellendrii as he swam about in the water. Gryphies are quite good swimmers. Ellendrii had been taught by his parents since they thought it was a useful skill to know. He could swim almost as though he was flying under the water, using his wings to steer and tucking his forearms under him while kicking out with his legs. He was very speedy and zipped through the water in an effort to wash off the mud. It worked very well and he was soon clean and swam back to the water's edge where Aro was lying down in the sun, enjoying it. Ellendrii climbed out and sat beside him, letting the sun dry his own body too. He sighed and looked up at the sky. He narrowed his eyes. Again he saw that odd mist. Not everywhere but in a lot of places. Not enough to impede the sun at any rate. And it appeared to be made up of some sort of cloud matter. No birds flew up there. Nothing seemed to be up there. He wondered if it was the heat of the sun causing some sort of heat to rise and create the mist. But he did have an idea. He would fly up to it. The next sun cycle. Try some sky exploring, see what was up there. It had been a good idea and he wanted to put it into practise and see what happened. He was fairly confident he could reach it.

"Hey Aro," he spoke up. Aro looked up. "See that mist up there?"

Aro looked in the direction Ellendrii's nose was pointed and squinted for a long time.

"Nope" he replied shortly.

"Look harder" said Ellendrii, now pointing with a finger.

Aro grumbled and stared more, gritting his teeth and squinting as much as he could without closing his eyes completely.

"Ok, I kinda see it?" His eyes were watering. "Why?"

"Cos I'm gunna fly up to it!" Ellendrii grinned. Aro looked at him like he was mad.

"Why would you want to fly up to somewhere you can hardly see? It's probably just thin clouds or something. I doubt there's anything interesting up there."

"Mostly to see if I can. It's higher up than any cloud I've ever seen. And partly because I'm curious. You did suggest going on an awesome long distance adventure!"

"Yeah, on the ground" replied Aro. "But if it pleases you, go ahead, see what's up there. Then come back and tell me. Bet you'll be disappointed though!" Aro stared up at the sky again. "Very disappointed" he muttered.

Gryphies have better eyesight than Lizariaouses. They have to, because they fly and hunt prey on the ground. Lizariaouses, while they do hunt, don't do it from such a distance. They also tend to eat things like cave cats that they can corner and catch easily. Although they can run a long distance, their heavy bodies prevent them from running long distances at higher speeds. They can only manage short bursts of higher speed. So it makes sense that they would prefer to sneak up on their prey rather than outright chase after it.

"Well if I'm disappointed, it's my own fault. It's not like you lose out" Ellendrii pointed out.

"And I can laugh at you!" said Aro brightly. Ellendrii gave him a withering look.

They sat chatting for a while longer while Ellendrii dried. He was in no hurry to go anywhere anyway, he hadn't much to do except ask Lunara about a container for the glowbugs.

As mid-sun hit, they decided to go back to the Forest and find Lunara.

When they got to her tree though, she wasn't in. Ellendrii and Aro waited for her to return.

Soon, Leida joined them.

"Hi you two, what are you up to this sun cycle?" she asked, sitting down with them.

"Waiting for Lunara to get back from wherever she's gone. I need to ask her about something" Ellendrii replied, a little secretly. He wasn't sure if he really wanted to tell his mother that he and his best friend were going to explore a stinky cave tunnel thing that moon cycle.

Leida wasn't that interested in knowing what he was going to ask Lunara and carried on the conversation without a second word about it.

"I just got back from a lovely romantic flight with your father" she smirked.

"Eww no, don't wanna know!" Ellendrii wrinkled his nose while Aro giggled and Leida smiled, knowing it would gross him out and he quickly changed the subject.

"Hey Mum, do you know what the sort of mist stuff is if you look up higher than the clouds?" he asked, now very curious.

"Yes, that's the realm of the Sky Gryphies. They live up on that mist. Few of us can actually fly up high enough to go see them. All of your father's squadron can but not many other members of the Forest. The air is very thin up there and it makes it hard to breathe, which also of course makes it hard to fly."

"Do you know anything about them?" asked Ellendrii, now fully interested.

"Not really, your father knows more than me. All I know is that they keep to themselves. They would have helped us in the war but only if it got so bad that it affected them in some way. They weren't prepared to help us for any other reason.

None of us have much of an interest in meeting them but we all live in harmony so it works well even so."

"Have you ever seen one?" asked Ellendrii, excited now. He'd only ever thought there were the Forest Gryphies and Mountain Gryphies and a few living in the valleys. Of course he knew of the Deamons because of his father having a Deamon mother and being half Deamon but he never could have dreamed about a gathering of Gryphies living in his favourite place; the sky!

"No I haven't. Your father has though, he can tell you more. Come over to our tree after you've spoken with Lunara and he can tell you."

Suddenly the glowbugs and Lunara weren't as important anymore. Ellendrii got up.

"She might be a while, why don't we go now? Aro can stay and wait for Lunara and let me know when she gets back?" he looked at Aro expectantly. Aro rolled his eyes.

"Yeah sure I'll wait. I'm not that interested in hearing what a Sky Gryphie is anyway." He was a little grumpy about his friend rushing off for something that Ellendrii deemed more important or more exciting than their moon cycle adventure but he tried not to show it. Ellendrii's obsession with flying sometimes ground on his nerves a little.

Ellendrii happily trotted off with Leida and they climbed their tree to where Diabloss was having a rest. He smiled and sat up when he saw his mate and son. Leida nuzzled him.

"Ellendrii has some questions about Sky Gryphies" Leida told him. She gave him a knowing look. Diabloss nodded, also knowingly. They both knew eventually that Ellendrii would find out about the Sky Gryphies and show an interest because of their high rise habitation.

"So, what would you like to know?" he asked his son.

"Everything" replied Ellendrii solidly.

"Ok, well, they live up in the clouds. Unlike us, their fur is blue and white, well; most of them have blue and white fur. It helps them blend in with the sky you see, the blue sky and the clouds. Their fur is quite pale and reflects the sky around them. They have markings on their bodies that resemble clouds. There are only two exceptions; their leaders. These are two Sky Gryphies by the names of Sierra and Reo and their fur is the colour of the sunrise and the sunset. They are the strongest flyers. That is what the Sky Gryphies rank around; strength of flight. They have a special rank of flyers called the Elite Flyers. These are the fastest and best flyers, similar to my own squadron. They are the best of the best flyers, performing near impossible tricks in the sky. It takes a LOT to get into the squad though and they don't even let any Gryphie simply compete. Only Sky Gryphies are allowed to compete to be a part of the squad. Which makes sense since no Forest Gryphies can withstand their thin air for very long anyway. So don't get any ideas!" Diabloss could see that Ellendrii was looking rather eager and interested at the idea of competing to be a part of a high flying flight squad of sky living Gryphies. It irked him a little that his son didn't have the same interest in joining Diabloss's own squadron. Diabloss continued.

"Sky Gryphies have scales on their bellies and their wings are a different shape to ours; more pointed for fast flight, as well as having near transparent skin between the wing fingers. They have very light bodies and are more streamlined for staying in the air longer. They also have feathery crests on their heads. I would say they look a little odd, but then look at me! I'm half Deamon so I can't really talk." Diabloss chuckled. Ellendrii was enthralled.

"How fast can they fly?" he asked.

"Faster than any of us. I've never met a Forest Gryphie who could match their speed in the air."

Ellendrii's eyes were wide now; fascinated.

"I knew there was something special about that mist!" he grinned.

"Not really. Though we live in peace, I've always found the Sky Gryphies to be somewhat stuck up and have sky high standards. Their heads are like where they live...in the clouds! That doesn't mean they are bad or nasty, they just aren't used to us. They look down on us in more ways than one."

"Have they ever visited the Forest? I'm guessing you've been to see them if you know much about them?" asked Ellendrii, still just as interested.

"I don't know if they've visited the forest. Some of us went to see them to see if they would join us in the war but of course they refused. We didn't stay long because of the altitude."

"Do they actually walk on the clouds?" Ellendrii cocked his head to one side, puzzled.

"No, they have sort of floating islands that they live on up there. They are scattered around, I don't know the exact placing of them. They are so high that they can't be seen from here, plus the clouds hide them. We don't even see their shadows on the ground like sometimes we see the shadows of clouds, simply because of the height. I dunno how they can live up there happily. And no, I haven't visited the islands. I only saw one at a distance. Where I met the leaders was at a separate meeting place. They didn't permit us to land on the islands. I guess there was no point because we couldn't stay long. We didn't want to get too comfortable. Nor did they want us to. I think they think we are contaminated because of our proximity to the ground. You know how some meal creatures are afraid of heights? Well I think Sky Gryphies are afraid of the ground!" Diabloss chuckled.

"Haha that's silly!" sniggered Ellendrii, "being afraid of the ground. That's where all the meal creatures are, well, except sea vultures. I wonder what they eat."

"Birds I imagine. I see them sometimes, up high, at a distance, swooping in on high flying birds. The larger birds tend to fly higher than the smaller ones and of course the larger ones make better meals so it all works out. I've seen them catch sea vultures. They'll take them off back to their floating islands to eat. I've never seen one eat in mid-air. I just see them swoop in and swoop away with their catch."

"Sounds cool! I wonder if I could meet a Sky Gryphie..." Ellendrii trailed off in thought.

"Probably not. Tranzoss tried calling out to one once, it just ignored her and flew away. They don't talk to us or come if we call them. They don't seem to want anything to do with us and we're content with that. We know that they would help if pushed and they aren't hostile. It's just like two different worlds."

"Two different worlds? Hardly! We live in the sky too…"

"Yes but we don't *live* in the sky like they do. We just visit it sometimes" replied Diabloss.

"It's similar though, we both fly! It's not like they own the sky. I don't see why we can't make better relations with them…"

"Our relations with them are fine. They aren't going to attack us, they keep their distance and that's fine. We're all Gryphies after all, even though they look a bit different from us." Diabloss explained.

"Maybe that's why they don't like us?" pondered Ellendrii.

"They don't not like us, they just prefer to do their own thing I think."

"What if I went to visit them" Ellendrii grinned.

"Yes well now I've told you about them, it only tempts you doesn't it? You can try to visit them, I won't stop you, nor will your mother, you're not a kitten anymore. But be careful. And understand that you won't be able to handle the altitude for long. If you stay up there for too long, you will black out, become unconscious. So make sure you don't stay up there long. Chances are you won't reach any of their islands anyway because you'll need to fly among the clouds up there to find them and you'll feel light headed long before getting anywhere useful." Leida came and sat next to Diabloss and nodded at all of this.

"Gee thanks Dad, ever the optimist!" Ellendrii mooched.

"I'm just warning you. I want you to be responsible and careful. Your mother and I have watched you over these sun cycles become ever more stressed about what to do with your life. If you want to go off and explore, you're old enough and we know you will do your best." Diabloss smiled. His son was not an idiot, he could be reckless at times but he never got hurt. He was proud of the kitten he and Leida had raised to young adulthood.

Ellendrii beamed, "Thanks Dad!" The fact his parents had faith in him made him feel very mature and he was determined not to let them down. He would be careful, he would also try not to let his excitement get the better of him and cause him to make mistakes.

Leida smiled. "You're not going to go off this sun cycle though are you?" She suspected the answer was yes.

Ellendrii opened his mouth to speak, then closed it, catching himself. He *had* wanted to go that sun cycle but then he caught sight of Aro still waiting for Lunara and changed his mind. Aro would probably be annoyed that Ellendrii was going on an adventure without him and Ellendrii wasn't about to make that any worse by also dropping the adventure they had planned that moon cycle. However the sun was warm in the sky, the moon cycles were shorter than they should be and he wasn't sure if he would be up for flying long distances the next sun cycle if he'd been up all moonlight. He decided to adventure with Aro this moon cycle and then leave it a sun cycle and go out the one after that so he would be well rested. So it was the sun after next that he would visit the Gryphies of the Sky.

"No, I won't go this sun cycle. Aro and I have an adventure to do this moon. I can't let him down. He's not going to be too happy that I'm going off without him anyway, you know how he gets about the fact he doesn't have wings. He often feels bad."

Leida and Diabloss nodded.

"Well, go off and carry on with whatever it was you were doing!" Leida ushered him off the branch and down the tree trunk. "Your father and I are going to relax till sundown."

Ellendrii bounded down the tree trunk and joined Aro at Lunara's tree. Lunara still hadn't returned.

"I dunno what's taking her so long" muttered Aro as Ellendrii approached him. He was getting bored and fed up. Aro wasn't one for sitting around unless he had a reason to. Waiting, he had decided, wasn't a good enough reason. He was getting that funny prickly feeling in his legs from sitting too long.

"I've no doubt she's doing something important like healing someone or collecting herbs or something" replied

Ellendrii. "Anyway, I've got something exciting to tell you!" He almost hopped from foot to foot in his glee.

"What is it?" asked Aro, curious now.

"I'm going to fly up to those misty clouds and see if I can find the Sky Gryphies!" Ellendrii was nearly exploding with excitement.

"Why doesn't *that* surprise me?" murmured Aro rolling his eyes.

"Hey, if I could take you with me I would." Ellendrii knew his friend wouldn't share his excitement but he didn't think he'd take it like this.

"Na it's ok" replied Aro, "I hope you find something nice up there or something." Even though he was jealous at times of Ellendrii's wings, he would never wish anything bad on his best friend. He just found it hard to be happy about an adventure he wasn't involved in.

"I'll try and bring you back something. I dunno what they have up there in the sky but if I can I'll bring you back something?" Ellendrii was trying to improve upon his friend's predicament.

Aro brightened a little; he knew Ellendrii was trying to make up for it. "Yeah sure, bring me back something neat!" He grinned. And all was well again.

Presently, Lunara returned. She was carrying two bags either side of her, thrown over her back like saddle bags, full to bursting with herbs.

"Hi you two, what brings you here? Have you been waiting long? I was out collecting fresh herbs to replace the ones I threw away when I cleared out the tree." She always knew when others were waiting for her to return; she could tell by the proximity at which they sat to her tree. The ones who sat closely to it were most likely waiting for her.

"Long enough!" said Aro. Ellendrii nudged him.

"Not too long. We have a question we wanted to ask" said Ellendrii.

"Ah great, come in and you can ask while I unpack and organise all these" Lunara headed into the tree and the others followed her, sitting down nearby as she slid off the bags and went about unpacking the contents.

"We were wondering if you could find a container to put glowbugs in?" asked Ellendrii.

"Hmm, that's a tough one" Lunara thought about it as she organised her herbs. "A gourd might work, with holes in it? No, wait, they would be able to get out of the holes…Hmm…"

"We need something they can't escape from but their light can still be seen" said Aro.

"So you can't just do what we normally do and spread nectar and tree sap on a nearby tree to attract them?" asked Lunara.

"No, we want to carry them with us and don't want them to escape so we need a thing to put them in. I can't think of anything though." Ellendrii explained.

Lunara paused in her work and looked thoughtful.

"Well you could get a large leaf and attract them onto it, then use a vine to tie it at the top and keep them inside? It would have to be a fairly thin leaf though so they gave off a good light and you'd need quite a lot of them inside it to be sure the light was good enough."

"Yes! That's a great idea, thanks Lunara! That'll work perfectly. We could tie a stick to the leaf bundle to carry them with when we umm…go exploring" said Ellendrii. He didn't want to tell Lunara or anyone too much about where they were going because he wasn't sure if they would try to dissuade them. In some Gryphies' eyes the pair of them were still very young, well they kind of were but they were old enough to make their own decisions as Diabloss had said himself. But the fact they were young made others think they would be reckless as a lot of young males were.

After thanking Lunara, Ellendrii and Aro bounded out of the tree and into the Forest to look for something with leaves big enough to use for their glowbug bundle.

It wasn't easy to find either, most of the ground growing leaved plants were bushes, ferns, shrubs, other things they weren't sure what they were but all of them with small leaves.

Ellendrii climbed up to look for any trees that might have larger leaves while Aro searched around the ground. A while later Aro exclaimed that he had found something.

"What is it?" asked Ellendrii, "Suitable?"

"You bet!" Aro showed him the plant he'd found with the large leaves. They were pretty much perfect size although they were a little thick but it didn't matter because Ellendrii said they could just use more glowbugs to compensate and so the light would shine through ok. Ellendrii pulled a leaf off and they took it back to the clearing in the Forest near Lunara's tree.

Evening had set in by now, the glowbugs were just coming out. But Ellendrii and Aro were hungry, they hadn't eaten since sunrise.

"Hey, Aro, you go catch us something to eat. We can share a forest deer if you like. I'll go about setting the trap for the glowbugs. I just need to wipe some sap onto the leaf and get a stick to tie to the top of the bundle once I've got the bugs inside it." Ellendrii told Aro.

"Sure, I'll catch a nice big fat one" grinned Aro, "Make sure to catch lots of glowbugs, we need a lot of light for this adventure. I wonder if it would have been a good idea to actually get two of those leaves so we could each carry a bundle?"

"Oh, NOW you tell me!" snapped Ellendrii, although it had been a good idea, it was just a little late. "Ok, while I wait for the bugs to land on the leaf and drink the sap, I'll fetch another leaf. It won't take long to go back and get another now I know where they are."

Aro nodded and went off to hunt while Ellendrii prepared the leaf to catch the glowbugs and went to get another one.

By the time Aro got back with his kill, Ellendrii was just tying the second leaf to its stick. It hadn't been hard encouraging the glowbugs to land on the leaves and eat the bait.

Ellendrii joined Aro in the meal after he'd tied the bundle to the stick. Aro had caught a young plump forest deer. It was tender and tasty although not very big. Ellendrii didn't complain though; he was too hungry. So they ate in silence. Aro could get a little greedy towards the end of a meal; it was his nature. Lizariaouses rarely shared their food and when they did, they always fought over the leftovers. He did try and restrain himself with Ellendrii though; another reason Ellendrii had had the leg the other sun cycle; because Aro hadn't wanted to get competitive over it so he'd just told him to take it and save it for later.

This time Ellendrii let Aro eat the rest of the deer while he went and picked up the leafy bundles containing the glowbugs. They cast a cosy glow over the tree trunks and what was left of the forest deer while Aro devoured it. Which kind of ruined the cosiness.

Ellendrii sat back on his hind legs and held the stick in his hand, stretching out his arm and slowly shining it over the Forest clearing they were sat in. He liked this; he would have to remember it for another time. It was a useful way of carrying light with them.

Aro finished and sat back, yawning.

"So, are we ready?" he asked.

"So long as you're finished" smirked Ellendrii. Aro nodded.

"Can't you see I'm finished?" Aro motioned to the ground before him. Lizariaouses always ate all of a kill, including the bones. Gryphies could eat smaller bones but tended not to, being more dainty eaters. Lizariaouses with their broad heads and strong jaws could crunch through anything. So all that was left of the unfortunate forest deer was a blood stain on the ground.

Ellendrii was being sarcastic but it had flown right over the head of Aro. Ellendrii shrugged.

"Yes I can see you're finished. So, shall we go check out this tunnel?"

"You bet!" replied Aro, excited now. He had no idea what to expect from the tunnel or where it would lead or even if it would lead anywhere but at least now with the glowbug bundles they would find out! Ellendrii was dreading getting muddy again. It would have been ok apart from the smell.

He handed Aro the stick he'd been holding and picked up the other one. Aro, not having hands, had to carry his in his mouth. Ellendrii walked upright on two legs and lead the way into the Forest and back to the strange tunnel.

Chapter 3
The Tunnel

As they walked deeper into the Forest, it got much darker. It was normally fairly dark where the trees grew up more thickly but at moon cycle it was nearly impossible to see unless there were glowbugs to help them. Normally the ones on the trees would be enough but of course the two of them were heading much deeper into the Forest than the bugs normally settled or the Gryphies coated the trees with sap and nectar. A few flew past here and there but that was about it.

However, with their glowbug bundle lights, Ellendrii and Aro had no problem finding their way back to the weird tunnel.

When they got there, Ellendrii dropped down onto all fours and held the stick in his mouth. He headed into the tunnel but Aro stepped on his tail and made him pause and look back at him. Aro took the stick out of his mouth.

"Hey can I go first, this *was* my idea" said Aro. Ellendrii took the stick out of his own mouth to speak.

"Sure, and if there's anything nasty hanging down impeding our journey, you can be the one to walk into it first and clear it back for me!" Ellendrii grinned. Aro was starting to regret his request. But he walked around Ellendrii and went in first anyway.

Ellendrii followed. The glowbugs lit the way very well although making their way through the tunnel was difficult at times again and they had to crawl.

Ellendrii wrinkled his nose. There was that horrid smell again. It really did smell like death. It COULD be damp but it was most likely something rotting. Ellendrii hoped it was only plant matter and that they hadn't stumbled across something more macabre.

Neither spoke since they were both carrying their bundle lanterns in their mouths. Ellendrii was quite glad of this, given Aro's excitement; he would probably be nattering away by now about their exciting situation had his mouth not been full.

Ellendrii followed behind him at a safe distance in case he stopped suddenly and smacked the Gryphie with his tail blade. He needn't have worried though as Aro ploughed through everything, determined to get to the bottom of the mystery and the tunnel. Ellendrii only hoped it was worth it and that it wouldn't lead to something really boring like just out the other end and back into the Forest.

Aro eagerly continued, not caring that he brushed through soggy cobwebs or the slime on the ground. It was quite slippery in places and he nearly stumbled. Ellendrii hated the mud and slime. Gryphies are much cleaner than Lizariaouses. They were both glad of the lanterns though, it was so dark that when they had entered before, they hadn't even been able to see their feet in front of their faces.

Presently, it got lower and they resorted to crawling. Both of them, more so Ellendrii, were trying to hold the lanterns up higher so they didn't drag on the ground and break. Without them they would have to back out and leave their exploration. But they didn't break and soon the ceiling got a little higher, although the tunnel was still narrow. Ellendrii held his wings in close to himself because the walls seemed to be oozing with mud as well and he didn't want to scrape them or get them dirtier than he had to.

Aro had trouble with his needles and the ceiling, so when they crawled, he had pointed them backward, flat along his spine. Another reason that Ellendrii kept a safe distance away! He was half afraid the Lizariaous would fire one off by accident, especially if something took him by surprise. But they seemed to be alone in this dark mucky tunnel. They couldn't smell any other creatures at least, only the dank damp smell and that of the rotting (hopefully) plants. Why would any creatures be stupid enough to enter this place anyway? That's what Ellendrii wondered. He looked at his friend's tail, illuminated by the leafy lantern. Was his friend so adventurous that he was stupid? Ellendrii pondered this as they crawled along. Not really, he thought. After all, Ellendrii himself wanted to visit the Sky Gryphies and get into their Elite Flyers. That was pretty crazy in itself! Crazy. Not stupid.

He remembered his father telling him of when he tried the crazy idea of reasoning with Zephirak back before the war. That wasn't stupid either, but it was crazy. Ellendrii wanted to be as bold and daring as his father but again, not stupid. There was a difference. Having no reasonable way to speak gave way for them both to think.

Aro was still thinking of nothing but what he would find at the end of the tunnel. The smell was getting worse now though; it stung his nostrils. He wished he could close them but then he would have to breathe through his mouth and that was a problem due to the stick he held in his teeth. He stared ahead as well as his eyes could see; which wasn't very well considering he was carrying a glowbug lantern. His eyes were adjusted to the light of that and not the dark of the tunnel. He saw nothing beyond his immediate surroundings, which was pitch black of course.

They crawled mostly, for a while and then suddenly Aro slipped and fell onto his tummy, sliding down a steep slope that he hadn't seen coming. He gritted his teeth but Ellendrii could hear his cry of anguish at being taken by surprise at the sudden change in the level of their current terrain. Ellendrii crawled more slowly at this but even he didn't see it coming and it was so slippery that no matter how slowly he was going, he wouldn't have been able to stop himself from sliding. And he slid after his friend.

He nearly opened his mouth to roar in surprise but remembered the stick so he gritted his teeth in the way Aro had done and managed to keep hold of it.

Meanwhile, Aro had found the bottom of wherever they were and slid to a halt. He was just picking himself up when Ellendrii slid right into him and sent him careening into the far wall of wherever they were. This caused Aro to drop his lantern and roar in surprise. Luckily both he and the lantern were unharmed. Ellendrii picked himself up.

"Sorry Aro, I slid right into you didn't I?" Ellendrii sat back, holding his lantern in his hand and shone it around for his friend, who he found a little way away near the wall, also picking himself up. Again.

"Yes, you did" replied Aro grumpily.

"I didn't mean to! I didn't know that incline was there. I tried to stop myself but it was too slippery! Blegh! My tummy's all muddy!" Ellendrii ran his other hand down his front and lifted it off, dripping with muddy goo.

Aro was too busy walking around and shining his lantern around wherever they were. There were holes in the walls, small ones. The smell was coming from them. Aro tried to peer into one with the lantern but the closer he got, the worse the smell was so he wasn't able to see much. All he could see was some sort of congealed goo at the far end of the little tunnel but he couldn't stand the smell long enough to hold the lantern there for as long as he needed to look in order to find out what exactly it was.

Ellendrii, sat on his haunches, reached his arm up to the low ceiling and shone his lantern around. The ceiling was too low for him to actually stand up tall on his back legs so he had to make do with sitting instead. He couldn't see much more than Aro. Just holes in the walls; all the walls. The walls were curved, the "room" they were in was a circular chamber. There were some places without holes but they were few. Ellendrii shone his own lantern into a hole nearby to him but this one was empty. He reached a hand bravely into the little tunnel but found nothing. Aro squirmed when he did this; afraid he would withdraw his hand with something horrid dripping off it. But nothing. This little tunnel was empty. What he couldn't understand was why some of the tunnels smelt of death in varying forms of pungency. Some stank of it. Others not so much. But the ones that smelled the most of course were the ones that they couldn't hold the lanterns near to long enough before they had to withdraw due to the smell, so those were the ones that they had no idea of the contents.

"This is SO weird, what the grik is in these things? I wish they didn't grikking smell so much!" Aro was starting to get annoyed. Now they were here, they *had* to solve the mystery of the place! He wouldn't leave until they had. Besides, his nose was getting used to it now anyway. Not that he enjoyed it any more though.

"I dunno. Let's have a better look at these tunnels. Check each one. We've ascertained that the smelliest ones contain something and the ones that don't smell don't contain anything. So, someone is putting things in these tunnels that smell. And some are just empty, which is why they don't smell. But what exactly are they putting in them?" Ellendrii would have continued but Aro gasped which cut off his speech. Ellendrii rushed over to his friend. The room they were in was pretty big despite the low ceiling.

"Look! A dead Furmine!" Aro pointed with a claw to one of the tunnels. A tail could be seen, the tip of which hung over the edge of the entrance of the little tunnel. Ellendrii looked at it and then gave it a tug, pulling out the contents of the tunnel. And it was indeed, a dead Furmine. Having gone through rigor mortis, the little animal was now limp and soggy due to its internal organs melting down inside it and it over balanced on the edge of the tunnel's entrance and flopped onto the ground below. Ellendrii had pulled it out too far and it had slipped. Its brown fur was dull and slightly maggoty. The two of them grimaced. Aro poked it with his tail blade. Because that's what you do. You know the thing is dead but the need to poke it is always there. Just in case.

The Furmine lay limply on the floor before them, eyes sunken in blindly.

"So this is a storage place? Someone is storing dead things here?" asked Aro.

"I dunno, let's have a look at some of the other tunnels" replied Ellendrii. The Furmine wasn't fresh but seeing it was making the Gryphie feel hungry.

They carried on looking and soon found another dead Furmine, this one was fresher and younger too. It had a broken neck. They assumed this was how it had died. Accident or predator? They didn't know.

"Well, whoever put them here isn't here now so why don't we tuck in?" Ellendrii suggested. Aro was really surprised. Ellendrii normally went by the rules. Normally it was Aro who suggested things like stealing food. But after all the two of them were wild animals anyway, even if the Gryphies were more civilised. And they were young and the young have less morals than the old. Stealing was naughty but they thought it couldn't hurt so they prepared to tuck into the freshest dead Furmines they had found.

Suddenly there was a loud squeal that made them both look round. At an entrance to the room they hadn't noticed stood a small brown Furmine looking very agitated.

"Please don't eat our dead!" he squealed. "If you do, I'll get in so much trouble! I'm supposed to protect this place and keep it hidden. Please don't snack on our deceased!" The little creature jumped about in fear, afraid also that the pair would snack on him as well!

"These are your dead?" asked Ellendrii. "You have a place you keep your dead?" This really surprised the both of them. Furmines were meal creatures, they didn't think they were intelligent enough to do anything like this, much less actually have a place they stored their dead, like a grave or what we could call a morgue.

"Yes! This is the Furmine necropolis. We store our dead here so they can't be taken by creatures like you and eaten! If one of us gets old or dies or even gets killed by a hunter like you, we bring them here and place them in a tunnel. It's called a grave chamber and this is the morgue of eternal rest, where they can sleep forever in peace. I am Flynn, the Morgue Master. Protector of the dead!"

Ellendrii and Aro looked at each other and put down the dead Furmines they were holding in preparation to eat.

"Sorry" said Ellendrii, "We didn't know. We just thought someone was storing umm…food here…" Flynn fluffed up in annoyance and offence when Ellendrii referred to the Furmine dead as "food".

"Here…" he pushed the two dead Furmines towards Flynn. "You can umm, have them back then…with our apologies." He looked embarrassed. Aro just sat there speechless. A meal creature with some sort of civilisation? None of it made sense to his dull carnivore mind. The Furmines had always been seen as something they just ate and that was that.

Flynn stamped in anger.

"Put them back where you found them! Respect our dead! Carry them carefully! Place them in their chambers!" He snapped with a growl and snarl. For something so small that could be killed so easily, he sure was feisty! Just so you know; a Furmine is about the size of a weasel. They also have long bodies like weasels too and long ears. Longer ears than a rabbit. They are mostly brown with cream bellies and faces and black spots. The colours can vary from Furmine to Furmine though.

Ellendrii, still taken aback, tried to find the right chambers for the dead Furmines. He got his own one right since he had found that one in the first place but he had no idea which tunnel Aro had got his from. Aro pointed to the one he thought it was. But it wasn't. Flynn knew it wasn't. He also knew that this pair weren't to be feared; they were pretty young, not children but not adults and still young enough to be intimidated. Especially due to the surprise they had admitted about the whole thing. So Flynn could intimidate them more. He wanted Ellendrii to put the dead Furmine back in the correct tunnel. Flynn knew which one this was and that that was the way that respect could be paid. At the dead Furmine's little funeral, her body had been put in the very tunnel that Ellendrii had pulled it out of and that was where she was meant to have her forever sleep. Unlike Gryphies, Furmines didn't believe that their dead lived on somewhere else after death; they merely thought they slept forever.

On the fourth try, Ellendrii got it right. Flynn was pretty much irate by this time.

"You say *we're* the stupid ones but you don't even know which grave chamber you took poor Chassia from! Use your nose and your head foolish creature!" snapped Flynn.

"HEY! Shut the grik up or maybe we'll dine on something a little FRESHER!" snarled Aro and leaped at Flynn with a snap. Flynn backed up but was cornered. He lost all of his intimidating confidence and shrank back into a defensive pose, snarling and whimpering.

Ellendrii stepped between them.

"That's enough! I put her back where I found her, Aro, we're not eating Flynn." Aro drew back with a grunt of annoyance.

"Why not! It would stop the little grikker mouthing off" he muttered.

"Because I don't want to eat Furmines now. This whole thing has put me off eating a meal creature that does something like we do."

"Like *you* do" muttered Aro, sitting down. "We just bury our dead, if that."

"Well ok, like Gryphies do then. Whatever. I don't want us eating Flynn. I've never liked eating Furmines anyway, no Gryphies do but we will if we're hungry. When you're hungry, you eat anything. Which is probably why Lizariaouses eat anything; they're always hungry!"

Aro nodded and grinned.

"Anyway, eating something that screams for mercy is unpleasant at the best of times. My parents always taught me that we feed on sea vultures or forest deer, ground birds if we can find them..."

"I've NEVER had a ground bird! I'm dying to try one!" Aro interrupted. "I hate that they're so rare, I heard they're really good. Mum got one for Dad a while back and I tried to nab some but they wouldn't let me. They said it was too small and rare to waste on a kid. I was pretty young back then."

"Yes well, I've only had one once and only cos I nagged Dad for it. He's good at finding them. But even he doesn't find them that often. That's why they're special. If we had them all the time, they would no longer be a special treat."

Flynn sat down and listened to the two of them talking, bored now with it all. He just wanted them to leave. They'd disturbed him enough.

"How did you even find the Furmine necropolis?" he asked them. "It's pretty well hidden; the smells and that horrid narrow tunnel have put off hunters up until now. Why in Shernaron did you decide to explore down here? Hunters are stupid but not that crazy, normally anyway."

Ellendrii ignored the little insult and answered the question.

"It was Aro's idea," he motioned to Aro. "He likes adventuring and exploring and we found this place so we decided to check it out. We made leafy bundles to carry glowbugs in so we could see our way. We did try to go down the tunnel without them but it was too dark."

"Hmm, yes that was the point. Well hidden, dark, smelly, unsociable. I never thought a hunter would be smart enough to actually put glowbugs inside something to see their way. I know you use them on the trees at moon cycle but that's about it."

"Maybe *we're* smarter than you give us credit for too." Ellendrii stated, sitting up straighter.

Flynn pondered this at length. "Maybe" he said.

"Come on, you must know we're not *that* stupid. You guys get around, you must see what Gryphie life is like" said Ellendrii.

"Yes, we see you burn your dead; you don't let them have their eternal sleep. You destroy them, turn them to ashes" retorted Flynn with a snort.

"That's because we believe that the light of Forever is over the water where no Gryphie has flown. That is where they go to fly forever free. The fire turns them to ash, which in turn does what the deceased Gryphie cannot; allows them to fly with the wind. That is why we burn our dead at the rock."

Flynn was silenced. Sure their method was different from the Furmines' but they still had their own rituals and respected their dead. Aro pulled a face at Flynn and stuck his tongue out.

"Well I don't know why *you're* being so cocky. The Gryphies might have the funeral fire for their dead but you just bury them…IF you can be bothered that is." Flynn scoffed at Aro.

"Actually," said Aro, pulling himself up to his full height and placing a paw to his chest, "We Lizariaouses KNOW that the dead go underground and if we leave them on the surface of the ground, they just go there anyway…by themselves. They don't *need* to be buried; they make their way there on their own."

"Well no, actually they just decay and rot. Where everyone can see them." Flynn said, wrinkling his nose. "It's respectful to bury them underground."

Aro sighed. "Well we just let them do it by themselves, like a final rite thing. It works for us, so why knock it?"

"Laziness" muttered Flynn with a small snort. Aro didn't hear so Flynn spoke up. "Fair enough, we're all different then. It's nice to know you hunters actually do something decent when your kind die. There is a tale we tell our pips…babies, then" he explained, "our kids, kittens, the young of our species. Anyway that tale is that when your kind die, you eat them."

The other two looked at him in horror and shock.

"Yes well, it's meant to scare them. It's a scary tale. To keep them in line if you like."

"How does telling them that we *eat* our dead keep them in line?" asked Ellendrii.

"Because they have to fear you, they mustn't be curious or wander too close or you'll hunt them. Well," he looked at Aro, "*you'll* hunt them at least. But we don't trust *your* kind either." He looked back to Ellendrii.

"It's better to be careful than overconfident" said Flynn.

"Well, Gryphies only eat Furmines if they're pushed. Why can't we form some sort of truce? We could all be friends" suggested Ellendrii.

"Oh we tried that. Then Mettalika came along. She ate mostly Furmines before she decided to eat Lizariaouses instead. She used to torture and torment us and tease us, make us beg for mercy and then kill us slowly. Or mutilate us so badly and slowly that we died from shock or blood loss or both. She even had a couple of us for slaves at one point. They only lasted a few sun cycles before she killed them, having grown bored of her little game. After that, the truce ended. We couldn't trust Gryphies anymore. And yes I know it was only one Gryphie but that was bad enough and in the worst possible way too; the things she did to my kind are unspeakable. I saw one once. A kill she did. It still gives me moonmares even now. It haunts me. She took out Texin's eyes and then toyed with him as he stumbled around blindly. And worse. I don't want to talk about it." Flynn's eyes were moist. "So no, we're not going back to getting along or a "truce" that is in the past and we will never be so stupid as to have that happen again."

"But surely you knew Mettalika was mad, why not just stay away from her?" Ellendrii had heard plenty of stories about the terrible Mettalika, whom Zephirak had killed eventually.

"You don't get it do you? When you are hunted, there IS no escape. The hunter is bigger and stronger than you. You don't understand because you're already big, nothing hunts you! You can't escape because they'll just smell you out. They will always find a way to find you." Ellendrii and Aro sat quietly, mulling this over. Flynn was right and they couldn't blame the Furmines for no longer trusting the Gryphies. They weren't to know what Mettalika would do and they couldn't possibly have predicted about how things would turn out with her.

"Ok, fair point Flynn. We can't blame you. And we're sorry if we've judged you and we're also sorry we tried to eat your dead." Ellendrii said, finally. They thought it was probably a good time to leave now.

"I accept your apology" replied Flynn.

"So, how do we get out of here?" asked Ellendrii.

"Not the way you came in. It is impossible to climb back up there. I will show you how to leave." Flynn stood and lead them to the entrance he himself came in by. He lead them through several more circular rooms full of grave chambers and their contents. The pair had to duck and crawl between the rooms though.

They still had their lanterns with them and they were undamaged too, for all the adventure they'd been through.

Finally the exit from the necropolis was reached and they went outside, glad to be out and able to stretch themselves and not have to duck and crawl all the time.

"You won't tell anyone about this will you? Because if you do, I will know it was you who told and I will call the other Furmines and we will exact our revenge on the pair of you." Flynn warned them. When he'd started speaking, he'd sounded a little meek and submissive. But then he'd issued the threat. It was a warning that even though the Furmines were small, they were still not to be messed with and had to be respected. Ellendrii and Aro were happy enough to do that.

"Don't worry, we won't tell anyone" said Aro, before Ellendrii could speak. Ellendrii was surprised he'd spoken up so fast. He wondered if Aro was secretly a bit scared of the little mammals.

"Thank you" said Flynn, with a bow of his head. Then he bounded back down the hole into the necropolis again and out of sight leaving the two young adventurers stood in the dark with their lanterns.

"Well, that was weird" said Aro. "I certainly never expected that to happen. Who'dve thought Furmines were *that* civilised?"

"Yeah, they're even more civilised than you!" joked Ellendrii. Aro shoved him in mock annoyance. In a way, Ellendrii was right.

"Anyway, let's get back home. I'm tired now" said Ellendrii and Aro nodded in agreement.

"Where are we?" asked Aro, looking around. They hadn't actually got their bearings after they'd left the underground graveyard and now they looked around, shining their lanterns. Ellendrii stood upright and held his lantern out, shining it around.

"Ahh, I know where we are. We're not far from the tunnel we went in by. That's odd. I wonder why the tunnel was so horrid and stinky, clearly a decoy and the other entrance to it is hidden but not as hard to find?" Ellendrii pondered.

"Because," replied Aro, "this entrance is further away from where you guys live so I'm guessing the Furmines wouldn't think it would be as easy to find." Aro sniffed. "Also this entrance stinks of death as well. No one in their right mind would think to go in here."

"Ah but someone in the right mind thought to go in the other entrance, which was the one that was far worse?" smirked Ellendrii.

"Of course! Adventurers always choose the right place to explore! The one that looks least like anyone would want to explore it because that one will always be the mystery!" Aro said proudly.

"I'll remember that" replied Ellendrii. "Because then I can distract you from the least appealing places!"

Aro laughed. "Yeah right, you'll never keep me from exploring the best places!"

They laughed together and walked back to the clearing. Saying goodbye to each other, Aro went on his way back to Dyarkroeen and Ellendrii went back to the tree he shared with his parents. They both still had their lanterns. Aro had taken his to see the way over the outlands. He didn't want to throw it away but he knew that the glowbugs would die if they weren't released. When he reached the edge of the Lizariaous territory, he released the little insects into the sky and watched them fly back to the Forest. They only lived in the Forest and not in Dyarkroeen, which was why they returned. Aro found something strangely comforting in the little procession of glowing bugs that flew into the moonlit sky and he watched them until they faded from view. The moon was half and high in the sky. It cast a good enough light that he could find his way back to his cave without the light from the lantern anyway.

Meanwhile Ellendrii had climbed the tree, passed his sleeping parents and up to his perch at the top. He released his glowbugs too. They flew onto the trunk of the tree and ate the sap there, sticking around to gently light the large branch Ellendrii slept on. He settled down. He'd enjoyed the adventure; he was glad he had a friend in Aro, the Lizariaous certainly made life more interesting. But of course in a couple of sun cycles, Ellendrii would be going to visit the Sky Gryphies. His biggest adventure was only just beginning!

*****

The next sun cycle, Ellendrii was up a little later than usual. Leida climbed up to see why he wasn't awake and dodging clouds like he normally did. She found him sleeping soundly, flopped over his branch.

"Are you going to get up and enjoy the sun?" she asked him, nudging him with her wing. He opened an eye.

"Just five more minutes, Mum" he murmured.

"It's nearly mid-sun. When did you go to sleep?" she asked him, concerned.

"I dunno, pretty late. Aro and I were exploring a Furmine necropolis! We found out Furmines also respect their dead and they put them in little underground tunnels called grave chambers."

Leida raised an eyebrow. "Really. Are you sure you weren't dreaming?" she asked, sceptically.

"No, seriously! Only, I'm not allowed to show anyone where the necropolis is. So I can't show you unfortunately." Ellendrii looked a bit downcast at this sudden remembrance.

"Well, if you say so" replied Leida. "Are you coming to eat?" she asked.

"No, I'm not hungry. I'm gunna go fly over to Dyarkroeen and see if Aro's about. I want to say good bye to him before I visit the Sky Gryphies."

"Oh yeah, the Sky Gryphies. I forgot you were going to visit them" said Leida.

"You're still ok with it aren't you?" asked Ellendrii.

"Of course! So long as you promise to stay safe and not get on their nerves and remember your manners. You know, all that." Leida grinned. Ellendrii grinned back. She knew he'd be ok and look after himself. He was a smart young Gryphie.

"Ok, we'll see you later then" she said as he climbed to the top of the tree and launched himself into the sky. He waved goodbye and set off for Dyarkroeen.

When he got there, Aro wasn't up either. He was sleeping in his cave, quite peacefully, on some dry grass at the back. It was dark and cool inside the cave, cooler than the hot sun outside. Ellendrii was never bothered about the sun making him too hot as he slept because the leaves on the upper parts of the tree shaded him. He'd been over to see Aro loads of times but the enthusiastic Aro usually came to the Forest to meet with Ellendrii.

"Hey Aro, it's mid-sun! Wake up! You gunna sleep all sun cycle? I'm off to see the Sky Gryphies in the next sun cycle and I'll be up early so we won't have a chance to catch up until I get back. I'm assuming you wanted to hang out before I went up there?"

Aro had stirred when he heard Ellendrii enter the cave and he lifted his head.

"Mid-sun already?" he asked sleepily. Ellendrii nodded and Aro slowly pulled himself into a sleepy sitting position with a yawn.

"Well then, we'd better get hunting! Wanna hang out over here instead of going back to the Forest? It's easier for you to fly back than for me to walk back over here." Aro wondered why he didn't invite Ellendrii over more often.

"Sure, let's go! I feel rested and ready!" In truth, Ellendrii was too excited for next sun and flying to see the Sky Gryphies. He really wanted to learn more about their culture and see if they would teach him any new sky tricks. But at the same time he didn't want to talk about it too much to Aro because the Lizariaous might get upset, since he already had a small jealousy for Ellendrii's wings and flying, though it was in a different way to how the other young Gryphies felt. So Ellendrii kept quiet about it. For now.

For their meal, they decided to catch cave cats. Ellendrii actually thought cave cats were sort of cute but they had a nasty scratchy streak if cornered so he was happy enough to flame grill one. Which he did. He cornered it in a cave and flamed it to a crisp.

Aro was a little jealous of that too. He liked raw meat but there was something appealing about cooked meat as well, which of course unless he asked Ellendrii to cook it for him, he couldn't have. He hunted a family of cave cats in another cave. A mother with a litter of seven kits. He managed to get one kit but the mother scratched him several times. His thick skin prevented too much of a deep wound but she still made him bleed. Like a paper cut, the kind that really stings and itches and bleeds a little. The smaller wounds always seem to hurt more.

They ate their kills sitting on top of Zephirak's old cave. No one lived in there but there was a tree that grew over it so they had some shade and a good view of the territory around them. Aro saw his sisters, Scit and Zixiniss playing together in the distance.

Scit was pale grey with blue scales and green eyes and Zixiniss was rusty orange like her mother but with purple scales instead of brown and also had green eyes. Neither of them were into adventuring or exploring.

"Hey you two!" a voice called up. It was Mordred.

"Oh, hi Dad" replied Aro, instinctively scarfing down the rest of his cave kit. Even parent Lizariaouses stole food from their kids sometimes. It was not unknown. But Mordred never had. Schaarl had a couple of times however. And for this reason Aro was defensive with his food around his parents.

"Up to much this sun cycle?" asked Mordred.

"Just hanging out before Ellendrii goes to see the Sky Gryphies" muttered Aro. So it *had* been on his mind.

"The Sky Gryphies?" asked Mordred, "aren't they the ones that live so high up no one can reach them and they never come down to the ground?"

"Yes!" replied Ellendrii. "Next sun I'm going to see them. They might be able to teach me something about flying or some new tricks or something."

"I heard they have the opposite of vertigo. That is, a fear of low places instead of a fear of heights" smirked Mordred.

"That's odd" replied Aro, "Why are they scared of the ground?"

"I dunno, I guess cos they're used to being up high?" Mordred suggested.

"How stupid, they have floating islands, if they land on those then they're on the ground" said Aro pointedly.

"Yes but they are still up high, think about it" replied Mordred. Aro thought and it dawned on him.

"Oh yeah" he replied.

"Well, good luck with it!" Mordred said to Ellendrii and left them sat in the sun.

After Ellendrii finished his cave cat (and Aro had eaten the bones) they went for a walk and chatted, mostly about the adventure from the previous moon cycle.

They hung out until the sun began to set and Ellendrii insisted on going back to the Forest so he could get an early sleep because he wanted to be up before sunrise. He had no idea how long it would take to fly up to the land of the Sky Gryphies or where he should even start flying from. He guessed he should fly back to where he saw the mist above the clouds and start from there. If he kept the mist in sight while he was flying, he was sure that he would be able to reach the floating islands eventually.

So he bid Aro farewell and flew back to the Forest.

His parents had got back to the tree with a fresh kill of a forest deer for their dinner. Ellendrii had caught a sea vulture on his way home and was carrying it in his hand, by its feet, as he flew. He didn't want too big a dinner because he had the long flight tomorrow. He would of course have to get breakfast and that would probably be another sea vulture since he had seen the mist somewhere near the coast. If they had floating islands, he assumed they might be over the sea because he had never seen them obscure the sun. Or that they were so high up, they just couldn't be seen and didn't affect the land below as his father had told him.

As he sat on his branch eating, he thought long and hard about what he was about to do. He suddenly had his first feelings of apprehension. What if the Sky Gryphies didn't like him? What if they were hostile? What if they chased him away because he was a Forest Gryphie? What if they attacked him? These were all worrying things to ponder and for the first time Ellendrii looked at the adventure from a different perspective. His expression hardened. No, he would not let it get him down or discourage him. If he didn't do this, if he didn't visit them and find out about them for himself, he would always regret it for the rest of his life. So he would visit them and he would overcome any problems he encountered. He would face any hostility they came at him with and he would conquer it. After all, they should be happy someone else wanted to learn about them and their culture. Unless they were really stuck up or something. Diabloss had told him they were quite full of themselves and looked down upon the Forest Gryphies in many ways. Surely in that case they would be happy to share their knowledge with him? He hoped so!

After his meal he settled down to sleep. He had said goodbye to his parents when he got back earlier, because he would probably fly out before they rose. He decided on flying out when the sun had just risen, so it was light enough to see the mist and catch his meal for breakfast. He found it hard to get to sleep for his excitement. He tossed and turned and squirmed and sighed and growled a little. He'd gone to bed early! He didn't want to spend half the moon cycle awake or it would have been for nothing.

However, finally, exhausted from all his wriggling and repositioning, he fell into a dream filled sleep.

Chapter 4
Into the Sky

The first light of the sun was just starting to shine down on the Forest when Ellendrii awoke with a start. His memory slowly coming back with his consciousness, he realized what he was going to do this sun cycle and hurriedly climbed up the tree, shaking himself fully awake when he got to the top before leaping into the sky and spreading his wings.

He flew to the coast and caught himself a sea vulture for breakfast. He dived on it, trying to catch one as fast as possible and as luck would have it, he found one by itself on the cliff, snuck up on it and broke its neck before it even knew what was going on.

He ate it maybe a little too fast and nearly burped it back up again. Only one thing was on his mind; reaching those floating islands he'd heard of and making contact with the Sky Gryphies! He wished he'd known about them sooner but then again if he had known about them when he was a kitten, he would have wanted to see them sooner and it might have clouded other things he'd wanted to do.

He looked up at the sky as he ate, thinking about where he should set off from. He saw the mist in the distance. It didn't seem that far but then again the metal mountains didn't seem that far but they were. Still, he knew by wing it was faster to get to a place than on foot. He wondered if it was the same with the sky and reaching places there. He also started to think about the altitude his father had told him about. He might not be able to handle it and he might not even be able to reach the floating islands. How disappointing that would be! Still, he would try his best. After all, other Forest Gryphies had been up there including his father. He thought about what Diabloss had told him about not being allowed to land on the islands themselves and he wondered where the meeting place was. He wished he'd asked his father first but this was something he really wanted to do by himself, with no help. Kind of a coming of age thing, something that would make him feel truly like an adult and not a kitten that needed help from its parents or friends. Of course he had no friends that could help anyway and he was happy that his parents had given him the freedom to do this.

Finally the time had come for him to leave. He leaped off the edge of the cliff, spread his wings, glided a little and then swooped upward to the sky, towards the clouds.

He turned in the air and faced the mist, heading for that. It was so far away. He reached the level of the clouds and flew through them, soaring and flapping his wings hard to gain altitude. The weather was luckily fine, no wind to hinder him, just a calm breeze which got a little stronger the higher he ascended.

Now he could feel the air getting thinner. Flying was becoming a bit of a chore. Before, when he flapped his wings, it had been easy; second nature. Now he was struggling but only slightly. He had definitely noticed the change in the air. It was harder to breathe. He'd never ever been up this high before. He'd passed all the birds and most of the clouds. He could see the mist getting closer but still not close enough to enter it. His muscles hurt from the exertion, his throat caught when he breathed. He felt a little bit like he was suffocating. But still his determination wouldn't allow him to give up. He needed to get to an island; he needed to find out more about these Sky Gryphies. He needed to rest. He decided to hover for a bit and see if he could catch his breath back. It wasn't working that well really. Hovering seemed to take up just as much energy. So he carried on. He'd flown up higher than the clouds now; he was getting closer to his goal! Just a little further and he'd be in the mist!

Finally, with a lot of flapping and struggling, he'd made it into the mist! Now he looked around for an island. He let go of the idea of getting to whatever meeting place was up there. He needed to rest and get used to the altitude so his main concern was finding anywhere to land.

He ascended higher and higher, feeling a little more at home with the thin air and saw an island in the distance. It was a strange phenomenon. On the top it looked like an island you might find in the sea but of course without the beach and with more rocks and trees. There was also a structure on it that shone in the sunlight and sparkled with ever changing light.

Ellendrii headed for it. He had no idea how long he'd been flying but it felt SO good to land and have a rest. He lay down on the ground after he landed, pacing his breathing and getting used to the atmosphere. He peered over the edge of the island, all he saw was mist. He'd not seen another Gryphie since he'd got here. In a way he was glad because they might have told him to get back or flamed him or something. It is easier to gain forgiveness than permission. That was something Aro had told him a while ago when they'd stolen some meat from one of the stocks the Lizariaouses kept in their caves. Aro always did this when he was too lazy to hunt.

Recovering from his flight and slowly gaining back his energy, Ellendrii looked at his surroundings. The island was full of trees. They got water from another cloud layer above the island. The air was cool and refreshing. The huge structure that had stood out to him earlier was some sort of cave with many holes in it. As he looked closer, he saw Sky Gryphies flying in and out of the holes. This must be where they live he thought. They were a marvel to look at. The scales on their undersides shone in the sun in a similar fashion to the structure he was now looking at. The base of the structure was fairly plain; a lot of it was hidden by the green trees. But as the great cave-like thing got higher, it was more and more ornamental. The upper part with the holes in was the most splendid and ornamental part. Each hole was decorated differently from the rest. Ellendrii supposed it was due to each individual's taste. There seemed to be no bottom entrance to the structure. So there was no walking into this cave; only flying.

He sat up, still gazing at this amazing thing unlike anything he'd ever seen before.

"HEY! HEY YOU!! WHAT ARE YOU DOING HERE??" a voice demanded and Ellendrii spun round, taken by surprise.

A Sky Gryphie whose fur was the colour of the sunset and spotted with cloud-like markings stormed up to him. The Gryphie had feathers about his head that flared outward in anger and long feathers at the back of his front and back legs, which also flared out in the same manner, although not as much as the ones on his head. He had small feathers dotting the base of his wings where the "arm" part joined his body, silver eyes and an elegant tail fin. His wings had only two fingers; a longer, tapered one and a shorter one, joined by a beautiful satin membrane that was pretty much transparent. All the feathers aside from the ones at the base of his wings were brightly coloured and Ellendrii immediately felt intimidated by him. He was covered in a short, soft, dense fur similar to the Forest Gryphies but he also had beautiful shimmering cerulean scales running from under his neck to midway down his tail. They shone in the sunlight in a spectacular way, with hues of purple.

"FOREST GRYPHIES ARE NOT ALLOWED ON THESE ISLANDS!! LEAVE NOW!!!" the Sky Gryphie snarled, hackles raised and a threatening stance taken up as he advanced upon Ellendrii.

Ellendrii backed up and showed submission, ears back and body close to the ground, wings gathered about him to protect himself and his tail between his legs. He didn't look his assailant in the eyes, but bowed his head to the ground instead.

"Please, I only came to find out more about the Sky Gryphies I had heard so many wonderful things about! I wanted to learn more about your life and culture. I love to fly, that is why I'm here. I wanted to learn your wisdom." Ellendrii spoke quietly.

"Our wisdom?" questioned the Sky Gryphie, "you heard wonderful things about us? Don't make me laugh, Forest Gryphie. Your kind is not welcome here. You can't even stand our thin air and it is absolutely forbidden to land on any of our islands. Our agreement with you dictates that only the meeting island is to be landed on."

"I couldn't find it. This was the first island I came across and I landed here to rest. If you will show me the way I would be happy to alight on the meeting island." Ellendrii's head was still bowed.

"Show you the way? Certainly not! You've already broken the code by landing here, why would I offer you anything more than chasing your sorry tail away from our lands? How long have you been here? No matter, even if you do stay where you are, you will have to return to the dreaded ground soon enough. No Forest Gryphie can stand our altitude for long. If you stay, you won't be able to breathe. And you'll die and I won't be knocking you off the island to save you. You can lay down and sleep forever. Only once you pass your last breath will I push you off." The Sky Gryphie snorted.

"So you'd have me "contaminate" this place with my death as well as my life?" asked Ellendrii, still avoiding eye contact.

The Sky Gryphie thought about this and couldn't answer. He'd made a bit of a fool of himself and didn't want to correct himself so he asked why Ellendrii was there instead, that is the real reason he was there since he didn't believe Ellendrii had flown all that way because of the "wonderful" things he'd heard about them. Forest Gryphies never had anything good to say about Sky Gryphies, any more than Sky Gryphies had good things to say about Forest Gryphies. Certainly the latter anyway.

"I came up here to learn more about your Elite Flyers" admitted Ellendrii finally.

"The Sky Gryphie Elite Flyers? Pfft you would NEVER be accepted into the league of the best of the best! Why would you even think you would have a chance? One of Diabloss's squadron tried to get into our Flyers and we sent her packing. It was a crazy thought, she could barely breathe up here! Wait, how is it you're breathing ok?" The Sky Gryphie advanced on him, studying him carefully.

"I got used to it after a while" replied Ellendrii simply. "If it's not too much trouble and since I'm not going to stop breathing and die here, could you show me around please? I would love to learn more and that structure over there is fascinating and beautiful."

"That is a Sky Temple. We have them on all the islands and that is where we live. Sierra and I have our own temple and our own island all to ourselves because we are the rulers of this realm" explained the Gryphie; Ellendrii's little compliments were now beginning to soften him a little. He figured this Forest Gryphie would leave if he was hospitable instead of hostile and explained it carefully in a way a stupid ground Gryphie could understand. Then he would realize why Forest Gryphies couldn't get into the Elite Flyers.

"Ah ,so you must be Reo" observed Ellendrii.

"Yes, my sister is Sierra" replied Reo.

"I'm Ellendrii, son of Diabloss and Leida" said Ellendrii. He maintained a slight amount of eye contact by this time, his confidence having grown somewhat.

"I see. Yes I guess only the son of Diabloss could be reckless enough to try to come up here." Reo snorted.

"Have you ever been down to the Forest?" asked Ellendrii.

Reo snorted again. "No. No Sky Gryphie would ever go down there. Why would we? The Forest is an ugly, dark place. There are no clouds and no sun and too many trees and there's…dirt." Reo shuddered.

"But there's dirt up here" Ellendrii pointed out, running a hand over the ground where he sat before Reo.

"Yes but this dirt is clean, it is of the sky! Not of the land or the filthy Forest" Reo spat with distaste.

Ellendrii was a little insulted he had to admit.

"Why do you guys dislike us so much?" he asked. "We've never done anything to you."

"True, but you come from down…there…" Reo pointed over the edge of the island and made a face.

Ellendrii thought he was really immature for a leader of a whole gathering of Gryphies. He hoped his sister was a little more amiable. He decided to ignore the racist remarks and ask more questions. That was after all, why he had flown up there; to find out more.

"So, tell me more about that extravagant looking temple over there" he said, desperate to change the subject.

"As I said, there is a Sky Temple on every island" Reo resumed, "where Sky Gryphies live. We have flight ledges and reside within the holes you can see in the walls there. The spaces inside are very large, perfectly big enough for families or ample room for single Gryphies. Each temple has

100 of these flight ledges where we can take off and land freely. We built the temples ourselves using white rock crystals found in some of the outlying islands. The facets of the crystals scintillate and shine in the sun, reflecting the heat very effectively. The colourful and beautiful inlays you can see around the ledges are down to each individual resident's preference. We moult the scales on our bellies and use them to decorate the ledges. Each resident uses their own scales on their own ledge and families will decorate them together. Ones that are passed down from generation to generation has each generation add to the decoration to create something beautiful and timeless. The shed scales never decay because they are hard and resilient. So the decoration will last forever. They also do not fade in the sun either. The decoration is like an heirloom for each family's ledge. And it also helps to make the temple look nice." Reo smiled at this. Ellendrii nodded, taking in every word.

"I bet your temple is even more impressive than this one though" marvelled Ellendrii.

"Yes it is" replied Reo with a smile. "And no I won't show you."

"Will you show me something else then?" asked Ellendrii. Reo thought about this for a moment and then nodded.

"I'll take you on a tour of the Skylands" he said finally. He figured also that Ellendrii would become intolerant to the thin air if they were flying and soon give up and go. With that, Reo leaped off the edge of the island they were on, spreading his wings and soaring into the sky. Ellendrii followed without much difficulty.

"Come on then, keep up. Each Skyland is a little way from the others. They move slightly and the distance between them is important, to ensure they don't collide with each other." Reo told him as they flew. Ellendrii annoyingly had no problem keeping up so Reo flew faster.

They flew to the next Skyland and around it as Reo told Ellendrii about the types of plants that grew there and the temple on that Skyland. This temple was a slightly different shape to the one before it. Ellendrii soon found out that each temple was unique according to the Sky Gryphies who had built them. They would build more on other islands as their population slowly grew over the years. Whereas Lizariaouses have "litters" of up to three or maybe even four kids, the Gryphies only ever had one at a time. They didn't have twins, triplets or any other multiples. Only one kitten and this was also true of the Sky Gryphies as well. They may have a kitten and then breed soon after for another one but it would still only be one that was born at a time. Some of the Skylands didn't have a temple on but instead were covered in trees and other plant life. Ellendrii wondered how trees could grow on them but some of the Skylands were quite big. Also the trees were smaller than the ones back in the Forest and couldn't really be climbed, much less alighted on.

They came to the Skyland where meetings took place with Forest Gryphies or any other meetings the Sky Gryphies might decide to arrange. This was a small, barren island and only had a few bushes growing on it. The rest had been cleared off to, in Reo's words, make it easier for stupid creatures (such as Forest Gryphies of course but he declined to mention that, nonetheless Ellendrii knew exactly what he meant) to find among the other Skylands. Also having no large plants on the meeting place meant that large gatherings could alight on it.

Reo and Ellendrii (who still didn't appear to be suffering the atmosphere) landed on the meeting Skyland and Ellendrii looked down. He couldn't see anything much of the land below. The mist shrouded the Forest, valleys, rivers, swamp, everything. The mist was cloudy and he figured it was because of this that there was more of a separation between the two kinds of Gryphies. They couldn't even see one another when they were all in their own territories so it was much easier to ignore the others' existence. Which was probably how the Sky Gryphies at least, preferred it.

"So, what do you eat?" asked Ellendrii.

"We eat the berries that grow on some of the trees here and sometimes we catch high flying birds. Due to the nature of the Skylands, being in the sky and all, there are no meal creatures on them. Anything living on them would probably have to fly and we've never seen anything of that kind. We sometimes eat bugs since they live in the trees and on the plants though."

Ellendrii wrinkled his nose at that. He'd never eaten a bug and didn't intend to. The Forest Gryphies were more for hunting properly. He had noticed how much slimmer the Sky Gryphie was to him though. They had slimmer legs and seemed lighter altogether so he figured they might not need to eat much or might indeed be slim because they didn't eat much. Or because they flew a lot and burned it all off.

Just then another Sky Gryphie alighted beside them. This one was female and the colour of sunrise, again spotted with cloud type markings in a similar way to Reo. She had golden eyes and much longer feathers on either side of her head than him although her crest feathers weren't as long. She shared his long leg feathers though. Her tail fin was a different shape but with the same thin membrane connecting the points of it, like her wings and her scales were a beautiful shade of aqua with hues of pink that shone in the sun.

"Ah Sierra!" said Reo and Ellendrii knew this was the other leader, Reo's sister.

"Who is…this?" asked Sierra, pointing to Ellendrii with distain.

"A Forest Gryphie who made his way up here, I'm showing him around" then in a lower voice Reo muttered to her, "I'm hoping he'll either get bored and go or the air will weaken him and he'll go." Sierra nodded. Then she walked up to Ellendrii and stood over him.

"I'm Sierra, Reo's sister. We rule over the Sky Gryphies and make sure everything runs smoothly. We run a good empire up here, good and pure."

"I told him that already" muttered Reo. Sierra held her wings out in a daunting manner, wordlessly telling him not to correct her because females have a habit of always being right. Reo shut up.

"I'm older than him and I'm smarter than him" she said, holding her head high. Reo rolled his eyes. His sister wasn't that bad but he could see she wanted to set a certain impression to the newcomer; that even though they were siblings, she was slightly more in charge than he was. Reo thought this was very immature; they *were* both adults after all.

"So, how did you come to rule? Were your parents rulers before you?" asked Ellendrii. He thought she was pretty.

"Yes they were. They are old now. When the leaders reach a certain age, the younger ones take their place. They are living a happy retirement in their temple." Sierra explained.

"Do they still get their own temple when they retire, like you do?" asked Ellendrii.

"No, they just go and live in one of the other temples with the other Sky Gryphies"

"But surely that would be stripping them of their authority?"

"Yes, but they aren't leaders anymore. So they have no authority. *We* have the authority." She motioned to herself and Reo.

"So who will take over from you then?" asked Ellendrii.

"Our kittens" replied Sierra, starting to find him a bit stupid now. "Obviously."

"Well you're siblings, surely you can't have kittens together" Ellendrii said cocking his head to one side in puzzlement.

"Well no, obviously we can't. There will be a ritual where one or other of us takes a partner to carry on the line. Most probably that will be me. It's normally the female since females of these colours" she motioned to herself and Reo, "give birth to kittens of these colours whereas if a male of these colours went with a regular blue female, the kittens would come out blue. The male who mates with me won't have anything to do with the raising of the kitten, nor will anyone know who he is. He gets his satisfaction from the honour of keeping the line going and creating more leaders." Sierra explained.

"And what if you have a boy kitten, would you have to have another, who is a girl?" asked Ellendrii.

"The first born is ALWAYS a girl" grunted Reo. Sierra nodded proudly.

"Because that ensures our line. The mother may choose to have more kittens afterwards like our parents did. The next kitten is normally a boy. If it's another girl, only the firstborn will go through to keep the line running. Normally though, the mother only has up to two kittens. Too many leaders and there will be fights. Many many seasons ago, we actually had four leaders. They ended up killing one another."

Ellendrii's eyes widened. "Wow, harsh" he said, "Did any survive?"

"Yes, our mother" replied Sierra. "Luckily"

"Then she had us" put in Reo.

Ellendrii found Reo much easier to get along with now his sister was here. She seemed much more amiable than him.

"Reo wouldn't show me but would you? The temple you two share? I don't want to go in or anything but to marvel at it from the outside would be truly awesome" Ellendrii said.

"Hmm, ok. You can see it." Sierra replied. Her brother gave her a "look" but Sierra ignored him.

"In that case," said Reo, "I'll be off, I have more important things to do." He gave her another look and then flew off. She knew he was pointing out that she was being too soft and making a mistake. But she had agreed to only show him the outside.

So the two of them flew off to the Skyland that the two leaders shared together.

It was a beautiful Skyland, not the biggest but not the smallest either. Most of it was taken up by the most beautiful Sky Temple Ellendrii had seen yet. It was huge and scintillated in the sunlight. It seemed to shine different colours at different angles and was nearly all the shining scales of the Sky Gryphies themselves. Sierra and Ellendrii landed before it and he stared up in awe.

"So do you live here all your life or just while you're leaders, until the next leaders are adults?" asked Ellendrii.

"We will live here until my kitten or kittens are fully grown and become leaders themselves. Reo will continue to live here with me as long as we rule and then we will leave. I will go and live with the partner I chose and he will live in the same temple as us. And before you ask, by the time I move in

81

with that partner, the rest of the Gryphies don't even think that he is the father of the next leader or leaders; it doesn't even occur to them since it is that far in the future. They all tend to think the ritual of the next leader being born is some magical thing. It's really not."

Ellendrii wondered why she was telling him all this since, being a "filthy" Forest Gryphie, he might tell. So he asked her.

"Pfft, they would never believe you" she answered simply. He looked back at the temple Sierra and Reo lived in and wanted to see inside so badly. So he asked this as well.

"Can I see inside, even if we just hover in front of one of the flight ledges and peer in?" he asked politely. Sierra sort of guessed this question would come sooner or later. She sighed.

"Ok, but don't tell Reo I showed you. He'd be totally grikked off with me." Ellendrii nearly jumped for joy. Sierra flew up to one of the ledges and landed on it and he followed but only hovered. She motioned for him to land, so he did, rather gingerly.

"You sure it's ok?" he asked. He was reminded of the many times he and Aro had been sneaky.

"I am one of the rulers of the Sky Gryphies and if I say it's ok, then it is. If you're worried about Reo, he can't do anything anyway. I have more authority than him. Now, come inside." She lead a rather surprised Ellendrii inside and showed him around.

The inside of the temple was a thing of beauty in itself. Although it didn't have the shining scales and the rock crystal wasn't white like outside, the caves or "rooms" within were spacious, airy, really lovely. There was a delicate smell of flowers in the caves within the temple and he soon found out it was because of the plants that grew in there, that Sierra took pride in keeping alive so the flowers bloomed and they gave a nice scent. She told him she preferred growing them because if she picked them, they would die quickly and the smell would not last. They only grew on the ground floor. The temple had a whopping twenty floors. Huge for only two Gryphies but it was an ornate, special place. Each floor had around eight caves. The walls were completely smooth and so shiny that he could see the outline of his body in them. They didn't reflect him precisely, like a mirror, but their forms could be seen reflected on the walls as they walked. The walls were brown stone, like marble.

Sierra lead him around and then up to the very top. They walked out onto the flight ledge and then flew off it and up to the top of the temple, alighting on the flat, white roof. They could see for miles up there. Skyland after Skyland in the distance.

"This Skyland we live on is actually at the centre of all the others so we can see a lot of them from where we are now. It's good to have our friends around us" smiled Sierra and lay down. Ellendrii sat near the edge, looking out with awe at his surroundings.

"You don't seem to be out of breath. How are you finding the air up here?" asked Sierra. Ellendrii turned around and faced her.

"I had some trouble at first but I seem to have adjusted now. I don't feel much different anymore to how the air is where I'm from."

"Interesting. Most Forest Gryphies can't stand the air here for even half as long as you have. How odd."

"Useful though! Because I would love to learn how to join the Sky Gryphie Elite Flyers!" blurted out Ellendrii and immediately regretted it because Sierra burst out laughing. Great. Just when he thought she was nicer than her brother and not a stuck up moron.

"The Sky Gryphie Elite Flyers? The best of the best? YOU! A Forest Gryphie?? I mean, yes you can handle the air up here but that is only the beginning. They have skills beyond anything a Forest Gryphie would be capable of. I mean, most Sky Gryphies aren't even capable of flying like they do. Most of those who go to the flight school of the Elite don't make it through, give up, end up crying like kittens, damage their wings beyond repair. Regret ever even dreaming of joining the Elite. And *you* want to join them? You have no idea do you. No idea at all." She snorted and laughed, nearly rolling around in mirth.

"I want to at least try" said Ellendrii quietly.

83

"For a start, a Forest Gryphie would never be allowed to partake." Sierra said, sitting up.

"And for another thing it would be bad for us too. Letting a, no offence, lesser sub-species enter our elite flying contest. Can you understand that?"

"No. And you're the leader so if you say I should join, they wouldn't argue."

"It would ruin my reputation as a ruler" spat Sierra. "But if you want to see what they can do, I will show you." She figured this would put him off. He had no idea the sorts of flying tricks and stunts they did and maybe if he saw the Elite Flyers in action, he would change his mind. Not that it had worked so far. But a part of her actually wanted him to enter so he would make a fool of himself. That would be funny. Seeing the humiliation of a Forest Gryphie who wanted to be as good as the Sky Gryphies.

"Please show me!" begged Ellendrii, "I would be honoured to see what they are capable of. I'm sure no other Forest Gryphie has."

"Diabloss did once" replied Sierra.

"He's my father" said Ellendrii. Sierra just nodded. It didn't mean much to her really. She knew Diabloss had his own squad of flyers but they were far inferior to the Elite Flyers.

"Come on then, I'll show you" she burst into the air so suddenly that it knocked Ellendrii backwards. He stared up at her for a split second and then joined her in the air.

They flew a fair way. So far that the Skyland they had been on was out of sight. They flew to pretty much the far end of the territory and a wide open expanse of sky with a small floating island at one end. It was only slightly smaller than the meeting place they were at earlier.

She landed on it, followed by Ellendrii. He looked around with wonder. Sierra smirked. Then she threw back her head and roared. Another Sky Gryphie soon flew up to them and landed with them. She had called him. The leader of the Flying Elite.

"Raediaxx, this is Ellendrii. He wants to see the Flyers in action. Think you can sort something out?"

84

Raediaxx looked a little surprised at the fact this was a "thing" from the Forest come to observe them but he would not disobey his ruler so he nodded and flew off.

"Now you will see why you would be useless in their flight" Sierra told him, snarkily.

Ellendrii frowned. He was still determined to do this and now even more determined because he was determined to prove her wrong. Raediaxx had been just a normal coloured Sky Gryphie. Pale blue, like the sky, with asymmetrical cloud-like markings all over his body. Each Sky Gryphie had different markings, which was how of course they told each other apart. And he had a normal sized crest and jaw feathers with feathers only at the back of his front legs, not the hind ones. Ellendrii noticed that only the leaders had the hind leg feathers.

Soon Raediaxx returned with a flight of nine other Sky Gryphies. And they began. And Ellendrii had never ever seen anything like it in his whole life. For a start they were powerful. Their wings were strong and the wind from them strong enough to knock him off his feet. For another thing they were completely without fear. They flew in formation and then broke apart, weaving in and out of one another so close at times that the tips of their fur touched. Or the tips of their wings lightly brushed each other. Then they all paired off, held on to each other's hands and feet and turned cartwheels in the sky endlessly, over and over again, swooping and diving at each other dangerously fast. They weaved their tails together and did amazing flying tricks and stunts working with one another to ensure they didn't hurt themselves or mess up. And then came the endless weaving, diving, turning and swirling in the sky as individuals. It was incredible and beyond anything Ellendrii could even have thought of. It certainly knocked spots off his cloud dodging. Another thing he was now worried about was that the Elite Flyers worked as a team as well as individuals. Who would he have to fly with? None of them liked him. And no one he knew from the Forest could come and fly with him. He wished really badly right now that Aro could fly.

When at last the show was over, Raediaxx bowed in mid-air and Sierra nodded to him. He flew off with the others. Some didn't fly far; they were out practising.

"So, do you still want to join the Flyers?" asked Sierra with a smirk.

"Yes" replied Ellendrii firmly. He wasn't going to come all this way and not at least try to conquer the thing he had decided he actually wanted to do with his life.

Sierra nearly fell over with shock and then shook her head in annoyance.

"You stupid Gryphie, are you blind? Were you not watching? Did you not see what they did?"

"I saw all of it and I want to try to do it myself. Where do I sign up?" after all, Ellendrii had nothing to lose. Well, he might get hurt in the process but he wasn't thinking of anything else but winning right now. Sierra growled in annoyance. Then her face brightened a little as a plan came to mind.

"Ok. Very well then. You want to try? Come back in…three sun cycles. You can enter the flight contest that's taking place then. If you beat every single one of the other flyers, then you can become a part of the Elite. Sound fair?"

"Yes!" replied Ellendrii. Sierra was finding him really really annoying by this time. Stupid determined young Gryphie. She wanted to clip his wings. Permanently. And she knew that if he entered this contest, he wouldn't stand a chance. In fact there wasn't a contest. Elite Flight School was how you got into the Flyers. After many seasons of hard training. But silly Ellendrii wouldn't know that. She could soon arrange a contest and put him against the absolute best and competitive Flyers.

"Very well. I'll allow you to enter." She looked calm but he could see her tail gave her away because it was swishing in a similar fashion to an irate cave cat. This amused him.

"So I just come here in three sun cycles?" he asked.

"Yes, come to this flight island. The contest starts at mid-sun. So be ready!" she replied. The hottest time of the sun cycle. That would make it even harder for him. Serves him right for being cocky! Ellendrii actually did jump for joy now. Finally he would have a chance to prove himself. He wasn't sure how he would do it and he was pretty sure he would lose but he wanted to at least try. He thought he would ask his parents for help. Diabloss especially would be a good help, he was a good flyer and he had his squad too, whom he had trained.

"Thanks for all your help and for showing me around" said Ellendrii. It was actually late afternoon and he was feeling a little hungry. He didn't much fancy eating bugs though.

"It's nothing" replied Sierra. Reo would be crazy when she told him. Mostly because they would be blessed by the Forest Gryphie's presence once again. She had been sure and he had too, that if Ellendrii was shown around and his questions answered, that he would go away and never darken their islands again.

"Come on" said Sierra and flew into the sky. Ellendrii followed. He suddenly remembered Aro as his train of thought crashed into thoughts of flying, telling everyone, telling Aro, Aro's gift!

"Oh, umm, I don't s'pose I could trouble you for a feather could I?" he asked her as they flew.

"A feather? You can't have one of mine! Why do you want a feather?"

"I promised my best friend I'd bring him back a souvenir from my trip up here and I thought a Sky Gryphie feather would be appropriate" Ellendrii explained.

"Oh, well there are feathers around" Sierra skimmed a nearby Skyland and pointed to the ground there, where a pretty feather lay. It was the same colour as the regular Sky Gryphie feathers; purple, pink and yellow. It was quite long so Ellendrii assumed it was a crest feather. He swooped down, doing a loop the loop as he did so, showing off a little of his skill and grabbed the feather. If Sierra had noticed his little trick, she didn't show it.

They landed on the meeting place and she sat down. Reo would *not* be happy.

"Well then, I guess I'd better go and train for the contest!" said Ellendrii brightly.

"I guess you should" replied Sierra. Not that it will help you, she thought.

"Thanks again and thanks for showing me around. You Sky Gryphies have a lovely place up here, it's just a shame we can't come up and visit you more often" said Ellendrii.

"It's not a shame, it's how things should be" replied Sierra, really wanting him to go now. Ellendrii shrugged.

"If that's how you want it" he said. He walked to the edge of the island and launched himself off.

"Bye Sierra, see you in three sun cycle's time!" he called.

"Bye, Ellendrii and good luck! You'll certainly need it!" she was inwardly amused at how he would crash and burn.

Ellendrii did a happy somersault in the sky and shot downwards like a bullet, causing Sierra to jump forward and stare down after him because of the speed of his movement. For a brief second she actually thought he might be in with a chance.

Chapter 5
Eager to Go

Ellendrii was elated. Not only had he had the chance to actually have a good look round the Sky Gryphie territory; he also had the rare chance to enter the Elite Flyers contest and get among the best of the best himself. He assumed he was the first Forest Gryphie to even be considered for entry and he found this to be a big honour. He was eager to get started with training but he was also hungry and food was the most important thing right now. He figured he would catch a bird when he was closer to the Forest. Or at least the sky above the Forest. He thought he would catch one in the air. He needed the practise and wanted the thrill of the chase.

As he descended, he found it much easier to breathe. Not that he had struggled a lot but the change was noticeable once he was out of the thin air and past the layer of mist that shrouded the Skylands. He was back among the clouds once more and felt much freer.

Now to find a bird to eat. Sometimes sea vultures would come inland from the sea. He was not near the sea right now but the birds would come in to look for food. They had a habit of padding about on grass to imitate rain so the worms would come up to eat. Mostly they ate fish but those who knew how, would eat worms as well. Inland though, there were birds who hunted sea vultures. Sea vultures were pretty nasty things. They had a beak full of horrible teeth and they also had bony spikes on their heads. They had grey wings and white bodies with pale coloured legs and feet, yellow beaks and nasty red eyes. They were really unpleasant creatures and they made a horrible screaming noise. They were very noisy on the cliff colonies. Another reason they were good to eat; it shut them up! Ellendrii was glad they didn't live in the Forest. Sharing his tree with those horrible birds would not be a pleasant thing. But at least there would be a ready food source in a similar fashion to the Lizariaouses' caves of cave cats. But cave cats were fairly quiet and easy to live with. Sea vultures were not. Inland, they were meal creatures not only for Gryphies but also Skreaks. A Skreak is a predatory bird with a long, thick beak and fast wings. They are brown or green and sea vultures don't stand a chance against them. A flight of Skreaks have been known to tear apart a flock of sea vultures. Literally rip them apart so there is nothing but feathers. Like sky piranhas! But sea vultures, although in some ways smart, are mostly stupid so they will unknowingly fly in the territory of Skreaks.

And Ellendrii had spotted both these birds flying a little way away below him. The Skreak wanted the sea vulture for its next meal. And so did Ellendrii. Ellendrii honed in on the sea vulture, hovering a little and then with one huge flap he propelled himself forward, folding his wings against his body in a torpedo shape and diving at the sea vulture. The Skreak had seen him too and took action, also going for the other hapless bird. It was too late for the sea vulture. While it might have escaped if there was one hunter after it; it didn't stand a chance at all against two of them.

As Ellendrii dived, he roared and flamed the Skreak, which screeched and dodged the blue fire. Ellendrii went for the sea vulture and caught it, swooping down, grabbing it around its body in his hands and soaring back upward again. The Skreak, angry at having lost its meal pursued him, screeching in rage. Ellendrii's prize was struggling and trying to peck him and it was impeding his flying so he lunged his head down and broke its neck, killing it instantly. Despite their nasty teeth and spikes, sea vultures were easy to kill by hunters who were bigger than they were.

The Skreak was now dive bombing Ellendrii and its pecks were hurting him. It was determined to get its meal creature off him. But Ellendrii was having none of it. He lashed his tail round and smacked the Skreak away with his tailspade. The bird squawked in pain and anger and resumed its pursuit of the Gryphie. Ellendrii roared threateningly and flamed at the Skreak but the bird still persisted. So Ellendrii flew a little way with the bird following him.

Suddenly as though on a pinhead, he turned arching his back as he passed the bird, allowing the long spikes along his spine to pierce the Skreak's underbelly and let lose a flood of

90

the hapless bird's insides. The Skreak soon followed, dropping like a rock; dead.

Ellendrii hovered in the sky, rearing his head back and roaring out his victory for all around to hear. It was HIS kill, HIS prey, HIS meal creature! He felt full of life after his little battle.

He heard a responding roar. It was his father. The roar Ellendrii had made was letting others know he was victorious in a battle, no matter how small. The responding roar was his father congratulating him. Ellendrii hadn't really had to fight over food before. A Furmine had tried to steal some bedding he'd been collecting when he was a kitten and he'd chased it away but nothing had outright attacked him for ownership of the thing he had. So he was even more proud of himself.

Diabloss hovered in the distance, watching his son and Ellendrii saw him, so after taking a bite of the sea vulture, he joined his father.

"I'm guessing since you're back so late and still alive that it went well up in the realm of the Sky Gryphies?" asked Diabloss.

"It went great!" replied Ellendrii excitedly. "They showed me around and in three sun cycles I'm going to be competing in a contest to become an Elite Flyer!"

Diabloss didn't look pleasantly surprised; he looked shocked. He knew that the leaders of the Sky Gryphies were playing with Ellendrii because he knew what they were like. And it bothered him.

"Who told you you could enter a contest to become part of their Elite?" he asked, concerned.

"Sierra, one of the leaders did. She showed me around. She showed me the Skylands and the temple she and her brother share and then she took me to the place where the Elite train and practise and they showed me what they can do. At first she laughed when I said I wanted to join them but then she agreed to let me enter a contest. I'm assuming there will be tests and trials and I have to overcome them."

"But the Elite Flyers get to where they are by going to a training school. You can't just enter a contest and be a part of them" said Diabloss.

"I think she was so surprised by a Forest Gryphie wanting to be a part of the Elite that she said about that. And what other reason would they hold a contest for?" asked Ellendrii, having another bite of his sea vulture.

"Er, maybe to compete against each other and train? I have contests with my squadron" replied Diabloss.

"Oh well, she said I could join in and I'm not going to knock that" said Ellendrii firmly.

"You do realize that you will probably fail miserably" said Diabloss.

"Yeah, I know that. But I am determined and I think even if I fail, I'll still be in with a chance if I enter. I won't have any chance if I don't."

Diabloss had to agree that this was a smart way of thinking but he was sure his son would get hurt in the process. Still, he was old enough to learn these things for himself.

"So, will you help me train, Dad?" asked Ellendrii hopefully. If his parents didn't help him, there was no one who could, well, maybe one of the squadron but they didn't know Ellendrii that well, nor he them so he didn't hold out much hope for that.

"Of course I will" replied Diabloss. After all, he wanted Ellendrii to be in with a fighting chance so if he showed him his techniques and tricks of the trade, he would have a better chance of even staying in the contest a bit longer. The Elite Flyers' skills far outstripped his own squadron's though. He'd seen them in action and even with his knowledge of the art of flying and his experience; he had been impressed beyond words at what the Sky Gryphie Elite Flyers had been capable of. And of course they were, because the sky was more their home than even the Forest or Mountain Gryphies.

"I forgot to ask them how they came to have a flying elite" pondered Ellendrii.

"I know why. It's because they have a lot to prove to themselves and each other. Since they live in the sky, they want to push their environment to its very limits. They love a challenge and they want to see for themselves what they can do in their environment. So as they worked themselves up and got better and better at what they could do in the air, then the best ones formed the Elite. Then they would strive to either be like the Elite or beat the Elite. And in the seasons this has been going on, the Elite get better and better as more Sky Gryphies surpass them. And...Ellendrii, what is that in your hair?" Diabloss was staring at his son in an odd and confused manner now.

"What? Oh, yeah, the feather for Aro. I got a feather for Aro since he wanted me to bring something back for him" explained Ellendrii.

"You didn't pull it out of one of their heads did you?" asked Diabloss, secretly thinking that would have been rather funny but also not wanting his son to endure the consequences of doing such a thing. Ellendrii laughed.

"Haha no, I found it on the ground. Sierra thought I was weird for wanting to bring a feather back for my friend" he shrugged. "I think Aro will be happy with it. Or I could have brought him back some fruit but he would have hated that. Did you know that Sky Gryphies eat bugs and fruit? Bugs! Who the grik eats bugs??" Diabloss frowned at him when he swore and Ellendrii looked sheepish, tearing another bite of his kill as they flew.

"Sky Gryphies, apparently. Although they do eat birds too I think" said Diabloss. Ellendrii nodded with his mouth full.

"Like us" he said, "in fact a lot of things they do are like us. They look like us too, except the feathers and scales on their tummies. I expected to find them completely different when you told me how offish they are. I mean, they have a lot of differences too and their culture is different but I still don't know why they can't come and visit us. Or maybe they're used to their own thin air and breathing ours would make them sick..."

"Hmm maybe it's because as I told you before, they are deathly afraid of the ground? And yes the different air would probably cause them problems much like their air causes us problems. I just don't understand how you managed to survive it and stay up there as long as you did"

"I have no idea but I'm glad I was ok with it! Maybe I was meant to be part of the Elite Flyers! After all, why else would I

93

be able to withstand their air? Sierra and Reo were pretty annoyed that I didn't collapse. I knew they were expecting me to at any moment and it amused me" Ellendrii giggled and finished his food.

"I'll bet they were annoyed. They think they are untouchable up there but now they know they're not. They think we're filth for living down near the ground and a lower species because we can't tolerate their air but now we are proving that we're not. I mean, we and they will never be close but at least it will shut them up, the fact that you want to prove yourself and in the unlikely event that you actually DO prove yourself and put up a good fight against the other flyers, it will really make them eat their words" Diabloss grinned now.

"Unlikely? Gee, thanks for the support Dad. You're supposed to be positive and encourage me"

"No, I'm supposed to look at this situation realistically. I will not fill your head with false hope and overconfidence because you will never succeed then and in the event that you do succeed, it will be with hope and humbleness and not pride and big headedness. Do you understand?"

"Yeah I understand. I also don't feel that confident, which is why I need a boost." Ellendrii looked at his father hopefully. Diabloss nodded and smiled.

"I will do what I can. By learning more, it will give you confidence and the will to succeed because you are sure of yourself. We can start training first thing next sun cycle if you like"

"That would be great Dad, thanks!" Ellendrii brightened up immediately and the old happy Ellendrii was back.

"I'm gunna go tell Aro about my adventure!" beamed Ellendrii. He was too excited about what he had seen and wanted to tell his friend. Diabloss was still very surprised his son had been able to get as far as he had with the Sky Gryphies, given their lack of patience for the Forest Gryphies.

"Off you go then" laughed Diabloss. "Make sure you're not too long. If you want to train for the contest, you need to sleep early. We will be up as soon as the sun rises tomorrow for me to start teaching you some of the things I know."

Ellendrii nodded and then flew off towards Dyarkroeen to see his friend. He found Aro sitting outside his cave enjoying the early evening sun. As soon as Aro saw Ellendrii he leaped up and greeted him.

"So, how did it go?" he asked eagerly.

"Awesomely! They showed me around, the leaders that is, and they've even allowed me to enter a contest to join the Elite Flyers!" Ellendrii bounced around in excitement.

"What?? Really??" Aro looked stunned. "I thought they hated Forest Gryphies! How come they were so nice to you?"

"They weren't really nice to me. Sierra is nicer than her brother, she is more tolerant and she showed me around mostly. But they are still stuck up and full of themselves and see us Forest Gryphies as lower than them because we don't live in the clouds like they do. That bugged me. But I think I'm in with a chance of winning the contest. They wouldn't have let me enter if they thought I was dreadful."

"Hmm, I dunno, they might just want to laugh at you" replied Aro.

"Aro don't be such a downer! I want to go into this positively." Ellendrii growled.

"Ok ok, well I hope you show them all that Forest Gryphies are better than they think. What was it like up there?"

"It was pretty amazing. Everything was so bright and warm. It seems to be sunny all the time. Sometimes a small cloud will float over but that's it. The air was a little hard to breathe but I got used to it. And they live in great towering caves on floating islands. They do eat bugs though, which is pretty gross."

"I've eaten bugs before" said Aro, "they're not too bad"

"Trust you to have tried bugs" laughed Ellendrii, trying not to let his stomach churn. "I wouldn't like something squirming inside me. I'm guessing you don't kill them before you eat them?"

"Of course not. You just eat them up" Aro shrugged. "They're ok, I've not eaten them that much"

"Anyway I'm gunna train for the contest. Mum and Dad are helping me. We'll probably be training at very high

95

altitudes so I can get used to doing strenuous stuff in thin air."
Ellendrii looked excited again.

Aro sighed. "I wish I could see what it's like up there. I wish I could fly. You get to see all the cool things. I can't even imagine what towering caves look like."

"You wouldn't have liked their attitude though" said Ellendrii. "They aren't that respectful and you would have lost your temper with them probably. Plus I think they respect Lizariaouses even less than Forest Gryphies. They see us as lower than them but you're practically meal creatures in their eyes."

"They eat Lizariaouses?" Aro looked shocked.

"No, they see you at the primitive level of meal creatures."

"Oh. Well they'd be wrong. I bet a Lizariaous could kill one of them easily!"

"Probably. They have thinner and lighter bodies than Forest Gryphies. A Mountain Gryphie would make a meal of them if it wanted to." Ellendrii sat down next to Aro.

"Ha! Well then they're nothing to be scared of! You'll easily beat those grikheads!" Aro laughed. Ellendrii nodded.

"Although what I saw Raediaxx do in the air was astounding. I really wish I could fly like that. They did things with their fire too. Like making a flame circle in the air and flying through it before it dissipated. They were SO fast! Faster than me I think. The shape of their wings is different; I think that's what gives them the speed. I'll have to improvise if I want to fly that fast and I've no idea how to do that."

"I'm sure your Dad can show you how" said Aro. "He's got his own squad so he must know a few things."

"Yeah you're right. I'll let Dad show me how to do it. Anyway I gotta go, my Dad wanted me to sleep early this moon so we can start training when the sun rises. I only have three sun cycles to train in and I want to do as much as I can."

"Good luck. Hey, did you get me anything? You said you would!" Aro looked at Ellendrii expectantly.

"Oh, yeah! I got you this…" Ellendrii produced the feather from his long mane.

"Neato, did you steal it from them?" Aro grinned and took the feather.

"No, I found it on the ground. They have feathers like this on their heads and legs."

"So, are they part bird then?" asked Aro.

"Maybe. They like high places and they are good at flying so yeah, maybe they are part bird. But they are a species related to my own so maybe I'm part bird too!"

"Well you can all fly so it makes sense. I wonder what sort of bird though" Aro looked thoughtful and studied the feather.

"I dunno. Do you like the feather? Sorry I couldn't get you anything more. I wasn't sure what to bring back. I would have liked one of their belly scales though; they were shiny and they used them on their sky towers."

"Yeah it's cool. You can get me a scale next time" grinned Aro.

"I think they use them on the sky towers whenever they shed one. I didn't see any lying around like I did with the feathers. They don't seem to waste the scales."

"Aww that's a shame. I wish I could meet one, I could just take a scale from it then" Aro grinned more.

"I don't think they would appreciate you threatening them or ripping their scales off"

"It would only be one!" Aro tried to look innocent but his violent Lizariaous ways couldn't be hidden. He liked the Forest Gryphies but the fact the Sky Gryphies didn't like them annoyed him somewhat. Ellendrii never boasted about his wings or his flying because he knew it would hurt Aro's feelings, so for the Sky Gryphies to do that annoyed Aro even more about them.

"We need to maintain a good relationship with them or they won't let me visit them" said Ellendrii.

"Yes but *we* don't need to maintain a good relationship with them" smirked Aro, referring of course to the Lizariaouses.

"We don't want another war. Can you imagine you guys against the Sky Gryphies? They are better flyers than the Forest Gryphies."

"But are they better fighters?" Aro grinned again. "With those weak little legs and bodies. Don't get me wrong, I think that war that happened was bad and shouldn't have happened but all the same, some creatures just make me want to bite them."

Ellendrii could see his point. But even so, fighting never solves anything. A lot of them died in the war, both Gryphies and Lizariaouses. And it was all wrong.

"Well you just have to maintain restraint. Besides, you'll probably never meet one anyway."

Aro nodded. "Yeah I guess not. But I'd still like to see where they live"

"Well I'm not trying to carry you while I fly again"

"I never asked you to"

"You were thinking it!" Ellendrii gave him a look. Aro looked sheepish.

"Well, maybe a little" he grinned.

Ellendrii shook his head, smiling.

"Anyway I gotta go now, it's getting late. I need to be up for training tomorrow. You can come and watch if you like but you gotta be up early. Meet me by my tree at sunrise." Aro nodded.

"Sure! I can watch you make an idiot of yourself."

"Gee thanks" replied Ellendrii and stood up, stretching his wings. Aro smirked.

"No worries" he said.

Ellendrii said goodbye to him and flew back to Shernaron. Aro watched him go.

Aro sighed. Ellendrii seemed to have such awesome adventures and Aro felt all he did was tag along at times. Then again Aro did find the best places to explore. They wouldn't have found that Furmine necropolis if it hadn't been for him. They both learned something new that moon cycle.

He was hungry so he got up and went to hunt for his dinner. He walked past a few caves sniffing as he went. He was looking for cave cats. Most of the caves he passed smelled like Lizariaous. Others smelled of nothing much. The cave cats lived in groups in their caves. They were small, either mottled or striped and very wild. Most of them were either brown or grey.

Aro paused, sniffing outside an oddly shaped cave. This one smelled promising! He entered the cave slowly, sniffing and looking around for activity. He smelled cave cat droppings and knew this was a place that they lived in. Something darted behind a rock and Aro followed, aiming his needles towards the movement. All his senses were on alert as he stalked his prey. Cave cats were fairly hard to hit with needles unless the Lizariaous was particularly adept at shooting his needles or the target was a large cat. But Aro aimed his needles at the movement just in case he needed them. His father had always taught him this. Aro slunk low to the ground, positioned himself and leaped over the rock, pouncing on and pinning a terrified cave cat that yowled in fear at him. He'd landed on its back so it was unable to get a claw out and scratch him. Aro sunk his teeth into its neck, twisting his own head and breaking the cave cat's neck, killing it. Dinner was served!

After his meal, Aro wandered around the territory a little. He passed his sisters but didn't go to talk to them. He rarely chatted to them. They often hung out together and he always got the feeling of being left out; the third wheel so to speak, if Lizariaouses knew what wheels were, which they didn't. Instead, he found his mother eating a plump rock hog. Rock hogs were another type of meal creature but they were big and stubborn and very temperamental. They would give all but the most experienced hunter a run for his money. They had bony plates along their backs and large horns and tusks. A true challenge for any hunter but a nice, filling meal if they could be caught and killed swiftly without injury to the hunter.

Aro couldn't help nagging her for a bit. Even though he was a young adult, when he saw his mother eating something, the kid part of him wanted some. He sidled up to her and looked hopeful, making a soft grunting sound which meant he wanted some of her food. Schaarl looked at him, raising an eyeridge which suggested to him that he was wasting his time. It told him, really, you're trying this at your age? Think again.

Aro gave up. But he did sit down near her.

"How's it going Mum?" he asked.

"Not too bad" she replied. "How are Ellendrii and his family?"

"They're ok. Ellendrii went to see the Sky Gryphies this sun. He's going to compete in a contest to try and join the ranks of their Elite Flyers. He gave me this" Aro showed his mother the feather. He'd tucked it behind one of his horns.

"It's pretty" she remarked. Aro nodded.

"He's got three sun cycles to train in. His parents are going to teach him. I'm going to watch if I can. I hope he shows those stuck up Sky Gryphies what's what!"

"I'm sure he will. He's a good flyer and dedicated to the point of obsession" replied Schaarl.

"Is the rock hog nice?" ventured Aro.

"Yes and no you're not getting any. I can smell you've just eaten a cave cat. Don't be greedy." Aro backed down.

"Sorry, it's just I can't catch rock hogs and they're so yummy!"

"You will one sun cycle when you're bigger. Your father will teach you. He taught me. I couldn't catch them either. Speaking of your father, here he is now."

They looked up and saw Mordred walking towards them. He looked tired.

"Are you ok?" asked Schaarl. Mordred grunted.

"A massive fight broke out to the north, I had to go and sort it out. One of the Lizariaouses had stolen another's food and they were pretty much fighting to the death over it. A low ranker was trying to get it off him. The injuries." Mordred shook his head.

"See?" Schaarl looked at Aro. "This is why you shouldn't nag for food. Catch your own!" Aro nodded sheepishly.

"Were you nagging your mother again?" asked Mordred. Aro looked down, his horns drooping a little.

"Yes, I wanted some of her food" he admitted.

"Well don't. Catch your own. Anyway, I've sent the injured low ranker to Jadariol to get fixed up." Mordred didn't mention the name of the low ranking Lizariaous. Low rankers have names but they are rarely used since the Lizariaous is too low for anyone to bother to even remember their name.

"Also, Muzzl got into trouble again. Low rankers have been stealing his food because of his problem. He's a higher ranker than these guys but they still get away with it since he can't defend himself well." Schaarl shook her head.

"Poor Muzzl. Even Jadariol and Lunara with all their remedies can't fix him."

"Well he shouldn't have been so rebellious when he was a kid. Answer back to your parents too much and it happens" Mordred shrugged. "You nearly did it to Scit, remember?"

"Ergh, Scit was a clawful. She went through this phase of always answering back. Remember when we starved her when she stole Aro's food?" Mordred nodded. Aro was still listening of course but saying nothing since his parents were talking and he didn't have anything to input.

"What was Muzzl called before he was Muzzl?" asked Schaarl. "I forget"

"Everyone forgets. After what happened, he was just nicknamed Muzzl and that was that. I don't know even if his own parents remember what they called him in the first place. Seems a cruel nickname though. Ever since it happened he quietened right down and is a shadow of his former self. All his confidence gone."

"He shouldn't have been so cocky when he was a kid. If only he'd listened." Schaarl shook her head.

The unfortunate Muzzl had been called Terixinn when he was born. He was always outspoken, rebellious, answered back and been a general bully to his three siblings and peers. Even his parents he'd snapped at a few times. Then his father snapped at him. He'd snapped his muzzle clean off. Just sunk his teeth into it and jerked his head back, crunching through the bone of Terixinn's skull and permanently disfiguring him. It's not unknown for Lizariaous parents to punish a kid in this way. Some of them don't even let it go as far as Terixinn's parents did. They were lenient. Lizariaous parents are short tempered and don't allow their kids to run riot. Now Terixinn had no muzzle. Just a hole where his mouth was and a few broken teeth. He couldn't smell at all and had to breathe through his mouth, having had his nasal cavities crushed. And so he earned the nickname of Muzzl. Because he had none. A lot of the younger kids were scared of him now. He had no friends and wandered around as a solitary and of course

101

couldn't defend his food very well. He had learned to shoot his needles more accurately though. There were a few hideous Lizariaouses with no muzzles around. That was what happened when kids screamed and whined and roared and stole and made nuisances of themselves.

Aro had seen Muzzl before. The first time he saw him, Aro was quite young and he had moonmares about the deformed Lizariaous. But this conversation was getting boring to him now so he decided to go back to his cave.

Bidding farewell to his parents, Aro went back to his cave. The sun was setting now and the wind whipped up a little.

Aro's cave was fairly large, being the son of the leader of the Lizariaouses, he got a nice home. His sisters did too. At the back, as with most Lizariaouses habitations, there was a bed of dried grass. It was similar to Gryphies really although not all Lizariaouses used it. Some of them preferred to sleep on flat rocks they had dragged in from outside. Others, like Aro and his family, had learned that grass was more comfy to sleep on. Lizariaouses are tough, with tough skin but even they enjoyed a little luxury at times.

Aro wandered in with a yawn and got onto his makeshift bed. He'd been exploring again. This time he'd wandered to the far side of Dyarkroeen and had a look around there. It was mostly caves and barren land. A few Lizariaouses lived out there as the pack had expanded over the seasons but there were more and more empty caves and eventually terrain that was too hard to cover by walking. It got rough, the ground rising up into points that got higher and higher as the land went on until eventually it was impossible to climb. Beyond that was the Dark Plains, the place where the Deamon Gryphies lived and no one dared venture. The Dark Plains were cut off from everyone else and no one really knew what it looked like except Diabloss, whose mother had been a Deamon Gryphie.

Aro hadn't found much this sun cycle though. A few dusty cave cats and a snaggle-beaked bird he didn't know the species of but couldn't catch anyway so didn't care about were about the only things of interest he'd discovered.

Settling down on his bed of dry grass, Aro curled up and closed his eyes. With a sigh he was soon asleep. The next sun cycles would be important ones!

***

When Ellendrii awoke the next sun cycle, Aro was already waiting at the base of the tree, looking up expectantly.

"Are we gunna train or not?" he yelled.

"Hey, *I'm* the one that's training!" yelled back Ellendrii with a laugh as he climbed down the tree. Diabloss caught breakfast for his family that morning. It was a large male forest deer with antlers. Aro had already eaten and, unable to persuade the Gryphies to share the kill, played with the antlers instead while they ate.

"Now, you know this will be hard. Intense even" warned Leida. Ellendrii nodded.

"And we will be training higher up in the sky than usual" said Diabloss. Ellendrii nodded again. Mostly because he was listening but partly because his mouth was full of food.

"Leida won't be up as high as you and I because she can't handle the altitude as well as us. I want you to show me exactly how long you can stay up there and how high you can go" Diabloss told a listening Ellendrii.

"First we need to know to what extent you can handle the thin air. Then we can begin training at that level."

Diabloss suspected that Ellendrii could withstand the same altitude as he could, however he was proved wrong when they got up there. Ellendrii could fly up and stay up much higher than his father. His father could fly to the same height but after a while he had to go back down again as he struggled to breathe. He marvelled at his son's odd ability to cope with the air up there. He figured it was down to Ellendrii spending so much time racing about in the clouds. That he was used to it. Diabloss himself had never had any reason to fly up higher than he needed to but he knew his son liked to push himself to the limit.

So they had to train lower down. Lower still when Leida was with them. Aro watched from the ground, occasionally joined by Leida when Diabloss was training Ellendrii at a

103

higher altitude. Aro got neck ache from looking up for so long. He shook his head and had to have breaks every so often to look down. Leida sent him to catch food, which kept him occupied in between watching Ellendrii training and kept their energy up with meat when they needed it.

First, after finding out what altitude Ellendrii could cope with, Diabloss asked him what sort of things Raediaxx and the others had done in the sky. Ellendrii told him.

"They would flame a circle of fire into the air and then fly through it before it dissipated. They worked as a team as well as individuals and they would also do things with their fire and never get burned due to their speed in the air. They did endless corkscrews in the air, trailing their fire behind them and creating patterns with it. It was really amazing. Like what Fire Masters do but without making images with their fire."

Diabloss rolled his eyes at this. So they don't have the talent to be Fire Masters so they just make patterns with their fire instead. And then they have the cheek to have the attitude of being better than Tranzoss. They had mocked her fire that time she went to visit them, saying things like they could create magic with their fire, the likes of which she couldn't even dream of. Odd then, that they would never show her this so called "magic" and only boast about it.

"What else did they do?" he asked.

"They sort of danced together with amazing precision and co-ordination and they raced each other as well."

"Hmm well you have no one to dance with so that's out; you'll just have to amaze them by yourself. This will mean working much harder though. I've seen what they can do so I've got a pretty good idea of what to teach you. You can weave around me. You have the experience of dodging and weaving and doing pretty incredible and precise flight work from what I've seen you do in the clouds, so instead of having someone else to dance with, you can just weave around all the other Sky Gryphies who are competing. That will really annoy them. It would mean that you have the co-ordination and talent to not even need a partner to fly with and that you can fly with anyone you like, without the predictability of knowing what moves to do. The ones who fly together will have practised together and thus know what moves the other is doing. For you to just work with anyone having had no practise with that individual would be very impressive. So you must weave in and out of the other competitors. Treat them as you do the clouds. Use your fire, when you aren't weaving and dodging the others. I will teach you some useful fire tricks. This sun cycle we will concentrate on the weaving. The next sun cycle will be to teach you tricks with your fire. The last sun cycle before the contest will be for you to work out a general order of what you have learned. Obviously you won't know an exact order of what you do but if you can work out what fire tricks you will do with what flying moves you do, then your confidence will be boosted. Knowing what to do is half the battle. When you are sure of what you are doing, you are more confident. And don't forget to finish with a really impressive display of fire!"

Ellendrii listened intently to his father and took it all in. He nodded every so often but never attempted to speak because he was too interested in what he was hearing.

So the training began.

The first sun cycle was pretty easy. Ellendrii already knew a lot of moves in the air from cloud dodging. He had to work on his speed and accuracy though, since of course clouds don't move as fast as flying Gryphies! He needed to be faster and able to dodge things sooner. At the beginning of the lesson, he bumped into his father a few times but as the sun cycle progressed, his flying, accuracy and reflexes got better. At mid-sun they stopped for some food that Aro had caught and then they carried on again afterwards. Diabloss was happy with his son's determination and quick learning. It was just as well he was a fast learner because three sun cycles really wasn't long enough to learn to the skill level of what was required. It was only good fortune that Ellendrii already had a lot of experience on the matter. The Sky Gryphies of course had known that it wasn't really long enough to learn what was needed for the contest. But then they wanted him to fail miserably.

On the second sun cycle, Leida taught Ellendrii a little of what she had learned from Tranzoss. Of course Leida wasn't a Fire Master but Tranzoss had taught her a few things that were easy for any Gryphie to pick up and use. Ellendrii would have to be careful not to burn the other Gryphies when he used his fire, which was why he couldn't use it when dodging the others, only when he was on his own. The Sky Gryphies hadn't been so mean as to insist that he had a flying partner. But they wanted to watch him humiliate himself without one. Which in itself was rather mean of course. Ellendrii didn't know this though. He was blinded a little by his obsession and need to prove himself. And this was no bad thing; it was just a love of what he did. He was also not fully aware of how much the Sky Gryphies enjoyed mocking the Forest Gryphies.

He had trouble getting the hang of the fire thing at first. He nearly flamed his mother. Luckily she protected herself with her wings. In the end she decided to make him land so he could get the hang of the fire tricks before using them in the air. Once he had the hang of them, it was easier to do them while he was flying. Of course, he struggled at first. If he'd ever used his fire while flying, it was never an organised, planned flame; it was to fry a sea vulture or something. So it would be an aimed blast at whatever meal creature he wanted to kill or cook. Actually trying to make some sort of pattern with his fire while flying was much harder, since it required much more concentration and co-ordination. Even harder was the fact he had to actually *avoid* hitting someone with it now. At one point he did wonder to himself why exactly he was bothering to do all this but then he remembered that he wanted to be part of the best of the best, the Sky Gryphie Elite Flyers! And since Sky Gryphies spend all their time up in the air, who better to become a part of than their flyers? So he carried on relentlessly, with determination and fire in his eyes.

On the ground, Aro occasionally got bored. He was still hunting for them when they needed food, just so they could get more training done and wouldn't need to spend time hunting, but when Ellendrii was too high in the sky to see properly, Aro fidgeted and looked for other things to do. Ellendrii would spend much of his time up high and by the time the second sun cycle came, Aro realized that watching his training wasn't quite as exciting as he thought it would be.

So he wandered off for a little time. Not too long, in case they needed him, but long enough that he could explore a little.

The training of Ellendrii wasn't taking place in the Forest but in the nearby training grounds where Strassor and his son Odax trained Gryphies in the art of flight and self defence. They didn't train as many Gryphies now, aside of course from the kittens in flight school. The kittens mostly went to them for flight training if their parents were too busy or couldn't be bothered. Strassor and Odax were paid in food to teach the youngsters. However, the training of Ellendrii was nothing they could help with. Neither of them had experience with Sky Gryphies or what was needed to become part of their Elite Flyers. They had trained a lot more Gryphies back when the war had been imminent. Nearly every Gryphie who wanted any kind of self defence in the event of the Lizariaous attack went to Strassor, Odax and Strassor's other son, Otuss, who had since left. Even though there was less business now, the father and son were still kept nicely busy sharing the things they knew to those who needed to know.

So Aro would go and watch the training nearby. He didn't want to wander too far, so properly exploring was a bit out of the question in case he got distracted and wandered too far when the others needed him for something. So he watched the kittens learning to fly. And laughed when some of them messed it up. He tried to keep his laughing to himself but at times couldn't help it. For example, two kittens flew right into each other and went spiralling out of control. They weren't hurt, luckily, but it was a very funny thing to see and Aro roared with laughter. The kittens got angry and flamed him and were promptly told off by Odax. Then Aro was told off by Odax for laughing at the kittens' misfortune.

Aro apologized and promised not to laugh again. He wandered further away, just in case he couldn't help himself again and so the Gryphies wouldn't see him laugh if he did.

After a while, and checking Ellendrii and his parents again in case they needed him (they didn't), Aro went to see who Strassor was teaching. He normally taught the adult Gryphies. He was teaching a couple of them self defence. Even though Gryphies rarely fought over anything, it was still a useful skill to know. The two Gryphies he was teaching sparred together perfectly; they were obviously advanced students who had been to a lot of lessons.

In a way it gave Aro a whole new appreciation for Gryphie fighting techniques. He always thought Gryphies were a little wimpy in the way that they didn't have thick skin and Lizariaous poison would kill them. But these two were truly formidable and Aro was entranced by them.

He stayed watching them for so long that he forgot the time and before he knew it, Ellendrii was next to him, poking him.

"Oh, you've finished? That was umm…fast…" Aro looked sheepish.

"You were watching these guys?" asked Ellendrii, motioning to the two Gryphies who were still relentlessly sparring with each other.

"They're awesome" breathed Aro, still watching them. "I didn't know Gryphies could be so advanced in battle. Look at the ferocity! I'm surprised they aren't tired yet. They've been sparring for ages."

"Well, when you really enjoy something, you keep at it and never tire of it" explained Ellendrii. "That is why they fight every sun cycle. It's what they live for, like I live for flying."

Aro nodded.

On the final sun cycle, Ellendrii was to learn his own routine. Putting together the flying techniques that Diabloss had taught him along with the fire techniques Leida had taught him. It was taking him time and thought to actually decide what to do. He had an idea of how things would go now and what to expect but still thinking up an order in which things would go, without knowing exactly what would happen, was more difficult. In the past two sun cycles he had been shown things and then done it himself. Now he needed to do it all by himself. His parents were still there to help and give tips though.

For the flying, he was of course going to use the techniques he had learned and had no way of knowing how it would turn out, just to be prepared.

For the order of what fire tricks to perform, he had decided to make the fire ring to fly through, which had taken some practise, then make a spiral of fire and weave in and out of it, spiral the fire out over himself and then down his body while spinning, which caused a corkscrew of flames to envelope his body, shoot fireballs in the air and then weave in and out of them and as a finale, create a wall of flame and slash it through with his tailspade to create a pattern, then billowing the smoke out with his wings and finally flying through the smoke to form it into the shape of Sierra and Reo's Sky Temple and shooting a ball of flame upward which would hopefully represent the sun and illuminate the Sky Temple shaped smoke in blue to represent the scales that were used to decorate the real thing. Originally he wanted the smoke to be in the shape of trees but Diabloss said it would probably get him more on the good side of the Sky Gryphies if he made something that they liked or that meant something to them. Diabloss thought afterwards that was only if Ellendrii got that far. He wished he could watch his son perform in the contest but sadly he wouldn't be able to stay up that high for long enough. Leida was sad she wouldn't be able to watch him either.

Aro was especially dejected that he wouldn't be able to see his best friend's performance in the all important contest. Ellendrii had to do it by himself. Aro only hoped that he wouldn't be totally humiliated and sent packing by the self absorbed Sky Gryphies.

Ellendrii was confident though. He had got that far. He could breathe their air with relative ease. He was not going to back down from this contest and he was above all going to do his best. It was after all, all he could do.

On the sunset of the third sun cycle, the four of them returned to the Forest together. Ellendrii and his parents were tired but happy. Ellendrii wanted to sleep early this moon cycle. He was excited and nervous all at once and really hoped all this training would pay off.

After a meal, which Aro had been invited to join in with since he had done so much hunting for them, Ellendrii and

Aro sat together under the tree and contemplated the recent events.

"I really hope you show them what you can do. Even if you fail, leave them speechless and go out in a barrage of blue flames!" Aro said to his friend.

"I won't fail" replied Ellendrii. "I can't. If I fail, I don't know if they will give me another chance to train and try again. I think they will laugh me right out of their territory. I don't think I'd be allowed back that's for certain. I can't even think about failing." Aro looked thoughtful.

"Well then I really hope you don't fail. And if you do, they treat you with dignity because if they don't, I will get up there somehow and tear out every throat in the place!" He snarled.

"Thanks Aro. If I do fail and I don't have the chance to go back, then that's it. I will join Dad's squad. It's better than nothing and it's certainly the best the Forest has. I know he wanted me to join anyway. He was sad when I didn't want to. I just thought there was more out there than what I know of here. And I was right but you know what? I really didn't even begin to imagine how hard it would be. These last few sun cycles have been so hard, I'm so tired already and don't even have much of a chance to rest because the contest is the next sun cycle. Still, at least everything I've learned will be fresh in my mind and I won't have forgotten anything. I just hope I don't panic or make a complete fool of myself up there."

"I'm sure you won't. I have faith in you. You'll kick all their tails!" Aro grinned reassuringly and Ellendrii was glad he was his friend.

A little later, Aro left to go home. He had been staying in the Forest while Ellendrii trained, just so he wouldn't have to keep walking back across the Outlands every sunrise. He had been sleeping at the bottom of Diabloss's tree. The base of it was hollow in a similar way to Lunara's tree although not nearly as big inside. It was big enough to sleep in though.

Aro had wished Ellendrii luck and Ellendrii had said he didn't need it. What would happen would happen and it would just be how things were. Aro really hoped his friend would succeed though.

So did Ellendrii.

Chapter 6
Unstoppable

Early the next sun cycle, Ellendrii was up and flying. He picked up a sea vulture for a quick breakfast and then headed straight up to the Skylands for the contest. It wasn't such a gruelling trip the second time round because he knew what to expect and he was also more used to it, with more stamina because of his training. Even with such little training, he was still better prepared now.

He'd said goodbye to his parents and again they wished they could come and watch him. It was difficult for them not being able to watch something their son deemed so important and support him.

The contest would start at mid-sun but Ellendrii wanted to leave early so as not to be late, just in case they used that as an excuse not to let him enter and he wasn't sure how long it would take him to get up there.

Also because he couldn't wait.

Again he felt the thinner air making it harder for him to breathe. This time he took it more slowly, so he would adjust faster and stopped just above the cloud and mist layer to hover for a while and adjust himself.

Then he carried on. He finally reached the Skylands and flew through them, looking for the flight island Sierra had told him to meet her on. It was just before mid-sun when he reached the flight island and there wasn't another Sky Gryphie in sight, much less the leaders of them. As he flew to the flight island, he had passed other Sky Gryphies. Most of them gave him dirty, disgusted looks. A few of them didn't notice him because after all, he himself was blue like they were but they usually picked up on his wing shape and avoided him. He was honestly surprised that none of them attacked him. Maybe they'd been told not to. Or maybe they didn't have the authority to. After all, it had been Reo who challenged him the first time he was up there; not a regular citizen of the sky.

Ellendrii alighted on the flight island and waited for one of the leaders to turn up or even Raediaxx or the other Elite Flyers.

Soon, another Gryphie did join him though. It was a stranger. She alighted beside him with a curious look on her face.

"Are you the Forest Gryphie who is here for the contest?" she asked. Whether she had been sent by the leaders, Ellendrii had no idea but she didn't seem threatening so he answered.

"Yes, I'm Ellendrii and I'm here to compete"

"I'm Verniy, I'm in the Elite Flyers. We were all asked to meet here at mid-sun for the contest. I'm guessing none of the others have arrived yet."

"How many are there?" asked Ellendrii.

"Altogether there are twenty three Elite Flyers. In this contest there will be ten. And you." She looked down her nose at him. She sat a little way away as well, which signified that she didn't really want to get too close to him, probably for racial reasons.

"Oh" was all Ellendrii said.

"Why the grik would a Forest Gryphie want to try his luck with us?" asked Verniy.

"Because I love to fly. It is my passion. So it's only natural that I would want to join the fleet of the best flyers in all of Shernaron. My father's squad, although they are good, are admittedly nothing compared to the talent that rests on the wings of the Sky Gryphie Elite Flyers. My life goal is to do something with my wings, so I wanted to join the best of the best. I'm very lucky to have been given this opportunity."

"You are," replied Verniy. "Because no other Gryphie other than a Sky Gryphie has ever applied to compete against us. Even most Sky Gryphies don't dare to fly with us. We're too much for them, too good." She leaned in closer to him and he could see every sharp tooth in her mouth as she spoke quietly and deliberately, meeting direct eye contact with him.

"And we will destroy you."

Ellendrii swallowed.

Presently they were joined by a couple of other competitors and Verniy moved away to talk to someone else.

Ellendrii felt small now. He wondered if Sierra or Reo had asked Verniy to threaten him. Then he remembered Aro.

"Even if you fail, leave them speechless and go out in a barrage of blue flames!" his friend's words echoed in his mind and he narrowed his eyes with determination, staring out across the sky. That's what he would do. He wouldn't let the threats of these bullies get to him.

He sat there solidly, ignoring the rest of the competitors who arrived.

Soon after, Sierra and Reo landed on the flight island and the competitors all lined up to attention. Ellendrii followed suite, feeling that if he did as the others did, he would look like he knew what he was doing.

Sierra walked along the line and stopped in front of Ellendrii.

"So you came then" she said. As if there was any doubt.

"Yes I did and I am trained and ready to compete!" replied Ellendrii, trying to look as confident as he could. Sierra was taller than him and Reo was even bigger than she was. He was glad it was her and not Reo. Even though Ellendrii wasn't fully grown and could well grow to be bigger than Sierra, he still felt intimidated by her. And rightly so. She could have him chased off the island if she wished.

"We'll see" she said and carried on walking. Well that was certainly the cold shoulder. Reo was following her and soon he came to where Ellendrii stood.

"I can't believe you actually turned up!" he said with a chuckle. "This will be fun"

Ellendrii figured that they would probably try to intimidate him and break his spirit before the contest even started and he was determined not to let them get to him. Reo had carried on walking, inspecting the rest of the competitors like his sister had done.

The Sky Gryphie who stood next to Ellendrii wasn't Verniy, much to Ellendrii's relief. He was a little worried she might try to start something or jeopardise his chances in the contest. The Sky Gryphie next to Ellendrii noticed that he was looking at her and she snorted.

"What are *you* looking at, commoner! You shouldn't even be on our islands. I have no idea why our leaders let you up here to compete." This Sky Gryphie was Ryuii and in truth, Sierra and Reo had told the others to rile Ellendrii up and wreck his confidence. After all, the contest was purely for Ellendrii's benefit and so the Sky Gryphies could teach a Forest Gryphie a lesson; that his sub-species would never be as good as theirs. It was all very immature but it was just how the Sky Gryphies were. They wanted to teach him a lesson he would never forget. And they would go so far as to do something like this to do it.

Finally, Sierra and Reo stood in front of the assembled group and spoke.

"Sky Gryphies …and ground bound Gryphie…you are assembled here this sun to partake in the contest to make it into the Sky Gryphie Elite Flyers. They are the best of the best and this contest will be no less than seeing you do your finest work. We want you to show us you are the best of the best. The flying will be freestyle. Anything goes. Do what you will to win! Any questions?" Reo looked around at the line of Gryphies waiting to fly. Ellendrii spoke up.

"Are there any rules to state what isn't allowed, such as attacking other competitors?" he asked, unsure.

"Sky Gryphies don't do such things. You are here to impress us, not to fight. It goes without saying that you won't attack each other in this contest. You must use your precious time to show us what you're made of, not waste it doing such things as that. YOU might attack and fight unfairly where you come from, Forest Gryphie, but we don't do things like that here. The rest of the competitors here this sun take their flying very seriously and we expect you to as well. You want to win, so show us what you can do." Sierra looked at them as a whole. "ALL of you."

"Now get ready" roared Reo.

The assembled Gryphies lined up at the edge of the flight island, ready to launch into the sky. Those with partners stood together and they all readied themselves. From what Ellendrii could tell, he was the only one without a partner. So this contest would be tough.

He looked out over the sky and suddenly felt a bit out of his depth. Glancing around at the others, he saw that they all possessed a confident air that radiated around them and really didn't help his situation. He sighed. He would do his best.

"NOW FLY HIGH! GO!" roared Reo. The assembled Gryphies launched into the sky as one unit, Ellendrii included and flew upwards, each pair peeling off from the group to go and do their own thing. Ellendrii was desperately trying to remember what it was he had learned and the order in which he would do things.

He started out by flying in cartwheels, over and under, weaving in and out of the other contestants but all the while somehow managing not to upset their own tricks. He was using all of them as obstacles as opposed to one single partner like they were using. He started his first fire trick, splitting off from the others in order to do it. The ring of fire. He blew it out and quick as a shot before it dispersed, he flew through it. The blue flames disintegrated into the air as he flew, his tail trailing smoke after it where his tailspade had purposefully caught the end of the fire ring. Then it was back to using the other contestants to work his flying magic and prowess. Oddly enough, once he got over the initial discomfort and under confidence and he got going, everything seemed to flow. In some ways even better than he had imagined. The next trick was the fire spiral that he would weave in and out of. He blew it out downward as he flew, looping over and flying in and out of the spirals as they turned and burned in the sky, moving his head in a circular motion to get the flames going right. The thin air certainly didn't affect his fire.

Somewhere during all this, Sierra and Reo had started to watch Ellendrii. They couldn't help themselves. He was so resourceful that they couldn't ignore him. He hadn't noticed their eyes on him though and after some more weaving and dodging the other competitors, to the point that he was actually moving with their own flight tricks and movements almost like he was a part of the team, Ellendrii did his next fire trick which was to engulf himself in blue flames, spinning around with a corkscrew of flames swirling around his entire body. He flew around a little and then did it again in a different place, this was mostly because one of the other pairs of flyers were getting a little too close to him but in the end it just made the trick have greater effect and be more impressive. Flying truly was his forte and the fire only added to it.

However, when he started weaving in and out of another pair of Sky Gryphies, they had different ideas. The other competitors had noticed Ellendrii's resourcefulness and they wanted to try and ruin things for him. So as he swerved around Ryuii, she purposefully turned at the last minute, throwing Ellendrii's preparations off and causing him to have to reverse, which of course took him right into the path of Ryuii's partner, Elyx. Elyx shoved Ellendrii, making it look like he had merely got in Ellendrii's way by accident since Ellendrii had been thrown off course. Ellendrii, trying to avoid Elyx flew upwards, right into the path of Verniy, who growled at him as she flew past him, narrowly missing him. Ellendrii tried to change course now, wanting to avoid Ryuii and Elyx completely but they wouldn't let him go. They pretended it was part of their act to fly all around him, letting him think he'd just got caught up between them. They spiralled and weaved all around him, having him stuck in the middle and not letting him escape. Every so often they would graze him with their wing claws while apologizing and then telling him that he was in their way and to get out of their way and that they couldn't break their formation because it was part of their act and if they did, they would jeopardize their chances of passing the contest. But still they wouldn't let him out. Ellendrii still tried in vain to get away from him but they wouldn't let him, still with excuses. They managed to hustle him away from the others, hoping to get him by himself and really hurt him. They couldn't let Sierra or Reo see, since they were still in keeping with the whole "no harming another contestant" rule. They didn't want Ellendrii to think they were being unfair; only that he was in their way.

As they got him further away, the little grazes they were causing to him became more violent. Ellendrii was doing all he could to avoid their claws but they were closing in on him. As they got closer, it became harder to avoid their scratches.

In a final act of desperation, Ellendrii flamed Ryuii in the face, only briefly but long enough to throw her off and for him to escape.

"Sorry!" he yelled at them as he flew away to join the others, "it was part of my act!"

They glowered at him but didn't trouble him again.

Next he flew a little way away from the others and shot fireballs into the air, flying as he did so and dodging them. He did this in an arc over the other contestants, then around and down and around the other side, doubling over and joining them again to weave in and out of them.

Sierra and Reo were astounded and annoyed at the same time as they watched him. He was doing WAY better than they thought he would and this was frustrating. Not only because they wanted him to do badly but also because he was proving them wrong and they might actually have to let him join the Elite Flyers, which naturally they didn't want him to do. Having a Forest Gryphie among their Flyers would destroy all that they vainly believed in and it would also make them look like massive hypocrites in front of their gathering. They both narrowed their eyes and continued to watch him.

Ellendrii himself had no real idea when the contest would be over. They hadn't given him a timescale. So he waited a little time before he did his finale. He didn't want to rush it but at the same time he didn't want to do it too soon either and then have to waste the rest of his time flying about. Luckily for him, the leaders announced that the contest would end soon, so to get the last tricks in and then land and they would find out if they got in.

So Ellendrii did his last trick. He blew out a wall of blue flames, slashing through them with his tailspade and creating a pattern as close as he could get to an image of the clouds. Then he billowed the smoke out with his wings, weaving in and out of it until he'd manipulated it enough to form a shape which resembled Sierra and Reo's Sky Temple, or at least was clearly recognisable as such. Then he flew in front of it and downwards, turning to face upward, aiming his head into the sky and shooting out a blue fireball that settled briefly above the smoke temple before exploding and illuminating the smoke in blue, to represent the temple's scales. Ellendrii flew up above it, hovering above with his wings spread out and roaring, making the other contestants take note of him before he landed on the flight island.

Soon, the others joined him and they lined up in a similar manner to how they had been before the contest for Sierra and Reo to judge them.

The two leaders walked the length of the line, looking down at the assembled Gryphies, assessing them. They stopped before one pair of them, nodding at them and smiling.

"You have made it into the Elite Flyers. Congratulations" they said. It was Verniy and her partner. She and the other Sky Gryphie nodded, bowed and walked off, past Ellendrii. She sneered at him as she passed. They reached the edge of the flight island and launched themselves off, flying down and away. Ellendrii looked after them in puzzlement. Verniy had told him she was already in the Elite Flyers. Unless she'd lied, but then why would she lie?

The leaders were going in no particular order past the contestants. They rejected the pair who were next to Ellendrii. The pair looked crestfallen, quite literally. The crests on their heads sagged downwards in disappointment. They left; heads down.

Then the pair reached Ellendrii.

"Now you" said Reo. "We were quite impressed with you. Do you still want to be in the Sky Gryphie Elite Flyers?"

"Oh yes, it's all I can dream of!" replied Ellendrii eagerly.

"Well, you're still not a Sky Gryphie but you did impress us out there" said Sierra, "So, you have been accepted."

Ellendrii's face lit up.

"Really? Wow, thank you!!!" He nearly bounced with excitement.

"However" interrupted Reo. Ellendrii stopped in his tracks.

"You are still NOT a Sky Gryphie, which would normally be the other condition in order to be accepted. So in order to

118

be fully conducted into the Elite Flyers, you have one more task to complete. Complete it and we will accept you, no arguments. No further requirements. Sky Gryphies need only to pass the flying contest. You are different."

"Whatever it is, I'll do it!" said Ellendrii excitedly. After all, he'd done the hard part right? He'd passed the contest. How hard could this be?

"Ah brilliant. Well then, your last and final task is to find the SilvaGryphie. Bring her to us, then we will accept you fully into the Elite Flyers." Reo smirked.

"The…SilvaGryphie…" Ellendrii was speechless. As far as he had heard, the SilvaGryphie was a legend, no one was even sure if she actually even existed.

"Yes" replied Sierra. "We Sky Gryphies have always wanted to meet our legendary predecessor. So we vowed that if anyone wanted to be in the Elite Flyers who wasn't a Sky Gryphie passed the flying contest, they would get the task of finding and bringing back the SilvaGryphie. And in return we would let them be a part of the Elite Flyers."

And that was the cruel plan the pair of them had concocted together. Of course there had never been this requirement in order to join the Elite Flyers. They didn't want him to join, so they were sending him off on a wild Skreak chase to find something that may not even exist. Even if he did go on this mission, he would never succeed and they would see the back of him either way. Forever. And they suspected this young Forest Gryphie would just be gullible enough to fall for it. And they were right. Knowing nearly nothing about the SilvaGryphie, Ellendrii assumed that because he was assigned with the task of finding her, that she must be around somewhere and the possibility of finding her was achievable.

"Where is she then? What part of Shernaron do I need to travel to in order to find her?" asked Ellendrii. The two leaders were mocking him inwardly.

"If we knew where she was then we wouldn't be asking you to find her, now would we? She isn't in Shernaron anyway. You can find her across the vast water. That is sadly all we know" replied Sierra while Reo had to look away

119

because he was sniggering. She kicked him in the tail with one of her back feet causing him to wince and shut up. He coughed.

"And you are SUCH a great flyer" continued Sierra, "That we know you will be able to make the journey to the other side where she resides. You proved your flying prowess when you were in the contest. We saw the miracles you worked out there. We never even *suspected* a *Forest* Gryphie could do those kinds of things. They *certainly* rival our own skills. Which is why we wanted it to be the other condition in order to join the Elite Flyers. We knew that someone who could rival our own flight skills would have much more of a chance of finding the SilvaGryphie than we would." Sierra was really piling on the flattery.

"And just think…you would also be a hero to our kind, finding the legendary Gryphie that we so badly want to meet! We would even let you live with us!"

Ellendrii pondered all this. She made it sound so easy. It couldn't be *that* hard could it? Except for maybe the fact that Gryphie law stated that the dead also reside the other side of the vast water. It's where Gryphie souls go after they die. No one knew what was over there and as far as he was aware, no one had ever attempted to fly it. But then again all the more reason why he should! He would be the first to do it! He would be a hero! The Sky Gryphies would respect him forever AND he would finally be in the Elite Flyers.

Mulling this all over, Ellendrii nodded with determination.

"Then I will do it. I will bring the SilvaGryphie to you!" Dead souls or no dead souls, he decided he wasn't afraid if it meant that he would finally get to do what he dreamed of doing as his life goal.

Sierra and Reo nodded. Neither of them were surprised in the least. Of course he would agree to do something so impossible. He was young and stupid and driven by a will to succeed but without the knowledge and logical thinking to realize that it was impossible and to just accept things were as they were and give up his silly dream. He could always join Diabloss's squad after all.

"Very well then" said Sierra, speaking again as her
brother was still a bit out of it, being too afraid that he would
snigger or laugh and ruin the whole plan.

"Go and find her, the other side of the vast water. She will
be there waiting for you"

"How will she know I'm looking…"

"She knows everything" interrupted Sierra. "Now GO!!"

She and Reo shooed him off the flight island. Taking
flight, Ellendrii heard them call after him;

"And don't come back without her! If you do, you will
NEVER be allowed into the Elite Flyers. We're relying on you
Ellendrii, fly strong!"

"I will!" he called back and flew off and away, feeling
determined about his new, impossible task.

Turning back to the others, Sierra and Reo addressed
them. Some of them were sniggering and trying to hide it.

"Well, the rest of you did good too, off you go" said Reo.
The others all flew off. Most of them were already in the Elite
Flyers anyway. As for the rest, they knew where they stood.

After they'd gone, Sierra turned to Reo.

"You stupid fool, you nearly gave away the plan!" she
snapped.

"Sorry, I know we'd already planned it out and I knew how
it would go down, it was just that stupid Forest Gryphie's face!
He looked so *convinced*! I couldn't help myself. In all honesty I
thought he would back down and say no."

"I *knew* he wouldn't say no. He's not that type of Gryphie.
Nor is he an adult. He's only just through his kitten seasons,
the fool! Certainly not as smart as his mother or father. We
won't be seeing him again. If he goes, he'll most certainly die.
If he stays, he won't be allowed to show his face up here
again. Either way he won't find the SilvaGryphie."

"Not that I care about the little grikhead or anything but
what if we've sent him to his death? What if he goes looking
for her and he's never seen again. No one knows what's the
other side of the vast water. Or if there is another side. We'll
have killed him."

"Brother, you're not usually like this. You're normally the
uncaring one. What's brought this on?" Sierra looked at her

brother accusingly. It was true that Reo had cared less for the hapless Forest Gryphie than she had. He had been the one to threaten him. She had treated him a little kinder.

"I may have the same views about the Forest Gryphies as you do but we're not killers, Sierra."

"Pfft, if he's *stupid* enough to go and try to find her then he deserves everything he gets. We didn't send him to his death. It is still his *own* choice whether or not he wants to take that chance. I'm sure his father will be able to convince him not to do it. He can settle for second best. He's naïve enough that he can be convinced of anything, I think. His father will talk him round." Sierra had little to no sympathy for Ellendrii. Forest Gryphies were just *so* much lower than Sky Gryphies. It would be akin to caring about the welfare of a meal creature. A mere bug crawling on a leaf.

"And what if…by any chance, no matter how remote…what if he actually *finds* the SilvaGryphie and brings her back here?" asked Reo curiously.

Sierra burst out laughing. It was malicious laughter and it lasted quite a while.

"HA! As if he would. To begin with, he has to actually FIND her. And THEN he has to CONVINCE her to come with him to see us. Even if he did find her, do you think the legendary SilvaGryphie would even want to come and visit US?? No matter how great the gathering of Sky Gryphies up here in the Skylands is, I seriously doubt she would want to come and see us. She would probably devour Ellendrii for having the very cheek to even dream of asking her such a thing! I can imagine she is powerful and with a short temper, that is IF she's actually real. For her to be asked the question of coming to visit creatures that are probably FAR below her would be cheeky in itself. She would flame him alive. Trust me brother, this is a foolproof plan. Nothing can go wrong with it. He doesn't find her, he's not allowed back. He tries to find her, he will perish. He manages to find her; he would never be able to convince her to come with him. She probably has far more important things to do with her time. I just needed something that would get rid of that stupid little Forest Gryphie for good and this is certainly the plan for the job."

Reo nodded. He couldn't argue with that, he guessed. It was certainly a very good plan.

As the sun began to set, they flew back to their Sky Temple.

Landing on one of the bottom flight ledges, they entered the temple and headed to the room used to store fruit. It was at the back of the temple, in a cool, dark cave that had no carved window.

Gathering some fruit each, they went and sat together at the top of the temple, looking out over the Skylands and watching the setting sun.

"And so what if he managed to bring her back?" Reo said quietly.

Sierra swished her tail in annoyance, glaring at him, a small snarl on her lips.

"Are we STILL going on about this?" she asked with a snap.

"You never answered my question last time" replied Reo simply. Sierra groaned and rolled her eyes.

"Then of course I would stick by my word and let him into the Elite Flyers. Obviously."

She angrily munched on a large, sweet fruit with a thick green and orange skin.

"And what effect would that have on everyone else?" asked Reo.

Sierra spun her head around in a short burst of temper.

"Having a pathetic Forest Gryphie in the fight squad that is universally considered to be the best of the best? Oh, they would of course lose ALL respect for us. They may even leave the Elite Flyers. We'll probably have no Elite flying squad left, which would in a way be good because it would mean that stupid Forest Gryphie would have to go back where he came from but at the same time would be disgustingly ironic because not only did the one thing we didn't want to happen, happen, but also the best of the best would no longer exist either, all because of a stupid decision and a plan that was not totally foolproof. In fact the only way we could have got rid of him for good would probably have been to kill him ourselves and start a war with the Forest Gryphies. Or even to have shot him down in the sky so no one knew who did it. Is that enough for you, brother, or do you want MORE??" She glared at him, her nostrils flaring and glowing blue as her fire lung heated up.

Reo cowered slightly, ears back.

"Ok ok sorry! Geez, I was only wondering what would happen if the plan didn't work. Of course it will work it's foolproof. Obviously, which is why we thought of it."

"Exactly. Now shut up about it." Sierra went back to eating her fruit, nostrils still glowing slightly blue.

"You're scared aren't you? You think he has a slight chance of actually finding her." Reo looked at his sister.

"Of course not!" she snapped. "Why would I even think that? She probably doesn't even exist! We Sky Gryphies gave up telling stories of her eons ago!"

"Because, given his talent for flying, you and I both know he has a chance however small."

Sierra pondered this. Yes, the plan was impossible, but some things do hold at least some possibility. After all, the SilvaGryphie was the creator of all Gryphie kind. She brought them all to Shernaron. There was no proof this had ever happened of course but there was also no proof that it hadn't. She may still be out there somewhere, watching over everything or whatever it was that she did.

In Gryphie society I suppose you could say that the SilvaGryphie was akin to a "God" in some ways. Not that anyone worshipped her or even talked about her every sun cycle but they did tell stories about her and there were some individuals who would have loved to meet her. Some of them even spent their entire lives hoping she would somehow appear to them. Every single Gryphie was aware of her although the kittens knew less about her than the adults, aside from what they had heard in stories. Lots of Gryphie parents would tell their kittens stories before they slept, much like human parents do. And she would of course feature in some of them. No one feared her, since she had always been portrayed in a positive light; however it was commonly thought that since she had never appeared to any known Gryphies, that she simply had better and more important things to do

124

with her time. She was just there, a part of life and had never been something to be sought after. Gryphies had other, more pressing things to think about like flying, hunting and being with their friends. And of course during the war times, learning to fight and defend themselves. It never even occurred to them that she would come and defend them; that would be foolish thought, perhaps even lazy.

"To be perfectly honest, Reo, if he actually did manage to come back with her, I would be so impressed that I would even forgive him for being a menial Forest Gryphie and would actually welcome him to come and live with us. Because can you even imagine? Actually *meeting* the SilvaGryphie of legend? It's not something I delight in admitting but I don't care what the sub specie is; if they manage to do something *that* impossible, it is worthy of respect. Even if one of those stupid Gryphers did it, I would respect them. Though I might not ask an animal like that to live with us. It certainly wouldn't be able to withstand our air anyway."

"Speaking of which," said Reo, "Isn't it incredible how well he breathes our air. Even though he's a Forest Gryphie, he certainly fits in well, even better than his powerful father. I'll give him that at least."

"You're very complimentary, which is unusual for you but I have to say that you're right. If only he wasn't a *Forest* Gryphie though. I mean *look* at them! Those cumbersome wings and bodies. We are far more elegant than they are; we are truly the masters of our craft; the air! I don't know how they could bear living in the trees like that or wandering through the forest. I heard in some parts it is *so* dense that you can't even see the sky. What sort of Gryphie would want to live like that? It would be like being blind. Being in a forest so dense that you can't even spread your mighty wings!"

"The Mountain Gryphies are worse though. They are even heavier" Reo pointed out.

"Yes but they do live in the High Mountains. It's not like living in a dreadful forest. I heard there is a swamp there." Sierra shuddered at the thought.

Sky Gryphies are fastidious, clean creatures. They pride themselves in beautiful fur and feathers. Well, most Gryphies are clean creatures; certainly cleaner than Lizariaouses. But Sky Gryphies are clean to the point of being vain about it. It was hard enough to convince some of the other flyers to join the contest once they heard a "filthy" Forest Gryphie would be contending too. That was most of the reason not all of them were already in the Elite. The Elite Flyers are particularly proud individuals. They are good flyers and they *know* they are the best of the best. Where Forest Gryphies are humble about their talents, Sky Gryphies are most certainly not. A few of them even refused their leaders and would not compete so they just ended up entering other good flyers instead. Most of the group had indeed been made up of the Elite Flyers though.

"I've had moonmares" Sierra muttered. "Moonmares about the Forest. Getting trapped in it. Unable to fly, no way out. It was horrible." She shivered, despite the warm evening.

Reo put his wing around her.

"It's ok, I understand moonmares like that. I've had them too. The very thought of the Forest scares me beyond all reason. But we will never see it outside of moonmares thankfully. I don't know how the Forest Gryphies can stand it either. Remember when mother first told us about them? We thought they were something from a scary story. Creatures that live in the very environment we fear. Creatures so similar to us." Sierra sighed and leaned on her brother.

"I don't know how he can stand it. And then to be so well adjusted up here as well. To be honest it makes me fearful for our future. What if more Forest Gryphies take after him and decide to try their luck up here? What if they find they can breathe our air as well as him and want to live up here with us? It scares me, Reo."

"It won't happen" Reo said firmly. "It's never happened until now. We know that our territory is better than theirs. Brighter, cleaner. More to the point we know that they simply can't breathe the air up here for long. Ellendrii is an exception. A once in a lifetime occurrence. We've never met a Gryphie like him until now, nor have any of our ancestors and I highly doubt there will ever be another like him again. We were just the unlucky ones who had to deal with it. And it's dealt with.

He won't be back. I think it was a great plan of yours. I'm sorry if I had any doubt. I just wanted to make sure everything was covered. And it is. Because of your cleverness."

Sierra smiled up at him and resumed eating her fruit.

"You're right. It won't happen again and we won't see him again. Let's put this all behind us and forget about it and him. If he comes back without the SilvaGryphie, we will have him taken care of. Either way, he won't have a future with us."

The two of them agreed not to let any of this bother them. After all, the Forest Gryphie was too young to survive out by himself seeking out the SilvaGryphie. It did occur to Reo somewhere in his mind although he never mentioned it to Sierra because he didn't want to worry her, but what if Ellendrii decided to take Diabloss with him. They were fully aware the huge, magnificent Gryphie was part Deamon and if anyone could help his son, Diabloss could. Even though they looked down on him, they were aware of his strength. He was one of the few Forest Gryphies who had visited the Skylands who actually impressed their leaders slightly. But Reo kept this to himself, wisely.

As the sun set, the two leaders enjoyed their fruit in peace, safe in the knowledge that their plan had worked.

Chapter 7
Unacceptable Defeat

Ellendrii had returned to the Forest excited and terrified at the same time. In truth, as he flew away from the Skylands, he began to wonder what in Shernaron had possessed him to accept such a huge and impossible task. He had accepted the challenge willingly but as he flew home, he started to think this might not be such an easy task.

To fly across the vast water? Where the souls of the dead went after they had died? That all sounded crazy. Plus he knew near to nothing about the legendary SilvaGryphie. How would he ever find her anyway? According to Sierra, she was just across the vast water waiting for him. Or at least he would find her the other side. He assumed she would be there when he reached the far shore. The only problem of course was that he didn't know how wide the body of water was. He couldn't see to the other side, it just stretched off ad infinitum. So if he flew it, he would get hungry. There would be no meal creatures out there. Or maybe there would be? Birds maybe? Sea vultures? He wasn't sure. Was it worth the risk? Maybe he could fish along the way. Yes, that would work. He could catch fish.

By himself? Yes. He needed to go by himself to prove to himself he could do this. His parents would freak he was sure.

Mulling all this over, he approached the Forest and landed in a clearing. He headed back to his tree, catching a small, young forest deer on the way. He thought this would make a good peace offering for his parents.

Approaching the tree, he saw Leida sitting at the base of it, talking to Lunara and Jadariol. Ellendrii breathed deeply and walked up to them, carrying the forest deer with him.

"Hi Mum" Ellendrii said, approaching. Leida smiled at him. Jadariol noticed his kill and looked interested. Typical Lizariaous. Even the adult ones couldn't resist someone else's dinner.

"Where's Dad?" asked Ellendrii.

"Out with the squad" replied Leida. "How did it go with the sky contest?" She looked at him brightly.

"I umm...I passed it" Ellendrii began.

"Oh great! They've actually accepted you? Brilliant! Your father will be so proud...and surprised! Not because you made it of course, he never doubted you for a moment, but obviously because they actually let you in and kept their word."

"Yeah but..."

"Did you bring that to celebrate with?" asked Leida as Lunara and Jadariol congratulated him as well.

"Sort of, I..."

"You're the first Forest Gryphie to even compete to be part of the Elite Flyers aren't you?" asked Lunara.

"Yes I..."

"WOW, how exciting!" Lunara beamed.

"Yeah, nice job!" said Jadariol. Ellendrii decided to give up trying to explain about his current plight. He felt remarkably alone and he quietly ascended the tree with the forest deer in tow. He could hear Lunara and Jadariol congratulating Leida on having such a smart son. Ellendrii sighed and sat on his sleeping branch, the forest deer draped over the branch next to him, untouched. He'd lost his appetite. He looked up at the setting sun.

First he needed to get all his thoughts sorted. He figured he would ask his father about the SilvaGryphie when he got back, maybe he would listen more than his mother. Then again she had been busy talking to Lunara and Jadariol when he arrived, which probably didn't help. He'd wait for Diabloss to get back and ask him about the SilvaGryphie. He would leave in the next couple of sun cycles. He didn't want to allow himself time to rethink or lose confidence over this. He'd overcome the contest, he could overcome this too. He wondered how he would tell his parents about wanting to leave on such a potentially dangerous journey. He hoped they would understand. He doubted they would understand. But he did need to know all he could about the SilvaGryphie, which was why he wanted to ask his father about her before he told him about going to look for her.

129

A while later, he heard the sound of someone landing in the top of the tree and looked up. It was his father. And he hadn't caught something to eat. Perfect!

"Dad!" called up Ellendrii. His father climbed down, using the stronger branches to support his heavy bulk. He gestured for Ellendrii to go further down the tree and sit on one of the sturdier branches with him. Ellendrii did so, carrying his, now cold, forest deer.

"I got this for us to share" ventured Ellendrii. Diabloss was only too glad of the food and accepted it gratefully. He had been planning to go on a hunt with Leida but this would keep him going and plus he wanted to know what his son had to say about the contest.

"So, did you pass? Did they let you in?" he asked eagerly.

"Yes" was the one word reply. Ellendrii didn't really want to elaborate on the subject because he hadn't actually got in yet.

"Wow, really? Well done son, I'm proud of you! Have you told your mother?"

"Yes I have" replied Ellendrii, "She was happy too!"

Diabloss nodded and smiled at his son. That would show those stuck up Sky Gryphies! He was about to ask his son what he would do next and what being part of the Elite Flyers would entail, when Ellendrii spoke again.

"Dad, I have a question though" ventured Ellendrii.

"What is it?" asked Diabloss.

"What can you tell me about the SilvaGryphie?" Ellendrii looked at his father, ready to listen intently to his reply.

"The SilvaGryphie? Well, that's a surprising question. You've never expressed much interest in her before" Diabloss looked a little taken aback at his sudden and rather random question.

"To be honest I never really paid much attention to the stories Mum told me about her. But Aro was asking the other sun cycle and I was curious. I'd forgotten about it until now and I told him I'd ask you. I've been so excited about the contest and everything that I hadn't thought further about it" Ellendrii lied.

"Well," began Diabloss, "The SilvaGryphie was the one who brought the Gryphies to Shernaron in the first place. She was their leader. She is a pearly white with an amazing fluffy ruff around her neck and along her back and beautiful beyond description. To look into her wings is to see into eternity itself; everything that has been, is and will be. They say that she formed the Gryphie race within her beautiful wings and then needed a place for them all to live, so she brought them here, to Shernaron. Some also say she herself created Shernaron with her own claws and mind and imagination. However, when she brought them here, she found all the different places like the Mountains, Valleys, Skylands and Forest and created a sub-species to live within each one, who would make good use of it and adapt to live in it properly.

But the Gryphies saw her as not only a leader, but also their God and they started to worship her. She didn't like that and said that even though she created them and brought them here, she was still their equal, even with her great powers and she tried to stop them from worshipping her. She just wanted to live amongst them and enjoy what she had created. But they wouldn't listen and wouldn't stop and so she left one sun cycle and was never seen again. By leaving, she wanted to teach them to live and survive on their own without her help or knowledge and they did but they never forgot her and she is still remembered through each generation. We still tell stories of her even now, especially in moonlit gatherings in the Forest. She has never been seen again. They say she might be across the vast water but no one really knows. No one really knows if she even existed at all but it's nice to think she did."

"Why would she want to live with the dead souls though?" asked Ellendrii.

"Well since she couldn't be with her Gryphies in life, she probably watches over them in death instead. After all, the dead are dead, they don't need to worship the living" Diabloss replied knowledgeably.

"I see" replied Ellendrii, looking thoughtful.

"Do you know if she's friendly?" he asked hopefully.

"I have no idea. No one really knows what she's like except she cares for her beloved Gryphies of course. Why are you asking me all these questions about her?"

Ellendrii sighed. Here comes the hard part. Better get it over with fast.

"Well Dad, I got into the Elite Flyers, only not quite. They have another task for me because I'm not a Sky Gryphie. And that task is to fly over the vast water and find the SilvaGryphie and bring her back to them."

Diabloss looked shocked and sat up, nearly dropping his food.

"What?! What in Shernaron are they asking you to do that for? That is an impossible mission. No one has even attempted to cross the water, let alone find something that may not even exist!" It was then Diabloss realized what they had asked Ellendrii to do was impossible for a reason.

"Out of the question. They asked you to do that because they knew it would be impossible and they don't want you to join their Elite Flyers. You need to give the idea up, Ellendrii and don't go up there again. They are clearly playing you for a fool and what is worse, you are falling for it! I am ashamed of you son, you have let your dreams cloud your reality. You are not going to even attempt to cross the vast water, you will die. Am I making myself clear? Do you understand me?" He looked at his son in the eyes.

Ellendrii huffed and frowned.

"Dad, I am old enough to make my own decisions. I know the task they gave me is seemingly impossible but what if I succeed? They would shut their mouths immediately if I brought her back. They even said I could live with them if I brought her to them. I know they don't really like me but I want to prove myself and if I back down from this, I will be accepting defeat and letting them win."

"Ellendrii, it is not a case of victory or defeat. They are laughing at you behind your back. If you do this and they get word of it, they will laugh even harder. You will never come back. Your mother and I don't want to lose you. Can't you understand that? You're our only son! We have worked so hard to raise you into what we thought was a sensible and mature individual. Clearly we haven't been doing our job right."

"But they will laugh at me if I don't do it. If I don't go back. They will never see me again and laugh because I gave up."

"But if they never see you again that means you could also have gone across the water and died and they will laugh anyway, they will laugh whatever happens!" Diabloss was starting to get angry now.

"But they won't laugh if I bring her back" argued Ellendrii.

"Are you blind? Have you not listened to a single thing I have said to you? You are NOT going across the water chasing after a false and stupid dream. This flying thing is just not worth it. Change your life goal, join my squad, do something else but I absolutely forbid you to go on a stupid quest like this."

"But I..." Ellendrii protested.

"No buts! The answer is NO. I don't want to hear another word about this." Diabloss snarled, eyes raging now.

"I'm old enough to..." Ellendrii snapped.

"NO!!" roared Diabloss, lunging at his son with a burst of angry flames and cuffing him across the ears.

Ellendrii, terrified at his father's sudden outburst took to the sky, tears streaming down his cheeks.

"You don't understand! You don't know what this means to me!" he yelled and flew off in an angry and upset rage.

"I DON'T WANT YOU TO DIE!" roared Diabloss after him. He made no attempt to follow his son; he intended to allow Ellendrii to calm down by himself.

Leida came rushing up the tree to see what the fight was about.

"What's going on?" she asked.

Diabloss growled and sighed.

"Ellendrii wants to go across the vast water to find the SilvaGryphie because the Sky Gryphies told him that was the other condition required in order to join their stupid flying squad. They are playing our son for a fool and Ellendrii is falling for it completely. I am ashamed of him and I am angry at them. So I told him he couldn't go and he snapped at me and flew off in a huff. He'll calm down. He needs to

133

understand that this flying thing can only go so far. He can join my squad. He is perfectly good enough to be a part of them. But of course the leaves are always greener in the other Forest and he wants to be in the Sky Gryphies' flyers. He needs to realize that it is an empty dream and that they are messing with him. I've let him go. He can think about it and sort his head out. He'll realize that I am right."

Leida sat down beside him and sighed.

"He loves to fly so much; it really is his one passion. I don't know how we can provide any other and better chances of doing something with his wings than your squadron. You have the best flyers in the Forest in that squad. But if nothing else, the Sky Gryphies must have been impressed by him in order for them to say he passed their little test."

"They could have just said he'd passed anyway in order to give him this stupid mission. They look down on us as it is, I can only imagine they think our kittens are even more stupid." Diabloss rolled his eyes and snorted.

"And he is playing right into their hands" he said with a sigh.

"I'm sure Ellendrii will calm down and sort himself out over it. He'll come to his senses" Leida reassured her mate, wrapping her wing around his shoulders and resting her head on him.

"I hope so" replied Diabloss.

Meanwhile, Ellendrii was seething. He had known Diabloss wouldn't be happy with him leaving to find the SilvaGryphie but he had hoped at least that his father would accept that Ellendrii was old enough to be allowed to. Well, his parents would just have to accept this particular decision he'd made. He calmed down a little and flew over to Dyarkroeen to tell Aro about it.

He found Aro hunting cave cats along the southern side of the territory. Aro was happy to see him and bounded up excitedly when Ellendrii alighted on the ground.

"So, how'd it go? Did you blow them all away or did it expire in blue smoke?" he asked eagerly.

"Well, I passed the test. I blew them away and they said I was accepted. However there was another condition I hadn't been aware of. Normally that condition is being a Sky Gryphie but because I'm not, they sent me on a quest."

"A quest? Sounds important. What do you have to do?" asked Aro.

"I have to find the founder of all Gryphies, the SilvaGryphie. And she lives the other side of the vast water." Ellendrii waited for this to sink in to Aro's reptilian brain.

"Ok, the vast water, not sure if you've said anyone's actually tried to go across that. Wait, didn't you say the dead end up the other side of that? And what's the SilvaGryphie anyway?" Aro plonked himself down next to his friend and waited for it all to be explained to him. Ellendrii sat down and told him.

"Yes, we believe the souls of our dead go to the other side of the vast water. No one has tried to cross it. The SilvaGryphie is the one who supposedly brought our species to Shernaron. She also created us as well. Dad said that when she brought us here, she made the sub-species for the sky and mountains and stuff but they started to worship her and she didn't like it so she left to live the other side of the vast water and watch over the dead souls instead."

"Worship her? Why wouldn't she want that? Her every need attended to, being waited on, all your meals caught for you, being allowed to laze about and have everything done for you. Why would someone not want that?" asked Aro, genuinely puzzled.

"Because she was *humble*, Aro, like all good Gryphies are! If she was a Lizariaous, she probably would have wallowed in worship. But she wasn't."

Aro put his head on one side and flattened his needles.

"How weird" he muttered, the whole idea a foreign concept to him.

"Anyway I asked Dad about her, which was how I found all this out but when I told Dad that I was going to cross the vast water to find her, he said no. Even though I'm old enough to make this decision on my own! Well I'm going. I don't care what my parents say. This is important to me and I must complete this quest or at least try. Flying is my life! If I don't do this, I will be accepting defeat. Because what if I *do* find her? If I don't at least try then I will never ever know and I will live the rest of my life wondering if I could have found her."

Aro nodded.

"Yeah go for it! Besides, it will be the ultimate adventure! I can't wait to find out what's the other side of the water!"

"When I come back, I'll tell you" smiled Ellendrii. Aro looked down.

"I meant I would come with you…you don't have to do this alone" he looked up, smiling.

"No, it's too dangerous; I don't want to put you at risk too. Besides, you couldn't swim across the water, it just wouldn't work. We don't know how wide it is, you wouldn't have the strength. I must do this alone."

"What? But we go on *all* our adventures together! I want to come with you on this one too! Don't you see how exciting it would be for me? We can find a way around the problem of me crossing the water. And you wouldn't have to travel alone. It's safer with two."

"No, Aro. I have to go alone. You'll…you'll slow me down. No offence."

Offence had been taken though.

"Slow you down?! Do I ALWAYS slow you down then?? Just because I can't fly?? Is that what you've been thinking the whole time we've been friends? That I've SLOWED YOU DOWN??!" Aro was standing now and aiming his needles angrily at his friend.

"I didn't mean it like that. I meant even if we did find a way for you to cross the water with me, it would slow me down. Flying by myself I can go faster; at my own pace. But it's not just that, I don't want to put you in danger. Can't you see? I'm doing this because I care about you?" Ellendrii was adopting a defensive position now. He knew how short tempered Lizariaouses could be.

"No. It's not because you "care". It's because you have wings and I don't. It's ALWAYS been about your wings. Everything we do. I'm sick of you and your stupid obsession with flying. Get real. Think about something other than your dumb life goal."

136

"You know what, Aro? You're just jealous. You always have been. The other Gryphies were jealous because I could fly better but you're jealous that I can fly at all! Jealous of my flying ability, jealous that I can get to places you can't when we go exploring, so jealous that I've had to try and CARRY you before. Do you know how that felt? Grikking HUMILIATING! Carrying your heavy bulk around, it wore me out quicker than flying to the Skylands. Who the GRIK carries a Lizariaous around? But I did it because I knew you were jealous and I wanted you to feel better, to let you see how I see, so you wouldn't feel so left out. I can see though, that it's just made your jealousy grow!! You're too blind to see that I won't let you come because I care about you and don't want you getting hurt. This is MY quest and MY sacrifice and I make it in the name of MY flying and MY life goal. It's none of YOUR business." Ellendrii's nostrils flared and glowed blue, wisps of smoke forming around his jaws as his adrenaline got going and his body prepared to defend itself.

"How grikking DARE you!!! Insult me AND my species? No wonder our species had a war. You Gryphies are stupid and blind and only YOU matter. Well I have news for you; you DON'T matter. You're vain and self centred. You and your stupid wings. Fly, go on! Fly up and I'll show you how easy it is for me to shoot you down!" Aro snarled.

"Shoot ME down? Look at you! Get you on your side and your poisonous needles are useless! How pathetic! Gryphies are far more graceful and resilient than Lizariaouses! I don't know why I ever wanted to be friends with you. I thought you would support me and wish me luck and be happy I was brave enough to want to do this. Do you even realize how scared I am of going out there by myself? No, because Lizariaouses don't know fear because they're too THICK and STUPID to know! You're a rock head, Aro, who doesn't care for anyone but himself and can't see past his own nose for the bigger picture." Ellendrii took to the sky.

"Go on then, Aro! Go, shoot me! If you can! If you can hit someone who is the best flyer in ALL the territories! What are YOUR talents, huh? NOTHING! You have no life goals; you never even grew up! You still only have any interest in

137

exploring like when we were little. Well the world has changed, we are older, and I have no time for your stupid little "adventures" anymore. I have bigger goals now Aro. And they don't include YOU."

Aro roared and snapped, firing off needles angrily and luckily for Ellendrii, badly. He couldn't aim properly because he was so mad. And even if he could, Ellendrii was right about one thing and that was the fact that he was excellent at dodging. Aro would never have been able to hit him anyway; he wasn't experienced enough to. Aro could only hit things on the ground and at close range that didn't move much because he had never felt the need to train himself to do anything other than using his needles to help him occasionally to catch meal creatures.

Aro easily spent all his needles shooting badly at Ellendrii and Ellendrii hovered in the sky laughing at him.

"You're wrong, my parents are wrong, I WILL find the SilvaGryphie. By myself. They can forbid all they like but I will go. Goodbye Aro, I'm only sad you weren't more supportive. Some friend." Ellendrii turned tail and flew away.

Aro pursued him for as long as he could before his legs got tired.

"Come back here and fight!!" he roared, running after the Gryphie but Ellendrii just laughed and carried on flying as Aro got angrier and angrier on the ground, growing more and more jealous of Ellendrii's flying ability.

In his mind though, Ellendrii was disappointed. He was very hurt that neither his parents nor his best friend would support him in something that he found to be so important. And he felt alone. Completely alone. He didn't realize that they'd only been like that about it because they cared. His father didn't want him doing something drastic and getting killed. Aro didn't want him to go alone; he wanted to be there, as his friend. But Ellendrii's determination and sureness that everyone was against him made him blind to the fact that they actually did care about him very much. He started to cry again and landed in a tree on the edge of the Forest when he reached it. It was a thick, full leafed tree and he hid among the leaves out of sight, sobbing.

138

Whether you're right or wrong about your situation, feeling alone is horrible. It feels empty and sad and you just want to escape it and have someone who understands. He mulled everything over in his mind and tried to work out a plan of action.

He could just up and go but he knew his parents would worry and whether they supported him or not, he knew that if he did that, it would hurt them and upset them even more. He knew he had to come clean and tell them he was going; nothing they could do would stop him because he was of age and old enough to make his own decisions. He didn't want them to control him; he was a free Gryphie! So he had to tell them. No question of that. And when would he go? The next sun cycle? The one after that? He didn't want to take too long over this because he didn't want his parents to try and sway his decision or talk him out of it. So he decided to leave as soon as he could. Maybe the sun cycle after next.

And what about Aro? The Lizariaous had been his best friend ever since he could remember and they had done nearly everything together. Were they still friends anymore? He didn't know. He tried to play through their heated conversation in his mind and work out from that if he would be able to stay friends with Aro. He had after all, insulted Aro's entire species. But then Aro had done the same to him. Maybe Aro would forgive him? At the same time, Aro had said some very hurtful things to Ellendrii and he was really upset by that too. Could Ellendrii forgive Aro? He assumed he would in time. When he got back from his quest, *if* he got back from his quest. If. It was a big if. A big and dangerous if. The if that worried Ellendrii more than anything. Ellendrii shook it off and wiped his tears away. No, he wouldn't let anything sway him. His parents and Aro would just have to live with his decision.

Back in Dyarkroeen, Aro was very angry. He stared, seething, at his fallen needles and clawed the ground in frustration as he walked back to where the argument had taken place. How could his best friend say those things and treat him like that? After all the seasons they'd been friends? Typical Gryphie, he thought. They never think of anyone but themselves. His tail swished in anger and he stalked back to his cave, sitting outside it and staring angrily up at the moon. Throwing back his head, he roared in frustration. He wanted to make Ellendrii pay but at the same time he didn't want to hurt him. He roared again and again, his thoughts and feelings mixed up and confusing. A few other Lizariaouses noticed his anger and stayed away. But his father heard him and came bounding to him, wondering and worried about what was wrong with his son.

"Aro?" he asked, approaching, "Are you ok?"

"It's that stupid grikfaced Gryphie Ellendrii!" snapped Aro. "He's going off on some stupid flying quest and he won't let me go with him! I hate him and his stupid wings! It's all he ever thinks about. He's completely obsessed and blinded by it and clearly our friendship over the seasons of our lives have meant nothing to him."

"A flying quest? Well, he was probably only thinking of you. I know you hate it but you can't fly and he probably didn't want you to feel left out or straggle behind. It's not like Ellendrii to be heartless or uncaring" said Mordred.

"Pfft yeah right. His father already told him he can't go. And he's right. This flying thing is getting over the top now."

"Where is he going?" asked Mordred.

"Over the vast water to where the dead souls go to find the SilvaGryphie, which was whatever created Gryphies, according to some stupid legend. No one knows if it even exists and he's risking his life to go after it? In the name of joining some dumb flying squad in the sky? I wanted to go because it would have been a nice adventure and he wouldn't have to go by himself cos he said it was dangerous. I dunno why I bothered to even care about that idiot" Aro spat angrily.

"Who would have told him to do something as fruitless as that? Going after something that might not exist? Why did he believe it?" Mordred looked incredulous.

"The Sky Gryphies. They said that he can't join their flying squad unless he finds the SilvaGryphie." Aro explained.

Mordred looked puzzled.

"It's not like Ellendrii to be that rock headed. Well if he wants to do it, you must let him. Sometimes someone has to

140

do something just to see if they can and find these things out for themselves."

"We had an argument" said Aro quietly. "I don't think we're friends anymore. I shot all my needles at him" Aro looked down in shame. He suddenly felt very bad about what he'd done. Mordred looked horrified.

"Did you hit him?"

"No I didn't. I'm a bad aim but his flying was too "good" anyway" Aro said the word "good" in a mocking tone. He was still mad at Ellendrii, even if he felt bad.

"Aro, I thought we'd raised you better than that. Shooting at a friend? Even shooting at a Lizariaous friend is bad. Our needles still hurt, even though the poison doesn't affect us. I can't believe you would do something so mean and stupid."

"I'm sorry, Dad! He just made me so angry that I lost my temper and couldn't help it. He mocked me, mocked our species! He called us thick and stupid."

"And what did you call his species?" Mordred looked Aro in the eye.

Aro sighed and muttered, "Stupid, blind, vain and self centred..."

"I see" said Mordred quietly. Aro knew he was in deep grik now. Whenever his father spoke quietly like that was the calm before the storm.

"Well, then clearly you are not the son I raised to respect others as I have done." Mordred tapped his war injured tail on the ground and shook his head. Aro hunched over, staring intently at the ground; wishing it would swallow him up.

"Did he say when he was leaving?" asked Mordred. The storm was too quiet.

"No. I never asked." Aro replied.

"Then I suggest you find out and wish him well on his travels before he goes. If he goes on this "quest" and doesn't come back, his last memory of you will be the fight you had. How do you think that would make him feel?"

"Sad" replied Aro.

"Yes, indeed. And a lifetime of friendship wasted on your petty little jealousy" Mordred looked at his son and snarled at

141

him, Mordred's scarred eye making him look even more threatening. Aro cringed.

"Isn't it?" asked Mordred, although it was really more of a statement that he expected his son to agree with.

Aro nodded quietly.

"ISN'T IT?!" snapped Mordred, his jaws cracking down inches from Aro's nose. "SPEAK UP, SON!"

"YES! Yes father, it is a lifetime of friendship wasted on my petty jealousy. And I'm sorry! I was angry; I didn't mean to be so horrid to him. But you don't understand how stupid and primitive I feel at times when I see him flying with such ease!"

"I DO! I do understand. That was part of the reason Zephirak wanted to control the Gryphies in the war. He saw they had fire and flight and all we have is our weight and needles and if we end up on our sides, we can't fight at all. But if you look at it, the Gryphies rely on their wings. A grounded Gryphie is as good as a dead Gryphie. Whereas we are perfectly at home on the ground. So we all have our strengths and weaknesses. Yes I would love to see what it's like up in the sky but I can't because I belong down here. They might have wings, fire and speed but we have our weight, needles, strong bite, tenacity. We have things going in our favour too, don't you see?"

Aro thought for a moment and then nodded with realization.

"Yes! Yes I do see. Even though I would love wings, I can see that Lizariaouses have good points like that too." He smiled, nodding. "I'd still like to go though, I know I can help him and a journey shared is a journey halved!"

"No, that's a problem."

"What problem?"

"A problem shared is a problem halved"

"Same thing. The journey is a problem and so is finding the SilvaGryphie. Surely with two of us it will make it easier to find it?"

"Yes it probably would but you're forgetting that your mother and I don't really want you going on a journey you might never come back from either."

"Oh. Yeah." Aro looked disappointed.

"But then again we know you'd be happier accompanying your friend on his journey. If you didn't go, you'd just be wandering around Dyarkroeen with nothing to do. You could make other friends but you've always preferred the company of Ellendrii and I know it wouldn't be the same for you. So, you can go if you want. Whatever Diabloss's choices are for his son; my own son's happiness is my top priority, plus I'm also taking into account that you are of age to do as you wish. I can't actually stop you if you really want to go. But before you do, you must spend some time with your mother. Go on a hunt with her. She will miss you when you go. If Ellendrii decides to let you go with him." Secretly Mordred hoped the Gryphie wouldn't let Aro accompany him on the journey. But he didn't want to be so mean as to not allow his son to have the choice.

"Thanks Dad, thanks for understanding" said Aro. "I only hope Ellendrii forgives me for what I did."

"If he's really your friend, he will. After all, you've never done it before. I'm sure he'll allow you a second chance at the friendship" Mordred smiled. Aro nodded and brightened.

"Now, come back to the cave with me and we'll tell your mother of your plan. You can stay with us this moon cycle" Mordred stood and smiled at his son, who followed him. Mordred only hoped that Schaarl wouldn't take the news too badly.

Back in Shernaron, Ellendrii had got over his tears and sadness and his head was clear now. He'd flown back to his parents and snuck up to his sleeping branch without letting them know he was home. He didn't feel like talking to them, especially his father. He would talk to his mother at sunrise. He knew his father would be going out to fly with his squad and his mother would be alone to talk to.

So the next sun cycle, Ellendrii awoke and climbed down to find Leida. She was dozing in the main sleeping chamber of the tree. Diabloss wasn't there and Ellendrii breathed a sigh of relief. Leida heard him climbing and lifted her head.

"Ellendrii?" she sat up and stretched a wing.

"Hi Mum" said Ellendrii, entering and sitting down before his mother.

"So you've calmed down now then?" asked Leida.

"Yes I have. And I still want to go, I'm afraid" said Ellendrii, straightening up to his full height in the hopes that it would make his mother see how big he'd grown and how ready he was to do this by himself.

Leida sighed.

"I thought you would. Your father and I both worried that even when he told you you couldn't, you would still want to. I know you are old enough to do this by yourself. You are not a kitten anymore. We can only advise you against it but we can't stop you and you know it."

Ellendrii couldn't help nodding at this. He knew that he could go and do this.

"Well then if it's something you really want to do, follow your dreams"

"Why are you so easily letting me when Dad was yelling at me?"

"What else can I do? We can't stop you from going. And I'm not in the habit of yelling. I am in the habit of letting others learn by experience. We are all in charge of our own lives. If you do this and die doing so, then it was your choice. But we, as your parents also know that we did all we could to change your mind. I don't want you to die and your father is terrified of it, which is why he got angry. He only knows to react in anger when he is afraid."

"He acts in anger most of the time" muttered Ellendrii.

"Well yes, he is rather grouchy, even when he's happy, he's gruff" smiled Leida, "But he does have your best interests at heart. We both do."

"I know" said Ellendrii quietly, "But you know I want to do this to prove to myself and I want to see what's the other side of the vast water as well."

"Then go, find out what's out there and please come home safely. If you fly and fly and can't reach the other side, don't worry, come back. Always know when to give up" Leida hugged her son close and nuzzled his head.

"I will, Mum, thank you" replied Ellendrii and hugged her too.

Chapter 8
The Journey Begins

Over the next couple of sun cycles, Ellendrii's parents got used to the idea that he was going on his quest and they did all they could to give him useful tips and ideas for survival.

Diabloss told him about living off fish if he was going to make the journey across the water. He taught Ellendrii how to catch fish with maximum efficiency and less energy use so he wouldn't tire.

Lunara made him a leather pouch bag to carry with him to keep food and water supplies in while he flew, so he could catch a bunch of fish at once, eat some and carry the others with him to eat later. And importantly, to ration the food and water.

"You mustn't ration too much or starve yourself or you will become weak, so be careful with eating. Not too much food and water and not too little. It will take a while but you will find a happy medium. You must ration the water extra carefully because unlike the food, it is unlikely you will be able to get any more." Lunara told him. She also gave him some herbs too, in case he got injured. They were wrapped in large thick leaves to keep the moisture off.

The main problem Ellendrii faced was resting. Flying over the water all the way would make him tired and he would have to rest. Not knowing how wide the water was, didn't help. He could land on the water and rest on it for a while but the problem then arose of sleeping and possibly drowning or getting dragged around by the tide and losing his way.

The sun cycle before he was due to leave, Ellendrii sat on the cliffs looking out to sea and wondered how he would rest. It was the only problem they hadn't managed to solve yet.

"Ellendrii…"

He spun around.

"What do *you* want?" he asked Aro.

"I came to apologize. I'm sorry for snapping like that at you and insulting your species and being so immature. I was just mad because I really want to come with you." Aro walked up to him. He hadn't been able to find out when Ellendrii was leaving, so he thought he'd just visit him instead and say what he needed to. He'd asked Leida where Ellendrii was but she didn't know so he'd just ended up wandering about and found his friend at the cliffs.

"I accept the apology. But you still can't come with me. I'm sorry too; I didn't mean to snap at you like that. Are we still friends?" asked Ellendrii.

"Of course" replied Aro. "Since you still don't want me to come with you, despite the fact that I can keep you company and help you on the journey, how's it been since our argument? Have your parents relented or are you just going?"

"They said they couldn't stop me but they and my other friends are preparing me to go. Dad taught me how to fish properly and Lunara has been providing survival tips and things to take with me. The only problem I'm having is a place to rest while I'm flying across the water. Since we don't know how wide it is, there's no way of knowing how long it will take and I can't just fly forever without resting."

Aro sat down and contemplated this. After a while he looked up and said, "Actually, I might have a solution to that problem! But you have to let me come with you!"

"You're so determined aren't you?" Ellendrii gritted his teeth and sighed.

"Ok, if you really want to come, what is your solution to my problem?"

"You have to PROMISE I can come with you and you won't change your mind on this!" said Aro.

"Ok, ok, fine, I promise you can come with me. Now what's your idea?"

"A float! Trees float right? We make a float out of wood and I can sit on it while you pull it. Then when you need to rest, you just need to land on it and rest. While you sleep I can stay awake and make sure we keep on course and don't turn around or anything and we can store food on it. We can make part of it like a cave to lie under while we sleep, or to shelter us from the rain or sun." Aro explained.

"Hmm, it sounds quite good but surely pulling it would tire me out more quickly?"

"It doesn't matter, because you could rest. You're in no hurry to find this SilvaGryphie so we don't need to rush anyway." Aro looked quite proud of his idea and Ellendrii had to admit that it was a pretty good one, for a Lizariaous anyway.

They went back to the Forest and asked Diabloss for help.

"So you want to go too then Aro? Have you asked your parents?" asked Diabloss.

"Yeah and they said I could!" replied Aro confidently.

Diabloss sighed. Lizariaouses had always been less bothered about their kids than Gryphies were about their kittens. He did suspect though that Mordred wasn't entirely happy about his son going off like that. And he would be right.

"I had the idea to make a float out of trees or something" said Aro, "So I could sit on it and Ellendrii could pull me. Then when Ellendrii needs to sleep, cos he will you know, it's a long journey, he can sleep on it while I paddle at the side to keep us going on our journey. We could make part of it under cover like a cave in case it gets too hot or rains and we have to take shelter, or for when we sleep." Aro looked very excited about his idea.

Diabloss looked thoughtful.

"Yes that can be done, though we will need help. I'll ask some of my squad to help as well. It will have to be quite a big float to fit you both on, are you sure you'll be strong enough to pull it, Ellendrii?"

"Yeah I'm sure, things are lighter when they're being pulled on water anyway" replied Ellendrii quickly.

"But what about rough water? Sometimes it gets stormy" said Diabloss.

"I have no other choice and Aro is right, I'd have to take something with me to rest on anyway, I dunno why I never thought of it before. So I'd still need to pull something. None of us know how long it will take or how far."

"You have a good point. You'll just have to do your best. But we will try and keep the size small to make it lighter for you. Trust me, after pulling something a long way, you will get tired and even more so with someone else sat on it."

"Ok" agreed Ellendrii. Diabloss nodded and they went off to find some others to help. They decided to fell a tree at the edge of the Forest. They needed something strong, so they couldn't fell a dead tree, which would have been easier. They found a decent size tree and Diabloss got the youngsters to wait by it for him while he went to find some of the squad to help build. The more help they had, the faster it would get done and Ellendrii really did want it done fast because he was dying to set out on his journey.

Diabloss found Tranzoss, Kayto, Xin and Cyrax and brought them back to help.

The first problem was felling the tree without damaging the trees around it. So they used strong vines to support the tree while Tranzoss and Xin flamed it to make the trunk brittle enough to break through. Tranzoss, the Fire Master, wrapped the trunk in her flames and seared the wood deeper and deeper. Since Gryphies' blue fire is more powerful than regular fire, it burned through faster.

Diabloss used his tailspade to slash the burned wood while the other two males, Kayto and Cyrax helped support the tree as the vines took more of the weight. The tree started to lean and Ellendrii and Aro helped out with supporting it too. They didn't want it to fall too fast and smash through the other trees. By letting it down more slowly, they could avoid most of the damage caused to the surrounding trees. A few branches were snapped off but the damage to the other trees wasn't nearly as bad as it would have been if the tree had fallen straight down and faster.

Finally the tree was lying on the ground and everyone had a rest. Now it was just a case of cutting it into smaller logs and getting them down on the beach. They had chosen a tree at the edge of the Forest that was nearer to the cliffs.

They cut the tree up in a similar way to how they'd felled it. By burning the wood until it was brittle and slashing it with their tailspades.

The squad members were big and strong and could carry quite a bit of the wood by themselves. Also, Diabloss carried a lot of it too. Ellendrii and Aro did their part but the wood was heavy. They could only carry one piece each. They left some where it was, planning to come back to it in case they needed more for the float.

The wood they used was mostly near the top of the tree where it was thinner. The tree's trunk got big and wide near the bottom and it would have been too heavy for Ellendrii to pull. They figured that they could just use more logs of the thinner wood as opposed to less of the thicker, wider wood. They gathered some strong vines so they could tie them together.

Reaching the beach, the Gryphies laid out the wood how it would be for the float. Ellendrii and Aro got onto it so the others had a good gauge for the size it should be and they put together the base of it first.

Then they gathered some more of the wood, burning and slicing it lengthways because of the thickness, to make the shelter part of the float. Again, the two stood on the float so they would know how high to make the shelter. They made it high enough that Aro could easily go under it without ducking. Ellendrii had to duck a little but he would only be going under it to shelter or sleep so it wasn't so important to make it too high.

Tranzoss shot down some sea vultures for their lunch and they all had a meal and a break and looked at their creation as they had made it so far. It was looking good. The base was made and bound together and the frame of the shelter had been put together too. Diabloss examined it. He wanted to make sure that the vines were bound and rebound so the strength of the sea wouldn't tear it apart if they ended up getting caught in a storm. He'd seen the power of the sea many times and it wasn't to be messed with. For this reason, he had had the idea to make a door for the shelter, so they could close themselves in if they were caught in a storm that was too strong for Ellendrii to fly in. He only hoped the pair wouldn't get turned around and lost during a strong storm. They had no idea where they should go other than straight and if they got turned around, then it would mean they would never get to the other side where the SilvaGryphie was. Obviously, given their ideas of what it looked like, everyone assumed that it was a vast body of water and there was land the other side, similar to a huge river and to get turned around would be the equivalent of going down that river into whatever oblivion may lay waiting for them. Straight was the *only* way to go if they wanted to reach where the SilvaGryphie and the souls of the dead went.

Ellendrii was starting to feel a bit nervous by this time. It was really happening! He was really going to go off, with Aro, and leave everything he knew behind. He felt a little scared but was determined not to let it show. After all, he needed to prove this to everyone, especially himself, in order to complete his life goal and do the thing he was truly passionate about.

Aro on the other hand wasn't nervous at all. Being a Lizariaous, he could just throw himself in and get on with it and didn't seem to know fear or anything like it. All he knew was it was adventure time and he would certainly be there to partake!

Later on, Leida joined the team and helped out as well. She had been taking care of some tasks but now she'd finished, she wanted to be a part of helping her son prepare for his journey once more. Ellendrii already had his carrying bag to put food and supplies in and Leida had brought along some more food and various other things to put in the float's shelter when it was built. She looked clearly worried about all this but also was determined not to let her son see it. She could sense his own worry and much as she wanted him to stay, she also knew that he needed to do this to prove himself in his own way so she respected that. After they'd eaten, the Gryphies got on with the rest of the shelter. Just after mid-sun it was finished and ready to go. Leida had twined a few lengths of vine together to serve as a strong rope for Ellendrii to pull the float. Now to test it out!

Diabloss and Kayto dragged the float into the water and Ellendrii landed on it, tying the twine around his body and chest like a harness. The sea was calm so it was easy to fly into the sky and pull the float around.

Next, Aro splashed over to the float and climbed on, sitting on it and letting Ellendrii see how different it was pulling the float with his heavy bulk on it. Ellendrii struggled a little at first but soon got the hang of it. He did worry how he would manage in rough water though. Diabloss saw this.

"If the water gets rough, land on the float and just paddle. If you get tired, you can always get Aro to tie it to himself and have him swim along pulling it." Diabloss suggested. Aro didn't look too sure. Although he could swim, it wasn't really a natural thing for barren Dyarkroeen living Lizariaouses to do.

"Just make sure you don't change direction" said Diabloss as Aro tied the twine around himself and tried to swim while pulling the float. They had spare twine in case what they were using broke.

Aro wasn't very good at pulling the float so they mutually decided to try and paddle for it if the water was too rough or at least keep an eye on it and make sure they didn't turn. If they ended up getting carried away by the current, they may never find the SilvaGryphie!

"I can fish, sorta…so I can probably try and catch food for us while you fly" suggested Aro.

"No, we'll make stops to catch food. We mustn't let our food stock get too low though, in case we can't stop and catch more for whatever reason. So when we see it's running out a bit, we'll catch a bunch more so we don't run out."

They pulled the float back onto the sand again.

"When did you plan on leaving?" asked Diabloss.

"Now" said Ellendrii, "I can't wait to get started!" And if I leave it till the next sun cycle, I might not want to do it he thought.

"It would be better to start next sun cycle" said Diabloss, "that way you will be able to get further before you have to sleep"

Ellendrii sighed. He'd kind of thought it might be like that. Then he had an idea.

"Ah but if we leave this sun then yes I might not have so long to fly before moon cycle but it will give me a chance to ease into it. I can fly for a shorter time and have a rest instead of jumping in with flying for a whole sun cycle and then resting. I'd have to rest anyway for a while, I couldn't just fly for the whole sun cycle and then rest."

"I know, I wasn't suggesting that. I just thought that you would get more travelling behind you if you started at sunrise. Before it got dark."

"But my idea is good too, right?" grinned Ellendrii.

Diabloss sighed.

"Yes it is a good idea too." In reality, he didn't want to say goodbye to his son so soon but he didn't want to let on. Diabloss had always been strong and tough but there were times when a softer side showed its way through and if he wasn't careful, now would be one of those times. These times only showed when it related to either his mate or his son though. Often during the war he'd worried about Leida.

"So I can then?" asked Ellendrii.

"Ok, yes you can. I can't stop you anyway. I just thought it would have been better to get more past you. Though I doubt you could fly to the other side in one sun cycle."

"Do you really have no idea at all how wide it is?" asked Aro.

"I don't, no. No one has ever wanted to fly across it. We can't see the other side so we've never been curious enough to try and cross it. We don't know what's out there and it's not worth risking our lives for" his eyes flicked at Ellendrii, who pretended not to notice.

"So you just think the dead go over there? Who came up with *that* idea?" Aro asked.

"It's always been that way. I don't know how it started. It's just what we believe, like your species believes the dead go underground. I mean, do *you* know how that started?" Diabloss asked, firing back the similar question at Aro.

"Oh it was one of our elders, ages and ages ago who came up with the idea cos the dead rot into the ground. He thought it would be a neat thing to believe so…meh" Aro shrugged.

Diabloss was speechless.

Leida was fussing around Ellendrii a little.

"So you want to go now?"

"Yes I do. The sooner the better, and just think, the sooner I go, the sooner I'll be back, with the SilvaGryphie!"

"Ok, well do you have enough food?"

152

"I have this" he showed her the contents of his pouch.

"We'll need to catch you more than that. Tranzoss, take the squad out and catch a few things to go in the shelter" Leida said to Tranzoss who was stood nearby. Tranzoss nodded and gathered Cyrax and Xin to catch a few small things to go in the shelter.

"I can fish too, remember?" asked Ellendrii.

"I want you to go out with plenty though, remember you said wanting to get as much travelling behind you as possible? Well with more food in the shelter, you won't need to spend so much time catching things." Leida told him.

"HEY!! CAN YOU CATCH A COUPLE OF CAVE CATS FOR ME?" yelled Aro at the disappearing Gryphies. Cyrax nodded and changed direction.

Leida gave Aro a "look". Aro looked sheepish.

"What? They're my fave! Who knows when I'll have another one" said Aro. Leida sighed and took a look at the shelter.

"Food can go in this corner. And I think you need to take the pouch off while you pull the float because you just don't need any extra weight than you already have" she said, gesturing for Ellendrii to give her the pouch, which he did.

"Hey I'm not *that* heavy!" protested Aro.

"I never said *you* but if you assumed that anyway well then you have a guilty conscience" grinned Leida. Aro quietened down. Ellendrii sat on the float as Leida arranged the pouch in the corner of the shelter near where the food would go.

"I'll miss you, Mum" said Ellendrii quietly. Leida looked round at him and came to sit next to him.

"I'll miss you too" she said, putting an arm around him.

"I know I've been determined to do this and I'm not having second thoughts but I am scared. In a way I'm glad Aro insisted on coming along." He looked over at Aro, who was trying to shoot down a sea vulture with one of his needles.

"At least then I'm not alone. I think I would have been more apprehensive if I'd been going by myself. I do want to prove myself but at the same time I'm fully aware I might not come back. You might never see us again. And if I die or don't

153

make it, Aro won't be able to make it either. There's no way he can make it across the water by himself. He can't fly and he wouldn't be strong enough to swim or paddle the float. So I feel even more responsible. It's not just me; I have to look after his life too."

"Yes I can see that's somewhat of a burden. Aro seems perfectly fine with going with you though. I'm sure if he had any second thoughts he wouldn't go."

"He would. To him it's just an adventure. I don't know if he would even care if he died doing what he loves. I don't even think it's occurred to him that if anything happens to me, that means he won't be able to come back. This is why I'm worried. I want to go but at the same time I'm so scared..." Ellendrii looked down at the wood and suppressed a tear.

"You still don't have to do it. After all, the Sky Gryphies aren't exactly going to come down here and mock you for not going. You won't ever see them again and in all honesty they'll probably forget about you. If it's only to prove them wrong, there isn't any point in bothering, there really isn't. You must do this for you, to prove yourself but again you don't have to. You know Diabloss's squadron is perfectly happy to take you on. What do the Sky Gryphies do that they don't?"

"Well, they're way better flyers than his squad. The main reason I wanted to be in the Elite Flyers is because I know they're up to my standard. No offence to Diabloss's squad but I outshine them all in the air. There wouldn't be any challenge. What challenge is there when you're the best at what you do?"

"There is still the challenge of improvement. And there is always room for that. Besides, Tranzoss is a Fire Master. But she's still in the squad because there is need for her. She's better with her fire than any of them but she doesn't let that stop her from being a part of them even though she outshines them in the fire department. There is always a use for her skills and in all honesty, Ellendrii, it's a little bigheaded to look down on others because your skills are better. She doesn't and you shouldn't either."

"I'm not. But I just want more of a challenge. I get that in the sky, among the clouds, I just think I could learn some

154

more skills with the Sky Gryphies, they could teach me and I could get better."

Leida looked thoughtful.

"Well," she said, "in that case you still don't have to join their Elite Flyers; you could just ask them for advice. They're bigheaded enough to give it to you if you butter them up."

"Yeah but I've already accepted this challenge. I can't go back there and say I don't want to do it and would rather have their advice instead. They'll just laugh at me."

"You could go up there and avoid the leaders and just ask someone else?" Leida suggested hopefully.

"No, the leaders would find out and I don't think any of the others would want to help judging by the looks they give me when they see me. It's no use; I have no choice but to do this now. Unless I just accept joining Dad's squad."

"So you don't actually want to do this now?" asked Leida.

"No, I do still want to do it. But I feel now more than ever that I *have* to do it. The only reservation I had, apart from failing miserably and not coming back was about taking Aro with me but of course he doesn't really care anyway; he's happy to be with me going on an adventure so I guess if that's the case then I don't have to worry so much anyway."

"You must do what you feel is best. After all, you are a young adult now and that is the adult decision you must make. We must accept responsibility for all our decisions in this life. And I will miss you and I hope you make it back, even without the SilvaGryphie. You need to know when it's time to return home and have the wisdom to give up when you have to. If you can't reach the other side or if you get there and can't find her, come home. Don't stay there and do a pointless search. Do you understand, Ellendrii?"

"Yes I do, Mum. I'll come back if I can't make it or I can't find her."

"Thank you, then I know you will stay safe." Leida hugged him.

Ellendrii nodded. It had never occurred to him that it might not be just about going out and finding the SilvaGryphie and that they might encounter other creatures to defend

155

themselves against. Since nothing hunted Gryphies, it also had never occurred to his parents either.

Presently the others had returned with food. Tranzoss, Cyrax and Xin had caught quite a bit, all were small though. And yes, Cyrax had managed to get a cave cat for Aro.

All together, the Gryphies had caught one Quadra-Felieon, six sea vultures, the cave cat and a Xole which is a small mole-like creature that only comes out into the open at certain times of the sun cycle. Xoles, like ground birds, are pretty rare. They are plump with plenty of meat on them so they make excellent rations since their meat is very filling.

Aro eyed the Xole as hungrily as he eyed the cave cat.

Leida and Ellendrii arranged the food in the corner of the shelter and Aro was given strict instructions not to eat any of it before they started. Or even after for that matter, since they had agreed to eat before they left.

Diabloss had caught some sea vultures and the two of them feasted on these while the squadron members bid them farewell and good luck and left. Only Leida and Diabloss remained to see them off.

"Is Mordred going to come and see you off?" asked Diabloss.

"No" replied Aro, "I spent some time with Mum and we hunted together and both of them said goodbye to me before I came here. They were obviously confident that I would persuade Ellendrii to let me go with him" Aro grinned. "My sisters never even said goodbye though. I'll chew their ears when I get back!"

"You do realize that you might not come back" said Diabloss, carefully.

"Yeah but we probably will, I mean, I'm with Ellendrii and he's THAT determined that nothing will stop him. I mean if you guys couldn't then nothing will" said Aro. "Plus he's got me if he gets stuck!"

Diabloss just smiled. Let him think what he likes. If he knows how difficult this could be, it would destroy his confidence. Maybe. Let him go into it with confidence and determination. At least Ellendrii was more aware of the risks. He was clearly going to be the common sense on this journey.

Maybe.

Finally everything was ready. The pair of them had had the food they needed to get started, all supplies were on board and they were ready to go into who knows what and who knows where.

Leida was getting teary eyed and trying to hide it and Diabloss had a wing around her as the two boys got the float ready to go. Ellendrii was getting himself into the twine harness and Aro had shut the door of the shelter and was starting to push the float out into the water. He was stronger than Ellendrii and Diabloss half thought that if Aro could fly, they may have a better chance of crossing however wide the water would be. Aro got the float into the water and climbed onto it and Ellendrii was checking the harness for strength and making sure it wouldn't slip from around him. He tightened it in a few places, since he'd had to loosen it to take it off and put it on and he pulled on it to make sure it was secure.

Next he checked where the twine was attached to the float and made sure that was secure as well. The last thing they needed was to be caught in bad weather and have the float come away from the twine and be swept away somewhere with the hapless Aro on board.

Diabloss helped Ellendrii do the checks since he was stronger and could tug harder on it to make sure it was secure.

"And don't forget to land on the float if the weather gets bad. Don't play the hero and try to pull it through the storm. You will end up hurting yourself and then you'll both be in deep water, quite literally, since only you can pull the float. So look after yourself!" Diabloss warned him.

"I will" said Ellendrii. His heart was beating faster and felt like it was slowly making its way up to his throat now. He was all nerves. It was really happening.

The late afternoon light of the summer sun cycle shone down warmly as Ellendrii and Aro prepared to set off.

Diabloss and Leida stood on the beach together, watching the pair and wishing them well on their journey. They both had a mixture of hope and worry on their faces. Ellendrii had never seen his father quite like this before.

Diabloss was strong and powerful but his son meant the world to him and he was sad to see him set out on such a perilous journey.

Ellendrii was sat on top of the shelter and he took to the sky, letting the twine run all the way out before pulling it taught as he flew forward, pulling the float through the shallow water with Aro sitting on it, waving to the watching parents on the shore.

"Good luck you two!" yelled Diabloss.

"We love you, Ellendrii! Stay safe, Aro!" called Leida, her velvety cheeks moist with tears.

"We will!" called back Aro, still waving. Ellendrii waved too.

"We'll be back before you know it!" he yelled. It sounded far more hopeful than he felt. Right now he had butterflies in his stomach and he was fighting the regret of his decision to do this. It had come on so suddenly when he'd been so confident before. He'd lulled himself into a false sense of security.

His wings were straining a little as he pulled the float into deeper water. The water got deeper rather suddenly. He only hoped that whatever strong Deamon genes his father had passed through to him would come into play and he would have the strength to pull the float across the vast water. This had better all be worth it! The Sky Gryphies had better not have lied! The legend had better be true!

They had gone out quite far now and his parents were steadily getting smaller back on the land. They would have flown out for a little way with the two boys but Leida felt too wobbly to do it.

She could be quite emotional despite her bravery. But after all, emotion is not a weakness. It just made her fly a little funny. Diabloss stayed with her to support her.

Finally Aro's foreleg was too tired to wave anymore and he stopped. He looked up at Ellendrii.

"How you doing up there? Holding out ok?" he asked.

158

"Yeah I'm alright. And I should hope I'm holding out ok, we've only just started!" Ellendrii chuckled. Aro was secretly happy that he didn't need to pull the float but he had a strange sense of guilt as well because there was nothing he could really do. He looked out at the water and the disappearing coastline. Ellendrii's parents were walking away together by this time. Aro thought of his own parents and wondered how they were doing. They knew that if he didn't come back to Dyarkroeen at sundown, Aro would have gone with Ellendrii and they may not see him again. At least they had the two sisters to soften the blow somewhat but he knew that his mother especially would miss the hunts they used to go on together.

"I'll see you soon, Mum" whispered Aro to the disappearing coastline. He shifted around on the float, which made Ellendrii look down as the float bobbed about a little.

"Aro, please don't move so much, you're throwing off its balance" Ellendrii scolded him and Aro looked up apologetically.

"Sorry Ellendrii, I'll try not to move too much" he replied looking sheepish. He decided to stare into the water instead. It was crystal clear but not so deep just yet that he couldn't see the bottom. He marvelled at all the different types of fish that were swimming around down there. The colours were incredible and he wondered what it would be like to eat one of them. He wondered if the colours would make them taste better or worse and he really hoped that the two of them would get a chance to catch some at some point.

He trailed a paw into the water while Ellendrii flew along, letting the ripples of the water play around his leg. It was cool and refreshing in the warm sun. Catching those fish was so tempting but he knew Ellendrii would be annoyed if he shifted about too much and he also wasn't sure about jumping in because it would hinder progress and he would knock the float around trying to climb back on. He sighed. He wasn't that hungry luckily. The food they'd had back on land was enough to keep him going. For now.

Ellendrii felt his wing muscles ache a little bit. Oh great he thought, my wings are aching already and we've barely left. I won't make it at this rate. I can't rest yet, we're not even into deep water.

He looked around as he flew. He could see nothing but water ahead of him. Behind him he saw the gentle curve of the coastline but it swept back and along, so there was no way that it would curve enough to meet at the other side. Ellendrii was a little disappointed at this. Still, the weather was nice, the water was calm and being after mid-sun, the sun wasn't as hot as it could have been so flying was fairly easy in that respect. He closed his eyes and swept back his wings in a huge, calm motion. The air felt good on his face and he laid his ears back, enjoying the flight despite his aching muscles. This was it, it had started, no going back now until they had reached their goal. His tummy felt better now they had actually started their journey and he felt more confident again. They *would* do this! They *would* find the legendary SilvaGryphie! They could do it!

On the float, Aro was now trailing his tail in the water. He wondered idly if he could skewer a fish on his tail blade. He swished it about a little, scattering the fish that did swim near. They were all too small anyway and the motion of the water seemed to push their light bodies away from him when he moved his tail. He turned and lay on his side, looking up at the clear blue sky. He couldn't lie on his back because of his needles and he certainly wasn't going to shoot them all off so he could lie on his back and sky gaze. He looked up at Ellendrii, who was still enjoying the cool ocean breeze and moving his wings in large sweeping motions which got more air behind him and helped him move faster and with less effort. The motions he made were quite slow. His father had taught him techniques like these so he could keep flying for longer. It was in fact his father who started out Ellendrii's love of the sky and flying. He would take little Ellendrii out and teach him instead of getting him to go to flight school like the other kittens, until he was older. Gryphies had no currency to speak of, so the flight school was free, but Diabloss had the time and knowledge to teach his son himself, so he did when he was very young. Sometimes two Gryphies would exchange something for something else, which was the closest they got to paying for things; fair exchange.

Ellendrii wondered what clouds and sky things he would find across the vast water. Maybe they would find clouds that were different to the ones in Shernaron. Certainly there *were* different clouds because of the large misty cloud covering that separated the Sky Gryphie territory from their own.

Ellendrii's mind wandered back to how peaceful and sunny it was up there above the cloud layer. Maybe one sun cycle he would be living up there. He only hoped it would happen if they managed to complete the quest and the Sky Gryphies accepted him. They'd better keep their word after all the trouble he and Aro were going to to complete this quest. He looked down at Aro, who smiled up at him.

Yes he was definitely happy to have a friend to travel with, even though he hadn't wanted Aro to accompany him at first. Ellendrii smiled back.

It would be a long journey but he would do his best. And his confidence grew with Aro by his side as well.

Chapter 9
Endless Water

They had been travelling for a while now, maybe a few hours. The sun was getting lower in the sky but it wasn't dark yet. Ellendrii hadn't stopped for a rest and his muscles were starting to burn. He sighed and flew down, alighting on the float next to Aro.

"You ok?" asked Aro.

"Yeah but my wings ache. I'm hungry as well. I'll have a rest and something to eat and then fly until sunset. When it gets dark, I'll rest and sleep. You need to stay awake though to make sure we keep going in the right direction.

"That's fine, I've been sleeping quite a lot in the sun before it got lower" Aro smiled. He fetched some food from the supply and they both sat and ate, looking out to sea as the float drifted slowly along. Luckily the current was with them but the float did have a habit of turning a little. Aro paddled with his tail just enough to turn it back around so it was facing forward again. They had it facing with the shelter towards the back and the sitting platform at the front.

Aro jumped on top of the shelter and looked back the way they had come.

"Wow, I can't see the land at all now" he remarked. Ellendrii took a look too.

"I can but only just. It's that line of land waaay over there" he pointed but Aro's eyes were just not good enough to see what Ellendrii could. Aro shook his head.

"Nope, can't see it" he replied and hopped back down onto the platform. He peered over the edge.

"Now we've stopped for a bit, can I have a swim? I really want to see if I can catch a fish…" He looked at Ellendrii hopefully.

"Yeah sure" replied Ellendrii. "But don't take too long. I want to fly a bit more before the moon rises" Aro nodded and dived into the water.

Ellendrii watched his friend swimming around chasing after fish. There weren't so many now that they were further away from the coast. But what he did find were bigger and easier to catch! He floated with his head out of the water so he could look down into it and spot the fish. Adjusting his body at an angle, he aimed and fired a needle down at a large fish that passed by, but he missed. The fish, frightened, swam away quickly.

"It's not as easy as it looks" remarked Ellendrii.

"No kidding" muttered Aro. He tried again but this time skewered a fish right through the middle.

"HA! You were saying?" he yelled, full of enthusiasm now and grinning. Ellendrii smiled.

Aro dived down and grabbed the needle between his teeth, hauling the fish up with it and plopping it up on the float. He climbed up afterwards.

"Nice catch" congratulated Ellendrii.

"This is great! I can catch fish for us!" yelled Aro excitedly.

"You can catch fish for you. I can't eat it, it's been poisoned. You're immune to your own poison. I am not" said Ellendrii. Aro looked sad.

"I hadn't thought of that" he said.

"It's ok, I can catch birds instead" replied Ellendrii.

"You're too tired to catch birds" said Aro. He had a point.

"Well then I'll catch a few each sunrise, for the sun cycle ahead, when my strength is fresh!" Ellendrii declared. Aro agreed that this was a good idea and tucked into the sizeable fish he'd caught.

After Ellendrii had rested, he took to the sky again and carried on flying and pulling the float. He hadn't taken the harness off; he figured he would take it off when he rested and put it on Aro instead just in case they needed to try and keep the float going the right way and Aro needed to pull it along while swimming. It wasn't such a good idea since of course he wasn't used to it but it was better than nothing and it made them both feel better about not completely losing control of their vessel.

The sun was setting. While Ellendrii flew, Aro rested and slept on the platform. He didn't want to sleep in the shelter just yet because there was no need and he felt the wind on his scales was soothing as he drifted off to sleep.

Soon the moon rose and Ellendrii landed next to Aro, nudging him awake.

"Is it that time already?" asked a sleepy Aro.

"Yeah, I need to rest, I'm tired" replied Ellendrii and headed into the shelter, closing the wooden door behind him.

Aro sat up and watched the moon high in the sky. It was high and bright and shone down, making the dark seem almost like sunlight. Aro marvelled at this. He'd seen similar back in Dyarkroeen when he'd sat outside his cave and moon gazed. The water was calm and the moon reflected in it like glass. Everything was so peaceful. It was hard to believe that the water could also be dangerous. Aro's tummy growled. He was hungry and Ellendrii was asleep in the shelter where the food was. He would have to be quiet and not wake him up.

Aro opened the door slowly and carefully and peered inside. The moonlight was good enough that it made it easier to see the sleeping form of Ellendrii and the food piled carefully into the other corner. Ellendrii however, moaned in his sleep when the moonlight shone on his face and he grunted, luckily rolling over. Aro closed the door a little, so that hopefully Ellendrii would go back to sleep and not be disturbed. Ellendrii had thankfully put his wing over his face, which would block out most light. Aro crept in and grabbed the nearest piece of food he could, which was a sea vulture and slowly backed back out with it in his mouth. The feathers tickled his nose in an annoying fashion and lo and behold he felt a sneeze coming on. He fell backwards, trying to close the door before he sneezed. He did manage to but unfortunately the force of him ejecting air from his nostrils made his body shudder, rocking the float quite violently. He slapped a paw over his face for what good it would do him and with eyes wide he stared at the door, afraid Ellendrii would come storming out and be annoyed with him. Luckily he didn't. In fact nothing happened. So fortunately, he had not disturbed the slumbering Gryphie again.

He dropped the sea vulture and breathed a sigh of relief.

Sitting on the edge of the platform, as far from the shelter as he could, he looked towards their destination, wherever that was, occasionally steering the vessel with his tail and

164

eating the sea vulture, bones, feathers and all. He looked up at the sky and admired what stars his eyesight could see. They twinkled and he noticed they looked different to the ones he was used to back at home. Seemed even the stars were different out here on the water. He wasn't sure why that was but he quite liked it. It made a change.

He spent the moon cycle just relaxing and checking to make sure they didn't divert from their course. Soon the sun started to rise again and he yawned, ready for sleep now. It was a long time since he'd pulled an all mooner, or even close. The last time was probably when they found the Furmine necropolis he figured.

The door opened and Ellendrii stepped out, carrying a sea vulture, which was his sunrise meal.

"Sleep well?" asked Aro.

"Yeah not too badly" replied Ellendrii, dropping the bird and yawning. He ate his meal fairly quickly, eager to get out and flying again. Aro took off the harness and gave it to Ellendrii so he could use it again.

Ellendrii was soon up and flying, their course set and still straight. Aro had done a good job of making sure they didn't turn around or deviate. Aro was now sleeping, though he chose to sleep in the shelter with the door open. He didn't want the full heat of the sun on his back while he slept.

As Ellendrii flew, something dawned on him. All this water. None of it was drinkable. He was thirsty. The blood of their food wasn't nearly enough to keep them going. He was surprised Aro hadn't mentioned this. Cursing under his breath, he landed on the shelter and climbed down onto the platform, poking his head through the open door and padding to the back, where his carrying pouch bag was. It contained two gourds which had water in them. One was marked with a claw mark, that one belonged to Aro and Ellendrii saw the Lizariaous had had a drink before he retired. However it was nearly all gone. Ellendrii snarled in annoyance. Aro hadn't been taught to ration water as well as food. The gourds were quite big but Aro had still drunk over half of his.

"Stupid swigger" muttered Ellendrii. He drank a couple of gulps of his water and put the gourd back in the bag. Then he returned to flying.

"I'll have to remember to tell him not to swig his water when he wakes up. That's if I can catch him before he has another drink. What if we run out of water?" Ellendrii asked himself. They had mostly been thinking about food. Water was never an issue back in the Forest. There were places to drink from and you didn't have to catch water anyway. Catching food was the hard part so it was more prominent in the minds of the Gryphies. But water can't be replenished here. He only hoped they could keep going if they ate lots of wet food like fish. He would have to catch his own though, if Aro still planned to use his poisoned needles to spear the fish.

Ellendrii stopped again at mid-sun and had some more to eat, then continued to fly. Aro slept the whole way through, which was a blessing in itself. Even though two is company, the fact that he was asleep meant that he wasn't eating or drinking. Ellendrii decided that they must rotate the sleeping. So he needed to sleep for whole moon cycles and Aro for whole sun cycles. They had to have equal times of sleeping and waking.

They ran out of food on the third sun cycle and had to catch more. This took a while.

Ellendrii flew around and caught a few birds. Some of them he didn't even recognise. Some were a bit like sea vultures but differed from them quite a bit, being larger and less vicious. Aro caught some fish but had to find a way of catching them without poisoning them so Ellendrii could eat them as well. Ellendrii had managed to catch him before he drank too much more water and he learned from his mistake because he had to ration even more carefully now.

Ellendrii's well meant plan of catching food at sunrise had backfired somewhat by a lack of available meal creatures and an urge to travel on.

Aro had to work out how to catch the fish without his needles. Since the poison ran through the needle from his body, he couldn't simply snap the end off the needle and use

166

the rest of it so he ended up managing to split a shard of wood off the float and fashion it into a spear.

It worked very well but he had to remember to put it safely in the shelter when he'd finished using it. He didn't want to lose it and have to keep making new ones or they'd have no float left!

Soon there was a sizeable pile of food in the shelter for them and they could continue their journey, after of course, eating.

By the fifth sun cycle, Aro's legs started playing up because he couldn't walk anywhere. He tried to pace up and down on the platform but it didn't really seem to help. The only time he'd really stretched his legs was when he was swimming after the fish when he was trying to catch them. So for a while he swam alongside the float instead of sitting on it. It was a pain for Ellendrii when Aro climbed back on it but it got his limbs moving again and stopped them from cramping up so badly. Also, Ellendrii had to fly a little slower when Aro was swimming.

However the good thing was that Ellendrii's wings weren't playing him up too badly anymore. His muscles had got used to flying for long periods like this and didn't ache and burn as much. The first two sun cycles had been the hardest for this. He was glad he was a good and strong flyer; he sure needed it for this journey!

He flew down lower as Aro clambered on for the second time that sun cycle.

"Hey we won't get anywhere if you keep getting off for a swim" he called down.

"Sorry! I won't do it again this sun" replied Aro and sat down.

"Good! Because I…" Ellendrii trailed off. "Aro, I can see something on the horizon!"

Aro went to the edge of the platform and gazed out ahead of them.

"I can't" he said, "You're imagining it! You've gone mad cos we've been out here so long!"

"I am not! It's only been five sun cycles anyway. And I *can* see something! It looks like land…"

"Land? This soon? I thought this water was endless or something" yelled Aro.

"I did too but I can definitely see something…" Ellendrii squinted again. Whatever it was spread across the whole horizon as far as he could see and looked very much like it could be the other side of the vast water. Unless of course somehow they had got turned around and it was the coast of Shernaron again but it certainly didn't look like it. It looked like a different coast. Maybe the land of the SilvaGryphie? Ellendrii sure hoped so!

Aro was sceptical. This was too easy. It couldn't be the other side. Even though it had seemed like moons since they'd left, he was sure it would be further than this.

He carried on squinting until his eyes hurt and then he gave up, lay down and dozed off. It was only his friend's excited cries that woke him up a while later and made him sit up and take notice of what was on the horizon now.

It *was* land!

It looked very much like they had reached the other side! It was still a long way off but it was gradually getting clearer as they approached it. And it wasn't Shernaron. There were no cliffs, just plenty of trees, almost like if the Forest stood on the edge of the beach instead of the cliffs.

Aro bounced around in excitement and Ellendrii scolded him because he was rocking the float and pulling on Ellendrii's twine harness. Aro sat as still as he could now.

"That was fast!" remarked Aro.

"We don't know if it's the land of the SilvaGryphie yet" replied Ellendrii. He had a point. But whatever it was, it really looked beautiful, especially to Ellendrii who loved anything that was full of trees and it really did remind him of the Forest. Neither of them had any idea what the land of the SilvaGryphie was meant to look like or how they would know when they found it but since it was the only place that was supposed to be across the vast water, they supposed this must be it. But reaching it after only five sun cycles was pretty fast. Still, they felt lucky for this and were glad of it.

As they continued towards the small line of green land, the sky started getting a little darker and it started to rain. Clouds had obscured the sun.

Aro went into the shelter; he was feeling rather cold now and very wet.

Ellendrii carried on although the rain was getting stronger and he was struggling to see. But he carried on; the longer he flew, the closer he would get to the land and he hoped that they would be able to reach it and find shelter from the storm that had now engulfed them.

However, things that look close can often be further away than they appear and he was starting to realize this.

Not only the rain but a strong wind had also swept up now. And it was not on his side. It was blowing strongly against him.

In the shelter, Aro crouched and shivered, worried that the float would overturn. It was getting pounded by the waves and Aro felt sick from the motion. Up until now it had been smooth sailing and seeing the land had given them a whole new sense of confidence about this journey. Now the weather was destroying that. Aro tried to hold his sickness in, clapping his paws over his mouth. He was not used to this or any kind of obscure motion. He wished he was back home in his cave. He closed his eyes and wished that this was all some horrid dream.

He was starting to seriously regret insisting on joining Ellendrii on this fool's errand.

With his paws over his mouth, he tumbled forward from the force of the waves and fell on his face. Swearing loudly he picked himself up and tried to wedge himself in the corner of the shelter. The food that had been stacked in the other corner was flopping around all over the floor. His stomach churned painfully as the dead fish rolled past him, followed by a sea vulture. Another dead sea vulture had got tangled up in Ellendrii's leather bag.

Aro was lurched forward and his stomach felt like it was stuck to the top of his chest. He moaned. This was not how he thought the trip would go!

Meanwhile, Ellendrii's wing muscles burned as he tried to keep on course. The rain smashed into his face and soaked his fur. His body felt heavy with the wetness. The wind swept him up and his harness nearly strangled him. He desperately tried to untangle himself from the twine that had wrapped around his neck while the wind blew him about. Ellendrii was scared and struggling to even keep in the air.

Suddenly there was a huge deafening crash and lightning lit up the sky. Ellendrii jumped and shivered and, panic stricken, he landed on top of the shelter to try and untangle himself there. The float bounced and spun in the water, the waves rising up and crashing into it, nearly knocking him off his perch. Ellendrii clung to the top of the shelter for dear life, not bothering with untangling himself anymore, lest he fall off and get killed from smashing into the float or drowning in the vicious waves. He shivered and cried, wishing he was back home, wishing his parents were there to protect him and bitterly regretting his stupid decision and naivety to be tricked into doing this.

His father had been right, his mother had been wise, he was stupid to do this and now he would die doing it, he would never return home to the Forest he loved and he would never see his parents again. Perhaps even worse, he had allowed Aro to come with him, much against his better judgement and now he would die too, because of Ellendrii and his selfishness.

The rain battered Ellendrii's body and the cold of it stung him viciously. The lightning lit up the sky again and the thunder rolled and crashed. The storm was very close; they were nearly in the eye of it he supposed in his terror and panic.

Meanwhile inside the shelter, Aro also shook and sobbed. He had heard Ellendrii landing on the shelter's roof and guessed he had given up trying to fly in the storm and pull them to the land. Which of course meant that they could be swept off anywhere now and go completely off course. That's if the storm didn't decide to completely smash the float and drown them both.

Ellendrii was struggling to hold on and in the back of his mind realized that he needed to get inside the shelter instead of clinging to the top of it. A huge wave swept up and tried to pull him off. He tried to wrap his tail around the shelter and dug his tailspade in between two of the wooden logs to try and maintain his grip. But his strength was failing him and with a powerful whoosh of wind, Ellendrii was tugged and pulled off the shelter and into the sky with only the twine harness preventing him from being swept away into the storm.

In the sky now, he saw the lightning strike and crackle around him and he screeched in panic and terror. He tried flying back towards the float but his wings were useless in this wind. He was tossed and swept like a little kite in a windstorm and couldn't control any of his wing movements.

For a while, he gave up and just let the wind take him until he noticed that part of the twine was starting to break and if it snapped, he would certainly be swept away. Not sure what to do at this point, Ellendrii wracked his brain desperately, not able to take his eyes off the tearing twine. Finally he settled on the idea of using the length of twine that attached him to the float to pull himself in and get back to the float. He would then get inside the shelter with Aro. He didn't want to pull himself in at the risk of snapping the twine though so he would have to grab the twine past the part that was splitting so it didn't put any more stress on it.

With the wind still buffeting him around, Ellendrii waited until a gust had passed and then with a huge sweep of his wings, he propelled himself forward and grabbed the twine as far down as he could.

By a small miracle, it worked and he managed to grab it past the weak spot. Now all he had to do was pull himself back to the float. Easier said than done. With the wind whipping up all the time and blowing him around, he was struggling to hold onto the twine, let alone actually place one hand in front of the other and pull himself. He couldn't afford to lose his grip and be swept out again because if that happened, the twine would almost certainly snap from the tension of having Ellendrii pulled back out again.

He pulled himself slowly back to the float. The wind whipped up and pushed him back many times and his hands slid up the twine, it hurt and burned but he was determined not to let go. He held the twine so tightly that his claws dug into the palms of his hands and made them bleed but he refused to let go of the twine. He used his wings to try and motion himself towards the float and help out with him pulling himself on the twine.

The effort was excruciating. Ellendrii gritted his teeth and carried on.

Aro meanwhile had no idea what was happening but because he hadn't heard or seen Ellendrii (he had been peering out between the logs of wood for a glimpse of his friend), he worried that the Gryphie had got blown away by the wind and that scared him even more.

That he could be alone in this storm.

However, he needn't have worried about that particular thing because the shelter lurched a little as Ellendrii managed to pull himself down and onto the side of it. He stood halfway on the platform and holding onto the shelter. He now had to open the door in order to get inside. The wind gusted and tried to throw him off the float again but he held on tight. The thunder rumbled and the lightning struck again soon after. The waves bobbed the float around, threatening again to throw it over. Ellendrii felt sick now.

With a great effort, he pulled the door open and managed to slip himself into the opening. He grazed his wings in doing so but at least he had got inside now. He found Aro, who was still sobbing and crouched next to him, wrapping his wings around his friend and cuddling close.

Neither said anything; the roar of the ocean was deafening. They just shivered and sobbed and hoped that this would all be over soon. Aro's needles were flat on his back, which allowed Ellendrii to hug him safely.

The two of them didn't feel like young adults. They felt like little youngsters. Alone, afraid and vulnerable.

For a while, the float bobbed around and swept up and down, causing Ellendrii and Aro to try to keep their balance.

Now he was inside, the feeling of sickness hit Ellendrii like a rock. Somehow, the wind blowing him around outside and the concentration he had needed in order to get back to the float had kept away any sick feelings that his stomach could conjure up. But now he was inside, his stomach churned like there was a tiny tornado in it.

Suddenly the whole float turned up and over, upside down. The pair inside rolled around and Ellendrii vomited violently. The float was now bobbing around with the shelter part under the water; the platform part was keeping it afloat.

Ellendrii and Aro floundered around, their paws and legs thrashing and trying to get out of the shelter before they drowned. The waves swept up again and turned the float back over and the two of them collapsed on the floor of the shelter, panting and gasping for air.

Aro choked and sputtered out the horrible salty water. It burned his throat and stung his eyes. And it was freezing cold.

Ellendrii wasn't in any better shape than he was. The two of them were at a loss of what to do. The only thing they felt they could do was stay in the shelter and try not to drown. And also try not to lose each other. Losing their way was no longer the most important thing in this situation.

Suddenly, there was a bright light, a huge crash and a deafening crack and crunch as the shelter was hit by lightning. The whole thing split apart like an egg and spilled out the contents into the sea. Which of course included Ellendrii and Aro.

Ellendrii managed to grab his leather bag before it floated away and he put the strap over himself. He couldn't lose that; if they survived, it would be an important asset. But the float was completely destroyed.

He looked around desperately for Aro and saw him a little way away trying to keep his head above the water.

The waves rose and fell and swept the two of them around as Ellendrii tried to get closer to Aro so he wouldn't lose him. Aro was panicking far more than Ellendrii was. Being a rocky wasteland living creature, Aro wasn't used to any sort of water really, apart from the river in the valley when the pair of them visited it sometimes and Aro very rarely ever swam in it.

Ellendrii got closer to Aro but suddenly felt himself being yanked backwards. The force winded him and swept him away. He still had the twine harness around him and it was still tied to what was left of the float. It dragged him through the water as the waves got ahold of the wooden log. By some unfortunate event, the twine hadn't snapped and it was now pulling Ellendrii away from Aro and off into the sea. Ellendrii roared angrily into the storm as the lightning flashed all around and the thunder rumbled ominously.

Ellendrii desperately searched for the twine so he could bite it and sever himself from the log. He managed to find it and as the water rolled him and the log around, he bit and tore at the strong twine, the motion of the waves interrupting his mission but every time he went back to it and carried on biting it until he was through and it snapped in half. The log floated away and Ellendrii tried desperately to find Aro again.

Aro was finding it hard to keep his head above the water. His eyes hurt and he had swallowed so much of the salty grossness that his throat was well and truly sore by now. He sputtered and coughed and tried to find Ellendrii. Right now though, his concentration leaned more towards not drowning. The waves carried him higher and higher and then crashed down, sending him tumbling and choking into the water. Every time he fought for the surface again but his strength was starting to fail him now. He wasn't sure how much longer he could keep this up.

The remnants of the float bobbed around him and he had to be careful not to get hit by the wood. He tried to swim away from it. The rain still stormed down and the sky crackled with lightning.

"ELLENDRII!!!" he called out, uselessly. Again and again he called, out of sheer panic now, knowing that his friend probably wouldn't hear but doing it anyway.

Some way away, Ellendrii didn't hear. He was using far too much concentration coping with swimming when he wanted to just take off and fly. Being unable to fly disabled him beyond all his comprehension. Without flight, he felt useless. Flying was always his go to for escaping things but now he couldn't. One of his wings also hurt him badly and he feared it might be badly damaged. He only hoped it wasn't broken. It was taking enough of his efforts, like his friend, to keep his head above the water's surface.

"AR..." he started to yelled but water swept into his mouth and choked him to silence. He listened to see if he could hear Aro's voice. He could! Though it was distant. He hoped Aro would keep calling and he thought he could see the needles of the Lizariaous poking out of the water some distance away. He swam towards it, the waves sweeping him away but every time they did, he kept going regardless.

As he got closer he realized it was not Aro's needles, but the remains of the shelter. The roof had been ripped clean off and the pointy things were the upright logs which had been split in half and the splintered wood stuck up skyward.

After floating around and fighting to breathe, Ellendrii was starting to get used to it but that didn't make it any less terrifying. He looked around; the land was nowhere to be seen now. Whether they were closer to it or not, he couldn't tell. He was too close to the surface of the water to see much but the water all around him and he surmised that because he couldn't see even a glimpse of the land that they had floated away from it. If he could only keep afloat and pass the storm out.

Aro was getting used to it too but he was still terrified and several times his heavy body had been pulled under the water and he had fought to get back up for air. He was tired and he allowed the waves to sweep him around; he didn't swim against them or fight them now. The only time he fought for it was to keep his head above the surface of the water. He was freezing cold and starting to lose the feeling in his legs. Though they are reptilian in form, Lizariaouses are not cold blooded. If he was, he would surely be dead by now.

He'd given up yelling and screaming for his friend. The waves swirled all around him and he felt tiny and insignificant and totally not how a Lizariaous normally felt. All the bravery and fierceness had left him. As he was pushed and thrashed around, he looked up at the sky. It was dark and cloudy. The thunder rumbles and lightning crashes had got far closer together and the wind was sweeping up in a monsoon. He was pushed and shoved up into the waves and thrown back down again into the water. He tried to ride the waves or find an easier way to move with them so they wouldn't throw him down quite so violently but it was all to no avail. His body hurt from being thrown into the water multiple times and he was sore and miserable. His thick skin did help to protect him from the bashing of the waves though.

Ellendrii was in a lot of pain. Gryphies have thinner skin, covered in a soft, dense and velvety fur and their bodies are not nearly as strong or hardy as Lizariaouses. He was trying to keep his wings close to him so the soft skin of them wouldn't be ripped apart by the waves. Being his greatest asset, he didn't want anything happening to his wings to prevent him from flying if he happened to survive all of this. He still held out the hope that he would in fact, survive.

He still couldn't see Aro or hear him either. The waves were still sweeping him around and he got it into his head to try and get into the sky again so he could hopefully fly above and see if he could spot Aro and at least go to him so they could try and survive this together. He was afraid of being alone as well. And he was worried and felt guilty about his friend. He *had* let him come along after all, even against his better judgement.

So he tried to take off. He floundered about, flapped his wings and tried to get back into the sky. But he was waterlogged by now and drenched right through. He didn't give up though; he tried and tried again. The idea to shoot a blast of flames into the air so Aro might be able to find him instead had occurred to him but he was so waterlogged that his fire wouldn't work anyway. He'd swallowed too much of the foul salty water.

He tried to jump out of the water at the same time as flapping his wings but he only succeeded in making more waves. Frustrated, he roared and kept it up until he was worn out and had to rest. After a while, he tried again, thrashing his tail to try and give him the thrust he needed to take off. This still didn't work. He rested and thought about it, the rain

176

driving at him and the wind and thunder howling around him. The waves swept him up and crashed him down and in this he formulated a plan. When a large wave swept him up, he pretty much fell back into the water. If he could take off in between the wave sweeping him up and him dropping again, he might be able to get into the sky.

So he tried that instead. He followed the waves instead of trying to escape them and he managed to swim into a huge wave. He prepared himself as it sent him higher and higher and finally crashed down. At it got to its peak, Ellendrii thrust himself out of the water, sweeping back his wings and launching himself into the sky. As if, weirdly, to help, a gust of wind swept him out of the water and into the sky at that very moment and he took off once again into the storm.

Lightning flashed dangerously close to him and he screeched in fear and tried his best to avoid it. He looked down into the sea briefly to see if he could spot Aro. But Aro was black and the water was also very dark and he could see no sign of his friend in the surge of waves that swept up and down.

Ellendrii flew lower but the wind was against him now and swept him away again. He was starting to lose strength again and couldn't stop himself this time. He'd used so much power just trying to take off out of the water that it was harder and harder for him to stay on course in the air. The wind took hold of him and picked him up; sweeping him away from the swelling ocean down below and making him lose control completely. He no longer had any strength to stop it and had no choice but to let it take him. It swirled around him, making him go with it round and round over and over again as he was caught in what seemed like a small tornado. Higher and higher he went, up to the soggy clouds and back down again. He closed his wings against himself to try and protect his body against the pummelling of the wind and of course to prevent any more damage to his precious wings. His legs flailed as he tried to instinctively fight what was happening to him. In the end he had to give up and let it take him, round and round and away. If it let him drop, he would simply fall into the water anyway and he hoped he would survive, so there was no point in using up the little strength he had left to try and prevent his own death. In the deafening roar of the howling wind around him, tears and rain streaming down his face, Ellendrii spoke quietly. So quietly he couldn't even hear his own words.

"I'm sorry Aro, I'm so sorry, I can't save us…" and Ellendrii was swept away into the stormy sky.

Down in the water, Aro was still desperately continuing to keep himself from drowning. He was glad the water was deep and they were out in the ocean. Although it meant he would probably drown, it also meant there would be no rocks for him to crash upon. It was the lesser of two evils really.

The wood was still floating around; he saw it every so often bounce past him in the water. The roar of the ocean deafened him as he floundered about gasping. He went up into the waves; he fell down into the water. He'd lost count of the times this had happened. His stomach lurched and he vomited until he feared that if he continued, he would puke up his organs.

The water swirled round and carried him and the wood through its depths. Every time the waves pulled him up and crashed him down, he used up more and more strength trying to get back to the surface. Now he couldn't feel much of his body at all. It was all cold, numb and in some places quite painful. The wood washed and swirled closer.

Then a large wave carried him and a piece of the unfortunate float up and over. Aro fell into the water first, followed by the log. Before he knew what was happening, the log fell on his head, knocking him out cold. The pain was excruciating and then everything went dark. Aro's limp body was carried by the waves, tossed around and swirled about into oblivion under the dark thunder ravaged sky.

Chapter 10
Washed Up

Aro saw only black but he had a massive headache. It seared into his unconsciousness and he started to become compos mentis again. He groaned. Was he dead? He *could* see only black after all, and under the ground *was* where Lizariaouses went when they died.

Then he realized his eyes were closed. He slowly opened them. He had grit in his mouth, which he later discovered was actually sand.

By some weird miracle, he was no longer floating in water but found himself flopped out on fairly solid ground. It was a beach. Looking around, he realized he had washed up on the mainland they had seen while travelling.

He tried to move but his body ached all over. He moved a leg at a time, to make sure he could feel them all and nothing was broken. He could move everything although it hurt to do so. He swished his tail and that was intact as well. Gritting his teeth, he slowly tried to stand but hadn't planned it well enough and fell back down again. He tried again, getting all his feet underneath him and pushing up from there into a sitting position. He managed this ok and sighed.

In the sat up position, he had a better view of where he was. Dense trees came down to the edge of the sand some way away and the weather was warm with a gentle breeze, as though the storm the previous moon cycle hadn't happened at all. He couldn't remember anything past the wood knocking him out and he was very surprised he hadn't drowned. He could only assume that he had floated in a similar fashion to how he had seen dead bodies float in water. Being limp let the water take you away but if you struggled, you started to sink. He knew this much from when he was learning to swim with Ellendrii.

Ellendrii! Where was he now? Aro knew he had to find him. He *must* have washed up onto land as well, surely?

Aro stood with some difficulty, his aching muscles burning. But the sand was soft and nice to walk on under his aching paws. He took a few hesitant steps forward, using his tail for balance. Groaning, he shook his head. He was starving and thirsty too. But he wanted to find Ellendrii first. Maybe he could find food along the way.

Aro walked along the beach, looking all around to see if Ellendrii had washed up there somewhere. He didn't find anything though, nor even any sign of their food supply. He found a few pieces of wood from the float. His stomach grumbled painfully so he decided to shoot himself down a bird. He had no idea what the birds were that were flying around and above him, they looked like sea vultures but they were a different colour. Some of them had landed near to him when he was lying on the sand but quickly flew away when he sat up. They were looking for food too and had thought Aro was dead.

Aro shot a few needles at some low flying ones. It missed one completely but caught the other on the wing, causing the bird to drop from the sky and low enough for Aro to jump up and catch it. The bird was pretty big, like a sea vulture, and it screamed and struggled. Aro quickly dispatched it and started to eat.

Even though he'd wanted to find Ellendrii first, he knew that if he didn't regain strength by eating something, he wouldn't be able to look for very long without stopping. Plus his tummy ached.

Once he'd finished, Aro continued along the beach. He was still thirsty but he knew that the water of the vast ocean wasn't good to drink and he had no idea how to find anything else. He only hoped he would find one of the gourds washed up too with some good water in. He found nothing of the sort. The beach was really long too and the sun was getting higher in the sky and hotter. Aro decided to go into the forest and see if Ellendrii had maybe flown into a tree or something or was looking for him in there. He guessed his friend must be looking for him like Aro was looking for Ellendrii. It was something Ellendrii would do. And being alone was a bit scary. Not that Aro was particularly scared, since Lizariaouses don't fear easily but he would at least like to be sure Ellendrii was ok.

The forest smelt different to the one back home that he was so used to. The animals in it were different too; a few fled as he passed by and they looked nothing like forest deer or Xoles or even ground birds, or Furmines. It was so new and alien to Aro. He used his nose to see if he could smell Ellendrii but the forest was so big and the trees were tall although not as dense as the Forest back home. Maybe he would find something like a swamp or something that he could drink from. He kept an eye out for this too as he wandered in deeper, sniffing out his friend.

Suddenly he smelled something similar to a Gryphie. It wasn't Ellendrii though and there was something off about it. There was something distinctly different about this but it still reminded him of Gryphie smell. It was getting stronger too and he came upon a large tree, the trunk of which weaved in a strange way into the ground, like lattice. The trunk was normal further up, but as it started to widen further down, it weaved, creating a hollow underneath. The smell was especially strong here.

Carefully, Aro advanced, sniffing. He could see no movement and no sign that the hollow was occupied. But someone *did* live there. He could tell that because there was a bed of leaves and some bones scattered about. And the smell was fresh too. Aro entered, looking around. It wasn't so dark he couldn't see though. The sun shone in through the wooden lattice. It was pretty. Well, he would have considered it pretty if Lizariaouses had any concept of what pretty was. He looked up and saw strange carvings in the roof of the hollow. They depicted stars and the moon.

Here and there, strange things had been tied to the latticework. They resembled what we would call dream catchers, with feathers and weaved twine that was so thin that the light nearly passed through it. Aro looked at these with wonder, lifting his claws up and gently touching one. The light danced through it and he couldn't take his eyes off it. He'd never seen anything quite like this before. Yes, Lunara had things in her tree that she hung off it to decorate it but nothing with the intricate twine weaving like this. The centres of the ornaments reminded him of delicate spider webs. He wondered if some creature had made them and the creator of the ornaments had just taken what the creature made and incorporated it into their work. But where *was* the creator? And were they friendly?

Aro turned to go and continue his search. And came face to face with a rather vicious looking draconic creature. Her eyes flamed orange and she snarled at him.

"Who are you?" she demanded, a snarl crossing her short, deep purple muzzle. She had bright green, tribal style markings on her face and body and they glowed brightly and angrily, though the sunlight detracted somewhat from the glow. She looked like a Gryphie but her muzzle was much shorter and her wings were different, having only three fingers and each one tipped with a black claw. She had a formidable looking silver tailspade with a black edge along one side and a black mane that started just behind her head to the first quarter of the length of her tail. Her fur was deep purple, short and dense like a Gryphie.

"I...I was looking for my friend..." trailed off Aro, backing up, unfortunately back into the tree hollow.

"You are trespassing!" snapped the newcomer.

"I didn't mean to, please don't hurt me" Aro warned, although his needles were aimed right at her head. Although he was being submissive, he wouldn't hesitate to shoot her if she came any closer. His ears were back and he was narrowing his eyes at her, ready to take aim.

"Midnyte, don't! He's my friend!" a voice suddenly yelled. It was Ellendrii!

Aro looked up momentarily ignoring his attacker, to see his friend stood by her.

"Ellendrii?" he yelped.

"Friend?" questioned Midnyte, looking round, her eyes turning yellow.

"Yes, please don't hurt him" said Ellendrii, dashing forward in an attempt to get between her and Aro. Midnyte hung back.

"Why is he in my home then?" she demanded, looking back at Aro, her eyes flaming to orange again in hostility.

"I was looking for Ellendrii" blurted Aro hurriedly. "If you attack, I won't hesitate to shoot you. I will run through your skull!" he aimed his needles at her head again and Midnyte snarled, her nostrils flaring green like her markings. It reminded Aro a lot of how Gryphies' nostrils flared blue before they flamed something.

"My needles are poisonous!" he snarled.

"And my fire will melt your skin off" growled Midnyte.

"STOP!!" cried Ellendrii, shooting out a small fireball between the two facing off. The pair looked at him, momentarily interrupted.

"Aro, get out of her home if it means she won't attack you" Ellendrii cried out. Aro complied and briskly removed himself from his position of trespass to a position next to Ellendrii.

Midnyte calmed down and her eyes slowly turned yellow again, her markings only giving off a dull glow now.

"What is going on??" demanded Aro.

Ellendrii sighed and then he spoke.

"I was swept away by the wind and ended up stuck in a tree here on this island. Luckily I still have my leather bag with me but unluckily it also got caught in the tree, making me even more stuck myself. I couldn't get free because my wings were caught as well and if I struggled too much, I would have broken one or both of them. I shot up distress flames because it was the only thing I knew how to do or that I hoped would bring help. Midnyte Comet saw them and came to my aid. She helped free me. She was bringing me back to her home to give me something to eat and drink. Then we found you."

"I was looking for you. I looked all along the beach and then the sun got too hot so I came into the forest instead. I found Midnyte's home, I could smell her and I was curious because it smelled a bit like Gryphie and I thought it was you so I came in. Then she found me...wait...island??? We're on an ISLAND???"

Ellendrii hung his head.

"Yes, Midnyte Comet told me"

Midnyte nodded. Ellendrii carried on.

"Once she got me down from the tree, she told me. It's just a really big island. It's not the mainland. When I asked how to get to the mainland, she said we have to cross the vast water again."

"Grik" muttered Aro.

"You still have several sun cycles' travel ahead of you if you wish to get to the mainland" said Midnyte.

"Our float though..." said Aro.

"I know" replied Ellendrii, "We'll have to build another one"

Aro sat down, defeated and hung his head.

Midnyte offered them both some food and they ate.

"Are you the only one on this island?" asked Ellendrii.

"Yes" replied Midnyte. "I haven't always lived here but I like it, it's peaceful and I like to sit and contemplate through my sun cycles. There is less here to distract and annoy me. Why are you looking to get to the mainland anyway? I've never met either of your kind. Where are you from?"

"We come from Shernaron. Well, he's from Dyarkroeen, which is another territory nearby and I come from the Forest. We're looking for the SilvaGryphie. We were told that she lives on the mainland, the other side of the vast water. So we travelled for five sun cycles on our float and then hit a storm and here we are."

"I haven't heard of the SilvaGryphie. What is it?" asked Midnyte.

"She's supposed to be the founder of my species, the Gryphies. I have to find her and take her back to Shernaron with me in order to get into the Sky Gryphie Elite Flyers. Apparently she's really beautiful and to look into her wings is to see into eternity itself."

"She sounds lovely but I've never seen anything like her before" replied Midnyte and offered them both a drink of water which she kept in gourds similar to Lunara's. They drank their fill, eagerly and thirstily and felt better.

"I'm sorry I trespassed" said Aro after he had finished drinking.

"I'm sorry I was so hostile, but no one ever visits this island so I was completely taken by surprise and I thought you were stealing from me" replied Midnyte.

"Would your fire really melt my skin off...?" Aro ventured.

"Yes, it's acidfire. It's bright green like my markings. It melts first the skin, then the body tissue and will even melt through bone if I breathe it with enough power" explained Midnyte. Aro swallowed. For once there was something he was afraid of.

"My fire's blue" said Ellendrii, "It's very hot you see." Midnyte nodded but didn't speak. Ellendrii shut up. He had hoped to impress her. She was older than he was but he thought she was beautiful and her glowing markings only helped to make that beauty more profound. He figured he would fly around and see if he could find any route at all to the mainland. Yes it was an island but he didn't know how far away they were from the mainland, around the other side of the island they could be quite close.

"I'm going to have a look around…if it's ok with you, Midnyte?" Ellendrii asked politely.

"It's fine with me" replied Midnyte. Ellendrii nodded and took off, weaving through the trees and into the sky.

Once he was in the air properly, his body ached in a similar fashion to Aro's. But the weather was nice and he wasn't about to let a few aches and pains get to him. Besides, he felt better now he had eaten. He flew up higher and saw the island went on as far as he could see. It was longer than it was wide but only just. It was huge! Most of it was covered by the forest he had been in. It had a beach all around but it stretched into the distance so far that he couldn't see and had to fly instead to find out. He flew lower though and went around the perimeter of it, following the line of the beach and most importantly looking under the water for any sign of a land bridge or any other way to any sort of mainland.

The water was clear and fresh looking, completely the opposite to the churned mess it had been the previous moon cycle. But as he had feared, there was no route to the mainland. He couldn't even *see* the mainland. Only endless water; the same view as he had seen from the coast of Shernaron.

While Ellendrii was looking around, Aro was getting to know Midnyte Comet better. Or as best as he could. She was very secretive. So he decided to tell her about himself instead.

185

"I'm a Lizariaous, I come from Dyarkroeen, which is the other side of the vast water err...that way" he pointed.

Midnyte nodded, listening carefully. She had been curious as to what he was as well, since she didn't actually know, having not met a creature like him before.

"Where I live, the land is barren with a few bushes and fewer trees. Lizariaouses are strong and vicious. We settle our arguments by fighting and the strongest always wins. I have two sisters. I don't like them though. My father is the leader of our pack. He got to be the leader because he killed the old leader, Zephirak. I heard Zephirak was horrible. He even started a war between us and the Gryphies, which is what Ellendrii is. As you can see though, now we're good friends. I was born after the war though, so I only know what others have told me."

"If you have few trees and bushes, where do you live? Surely the land is open and unprotected?" asked Midnyte.

"We live in caves" explained Aro. "We have a reservoir where we drink. Where we live is completely different to the Gryphies"

"I can tell" remarked Midnyte.

"How old are you anyway?" asked Aro.

"Older than you" replied Midnyte.

"I can tell" replied Aro with a frown. Then he remembered something he wanted to ask.

"What are those things that hang in your tree?" he asked, pointing to the ornate decorations that hung from the wooden lattice.

"Ah, those are supposed to protect me and bring good fortune. I made them myself. They're something someone taught me how to make a very long time ago." Midnyte looked nostalgic and misty eyed.

"Who taught you?" asked Aro.

"Someone wise. My mother" replied Midnyte.

"That's cool. My mother taught me to hunt. In fact we used to go on a lot of hunts together. Used to..." Aro trailed off and suddenly felt very small and vulnerable. He wondered where his mother and father were now and if they were thinking of him. Well, obviously they were in Dyarkroeen but his home and his fellow Lizariaouses seemed so far away now, like some sort of distant dream or memory. Well, obviously they were in his memory but it seemed almost as if his life hadn't existed beyond where he was now. It scared him.

"Are you ok?" asked Midnyte.

"I guess so. It's just, we've travelled so far, I've never walked more than I could in a sun cycle. When I go somewhere, it doesn't take sun cycles; it only takes a short time. This is further away from home than I've ever been before. I guess it took a while for it to sink in fully." He sighed.

Just then, Ellendrii returned.

"Well I can't find a land bridge or even see land. I've flown all the way around the island" he reported.

"I told you that. We are sun cycles away from land here" said Midnyte.

"Yes but I thought there was maybe a land bridge or something" Ellendrii felt stupid. He had looked purely out of desperation.

"It would have to be a very long land bridge" said Midnyte.

Ellendrii sighed and sat down. He looked at Midnyte. She did look a lot like a Gryphie, apart from the claws on her wings and the shortness of her muzzle and her hands were more like paws and she had opposable thumbs on her back feet, similar to a Lizariaous. He could have sworn their species were related somehow. After all, the sky and mountain Gryphies were related to his own species.

"Are you ok?" she asked him as she noticed him comparing her paws with his hands.

"Sorry, it's just that you remind me so much of one of my own" he said.

"I can assure you that our species are not related in any way" she said. "I am different to you in more ways than you can imagine. Do any of the Gryphie species have glowing features? Do they all breathe blue fire? Those are the questions you must ask yourself. Look at what connects you all"

"Well no, none of them glow and we all breathe blue fire...I guess we're not related then. But you just seem so close to me…I guess it feels reassuring to meet someone who reminds me of my own back home"

"I guess it must be" replied Midnyte.

"So I don't remind you of your family?" asked Ellendrii.

"Not at all" replied Midnyte. Ellendrii looked disappointed.

"Never mind then" he said quietly.

Midnyte quickly changed the subject.

"Your friend here was telling me about where he lives. What about where you live?" she asked.

"I come from the Forest in Shernaron. It's a forest full of big trees, bigger than the ones here and we all live in them. There are valleys and mountains in Shernaron too and the swamp. And also the cliffs. That's where the beach is that leads to the vast water and where we set out on our float, which got destroyed in the storm." Ellendrii told her. Midnyte listened and nodded.

"And you're looking for something that you're not sure exists?" asked Midnyte.

"How do you know that? I never said that I questioned her existence" snapped Ellendrii.

"Her existence seems questionable from how you described her" replied Midnyte.

"She does exist. There are too many stories and legends around her from too many different sources to deny her existence" said Ellendrii. "And plus, why would we go on this journey if we thought she didn't exist?"

"That's true. Unless you're just a stubborn creature who thinks he's always right"

Aro sniggered at this. Ellendrii snorted.

"I AM right. And I will prove that I am! Besides, how would you know? You didn't even know what she was until I told you."

"You're right, I didn't. And who knows anyway" replied Midnyte.

"While you're here though, let's go down to the beach and I will show you the smaller islands around here. They're very interesting and yes, both of you can get to them." She nodded at Aro who had looked unsure.

188

So the three of them went down to the beach on the far side of the island and Midnyte showed them four smaller islands just off the coast. They could easily be reached by swimming and one had a little land bridge that was out of the water since the tide was low.

The islands themselves were very small, not at all like the main one Midnyte lived on. They were just lumps of land stuck out of the water. But all of them were quite tall; in fact Aro struggled to climb the tallest of them.

Ellendrii perched on top of it beside Midnyte while they waited for Aro to make his way up it.

"I often come and sit here and watch the sun set" said Midnyte quietly. "It's so peaceful just listening to the water."

"It's not so peaceful back home on our cliffs" said Ellendrii, "The sea vultures scream and fly around them, it's where they nest. We go there to feed but we don't go there if we want some peace and quiet! We go into the Forest for peace and quiet, or to the valleys. There are a few Gryphies who live in the valleys but not many. They make their homes on the higher ground where there is shelter from the elements. I like to sit by the river and just watch it flow or watch the fish swimming in the clear water. It's very relaxing."

"It does sound it" replied Midnyte.

"Have you done much travelling?" asked Ellendrii.

"Not much" she replied, "Only from home to here. That's about it really. And this island is so big that I don't need to travel any further than I am now. I can be on a part of the island in the forest and if I look around, I can't see the water; it's like I'm on the mainland again."

"Does your island have a name?" asked Ellendrii.

"No, because it's not *my* island" replied Midnyte. "It belongs to all the creatures and plants on it. I'm just staying here until the end of my life. I don't need to give it a name because I don't need to tell anyone how to get to it or refer to it as anything other than my home."

Ellendrii nodded. Aro had finally reached to them and nearly collapsed beside them, panting.

"That was one grik of a climb!" he panted. Ellendrii smiled but said nothing. He didn't want to bring up flying VS walking again and upset his friend.

Aro sat down next to them.

"Nice view" he said, looking around.

Midnyte nodded and agreed. Aro wasn't used to sitting in high places. Everything was pretty much on the same level back in Dyarkroeen. He lay down and relaxed.

They spent a good time longer sat on the high island in the sea. They chatted and sat in silence. And Ellendrii and Aro relaxed. They stayed until the moon was full and bright in the sky, just relaxing and hanging out. Midnyte didn't reveal much about herself but by the time the sun set, she knew a good bit about the other two and why they had been washed up on her island.

Ellendrii looked over at Midnyte as some clouds obscured the moon and he gasped. Her wings were folded but he could just see the undersides of them. They appeared to be dotted and flecked with stars and light. He moved closer to get a better look and she glanced down at him.

"Yes?" she asked.

"Umm...can I see your wing...it looks like..." but he didn't know how to describe it and he felt silly. However, Midnyte obliged and opened out her wings. In the darkness of the moon cycle, Ellendrii saw the inside of her wings were alive with stars and flowing aurora lights. Constellations and galaxies that he could not name because Gryphies aren't aware of outer space. Planets burned and swirled and stars twinkled and flickered in the ever changing flowing colours and darkness. It was like the moon time sky within her wings. To us it would look like an ever changing window to outer space. Ellendrii hadn't noticed this in the sun cycle but now it was dark, the beauty of her wings showed so clearly. He was rendered speechless and just stared. Aro, who didn't know what he was looking at since he was sat a little way away, came to have a look too and stared, mouth open with an astounded gasp. Midnyte let the two of them look for as long as they wanted. She was used to others being blown away by the unlikely beauty inside her wings. During the sun cycle,

190

although it could all still be seen, it wasn't as noticeable due to the sunlight.

"How…" breathed Ellendrii.

"It's just always been; my whole life" Midnyte replied, as if that was obvious.

Ellendrii still couldn't take his eyes off her wings, entranced. She was becoming ever more beautiful in his eyes with her magical space wings and glowing markings. He was starting to get a small crush on her. He'd never had a crush before as he'd never had time for such things, given his obsession with flying and the adventures he went on with Aro. He never paid attention to the young females of his age. But now he was very much interested.

Aro lost interest after a while and went back to lying around on his belly. Ellendrii only stopped staring because it suddenly occurred to him that she might find him rude for staring so long. He coughed and sat back.

"Are you finished?" asked Midnyte.

"Sorry" muttered Ellendrii, "I didn't mean to stare for so long"

"It's ok" replied Midnyte, my wings often astound others.

"You seem so much like a Gryphie sub-species" Ellendrii observed once again. "*Are* you?"

"It's not for me to say" replied Midnyte mysteriously.

"Do you know what you are?" asked Ellendrii.

"What do *you* think I am?" asked Midnyte, replying with a question.

"Beautiful" said Ellendrii before he could stop himself. He swore mentally to himself for saying such a thing while he blushed bright red. Luckily the change of colour in his cheeks couldn't be seen in the darkness.

"Well, thank you" chuckled Midnyte. "It's always nice to receive a compliment"

"Uhh…you're welcome" mumbled Ellendrii.

They sat in silence for a while until Aro's yawn interrupted it.

"I think we all need to sleep" said Midnyte and she lead them back to her home in the forest.

Ellendrii climbed up her tree and slept in the branches while Aro slept in the opening of the hollow. Midnyte had offered him her bed but he was trying to be polite and said he would sleep in the entrance instead. She had been very helpful after all and manners were something he had sort of picked up from Ellendrii. When he remembered to use them that is. Ellendrii stayed awake for a while, thinking about Midnyte and his growing crush on her. He wasn't sure about these feelings. He'd never felt like this before. But she was so beautiful! He really wanted her to travel with them. He supposed she would say no though. She seemed to like being alone. He wondered what sort of creature she was and he also wondered if, since he'd never seen anything like her before, that maybe she was the last of her kind. He was a little annoyed that she wouldn't tell him what she was, no matter how much he guessed or asked. But he didn't want to annoy her so he figured he'd stop asking. She wasn't going to tell. He wished he knew where she came from. They may never see her again after this. He wondered if he could visit her sometimes but of course it was so far to go and flying by himself he would never make it without a float to rest on and the storm…they were lucky to survive it this time so he put the idea out of his head. He decided to make the most of her while they were staying with her and then say goodbye when the time came. He listened in the silence of the moon cycle with nothing but a full moon to light the sky. He looked up at the sky and even harder the time when the clouds obscured the moon.

Midnyte's wings were more beautiful than the moon time sky itself! The whole flight from the island back to the beach, which wasn't very long, he had flown just below her so he could marvel at her wings. She seemed to be used to others staring anyway so surely she wouldn't mind? He hoped she wouldn't mind.

From his position flying beneath her, her wings were in shadow so he could see the beauty underneath them. He almost wanted to reach a hand up and touch them, to see if they really were a portal to the cosmos. Of course they weren't. She let him touch her wing when they landed and he only felt the soft skin, similar to his own. He was a little disappointed to say the least but then again being able to pass through a part of someone else's body into another world was totally farfetched and silly.

They'd waited for Aro to reach them. He found it easier to climb back down of course. Ellendrii concentrated on staring out to sea and not at Midnyte's wings, out of politeness and in case she got annoyed at him.

Now he lay on his back on the sturdy branch of the tree and gathered his thoughts. Well, he tried to. He couldn't stop thinking about how magical Midnyte was!

He sighed and tried to get more comfortable. He closed his eyes and tried to get to sleep but his mind was racing and he still couldn't get her out of his head. Finally he fell into a deep sleep full of dreams about flying with her and then the dreams warped and changed and she turned into the SilvaGryphie. In his eyes she was magical enough to be her.

By the time the sun rose, Ellendrii's mind was twisted around and confused and he nearly fell out of the tree as he gained consciousness.

Down below, Aro and Midnyte were still asleep. Ellendrii nearly fell out of the tree again while he was climbing down the trunk. He ended up taking the last bit a little too fast, missing his footing and falling on top of Aro, who had moved further out of the hollow in his sleep.

Luckily the Lizariaous was lying on his side and not on his tummy or Ellendrii would have been impaled. But Aro *was* pretty angry at being squashed awake.

He jumped up and snarled; lunging for Ellendrii before he even knew what he was doing and shooting needles at him in a state of half conscious confusion. Ellendrii dodged and yelled for Aro to wake up.

Finally, Aro snapped awake properly and hung back, stunned.

"W…what's going on?" he asked. Midnyte was also awake by this point and had rushed outside to see what was going on.

"Sorry, I fell on you…I …I had a moonmare" lied Ellendrii.

"Can you not..." trailed off Aro as Midnyte came rushing out.

"What are you doing?" she demanded.

"Nothing, sorry, I fell out of the tree" replied Ellendrii. Midnyte rolled her eyes and sighed.

"He fell on *me*" snarled Aro, glaring at Ellendrii. Ellendrii backed away submissively and apologetically. Suddenly all thoughts of Midnyte Comet being the SilvaGryphie melted away in a goo of stupidity.

"Let's get something to eat, shall we?" suggested Midnyte and the other two agreed.

The three hunted together. They caught a drixell, which looked like a brightly coloured Furmine, a carxilo, which looked like a tropical armadillo (to us anyway) and a large deerwig (it's like a cross between a deer and an earwig, very odd, but it somehow works). Aro had seen none of these creatures when he was looking for Ellendrii the previous sun cycle and somehow the familiarity of a few of them helped make him feel more at home.

The deerwig was Midnyte's. It was difficult to bring down because it had huge pincers in the place of antlers and it was a male as well, which meant it was larger and stronger than the females. The other two meal creatures were small and meagre in comparison. Aro finished his first and tried to have a nibble of the deerwig's hind leg but Midnyte nearly flamed his face off so he decided he wasn't so hungry after all.

The food of this strange and new island was just as tasty as the food back home and the two travellers enjoyed their meal.

But Ellendrii knew they needed to leave at some point and carry on. He didn't want them to outstay their welcome even though his feelings for Midnyte were growing.

Aro went to go hunting again. The drixell he'd had just wasn't filling enough for him. Luckily even though they looked like Furmines, drixells couldn't speak. But they were small and skinny and not enough to satiate his appetite.

He wasn't really used to a hunting ground like this. He had hunted in the Forest before of course but the layout was different here than what he was used to and it was more open. Something scurried up a tree and he watched carefully to see if he could see what it was. He spied it further up the trunk. It was watching him with small beady eyes. It wasn't moving. In fact it blended in pretty well with the tree trunk. It looked like a flat squirrel. Aro took aim and shot a needle at it. The needle missed and the thing scurried further up the tree with a little squeak. Aro growled and shot another needle at it. This one hit it dead on and it fell to the ground, poisoned.

Aro pounced on it and devoured it hungrily but it still wasn't much. It tasted sort of bitter as well.

Nevertheless, he went back to the other two and didn't continue his hunt, just in case he was missing out on anything they were doing. They weren't doing much. Ellendrii was sat down after his meal and Midnyte was just finishing hers.

Aro sat with them as they watched the sun rise together.

Chapter 11
Rebuilding

"So, what are you two gunna do then?" asked Midnyte.

"Build another float and carry on" replied Ellendrii. Aro nodded.

"Hmm, you'll need help" said Midnyte. "I'll help you build it. I'm good at making things"

Ellendrii brightened.

"Thank you so much!" he said gratefully. Midnyte smiled.

"How did you make the last one?" she asked.

"Wood, we used a tree" replied Ellendrii.

"Well then, let's find a tree and fell it. We'll pick one near the beach so we can just drag it onto the sand and build it there" said Midnyte.

The three of them set off and found a tree.

Midnyte flamed it from a direction behind the tree so it would fall forwards onto the sand. She shot a spear flame through the trunk and it melted straight through it, searing the wood and allowing her and Aro to push the tree trunk forwards and down. The tree felled with relative ease although it was not as broad in circumference as the tree from the Forest had been.

Ellendrii was a little jealous of her fire. It had taken much more flaming to fell the tree in the Forest.

She sliced the tree with her fire and Ellendrii gathered the vines needed to tie the structure together. Midnyte fixed it all together with the vines. She tied it strongly and intricately and it was put together so well that it was almost like it was all one solid structure. Once again they made a shelter as well as the platform and Ellendrii found more twine for a new harness.

By the time they had finished, the moon had risen fully and they were all pretty tired.

They sat on the beach in the moonlight enjoying some fresh fish. Midnyte Comet's markings glowed brightly and she looked up to the sky peacefully. It was quiet; the water gently swelling and falling and the tide going slowly out.

Ellendrii stared at her wings again, he couldn't help himself! He wanted to ask her to fly with him just so he could see them. They fascinated him so much! His mind drifted back to the idea that she could be the last of her kind.

All the more reason to be with her then, to carry on the species! He told this little voice to shut up. He had bigger things to do; he had to find the SilvaGryphie. He wasn't going to let natural instincts stop him or distract him from his goal. Besides, he was too young to start a family of his own. He adjusted himself on his branch and closed his eyes. They would have to set out next sun cycle, although part of him really wanted to stay.

"Hey Midnyte, are any of the fish dangerous?" asked Aro. "I need to know, just in case"

"Stay away from the red and blue ones" replied Midnyte. "And don't try to hunt the ones with teeth. The water is their natural home, not yours, so you will fail in hunting them unless you can get far away from the water. Getting onto the float is not good enough; they can jump."

Aro swallowed. He'd never met creatures that could seriously hurt a Lizariaous before. He didn't like not being top of the pecking order.

Midnyte lay down in the sand and Ellendrii lay next to her, glancing at her every so often. She just looked peacefully out to sea and didn't seem to notice his glances. Finally he spoke.

"We're not disturbing or annoying you are we?" he asked.

"No, not at all. I know you will be gone soon" she replied.

"What's the longest anyone has stayed here?" he asked her, curiously.

"Eight sun cycles" she replied.

"Well if you can't tell me about where you're from, could you tell me more about who has visited you here?" Ellendrii was curious and he wanted information about who had passed through here and what way they were going. If they flew or swam. If any Gryphies had been through, although he guessed not since Midnyte was not familiar with his species.

"Not all of them have been friendly like you, although most just pass through and only stop briefly here for a rest. They don't even sleep here. Most of the passers through are just creatures, birds and things like that. They fly through here when they go to warmer or colder places in certain seasons.

However, a couple of others came through here a few seasons ago. They could fly and were vicious. They didn't look like you. Of course, foolishly I greeted them and paid the price. They tried to hunt me. Well, they *did* hunt me, they just didn't catch me. That was part of the reason I was so hostile to Aro when I found him in my tree."

Aro nodded, though he had forgiven her for her mistake in assuming he was hostile. Midnyte continued.

"I saw them arrive. They looked more like birds in the face than creatures like us. And they had reptilian bodies with huge bat-like wings. I suppose I should have known they were nasty from the sight of them. But I didn't. I greeted them and I tried to help them. They could speak but their language was limited. Or at least the language I understood was limited. They seemed perfectly at home speaking to each other fluently in another language. And they were hungry. So I showed them some food. I even gave them some of my own food so they wouldn't have to hunt for it. I was already afraid they would take offence at the slightest thing. They didn't, until they tried the food and didn't like it. They said it wasn't fresh enough. I said I would hunt for them, again, to stay on their good side, but they told me that where they came from, they ate things that looked like me. None of the creatures on this island that they had seen so far were big enough to sustain their appetites so they wanted to kill and eat me and live here themselves, which I could see no sense in since it was contradictory. So understandably, I fled. I was ready to leave this island and go back to the mainland but then I remembered that it had taken so long for me to even find a place like this and I didn't want to give it up so easily. So I fled but I formulated a plan as well. I had to find a place to hide and I ended up hiding on one of those islands the other side of here. It wasn't that sheltered but I found a small cave the other side of it that I could hide in. I hunted fish that washed into the little inlet there and I lived there for several sun cycles. Luckily the island was so big that if they were looking for me, they would be spending ages there while I hid in relative safety. It gave me the time I needed to formulate a plan.

I had quite a few ideas for what I should do. For one, I *could* just attack them. My acidfire would easily burn through their bodies. Well, I thought it would. I wasn't too sure though, given their skin type. I didn't want to rush in there fire blazing and then have them kill me in some way I hadn't been aware of. I didn't know what they were capable of, having never seen their kind before. They had sharp claws and they were pretty fast and strong. It had only been sheer luck I'd been able to escape them when I flew to hide.

Living in the trees, I've learned how to fly among them and how to twist and turn to avoid them. Wherever these two came from, the land clearly wasn't the same because they couldn't weave in and out of the trees; they were unfamiliar to them. But attacking them wouldn't work, I decided.

What else could I do? Maybe I could scare them or set up a trap for them. Setting up a trap would be fairly easy. I could lure them into it with ease because they wanted to kill me, so they would just chase me into it. But then what would I do with them? I could kill them, or poison them. I could fill the trap with snakes and they could kill them for me. But I don't much like killing and where would I put the bodies? Throw them into the sea? What if others of their kind came along and found out I'd killed them and took revenge on me? I couldn't be sure that wouldn't happen. I supposed I could eat them but they might be poisonous themselves or bad to eat and make me sick. So that was out of the question.

Scaring them. That was becoming my only option. I wasn't sure really how to go about it though or what they were scared of but how would I get them off my island otherwise? I thought maybe I could trick them but they had called after me when they found out they were losing me that next time they saw me, they would kill me on sight. So I figured if they saw me again they would attack first and not ask questions later.

I thought and thought. I spent all my time thinking because the longer they were on the island, the more at home they were making themselves and the less they would want to leave. Also, the more they would learn about the island too and the less easy it would be to trick them into thinking there was something sinister here. I was starting to come up with a plan. I would disguise myself and warn them away from the island. I would do it during the moon cycle so they wouldn't be able to see me as well. Of course, my glowing markings would give me away so I covered them with mud. I only hoped that it wouldn't start raining when I went to put my plan into motion. Being as they'd chased me away during the sun cycle, they hadn't seen my wings so I could use them to my advantage. No creature likes the possibility of danger threatening their existence so I decided to use that to my advantage. Secretly, I went around the island looking for the things I needed to disguise myself. Mud of course, I put that on first. I made a thing for my head out of large leaves. It would make me more imposing if I had some sort of thing on my head that looked like I could make myself bigger. Plus I would look less like myself. I used gourds as well, large ones; I tied them to my tail and covered my tailspade with them. The gourds I tied down the length of my tail to make it appear different. I wanted to look like an entirely different creature and certainly one they had never encountered before. If it was new, it was unknown and the unknown is something most creatures fear the most. They hadn't seen my acidfire either, so I could use that to my advantage as well. Finally my disguise was ready and I was ready to trick them!

First though, I had to find them. And I had to do it quietly, so as not to give myself away before I intended them to see me. The sun was going down, which made it easier. I dreaded to think what they had done to my home. If they had chosen that place to live in that is. So, I headed to my tree and to my relief, they weren't there. There was no sign of them actually being there either. Clearly after they had chased me off, they'd not returned to my tree. They were somewhere else. I had to go on foot. I couldn't fly, or they might have seen me. Quietly, I searched for them.

The moon was starting to shine when I found them. They were on the beach, fishing. It seemed fish was the food they preferred now that they couldn't find anything like me to eat. I suspected they'd probably searched the island to see if there were any more of my kind around and of course come up empty clawed. There had been two when they had chased me away but I noticed to my horror they had been joined by three more and there were now five of them. So now I knew where they were, I had to put my plan into motion. I went back to my tree and found some meat I had buried in the back. It was rotting a bit and smelled bad, which was perfect for what I wanted to do. It was also whole, it was a carxilo. It was good it was whole because I wanted to partly melt it so it looked like it had died of some sort of sickness. So I flamed it and melted off some of its shell. It ended up looking pretty gruesome and just how I'd wanted.

I returned to the beach. The creatures were still there, eating the fish they had caught and a couple were catching more. The pair who I had encountered seemed to be the ones in charge. They were more dominant than the other three and it seemed the other three were the ones catching the fish for the first pair. They had not yet eaten and were griping a bit about having to catch fish for the other two. This was resulting in the other two threatening them although they never carried through on their threats. Probably because if they did, they wouldn't have anyone to catch fish for them.

Anyway, now was my chance to try and trick them. I wanted them to think the island was cursed with sickness. I had thought about draping some sort of seaweed or something on myself so it looked like I was infected as well, but they might just have ended up simply killing me to get rid of it. I only hoped the unfortunate carxilo would be enough to convince them.

So I went stumbling out onto the beach in the faint moonlight. It was not enough light for them to realize who I was and my disguise worked perfectly. I had after all, only one shot at this. I carried my wings close to my body so it looked like I was more bulky than anything else and I hobbled a bit so they would think I wasn't a threat. I had the carxilo with me although the smell was starting to get to me. I had an idea for that though. I called out to the newcomers and they all looked round.

"Cursed! This island is cursed with sickness!!" I called.

201

"What do you mean?" asked the largest of the two in charge.

"If you stay here it will infect you too, it may already have infected you! Look! This carxilo has the sickness!" I made it look as though the carxilo was still alive by moving it with my tail. It was dark enough that it tricked them into thinking it really was alive.

"Your skin falls off and you smell terrible when you get it!" I called, still moving the carxilo. By this time, the three subordinates were looking very nervous and worried and had stopped fishing, staring at the carxilo. One of the others went for a closer look but I warned him away.

"Don't go near it! It is very catching!" I warned.

"How come you don't have it then? You're stood right by that thing" snapped the larger of the two.

I had to think fast. I didn't think they would be smart enough to ask me this. I wanted to say I was immune but that might make them think they could be immune too and I wanted them to think it would definitely kill them if they stayed. I took a chance to say I was infected.

"I have it too. In fact this island was populated by my kind until the sickness came. Now we are all dead and I am the last of my kind. I'm warning you that if you stay, you will catch it too. It will wipe you all out. Don't take the risk!"

The smaller of the two leaders looked convinced. She wrinkled her nose.

"It stinks. Is that smell to do with the sickness?" she asked me.

"Yes, it starts with a smell. Your body starts to decay while you're still alive and then you just fall apart. It's very painful" I told her. She looked frantically at the larger one. He was starting to look convinced too. I decided to up the pretence.

"That creature I saw you chasing the other sun cycle. The purple winged one. She died. I found her corpse the other side of the island. It got washed away by the tide in the end…" I added the last bit in case they wanted to go and find my corpse.

202

"How do we know we're not already infected with it?" yelped one of the subordinates in fright and anxiety.

"Oh it's ok, you don't look infected. The first signs of being infected are seeing things. For example, my wings are just black. You *can* see only black can't you?" I opened out my wings and of course the five of them saw the stars and colours inside them and they freaked out.

"We're infected!!" screamed one of the smaller ones.

"Can we stop it?" demanded the largest one.

"Only by leaving the island. Staying here will only make it worse. If you leave the island and don't come back, the sickness will get better and you won't die from it, though you may still smell bad for a while." I had barely finished speaking when the five of them took to the sky in panic, nearly flying into the line of trees as they hurried to get away from the "cursed" island.

The largest one called down to me.

"Thanks for the tip! We're not coming back here, no way!" he called. The other one in charge suddenly complained that he didn't smell very good and that made them freak out even more. They were nearly gone before I could blink. I sat down in relief. I was so glad it had worked! I went back to my tree after that. Mostly because I needed to get away from that stinky carxilo."

"Wow, it must have been pretty frightening talking to them when you knew it might not work" said Ellendrii with awe.

"It was a bit, but I found that being in disguise gave me more confidence. They had no idea who I was and I made it so they wouldn't need to come closer to me, just in case they saw through my disguise. I had to stop myself from laughing when they looked at my wings and started really freaking out" Midnyte chuckled. "It served them right. How dare they come to my island and push their weight around! Until them, all the visitors I've had have been pleasant and certainly none of them have tried to get rid of me and live here themselves."

"Have any of them wanted to actually live here with you though?" asked Ellendrii.

"A few have, but as soon as they find out how badly the weather can affect this island, they change their minds and leave. Just as well really."

Ellendrii nodded.

Aro was making something with the sand. He was digging and forming the sand into the shape of a cave. He dug a moat around it and the water flowed gently in and out of the moat with the moving tide. Because the tide was going out though, his moat never really filled up.

He didn't understand this.

"You need to make it closer to the water if you want it to fill up" said Midnyte.

Ellendrii sat up with an idea. Aro's sand cave had inspired him! He set about trying to make a sand Gryphie. He couldn't make one with its wings out but he made one that was sitting down with its wings folded. Halfway through, he decided it wouldn't be a Gryphie but a little sculpture of Midnyte. His hands were far more deft than Aro's paws and he could make the sculpture quite detailed. He even gave her claws on her wings. When he finished, he sat back and admired his creation. Aro hadn't really noticed that Ellendrii was better at making things in sand than he was. He'd made the thing he wanted to make and Ellendrii had made the thing he wanted to make. Ellendrii looked at Midnyte.

"It's you" he said simply, pointing to the sculpture.

"It's very nice, it looks just like me" smiled Midnyte, looking at it. Ellendrii blushed deeply and hid his face.

Aro yawned.

"I'm going back to the tree" he said. The other two agreed that it was late and they had a long journey ahead of them the next sun cycle as well. So they all set off back into the forest.

"Midnyte, can we fly back to the tree?" asked Ellendrii. He wanted to see her wings again.

"What about Aro?" asked Midnyte.

"I really don't care what you do" said Aro. "I'm happy to walk back and go to sleep. Besides, if Midnyte gets back before me, then she will be already settled at the back of the tree and won't have to step over me or disturb me. So, go ahead" he smiled. Ellendrii was taken aback a little by his attitude but he didn't question it. He and Midnyte took to the sky and flew back to her tree. All the time, he flew a little under her again, just to gaze up at the beautiful view of space that the underside of her wings showed. Midnyte had noticed this but said nothing. She let him have his moment of fantasy. It would probably be the last one he had before they left.

When they reached the tree, Ellendrii landed on his sleeping branch and Midnyte landed on the ground down below and they retired for the moon cycle.

Ellendrii lay back, looking up at the sky. Still not half as beautiful as her wings! Soon he was asleep, only this moon cycle he didn't have such odd dreams. He did dream about mysterious visitors to the island though.

***

The sun was just coming up when Ellendrii awoke the next sun cycle. He shook himself, momentarily disoriented and wondering where he was. Oh yes, of course, he was on Midnyte Comet's island. Midnyte Comet! Her beautiful wings! He nearly fell out of the tree again.

Down below, Aro was already awake and had caught himself some breakfast in the form of something that resembled a fat groundhog but of course wasn't. It was blue for one thing. Midnyte was up too and eating some food she had in storage. She had buried it under the earth at the back of her tree hollow. It was wrapped in leaves so it wouldn't get dirty. She had standards!

"Morning Ellendrii!" yelled Aro, his mouth full so his words sounded rather muffled.

Ellendrii rolled his eyes at his friend's lack of manners and said good morning too.

Ellendrii went out to hunt for some food but came back empty handed. He had no idea what was good to eat here. All the creatures looked rather bright and dangerous.

Midnyte gave him some of her food instead and that only made him blush furiously and turn away while he ate.

"We'll catch some food for you to take with you" said Midnyte to Ellendrii's back.

Ellendrii nodded, his mouth full.

"Thank you" said Aro. "We'll need new gourds for water too" he said in a moment of clarity and intelligence.

"I can get you some of those" said Midnyte. "I'll fetch some large ones for you; they will hold a lot of water. I'll fill them at the stream. The water there is fresh." She left in search of gourds.

Aro sidled up to Ellendrii.

"You *like* her, don't you?" he smirked with a knowing look and a quirk of an eyeridge. Ellendrii nearly choked.

"What do you mean? I…err…of course I like her, she's helping us!" he blurted.

"Ha! I can read your body language and you smell different too! I can tell you like her!" Aro laughed.

"So? Aren't I allowed to like someone?" asked Ellendrii defensively.

"Of course but isn't she…too old for you? She's like…an adult…you're barely out of your kitten seasons. She's old enough to be your mum!"

"Shut up Aro."

Aro collapsed into fits of giggles. Ellendrii frowned at him.

"I…I saw you last moon cycle…" laughed Aro. "Staring at her wings like this" he stared at Ellendrii, his eyes wide and dumbfounded.

"I mean they were cool and everything but you didn't start getting a crush on her until you saw them, which means you only like her for her wings. How shallow of you! I really thought you were better than that Ellendrii!"

"Shut UP!" yelled Ellendrii and shoved Aro over in the grass.

"HEY! No need to be like that, geez" muttered Aro, getting up.

"I'm NOT shallow ok? I just like her, that's all. Yes her wings are unusual but that's not the only thing I like her for. I like her cos she's wise and kind and pretty…and helpful, unlike you! Why are you being so mean about it?"

"I'm just having a laugh. I didn't mean it nastily. I was just surprised that your first crush should be someone so old."

"Age doesn't matter" replied Ellendrii with his nose in the air. Aro just shrugged.

"Well you can't be with her anyway; we have to go this sun cycle"

"You think I don't know that? I thought she might come with us but she seems to like being here"

"She does" said Midnyte. Ellendrii and Aro spun round.

"Oh…err…sorry! H…how long have you been there?" blurted Ellendrii looking flustered.

"Long enough to know you want me to go with you but not long enough to know why" replied Midnyte.

"Er…cos you're really smart and stuff, so it would be an advantage to have you travel with us" Ellendrii said, hoping it was true that she hadn't heard any more than the last part of what they had been talking about.

"Well you're right, I wouldn't come with you. Some journeys you must make by yourself" she replied, sitting down and rolling three gourds towards him.

"I thought you two would like to come with me to fill these, so you can have a good long drink before you leave. You'll need it"

The pair nodded and stood up.

"I can show you around a little along the way, so you can spend more time here before you go" she said. Ellendrii then wondered how much more she had heard of their conversation. But it could still just be a coincidence.

The three of them trekked into the forest towards the stream. Birds of many colours sat in the trees, singing and a gentle, fresh breeze rustled the leaves of the trees. Aro and Ellendrii looked all around them with interest as they followed Midnyte.

Ellendrii was thinking about Midnyte. Aro was taking in the sights all around him with awe. This forest was far brighter than the one back home he thought.

"This place is huge" said Aro.

"Yes, that is probably why you thought you'd hit the mainland. I've met others too who thought this was the mainland. They are always headed somewhere and never stay. Not that I wish they would stay. I am perfectly happy here being the master of my own little world on this island. There are still parts I've yet to explore and I have lived here more seasons than I can count. That gives you some idea of the sheer size of this place."

"Is there anything dangerous here?" asked Aro.

"There is a type of snake with a bite that will kill you" replied Midnyte. "I've seen it hunt before, which is how I know. When you live by yourself with no one else to talk to or hang around with, you learn a lot about your surroundings and the things that live within them. I've watched this snake hunt and I know to stay away from it if I want to live."

"What's a snake?" asked Aro dumbly. She had mentioned them before.

"A creature with a long body like a vine. It makes a hissing sound like this" Midnyte mimicked a snake sound.

"Sounds creepy" said Aro. "I hope we don't meet any of those. Is it poisonous then?"

"No, it is venomous. That's similar to poisonous though; it will still kill you."

"I shoot a poison through my needles that will kill you" said Aro. "That's why I threatened to shoot you when we met. That, my claws and my teeth are my defence."

"My fire is my defence" replied Midnyte. "And also my wings of course"

"Your beautiful wings" muttered Ellendrii.

"Huh?" questioned Midnyte.

"Oh, nothing" replied Ellendrii hurriedly. She actually hadn't heard him so he needn't have worried. Aro heard him though and sniggered.

"Midnyte, did you create that neat weaving effect with your tree yourself?" asked Aro, curiously.

"Yes I did, though it took a very, very long time. I found that trees grow around obstacles. I discovered this when I saw a tree in another part of the forest that was a funny shape and I thought I would try the same on a tree myself. So I weaved vines and twines around the tree and it grew around them. The effect was great and I have my own little light sources in what would otherwise be a very dark home."

Aro listened, fascinated.

"Do you only sleep inside the hollow of the tree?" asked Ellendrii.

"Sometimes I sleep further up, but I feel too exposed up there. The weather here is unpredictable and storms come but you never know when until it is too late. I prefer to sleep in safety. Even though the island is big, the weather still damages the trees here, mostly because they are not so dense as to protect each other. They blow around."

"Where did you live before?" asked Ellendrii.

"Somewhere else of course" replied Midnyte mysteriously. Ellendrii wondered why she wouldn't tell them of her past or anything else for that matter, aside from information about her current home. He really wondered what sort of creature she was too.

Finally they reached the stream and filled the gourds. It was time to head back to the beach.

"Let me show you something, Ellendrii" said Midnyte and took to the air. Ellendrii followed.

"What about me?" asked Aro.

"We won't be long" replied Midnyte.

Aro sat down in annoyance. Stupid flyers. He wondered if they were going to court or something. Lizariaous courtship was far different to Gryphie courtship. For obvious reasons, Lizariaouses couldn't mate with all the needles on their backs. So a couple would shoot them all off in a courtship display. They would fire them into the air in a particular way, at particular angles, which signified their affection (love would be too strong a word) for each other. And they would fire them off together, at the same time so the needles crisscrossed in the sky. No training or teaching was needed for them to know this; it just came naturally, by instinct. And of course after all their needles were used, they could then mate comfortably.

Gryphie courtship was different of course. They used their fire and courted in the air. They would shoot fireballs and other styles of flaming into the sky, again in a ritual like the Lizariaouses. They may mate in the air or go back to the privacy of their tree or another private place, depending on if they were show offs or not.

Aro looked at the pair of flyers disappearing from sight and grumbled.

But of course he was wrong. Midnyte wanted to show Ellendrii something entirely different.

She lead the way to a small mountain range. They were smaller than the Metal Mountains that Ellendrii was familiar with but they still looked impressive. They were high enough that the tops were misty. She landed on an outcrop that looked over them and Ellendrii landed beside her. He hadn't seen these when he was looking around on the island the previous sun cycle. He'd flown lower and mostly along the beaches then.

"Aren't they beautiful?" she asked him.

"Very" he replied, looking across the mountain range with awe. "But why are you showing them to me?"

"Because I wanted to show you something that very few have ever seen before. To share it with you before you leave so you'll always remember. I know you have a crush on me" she looked at him and he hid his face with a wing.

"And I can't offer you anything of that sort but I can leave you with a memory that few others in this world have. And that is these. The beauty of these mountains. See how the sun casts the tops of them in pink? At sunrise it really is a special sight."

Ellendrii nodded and took in all that he could see. He was sitting so close to her that his body touched hers.

"Why *do* you live alone, really?" he asked, hoping she would tell him some secret or something personal and share that with him too.

"Because I've chosen to. I found life back home was too noisy and hectic. And I'm not lonely so don't worry. The creatures on this island are enough company for me. Besides, if I didn't live here, who would help those who are lost like you were? This island is the halfway point and I am its keeper, to help travellers who need to find their way."

"But I've never known anyone come to Shernaron from the other side. We always thought that was where the souls of our dead go." Ellendrii said. "Not that you helping travellers find their way isn't a good thing of course" he added hurriedly.

Midnyte nodded, understanding.

"You'll see what lies the other side of the vast water. It's not my place to spoil it for you. But great things are waiting for you and new creatures and new adventures. And it is all for you to discover for yourselves."

Ellendrii felt reassured and happy about continuing his journey now, although he would still miss Midnyte, at least for a while.

The two of them flew back to where Aro was waiting.

"Have fun?" he asked sarcastically.

"I showed him the mountain range, that's all" said Midnyte. In truth, Aro could smell nothing else had happened but he still felt jealous that he hadn't been included.

The three of them made their way to the beach, stocking up the food supplies for the shelter and putting the three gourds in with it. Along the way, Midnyte found some healing herbs and other things to put in Ellendrii's bag since some of the others he had been carrying had got wet and destroyed in the water during the storm.

"I didn't know you knew about these" said Ellendrii, impressed with her knowledge. He would have looked for some himself, but of course he was in a strange place and had no idea what plants to use since they all looked different to what he was used to.

"I have to know what will heal and help me. Living on my own, I need to survive" she had replied. Ellendrii nodded, still impressed.

It was nearly mid-sun when they were finally ready to set out again and the ocean was calm. Of course the float had been built on the beach the opposite side of the island so they could continue on their journey. Looking out across the water, once again they saw nothing but water. They both hoped they wouldn't encounter another storm. It had been terrifying enough the first time and if it had caught them in the middle of the water with no land nearby, they would have died.

Ellendrii secured the harness around himself. It felt weird to be leaving, he felt like he'd been on the island far longer

211

than just a sun cycle and a moon cycle. He wondered how many lunars they would be travelling for before they returned to Shernaron. IF they returned to Shernaron. It was still a big if.

"Are you ready?" asked Midnyte.

Ellendrii knew if he stayed longer, he would find it even more difficult to leave. He still had a crush on her and he couldn't help that and he couldn't help his worry about setting out once again.

"Yeah we're ready" he said finally and took to the sky. Midnyte flew up beside him.

"I'll fly with you two a little way if you like" she said. Ellendrii felt overjoyed. But it would still be hard to say goodbye when the time came.

"Let's go then" Aro called up to them and off they went. Aro's body still ached from being thrown around in the sea but he did feel better this sun cycle than he had the previous one.

Ellendrii felt the old familiar strain return to his wing muscles as he pulled the float into deeper water.

Midnyte flew with them for quite a while but still would not tell either of them what lay ahead. Aro liked surprises but he was also a bit worried. She hadn't known what the SilvaGryphie was and she had apparently come from the mainland. He only hoped it was a different part of the mainland to whatever part the SilvaGryphie resided in. He still had doubts as to whether or not the SilvaGryphie actually existed but if he ever spoke of it to Ellendrii, Ellendrii would simply tell him that of course she existed, she HAD to. Yeah she did, or this would all be for nothing and Ellendrii would be the biggest fool in Shernaron.

"I will leave you here" said Midnyte. They were quite far away from the island now.

"Ok, thank you so much for coming with us this far" said Ellendrii gratefully.

"You're welcome" replied Midnyte. "Both of you take care and goodbye!"

She flew up into the air with a respectful flame burst of her bright green acidfire.

Ellendrii replied with a burst of his own blue fire. Aro shot a couple of needles into the air in a sign of respect too.

They bid farewell to Midnyte Comet and her beautiful space wings and carried on their journey into the endless vastness of the water.

Chapter 12
Sailing Again

Ellendrii did look back a couple of times and his heart ached as he saw the figure of Midnyte Comet disappearing back to her island. Maybe they could visit her again on the way back. He really hoped so. He hadn't said they would see her on the way back just in case they didn't make it back. It would have been too big a promise to keep and too unsure.

"I'm gunna miss Midnyte" said Ellendrii to Aro, who was sat on the float looking out to sea.

"Don't be so silly" replied Aro. He really couldn't see her beauty like Ellendrii could. To him, she was just another flying creature. He really wanted to meet a creature that was ground bound and couldn't fly, so he would have someone to relate to and not just Ellendrii all the time. Ellendrii and his Sky Gryphies and Midnyte Comet. Aro snorted.

"I'll probably never meet anyone else like her" muttered Ellendrii. Sure she had known about his crush but it didn't matter to him. She could see the truth and didn't mind it. He remembered what she had said about the adventures they would have and the new creatures they would meet. It made Ellendrii excited but at the same time he really missed Midnyte. He was currently torn between his quest and missing her. He tried to put her to the back of his mind. He had bigger things to worry about. She hadn't known what the SilvaGryphie was and they may be in for more storms, despite the current nice weather.

They travelled for a while and then Ellendrii stopped for a rest and some food. The fact they had three gourds now was very useful and Aro had learned how to ration. Sort of.

"Still *missing* her" chided Aro.

"A bit" admitted Ellendrii, ignoring his friend's sarcasm. He looked through the leather bag and found the herbs that Midnyte had put in there for him. Delving deeper into it, sniffing the scents of the herbs, his hand landed on something that was strange. Lifting it out, Ellendrii found that it was one of the curious ornaments that she had had hanging in her hollow tree. Ellendrii held it up and admired its intricacy. Aro spoke up.

"Oh that's for protecting and bringing good fortune" he said.

"How do you know?" asked Ellendrii.

"I asked her while you were off scouting about the island needlessly for a land bridge" he replied, taking another bite of his meal. Ellendrii frowned.

"It wasn't needless. I needed to be sure. Dad said to always check things out for myself just in case" he said. Aro shrugged and carried on eating.

"It was nice of her though, to put this in my bag for me. Protection." He looked at the ornament and sniffed it. It smelled of her and he smiled. Aro noticed the flush on Ellendrii's cheeks and rolled his eyes.

"Get a grip on reality, El. Put that thing away. It probably brings better fortune when it's inside the bag, not out"

"Fine. I'll put it away. You have no romance, Aro." Ellendrii spat, putting the ornament carefully back in his bag.

"What's romance?" asked Aro. He genuinely didn't know.

"It's to do with love" replied Ellendrii, "And the things we do when we love someone. But you wouldn't understand anyway"

"Nope. Makes no sense to me" said Aro. He meant that entirely honestly. It was a completely foreign concept to Lizariaouses. Ellendrii sighed, had a drink and took to the sky again.

Aro went back to looking out to sea. Ellendrii often looked back towards the island until he couldn't see it anymore. He wondered a lot if Midnyte was thinking of them or if someone else had come to the island to take her mind off them. He also wondered if someone would come to the island who she would fall in love with and want to be with. He felt pangs of jealousy just thinking about things like that. It made him want to fly back and just make sure no one else would do such a thing. It never occurred to him that maybe it would be nice for *her* if she had someone instead of being alone, so selfish his feelings were becoming. Since he had nothing much to do while flying, his mind played out constant scenarios of what might happen.

He could fly back to the island and just spy on her, watch over her until the end of his sun cycles. Because even if he couldn't be with her, he could at least watch her. Like a creepy stalker. Not that this was the way he was thinking of being but it would almost certainly come off that way.

Or maybe he could go see her again when he was older and be with her then.

Or maybe just watch over her and keep other males away because she was *his* and his alone!

Or if they didn't find the SilvaGryphie as soon as they reached the other side, he could just suggest they turn around and then go back to the island and be with her. He would take Aro home if he wanted and then he could go live with Midnyte. They say love is blind. His feelings were starting to blind him. This mission was his entire world and he was willing to jeopardize it all just to be with a creature he barely knew. Young male Gryphies often can't help their hormones running off with them.

And how much longer would it be? Maybe he'd leave it for a few sun cycles and then just go back to the island if they didn't reach the mainland fast enough. Aro would lose all respect for him of course but that doesn't matter. What is a Lizariaous's respect anyway? They don't even respect one another!

What are you thinking? He asked himself. His thoughts were running away with him and not in a good way. It was probably good he wouldn't be going back to see Midnyte. Part of him hoped he would never see her again. These thoughts and urges were scaring him a little. Flying had always been his passion and he was letting thoughts of a female get in the way of it!

No, he must wait until he gets home, after he has completed his quest. He could find a nice female Sky Gryphie. Wait, Gryphies don't interbreed, do they? No, of course they did! His father had a Deamon mother. And she had been banished from the Dark Plains because of her love for her Forest Gryphie mate. But it wouldn't be the same for

Ellendrii's mate surely? Because he would be part of the Sky Gryphies too! He would probably impress every single one of them, including all the females when he returned with the SilvaGryphie! He'd have females chasing after *him*! It wouldn't be hard to find a mate then.

But she wouldn't be like Midnyte. She wouldn't have those astounding wings. He wouldn't be able to lose himself in her beauty. Maybe she'd have pretty feathers? He sighed. Still nothing compared to those wings that he couldn't get out of his mind.

Wait, *did* he only love her for her wings? Had his opinion of her changed so drastically since he'd seen them? He'd always thought she was pretty since he met her but he had to admit that his crush and admiration for her grew tenfold when he saw the insides of her wings.

And *was* she the last of her kind or just someone who liked to be alone? Maybe they would encounter more of her kind along their journey! He would be sure not to tell them about her though. She had obviously left because she'd had enough of her peers so he wasn't going to ruin that for her. Unless of course they weren't bothered about finding her again. Maybe her kind didn't have life mates? So even if he had wanted her, she wouldn't have stayed with him. Just cos she looked like a Gryphie didn't mean her lifestyle would be the same as his. If he didn't encounter any more like her, he would ask his father about her when he got back home. IF of course he made it. He never ignored the fact that they might not make it even now. Midnyte had said the mainland was several sun cycles away but it WAS there. So at least they knew that much.

Meanwhile, Aro's thoughts were enjoying their own little internal dialogue.

He wondered what Zixiniss and Scit were doing. He never got along with his sisters but now he was no longer with them, he missed them a little. He supposed they were just going along with life as normal now he was away. Probably hunting with their mother or something. And his father? He guessed Mordred would be missing him or at least thinking of him. Lizariaouses didn't normally "miss" each other.

217

And Ellendrii. Him and his stupid crush. He really was pretty intolerable at times. Aro was sure Ellendrii would lose interest in Midnyte and he would probably be right, since Ellendrii would probably never see her again. Out of sight; out of mind. Aro was glad of this. He didn't want his best friend crooning over some female. Aro really wanted them both to remain young forever so they could go on adventures together. He was more immature than Ellendrii. Ellendrii's immaturity came from lack of knowledge about the world. Aro's came from a lack of eagerness to grow up. Adults had to have life goals and do the same tedious thing every sun cycle. He didn't want to be like that. Maybe he would just go adventuring and when Ellendrii lost interest in it; he would go by himself.

The sea was calm this sun cycle. Aro was glad it wasn't choppy like it had been. He got seasick so easily.

The two of them travelled for four sun cycles, talking, joking sometimes and other times just thinking to themselves.

Ellendrii often thought about Midnyte Comet but only when his mind started to wander. He had resolved to try to think about her as little as possible, having finally realized that any relationship with her was doomed to failure. So he was determined to just drop the whole thing. Aro was glad of this.

At mid-sun, Ellendrii and Aro caught some more food to stock up their little supply.

"Well, it's been four sun cycles, we must be near the mainland now" said Aro, "It was around this time that we found that island before" He was careful not to say "Midnyte Comet's island" for fear it would turn his friend's mind to her again.

"Yeah it was but I see only water ahead of us now" said Ellendrii.

"Grik" muttered Aro, "I thought with your good vision that you would be able to see something at least on the horizon." Ellendrii just shook his head and carried on eating.

By the sixth sun cycle, they were starting to run out of water. They had only half of one gourd's full left.

Aro was freaking out a little.

"WHEN are we going to hit land?? Do we have to wait for another storm again?" his voice cracked and broke while he freaked out. He paced around irritably and rattled his needles.

"Calm down, we'll get there" said Ellendrii but he really wasn't sure of his own words.

"She said A FEW sun cycles, A FEW, Ellendrii!! We'll starve before we hit land!" snapped Aro.

"Starve? We won't starve; we've plenty of food here"

"I'm SICK of fish. We hardly find any birds anymore either. Fish makes me SICK, Ellendrii!"

"Please calm down, Aro. You're rocking the float"

"ROCKING IT???? I'LL SHOW YOU GRIKKING ROCKING IT!!" And Aro started swaying around, making the whole float rock from side to side so much that Ellendrii had to hold on to stop himself from falling into the water.

"Aro, please stop!" he yelped, clinging to the wood. But Aro didn't stop. In fact he rocked it so violently that the hapless Ellendrii fell in. Aro stopped rocking it then and went to the edge to see where Ellendrii had gone. His yellow eyes rolled about madly and he snarled.

Ellendrii floated in the water, not sure what to do but knowing he couldn't spend too long in the water or he would get waterlogged and have to dry out before flying again. It had taken this long; it really didn't need any more hold ups. But Aro looked very much like he was guarding the float and wouldn't let him back on. Ellendrii attempted to climb back on anyway but Aro just pushed him off again.

"Aro! What the grik is wrong with you??" Ellendrii demanded but Aro wouldn't reply; he just snarled and snapped at him. Ellendrii saw that Aro was salivating and panting. He kept retching as well and Ellendrii could only assume Aro had eaten something that hadn't agreed with him.

Ellendrii swam around to the part of the float that was behind the shelter and tried to climb up the back of the shelter in order to get back on board. At the moment, Aro was looking for him. To Ellendrii's advantage, it seemed that the Lizariaous couldn't properly focus on anything so he was confused, thinking Ellendrii had disappeared.

Ellendrii finally got on top of the shelter and lay down so Aro wouldn't see him. He needed to work out what was wrong with his friend and how to fix it before one or other of them got seriously hurt. Most probably Ellendrii.

As he looked down, Aro was pacing around on the platform, looking over the edge into the water and growling low in his throat. A Lizariaous is far worse than a Gryphie when it's in a bad mood. Ellendrii tried to clear his panicking mind long enough to actually focus on the problem at hand.

They'd just eaten. They'd been sat chatting when Aro threw this wobbly of a temper. What had he eaten? Only the fish they ate normally. They tended to always catch the same kinds of fish because they knew they were good to eat. So far this food hadn't done them wrong.

Ellendrii looked down onto the platform. There were the remains of the fish they had been eating and nothing else. The other food and supplies were inside the shelter. Ellendrii's bag was inside the shelter. Maybe he could get inside and get something from it that would heal Aro. If only he knew what the problem was.

He decided to wait until Aro was the other end of the platform looking out over the water and try to sneak into the shelter while he was there. If Aro saw him or knew what he was doing though, Ellendrii was sure he would attack. But it was worth a try anyway.

He crawled on his belly to the front of the shelter's roof and watched Aro carefully. Aro was still growling and drooling in a rather unwholesome manner. He was still, luckily, looking down into the water. Ellendrii waited until his pacing took him to the other side of the platform and carefully pushed the door open by hooking his fingers into the crack at the top where the door met the shelter. He pushed it open ever so slowly and softly. As soon as Aro's back was turned, Ellendrii clambered down, pushing the door open and all but falling inside the shelter. He closed the door quickly behind him. But Aro had seen the door close and he was charging over to attack.

"ELLENDRII!! GET OUT HERE AND FIGHT!!" he roared.

"Not until you tell me why" Ellendrii growled back fiercely.

"I'M SICK OF THIS!! WE'RE NOT GETTING ANYWHERE AND WE'LL DIE OUT HERE! I WAS A FOOL TO WANT TO COME WITH YOU. NO, I WAS A FOOL TO WANT TO BE YOUR FRIEND!! THERE *IS* NO SILVAGRYPHIE, THERE *IS* NO MAINLAND!!"

"Tell me what's wrong with you, Aro! What have you eaten? Why are you so mad at me? I don't understand. Why are you drooling like that? We've been friends since we were youngsters, why now do you hate me?"

"I'VE EATEN FISH. STUPID GRIKKING FISH. I **HATE** FISH, ELLENDRII!! I HATE YOU TOO!! WE'VE NEARLY RUN OUT OF WATER TOO, I DON'T KNOW WHY I EVEN CARED TO HELP YOU SURVIVE!"

"Help me survive, what do you mean?"

"WE WERE RUNNING OUT OF GOOD WATER SO I DRANK THE NASTY WATER *JUST* SO YOU WOULD HAVE MORE TO DRINK AND LIVE LONGER. BUT I WAS WRONG, I WASTED MY TIME. GET OUT HERE AND **GRIKKING FIGHT ME**!!" Aro's voice cracked and rose again on the last part because he roared it so loudly.

Ellendrii finally realized what was wrong. Aro had drunk the nasty salty sea water and now he was going mad. Knowing him he probably took huge Lizariaous sized swallows and gulps of the grikking stuff to sate his thirst. Ellendrii groaned. The idiot! He would have to give Aro what was left in the gourd in order to water what he had drunk down enough to make him better. And Aro was seriously angry, not to mention volatile and unpredictable. If Ellendrii put one foot out of that shelter, Aro would attack without hesitation. He had to somehow reason with him.

"Aro, I know what's wrong with you! Please calm down and let me help you!" Ellendrii called to him.

"Please come out here and let me KILL YOU" snapped Aro in a mocking tone, mimicking Ellendrii's voice only with spite.

"Aro, I can make you better. Please just listen and calm down! You've drunk the bad water of the vast...water..." too many uses of the word "water" thought Ellendrii.

"It's full of salt and it's messing with you, making you sick. I can fix it. I can make you feel better. Please just calm down and I'll come out."

"Come out then, let me kill you!" replied Aro, surprisingly calmly.

"Sure, I'll come out and you can kill me any way you wish. But first I want you to drink from the gourd. Then you can kill me."

"Why? I was drinking from the vast water so you would have more of that stupid gourd water" snapped Aro.

"But if I'm dead then I won't need the gourd water will I? And you can drink it all yourself!" Ellendrii only hoped Aro would be stupid enough not to mention rationing it. He would have to drink a large amount of it to water the other down well enough that he would regain his senses.

"FINE. Just get out here" snarled Aro.

Ellendrii complied and opened the door a crack, offering the gourd to Aro. Aro snatched it away and drank down the whole thing, swigging it greedily. Once he had started drinking it, it felt good and quenched his thirst and made him want more. Oddly, the liquid of the vast water had only served to make him thirstier; he had never quite understood that. He thought that if it was wet, it would quench thirst, not make it worse.

Ellendrii was still mostly behind the door, peering out. Aro threw the gourd onto the float with finality when he'd finished. Then he sat down and then he suddenly threw up. Seems he had drunk it too fast, however in throwing up, he also ejected the bad water from his body and fixed himself.

"A…Aro?" ventured Ellendrii, "You ok?"

Aro was sat there swaying gently from side to side and looking queasy. Ellendrii thought he might puke again but he didn't. He put a paw to his head and groaned.

"Aro?" asked Ellendrii again, opening the door a little wider and poking out his head in order to see better.

"What?" asked Aro.

Ellendrii came out fully and went over to him.

"Are you feeling better?" asked Ellendrii, looking worried.

"Yeah I am, thanks. Sorry I went a bit mad back there. I felt awful and it made me very irritable. I dunno why the water made me like that. I thought it just tasted bad but would work in the place of the fresh water. I didn't know it would hurt me. My stomach is killing me" he groaned again.

"It's got a lot of salt in it. I know you had good intentions though and I'm grateful but unfortunately in trying to do the right thing, you ended up drinking ALL the rest of our water. Now we have none at all."

"Grik" muttered Aro and mentally kicked himself. "I'm so STUPID!"

"You're not, you meant well. But I dunno if we *will* survive now" Ellendrii looked as upset as Aro felt. Aro felt his eyes getting moist.

Ellendrii patted him on a spiky shoulder. "I'd better get back into the sky if we want to survive" he said and flew into the air. It was more important now than ever that they reach land. Any kind of land with water. He intended to fly until he was worn out. He wanted to do this now, as opposed to waiting until they were desperate for something to drink and then keel over while he was in the sky.

So he flew.

And he flew.

And for a whole sun cycle and moon cycle he flew. Six sun cycles became seven and seven became eight.

Ellendrii was nearly dead in the sky. He had eaten but he hadn't stopped to rest. He had merely flown down to have something to eat quickly and then taken to the sky again.

Aro sat the whole time on the float. No getting off and swimming or doing anything that would slow them down now.

They were both starting to become dehydrated and feel dizzy, Ellendrii especially. The hot sun was not kind to him. He thought that even his eyeballs were drying up. And he was starting to see things, so he was starting to fly with his eyes closed. For one, he felt they wouldn't dry up if they were closed and for another, he knew he wouldn't see anything bad if they were closed. But then he started seeing things behind his eyelids too and had to open them again. The images in the darkness of his closed eyes were even more vivid than the images he was starting to see before him with his eyes open.

He was seeing a long line of white on the horizon. It looked a bit like cliffs but there was something very off about it. It was weird shapes. He thought he was imagining land and couldn't help it; he *had* to stop for a rest.

Aro was lying on the platform, listless and thirsty. He hadn't drunk any more of the awful vast water though.

"I'm sick of this, El. When are we gunna find land?" he was no longer clouded in the mind and angry at his friend. He felt just as helpless as Ellendrii.

"I dunno. And if we don't find it soon, we'll die. I don't have the strength to fish. I barely have the strength to pull the float."

"That's cos you went all out and full pelt on pulling the grikking thing. If you hadn't gone so mad and conserved your energy more, you would be able to hunt." Aro sat up but felt dizzy so he lay back down again.

He looked out to sea and the way they were going. And he squinted and saw the weird white on the horizon. He squinted more, thinking he was seeing things like Ellendrii had done but the white thing continued to be there.

"El, what is that on the horizon?" he asked.

"It's nothing" replied Ellendrii, "Wait, you can see it too?"

"Yeah. It looks like it's full of holes or something. The shape is really odd to me" Aro squinted more.

They could both see it. That meant it had to be there right? Ellendrii just needed the strength to pull them to it. But it seemed a long way away so it must be even further than it seemed. Land had an annoying habit of being like that. It looks much closer than it actually is.

If Ellendrii went for it, it would be the last thing he probably did. It would take all his remaining strength to get to it. He stared out determinedly and spread his wings. He took to the sky, a little wobbly and hoped that there wouldn't be another storm. But there wasn't. The weather was fine and warm. A little *too* warm at times.

The sun got lower in the sky as he travelled though and made that aspect of it a little easier for him. Several times he faltered in the sky and fell a little way before flapping his wings and gaining height again.

Aro was looking at the land that got ever closer. Slowly but surely. What it appeared to be now was vast white plateaus. There was something unusual about them. They seemed to be tiered in terrace formations, not like any cliffs Aro had seen and certainly not like the ones he was used to. But at the same time they were fascinating. He watched as they got closer.

Meanwhile Ellendrii was focusing solely on reaching these terraces. He stared at them in determination, using every last ounce of his strength. They HAD to make it. Not just for him but for the two of them. Aro's life depended on him once again.

He was formulating a plan for when they reached the plateaus. They needed to find water. It seemed though, that water was flowing over these curious white terraces and pooling in the formations on each platform. *Was* it water though and *would* it be good to drink? Ellendrii desperately hoped so. And would there be inhabitants that needed to be watched out for? Ellendrii tiredly hoped they would be friendly and not hostile. They hadn't met anyone hostile yet and he hoped it would remain that way. They were not close enough to see if the terraces were inhabited. He couldn't see any little figures or anything on them that might denote life but they weren't that close yet.

So, when they reached it, the first thing he figured they would do was look for water. Then rest. Then eat the rest of their supplies and then find out if there were any locals they could talk to and ask about the whereabouts of the SilvaGryphie. Or maybe this *was* her home? Maybe the plateaus were where she resided? He wondered if she had friends or just lived by herself. She probably had friends. She seemed nice.

His wings were starting to ache again and he was feeling immensely fatigued. But he kept on going. He was determined to get there. And slowly but surely, the land was indeed getting closer.

The sun was going down by the time they reached the plateaus. Ellendrii was just about ready to drop and when they reached the land, he all but nearly did.

Aro got off the float and went to the back and pushed it up on the shore. This wasn't a beach though; it was the same white rock of the beautiful terraced plateaus that rose up before them. Aro pushed the float up as far as he could, so the tide wouldn't take the float away and Ellendrii managed to get himself out of the harness. He went into the shelter and got his bag and they used the twine that attached the harness to the float to tie the float to a white rock that stuck out near the base of the cliff. There were a row of shallow caves all along the bottom of this high terraced cliff that overlooked the sea.

Now the pair were out of the water, they felt less sick and more like exploring but they were still very dehydrated and very thirsty. They both moved slowly and stumbled a little with their steps. They were looking solely for water; nothing else mattered at the moment. Aro went up to the shallow caves and looked in each one as he walked past them but they were empty and there was no water.

"We need to climb higher, to where the pools are" said Ellendrii quietly. It was still light enough to see but the sunset cast a pretty pink glow on the white plateaus and the shadowed parts were darker than they would have been during the sun cycle.

"I don't think I can climb" said Aro. "I'm too thirsty"

"Well you'll have to because I'm not dragging you up there. In fact, you should be dragging me. I flew your butt this far!" Ellendrii was getting short tempered but he had found a natural path leading up higher onto the cliff and from there they would be able to be high enough to see where the nearest pool was and see if they could drink from it. If they couldn't, they would have to continue the search next sun cycle. After a rest, they would probably feel better. After his long flight without much rest, Ellendrii was nearly dead on his feet. He wanted so badly to sleep but drinking was more important right now.

Aro followed him up the natural path and higher onto the cliff. Now they had a better view of everything. But the growing darkness was preventing them seeing properly. Ellendrii was too tired to take to the sky and see if he could find the pools that way so they carried on walking higher and higher until Ellendrii fell into water and they'd found their first pool.

Aro waded in and took a tentative sip but it didn't taste salty or bad and it was warm as well. Ellendrii thought the sun had probably warmed it. They both drank their fill once they found it was safe and then nearly collapsed into sleep right then and there but Ellendrii wisely said that they should find a place secluded to sleep. He didn't know if the inhabitants, if there were any, were friendly and he didn't want them to take the risk of being killed in their sleep, especially after making it this far.

So they both headed down the cliff side again at Aro's recommendation of sleeping in the hollowed out caves near the vast water.

Ellendrii would have argued about the possibility of the water coming in and drowning them in their sleep but he was too tired to say anything right now and besides which, there was nowhere else he could think of, short of looking further in the dark and possibly falling in a deep pool and drowning that way.

They both crawled into a couple of the caves that were next to each other and went back fairly far so they could hide themselves better and curled up to sleep.

The white rock was smooth and oddly comfortable for something so hard. They had thought about hiding away and sleeping in the shelter but they figured that since it was a strange new object by the water, that if anyone did live there, they would search that first for newcomers.

Ellendrii closed his eyes. Finally. They had made it to the mainland. Midnyte *had* said it was the mainland and there were no other islands around there and Ellendrii was pretty sure they hadn't got turned around, so this must be the place. The next thing they would have to do would be to eat and then to find the SilvaGryphie. She must be here. Maybe she even lived in a cave like this, only more ornate and pretty and less damp. They only had a little food left in the shelter so they would have to make do with the rest of that and then travel on. He only hoped that their float would remain where it was for the duration of their search on this mainland so they could get back to Shernaron again. The tide could still carry it off, despite that it was tied to a rock. What if the twine broke? Ellendrii decided not to think of things like that just now and promptly drifted off to sleep.

Although he was tired, Aro was not as sleepy as Ellendrii. He was worried about his friend. Ellendrii had put himself under a lot of stress by making that last mad dash for the mainland and Aro was scared that he might have done himself damage. And they were not alone either. He smelled that they weren't alone. There had been others around that pool. He could smell where their feet had stepped on the rock. They didn't smell hostile but you never know. Now that there could easily be things that would hunt a Lizariaous. This place was certainly different. It reminded him a bit of Dyarkroeen but with more water and less dirt. It all seemed terribly clean. It made him feel dirty for the first time in his life. A creature that had never thought or bothered about being dirty until now.

Aro's stomach grumbled. He sighed and turned over, trying to ignore it. But it wouldn't go away. It grumbled again; more loudly and painfully this time. Aro grumbled quietly. His verbal grumbles were quieter than his stomach ones. Cursing his digestive system, he decided he'd just have something small to eat. He'd never sleep otherwise. So he padded out of the cave and over to the float and went into the shelter looking for food.

There were a few fish left and that was it. Two of the three gourds remained. He supposed that water wouldn't be a problem anymore because they were in a place where there were plenty of pools to drink from. He sat quietly eating a fish. He made himself swear that he wouldn't eat more than one. Despite still feeling hungry, he kept his word to himself and only had one. He left the shelter and closed the door behind him. Hopefully no other creatures would smell the food and come looking around. Until they were more familiar with this new land, he and Ellendrii would have to make do with what they had. He was sure there were things here that were good to eat though. But for the first time in his entire life, he did envy creatures who could just eat leaves or grass. So much less stress to just lean down and nibble leaves than to waste energy hunting things that would fight back. Sure, he loved his meat but he was also sick of trying to hunt things that he didn't know what they were and that could probably kill him.

He wandered along the strange sandless beach and went back to his cave. He felt too exposed outside for some reason. Things had become too uncertain for him now. There was no assuredness of his dominance like there had been back in Dyarkroeen or even the confidence he had in the Forest knowing there was nothing that would hurt him and the Gryphies were either strangers or friends but never enemies.

He looked out at the moonlit ocean. It was so peaceful but at the same time it was as though there was nothing the other side of it. It was just like looking out over it *from* the other side. The same view only he was on the opposite side of it now. He was sure that anyone who lived here probably had the same view of it that the Gryphies had. That there was nothing the other side of it because they couldn't *see* anything the other side of it. Which just went to show that you shouldn't assume something's not there just cos you can't see it! Aro wondered if there were actually dead souls here like the Gryphies thought there were. Did dead souls have a smell? Were they invisible? Did they hide and watch you? What did they actually look like anyway? Ah, the late moon ramblings of an active mind with nothing better to do than question the universe it resides in!

Aro lay down and sighed. He was starting to feel a little sleepier now at least and being in a cave again felt good. It felt like being back home. They had travelled a total of thirteen sun cycles, which was nearly more than Aro could count. He wondered what his father would say if he knew how far they had gone. He looked up at the sky. He saw a bright, sparkling shooting star and pricked his ears up, wondering what it was. He'd never seen anything like that before and it was interesting to him.

In fact, all the stars looked different here. They were closer somehow, it was weird. Sleepily, he looked out at them and tried to count them. It had the same effect as counting sheep does of course and he was soon fast asleep, dreaming about ghosts and stars and other things that came out and then disappeared into the ether just as mysteriously as they had arrived. Silent things that never spoke but for some reason had a smell to them.

Ellendrii and Aro slept peacefully as the moon shone into their caves, silently watching over the two brave adventurers resting within.

Chapter 13
The White Plateaus

The sun shone down and warmed the two sleeping bodies inside their caves. But it didn't wake either of them. They continued to sleep and rest peacefully, so worn out they were from their journey.

Presently, there was movement on the rocks as three young creatures came tumbling and playing together. They bounced and laughed and gambolled along the smooth white ground where the water touched the shore.

Each one was a single pastel colour; mauve, blue and yellow and they each had unique, black, symmetrical markings here and there on their bodies. The mauve one had noticeably less markings and was younger than the other two. They all had yellow eyes with slit, cat-like pupils and black scleras. They were quadrapedal and dog-like in appearance with longish, flowing ears and tails and their claws were large, chunky and black. They had three claws on each foot and a smaller dewclaw on each front foot. Their muzzles were fairly short and they had two serrations on each side of their mouth and black triangular noses. They had tufts of fluffy fur at the base of their jawline and on the back of each leg.

It was the younger, mauve one who found a sleeping Aro. She jumped back when she discovered him and then went for a closer look, sniffing him. Aro rolled over and rattled his needles and the little creature yelped and ran back out of the cave.

"Addis! Kaisey! Come and look at this! There's a strange creature asleep here!" she called the other two over.

Addis, the blue one, went to have a closer look too. Kaisey warned her back.

"It might be a gift! It *is* in a donasis cave…"

"Kaisey, we leave things in the donasis caves, we don't receive things from them, that would be backward" Addis scolded her. "They are gifts we give, not ones we receive"

The mauve creature joined her friend in examining Aro.

"Sarris, don't go too close to it, it might be hostile" warned Addis. Sarris didn't step back much; however, when she did step back, it happened to be on Aro's tail. And of course it woke him up painfully. He shot awake with an angry roar and spun around. Sarris had bolted, Kaisey was nowhere to be seen but the unfortunate Addis was trapped in the cave with Aro. And he had seen her. He pinned her to the back of the cave and snapped his teeth within inches of her snout. She whimpered and shut her eyes, waiting for him to bite her.

Holding her pressed up against the back of the cave with his powerful paw and claws, Aro spoke.

"Who are you? What are you doing?" His yellow eyes flamed at her in anger and Addis started to shiver in fear.

"I...I live here, please...d...don't hurt me! My sister stepped on your tail by mistake, s...she didn't mean to..." Addis managed to whimper out.

"That's unfortunate. Cos I'm hungry and you'll do as a nice meal for me and my friend!" growled Aro with delight. He grinned at her, showing off his sharp, sickle-like teeth and prepared to tear her throat out.

"ARO!"

Aro looked around.

"Can you not, El! I'm trying to get us a meal!" he turned back to Addis but Ellendrii grabbed his tail.

"We DON'T eat those who can speak!" roared Ellendrii. "Put her down! She lives here and we don't want to anger the locals by eating one of them!" Aro grumbled but dropped Addis, who nearly flew out of the cave in terror.

"I just thought it would be nicer to have a fresh meal than the cold, nasty food we have in the shelter" explained Aro. "Maybe we can eat her sister...maybe her sister is too young to speak..."

Ellendrii looked around. The creatures hadn't left but they were hiding in fear. He could see a tuft of yellow sticking up from behind a white rock. Clearly they thought they didn't have enough time to run back up the cliff but they could at least hide and hope they weren't found. They could see Ellendrii could fly and would pick them off if he wanted to.

"Let's not eat any of them. Maybe they might know what's good to eat?" suggested Ellendrii.

"That would mean waiting longer for food" grumbled Aro.

"Then you'll have to wait. They look like youngsters. If you kill one, I'm betting the parents will be bigger and meaner and kill us. We're in their territory and must try to remain peaceful."

"Ok whatever" muttered Aro and sat down where he was, to let Ellendrii try to talk to the creatures by himself.

Ellendrii went slowly up to the rock that Kaisey was hiding behind.

"I'm sorry for my friend's outburst. Please don't be afraid of us, we mean you no harm" he ventured.

Kaisey's face appeared over the top of the rock.

"He was going to kill Addis and you say you mean us no harm?" she said. Ellendrii sighed.

"He didn't know you were intelligent and could talk"

"Yes he did. She pleaded for mercy and he was still going to kill her"

"You frighten us" said Sarris quietly.

"I'm sorry" said Ellendrii and sat down. "I'm just a kitten like you" he explained, in the hopes that that would put them more on the same level.

"We're not kittens" said Sarris, "We're houndlets"

"Are you the kids of your species?" asked Aro, stepping up.

"No, we're houndlets" repeated Sarris. Aro grumbled in his throat and Sarris hid behind her rock again.

Addis jumped up suddenly.

"Don't scare my sister" she barked but quickly shrank back down again when Aro snapped his head round and snarled at her.

Ellendrii groaned. They were getting nowhere.

"You seem young. Are you youngsters? Do you have parents who are older?" he asked Addis.

"Yes" replied Addis.

"Ok so that means we must all be around the same age. You're youngsters, not adults and we are too. Kittens, kids, houndlets, the same yes?"

Addis nodded. Ellendrii continued.

"We're travellers. We came to your shore looking for the SilvaGryphie. I am Ellendrii, the Gryphie and this is my friend Aro, the Lizariaous. What creatures are you?"

"We are Wind Hounds" said Addis. Ellendrii nodded.

"Ok, well I'm pleased to meet you. I'm sorry again about my friend. We're hungry and we were very tired when we arrived last moon cycle. We travelled on the water for eight sun cycles to get here and we ran out of things to eat and drink. We promise we won't try to harm you again. We would love to see where you live and learn more about Wind Hounds."

Addis looked unsure. Ellendrii mentally cursed Aro and his natural Lizariaousness. He could well have damaged any chance the two of them would have at making friends with these houndlets or seeing where they lived. They most certainly didn't look like they trusted either of them. Aro spoke up.

"Hey, I'm sorry too ok? When you're hungry, you sometimes get desperate and act out of instinct. I didn't mean to scare you. I was pretty scared too; I thought I would bite first and ask questions later."

Addis still looked unsure. It was Sarris' turn to speak up.

"Well we can take them to see Lord Scerniss. He'll kill them himself if he deems them to be untrustworthy" she said.

Finally, Addis nodded. Kaisey came out of hiding too.

"Yes" she said, "He'll see whether they're worthy or not"

In hindsight, Ellendrii thought it may have been wiser to just say they had appeared in the cave. He'd overheard the conversation from earlier about the donasis caves and things just appearing in them might make these houndlets respect the newcomers or think they were something special. But then again that would be a lie and it would probably backfire on them eventually so it was probably better to tell the truth.

Ellendrii and Aro followed the houndlets up the cliff and out onto the terraced plateaus.

"It's a very beautiful place" observed Ellendrii. He wasn't lying; it was beautiful but it also helped, he felt, to compliment the territory of the locals.

"Yes it is" replied Addis, "We are happy to live here. This is where our rituals take place."

They climbed higher and higher and soon left the vast water behind as they made their way through the white terraces with their beautiful blue pools. Some pools were larger and deeper than others and many had Wind Hounds in them. It did indeed look like these dog-like creatures were performing rituals around the pools. Ellendrii watched with interest as they walked.

"It's a washing ritual" explained Sarris. "Wind Hounds don't groom themselves; they prefer to wash in the naturally heated spring waters that come up through the rock and fill the pools. Every sunrise, we wash like this. Some of us wash later than others but it is generally in the sunrise. If, during the sun cycle, we get dirty, then we do the ritual all over again. Not every pool can be washed in though; only the ones that are marked for it. They must be a particular size and deepness. You cannot wash in something that is shallow."

Ellendrii was fascinated, having enjoyed washing himself in water many times; he liked the idea of this very much. Aro was just a bit bored but didn't say anything.

The adult Wind Hounds were pastel colours like the houndlets but as a general rule, they had more symmetrical black markings. The older ones had even more markings. Ellendrii suspected that they gained more markings as they aged. The adult ones had longer, slimmer legs and bodies than the stubby houndlets and longer muzzles too. The fur on their ears and tails and the backs of their legs was longer as well. They all looked immensely graceful and beautiful.

Going further up the terraces, the pools disappeared and the ground was flat and white. Looking ahead, huge tall structures rose up out of the ground. It was as we would see it, a partly naturally made "city" of white stone. There were steps leading into each "building" and holes where the windows of the "buildings" would be. The wind blew through these gently, creating a peaceful sound that calmed the minds of the two travellers and made them feel at ease. There were no coloured decorations or gemstones on these buildings; all were just plain and white. But each one had carvings on it and all the carvings were different. As they passed, Ellendrii saw the Wind Hounds using the carvings as a way to communicate with each other. For example, a Wind Hound would go to the abode of another Wind Hound and run their large claws gently over the carvings at the entrance. The sound carried to the occupier so they knew someone was waiting to enter or call for them. Ellendrii had never seen anything like it. It was new and obscure to him but also amazing at the same time how different another's culture could be.

The five of them headed past all these structures and towards a huge formation which, unlike the rest of the natural "buildings" was long instead of tall. The carvings were extremely abstract and complicated on this one and it was difficult to make any single carving out. It had several entrances lining the front of it and the houndlets lead them to one at the far end.

Addis ran her claws over the carvings around the entrance, touching only certain ones and in a particular order. A delicate sound rang out. It sounded like the wind and soft singing.

Then they waited. For what, exactly, Ellendrii and Aro weren't sure about. The houndlets never explained what the sounds had meant. Clearly they had "said" something to the structure by running the claws over the carvings like that.

There was movement inside the stone palace. A tall, regal Wind Hound walked proudly down the stone steps, his head held high and his long ears held behind him, over his back. The tips of them curled round and under.

He looked far different to any of the others and Ellendrii guessed this must be Lord Scerniss, their leader.

His face was proud with a hint of arrogance and his eyes narrowed as he spotted the newcomers. His ears and tail were much longer than all the other Wind Hounds but what was most noticeable were his markings. Unlike the others, Lord Scerniss wasn't just a single pastel colour with the black markings, but mostly black with only his tummy and back legs a colour. It was lilac. His head, front legs, along his back and his tail was black with stunning bio-luminescent tribal markings. Again, these were symmetrical. They glowed turquoise against the black of his fur. He had a flash of white running up his snout to the base of his ears, which had black markings on it; circular ones going up and over his head. The fur on the backs of his legs was longer too.

The houndlets all stood tall and respectful when he approached, so Ellendrii and Aro mimicked them, hoping that they would show the right idea and not insult or anger him.

The king of the Wind Hounds spoke.

"Where did you come from?" he asked. Ellendrii was a little sad there was no "Welcome to Wind Hound Territory" or anything like that but he did his best to answer accordingly. Thankfully Aro had left all the talking to Ellendrii.

"I am Ellendrii the Gryphie and this is Aro the Lizariaous. We come from the far away land of Shernaron. We have travelled for a total of thirteen sun cycles on the vast water to reach your beautiful territory and we have come in search of the SilvaGryphie." He didn't mention the island, somehow a part of him wanted to keep Midnyte Comet to himself.

Lord Scerniss eyed him curiously.

"That is a long way to come. This is Kazétos, the windy city. We are the Wind Hounds and we reside here. Our culture is based on respect and rituals. If you treat us with respect, you will receive the same in return. However..." he moved closer to Ellendrii and Aro, "If you aren't respectful, I will kill you myself." He flexed his claws and up close, the pair could see how dangerous they were. Despite being chunky, they were not by any means blunt and they could probably tear a stomach out with one swift swipe.

Ellendrii bowed.

"We will show the utmost respect, Lord Scerniss. We are only passing through; we are merely looking for the whereabouts of the SilvaGryphie. Does she live here?"

Lord Scerniss straightened and shook his head.

"No, I have not heard of her. She doesn't live here. You will have to travel further."

"Thank you for the information. Could you please tell us where we might find something to eat? We are both very hungry" said Ellendrii. As if to confirm this, Aro's stomach grumbled. It was true they had the food back at the shelter but it was a long way away now and Ellendrii really wanted to know what was good to hunt here.

Impressed at the politeness of the young Gryphie, Lord Scerniss was happy to help them.

"We eat little creatures called rockrats. They are small and they hop. There are plenty of them around here since this is their habitat. They are white, so they blend in well with the rock but it's easy to find them if you run your claws over certain carvings on the rocks near where they reside. They like the sound and will come out, entranced by it. Then you can kill them. We tend to just pick the nearest one up and eat it whole. As I said, they are not very big. The sound paralyses them and they don't notice you coming until it's too late. If you try to catch them without the aid of the sound sign, you won't succeed. Their main defence is their speed. I will show you how to catch them." He walked past Ellendrii and Aro and the two turned and followed him, walking respectfully just behind him. The houndlets hung about for a bit but wandered off by themselves before too long.

The pair followed Lord Scerniss away from the stone structures and down one of the terraces. The rock here wasn't so pristine and was darker in places. There were also tiny holes in the rock where it overhung the rock below it. Lord Scerniss stopped and so did they.

"Watch" he said and they complied.

As they watched, there was movement and a couple of small white creatures bounded past them. They had large ears and long, fuzzy tails. Their back feet were large and their fur was bright white. They had large eyes and long whiskers and judging by the speed at which they did even relaxed tasks; they were certainly too fast to catch without help of some kind. They ran into their burrows, the holes in the rock, as Lord Scerniss moved to some carvings on the ground near their little homes. He ran his claws delicately over the carvings and a few rockrats came out of their holes, their bodies swaying as if they were dancing. They came as close to the source of the sound as they could and then just stood there, entranced, their ears twitching and their expressions peaceful.

238

Lord Scerniss reached a clawed paw down and picked one up by its tail. He tilted his head back, opened his mouth and popped the unfortunate rockrat in his mouth. Before it could even squeak, he had closed his mouth and there was a crunch as its body smashed in his jaws while he chewed. As the sound of the carving died down and disappeared, the other rockrats regained their senses and disappeared promptly into their holes.

"They are very filling. You won't need past one or two despite their tiny size" explained Lord Scerniss, "Which is just as well considering it would take longer to catch more of them. One sound is enough to bring them out and get one. You try."

Ellendrii let the apparently mute Aro do this. Aro ran his claws over the intricate carving on the rock. Nothing happened. Aro tried again but nothing happened. He tried a little harder, still nothing happened. He went to try harder again but Lord Scerniss put a paw on him and stopped him.

"Gently is all that is needed" he said, "But it appears that you cannot do it. You try, Ellendrii."

Aro sat down grumpily but he did start to smile when Ellendrii appeared not to be able to make the sound either. All that came out was the scraping of his claws on the rock. No peaceful music, nothing.

"What do we do?" asked Ellendrii. "We can't hunt without being able to make the sound."

"You will have to ask others for their help then" said Lord Scerniss. "They will be happy to assist with an enquiry of politeness. When you need to eat, just go to where the rockrats reside and ask someone to make the sound for you. Or take a rockrat when someone else had made the sound. Groups of us sometimes hunt together. One touches the sound signs and the others can then pick up a rockrat each before the sound has died."

Lord Scerniss ran his claws over the sound sign again and once more, the rockrats came out to enjoy it. Ellendrii and Aro both picked a rockrat up each and ate them. Aro was sure he would want another, since they were so small but that was not the case. He was full after just one.

"Could you show us around Kazétos please, Lord Scerniss? We would love to learn more about your culture" Ellendrii asked politely. Lord Scerniss nodded.

"Your interest in my kind impresses me. I would be happy to show you both around."

"Thank you!" replied Ellendrii.

They followed Lord Scerniss and he showed them around, telling them more about his culture and home.

"Kazétos is the windy city; it is the place with the natural rock structures where we live. The structures, although they form naturally from the ground, are modified by us for the purpose of living in. It is called the windy city because the wind blows through the holes in the structures and makes a sound. We can tell the mood of our home by listening to the sound the wind makes. It tells us when the bad weather is coming and when there will be plentiful rockrats to hunt. It tells us many things. I live in the largest structure; it is my palace. I am a Lord. Lords are born, not made. If a houndlet is born with the markings like mine; it means they will grow up to be a Lord. The current Lord will step down and the new one will take their place when they are old enough, which is usually when they get their first ten bio-luminescent markings. A new Lord is only born when the current Lord is older. I am quite young. Lords can be born to anyone; it does not take special breeding or anything. When a Lord is born, they do not have the bio-luminescent markings; they come when the Lord is older. Getting your first marking is coming of age here. All houndlets are born plain. The Lord is the exception but only in as much as the markings are black like mine and a colour. The black marking is always the same as mine but the colour may vary. The last Lord had orange as their colour, not lilac like me. The black like mine is known as the "cape" and only Lords are ever born with it. As we mature, we get more unique markings. Each one means something and is unique to the owner of it. The meaning could be to do with something the Wind Hound has done, seen or more personal, like a subconscious thought that creates the marking. However, we cannot create our own markings at will. They will always appear of their own accord. You cannot think in a particular way in the hopes of getting a certain marking. It won't happen because our markings are as unique as we are. When a houndlet gets his or her first marking, there is a celebration by their family and we all join in a special ritual at the pools."

Ellendrii and Aro listened and paid attention. Even Aro was interested in these alien rituals and different culture.

As they walked, they passed a breeze (group) of Wind Hounds who were running their claws over some sound signs at the entrance of one of the structures, each of them working together to make the sound. Another breeze of Wind Hounds passed by talking amongst themselves and nodding respectfully to Lord Scerniss. In fact every Wind Hound they passed acknowledged him in a respectful manner. Since Ellendrii and Aro were with the king, the Wind Hounds didn't bat an eyelid at them. Before, when they had been following the houndlets, the other Wind Hounds had regarded them suspiciously.

"Lord Scerniss, what is the meaning of the different sound signs on the white stone?" asked Ellendrii, "I see Wind Hounds running their claws over them in a particular way each time they use them"

"Each sound sign means something different. By running our claws over them, we use them to communicate. For example, when that breeze of houndlets brought you to my palace, they used the far right entrance and made the sound for arriving with visitors from another place. The sound signs there would also have allowed them to make the sound for arriving with visitors from another part of Kazétos or either a friend or family member arriving or arriving with a friend or family member. By moving our claws in a certain way, we can communicate the sound we mean. Because of the size of my palace, I can have several entrances with different sound signs around them, which makes them less cluttered and more attractive but the other Wind Hounds have only one or maybe two entrances to their abodes and many different sound signs around each entrance so it is important to pay attention to what sound you are making with them."

"Forgive me for asking" said Aro, "But why don't you just call up to the Wind Hound inside and tell them what you're there for?"

"Because it is not as respectful and wouldn't sound as nice" replied Lord Scerniss. Aro nodded, though respect and sounding nice weren't really things that Lizariaouses favoured, except maybe respecting their leader or those who could kill them.

They continued to walk and came to the impressive terraces of white with the pools of thermal water.

"Here you can see breezes of Wind Hounds partaking in the cleaning ritual and other water based rituals. There are also rituals for drinking, swimming and paddling in shallow water." Lord Scerniss explained.

The three of them looked out over the pools. Most of the carvings were around the deeper pools but there were also a few around most of the other pools too. A few pools had no carvings at all.

"Do you use the pools that don't have sound signs?" asked Ellendrii.

"No, they are not in pleasing positions. The sun needs to hit the pool just right. Or the shade, or the wind. It needs to be pleasing to be in and around the pool and some of them just don't feel right so we don't use them."

"What are your deepest pools?" asked Aro.

"The deepest ones our feet don't touch the bottom. We can't go underwater for very long though, so we have never explored them to see where they go or how far down. Some of the unfavourable ones are deep ones. Houndlets are not allowed in pools where their feet can't touch the bottom. We fear them drowning."

"That's understandable" replied Ellendrii. "I can swim pretty deep but I can't hold my breath for long, so I probably wouldn't be able to see where they lead either"

"We do not expect you to" replied Lord Scerniss.

"Last moon cycle, we had a drink from one of the pools, is the water safe to drink?" asked Aro.

"Yes it is fine. Some of the pools are actually meant for drinking", Lord Scerniss lead the two of them to a pool that only had one type of sound sign around it.

"This is a drinking pool. Look for this sound sign if you wish to drink. We do not drink where we swim or bathe. We can drink from the shallow pools that are too shallow for other uses."

Ellendrii and Aro had a drink. They were both pretty thirsty. Despite the fact that it was sunny, there was still a constant wind over where they were; most likely because of the wide open spaces. Ellendrii had noticed there were no birds and he suspected that this was because there was nowhere for them to really land or nest. He had only seen one bird and a Wind Hound had chased it away. Ellendrii surmised that this must be because of the birds contaminating the pools with their droppings. This thought reminded him to ask the question.

"Not to be rude, Lord Scerniss, but where do we..." he trailed off, struggling to find the right word that didn't sound impolite. He wanted to know where the bathroom was but the word wasn't the same for Gryphies, since they do not know of bathrooms and he had never asked where he should go to the toilet before, so he was really struggling.

"Where do we what?" asked Lord Scerniss, cocking his head to one side questioningly.

"When we have digested our food and need to get rid of it, or our water. I haven't seen anywhere I could use without spoiling the beauty of something..."

"Oh, you mean where do you excrete" said Lord Scerniss, helpfully.

Ellendrii nodded, he guessed so.

"When we need to go and release our waste, we generally either do it in a section of our own home or wander further away from Kazétos and do it there. It is absolutely forbidden to release waste on the sacred terraces or in the pools. It is a crime punishable by death. Even passing liquid waste into a pool will mean death. It is forbidden to contaminate the pools with anything like that. That is why birds are chased away. The rockrats don't go near the pools here so they never cause this problem. They have their own drinking pools near their holes, which I suppose they must bathe in too. None of us have ever observed them since they are only food to us and nothing more than that."

Ellendrii nodded, understanding and he glanced at Aro. He hoped Aro was listening to this vital information and didn't decide to secretly pee in one of their sacred pools. Ellendrii found it would be easy enough for himself to find a place to go to the toilet; he could just fly a little way away. He also hoped Aro wouldn't get lazy or let himself be caught out with desperation for the "call of nature" so that he wouldn't be able to hold himself the required amount of time to get somewhere far away and go there.

"What are those little caves near the vast water?" asked Ellendrii, "I heard the houndlets refer to them as donasis caves?"

"Ah, those are small caves we dug with our own claws. We leave things in them as a sign of respect to our land. The things we leave disappear so we know the land is happy with us. If several sun cycles go by and the things we leave haven't disappeared, we know the land is angry with us because it didn't accept our gifts and we must then work harder to care for our land and look after it. We respect our land and gain respect in return. Recently, the land has been happier with us and the things we leave are taken over the moon cycle."

"You must have very strong claws if you can dig through rock like that" observed Aro.

"We do. We make all the sound signs in the stone with our claws. The stone is hard but an experienced carver can make the signs with relative ease."

"That's awesome" breathed Aro. Lizariaouses also have strong claws and some of them are tasked with digging out new caves.

"We damage the rock though and that is why when we run our claws over the signs, we do it so lightly and gently. For one reason, this is our apology for damaging the rock. For another, the lighter touch always sounds better."

"What sort of weather do you have here?" asked Ellendrii.

"Always a breeze. The air is never ever still. Mostly sunny. But because the city is so exposed, sometimes storms will be bad. However, the rock is so solid and strong that the storms don't damage our homes. There was only ever one storm that damaged anything and that was because there were things flying about in it and one hit one of our homes and smashed the top off it." He turned and pointed towards Kazétos.

"See that one there? It's much shorter than the others. That is the one that was hit"

Ellendrii and Aro looked out and saw the broken structure. Ellendrii squinted and looked beyond the windy city, though the amount of stone structures blotted out much else.

"What is beyond Kazétos?" he asked.

"We never go beyond our city. There is another place that way. We call it the Forest of Foreboding and we don't go there" replied Lord Scerniss. Ellendrii didn't like the sound of that.

"Come, I will show you the rituals of the pools" said Lord Scerniss and lead the way along the serene white terraces. He stopped at a breeze of Wind Hounds who were swimming in one of the pools. Before getting into the pool, they would run their claws over the sound signs to make a particular sound.

"It is a mark of respect for swimming in the water. Also for the others who are swimming with them. We each take our time with these things; we never rush" explained Lord Scerniss. "Before getting into the water, first we run our claws like this" he showed them, "Then like this for paying respect to the water and like this for paying respect to anyone else in the pool. If the pool is empty, then we don't do the last sound. We do similar sounds for washing as well. We swim in pools like this. They are larger. We wash in the smaller pools with a deepness only so far that we can touch the bottom of the pool with our feet. You need to stand in order to wash, of course. But the larger, deeper pools we swim in, it's not so important for our feet to touch the bottom. Each pool slants gently into the water, so you can walk in, test the depth and if it is too deep, you don't need to proceed further. When the cold weather comes, we spend more time in these pools. We don't feel the cold easily but it is always pleasant to be in a warm place on a cold sun cycle."

He lead them to another, shallow pool where a breeze of Wind Hounds were drinking.

"This is one of our drinking pools. As you can see, they are not near the pools we swim and wash in. They are on the outskirts of the terraces where the pools are shallower. Before drinking, we make this sound with the sound signs and then after drinking, this sound." He showed them the sounds and Ellendrii tried furiously to remember them, despite that his claws didn't make the right sound on the carvings.

"What if you drink from a swimming or bathing pool?" asked Aro.

"Then that is up to you. But Wind Hounds never do. It is unclean" replied Lord Scerniss and wrinkled his nose.

"Come, let us go swimming" he said and headed to a pool. He ran his claws along the sound signs and elegantly stepped into the pool. The others stood and watched but made no move to follow because they couldn't make the sounds. The pool was empty and it was a huge one as well.

"Come in then" said Lord Scerniss, "This is my personal pool. Only I and those I choose may bathe in this pool. You have my permission."

Ellendrii and Aro followed him, trying to look as dignified as possible. Aro soon lost interest in the dignified and plodded in, splashing water everywhere. Lord Scerniss regarded him with mild horror.

"Aro!" muttered Ellendrii, "Don't splash like that!" Aro stopped only when he saw Lord Scerniss' face.

The magnificent Wind Hound swam gracefully into the centre of the pool and round to face them. Ellendrii swam under the water, using his wings to help him while Aro doggy paddled clumsily, his needles rattling. Lord Scerniss trod water like a pro, as did Ellendrii. Aro had a few problems though and ended up just swimming around to disguise the fact that he didn't know how to tread water.

"Does your kind not swim normally?" asked Lord Scerniss.

"I come from a barren, earthy place. I'm not that familiar with water although I can swim" replied Aro, swimming in small circles in the water.

"No, I meant do you not swim *normally*. I am swimming normally, as is Ellendrii. Can you not?" Lord Scerniss asked. Aro knew now that he meant his inability to tread water.

"I don't swim much" muttered Aro feeling small and stupid.

"It's true, he really doesn't" said Ellendrii sticking up for his friend. Lord Scerniss merely nodded and carried on delicately treading the water, the long fur on his legs flowing out like ripples.

"So, you have pools for swimming, pools for bathing or washing and pools for drinking?" asked Ellendrii.

"Yes and we also have pools for the houndlets that are deeper than drinking pools but shallower than swimming pools" explained Lord Scerniss. Aro wondered if the houndlets were allowed to splash. He had seen them splash, certainly. Maybe adults weren't allowed but the houndlets were. Or something. He was annoyed that he had got into trouble merely for splashing a bit. He liked splashing in water. Lord Scerniss was so serious. How could one be *that* serious? Maybe it came with being a "Lord" or something. Maybe he was born serious because of those markings. Either way, Aro was seeing that Ellendrii got along with the king of the Wind Hounds far more easily than he did. He was still terrified of saying or doing something wrong.

As Ellendrii and Lord Scerniss chatted, Aro just swam around looking into the water. He tried to be invisible, which was no easy task considering that Lizariaouses are commonly loud and obnoxious. He felt relieved when finally Lord Scerniss decided that was enough in the pool and beckoned them to follow him back to Kazétos. Which they did.

The next task was finding them a place to stay. Aro thought maybe they would stay with Lord Scerniss. No such luck. Or lack thereof. Aro was still unsure about the king and part of him did indeed feel relief when Lord Scerniss showed them to a structure nearby that was uninhabited by Wind Hounds.

"I will leave you to get settled in. I've no doubt you will need time to plan the next step of your journey" said Lord Scerniss and left them alone outside the "building".

"Well, we may as well explore this place and find a part to sleep in" said Ellendrii heading inside. The structure was light and airy and felt fresh and good. They soon found a couple of chambers in it they could sleep in although neither had any bedding. Ellendrii supposed the Wind Hounds just slept on the white stone. And why not? It was surprisingly comfortable for something hard. There was a certain relaxing aspect of it that he couldn't quite work out.

So the two of them didn't bother to try and find bedding. They did explore the rest of their little abode though and found a total of eight chambers, two on each level with crooked stone steps leading up to each one. One of them had a little balcony. It was the third level up and Ellendrii liked it because it gave him a platform to take off from if he wished. Perhaps that was Lord Scerniss' idea in giving them this particular place to stay. Not many of them had balconies. Some of them had one chamber extra on the bottom level and steps leading up so one could walk on the roof of that chamber. These had a short wall around them and Wind Hounds liked to sit out in the sun on these little "patios".

After exploring their temporary abode, Ellendrii and Aro decided to explore the city also. Lord Scerniss had only really been concerned with showing them the sacred, ritualistic place of their home but not the city itself. After choosing a chamber to use as a toilet, they set out to look around.

Once they were walking among the stone structures, exploring in between them and up and down the streets, the structures seemed a lot bigger. There was a kind of square in the centre of the city where the palace was. The rest of the city consisted of a labyrinth of streets and lots of the stone structures all around. The streets were the same white stone as everything else was and it seemed a bright, clean place, even in the shade.

The Wind Hounds walked with a regal air and always had their heads held high. After a while of wandering around, looking at everything (although there wasn't much to look at because unlike human cities, there were no shops or anything else other than Wind Hound homes) and peering in through the holes of the structures to see what was happening inside (occasionally a Wind Hound had snapped at them for this), they came to an open place with long lines carved into the stone. Here, there appeared to be some sort of competition going on. They seemed to be trying to find which of them was the fastest.

Ellendrii stared in awe. He'd never seen a Wind Hound run before. They ran literally, like the wind!

One of them appeared to be faster than the others and each one was going up against him in an effort to beat him and failing miserably. They raced from one end of the lines to the other and with the start of each race; another one would rake his claws down a wall, making the sound for them to go. Through watching these races with the other spectators, they soon found out that the champion's name was Razzn. He was pale red with striped markings that went down the length of his back and sides and also down his muzzle, tail and ears. Razzn was the word that meant fast and he had been born into speed, always looking to race others, according to another Wind Hound who stood nearby who Ellendrii asked. Ellendrii was sorely tempted to race him but knew the wings VS legs thing probably wouldn't be a fair race anyway.

After beating yet another challenger, Razzn looked around asking for anyone else who thought they were brave enough to step forward and accept his challenge. There was no prize other than satisfaction. A female Wind Hound stepped forward who was called Clixm. She had pale yellow fur and intense markings around her face but fewer on her body. She was younger than Razzn but raring to go!

They both stepped up to the starting point and the sound was made for them to go. The sound echoed around everywhere and as the two of them shot into action, it was almost like they were actually racing the sound to the other end of the lines. Razzn won again. Clixm got tired about three quarters of the way through and started to slow, which was a shame because when the two of them had begun the race, she was actually ahead of him. But she was no match for him.

"Some say" said the Wind Hound who was stood next to Ellendrii and Aro, "That his markings went in a line like that because he runs so fast that he blurred them out with his speed."

Ellendrii looked at him and the Wind Hound looked back at Ellendrii perfectly serious. Meanwhile, Razzn was looking for another challenger. Ellendrii idly wondered if Lord Scerniss had ever raced Razzn and what would happen if Lord Scerniss lost.

Suddenly someone called to him.

"Hey you, you look like a weird challenge. Want to race?" it was Razzn and he was looking right at Ellendrii.

Chapter 14
Research

Ellendrii stared back at Razzn, thinking he was talking to someone else but when Aro shoved Ellendrii forward with "Show him how it's done!", Ellendrii knew it was him.

He walked down to the lines and swallowed as he approached the confident Razzn. Despite having raced countless others, he wasn't even panting. Ellendrii swallowed again.

"You want to race *me*?" he asked.

"Yeah, I've never raced anyone who could fly before" said Razzn, confidently.

"But I'm sure to beat you" said Ellendrii.

"You haven't seen me at full speed" said Razzn without missing a beat.

You haven't seen me at full speed either thought Ellendrii but what he said was;

"Well, then it will be a nice challenge for both of us" and smiled. Razzn nodded.

"Well then, are you ready?" he asked, standing at the start line. Ellendrii hovered in the air next to him and looked down the lines. The finish line was a long way away from where they stood now. It was a massive square, similar to what we would call a market square but without all the stalls. Ellendrii knew it wouldn't be a challenge though. He'd seen Razzn race and thought he knew the Wind Hound's technique.

The referee Wind Hound asked if they were ready and counted down the start of the race.

"3, 2, 1, GO!!" he yelled and there was a rush of wind, almost as though it launched Ellendrii and Razzn off the start lines.

The two shot out; Ellendrii looking down to see how Razzn was doing. He wasn't flying that high up and he wasn't flying over Razzn either, but next to him and obviously high enough that the beating of his wings wouldn't affect the Wind Hound. They seemed fairly equally matched which surprised Ellendrii; he was sure that flying was faster than running. Well, usually it was. But this was a Wind Hound and they are fast runners.

Ellendrii decided to *really* show what he was made of and he suddenly shot ahead of Razzn. It was time to knock Razzn back a peg or two and show him how it was really done!

Razzn, seeing Ellendrii shoot ahead like that, sped up instantly and was soon matching him again. They were about halfway to the finish mark now and Ellendrii was very much surprised his rival could outpace him seemingly so easy.

Aro cheered for Ellendrii and everyone else cheered for Razzn. He really was the best of the best. But Ellendrii had beaten the best of the best of the Sky Gryphies and he was determined to beat Razzn too. There was no prize but satisfaction.

So he flew at full speed, his wings flapping faster and with larger sweeping motions. The larger motions, like an increased gait, pushed him forwards much faster than before. Ellendrii looked straight ahead now. There was no point in looking down to see how Razzn was doing; Ellendrii was going at full speed anyway so if Razzn could run faster, there was nothing he could do about it.

The crowd's attitude had changed though; instead of cheering, they were booing. Razzn could be losing. In fact, Razzn was almost matched to Ellendrii but the Gryphie was outpacing him by about a head. Razzn narrowed his eyes and ran until his muscles ached. He had never had a challenge like this before! In truth, he would easily have outrun a normal flyer but the fact that this was Ellendrii he was racing and not just any normal flyer really put Razzn at risk. Flying *was* Ellendrii's passion. He could already fly faster than any other Gryphie in the Forest and outpace the Sky Gryphies, so the Wind Hound wasn't so much of a challenge in the end. But it *had* caused him to fly at full speed and he had never had to do that in order to outpace a ground runner before.

Ellendrii reached the finish line by a whisker, followed by Razzn who was looking rather flustered. Flying at such speeds meant that it took a while for Ellendrii to stop. He used his legs and tail to slow down and then he landed, almost on the front row of bystanders in the crowd.

He turned away from the disgruntled onlookers and went towards Razzn. The Wind Hound *was* panting this time and he had sat down to catch his breath. Ellendrii wondered if Razzn would be angry with him for outpacing him. But he wasn't. He looked at Ellendrii, impressed.

"Wow, that was the best race I've ever had! I love a challenge! How fantastic!" he barked happily. "I race others all the time but never have I raced against someone who caused me to run at my own full speed. I ache and it feels wonderful! Thank you…err, what's your name?" Razzn had never bothered to get Ellendrii's name because at the beginning, all he had regarded him as was another creature to race. He had assumed he would beat the Gryphie and not even talk to him.

"Ellendrii" replied Ellendrii, "Pleased to meet you, Razzn and thank you for the challenge too. I was flying at my own full speed. I've NEVER had to do that against someone who couldn't fly."

"How did you get so fast before though?" asked Razzn. "I mean, I wanted a challenge but you were off the rocks!"

"Flying is my passion" replied Ellendrii. "I've raced all the other young flyers in my own territory. Are you like me? Is running your passion?"

"Yes! I love to run! I've run and raced nearly everyone in Kazétos and beat them all too. I didn't know it was a thing in other places as well."

"Are there often travellers passing through here then?" asked Ellendrii.

"We do get a few or those who just come to see our city and learn our culture and rituals. I usually try to race one or two, just to see. We had some come a few lunars ago who were pretty fast but I still beat them"

"Am I the first who's beaten you?" asked Ellendrii as Aro came running up excitedly.

"No, I was beaten a fair bit when I was a houndlet, when I was just learning" replied Razzn. "Who is this?" he asked of Aro.

"I'm his best friend, Aro!" replied Aro, "Congrats Ellendrii, nice race!" he grinned at his friend and Ellendrii grinned back.

"I won't ask to race you too" said Razzn, "No offence but that's enough racing for me for this sun cycle. I definitely need to rest now!" Razzn also suspected that Aro wouldn't be as fast either, looking at his sturdy bulk. Lizariaouses are sturdy but not overly chunky unless the individual is built or trained like that.

"Oh, I don't want to race anyway, so no worries" said Aro hurriedly.

The two kindred spirits of Razzn and Ellendrii chatted into the moon cycle and Aro went to explore a little more. He went to where the rockrats were and managed to persuade a houndlet to catch him one. Since the houndlet had obliged, he stayed a little and listened to her stories of Kazétos and the sacred pools. He didn't say much; since Ellendrii had warned him not to if he went off by himself, just in case he upset anyone. Lizariaouses often say what's on their mind and don't care who gets upset because of it.

The moon came up high in the sky and the sky filled with beautiful lights and colours that reflected in the glass-like stillness of the pools and Aro was truly rendered speechless.

"Now is the time when we sing" said the houndlet, whose name was Orixx. She ran her claws over the carvings at the edge of the pool where they sat and other Wind Hounds did the same at their pools. The sounds all complimented one another to create a beautiful sound like soft gentle music that sounded out and rose into the moonlit sky with its beautiful lights and colours. The music rose almost as if it painted a picture in the sky with sound and colour. The colours seemed to turn and flow into shapes created by the beautiful sound and Aro felt his eyes tearing up from the sheer beauty of it all. He was moved beyond words. Despite his Lizariaous soul, he was knocked back and blown away by such stunning brilliance.

The Wind Hounds all looked to the sky and let their claws just move with the rhythm and sound of the music. They didn't themselves sing; they let the sound signs sing for them. Each sign was a different "voice" which rose to the sky to harmonise with the rest of them. The houndlets' signs gave off a lighter, higher note. The male Wind Hounds' song was deeper and the females' helped to wrap them all together in a sweet serenade of the moon. Aro had noticed this. He had noticed that whenever a single Wind Hound used the carvings to make a sound, it was always unique to that individual; almost as if it was that Wind Hound's voice.

The mirror pools, the music, the lights, the moon, the serene creatures sat all around him lost in the moment. Aro felt completely at peace. He thought of nothing else but that very moment he was experiencing. Soft tears dampened his cheeks but he didn't notice. He was so moved. He didn't even wonder or think that this was strange; he just enjoyed the moment.

Ellendrii and Razzn had finished chatting and Ellendrii went to find Aro. He heard the sound echoing over the plateaus and into the city and followed it out of sheer curiosity. The lights in the sky painted all the homely structures with colours, colouring the white of the stone. The city was alive! Everything was so calm and still and beautiful!

Ellendrii stood at the top of a terrace, looking down at all the pools with their own reflected colours and the Wind Hounds sat around them. He saw Lord Scerniss and went to sit next to him.

Quietly, he looked up at the king of the Wind Hounds and then up at the sky, following Lord Scerniss' gaze. And like Aro, Ellendrii too was lost in the beauty of the sky and he felt himself crying from the serenity and beauty of the moment.

"It is the song of the Wind Hounds" said Lord Scerniss quietly. Ellendrii could only nod in reply.

Long into the moon cycle, the pair sat with these strange and majestic native creatures and enjoyed their ritual.

Finally, the two friends went back to their temporary home feeling at peace and rested even though they had not slept. They went into their separate chambers and curled up, falling into a deep and restful sleep.

The sun rose early the next sun cycle but neither of them rose with it. They slept for quite a while and finally woke up feeling completely refreshed and rejuvenated. In fact, they felt like the previous moon cycle had been a dream. It had been so amazing and beautiful!

"I feel great" said Aro, stretching before they left the building in search of something to eat. Well, a rockrat, since that appeared to be all Wind Hounds ate.

"Me too!" last moon was magical, I can't believe it. If that's how these guys live and what they do every moon, I wouldn't mind living here myself!" said Ellendrii enthusiastically. Aro nodded but both of them knew they had to continue on their journey. This sun cycle would be the one for their research, or at least some of it. They found they didn't want to leave Kazétos in such a hurry!

They went to the rockrat holes and asked a couple of the other Wind Hounds to catch them one each, which they did obligingly.

Tucking into their breakfast, the pair looked around.

"We'll have to ask questions" said Ellendrii, "I was thinking about asking Lord Scerniss, since he is probably the most knowledgeable"

"Asking me what?" Lord Scerniss stood just behind him, having come for his morning food too.

"Oh! Asking you more about places round here, where we could go next and if you know about the SilvaGryphie or have heard of her" replied Ellendrii.

"I know little of the places outside Kazétos" replied Lord Scerniss. "You would have to fly around and see for yourself. I'm sure you can see far more from up in the sky than I can down here. Even though we have high places like the top of the terraces and tops of the structures we live in, it would still be easier to fly and look for yourself."

"Hmm, yes you're right. Have any of you ever been out of your territory?" asked Ellendrii.

"A few of us have tried to look for other places. Usually houndlets who think the grass is greener elsewhere. And they always come back too. The only place I know of, I told you about. It is the Forest of Foreboding. We never go there. There used to be a path around it but that was many seasons ago and now the only way, unless you can fly over the top of it, is to go through it."

"What happened to the path?" asked Ellendrii.

"It fell away. It was on the edge of a ravine. There was a storm that destroyed it and filled in the ravine. The forest then took it upon itself to expand into what was left and there is no way around it now. Horrible, unspeakable things exist in that forest. If by flying, you can find another way then I would strongly advise you to go that way. I would advise against going through that wretched forest."

Ellendrii shuddered. The forest sounded horrid and dangerous. But he couldn't fly over it. What about Aro?

"Will you show us around a little more?" asked Aro.

"Of course, I would be happy to show you more of our home and culture" replied Lord Scerniss.

They walked with him after he had finished his breakfast and he shared more of their culture and life with them. He was quite amiable but at the same time they still showed him respect. They never tried to joke with him or take him lightly and he admired them for that. Youngsters could so often take liberties and be disrespectful.

He lead them to some amazing white cliffs that went up so high, the other side of the city. At the top it looked barren but he told them that was where the Forest of Foreboding was that none of them went. The forest apparently started a few miles away from the top of the cliffs so there was no fear of the Wind Hounds climbing up to attend the places that they had carved in these magnificent cliffs getting too close to the forest for comfort. They had carved tombs. High rock tombs with intricately carved entrances that could be seen from all around.

"This is where we place our dead. We are all equally important here, so everyone who dies gets a tomb. Sometimes families will choose to have one tomb for the whole family. The entrances are all different; each pertaining to the individual who rests there. We carve holes, shapes and windows at the entrance and then when the wind blows, the tombs sing songs of death and life. It is the voice of our ancestors speaking to us. If you listen closely on a windy sun cycle, you can hear their voices guiding you. We go and listen to our relatives and what they have to say to help guide us through life."

Ellendrii and Aro looked in awe at these tombs. The rock face was covered in many of them, with paths leading to them and a few Wind Hounds here and there either carving new ones with their claws or sitting outside existing ones and listening to what they had to say. It was definitely a very auditorial culture. Everything seemed to revolve around wind and sound.

"Follow me and I will give you a closer look" said Lord Scerniss and they followed him up one of the narrow paths and along a row of tombs. These were pretty high up in the rock and Aro felt a little vertigo at such heights. He was usually fine with heights but the fact that the path was narrow and he felt he could fall at any moment really didn't help him.

As they walked along the row of carved tombs, they passed several other Wind Hounds sitting in the entranceways of them. They each had some steps leading into them and this is where the Wind Hounds sat, so they wouldn't get in the way of others who were walking along the pathway outside. It was easy to see into the tombs as they passed. They each had pillars either side of the entrance. They weren't round but rather, flattish with carved holes and shapes in them in a variety of intricate patterns. The wind often caught and whistled through these. The tombs went back a fair way into the cliffs, some more than others. At the back there were plinths and on them sat stone coffins, again, all carved and decorated with sound signs. The walls and ceilings of the tombs were decorated in a similar manner. Some Wind Hounds sat on the steps and others sat inside, some with their paws on the coffins and heads bowed in respect and reverence.

Lord Scerniss lead them into a large and magnificent tomb with a smoothly carved and beautiful floor. He sat down before a fantastic coffin and bowed his head before speaking.

"This is the tomb of my ancestors. None of them are related to me; they are Lords who came before me. They are who I have learned from. When a houndlet is born with the Lord markings, he spends his young seasons learning from his predecessor. Here lies Lord Xzenirax who taught me much of what I know about leading the Wind Hounds and all my responsibilities as a Lord."

"This tomb is so much more intricate than the others" breathed Ellendrii, looking around.

"They are signs of respect and the life stories of each individual Lord. The signs tell of their journeys through their lives and their greatest achievements, starting from birth. You can see here that since this is classed as a "family" tomb, there are still walls that are blank. There are other Lord tombs because of course you couldn't fit all the Lords who ever existed in just one tomb. But this is the most recent one. Listen…" Lord Scerniss ran his claws over some of the carvings and a sweet tune echoed around the room.

"This one tells us that Lord Xzenirax was born of Tiferinn and Sazziros and got his first glowing marking when he was eight seasons old. He got his second marking a season later and started learning from his predecessor when he was fourteen seasons old. He was very young when he started to learn but young minds soak up knowledge so much more easily. It then goes on to tell us what he learned and when he learned it and when he came to power. The next set of sound signs will tell us what he did when he was in power and when he started to train me up."

"You must have very good ears" remarked Aro, "To hear all that from the sounds the carvings make"

"We are just in tune to sound since our culture revolves around it" replied Lord Scerniss simply.

"I think it's amazing" breathed Ellendrii.

"Thank you" replied Lord Scerniss with a small nod of his regal head. "We think so, too."

They sat a while more and talked about the tombs and rituals of burial.

"We will have a funeral ritual soon, they are preparing a fresh tomb for someone who passed away a few sun cycles ago. You may join us if you wish" Lord Scerniss said and the others agreed that that would be a nice thing to see since the rituals were so important to the Wind Hounds and so far they had only seen the water rituals. Seeing one that related to other aspects of their lives would be interesting.

Leaving the tombs, Ellendrii thought up a plan of action for what they should do next. They needed to research where to go next, which he would do and Aro could go around and talk to the locals and ask if anyone had heard of or even seen the SilvaGryphie.

They bid Lord Scerniss farewell for now and went about the business at hand.

Ellendrii took to the sky to get a proper look at Kazétos and the sacred pools on the plateau terraces.

It was a HUGE territory. First there was the coast of course, then the cliff rising to the pools and terraces and along the plateaus. Beyond these, the city of Kazétos itself rose up, with its crawling streets and tall, narrow housing structures. The city was placed quite high atop the plateau which was why the wind caught it coming in from the sea. Beyond the city, the carved cliffs with the tombs rose and on top of that, a few miles away the forest began. Ellendrii flew over it a little way. It was dark and ominous looking with sharp, nasty looking trees. It spread as far as the eye could see and was vast. He saw where the ravine had been and the remains of the path that had once been there just lead into the forest now. Any way around the forest that there might have been was certainly impassable now. There was nothing else. Short of walking around the coast but that was also impossible as the white rock that served as a beach fell away some way around and there was no way to make it on foot. There was no way that Ellendrii could carry Aro around and he gave up flying around and trying to follow the coastline because it seemed that the forest was endless and he could still see it high above him as he flew. It would be SO much easier if he was alone. But it would also be so much lonelier.

Meanwhile, Aro wasn't having much luck asking the Wind Hounds about the SilvaGryphie. He asked everyone he met but no one knew anything about her. It was also unfortunate that Aro didn't really know what she looked like. Well, neither did Ellendrii, but at least he could say that she was something that resembled himself. Aro had to say that she looked like Ellendrii and if the Wind Hound in question hadn't seen Ellendrii, then Aro had to go through the trouble of trying to

260

describe what a Gryphie looks like. Which was difficult considering it was something he'd never had to do before and that Lizariaouses are not good at describing things with any sort of clarity. Most of the time he just confused whoever he was talking to.

Only one Wind Hound had seen something like the SilvaGryphie but it turned out that he had just seen Ellendrii and been mistaken. He was quite old and his eyesight was bad, so he was confused between who Aro was looking for and who Aro described. Mostly because instead of giving an idea as to what the species of Gryphies looked like, Aro was telling those who didn't know; what Ellendrii looked like. Then if they had seen Ellendrii, of course they would say yes. And then Aro got his hopes up for nothing.

Finally, Aro sat down defeated. He was tired and his brain was even more tired from describing Gryphies to everyone (he'd had to change his tactic and not specify a fur colour in order to lessen the confusion). He hoped Ellendrii would get back from his exploration soon because now he was getting bored.

"Hey there…" came a voice and Aro looked around. It was Sarris, the little houndlet he had pondered about eating back when they arrived.

"Hi" replied Aro, too tired to really say much else. He was tired of describing the SilvaGryphie by this point.

"How do you like our territory?" asked Sarris.

"It's cool. Sorry I was so threatening to you and your friends by the way. I didn't mean to be. It's in my nature to be like that" said Aro.

"It's ok. Wind Hounds forgive little things like that" said Sarris, sitting down.

"That's good. Lizariaouses don't" smirked Aro. He suddenly felt rather homesick.

"Are you ok?" asked Sarris, picking up on this.

"I guess. I miss my parents" said Aro.

"Then go home" suggested Sarris, not unkindly.

"I can't. I have to help my friend find the SilvaGryphie and prove himself" replied Aro.

"But it's proving harder than we thought it would be. We thought we would get here and just find her hanging about and take her back with us. We were wrong. She's not here and no one seems to have heard of her. Hey, have you heard of her?" he asked hopefully.

Sarris shook her head.

"No I haven't" she replied, "I'm sorry"

Aro sighed. He guessed she probably wouldn't have heard of her.

"I'm starting to lose hope" he said.

"Don't lose hope. If she's here somewhere and several have told you she's here, then she must be here. If a lot have told you she's here then they can't be wrong."

"They might be. I only heard that she lives over here, no one has actually visited her or even seen her."

"How silly, she might be somewhere else then. Who knows." Sarris shrugged.

"I wonder though; what if she doesn't actually exist and is just a story?"

"Believe in the stories. They help us and give us faith" said Sarris wisely. "If several know about her and have told you she's here somewhere then she's bound to be here. You just need to have faith."

"Lizariaouses don't really have stories. Well, maybe ones about the war but that's history."

"Some stories *are* history. Or inspired by it. Like when we listen to the sounds of our ancestors and they tell us what their lives were like. Those are still stories. They aren't all made up and they all have some base on life things and reality. If this SilvaGryphie ends up looking nothing like you think but still exists, then it's all worth it."

"But if she looks nothing like we think then how will we find her? What if creatures over here *have* seen her but know her under a different name? All this time I've been asking for the SilvaGryphie and the Wind Hounds might have seen her but know her under a different look *and* a different name."

"Well then you really are stuck!" giggled Sarris.

"Gee thanks" muttered Aro.

Presently, Ellendrii returned. Aro was glad of this. The little houndlet was starting to confuse him. The SilvaGryphie not looking like a Gryphie and being called something different? Lord Scerniss could be the SilvaGryphie for all he knew. He secretly wondered if she was trying to confuse him on purpose as revenge for him nearly eating her sister.

"How did you get on?" asked Aro.

"Not so well. Lord Scerniss was right. There's no way around the Forest of Foreboding but through. I thought we could walk around the coast and then get back up inland later on, past the forest but no. The coast path drops away a little way past the terraces. So that wouldn't work either. Lord Scerniss was also right about the path that fell away as well. It's just forest now, nothing else and no way through other than through the forest. And it looks horrible. All the trees are dark and sharp looking. And thick. I don't know how we'll find our way through it either. There are some nasty looking birds with sharp beaks flying around them. If all the creatures are like those then we're going to have some trouble going through there."

"What about just getting back on the float and riding round the coast?" asked Aro. It was certainly a good idea.

"I'd thought of that but it won't work either. The water gets rough further around. We'd crash against the rock and the float would be torn apart. I don't know if it's something under the water that's causing it but despite the rest of the water being calm, this is always rough and turbulent so we couldn't possibly get through with the float. We'll need it for going home anyway; I really can't risk destroying it a second time. That reminds me, we need a place to store it. We can't leave it where it is in case the water gets high and breaks it on the rocks" said Ellendrii.

"Ask Lord Scerniss, he can tell you where to store it" said Sarris.

"Thanks, we will!" replied Ellendrii. "Have you had any luck, Aro?"

"No. And Sarris is no help. She said what if the SilvaGryphie looks different and is called something different over here?"

263

"She might be called something different but she definitely won't look different. She looks like I do. Otherwise she wouldn't be the founder of our species. She is the SilvaGryphie. That is who she is and so she couldn't possibly not look like one of my kind."

"Well either way, no one's seen anything that looks like her except for you" replied Aro looking defeated.

"So much for her being just the other side of the vast water" muttered Ellendrii with a small snort.

"Sorry" said Sarris, "I wish we could be of more help to you"

"It's not your fault. I just wish this was all easier. Never mind. We WILL find her!!" Ellendrii looked confident. After all, they had made it this far. Traversing the Forest of Foreboding probably wouldn't be easy but at least there was no water to hold them back and if there was a storm they would be sheltered. He hadn't suspected that there might be something that ate Gryphies in the forest but he did think there would be dangerous creatures in there who would attack them so they had to be fit and healthy before they went in.

Next, they went to find Lord Scerniss. Sarris told them that at this time of the sun cycle, he would be in the sacred pools relaxing. Wind Hounds seemed to do a lot of relaxing and none of them appeared to have many life goals but that was only what they had seen so far. It was still a lovely culture.

They found him at the pools as Sarris had said and walked up to him quietly, in case they disturbed him but he was amiable as usual and easy to talk to.

"Lord Scerniss, we came here on a float that goes on the water. We have left it down by the donasis caves, would it be possible to store it somewhere while we go on? We might come back this way and if we do, we will need it to go home on" said Ellendrii.

"Of course. You may take it and leave it where you are staying. When you leave, leave it here and it will be waiting for you if you return. We are in no dire need of the structure you are staying in, so it will be safe there until you come back" replied Lord Scerniss.

The two friends thanked him and went to get the float.

Upon reaching the rocks, they found a slow and small breeze of Wind Hounds heading to the donasis caves to leave a gift in them. The breeze walked regally and respectfully, the Wind Hound at the front carrying some small trinkets and then stopping outside the desired cave and placing them within. After he had set them down, he ran his claws over the carvings either side of the cave's entrance and they all paused to listen, heads bowed. Ellendrii and Aro stopped too. They didn't want to make any noise in case they disturbed the ceremony.

After a while, the breeze moved away and headed back up to the terraces. Ellendrii and Aro watched them go and made sure they didn't go too close to the donasis cave that the trinkets had been left in, lest they annoy the Wind Hounds or make them think they were stealing from them. Instead, they ignored the donasis caves and went to the rock that they had tied the float to and untied it.

"I'll wear the harness and pull the float up the rocks. You can push it from the other end" said Ellendrii. It was easy for Aro to push the float, since the shelter was the other end of it and it gave him something to press his body weight against.

And pushing the float was easy too. At first. Until they got higher up the rock face and then started to struggle with the steepness. Even without pulling the large float it was tiring to climb up to the plateaus. Luckily the path was wide enough to take the float but it did narrow at points and they had to be careful the float didn't tip over and fall off.

They had reached a particularly narrow part in the path, which was plenty wide enough to walk on but of course not wide enough to really accommodate the float. Aro was pushing from the outermost side of the float in an attempt to try and stop it overturning and falling off the path. Ellendrii was flapping his wings and straining as hard as he possibly could to try and move the float faster and lessen the chances of it falling off and back down the rock face. If they let it fall, it would surely smash on the rocks below.

But then the float caught on a small piece of rock that stuck out of the path and the whole float tipped forwards as

Ellendrii pulled. It nearly fell on top of him and Aro nearly ended up underneath it. Losing their grip and their concentration, the float tilted dangerously over the edge of the pathway. Ellendrii flew in the other direction to try and pull it back up but it was no use; it started to fall!

"ELLENDRII!! WE'RE GUNNA LOSE IT!" roared Aro in a panic.

"I can see! I'm trying to pull it back onto the path but it's not wide enough for me to fly, I'm up against the rock face and nowhere else to go and it's still tipping! I'm going to have to fly around and push it back on and I'll have to be fast about it!"

Aro's eyes were wide with panic and he was losing what little grip he had on the wayward float. He dug his claws in as best he could. Ellendrii would have to stop pulling and quickly fly round to the side that was falling and push it back onto the path. However in doing so, he would have to let the twine slacken, which would inevitably allow the float to fall right off the path and down onto the rocks below if Aro wasn't strong enough to hold it up, which of course he wouldn't be. Ellendrii had seconds to judge the distance and dash round to push it back on the path. He narrowed his eyes and swiftly prepared himself, then he pushed his body off the cliff face so he could dive around faster to the other side of the float and push it. Aro didn't know what to do, so he continued to dig his claws into it in a vain attempt to keep it something like where it was. But if it fell, it would surely take him with it!

Ellendrii swung round and shoved the float hard back onto the path. It tipped and tilted but stayed on the path by some miracle. Ellendrii was panting and panicking.

"We need to pull it up past this part of the path, FAST!!" he called to Aro. Aro had no complaints about that; he didn't want any more trouble with this!

They managed to pull it past the narrow part and carried on. It took them a while but they finally got it near the top and then over and onto the plateau.

They stopped for a rest then. A few Wind Hounds looked at them but none of them offered to help. Not surprising thought Ellendrii; they don't look that strong anyway.

The two of them dragged the float past the pools, going around the outside of them instead of through the middle, in case they upset any of the rituals. Some rockrats ran for it when they saw them coming.

Finally, they reached the city and stopped for another rest. After all, there was no hurry to get it to its destination. They were very hot and thirsty though so they left the float temporarily while they went to a drinking pool for refreshment.

When they came back, they found some houndlets playing in the shelter. They wanted a ride when Ellendrii put the harness back on but he had to decline them, since it was heavy enough without them in; they didn't need any more weight on the float.

"Hey if we let you ride, then I would have to sit on and ride too" joked Aro. Ellendrii shot him a poisonous look and Aro and the houndlets laughed. The breeze of houndlets ran alongside them as they pulled the float through the city. Sometimes they helped Aro push the float when the paths got narrower. They had to be careful what paths to take as well; the float had to fit through them. At one point they went down a path that ended up being too narrow for the float and had to backtrack. However, Ellendrii and Aro were learning the layout of the city or at least the part they resided in pretty fast and they soon found their way back to their residence.

Getting the float into the building though, was much harder. It wouldn't fit through the doorway. In the end they pushed it around the side and left it there instead. Beside their temporary home was a shelter of sorts; well, it had a stone overhang so they thought the float would be kept enough out of the elements under there until they got back, if they came back this way.

They had a long rest on the little balcony of their building after that.

"I don't EVER want to do that again" said Aro.

"Well you will if we come back this way" Ellendrii told him.

"By that time we might have the SilvaGryphie to help us" said Aro.

"I couldn't ask her to do such a menial task, she's like royalty to us" replied Ellendrii.

"Well maybe she'll *offer*, what would you say to that?"

"I'd say no of course! Politely though"

"So you'd make us do all that again when we had the offer of help? Surely it would be *rude* to refuse"

"It would be easier to push it back to the water going back though" Ellendrii pointed out.

"So we probably wouldn't need the help"

"Any help is better than no help" muttered Aro, a little put out by his friend's attitude on the matter.

They headed back out into the city a little later and bumped into Lord Scerniss.

"Did you manage to get your float back to your abode?" he asked.

"Yes but it was hard" replied Ellendrii, "We got there in the end though"

"I would have got some of the Wind Hounds to help you" said Lord Scerniss.

Now he tells us thought Aro with a snort.

"Oh, we managed. But thank you very much for offering" said Ellendrii.

"Happy to accommodate you" replied Lord Scerniss and went on his way with a nod and a smile.

Aro and Ellendrii went to the sacred pools for a swim. They weren't very good at performing the ritual of the pools though but they ran their claws over the sound signs in some sort of an attempt at performing it even though it sounded like scraping and didn't make much sound. Some of the Wind Hounds nearby looked at them in approval because they were making an effort. They stepped into the warm, relaxing water and just floated for a while, enjoying the peace around them. All they could hear were the gentle sounds of the other pools as the Wind Hounds did their rituals and all they could see were fellow creatures enjoying the same peace. They heard the quiet sounds of the sea nearby. The salt water never made it as far as the beautiful pools because the cliff was just too high for the tide to reach. It barely made it halfway up the white rock face even at the highest tide. So the water in the pools was always pure and untouched by the undrinkable sea water. Also the tides were never particularly rough, so even when the water swelled up and dashed against the rocks, it never ever made it as far as even the closest pool. The weather there was nice most of the time, they had been told. Sometimes there was a storm but it wasn't often. Normally the sun shone and the wind blew gently. The wind was a little more inland since it whipped up over the plateaus and through the city.

"I could live here" said Ellendrii again. "It's just so beautiful; I don't feel stressed or worried at all here. And last moon cycle, those lights! They were amazing! I wonder if that happens every moon…"

"Maybe" replied Aro. The warm weather and water was making him sleepy after all the trouble they'd gone to to get the float to their residence. He lazily splashed the water a little with his tail and then gazed deeply into the pool they were in. The water made the white rock look blue. It really was quite stunning.

"Well, it was certainly a nice place to come across as soon as we got here" said Ellendrii,

"It could have been worse. We could have come across a territory full of horrible creatures that wanted to eat us. I hope all the places we visit will be like this"

"I doubt the Forest of Foreboding will be" said Aro.

"You don't know that. Maybe it only looks bad but isn't actually and anyone who's been there has just been put off by how it looks so they haven't given it a chance and just run away."

"That's wishful thinking" replied Aro. "It'll probably be just as horrid as they say it is."

"I want to find someone who has left Kazétos and ask them what it was like" said Ellendrii.

"Good luck with that. I couldn't even find anyone who knew who the SilvaGryphie was and she's *meant* to be here, according to the stupid Sky Gryphies. Are you SURE that they weren't just pulling your leg about her?"

"If they were, more fool me" sighed Ellendrii. "But we're here now so we have to make the best of it. I said I'd come back with her and I will. We won't be going back without her."

"We might spend the rest of our lives looking for her" said Aro, "Then when we go back we will be old."

"But at least we will have found her!"

"But our parents will probably be dead."

"Don't talk like that, Aro!"

"It's true."

Ellendrii sighed. Yes it could be true. But he was determined not to think like that. He didn't want to get down and upset. So far things were going well. They were in a territory full of friendly creatures and it was a nice and pleasant place to stay so they were lucky. Things had started well; Ellendrii only hoped that they remain that way.

Chapter 15
An Accidental Insult

Ellendrii and Aro stayed with the Wind Hounds for several sun cycles. In that time they learned much about their culture and they also told them about where they were from as well.

They also asked Lord Scerniss about the Wind Hounds who had travelled away from Kazétos and what had become of them.

"A few unwise Wind Hounds have travelled outside Kazétos but they've always come back. Those who made it through the Forest of Foreboding of course. They were always unimpressed with the lack of civilization anywhere other than here. Our culture is so refined and our rituals are so important that to live somewhere else is beyond blasphemous and it's also rather confusing too. Think about it; to live in a culture such as ours and then go somewhere else with no culture at all is very confusing. Not many of us, thankfully, seek out places like that, since we are smarter than to question our existence here" he explained.

So clearly, (despite Aro thinking Lord Scerniss was a little up his own) the Wind Hounds were so strongly involved in their culture that they struggled to exist anywhere but their home.

"Those that went beyond the Forest of Foreboding, what did they learn? What was beyond it?" asked Ellendrii, wondering if maybe they had encountered the SilvaGryphie.

"Only two made it through the Forest of Foreboding and managed to get back again. Going through it once is a risk and would probably kill you as it has the rest of us who ventured out. But going through it twice is fatal. Kraarz and Zakk are two daring brothers who made it there and back. It's not normal for a Wind Hound to be warrior-like, such as they are. The two of them have always been too big for their claws and too brash for their own good. But going through the Forest of Foreboding and coming back has humbled them and they are no longer as overconfident as they used to be. You are welcome to find them and speak to them but I doubt they will be much help. They refuse to say what horrors they saw within the forest and haven't said much about what was the other side either."

"Where do they live?" asked Ellendrii, as he needed to know an approximate area they may be in order to narrow down their location.

"They live to the south of Kazétos and never ever go near the area where the forest is now. Ask around. Their abodes are next to each other down the third street near the coast."

Ellendrii and Aro headed over to try and find them. It wasn't that easy considering most of the "buildings" looked the same. The longer they had stayed there though; the easier it was to tell the difference between things and learn their locations.

"He said down here didn't he?" asked Aro, pointing down one of the streets.

"No, I think it was this one" replied Ellendrii, pointing down an adjacent street.

"I've counted, it's this one" said Aro.

"No, it's this one. I'm a better counter than you, Aro" argued Ellendrii.

Finally they settled on taking a street each and asking around.

It was Ellendrii who found them. He found Kraarz lying in front of his abode.

"Excuse me, do you know where Kraarz or Zakk live?" he asked.

"Why do you want to know, outsider?" asked Kraarz. Lord Scerniss had neglected to tell the pair that these two Wind Hounds, due to the suffering they had experienced now disliked anything from anywhere beyond Kazétos or the sacred pools. Mostly because they feared the things from other places now.

"I am looking to find out about their experiences. My friend and I are planning to leave Kazétos and venture into the Forest of Foreboding since we have no other choice on our journey" explained Ellendrii.

"Why would you want to leave? You are better off here or going back where you came from. I've seen you and your friend around and you are both fools to think about going through that forest. Nothing is *that* important that you need to risk your life or your mental state by putting yourselves through that."

"You sound like one who knows these things" replied Ellendrii, gently probing now.

"I've *heard* things. It's too big a risk. It changes you. Don't do it. You don't *have* to listen to me but don't come crawling back here mindless and fearful if you venture through that terrible place."

This Wind Hound was a pale minty green and he had a hideous scar down his face. There was really no hiding who he was, or at least the fact he could possibly be one of the two brothers and Ellendrii rightly thought that he had a chance with this guy in finding out what had happened. So he pressed a little more.

"All the same, Kraarz and Zakk must have been pretty brave to want to go there and see what was beyond the Forest of Foreboding" said Ellendrii.

"Pretty stupid. Are you going to leave me alone now?" asked Kraarz.

"Well, only if you really *can't* tell me what you saw there..." said Ellendrii with a wry smile. Kraarz sighed and snarled a little, his longish ears tucking behind his head in annoyance and his tail flicking.

"Fine" he said, running his large claws into the dirt in frustrated scratching motions with one paw.

Ellendrii sat in front of him and waited patiently for his story.

Kraarz began.

"It was thankfully a good few seasons ago now. I say thankfully because time tends to fade memories and things heal. My brother, Zakk and I were always a bit delinquent. We got into fights, which is something greatly frowned upon here. If you fall out with someone, you're supposed to walk away calmly to think and then when your head is clear again, go and talk to them. But we didn't. We would fight and since it was frowned upon, we would always win since the other Wind Hound would back down. Then I had the stupid idea one sun

273

cycle to go into the forest that everyone else feared so much. There couldn't be anything there that we couldn't handle, surely? They told us not to, they warned us but we didn't listen of course. So in we went. The horrors that lurk there are unlike anything you could possibly imagine. I got this awful scar there. Wind Hounds NEVER get scars since we don't fight and as a result I am considered to be tainted and the others don't talk to me. I was always the dominant brother anyway and I freely admit that I got both Zakk and myself into a lot of trouble. He is younger than me and I am pushy and tend to drag him along with me because he looks up to and admires me. So he would do whatever I wanted him to, because he wanted to prove himself to me and how strong and brave he could be like me.

Even now I'm still the brother who is in charge and it griks me off that the other Wind Hounds look at me so distastefully now. Before we went into the forest, we both had life partners. Mine left me when we came back because she thought I was hideous. Zakk still has his. She hates me, of course, for what I "did" to Zakk. I didn't do anything to him. He came with me willingly. I would have gone by myself if he hadn't come along, but I doubt I would have survived in there by myself. There are things in there that will send you mad, give you moonmares for the rest of your life. I found the corpse of another Wind Hound in there. He had smashed his head open on a rock and bled to death. Who knows what happened to him. It was horrible. I can only assume he was trying to get the forest sounds out of his head and it had driven him to do that. We ran after we saw that. I should have hidden it from my brother, really. But I thought that showing him would make him fearful and more careful with his senses so he would run with me and not question me. Zakk still has moonmares about that. Wind Hounds never die in horrible ways like that. We die of old age or in our sleep or sometimes of an illness but we remain in our abodes if we are ill, so it doesn't spread. We die peacefully. To see a Wind Hound in that condition traumatized both of us more than we thought.

I...I can't talk about what I saw in there in too much detail. If you are determined to go in there, beware of anything that flies. We tried to get through the forest as fast as we could. We didn't hang around. We ran pretty much the whole way through it but even then it took us four sun cycles. I think it was four. It's hard to tell since the forest is so dark and horrible. The trees are black. The wood is black. The leaves look black. The ground is grey and poisoned. Take water with you. The water in there is rank and murky. It stinks of death. Trust nothing you see or hear. Don't listen. Because it will get to you. It will drive you mad. The sounds. The sounds of fear and terror and losing control. Unlike anything we've ever heard before. Since much of our culture is based on beautiful sound, it was even more shocking. We were not used to hearing sounds that ripped through our bodies like claws on a flint. Screeching, searing, burning our ears. DON'T look up into the trees. I did, once. I never did it again. There are *things* up there, lurking in the branches. *Watching* you. Once you look up there, you will forever feel their gaze upon you. Just don't do it. They slither and rustle and you can hear every inch of their filthy, horrid bodies sliding over the branches as they follow you. Waiting for you to go mad and drop dead from insanity. If you see a red light in the air, turn away and go back. It's like a flying glow bug but it has a searing shriek and comes right up to you. The nearer it comes to your face, the more it blinds you. You see everything in a red tone after that. I still do. Nothing is normal colours for me anymore. Like looking through red all the time. This is why we ran. We couldn't walk. Every fibre of your being is telling you to run and escape. There is a creature in there we dubbed a Repulsator. They are a bit like rockrats in appearance but larger and mostly brown and they float in the air. They only have half a body, like they've been ripped apart and they drip blood. But that isn't the worst part…" Kraarz suddenly trailed off. He clenched his eyes shut and shook his head. When he opened his eyes, they were wild with madness, staring at Ellendrii. The Wind Hound spoke slowly.

"Don't…go…near…them. They will…take…your eyes…" he said.

Ellendrii felt his stomach churning. This forest sounded horrible. He figured the only way to get through it was to do as the Wind Hounds had done and run and not dawdle. He was also not sure if it was entirely a very good idea bringing these terrible memories back to the front of Kraarz' mind. He was going mad even talking about it.

"I got the scar in there" he continued and Ellendrii closed his mouth which he had opened to say something to the Wind Hound.

"There is a…creature…it…takes your being…who you are…it drains you…it…latches on to you…it did this to me. I hope you never encounter it."

"What does it look like?" asked Ellendrii, needing to know what to look out for.

"Your worst moonmare. Both of us saw that when we looked at its face but we both saw something different. It was our worst fears. It's hard to explain…I…I'm sorry. I can do no more than tell you that. I can't think about it or it will get into my head. It will get me…get me…" he started panting with stress and placed his paws over his head, lowering his head to the ground and looking around with stark craziness in his eyes; his slit pupils getting narrower.

Ellendrii wanted to change the subject and fast!

"What about the other side of the forest? What did you see there? There's no need to tell me more about the horror in the forest. It's ok. What was beyond it?"

Kraarz was still panting and it took him a while to regain his composure. Ellendrii waited patiently. Kraarz' hackles were raised up completely, making him look rather odd since their fur is fairly long and silky. Ellendrii had never seen a threatened Wind Hound do that before. Even his tail was fluffed up, similar to a cave cat.

Finally, Kraarz continued.

"Beyond the forest there is another land. It is fairly flat and there are a lot of trees but they are not so densely packed as a forest would be. And it is green. We didn't go much further. There was a settlement of creatures there. They weren't very civilized though and they were primitive. My brother and I decided to turn back because we hadn't found what we were looking for. These creatures wouldn't let us past them for some reason. I don't know why. We didn't speak their language and none of us could understand each other. After going through the forest and then encountering these creatures, we couldn't take it anymore. We'd lost our will to live. So we went back through the forest again. At that point, we didn't care if we lived or died. We'd learned enough about the forest to be able to fair a bit better and knew what to look out for as we travelled. We just wanted to be back home by that point. It was still just as terrifying going back through though and we did encounter some more unpleasant creatures and things we hadn't encountered the first time we went through there. Our fear helped us in a way because it made our senses more alert. It took us a little longer to get back though because we were tired and hungry and fatigued from running all the time. Some of the forest is hard to get through as well. There are bushes that grow up and you have to force your way through them. And there are filthy, boggy parts with deep black mud. And don't even think about trying to fly up through the trees to place where you are and where you need to go. If you can even manage to break through to the outside; the creatures in the trees will kill you before you even hit fresh air. There is no way past but through. No way around either. You're both fools. You have no idea what you're going to put yourselves through. No idea at all."

Ellendrii noted with slight irritation that Kraarz had gone back to talking about the forest again. He wanted to know about the creatures the other side.

"What about the creatures the other side? Can you tell me anything about them, to better prepare ourselves?"

"They wear these things on their faces. They never take them off. The things on their faces are white. They have flat faces too and large ears. Some have bushy tails, the males I think. The females have thin tails. The things on their faces have carvings on them and their eyes glow. When we first saw them, we thought their culture might be a bit like ours. Though not as refined of course. But we were wrong. They spoke in noises, like squeaking and chitters. Most of them were black, some were grey and a few were brown. Others had broken markings on them. Spots and blotches. Clearly they were primitive like meal creatures. They were nothing more than large rockrats. But they would not let us past. They attacked us and in the state that we were in, it was no state to fight. All that for nothing. There was nothing better across there than Kazétos. I'm warning you now that the trip will be fruitless."

"What was beyond their territory, did you see?" asked Ellendrii.

Kraarz sighed and thought about it.

"Ergh, I don't know. We couldn't see much past the trees these things lived in and around. Even though it wasn't a forest and the trees weren't tightly packed, I guess it went on for a while, their territory and what was beyond was just too far to see. They were small creatures but tenacious and they would gang up on us if we tried to make any progress through their land. They had little wooden houses both in the trees and on the ground. They were good climbers and they were fast and they would jump on us and push us back. Even when we tried to run through, they would pursue us and others who were ahead of us would jump down and push us back. Hateful things. We didn't mean them any harm. Well, not until Zakk killed one by accident because he lost his temper. They flew at us full force after that. Until that point all they had done was restrain us. Now they bit and clawed at us and we had no choice but to go back to the forest. We were both SO angry and frustrated. But we knew that the domain of the Wind Hounds was where we belonged. Nowhere else. So we came back here.

It was not a warm welcome either. Well, not for me. My brother was forgiven because he had basically always done things because I did them and because he wanted me to respect him. And he didn't have an awful scar across his face. Then my life partner left me and that's the end of the story." Kraarz sat up.

"Thank you very much for telling me. I'm sorry if it brought back bad memories for you" said Ellendrii.

"If it helps you then it was worth it. But I really don't think the trip will be worth it because those creatures will stop you when you reach the other side. There might be a way to go around their territory that they don't know about but when

Zakk and I tried, they still pushed us back. And you won't understand them so don't bother trying. If I was you, I would flame them. If we could breathe fire, it's what we would have done. Maybe you can eat them afterwards."

"I have one last question, if I may?" said Ellendrii.

"You may" replied Kraarz.

"Did you see anything that looked like me at all the other side of the forest?"

"No. Nothing. Only those little creatures with the white faces. We may have done if we'd gone further but of course we never got that far. Why? Have you lost someone?"

"I'm looking for the founder of my species. She's known as the SilvaGryphie and all I have to go by is that she's a Gryphie so she must look in some part like myself. And also very beautiful as well. And I was told she lived over the vast water but none of the Wind Hounds have seen her, so she must be the other side of the Forest of Foreboding too."

"Is it *that* important to find her? Surely if she's the founder, she must be dead? Or do your species live forever?"

"She does. So I heard."

"So you are going to pass through the Forest of Foreboding on a whim? Because of something that may not be the other side of it? Why? Surely it's too big a risk to take for fear of failure?"

"That's what everyone says but my life goal is at stake here! In order to get into the Sky Gryphie Elite Flyers I must find her! That was the final condition I had to meet; to bring back the SilvaGryphie. And yes I am aware they may not be telling me the truth and she might not be out there but there's no harm in trying. If you don't try, you don't know and I have nothing to lose. This is my life goal; to be in with the best of the best flyers and they are the Sky Gryphies. If I didn't do this, I would spend the rest of my life wondering if I could have succeeded and it would be an awful existence. So here I am. And already I've made memories I would never have otherwise; meeting the Wind Hounds! Seeing those lovely lights in the moonlit sky, sharing your rituals, learning how others live, broadening my horizons. If I hadn't set out to find her, I wouldn't know what I would be missing. So far it's been worth it."

"Well yes, because you met us first. But what lays beyond here won't be as nice."

"Actually we met you second. We ended up on an island in the middle of the vast water first and met a beautiful Gryphie type creature called Midnyte Comet who had incredible wings that were like a window into space..." he trailed off and became misty eyed. Suddenly he missed Midnyte so much. They could have stayed with her of course. But no. That was not their mission.

Kraarz chuckled.

"Like me with my life partner. She was so beautiful. Completely the opposite of how I am now" and he became misty eyed too. For a moment the pair of them sat there thinking of females they loved. Then Aro turned up.

"Ah there you are. Is this one of the Wind Hounds who saw the Forest of Foreboding?" he asked, bounding in loudly as usual.

Ellendrii shook himself out of his love struck stupor and Kraarz did similar.

"Er...yes, yes this is Kraarz and he's been telling me all about what lurks in the Forest of Foreboding. And it won't be pretty. Not at all. I'll have to tell you about it later. We need to both be prepared for it."

"Great. MORE trouble. Well it had better not be like that awful water. I spent most of those sun cycles feeling sick."

"It's not. But Kraarz said you can't drink the water in the forest so we have to take our own again"

"Oh great, what if we run out?"

"We won't. It doesn't take as long to get through the forest. What was it, Kraarz? Four sun cycles?"

"Yes. But we were running and we can run faster than you."

"Well we will still try" replied Ellendrii, "Won't we, Aro?"

"Of course" said Aro, nodding his head.

"Then I wish you luck. Remember what I told you and I hope you survive" said Kraarz.

"Thank you for all the information you've told us" said Ellendrii, gratefully. Kraarz nodded and smiled and lay back down in the sun.

Ellendrii and Aro left him and went back to their abode to talk about what Kraarz had told Ellendrii.

They sat on the roof of the structure away from everyone else and Ellendrii spoke.

"I gotta say I'm starting to regret coming on this journey. Up until now we've met friendly creatures but that will all change whenever we venture into that wretched forest. From what Kraarz said, it's terrifying. There are horrid creatures in the trees and nothing to drink, noises that send you mad, a thing that sucks out your being, floating rat things with only half a body that steal your eyes, red lights that scream at you…not to mention the things he didn't mention cos he didn't mention them. He and his brother basically ran all the way through and still got injured. He got that awful scar on his face from a creature of the forest. And when they finally got out the other side they encountered these little things that spoke a different language and they wouldn't let them past. The Wind Hounds tried all they could to get through this territory but the creatures wouldn't let them and kept pushing them back. I can only assume it's because they thought the Wind Hounds came from the forest and they assumed they were a threat because they didn't speak the same language."

"Maybe it's because the Wind Hounds have such a defined culture and they couldn't understand anything beyond that. We'll probably have a better chance of getting through to the creatures and having them let us past. We're more understanding" he lowered his voice to a whisper, "And more open minded"

"Hmm, you're probably right" replied Ellendrii. "We will see."

"When will we leave the windy city?" asked Aro.

Ellendrii pondered.

"I don't know. I think I'm gunna have to work myself up to this."

"I know what you mean" replied Aro.

"We'll give it a few more sun cycles" said Ellendrii. Aro agreed that this was a great idea.

They were putting it off.

Soon, the time came for the burial ritual that Lord Scerniss had told them about. By this time, Ellendrii and Aro were becoming quite a part of the community and getting on well with the Wind Hounds. Lord Scerniss still very much enjoyed the interest they took in the rituals and culture.

They had also become friends with Addis, Kaisey and Sarris, the three houndlets they had met when they arrived and all the initial threats and fear between the five of them had been forgiven.

Lord Scerniss himself showed them how a body is prepared for the funeral. It would be put in a coffin that lay in the back of the tomb. Or in the case of family tombs, stacked with other coffins.

A team of Wind Hounds prepared the body in a manner that reminded Ellendrii very much of how Gryphies prepared theirs. They used leaves and flowers from the few plants that grew up here and there in the territory. All the flowers were highly scented, which helped to hide the smell of death. The tomb was also prepared with scented flowers as all the tombs were that had fresh bodies in. Of course the smell didn't really come out of the coffin once the body was inside it but the smell infused itself into the coffin if the flowers were regularly put into the tombs. The coffins also had scented flowers put inside them and left for a few sun cycles to freshen the coffin for the deceased. The flowers lasted a long time and stayed scented for a long time too. Lord Scerniss told them that was because the heated springs and fresh water provided healthy nutrition for the plants so they lived longer. Much like the Wind Hounds themselves as their life spans easily matched those of Gryphies and Lizariaouses and went on longer as well.

The Wind Hound's body was treated very carefully. It was not messed with, injured, taken apart or changed in any way since the Wind Hounds considered the bodies to be just as sacred in death as in life. So the body was laid out with flowers in a funeral room in a special building meant to house the dead before they were placed into their coffins.

Of course, most deaths happen without warning so the carvers who carved the tombs had to work very hard when the Wind Hound died because the longer the body was left out, the more it succumbed to decay.

Lord Scerniss took them to see what the carvers had done at the entrance to the tomb after they were shown the body. He showed them the sound signs, which told the name of the Wind Hound who was in the tomb and then inside, the story of their life. It was of course greatly abridged but it told of their most important achievements, life partners, houndlets if they had any and it also showed a little map of what markings they had, since they got markings at different times in their lives depending on what they did with their lives and all the markings on every Wind Hound are different. So every marking map was different. If a Wind Hound wanted to hear what we would call a bullet point list of the important things in an individual's life, then all they had to do was run their claws over the marking map.

The life partner or houndlets of individuals were buried in the same tomb so the marking maps became like a family tree as well as a record of their lives. Wind Hounds called their mates "life partners" because they deemed the term "mate" to be too primitive.

"Mate is what we do with them, not what they are. They are our partners for life" explained Lord Scerniss and Ellendrii agreed that this was a much nicer and less blunt way of putting it. He decided to use the term "life partner" for himself from now on, if he could remember to, as it meant taking a little Wind Hound culture with him after they left. He decided to do this with all the nice places they visited and creatures they met who left a positive impact on him. It was crossing cultures and bringing far away creatures closer together in a way and he felt there was no harm in introducing some new ideas to his own Forest. That way he could hold on to his experiences, provided they were positive of course!

"When the ritual of death takes place, the individual's family and friends are all there and we all gather around at the base of the tombs for the Ritual of Parting. This is where we part ways with the individual on a physical level. As you know, with the sound signs they can still speak to us but we can no longer see them. They are however, never really gone" Lord Scerniss explained.

"Then, the procession takes the coffin to the tomb. The body is already in it. It is placed in the coffin back at the preparation area. The lid is placed on the coffin only after the Ritual of Parting takes place. The lid is on the coffin as it is carried up to the tomb. It takes strong Wind Hounds to carry the coffins and each coffin is flanked by eight of them; four either side. The reason the coffin is brought to the base of the tombs with the lid off, is so the air can get to the body one last time and also so the family can know that the body is indeed inside the coffin and they aren't just bringing an empty coffin to the tomb. A bereaving family needs closure and they get this during the Ritual of Parting. They will gather around the coffin for their last few words to the individual, if they wish to say them, before the lid is put on.

When the coffin reaches the tomb, it is carried in and placed carefully where it will lie for the rest of time. The family of the deceased follow the coffin carriers and I lead them all to the tomb. I oversee all the funerals."

"You must be very busy" observed Ellendrii.

"I am, but I still have time to rest. Funerals don't happen every sun cycle."

"Does everyone have a funeral ritual?" asked Aro.

"Yes, why wouldn't they?" asked Lord Scerniss.

"What if they didn't like the one who had died?" said Aro.

"They still have a funeral and the Ritual of Parting out of respect. Besides, not everyone in a family dislikes a member of it. It is normally just one individual the deceased had a disagreement with who might not like them. In which case, that individual may not come to bid them farewell, which is the most disrespectful thing one can do, since it prevents closure. We don't fall out very often here since we are all equals and because there simply isn't any point in fighting. We settle our differences with thought and care and if the ones arguing still can't settle their differences then they call me to do it for them. And my decision is final." Lord Scerniss looked straight at Aro imperiously and Aro said no more on the matter.

"Do funerals happen at any time of sun cycle?" asked Ellendrii.

"Yes, whenever the family of the deceased has decided to say goodbye to them. I know when all the funerals are taking place. The preparation area has sound signs and they will let out the sound to tell me when the next few funeral rituals are, so I am aware and can prepare accordingly."

"I admire how organized you are" said Ellendrii and Lord Scerniss smiled.

"Thank you" he replied with a small nod of his head.

"This funeral ritual will happen when the sun is just past its mid point. Until then, let us bathe in the sacred pools"

"Do we have to prepare too?" asked Ellendrii.

"No, you and I just have to be there. And of course I have to lead the ritual but I have done it many times and I don't need to prepare what to say. It's generally the same for everyone, with only things like names and life experiences changed. I look at the deceased and see their markings and then I can lead the ritual. It's a quick way of learning about someone."

"I wish I knew what all the markings meant. It must be easy to know someone when you can see it on their body" said Ellendrii.

"You would think that" said Lord Scerniss as the three of them made their way to the pools.

"But it is harder than that. The markings only tell me what has happened to them or what they have done. They tell little about their personalities or who they are. There are other ways to tell that. Body language; how someone carries themselves. But it is still hard. I know most of the Wind Hounds who live here but there are some of course who I have never met. However I do say goodbye to them all when they leave."

The three of them relaxed in one of the pools until the time came for the funeral ritual. They headed to the preparation area. This was a large "building" adorned with flowers and scented plants and several levels to it. Inside were plinths where bodies were laid out with flowers to

285

decorate them. It was strangely beautiful even though it was also rather macabre.

To the side of the building, a breeze of Wind Hounds gathered. Ellendrii assumed they were the relatives of the deceased. They all looked very sad with their regal heads held low and their eyes closed. The body was being placed into the coffin, very carefully and then flowers were laid atop the corpse, arranged with care. The body had been placed in a laying down position, as though the individual was simply sleeping with her head rested peacefully on her paws.

This preparation area was near to the rock tombs so they didn't have far to walk to get to the base of the cliff they were carved into.

The eight Wind Hounds who were the coffin carriers lifted the coffin carefully and Lord Scerniss lead them all to the base of the rock tombs. The breeze walked slowly (mostly because the coffin carriers did; the coffin was white stone and very heavy!) with Lord Scerniss at the front. Ellendrii and Aro were at the back, not wanting to impose too much on the procession.

Lord Scerniss had also told them that the coffins were carved as well. In more detail than the tomb wall. But they were only carved on three sides. Not the side that would be against the wall of the tomb and not be seen because the coffins were never moved once they were placed. This coffin was going in a fresh tomb. The carvings on it were so delicate and intricate; Ellendrii had marvelled at them.

They reached the place where they would do the Ritual of Parting and Lord Scerniss spoke his piece. It was all about the life of the departed and what she had done and the things she had achieved and many other things, all of which Aro found pretty boring and after a while he started to shift about.

They were near the front; near Lord Scerniss, since they had wanted to hear what he was saying properly. The coffin had been placed at the bottom of the path, ready to be carried to its tomb and the coffin carriers awaited their signal to take it to the tomb, which would be Lord Scerniss starting to make his way up the path after the family had said goodbye to their relative in the coffin. The lid had been carried as well; it was less heavy so only four carriers had taken it and they had followed the ones bearing the coffin. Because they were quadrapedal animals, the Wind Hounds had a special setup with harnesses supporting the coffin so they could carry it with relative ease since of course they couldn't walk on two legs, which in Ellendrii's opinion would have been easier.

Aro sighed. Ellendrii looked up at Lord Scerniss who was stood on a white stone plinth, this also being decorated with sound signs. The wind whipped up and blew through the holes in the tomb entrances and there a sweet music wafted past. Ellendrii was lost in it. He suddenly felt a deep sadness but at the same time, a deep feeling of overwhelming respect for the deceased even though he had never met her.

Aro didn't.

"Ergh I dunno why this has to be so long" he muttered to Ellendrii, "why can't they just bury them in the ground like Lizariaouses do. It would be much quicker instead of all this faffing around. I thought it would be a *short* speech. My bum's gone numb from sitting for so long"

But Lord Scerniss had heard him and was now glaring down at them both.

"WHAT did you say?" he demanded. The other Wind Hounds were also staring at them.

They couldn't *all* have heard thought Aro. He was sure he'd only said it quietly to Ellendrii. He hadn't noticed Ellendrii motioning for him to shut up as Lord Scerniss had heard him. Wind Hound ears must be better than he had first assumed. He figured he was in deep enough trouble as it was so he decided to tell the truth.

"I said that it would be easier to just bury the dead in the ground instead of dragging out the mourning in this long ritual. Or maybe just take them up to the tombs or something? Lizariaouses bury their dead and that's that. It doesn't take half as long and then they can get on with happier things" Aro said. He wished he hadn't. Lord Scerniss was fuming mad!

"How DARE you!! HOW DARE YOU!!" he roared, "You come to OUR territory, you take part in OUR rituals, we give you the honour of being a part of OUR community and then you have the utter cheek to say something like that? How disrespectful!!"

There was a low rumble all around. Ellendrii thought it was thunder rumbling at first but it wasn't. It was the low growl of the assembled Wind Hounds. And it was directed at them.

"I…I'm sorry! I come from a place where we do things differently and I was saying it to Ellendrii, I wasn't aiming it at you or anyone else here" blurted out Aro.

But Lord Scerniss was riled up by now.

"But I still heard it! And you still said it! I thought you had open minds. I accepted you here because you were respectful but I can see that was all just a front. You were probably both mocking our rituals behind our backs!"

"We weren't!" spoke up Ellendrii, "We have a great respect for you and your rituals! My friend speaks before he thinks and he is very sorry!"

"I am! I really didn't mean to, please forgive me!" yelled Aro, shaking now. Even though he could probably hold his own in a fight against a Wind Hound, Lord Scerniss was powerful and those claws would be dangerous.

"Too little too LATE!" roared Lord Scerniss. He lunged at Aro, missing him by inches as the hapless Lizariaous dodged only just in time and started to run. Ellendrii instinctively took to the sky. He wanted to flame the Wind Hound for attacking his friend but he knew it would make things worse.

"RUN, ARO!!!" But Aro was way ahead of him although he wasn't sure where to run and Lord Scerniss would soon outpace him. The Wind Hound snarled and snapped at Aro's tail, slashing out with his powerful claws whenever he got the chance, hoping to dig them into Aro's hind quarters and bring him down. The other Wind Hounds all joined in at this point and the funeral was abandoned. Aro had insulted not only their rituals and culture but also their dead relative and they were all out for his blood now.

Ellendrii saw Aro heading into Kazétos but he knew there would be no way out that way. It would lead back to the coast and Aro would be trapped.

"TO THE FOREST, ARO!! THEY WON'T GO IN THERE! THEY WOULDN'T DARE!!" yelled Ellendrii and Aro quickly changed his course. Swerving wasn't one of his strong points and Lord Scerniss could pretty much turn on a leaf he was that supple. His claws caught Aro as he turned but Aro charged onward. He had to run up the huge cliff where the tombs were in order to get to the top and then to the forest. This was *not* how either of them had expected to go onto the next part of their journey!

The breeze of furious Wind Hounds lead by Lord Scerniss chased Aro up the narrow paths of the cliff. Past all the tombs he rushed, nearly tripping and falling a few times since of course the narrow path made him nervous. The Wind Hounds looked expectant when they thought he would fall and disappointed when he didn't. Aro didn't want to hang around and find out what they would do to him should they catch him. He'd never seen them angry before. They had seemed so peaceful. He felt beyond bad for what he had done and who knows what Ellendrii would do to him either for blowing their chances at being friends with the Wind Hounds.

Aro and his stupid big mouth and dumb reptilian brain. Had he learned nothing from the time they had spent with the Wind Hounds? To wait before he spoke, to think before he acted? Ellendrii half wanted the Wind Hounds to catch and punish him. He had no idea either about how they would dole out a punishment. Would they imprison him? Kill him? Maim him so he had to live with the scars? He was so *stupid*! Of course, Ellendrii didn't *really* want his friend to be captured but he was mad enough with him that he would rebuke him when they were safe again. Maybe singe his ears or tail a little.

Aro was nearing the top of the rock tombs now. Not much more of the path to go but he was clearly tiring. Not only was he running at full, fearful pelt for a Lizariaous but also uphill as well. The Wind Hounds were not tiring at all. The noise of the wind whistled and echoed all around and it didn't sound peaceful anymore. It was almost as if the very ancestors of the Wind Hounds were angry at Aro as well.

Great. He'd angered the dead as well as the living. COULD this get any worse?

Finally reaching the top, Aro was now running on flat, sparsely grassed land. The ominous Forest of Foreboding stretched out in the distance. Now he could at least run a bit faster, no longer uphill. However, so could the Wind Hounds and they were fast gaining on him. Lord Scerniss was the fastest but the others were coming up behind him swiftly. They were snarling and snapping angrily; their anger fuelling them into a rage and keeping them going.

Aro was sweating and starting to stumble. Lizariaouses don't pant; neither do Gryphies. Both sweat. He broke into a frenzied gallop, desperately racing for the forest. It was the lesser of two evils, really.

Lord Scerniss didn't speak or call after him. There were no barked threats. They were saving that energy to put into running.

Then Aro stumbled and fell. Lord Scerniss went to leap on him but Ellendrii swooped down and flamed the Wind Hound, giving Aro time to get up and carry on.

With singed fur and even angrier, Lord Scerniss resumed the chase. The others looked angrily up at Ellendrii. Flaming their king?? Insult!!! Ellendrii had had no other choice. It was that or let his friend get possibly torn apart.

Aro's leg throbbed where Lord Scerniss' claws had struck him. The injury wasn't bad but of course it's that old saying the smaller the cut; the worse it hurts.

"NEARLY THERE, ARO!!!" called Ellendrii.

Aro had reached the edge of the forest now and dove in. Ellendrii remained hovering but the Wind Hounds had skidded to a halt. None of them dared venture into the Forest of Foreboding.

"Come back here and face your punishment!!" roared Lord Scerniss into the forest.

Aro hid under a horribly uncomfortably spiky bush quietly and shivering.

Lord Scerniss waited.

"No matter" he said, "The punishments the Forest of Foreboding will dole out would be far worse than anything I could do." He looked up at Ellendrii.

"If either of you ever come back to Kazétos again, we will kill you" he barked to him. Ellendrii said nothing. No apology would be enough.

The Wind Hounds turned and walked away. Ellendrii waited until they were most of the way back to the cliff before alighting and looking into the terrible black forest.

"Aro? Are you in there?" he called. He knew the Wind Hounds had all gone; none of them had remained to tackle either of them.

There was a pause and then Aro crawled out from under the bush and came to the edge of the forest.

"I'm *so* sorry" he said to Ellendrii, head low and ears down. His needles and tail drooped too.

"I really didn't mean to" he muttered.

"Yeah, well you did. And now it's too late. Now we're going into the forest without provisions and no water with us" Ellendrii stalked past Aro and headed into the forest without another word.

The Lizariaous followed him, quietly.

Chapter 16
The Forest of Foreboding

Ellendrii said nothing to Aro for some time. He was trying to work out if there was any way to fly back to Kazétos and nab some water. They still had the gourds in the shelter of the float and he could try and get the water that way. Surely not all the Wind Hounds would know what they had done. Surely he would have a chance? But the longer he left it, the less chance they would have. He stopped in his tracks.

"Aro, I have to go back. I need my leather bag and the gourds with water. We can't go in here without those. I have healing herbs in the bag. We'll surely die if I don't go back and get our stuff"

"They'll kill you" said Aro, "Because of me"

"Yes it IS because of you. But the longer I leave it, the more Wind Hounds will find out what you did. I need to go back before that breeze reaches Kazétos and Lord Scerniss spreads the word about us. It just griks me off that I get blamed for something YOU did!"

At the word "you", Ellendrii poked Aro's snout roughly with his finger. It hurt but Aro did nothing. He didn't even rub it; merely wrinkled it.

"Wait here, fool. I'll go get what I can." Ellendrii rushed off. He didn't have that far to walk since they were only a little way in. When he got to the edge, he flew. He flew up high, so high that the Wind Hounds would have trouble spotting him unless they were looking up for a while. He decided to fly to the east of Kazétos so that the breeze of Wind Hounds who were heading back down the rock paths now to carry on the funeral wouldn't see him. The funeral gave him a little time at least. Lord Scerniss wouldn't abandon that; he would see it through to the end and then go and tell everyone about the two "outsiders".

Flying over the city itself, Ellendrii landed in one of the streets. The passing Wind Hounds paid him little or no heed and he went straight to the place he and Aro had stayed and into the shelter of the float. Putting the leather bag on swiftly, with the gourds and other needed items inside it; he flew to the drinking pools to fill the gourds.

There, Sarris found him.

"Are you leaving?" she asked. He hadn't noticed her stepping up beside him. He decided to pretend all was ok.

"Sadly yes, it's time for us to go. We've stayed here long enough and I don't want us to outstay our welcome" replied Ellendrii, filling up the gourds with the delicious water.

"Oh you could never do that. Lord Scerniss really likes you. He puts a lot of effort into showing you our ways and he never does that normally. You're so respectful and interesting" she beamed.

Ellendrii felt sick.

"Thank you" he said, filling up the last gourd and putting it in the bag.

"Could you catch a few rockrats for us please? I can't make the sound that brings them out" he was pushing his luck sticking around for her to get some rockrats for them but he decided to take the chance. He could always get away with ease now and he had the things they really needed. Anything else was a bonus.

"Of course!" barked Sarris and they headed to the place the rockrats lived.

She made the sound and out the little creatures came and the two of them caught a few. They gathered ten altogether. Ellendrii wanted it to be an even number so they could share fairly, even though that idiot of a Lizariaous didn't deserve any at all.

He put the rockrats in his bag and thanked Sarris for helping him.

"Oh, please don't tell anyone you saw me" he said.

"Why not?" asked Sarris, puzzled.

"Oh, because it will make them sad to hear that we left" Ellendrii lied hurriedly.

"Ok. It was lovely meeting you" said Sarris and touched Ellendrii's hand with her clawed paw gently in a sign of respect and farewell. Ellendrii did the same and smiled. Then he took to the sky.

"Goodbye Sarris! Take care!" he called and headed back to the forest. She waved after him.

At least his last moment in the territory of the Wind Hounds had been a pleasant one. After all, none of this was *his* fault. He flew around the coastline and then inland and up and over the rock tombs. He could see the tiny figures of the Wind Hounds bearing the lidded coffin to its tomb.

"Bye, Lord Scerniss" muttered Ellendrii, "I'm sorry it ended so badly."

Ellendrii reached the forest and headed in. Aro was where he had left him, staring out into the light and making the most of it before the darkness and terror enshrouded them both.

"Did you get the water?" he asked.

"Yes and I got us ten rockrats, five each, with Sarris' help, not that you deserve any" snorted Ellendrii and pushed past him, heading into the darkness.

So, he was still upset thought Aro. He followed in silence.

The deeper into the forest they got, the darker it became. The paths were narrow and rarely trod. As Kraarz had told Ellendrii, some of the paths were blocked by bushes and other prickly plants and they had to watch themselves.

They took it in turns to lead since the leader had to clear the path for the other one. It wasn't so dark that they couldn't see anything, luckily.

When Ellendrii lead, he used his wings as a shield around his body. When Aro lead, he just pushed through, allowing his tough skin to take the brunt of the damage and his head lowered so he didn't poke his eyes out. The branches of the plants and bushes only grazed them but they both soon tired of the irritation and pain.

Ellendrii wished he had asked Kraarz more about the plants and things in the forest and if anything was poisonous or would hurt them in any other way but the Wind Hound had been so traumatized by having to bring back the memories of the place that Ellendrii hadn't the heart to push him with questions.

He had been right about the noises from above though.

"Don't whatever you do, look up when you hear those noises" he snapped at Aro. He was still annoyed with him but he felt it fair to warn him about the things that lurked up there. He didn't want a mad Lizariaous on his hands. A normal one was bad enough. A mad one would be deadly. He had no escape should Aro decide on an unprovoked attack for whatever reason.

The trees in the forest did indeed have black bark. It was so odd. The leaves of all the trees and plants looked black like Kraarz had said and the earth below their feet was ashen grey. They could hear things skittering around them and didn't want to know what any of the things were. They had no urge to find out whatsoever. The only thing they could concentrate on and they did indeed concentrate all their mind on it, was heading forward in as straight a line as possible so they didn't get lost forever in this shroud of morbidity. Aro was starting to miss the water. At least there was nothing there that would kill them. Except the weather of course.

They were both terrified of the thought of this place sending them mad but it was ok so far. Ellendrii started to think that maybe it wasn't so bad. Sure it was dark and dingy but nothing had attacked them despite the odd noises they heard in the canopy. Slithering and scratching. Tiny screams that reminded him of when the Wind Hounds killed the rockrats. The screaming of the creatures as the Wind Hounds' teeth cracked their tiny fragile bones while they ate them. Ellendrii had never quite got used to that. He had always tried to bite the heads off them as he ate them before they knew what was happening. Aro had just been amused by it. Cruel creature!

They walked for a long time. They didn't know when the sun was up in the sky or when the moon took its place. Which was probably just as well. All they focused on was getting out alive. They came to a small clearing and stopped for food. One dead rockrat each was enough to keep them going and Ellendrii was thankful for the satiating qualities of the little rodents.

Aro said nothing while they ate. Luckily eating didn't take long. They both had a drink afterwards and carried on in silence.

Aro wondered when Ellendrii would talk to him again.

They walked until they got tired and then they slept. They went off the path a little way and slept in the relative shelter of some bushes. They didn't want anything to try and attack them while they were asleep. Aro had the idea of one of them staying awake while the other rested but Ellendrii argued that that would take longer than both of them simply sleeping at once. So they slept and then they carried on.

Even though Ellendrii had been right, Aro partly thought he had argued the point with him because he was annoyed still.

It was then that things started to go strange and terror found its way in.

Aro was leading when Ellendrii heard something that sounded like a wounded Gryphie. He instinctively looked upwards into the branches of the dark trees above them and instantly wished he hadn't.

His heart skipped a beat in sheer fear as he saw them. Crawling, writhing, creeping along the branches of the trees, their red eyes glowing and gleaming in the dark, watching him. They made strange slithering noises and crackling sounds like breaking bones.

Then he heard it; whispering. He couldn't understand what it was saying but he heard voices whispering near him. Right next to his ear. He shook his head and flicked his ears, grumbling. Aro didn't hear him; he was too busy forcing a path through for them between the horrible dark bushes.

Ellendrii couldn't quite make out what these things were. Their bodies had no particular detail; they were just shapes in the trees, moving. Some things were discernible though, such at their sharp claws, eyes and occasionally their gleaming teeth. And the strange whispering, which was weirding him out.

"Aro, stop a minute" called Ellendrii and Aro stopped and looked round at him.

"What is it now?" he asked, sure Ellendrii would scold him again for what he'd done.

"Do you hear that?" asked Ellendrii. Aro listened.

"No I don't" he replied.

"Listen harder" said Ellendrii, although the whispering was loud enough that he couldn't possibly ignore it and he wondered why Aro couldn't hear it. Aro listened again.

"I really don't hear anything except the wind blowing in the trees" he said, puzzled. "What can you hear?" he asked.

"I hear creepy whispering. I can't make out the words but it's all around me. It's stopped now but it was right by my ears and there's nothing there."

"You're imagining it. I can't hear anything. It's your paranoia cos of the stuff we've heard about this forest. Just try and ignore it. Want to lead for a bit?"

"Yeah, sure, thanks. Maybe the sound of the bushes will shut out the sound of the whispering" agreed Ellendrii. Although he thought it was too real to be paranoia.

So he lead for a while and Aro followed.

Aro didn't notice any noise. But then he hadn't looked up at the trees. They had both been warned not to. It was only Ellendrii's shock and the conclusion he had jumped to that had made him look up, after all. Aro just concentrated on following Ellendrii and not getting smacked in the face by the Gryphie's tail.

Ellendrii had his wings shielding himself and he concentrated on the task at hand. However, though he thought it was going ok for a bit, he started to hear the whispering again. Almost as if something was sat on his shoulder, whispering in his ear. He shook his head and growled. This was getting on his nerves now. But it didn't stop. It kept on irritating him.

Finally he had had enough. It had been creepy to begin with but now it was annoying. He stopped, causing Aro, whose head had been down, to nearly bump into him.

"What is it? Found something that you need me to push through instead?" asked Aro.

"No, it's the whispering. I've had enough of it. I think it's whatever's in the trees. DON'T look up. I want to try something. I didn't hear the whispering until I looked up into the trees. I saw all these weird things crawling about up there. Like Kraarz told us. I want to see what my fire will do."

"You sure that's wise? The trees might burst into flames…"

"Yes and that's why we use glowbugs in the Forest back home instead of our fire. But here it doesn't matter."

"Ok, go for it" Aro sunk low on the ground in case anything bad happened. Ellendrii studied the beings up in the trees. They were still there, slinking and sliding, creeping and crawling around and peering at him. He aimed at some of them and then flamed into the trees.

Immediately they were surrounded by high pitched, deafening screams as the things were burned by the blue fire. They ran around through the trees trailing flames after them. But none of them jumped down onto the pair below. Even lit up by the blue fire, they still seemed like shapes without much detail except teeth, claws and eyes.

But the screaming and shrieking was deafening! Aro and Ellendrii both had to cover their ears.

"What the grik did you do that for? I thought you were just gunna flame into the trees and scare them, not set them alight!" roared Aro over the sound of the screaming.

"I didn't realize there were so many of them up there!" roared back Ellendrii.

"Let's get out of here!" roared Aro and they both ran for it, Aro leading because he was stronger and bulkier. Crashing through the undergrowth, their hearts beating furiously, the pair of them ran to get away from the screaming that rang in their ears. The longer they ran, the further away the screaming became, thankfully. But even after it died away they kept running, out of sheer fear.

Finally they stopped, sweating. They were exhausted and needed to rest. Aro sat down.

"NEVER do that again" he said.

"Don't…worry, I…won't" panted Ellendrii.

They rested for a while and carried on. The forest had slowly got darker and they could only see outlines of shapes via what little light filtered in through the trees. Which of course, they didn't dare look up at.

All sorts of different plants grew around them but the leaves were all black. Or looked black at least. They could have been very dark green for all the pair knew.

After a while, they came across a dark stream. The water flowed and sloshed across their path. It was narrow enough that they could jump over it though. Aro looked into it as they were about to cross it and leaped back.

"El…there…there's something in there…"

Ellendrii leaned down for a closer look and sure enough, he saw something. And the "stream" was far deeper than it appeared. He picked up a rock and tossed it in. Watching it, it disappeared into the depths of the water and didn't appear to hit the bottom although it was rather hard to see. The water rippled after the rock had sunk and it continued to ripple, almost as if the water itself was a living entity. Ellendrii shuddered.

"Probably best to just jump over it and not touch it. Don't even dunk your tail into it" he warned Aro.

But it was too late. The curious Lizariaous had dipped his tail blade into the water and was splashing it around slightly, wondering idly if it was safe to drink.

Suddenly, he felt something tugging on his tail, yanking it over and over, trying to pull him in. Aro panicked and scrabbled away, managing to pull his tail free. As he pulled, something rose out of the water for a split second, holding onto the end of his tail. It was black and oily looking. It quickly retreated back into the water and disappeared. Or it could have been lurking just below the surface; neither of them wanted to find out.

Aro and Ellendrii jumped over the stream and carried on quickly. It didn't do to dawdle in this place.

"Why does it all have to be creepy? Why can't there be something, at least a little thing that's nice? Even a friendly creature or at least a harmless meal creature or something?" said Aro.

"Cos it's the Forest of Foreboding and they wouldn't call it something like that unless it was scary beyond all reason" replied Ellendrii. Aro sighed and they carried on. They went swiftly, running would use up more energy and they didn't want to tire in case they needed to get away from something fast, so they walked or trotted in the clear parts and then forced their way through the overgrown parts.

As they got further in, oddly, there were less parts that were overgrown. It was almost like the forest was trying to keep things out, the way it was more overgrown around the outside as opposed to the inside. The two of them came across whole clearings that were just ashen soil and a few bushes here and there.

They still continued to go in a straight direction or at least as straight as they could. Sometimes they would come across an obstacle that blocked their path and they would have to find a way around it. It wasn't so bad with the smaller obstacles like impenetrable bushes that they could just push their way around and not through, but it became difficult when the obstacle was something larger.

At one point they came across a cave. Their straight line dictated that they had to go through it but neither of them wanted to do that so they had to find a way around it. Climbing up the side proved difficult and Ellendrii couldn't spread his wings to fly Aro up and over it because the trees were too closely packed. So they had to go right out of their way to get around it and then hope that they would continue in a straight line afterwards. They figured that if they kept going in the same direction, they would reach the other side of the forest eventually. They would know if they had gone the right way because of course of the little creatures in their trees they should meet on the other side. They would have been happier if they were able to just go through in a straight line though but as far as they were aware, they hadn't got turned around or anything so they were on the right track.

Still having no real idea of time, sun or moon cycles, they carried on, only eating when they were starving and drinking a little more often than that.

They stopped again for a rest and a meal and then slept a little. Then they carried on.

After a while and not having been attacked by anything, they became more relaxed in the forest. Sure it was a horrible place, smelled weird and sounded weird, but if they could ignore that then it wasn't so bad.

Aro decided that since it had been a while, to talk about when Ellendrii fetched his bag and the gourds.

"When you went back to get the gourds, did you see anyone other than Sarris?" It was more to start a conversation since they hadn't really talked at length since they entered the forest.

"No. Well I didn't see anyone who tried to chase me or knew what you did. I flew up high when I passed Lord Scerniss and the others. Why the grik did you say something negative about it when Lord Scerniss was right near us?" asked Ellendrii.

"I only meant for *you* to hear it" muttered Aro.

"But you *knew* that their culture revolves around listening. Did it not even occur to you that the ears of the Wind Hounds were very sensitive? If he hadn't heard, one of the Wind Hounds stood near us would have."

"I know, I know. I was stupid. I regret it even now and I've never regretted insulting others before. We do it all the time in Dyarkroeen. But don't you think Lord Scerniss was a bit full of himself at times?"

"A little. But he *was* their king. What did you expect? Sierra and Reo are full of themselves and they're the leaders of the Sky Gryphies. I guess it's a leader thing. I thought he was pretty kind and he respected us cos we respected him. Until of course you messed up."

"Yeah, well my Dad is the leader of our pack and he's not full of himself at all. Being a leader doesn't mean you *have* to be stuck up."

"Yes but these are different cultures than what we're used to, we have to respect them. What if the Wind Hounds had caught you? What if they had injured or maimed you or punished you in other ways?"

"You could have protected me with your fire. And if they'd dared corner me, then I would have poisoned a few before I went" Aro snorted and snarled.

"They would still have killed you though. You'd have run out of needles and what good would that have done?"

301

"I would have taken some with me. And not just with my needles, with my teeth and claws as well. I would have left the image of sheer carnage in their minds and memories because they had dared attacked me. So even if they killed me, they wouldn't have completely won. They would've had to live with that mental image."

"Hmm I guess. But all the same if we bump into any other advanced cultures, PLEASE don't say anything negative. At all. Not even privately just in case someone hears. Because next time you might not be able to outrun them. You nearly couldn't this time."

"Ok, ok. I'll hold it next time. It was only an opinion though; I still think he overreacted. It wasn't like I went up to him and said his culture was awful or his species were dumb. It could've been a whole lot worse."

Ellendrii groaned.

"But you KNEW how much their culture meant to them. It wasn't just insulting the funeral; it was insulting their very rituals. And that *was* even worse."

Aro still didn't understand really but he didn't want to argue anymore, just in case his friend stopped talking to him again. After all, most of their journey in the forest so far had been done in silence. He decided to change the subject.

"What do you think of the forest so far?" he asked.

"Not much. It's a dismal place, just like Kraarz said it would be. I'm a bit less worried about dangers here though since we haven't encountered much. And it's less overgrown now too. Those bushes scratched my wings. I just hope we don't run out of food. Rationing is hard. But those rockrats seem to satiate me for long enough. I haven't slept well since hearing that whispering though."

"Did you ever manage to make out any of the words?"

"Nope. It's weird. Maybe they spoke a different language that we can't understand, you know, like a sea vulture or a forest deer. They just make noises but I'm sure they can understand each other. Whatever it was, it sounded creepy and foreboding and it had threatening undertones as well. Like they were telling us to get out and leave them alone or I guess they could have been warning us…"

"And then you flamed them" sniggered Aro.

"I needed them to shut up. I know they're everywhere. I know they're up there right now watching us but at least they aren't whispering to us."

"I wonder what I would make of the whispering though…" mumbled Aro.

"Don't you DARE look up there. We don't need more problems. At the moment it's ok, there's nothing bothering us or attacking us but who knows what might happen if you look up there. Don't grik things up again, Aro."

"Ok, ok, fine" Aro mooched. "It's not like I mess up all the time. It's not like I'm always doing things wrong. I did ONE little thing wrong and you're never going to forgive me are you?"

"No, Aro, you don't get it. You did ONE little thing wrong and that ONE thing messed up our friendship with a WHOLE species. If we come back this way, they won't let us pass without a fight. What's more is that they've probably destroyed our float to make sure we don't make it back across the vast water. Do you see how badly you grikked up NOW??" Ellendrii snapped at him.

Then it finally dawned on Aro and his face paled slightly.

"Grik" he said, "I do. I really need to keep my mouth shut. To be honest, I did to begin with but they were so nice to us that I relaxed and then I forgot to keep my mouth shut."

"Well next time, DON'T forget!" growled Ellendrii.

"I won't" said Aro quietly.

They continued on a while before Ellendrii spoke again. Mostly to change the mood.

"I wonder how much longer we'll be in here. We haven't encountered any of the other scary things Kraarz told me about yet. Like those rat things that steal eyes. Ergh, they sound horrible."

"Probably just as well. But then again I wouldn't be scared of something like that. Rockrats aren't scary, they're too small to be scary so these other rats can't be scary either."

"He said they float though…and bleed all the time and only have half a body…" muttered Ellendrii.

"Pfft, they sound silly. They'd bleed to death if they bled all the time. He must've imagined it."

Ellendrii suddenly turned to him, looked him in the eyes and spoke in a low tone.

"Maybe they *are* dead…" he said. Then they both laughed. What a silly notion!

They carried on for a while. Then they heard something. It sounded like rain but nothing in the forest was wet. It was all still dry and the earth was still ashen and grey. It was raining above the canopy and the trees were so densely packed that the rain wasn't getting through. Ellendrii wanted so badly to look up at the source of the rain noise but he knew better and so did Aro. Aro was determined not to mess up again with any of his actions. So the pair of them listened and didn't look. The noise was strangely calming. It reminded Ellendrii of his home back in the Forest and he suddenly felt very homesick. Even though this place was a forest also, since it looked nothing like the Gryphie Forest, it hadn't really reminded him much of it. But now he heard that sound, he thought of his home and his parents. Of Lunara as well and the things she taught him before they left.

"I miss home" he muttered to Aro, "I want to sit in the trees but these ones I can't even climb or I might be attacked. I've been two sun cycles without flying. I think I'm getting withdrawal."

"We'll be out of here soon. How many sun cycles did that Wind Hound say this would take? Four?"

"With running" replied Ellendrii.

"Well then let's run" suggested Aro.

"We can't, you know we can't. We need our speed if something attacks us. I miss flying so much. I've never gone even a single sun cycle without flying, not even when I've been sick."

"We can run for a bit though can't we? If it means we won't tire ourselves out?"

"Ok. It would make me feel better. We'll run. Not too fast. We'll pace ourselves."

So they ran for a bit in a similar fashion to what we would call jogging. Since the paths were clearer further in, there wasn't anything to impede their journey. And since they didn't run that fast, they didn't tire much either and could run for longer.

Finally they stopped and walked a little more.

Ellendrii pricked up his ears.

"Aro, do you hear that?"

"Not more whispering" Aro sighed. "Just ignore it"

"No, no not whispering. More like wheezing, like a shuddering sound. Like something that's struggling to breathe or when it's cold and you shudder or shudder from fear…"

Aro pricked his ears up too and paused from his walking.

"Yeah actually I do hear something but it's faint…"

The two listened, hardly daring to breathe, so they could hear better. They strained their ears at the sound. It was faint and didn't seem to get any louder. Eventually Aro got bored.

"It's no threat, come on, let's continue. We don't want to wait around too long in case something finds us and attacks us. I know nothing has yet but I feel better if we keep moving."

Ellendrii agreed and they continued. They still heard the sound on and off but it never got any louder and in the end it just became like any other sound in this weird place and they ignored it.

When they first arrived in the forest, any little movement or noise put them on edge but as the sun cycles wore on, they got ever more relaxed about it. Of course it would have been foolish to drop their guard completely and they still slept in rotas with one watching while the other slept but they gradually felt more at ease. They found that if they ignored the noises and didn't let the sounds get to them, that they could get on perfectly well.

They chatted and Ellendrii sang a little as well. Aro tried to sing too but his singing was pretty bad. Sometimes Gryphies sing, for sheer joy of being alive or flying or being in the trees or a good hunt. They are good singers and should really sing more often but it is just to show their emotions. This time, Ellendrii sang more to take their minds off the noises around them when they had nothing else to talk about.

They played a few verbal games too, ones similar to "I spy". They thought briefly about playing a game for hearing but decided swiftly against that. After all, some of the things they had heard were pretty disturbing. A scream, for example, not to mention the wheezing and shuddering noises.

Ellendrii tried to tell Aro some jokes and vice versa but neither of them found the other's jokes very funny so they stopped that.

It was then that they stopped dead and stared in horror at the ground. Until now, the ground had just been the ashen grey and dusty, as though it got no water at all. However, right here and blocking their path was a vast patch of red, fresh blood. And the smell. It was an overpowering smell of death. They stared at the blood. They couldn't walk round it and it was too wide to jump across. And what would they find the other side? The thing that had caused the blood? And it wasn't just a light patch either; some of it was fairly deep and there were…things floating in it. Unspeakable things that filled the pair with pure fear when they looked at them. They could only guess that these things were something to do with the innards of a body that had been killed. But there was SO much blood. It had splattered on the bushes and tree trunks surrounding the patch. What could have made so much blood? This wasn't just a killing. This had been done in such a way that whatever had killed this thing had played with it. It had literally taken it apart to create the biggest mess it could. A normal killing would not make this much blood. It was almost as if the creature had exploded right there where it had stood. This also worried the pair.

"What do we do, Aro?" asked Ellendrii. Aro usually had a better stomach for these things since Lizariaouses were sometimes known to play with their food. But this wasn't anything like that. Whatever it was had been torn apart.

"We'll have to walk through it" said Aro.

"Ergh, really? Well I guess you're right, there's no way around it. Have you ever seen anything like this?"

"Nope. We kill in a similar fashion sometimes; we tear the food apart if it was particularly hard to catch. We tend to take our temper out on it. But not like this. This is like the hunter wanted to count the organs of the meal creature or something. It's been messily dissected" Aro observed.

"Ok, well if we dash through it" said Ellendrii, "We might get less on us"

"If we dash through it, it will splash everywhere" replied Aro.

"Fine, then I guess we go slowly…" Ellendrii rose up on his hind legs. May as well walk two legged; no point in getting everything dirty. But when he put a foot in the putrid, stinking red goop, he pulled it out fast with a yelp.

"Agh! It burns me!" he yelped. Aro rolled his eyes and put a foot in it. It wasn't long though before he had to pull it back out. His paw was burning badly and the feeling didn't go once he'd taken it out.

"Grik. How do we get across? We could dash but it would splash onto our bodies. I don't have enough room to fly and walking over it won't help at all." Ellendrii growled at the red puddle of unwholesome evil. As if that would help.

"We'll have to cover it first" suggested Aro. He started to dig up the dirt at the edge of the puddle and kick it in, in an effort to build up a layer of dirt they could walk across. But the dirt just sank in. It would take a LOT in order to actually get enough to walk across it unscathed.

"Aro, Aro!! Stop. It's not working. We'll have to find something else to put on it to get across it. Like some fallen wood or something. Leaves won't work. Look for logs or rocks we can put in it" Ellendrii said, putting a hand on Aro's shoulder to stop him digging in vain.

So they looked for something to help them cross the blood puddle.

Neither of them had ever encountered anything like this before. Blood didn't burn you! What kind of creature had made this?? Ellendrii was glad they had bought food with them. He assumed that the acidic blood was some sort of defence mechanism a creature could use as a last ditch effort to survive. Maybe that was why the hunter had spread it around. Maybe the hunter had got the blood on themselves and panicked and that was why it had gone everywhere? Ellendrii pondered this as he looked for rocks to put down and cover over the blood puddle. Even though it was too wide to jump without hurting themselves, it wasn't so wide that they needed a lot to cover it and make a path across.

Aro had found a large log and was pushing and struggling with it to get it over to the puddle. He managed to, uprooting a load of bushes and plants in doing so. He pushed it into the bloody puddle and shoved it as far as it would go before his paws would touch the sickening mess. Ellendrii followed with some rocks. They could now get across it.

The two of them rushed across swiftly. Ellendrii was a little worried what they had put down would sink. He was nearly right. Although it wasn't deep enough to sink in; the blood was slowly eating away at the rocks and log and they soon dissolved into it. The two friends shuddered in horror. Ellendrii wondered if there really *was* something that had that inside its body. It was hard to believe after what they had just witnessed.

"I hope we never encounter anything like that again" said Ellendrii quietly. Aro nodded in agreement.

After a rest and some water, the two of them continued on their way. At times, the murky, horrible forest made Aro regret going with Ellendrii and it made Ellendrii regret going on this silly journey. Quite often the two of them were filled with doubt but they just continued on because they couldn't stop and couldn't go back. Not that they wanted to now. It would have made their journey so far into the Forest of Foreboding a waste of time.

"This place is massive" said Aro, "I think we've been in here more than four sun cycles. The Wind Hounds were running and they are much faster than us. They have more stamina too. I've lost count. I don't know when it's sun or moon. It all seems the same in here."

"I know. It's really disorienting. I don't like it but what can we do? There's no way I can fly up and have a look. I haven't even looked up into the trees since that whole awful encounter with those whispering ghouls up there. I'm just glad they don't come down here."

They had heard the things running around in the trees but they had got so used to it by now that it was just background noise like everything else and they just ignored it.

Sometimes when they rested, they played games to raise spirits. Ellendrii and Aro played "Which One?" which was a game in which Ellendrii would hide a small item under one of his hands or feet and Aro would have to try and guess which one it was hidden under. The Lizariaous grew bored of it after a while though.

"I'm scared about when we run out of food. There's only two rockrats left" said Ellendrii.

"We'll just have to keep drinking and keep going. We can go a while without food. I hope we reach the end of this stupid forest soon though. It got boring ages ago" retorted Aro. They had one gourd of water left and decided not to eat the last two rockrats unless they were really hungry. And they would share each rockrat. So, half each. It would help them last longer. Maybe half a rockrat was just as filling? They sure hoped so!

Up ahead, Ellendrii saw something and perked his ears up.

"What's that?" he asked, even though Aro probably wouldn't know.

"I dunno" replied Aro, predictably.

Upon closer inspection, the two discovered it was a vast structure. Maybe a temple or something? They weren't sure. Up until meeting the Wind Hounds, the two of them had rarely seen things that had been built by individuals. Trees and caves such as the two of them lived in were natural things. The closest either of them got to building was digging, in the case of Lizariaouses making more caves. This thing reminded them a little of something that was lived in by Wind Hounds. Like Lord Scerniss' temple. Only it was dilapidated. Black vines twisted their way around it. Some of it was only held together simply because the vines bound it together. The roof was missing in places and other parts were crumbling. The temple was made of a dark grey stone and looked just as foreboding as the forest it resided within. There were no carvings upon its walls but they did find a hideous carved sculpture at the centre of it. It featured a creature in a threatening stance with a horrible face, long arms, horns on its head and a wide, terrible mouth full of sickle-like teeth surrounded by wide, nasty looking lips. Two hollow, black eyes stared out at them and it had a sunken, grotesque nose. The two of them shivered looking at it and when they turned away, the face of the thing seemed to be imprinted under their eyelids so they could see it when they blinked.

"Who do you think lived here?" asked Aro, "That thing?" he motioned to the statue but didn't look at it. It was too hideous to look at for too long. The thing was crumbling a little but no vines grew on it like on the rest of the place. It was almost as if the very plants were scared to go near it.

"I dunno. But whatever did live here isn't here anymore. This place has been abandoned for many seasons. I can't smell the scent of anything living here. Only death, plants and blood." Ellendrii replied.

"Speaking of blood…" Aro trailed off and pointed to the ground. Ellendrii looked. There were spots of blood here and there, as though something had been injured and dripped blood in places.

"I hope it's not the burning kind that we encountered before" muttered Ellendrii. Aro touched it gingerly.

"Nope. It's just blood. As harmless as ours I reckon."

"Thank grik for that" replied Ellendrii. "We don't need any more weird things happening for the time being. Some of it looks fresher than other spots. Almost as if whatever dripped it wandered around a lot and kept coming back here."

The two of them observed the blood patches for a while before wandering on, exploring the temple. It was different so they took a little time to look around. They had become tired with wandering through the forest and seeing nothing but plants and trees all the time and the occasional obstacle in their path.

Gradually, the pair split up to look around. Ellendrii was walking up some stone stairs when he heard it. The strange rasping, wheezing, shuddering sound they had heard before. Only this time it was much louder. He pricked his ears up and looked around.

And then he saw it.

Chapter 17
Running from Repulsators

Ellendrii stared at the thing that floated before him. He couldn't take his eyes off it. It was hideous and obscure. It was just like Kraarz had said. It was a brown rat with the lower half of its body ripped away under the front legs. It had a ribcage but below that, there was nothing. Where the body ended, it was as though it had been ripped in half. The flesh was shredded and sodden with fresh blood. The spinal cord carried on past where the body had ended and it hung down white and bony. A few internal organs could be seen hanging just below the shredded flesh and they dripped with blood. That had been the blood spots the two of them had seen around this horrible place. The rat's eyes were atrophied and shrivelled, completely blind. But in its mouth, held in place by its yellow/orange incisors was a bloodshot eyeball that swivelled around to look at its surroundings. Not a rat eyeball, which would have been mostly black, but an eyeball from a different creature. This one resembled a human eyeball if we were to look at it. A bloodshot white sclera with a green iris and black pupil. The pupil dilated and retracted in a horrible manner as the creature focused on Ellendrii. The forepaws scratched the air, reaching out for him as the Repulsator floated closer. Its nose twitched and sniffed the air, the whiskers quivering. And it made a horrible shuddering, wheezing sound like it was breathing its own internal fluids.

Ellendrii growled at it and charged up his fire as it got closer. It didn't seem to listen to his warning growl though even though its ears looked sensitive. So he flamed it. Only a short burst just to set it alight. He didn't want the same thing that had happened before to happen again. The Repulsator crackled and choked at him, the blue flames engulfing it but it wasn't burning. The fire soon went out and the thing continued to come towards Ellendrii.

That was it; Ellendrii wasn't sticking around to learn any more about this terrifying creature. He turned tail and fled down the stairs. He needed to find Aro so they could get out of there.

Aro though, had his own grisly encounter. He had been wandering through the rooms of this weird temple, looking out for any other hideous statues or the thing that had caused the blood. He was wandering along a crumbling hallway when he heard a whimper and yelp. Worried that it was Ellendrii, he went to check it out. Standing in the entrance to the chamber where the sound was coming from, he saw the source. He didn't dare go to help though.

A creature lay prone on its side on the ground. Surrounding it were Repulsators. Three of them were slashing at the creature's belly while another two were gouging out its eyes. Nearby another Repulsator lay on its side, occasionally twitching or reaching for its comrades. It squirmed and flopped, looking like a regular Repulsator but minus the floating and the eyeball in its mouth. Its mouth opened and closed with an unnerving eagerness and its blind, shrivelled eye sockets blinked even though they couldn't see.

The two who were busy removing the eyes of the creature finally managed to pop the eyeballs out one by one and carried them in their paws to the blind one. They floated over it quite low, placing an eyeball near its mouth. The blind one's nose twitched eagerly and it pulled its half body over to the eyeball, taking it gently in its mouth and securing the eyeball with its incisors. It lay there for a moment, the eyeball remaining unmoving in its mouth. The body of the Repulsator throbbed and twitched as though things were being rearranged inside and the eyeball in its mouth started to swivel around, looking at its surroundings. The thing rose slowly off the ground and joined its brethren in the air. The others all looked at it and shuddered with what Aro could only assume was glee. The one who had the other eyeball floated off somewhere, Aro presumed to another eyeless Repulsator. Aro didn't move. He thought he could take these things on. They seemed feeble. But the creature that was dead was much bigger than the Repulsators and looked quite capable of looking after itself. He wondered if they had found it there or brought it down themselves. Luckily the room they were in was missing a wall so they flew through that and didn't head out of the entranceway where Aro stood.

He didn't wait around either though; he needed to find Ellendrii and fast!

Ellendrii meanwhile was of course looking for Aro. This place was bigger than either of them had first assumed. He saw more Repulsators flying around overhead. They could fly pretty high but they didn't fly above the roof of the place or at least, where the roof would have been in the parts where it was missing. Now he had seen one, he seemed to see more of them.

Turning a corner, he saw a group of Repulsators gouging out the eyes of a living creature. To us, the creature would have looked like a monkey. Ellendrii had never seen anything like a monkey before though and this was a new creature to him. The poor thing was covered in Repulsators that held it down and scratched and slashed it into submission while two others took its eyes. They all flew off after achieving their vile goal and left the poor monkey-like creature to stumble around in pain and confusion and fall off the wall it had been atop of, to the ground to fumble around in the dirt, pawing at the bloody holes where its eyes had been.

And the screaming. Ellendrii couldn't take it and he ran to get away from it.

He wanted to call for Aro but he was afraid the Repulsators would hear so he didn't. He just ran around swiftly, hoping he would bump into his friend. And once again flying would do him no good since the Repulsators could fly and they would find him all the more easily if he tried that tactic. All the time he kept looking up to see what was above him. This was a time when he *could* look to the sky. Not that he could see the sky. Again, it was either the ceiling of whatever room he was in or the trees or vines covering the rooms that didn't have ceilings.

The shuddering sound was all around him, coming from all directions at this point. He didn't know if there were more of them around because of the time of sun cycle, because it was their hunting time, because they knew he and Aro were there or simply because they had reached a part of the derelict temple where the awful beings resided.

Aro was getting very unnerved by these rat-like monstrosities. One came right at him at one point and he smacked it to the ground with a powerful swipe of his paw. The Repulsator simply floated back up into the air again and went towards him, shuddering and wheezing. Aro shot a surprisingly well aimed needle at it, which impaled it right the way through but the creature still came at him, only now with a needle going through its horrible sagging body. It did seem to gargle and shudder more angrily at him though. Soon, another found them and pursued Aro as well. He ended up managing to lose them by hiding in a small alcove. He sat there in the dark for a while, glad of his black skin to hide him in the shadows. He somewhat selfishly hoped that Ellendrii would find him. Then again Ellendrii could be hiding and waiting for Aro to find him also. Aro was willing to take the chance that he wasn't though. Because Aro was very scared right now. The mere sight of the Repulsators was enough to send a shiver down his spine, let alone the sight of one coming towards him with that awful eyeball swivelling in its jaws and that twitching, whiskery nose and those reaching handlike paws, clawing the air almost as if Aro's very eyes drew the creature to him like a magnet.

Aro didn't want to admit even to himself that he was scared. He kept telling himself that he was hiding not out of fear but out of common sense. He couldn't kill these things so he was hiding from them. They might go away after all, who knows?

Ellendrii was running around desperately searching for Aro so they could get out of this dreadful place. He had seen more Repulsators hunting and had encountered a few more of them too but still couldn't seem to be able to kill them. It was like they were halfway between the living and the dead and he could hear them all around him. Luckily the ones he had encountered had only been one or two and not a group of them. He had no idea how he would defend himself against several of the vile creatures.

Some time had passed though and he still couldn't find Aro. He was trying to sniff him out but all he smelled was blood and decay and it made his nose sting and run. He coughed a bit. Then of course he started to worry. What if they'd got Aro?

He needn't have worried for long though because it was at that very moment that he tripped over Aro's tail. Turning around, he saw the hidden Lizariaous in the alcove. Aro dared not speak in case the Repulsators heard him so he had put his tail out for Ellendrii to trip over. Not the best way of getting his attention. It had hurt both of them a little.

"There you are! I thought those awful things had got you!" said Ellendrii in a low voice as he joined Aro in the alcove.

"They didn't but it was close. I saw them taking a dead animal's eyes to put in one of their own kind. It was horrid" muttered Aro.

"You're lucky you saw them take eyes from something that was already dead" said Ellendrii and Aro stared at him in horror.

"I NEVER want to see anything like that again in my whole life" said Ellendrii with a horrified shudder.

"My poison doesn't work on them" said Aro quietly. "I tried to lash out at one but my claws did nothing to it. I don't know how to kill them."

"Neither do I. We'll just have to make our way out of here as fast as we can. Unfortunately I'm not sure which way we have to go to get out, nor am I sure of if we're even heading in a straight direction anymore. We may have got turned around somewhere in here. I can't smell anything, I can't smell our way out of here and if I fly up, they'll see me and probably swarm me like I've seen them do to other creatures. Let's hurry and sneak out. Aro?"

Ellendrii was about to go when he realized his friend wasn't following him.

"Aro, come on!" he said but Aro didn't move.

"I...I'm scared. We can't kill them. How do we escape if they attack us? What if they gouge out *our* eyes too?" Aro was very embarrassed to admit that he was scared but right now he felt safe sitting in the alcove. While he'd been there, he'd seen Repulsators floating past and none of them had looked in there for him.

"We have to take that chance. There must be *some* way to kill them. Nothing is unkillable. Besides, you can't sit there forever. We need to go. NOW!"

But Aro still sat where he was and didn't move.

"I...I can't. I'm tired. I'm sick of this place. I..." but he was cut off when his friend unceremoniously bit him on the leg. Aro leaped up with an angry roar.

"WHAT THE GRIK??" he roared and automatically lunged at Ellendrii, who fled. Aro chased him before he knew what was happening. And that was precisely why Ellendrii had bitten him. He knew Aro would bite back first and ask questions later.

Unfortunately, the roar that Aro had so loudly let go also made their presence known to the Repulsators around them and a few were now also pursuing Ellendrii as well as Aro was. The two of them ran around all over the place with their creepy halfbodied enemies in tow. The Repulsators all shuddered in unison, which scared Ellendrii and Aro even more. Because they were now fleeing the Repulsators, they were no longer paying as much attention to where they were running and instead of fleeing the temple; they were getting more and more lost within it.

I really wish I'd asked Kraarz more about these things or how he and his brother escaped here. I thought these rat things would be in the forest and we could just run from them. We're getting more and more lost in this place. And it all looks the same as well. I can't tell if we've run past this part or that part over there or if we've doubled back to where we came in although I haven't seen a way in or out of here.

Suddenly Ellendrii skidded to a halt as a Repulsator came right at him, clawing at his eyes and shuddering in excitement. The horrible eyeball in its mouth rolled around, the Repulsator's saliva keeping it moist in the place of blinking. The thing drooled at Ellendrii and wheezed. Its hideous death rattle filled his head.

Ellendrii flamed it but the same thing happened as before and his flames just ended up going out, leaving the Repulsator unscathed.

"GRIK!" roared Ellendrii and pounced on it, biting its neck in the way that one would normally kill one's prey. He bit and tore, twisting his head and breaking its neck with a nauseating crack as the bones came apart.

Panting, he backed off.

"Take that!" he snapped at it, growling. The thing curdled and gurgled, unable to move its broken neck. The eyeball looked up at Ellendrii and the spinal column lay limp. Then the body started to pop and crackle and the Repulsator rose into the air, lifting its head like it had never been broken. It shook its head and hissed at Ellendrii, clawing at him and coming towards him again.

Ellendrii was getting very pissed off by this time. He dived on it again, ripping and shredding it, breaking its neck again and ripping off its forelegs. He pushed it into the ground, crushing its body beneath his weight, feeling the crack of its delicate ribs. Over and over he lunged, stamping on it until it was nearly flat, embedded into the ground. He'd crushed its skull as well and torn one of its ears off.

He threw his head back and gave off an earth shattering roar in anger and victory, nostrils flaring with a blue fiery glow. Eyes burning and his body heaving with the effort of his recent victory, he stared down at the shattered body of the Repulsator and he growled low in his throat, just daring it to come back to life after *that* level of destruction.

But his eyes grew wide and he stepped back a pace when the Repulsator's body was pulled up out of the ground by some unseen force and floated into the air again. Ellendrii shook his head in disbelief. There was NO way that the thing could come back after he had completely decimated it. But sure enough it was. He heard its bones cracking back into place. Popping and churning inside its body and the forelegs floated to it, re-attaching themselves. The eyeball in its mouth swivelled around and glared at him angrily, the pupil retracting to a slit.

Ellendrii thought quickly and came up with a plan. Diving at the Repulsator again, he tore it apart, scattering its organs around the ground, crushing its body, ripping off its forelegs and decimating it as he had done before.

He stood back and waited and sure enough it started to reform itself again. Only this time he didn't let it. He leaped up into the air, caught it down, and destroyed it again. It ended up being barely recognizable as a rat, or any other creature for that matter.

With every leap, every pounce, every stamp into the ground, Ellendrii yelled "DIE!! DIE!!!" because by this time he was beyond wound up and he was sure that if he got the thing while it was trying to regenerate that he would get it for good.

He sat down on his rump, panting and staring at the mess that he had made. That was it! It had worked! That was what they had to do to kill these things! No, wait…was that movement? No, couldn't be. His imagination. No, wait, it was! The wretched thing is coming back to life again! Mustn't let it!

He pounced on it again but this time it floated up out of his reach and away, almost as if whatever was controlling it was trying to get it away from him so it could heal. Ellendrii couldn't understand it though. He'd broken all its bones, he'd smashed its body up, he'd spilled its guts all over the ground. HOW could it possibly come back from that?? So you couldn't kill these things.

Nearby, Aro was having no better luck. He had also found out that the Repulsators could regenerate and heal themselves. He was ripping them apart and shredding them, destroying them but every time they healed themselves and came back at him again. Neither of the friends could understand how these things could do that.

"They must be ghosts!" yelled Aro, "They can't be killed. We'll just have to run for it. If they attack us, throw them off and run faster!"

Ellendrii agreed that this was a good idea.

However, because the pair were putting up such a fight, the Repulsators thought all the more that they had especially good eyes and were worth pursuing. Instead of being put off by the challenge, these creatures chased them all the more and wouldn't stop or give up.

Ellendrii really wanted them off their tail so he could concentrate more on where they were going and how to get out. Right now they were just running in any direction to get away from their attackers. And they were inevitably starting to tire.

"I can't keep running forever" yelled Ellendrii, "We have to rest!"

"But…how?" breathed Aro, "Without being attacked?"

"We have to figure out how to kill them or at least disable them long enough that we can lose them!" yelled Ellendrii.

"Well, the only weakness is they have no legs but we both know how they've got around *that* particular problem" yelled back Aro.

"Eyes are important to them though" yelled Ellendrii, "Maybe if we blind them?"

"What, by ripping out their eyeballs or something? Cos their actual eyes ARE blind" roared Aro.

"Yes, let's do that!" called back Ellendrii and now they had a plan. There was a swarm of Repulsators following them now so it wasn't hard to slow down, turn around and pick one to blind. However, when the pair slowed down and turned, it enabled the Repulsators to dive on them and start clawing them into submission.

"You sure this was a good idea?" growled Aro in frustration.

"Just grab one and blind it!" roared back Ellendrii. Aro grumbled and tried to pounce on one nearby but the others were dragging down his body by now and it was a problem trying to jump into the air to get one.

Ellendrii was having less trouble on account of because his wings helped him. He was batting the creatures away with his wings and so it gave him a better chance of grabbing one. However, the swarm was getting bigger and in order to concentrate on blinding one of them, he would have to leave his body undefended. As soon as he'd grabbed a Repulsator and used his hand to grab hold of its eyeball, the rest of them that had been following him flew down and started clawing him viciously. And it hurt! A lot!

Ellendrii tried to ignore it and yanked on the eyeball of the one he was holding. The thing screamed at him and tried to claw him with its forepaws. He held the forepaws together with one hand and used his other hand to pull out its eye.

"Let's see how YOU like it" he growled and pulled harder. It was amazingly well attached to the creature though and he had to put quite a bit of strength into it. Again, the damage the others were doing to him really wasn't helping. His body felt raw. But with one final yank, he pulled out its eye.

With the eye came everything else. Like all its other organs were attached to the back of the eyeball and so in pulling out its eye, he gutted it as well.

"ARO! DON'T WASTE TIME!! PULL OUT THEIR EYEBALLS!" roared Ellendrii and set upon another one.

Aro was a bit better at it simply because he used his jaws, which were stronger than Ellendrii's hands. Ellendrii had used his hands because he didn't really fancy putting his mouth near such a horrible creature.

Aro pounced on one, held it down with his paws and pulled its eye out. A strand of glistening internal organs followed and Aro spat out the eye in surprise and disgust.

Even though the pair of them had killed their fellows, the other Repulsators didn't let up. They knew, as with most predatory animals, that sometimes you lose a few before killing something truly worth it.

Aro dispensed with all the Repulsators who were attacking him with relative ease. Then he went and helped Ellendrii with the ones who were attacking him.

Ellendrii had killed a few of them but he was hurting pretty badly from the claws and scratches the rest of them had inflicted upon him.

However, soon the pair of them had killed all their attackers and were sitting in the middle of a ratty battle field, amidst the carnage of death and entrails.

"It was a good idea of yours to kill them that way" said Aro. Ellendrii nodded but it was too painful to speak. He turned to his leather bag and unfastened the flap on the front, lifting it and looking inside for some healing lotion Lunara had made for him before they'd left.

"Not here" said Aro, seeing Ellendrii try to rub some on. Ellendrii looked up.

"Let's go somewhere cleaner and less bloody" suggested Aro and helped his friend to a low wall a little way away where they could sit and Ellendrii could see to his wounds more easily.

He first washed his hands with a little water, though he was loathed to use their precious water for that but he didn't want to infect himself with unclean hands. Aro did the same with his paws and rubbed the lotion on parts that Ellendrii couldn't reach.

The two of them then rested awhile.

"Now we know how to kill those things, we can concentrate on getting out of here and away from them" said Ellendrii.

"I think we heard them in the forest though" said Aro, looking around.

"No, it was only because we were getting close to their territory. I think they only reside in this derelict temple. We could hear them from in here. I didn't realize this place was so big."

Ellendrii looked around. Here and there, Repulsators floated around but didn't attack either of them. It seemed that they only attacked en masse if they thought the victim was worth it, or had good eyes or if they actually *saw* the victim. After all, they didn't attack for food it seemed; but because they wanted to make more of themselves. Like breeding, only in a weird way.

"I wonder how they eat" muttered Aro, looking up at the few that floated around in the distance.

"I have no idea and I don't want to find out" replied Ellendrii. "Having them attack us for our eyes is bad enough. I don't think they *do* eat, you know. They can't, with an eyeball in their mouth."

"Then how do they live?" asked Aro.

"They bleed constantly. How do they live with *that*?" replied Ellendrii.

321

"Ok, point taken. Maybe this is all a dream and we're asleep back in the Wind Hound territory and we never went here after all. Because none of this makes sense."

Ellendrii agreed that it was all rather odd. And creepy. Living all their lives in Shernaron and Dyarkroeen seemed rather sheltered compared to the things they were experiencing in the big wide world.

"So now we know how to kill them, it shouldn't be too hard to get out of here" said Ellendrii, pondering.

"Ergh this place is like a maze" grumbled Aro, "How are your wounds doing?"

"Itchy, but ok. The lotion will keep them clean and free from infection" replied Ellendrii.

Aro smiled. At least one thing was going right.

"Ok, according to my instincts, we need to go in that direction" said Ellendrii, pointing.

"Well then, let's get going before those creatures decide they want our eyes again" said Aro.

The pair set off again. This temple seemed more like a derelict city the way it went on and on like that. But it was only one structure. Repulsators watched them from the shadows and cracks in the walls, their creepy eyeballs swivelling in their jaws as the pair walked past them. Maybe word had got round that these two knew how to kill Repulsators. They were generally left alone now but occasionally, a small swarm of the horrible creatures did try their luck. Aro and Ellendrii fought them off valiantly but Ellendrii still got scratched badly from it. Aro's skin, being thicker and tougher stood up to the clawing much better. So they had to stop and apply more lotion to him. Luckily they only needed a small amount of lotion so they wouldn't use it all up. Lunara had made sure she mixed a batch of the most potent healing lotion that she could, for that very reason.

Presently, they came upon a large room that contained more creepy statues. Some of them had some sort of gemstone inlaid into the eyes. One had two huge round red crystal eyes that stared at them and a hideous mouth similar to the previous one they'd seen. Its paws were raised in a threatening manner again and it appeared to have four arms, although some of the paws were missing. The statues lined the room facing each other, so the two friends would have to walk through the statues. They headed along the room, with statues on either side of them, glaring at them menacingly.

"I wish those rat-things would come and take the gems out of these statues' eyes" whispered Aro.

"I know; they're *so* creepy" murmured Ellendrii. For some reason they didn't want to speak loudly. That is until Ellendrii tripped up and yelped. His voice echoed around the room and there was a grinding sound. The statues were starting to move. Towards them!

On either side the statues slowly ground towards them, their creepy clawed paws reaching out for the pair and the gem eyes glowing.

"What the…" Aro stared at the nearest one, stupidly transfixed.

"Aro, MOVE!" roared Ellendrii and shoved him forwards. Aro snapped out of it and the two of them ran out of the room. Looking back, the statues were now interlocked together and would have crushed the two of them if they hadn't run out in time. The heads of the two closest statues swivelled around and looked at the pair, eyes still glowing.

Aro and Ellendrii yelped and ran for it again.

Once they were far enough away from the room, they stopped running and caught their breath.

"What the grik was that?" asked Aro.

"Contrary to your belief, I do not have all the answers" said Ellendrii, scowling at him.

"Well I didn't think you actually *knew*, I was just you know, saying, cos I didn't know"

"That makes no sense" replied Ellendrii.

"I know" said Aro and hung his head.

They carried on in a fairly straight line if they could but some of the rooms and corridors were a bit twisty and turny and Ellendrii could only hope that they were headed in the right direction. They still encountered Repulsators but killed them with ease now they knew how to and the creatures rarely bothered them anymore. They did see plenty of them floating around though.

Ellendrii tried climbing to a higher part of the temple to see their way out but his sight was always hindered by walls that went higher than his height and so blocked his view any further.

"I really don't think the Wind Hounds only took four sun cycles to get through this forest. We've been in here way longer than that" said Aro.

"I know. Even if they ran, they wouldn't be *that* fast" agreed Ellendrii.

"I think we've been going round in circles. It can't be that big here. It's only a temple after all" said Aro.

"I dunno, I haven't seen anything I recognize, which makes me feel that we aren't going round in circles. Either that or we're taking the long way around here!" he tried to joke but Aro didn't laugh.

They rested, drank a little and headed onward.

Finally, Ellendrii started to see an end to the ruins or at least part of them that was in bad shape and smashed up and crumbled. This could mean the end of the temple. Maybe an outer wall or something. They both hoped so!

Their hope didn't last long.

Something was blocking their path. A Repulsator that had its back to them. A few others floated around nearby and as the pair approached the one that was facing away from them, the others came closer.

Ellendrii squinted at the Repulsator. There was something wrong with its head. No, wait it was actually two Repulsators. The angle and perspective made it an optical illusion. It was two, one behind the other. Two heads, two Repulsators.

Then, the creature turned around.

Ellendrii and Aro stopped in their tracks and stared in utter horror.

The thing that floated before them was a Repulsator alright but it had two hideous heads, each with a bloodshot eyeball in its mouth. The mismatched eyes watched the pair. Somehow seeing one with two eyes was far freakier than the cyclopsian things they had seen so far. And this one was bigger than the others too. The eyes could move independently of one another as well, which somehow made it worse. The creature shuddered deeply and its ears pricked towards them, noses picking up their scent. Other than its two heads, its forelegs were also deformed. An extra foreleg sprouted out from where its elbows were. Its ribcage heaved as it breathed, rattling with that same awful death rattle they had heard some of the others make.

The smaller ones now swarmed around what Ellendrii and Aro could only guess was their master. The one in charge. The heads were partially conjoined but still managed to move a little to enable the eyeballs to face forwards. The little blind shrivelled eye sockets in the heads blinked and winced and the noses wriggled grotesquely. Like the rest of the Repulsators, its innards draped a little way out of its destroyed halfbody and the spine hung down below that. Their spines could also move in a similar fashion to a tail and this one's spine whipped and trashed angrily. It knew. It knew what they had done to the other Repulsators.

It knew they had killed them.

And it was angry.

"We'll have to stand our ground. That thing is blocking the way out and I'm pretty sure if we run, it will follow us. We can probably kill it in the same way to its comrades but I don't want to mess around with killing it. We need to charge past it as fast as we can and get out of here. I'm pretty sure that's the end of the temple back there" Ellendrii pointed.

Aro was getting himself pumped up to run. Feeling the adrenaline and anger coursing through his body. He made himself get angry about these creatures that had attacked them and tried to stop them and hurt his friend Ellendrii. And he was ready for this last dash.

"Let's go!" he roared and charged forward. Ellendrii was a little taken aback at his sudden motion but followed and they both sprinted forward, hoping to dash through the Repulsators that were blocking their path. Both of them terrified and pumped up in equal measure. Running into danger like that went against everything their instincts told them to do but they ignored it this time and charged forward anyway.

Looking back on the events that followed may even have made them laugh but in the moment it looked as though they had failed.

The large Repulsator was dripping a lot more blood than the others were and it had been stationary for some time. And there was a large puddle of blood under it. And they both slipped over in it and ended up skidding on their faces.

Immediately they were swarmed by the smaller Repulsators while the large one watched over the whole thing, shuddering in glee and wiggling its horrible little claws. It had one eye on Aro and the other watching Ellendrii. Nearby some eyeless Repulsators mewled and wriggled; eager to get their eyeballs and float like their friends.

The two friends roared and struggled with the horrible scratching, clawing creatures that threatened to overpower them. Ellendrii was a bit better off because they were having trouble holding down his wings. There needed to be more of them than there was in order to get Ellendrii down and keep him there.

But Aro had been forced onto his side by the number of Repulsators that were attacking him and two of them were preparing to gouge out his eyes. He closed his eyes tight and turned his head every which way to stop his relentless attackers from injuring his precious eyes. He didn't want to be rendered blind from this if he managed to escape. He thrashed around, smacking some of them off his body with his tail blade. He'd de-eyed quite a few but more and more were swarming around, obviously called by their master to attack these two who kept escaping.

Ellendrii was no longer using his hands to rip out their eyes but had resorted to using his more powerful mouth and jaws. His wings and tail were aiding him well as he batted the creatures off him. Unfortunately one of the creatures had almost ripped one of his precious wings when it clawed him. This made him even more determined not to let the Repulsators get a grip on him.

Since the other Repulsators were having trouble pinning down Aro, their leader was now trying to help. Its creepy little paws and claws held him down with surprising strength and because it had conjoined arms and four paws instead of two, it could hold him down with better effect. It leaned over his face and the eyeballs both glared at him as it shuddered and rattled in his ear. Aro shut his eyes and squirmed for all he was worth but now he couldn't escape.

Luckily the Repulsators were still having trouble pinning down Ellendrii and he managed to break free but only through sheer strength and the will to save his friend.

He leaped on the lead Repulsator and threw it off Aro, then attacked the others, forcing them off his friend. Ellendrii was still being swarmed and a brief glance around alerted him to the fact that more and more of the vicious rodents were coming to their master's aid.

As soon as he could get up, Aro fled with Ellendrii and they reached the edge of the temple and rushed into the forest, not looking back, not stopping until they couldn't hear that terrible shuddering anymore.

Panting, the two of them collapsed on the now familiar grey soil and rested. Their bodies ached from running full out but they had made it; they were safe!

Aro rubbed his eyes, partly to make sure they were still there. When he had caught his breath, he spoke.

"I thought I was done for. I thought they were going to take my eyes. Even now I can feel their horrible little claws digging at my eye sockets. Are my eyes ok?" he asked Ellendrii in fear. His friend looked at his eyes and nodded.

"Yeah they're fine. It's a good thing I had my wings or we wouldn't have got out of there with our eyes intact and we'd never be able to find the SilvaGryphie."

"I'm surprised I haven't seen more creatures around here with no eyes" said Aro.

"They probably starve to death or bleed to death. Unless they resort to using their nose to hunt, I doubt most creatures who are used to sight hunting would survive without their eyes. I should think most of them die of shock anyway. Still, I can't see any of those horrible things here." Ellendrii looked around and to his relief saw not a sign of a single Repulsator anywhere around the two of them.

"I bet they don't leave that wretched temple they live in" muttered Aro with spite.

"Let's hope for our sake that they don't" replied Ellendrii.

They rested a while and then headed onward.

"Hey, Ellendrii?"

"Yes, Aro?"

"Let's not go exploring any more derelict places."

Ellendrii nodded. They knew to keep away now. He only hoped they wouldn't find any more places like that temple around here. He wanted the journey to continue how it had been going before they discovered the temple. Smoothly and with minimal danger.

He was a little sad in a way though because the temple had been interesting at first. He had been having fun enjoying it before he'd encountered the Repulsators. It was a little break from the humdrum of the forest and its blackened plants.

Aro had enjoyed exploring it too, at first that is. But now he knew places like that were dangerous. They both knew that now. And to keep a better ear open for odd and strange noises. Anything like shuddering was to be avoided at all costs.

Ellendrii regretted not asking Kraarz if there had been more places in the forest with Repulsators. He hoped there was only one place with them and it was past and over now. After stopping and sharing a rockrat, Aro got pondering.

"We're gunna run out of food soon. I wonder if those Repulsator-things would have been any good to eat?"

"Hardly, Aro. We aren't even sure if they were alive or dead. Their flesh was probably poisoned. You could have snacked on one if you'd wanted but I refuse to be held responsible for what happened to you because you'd got greedy."

Aro sighed.

"Yeah, you're right I guess. We've still gotta be careful." He frowned and growled.

"I HATE this place. I want to be out of here now! I feel trapped."

"I've been feeling trapped for sun cycles now" replied Ellendrii, "So join the club! Anyway, sitting around won't help. Let's keep moving."

Aro nodded in agreement and they headed onward. Ellendrii still dearly hoped that they were still going in a straight line and hadn't got turned around. He really wished they could meet someone that they could ask or who could guide them. Even if they met someone who would tell them how much further they had to go in this dreadful forest would be of some use. But so far they hadn't met any friendly creatures; only hostile. He guessed that was to be expected. It *was* the Forest of Foreboding, after all.

After a while, the pair of them started to notice that the bushes were growing up more thickly and the forest was getting darker again.

"Oh great" muttered Aro, rolling his eyes.

The pair had to push and force their way through again.

"Maybe we're going the wrong way" said Aro as he followed Ellendrii in a similar fashion to how they had forced their way through at the beginning.

"Let's hope not! Besides, if we are, there's nothing we can do" replied Ellendrii.

Aro grumbled and they carried on. Everything was so dark and dismal now. Well, it had always been pretty dark but this was getting more worrying. There were now no gaps of light between the trees at all anymore. Not even the usual small ones that light filtered through.

But the pair trudged on because it was all that they could do. They only stopped occasionally for toilet breaks and they didn't rest. Their fear instinct wanted them to keep going and get far away from that awful temple and its creepy residents.

So they kept going. They changed places and Aro walked in front when Ellendrii got tired. Since neither of them could sleep properly anyway, they started to take less and less breaks for sleeping and only stopped to rest. It was like they both had insomnia. Because the problem was that when they went to sleep, it was fine, they could escape their current situation. But when they woke up, the realization of their current situation came flooding back anew and it didn't do to let anything get them down any more than they were already becoming increasingly more miserable at the lack of light and increasing lack of hope of getting out of this awful forest.

Chapter 18
Deeper and Darker

Soon, they had to eat and shared the last rockrat. And then they ran out of food, so they had no choice but to try and find things that were good to eat or they would surely starve. How to go about this was more difficult, however. Aro had the idea to see what other creatures ate and eat something like that but they hadn't even seen any other creatures that weren't hostile so that was easier said than done.

"We could just try and find something that looks like what we're used to eating?" asked Aro.

"Yeah of course we could. Cos we've seen a lot of creatures that look like cave cats, forest deer and sea vultures" replied Ellendrii with sarcasm.

"It was only a suggestion" snarled Aro, frowning.

"Sorry" said Ellendrii, "I honestly thought that we would have been out of here before we ran out of food." He sat down with a sigh.

It had also occurred to him that even if they saw another creature eating, that food may not be suitable for the two friends to eat.

"There doesn't seem to be any plant life we could eat. It's all blackened and horrible looking" Ellendrii said, looking around.

"I wouldn't want to eat plants anyway, blegh!" spat Aro.

"It's better than nothing" said Ellendrii, "You'd rather eat plants or fruit than starve."

"I guess" mooched Aro.

Ellendrii stood up.

"Let's keep moving. We'll see how far we can get before we have to eat. We still have some water left, luckily. We'll keep going."

At that moment, Aro's tummy grumbled.

"Let's move fast then" he said.

They headed onward.

It was ok for a while. They didn't feel hunger pains and their fear kept them going. After encountering the

Repulsators, they realized that they must keep their guard up and carry on. They decided against exploring anything else they came across and just keep going in what they hoped was still a straight line. In truth they had got a little turned around now and instead of heading straight out of the forest like they had planned, they were going at a curve and so would inevitably end up spending a little longer in the Forest of Foreboding.

It was still just as dark as before and some of it was harder to get through than other parts but they kept going relentlessly, still not stopping to rest much or sleep. They were now afraid that if they stopped to sleep, they would wake up starving hungry and thus waste the time that they weren't hungry. The hunger would grow as they slept.

This caused both of them to be slightly fatigued but they kept going. Whenever they got too dizzy or felt the urge to sleep, they would have a little drink from the ever lessening gourd water. Aro was tempted at one point to have a drink from a stream they crossed. He was *that* thirsty. But Ellendrii quickly pulled him away and kept him going.

Ellendrii was a good crutch for Aro. Aro was easily lead by his more primal instincts and Ellendrii kept his mind much straighter than it would have been if he was in the forest by himself. If Aro had made this journey by himself; he would have got eaten or lost a long time ago. He was brash and bold but he wasn't that smart. He had the better weapons, arguably that is. Gryphie fire was strong but not everything could be killed by it. Lizariaous poison had so far killed everything the Lizariaouses had ever encountered. Granted that was only Gryphies or meal creatures but Aro swore by his needles and rightly so.

Ellendrii was doubtful, on and off, which made sense considering their current place in this strange new land. But he had Aro and needed to make this journey for both of them; to find the SilvaGryphie but also to keep his friend safe. If Ellendrii had done this by himself, he may have given up. Having someone else there too was a great help to keep someone's spirit up.

Even if they did argue sometimes.

Neither of them looked around much beyond the path they were taking after they had decided not to look for food. Ellendrii was worried they would starve. Carrying on was a good idea but there was also the risk that they wouldn't make it to the other side before they got too hungry that they were too weak or tired to hunt or fight. So far nothing in the forest except the Repulsators had attacked them. He didn't count the shadow creatures since they remained in the trees and didn't come down at all.

But if they made it back, what stories they would have to tell to the others! Meeting Midnyte Comet, learning the ways of the Wind Hounds (he thought he would leave out Aro's little *faux pas*), surviving the attack of the Repulsators and all the weird things they had seen in this forest so far.

The plant life in the forest was unusually odd to Ellendrii. He was used to seeing flowers and colour with plants; not the black withered things he was seeing here. They all seemed to be dead. And yet they weren't. When he looked closer, he could see that they were very much alive and some even had flowers but they were horrible crusty looking things. He surmised that the reason they had no colour was because they had no sunlight. However, how could they survive with no sunlight? His bored mind pondered these and many other things as they walked. He missed flying. He wished once more that they had stayed with Midnyte. He secretly knew she may not have appreciated that.

Aro didn't care about plants. Dyarkroeen had hardly any anyway. But he was feeling hungry, having more of an appetite than Ellendrii did. And a larger one too. He secretly hated the fact that he had been afraid of the Repulsators and hidden. He wasn't afraid of anything back home. Well except for maybe if his parents were mad at him. He knew that Mordred had lost half his tail killing Zephirak and if his father had the power to kill who was universally known as one of the most powerful Lizariaouses of all time, he was certainly not to be trifled with! Given the fact that some Lizariaous parents do considerable damage to their kids if they get angry at them.

The two of them were secretly sure this horrible forest would haunt their moonmares whenever they did decide to sleep next.

Aro yawned and they trudged onward.

They were walking in silence when suddenly Aro lost his footing and started to slide. He was leading at the time. His paws and claws slid out of control from underneath him and he fell into a deep dark pit. Ellendrii tried to grab him as he fell but he couldn't; it all happened so fast. Neither of them had seen the pit because the forest was dark and this part was covered in the nasty black leaves from the trees. It was hidden.

Aro scrabbled to his feet at the bottom of it and tried to haul himself out of the pit. Again and again he tried but the sides were just too steep. Ellendrii peered down at him from the edge of the pit.

"ARO! CAN YOU CLIMB OUT?" he yelled down.

"NO!" roared back Aro and continued to try and get out in vain.

"I'LL FIND SOMETHING TO GET YOU OUT!" called down Ellendrii.

Aro still tried to clamber out but Ellendrii yelled for him to stop. It was just too deep to get out of. Ellendrii worried that this pit might be a trap of some kind and he wanted to get his friend out of it fast just in case it was. Whoever set the trap might come back or even worse, whoever set the trap might be waiting down there with Aro. Ellendrii went to look for some vine or anything he could hang down to get his friend out.

Aro paced around at the bottom of the pit. He was annoyed with himself for not paying attention to where he was going or where he put his feet. He'd felt the ground give when he placed his first foot down in front of him but paid no attention to it because the leaves made the ground squishy and give a little. And he cursed his own weight, as it was too late now and he was stuck. He only hoped that Ellendrii would find something to get him out.

Ellendrii was looking around but with some trouble. It's not like he could look up into the trees to see if anything useful was hanging down that he could use to get his friend out. The shadow creatures were up there and they could sense something was up with him and Aro.

So they were gathering.

Meanwhile, Aro was looking around the pit. It was pretty sizeable. He could stand in it with his tail held almost straight behind him. It could just be a natural pit where the ground had subsided but he worried that most probably it was a trap. Then he saw something move out of the corner of his eye...

Ellendrii had wandered a little way away. He was looking now in a slight panic. If he didn't find something to help his friend out, then he wouldn't be able to rescue him. He really needed something to help. His mind was mulling over the possibility of him not finding something and also thinking that if this happened, what he would do. He thought he would dig the side of the pit down and see if he could get it low enough so maybe Aro could pull himself out if he jumped. Aro probably wasn't very good at jumping but that was a trivial thing right now. Ellendrii looked for branches, vines, even logs. Maybe he could throw down a load of things and pile them up so that Aro could use them to climb out. At the risk of the falling objects hitting Aro. The bottom of the pit didn't look wide enough for them to avoid hitting him.

Aro had backed into a corner now, needles aimed at whatever it was that he had seen move. The thing came closer and he could see its shape in the dim light. It was lithe and it moved carefully.

"Get back!" growled Aro. "Or I'll hurt you..." He snarled at the thing. It didn't speak back to him but continued to approach. Aro wasn't taking any chances. He shot the thing point blank with a well aimed needle. The thing fell over and writhed for a little, then lay still. Another soon followed it and Aro shot that too.

Suddenly he felt a sharp pain in his back leg. Another had got close enough to bite him. More were coming out from who knows where as well. Aro could only assume that these creatures could dig. They had bodies a bit like Furmines but they didn't have fur. Instead they had smooth skin. He guessed fur would only impede them if they lived under ground. The weaselly things carried on trying to attack him and he fended them off, shooting off his needles and killing the rest with his teeth and claws.

"ELLENDRII, I COULD REALLY DO WITH YOU HURRYING UP!!" he roared, hoping the Gryphie could hear him. He was down to his last two needles.

Ellendrii had sort of heard him. He'd heard Aro's voice but not his words. He had also finally found a strong vine to dangle down and hope his friend could use it to climb up. He rushed back to the pit and called down.

"ARO! I FOUND A VINE, I'M THROWING IT DOWN NOW!" He looked around and found a nearby tree to tie the vine around so it could be a bit more supported. Hurriedly, he tied it around the tree and then trailed it back to the pit and threw it down, hoping it would be strong enough to support Aro's weight.

Aro saw it come down and thought he could reach it, though he would have to stretch and it meant that the rest of his body would be open to attack by the creatures. He used his tail to defend his back end while he reached forward with his teeth. He was up on his back legs, front legs leaning on the side of the pit and reaching out with his teeth. He had no clue if he could even do this. It wasn't something Lizariaouses were used to doing. He reached up with a clawed paw and grabbed the vine. Maybe this would work better?

"HOW ARE YOU DOING?" called down Ellendrii.

"YOU COULD'VE FOUND A LONGER VINE! OW!!" yelled back Aro.

"WHAT WAS THAT?" asked Ellendrii.

"I'M NOT ALONE DOWN HERE. WHATEVER SET THE TRAP IS ATTACKING ME WHILE I'M TRYING TO CLIMB UP" roared back Aro, thrashing his tail and knocking some of the creatures flying backward.

"STAY STILL" roared Ellendrii, "I'LL USE MY FIRE!"

He flamed down into the pit, narrowly missing Aro because the pit wasn't that wide but flaming some of the creatures. They screamed at him and retreated into the dirt. Being soil dwelling creatures; they didn't like bright light of any kind. Ellendrii continued to use his flames when the creatures attacked Aro.

Aro had grabbed the vine and was using it to pull himself out but he was having difficulty. He pulled himself up a little and then fell back down a little so the process was very slow indeed and the creatures kept nipping his tail in between Ellendrii flaming them. They were determined to try and keep their meal. They would be out of luck though.

Aro pulled and strained and struggled but he was halfway out when one of the creatures decided to jump on his back. Since he had no needles there now, as he had used them all up and the new ones hadn't had time to grow, the creature had no trouble grabbing hold and clinging to him, ready to give him a bite.

Ellendrii didn't want to risk flaming this one in case he got Aro instead. The other creatures cottoned on to this and joined the first one, clinging on and nipping Aro's back. Luckily Aro's thick skin prevented most of them making much of an impact on him but a couple of them hurt him and he roared in pain, wanting so badly to throw them off but not being able to since he was holding on to the vine.

Ellendrii wanted to throw something at the creatures but again risked hitting Aro. All he could do was stand there dumbly and cheer his friend on. He growled at the creatures but they ignored him and carried on biting at Aro in the hopes that he would fall back down into the pit. A few more had gathered in the pit now as well and were making their little eager noises at their comrades.

Finally Aro was nearly at the top and Ellendrii swept his wing across and knocked a few of the creatures off his friend. Aro clung on to the edge of the pit with his claws and Ellendrii helped him pull himself out of the pit. Ellendrii knocked the rest of the nasty little creatures back into the pit as Aro pulled himself out. Aro lay on the ground on his belly, exhausted from the effort.

"You ok?" asked Ellendrii, concerned.

"Yeah I'm alright" Aro panted and regained his energy a little before the two of them leaped over the pit so that they wouldn't risk falling in it again.

"Let's be careful as we continue" said Ellendrii. "I'll go first and make sure there are no more of those pits around."

"Great, another danger to look out for" murmured Aro, rolling his eyes. "Those creatures down there were..."

"Don't tell me, horrible." Ellendrii filled him in.

"How did you know?" grinned Aro. He felt much better now.

"Pity you used up all your needles though" said Ellendrii.

"I didn't have many to begin with. I wish I'd hurry up and grow some more"

"You will as you get older" said Ellendrii.

"Yeah but I want them now!" roared Aro impatiently.

As a rule, Lizariaouses grow more needles as they age and their bodies get bigger. Obviously, the larger the body, the longer the back, the more needles will grow. The largest of Lizariaouses can have up to fifteen needles. Of course the amount of needles a Lizariaous has doesn't mean more power. That's all down to fighting ability. Zephirak only had eleven. The more they have only means they have more to use and might last longer in a fight if they know how to use them. Aro of course had eight needles. But at the moment he had none since they hadn't regrown just yet. It wouldn't take long for them to regrow though.

As they walked, Ellendrii found a few more pits and they leaped over them. Ellendrii was *so* tempted to use his wings when he jumped but he used them only for gliding. He wanted to make sure the pit was cleared before letting Aro jump over. Once Ellendrii had cleared it, he felt his way back to the edge so that Aro would know how far to jump. Luckily the pits weren't very wide and they were all similar so Aro could easily clear them himself when he jumped over. But this did slow them down quite a lot. Ellendrii wondered why the Wind Hounds hadn't come this way. Kraarz hadn't warned him about the pits. But of course since the pair were walking a curve now instead of a straight, some things they would encounter would be new.

Naturally, some pits could be walked around but most of them filled the pathway and it was hard to walk around them because of the bushes and undergrowth all around. Some of which were rather sharp. There was only one pit that caused either of them a problem and that was a particularly wide one that Ellendrii nearly fell into when he landed the other side. This was too far for Aro to jump. He had to back right up and take a running jump and he nearly fell into it too! Luckily he made it. Ellendrii, being lighter, didn't have much trouble being able to climb out the part where he had nearly fallen into the pit.

"When will these pits end? We're not getting anywhere very fast" said Aro, stating the obvious. Well, someone had to.

"I dunno. Let's keep going though" replied Ellendrii, getting tired now.

They continued and in time the pits ended. Some of them had already been triggered and there were bones in the bottom of them or more of those unwholesome creatures. Ellendrii had flamed into the open pits to see what was in them. The pair were curious. The creatures would retreat quickly if they were spotted or disturbed by the flames.

They could carry on faster once there were no pits to look out for.

As they continued, they felt ever hungrier. They carried on having a few sips of the water but that was starting to run low as well and they were getting very concerned over it.

"I really wish I could fly up past the trees and see how much further we have to go, but I know those things in the trees will attack me or worse" said Ellendrii. Aro sighed and agreed although he secretly wondered if Ellendrii could just try anyway. After all, he didn't know for sure that the things would attack. They both knew that the things were still up there though. Ellendrii carried on leading because of the pits. Even though they hadn't come across any more for quite a while, he still felt it would be safer if he lead them because he was more careful than Aro. Aro didn't complain. Mostly because if they got into trouble it would probably be Ellendrii's fault!

"Aro, stop a minute" said Ellendrii quietly, standing still.

"What is it?" asked Aro.

"Look at that" said Ellendrii, pointing.

There before them, a little way away and with its back to them was a small black creature that looked a lot like a cave cat in appearance. It was covered in soft fur with soft little ears that twitched and listened and a mid-length tail that curled around its body. It was sat there quietly soft and downy; a little cave kitten!

"Hmm…I wonder if it's edible" pondered Aro.

"It's the first thing I've seen that isn't evil or threatening. Look, it's so cute and fluffy!" said Ellendrii.

The cat creature's ears twitched as it heard him and it sighed softly. They watched it for a while, happy that there was something at least that was some sort of reassuring. They were just about to head onward when the little creature turned around and looked at them.

The pair suppressed their screams of horror. The cat creature had no face. The black fur ended at its cheeks. The whole of its face was skin and bare.

"A Narg'tok" murmured Aro.

"What?" asked Ellendrii.

"Dad told me about them, when he told us stories as a kid. Only a couple of times. It sucks out your soul. I didn't think it was real. I thought it was just made up to scare us."

The Narg'tok's face seemed to swirl and two black pits appeared for its eyes. Ellendrii stared in horror. Neither of them could move. It was as though its face showed their deepest, darkest fears and it paralysed the pair of them to the spot. They couldn't do anything to stop it or turn their heads away.

The creature stood up, tilting its head to one side. A hole started to appear where its mouth should be. The hole grew larger and rounder. Still they couldn't move. Ellendrii's ears were pinned back against his head in sheer terror and Aro's eyes were the size of saucers as he failed to fight the fear that filled his very being.

Slowly the Narg'tok approached them, the hole for its mouth filled with razor sharp teeth. The teeth went all the way around the circle it had for a mouth and a strange hypnotic moaning sound emanated from it.

Still, they were rooted to the spot. They both knew they should move but they were frightened that if they did, the fear would become worse. To each of them the Narg'tok's face still distorted into an image of intense terror to the individual who was looking upon it.

340

Whatever it was that triggered their innermost fears was reflected in the creature's hideous face. It placed one soft paw in front of the other, still slowly approaching them. It had them under its unholy spell and there was no hurry. They wouldn't be going anywhere. The creature's tail was raised behind it and its ears leaned eagerly towards Ellendrii and Aro as it came closer to them. Its fleshy face distorted out towards them as it got closer. Neither of them could see the circle of a mouth that had appeared; they could still only see their own fears.

The Narg'tok went for Ellendrii first. It walked slowly up to him, taking its time. The eye holes blackened into oblivion and the horrible circular mouth of teeth started to stretch outwards, latching on to Ellendrii's chest. The teeth broke his skin and clung on to him. His head leaned back and his eyes turned white, a strange glowing smoke leaving his body and being drawn into the Narg'tok's mouth.

Aro was still staring in horror but the feeling of fear wasn't quite as intense as it could have been since the Narg'tok was busy with Ellendrii. The Narg'tok's idea had been to paralyse Aro with fear while it fed off Ellendrii's life source. Perhaps it was the lack of intelligence in Aro or just the fact he could see this horrible creature feeding off his friend but he could feel the fear subsiding just enough for him to regain some sort of movement in his body. It was difficult but he was no longer completely pinned to the spot he stood in.

He tried to move one paw forward to help his friend. If he didn't hurry, Ellendrii would be dead! It took every ounce of his concentration and power to move even one paw and Ellendrii was several steps away from him. He couldn't fire a needle at the creature either because they hadn't grown back yet.

Ellendrii felt his life force being sucked out but he couldn't do anything. He was in too much pain and fear and he was completely paralysed. He was blind as well; all he could see was black despite the light that was emanating from him.

Luckily (or not luckily for the hapless Gryphie), the Narg'tok was too busy feeding to notice Aro getting slowly closer.

Aro gritted his teeth and slowly approached. Finally he was close enough to actually reach the Narg'tok. However, the next problem he had was to get the Narg'tok off Ellendrii without hurting the Gryphie. He wasn't sure if pulling it off was a good idea since it might tear off a chunk of Ellendrii's flesh with it. It was literally suckered onto him. He figured he should hurt it somehow and get it to let go that way. However, he needed to actually kill it or it would just cast its spell on him again and maybe even attack him this time so he wouldn't be able to do the same again.

He got closer to the Narg'tok and thought with difficulty about his next move. He would be too slow to lunge his head down and bite its neck. It would know what he was doing. He hoped that if he hurt it, it would fall off Ellendrii and be a little stunned, long enough for Aro to attack and kill it.

He tried not to look at the hideous Narg'tok as he moved closer to it, near enough to its leg to bite it. This would hopefully shock it enough so that it would let go of Ellendrii. Closer and closer Aro's face went to the soft black fur of the little Narg'tok. Aro's lips curled back in a snarl as he prepared to bite it. It was all going so painfully slowly. He was sure the creature would see him. But it seemed to be distracted while it fed, that's if it could even see with those pits it had for eyes.

Aro's jaws closed around the Narg'tok's leg and he bit down hard, hard enough to crunch through its bone.

The creature let go of Ellendrii and the Gryphie collapsed, while the Narg'tok made a terrible screaming sound. It was halfway between a scream and a roar of anger. It flew backwards but didn't retreat. However, when it let go of Ellendrii, it also lost its hold over Aro and he felt his senses coming back to him again. He felt great relief to be out of the dark, dismal place the creature was holding his mind in.

The Narg'tok wasn't going to go without a fight, though. Aro surmised that since there was a lack of decent food in this place, it struggled to find things to feed upon so it wasn't keen on letting either of them escape. However now, it was injured and in pain and its powers of fear weren't as strong as they had been before. Aro was careful not to look at it. You could lose yourself in its swirling, hideous face and bottomless eye pits and it was unwise to look at it directly.

So he charged at it, having his speed back now and able to move properly, he didn't want to waste time standing around. He wanted to kill it quickly. It had a soft, weak body, clearly relying on its svengali powers to trick its prey into not attacking.

Being a bit block headed made it fairly easy for Aro to charge at it, without even thinking and get his jaws around its neck. The Narg'tok's mouth tried in vain to latch onto his head as he did this and he squirmed around to get out of its way while he bit down hard and fast. He felt its neck crack and its warm blood seep out onto his chin and it was dead. He dropped it and its body fell limply to the ground and lay there lifeless.

Without wasting any time, Aro rushed over to his friend who was barely conscious; and barely alive.

"ELLENDRII!! Are you ok?" he asked. He knew the answer but there wasn't much else to say except this.

Ellendrii didn't speak; just blinked weakly at Aro. He was barely breathing. The fur on his chest was sparse where the Narg'tok had been latched onto him.

"Don't die! Please don't die!" Aro yelled, panicked. He looked around as though the answer to the problem would just come out of the trees. The two of them were too weakened by lack of food and sleep and Aro's vision was becoming a bit blurry because of fatigue. Aro looked back at Ellendrii and saw the Gryphie's eyes had closed now. Aro shook him, hoping to wake him again but Ellendrii lay still on the ground, breathing weakly. His eyes were no longer white but that didn't really mean much to Aro.

Aro called out distress roars into the forest, completely at a loss. Ellendrii was dying and there was nothing he could do! He didn't know where to take him; he had no food to give him and no cure. Frantically he looked in the leather bag at Ellendrii's side to see if there was anything in there he could use. It was all he could think of.

He found the gourd of water and offered it to his friend. Ellendrii remained with closed eyes. Aro nudged him and

343

splashed a little of the water onto Ellendrii's snout but the Gryphie didn't respond. Aro splashed a little onto his head too but nothing happened. He looked back in the bag again.

Next he found some strong smelling herbs and put them under Ellendrii's nose. The Gryphie wrinkled his nose slightly so Aro pushed them closer, so they touched his nose. Ellendrii didn't do anything this time. Aro rubbed the herbs on Ellendrii's nose but no response at all. Aro started to breathe faster, panicking more. He rifled through the bag for anything else and tried several different herbs under his friend's nose but Ellendrii didn't respond anymore.

Aro started to cry, choking back tears and not knowing what to do. He put all the things back in the bag and looked around him again. Not seeing anything of any help, he decided to try and carry Ellendrii to somewhere where there might be something, anything that might help him. If nothing else it would get them both out of this area in case another Narg'tok appeared.

Hoisting Ellendrii over his shoulder, Aro managed to get the unconscious Gryphie onto his back and carry him. It was hard going and he was weak from not eating but he carried on as best he could.

Aro felt so alone. Even with the warm form of Ellendrii on his back, because the Gryphie was unconscious, Aro felt totally alone in the forest. He didn't know really if Ellendrii had died while he was carrying him. The Gryphie was heavy and since his breathing was so shallow, it was hard to tell if he was still alive. Aro couldn't help sobbing as he walked, or talking to Ellendrii either. Somehow talking to him made him feel as if his friend was still listening and he felt less lonely.

"Come on, I'll find something to help you. I'm sure we can find something that will help. Not far now, we might even find our way out of this forest" Aro chuckled but it was watery and sad, without any mirth at all. His friend felt like a dead weight and Aro tried not to think so much about the idea of him dying.

"It'll be ok, I'm here for you. I might not be much but I'm here and I'll...I'll make sure you don't...d...die..." Aro started to sob. He stumbled a little but kept going.

"I'm sorry I…I wasn't faster, I couldn't g…get there sooner…to you…you're my…my best friend and…and I won't let you…d…die…"

He carried on determinedly, not letting the bushes or anything get in his way. He thought if they could make it out of the forest, if he could find food or water, anything, if he could make it out with Ellendrii, his friend would have a chance of survival.

His legs ached but he carried on, still stumbling a little as he went.

Then he saw something through the trees, something he hadn't seen in a very long time. It was sunlight! Aro gasped with disbelief. It was as though something somewhere had helped him. Sun, in this forest? It was unheard of and yet there it was.

Aro carried on with renewed determination towards the sun. Maybe this was it! Maybe they'd got to the other side of the forest? Maybe they had made it!

Wishful thinking.

They hadn't made it out of the forest. What they had made it to was a sunlit dell with a small stream that sparkled in the sunlight. With the light of the sun, Aro felt safer somehow. There were no shadows here and nowhere anything nasty could hide. He stumbled to the stream and put Ellendrii down beside it. The Gryphie looked dead. Aro started to panic again.

"Ellendrii! Ellendrii!!" he whimpered but Ellendrii didn't move. Aro got into the stream and used his tail to splash water over his friend. Ellendrii squirmed weakly; he was still alive! Aro breathed a sigh of relief.

He looked around. He still couldn't see anything to eat but the water of the stream smelled fresh and clean and he had a drink. After all, if he died, well his friend was nearly dead anyway and he didn't know how to save him so he was prepared to take the risk that the water might poison him. At least if that happened he could lie down and die beside his friend.

The water wasn't poisoned though.

Aro felt refreshed. He wished Ellendrii would drink. He sat next to him to think and get his head straight. While he sat, he looked around. This area looked different to the rest of the forest. The grass was green and the flowers were pretty colours. He didn't hear any birds or other animals but at least the foliage looked nicer than the rest of the place. Occasionally a butterfly would flutter around and land on a flower. This place seemed to be so uplifting and all of it was neatly kept and seemed as though it was cared for. The stream had small fish swimming in it and Aro watched them. He wanted to catch one but he was afraid that something nasty might happen as it had with that river that nearly tried to pull him under and the strange creatures in it. He looked at Ellendrii.

"I really wish you would drink something" said Aro quietly to his friend. This place seemed so peaceful and calm. Aro felt himself getting sleepy as the sun warmed him. It was just a little sunlight but it was warm enough to feel. And it felt so good after who knows how many sun cycles they had been in that forsaken forest. Aro really wanted to look around but he was reluctant to leave Ellendrii by himself. He was worried that some hunter would take advantage of an easy meal.

Aro took a deep breath and looked up at the sky. Nothing happened. No whispering, no horrible shadow creatures from the trees. Just blue sky up above. The trees still made a small effort to try and block the sun out but the spindly branches easily gave way to the sunlight.

"Ellendrii, I don't know what to do. What if you don't make it? Should I carry on and look for the SilvaGryphie myself? I don't think I'd make it without you. This is your quest, you have to live and complete it! You know how much this means to you. I wish I knew what to do or how to help you. I wish you could tell me. I…I'm not as smart as you. I guess I always knew that deep inside. I never wanted to admit it. And being jealous of your flying ability. I'm so sorry. I should never have been jealous of you. You're my friend. It's just, we were raised so differently. I guess that's why I let my jealousy get the better of me. Can you even hear me right now?" Aro looked at Ellendrii but Ellendrii made no sign that he could hear him.

Aro sighed and grunted and then got up.

"I'm going to look around. Don't worry; I won't let you out of my sight. I'll keep my eye on you and make sure nothing attacks you. I won't go far."

Aro wandered away from Ellendrii, keeping one eye on him while looking around to see if he could find anything that might be good to eat or any small creatures he might be able to catch for them. He was starving now. In fact you could see the ribs of both him and Ellendrii; they were so malnourished. His hunger was driving him to find food before anything else. Walking made his legs ache but he had to find something and try to find something for Ellendrii to eat as well. He felt he had to get his friend to eat. If Aro was hungry, it surely meant that Ellendrii was in the same predicament.

As he wandered, in ever increasing circles around Ellendrii, he saw a lot of reassuring things. Plants, flowers, grass, even an odd bird, though the birds still didn't sing. Maybe they didn't dare to in case they got eaten. Aro sniffed and searched for anything edible. He didn't have much knowledge of food other than living creatures. Even if there had been fruit or berries to eat, he wouldn't have noticed. But at least there were no bad smells. The Repulsators had smelled bad. Of blood and decay.

Finally he wandered back to Ellendrii again. The Gryphie hadn't moved. He still lay there with his eyes closed and still barely breathing.

Aro turned his attention to the stream and catching a fish.

"Looks like we're going back to a fish diet" said Aro with a half-hearted chuckle. He couldn't even get himself to smile properly.

He stood at the edge of the stream. It was shallow enough that he could get in and fish, so he did. Tiredly he got into the stream and stood quietly and still, waiting for the fish to get used to him being there. He waited for what seemed like ages and finally the fish started to swim closer. He knew that if he moved, he would have to wait again for the fish to get used to him being there so he wanted to catch a fish on his first try. He stood in the stream purely because he was too tired to reach the fish from the shore.

A fish swam close and he pounced on it. He missed because of fatigue but he simply tried again. He was too tired to even focus properly by this point but he still kept trying. Again and again. Finally he caught a fish. He wanted to catch more but he was just too tired. He carried the fish over to Ellendrii and placed it in front of his friend's mouth.

Aro lay down next to Ellendrii and pushed the fish at his mouth, wanting him to eat it. Ellendrii did nothing. His nostrils sniffed weakly but he didn't move.

"Please eat. I caught it for you. I can go without. I just need to sleep. Please eat it…" Aro continued to push the fish at Ellendrii but the Gryphie didn't respond at all. He seemed nearly dead.

Aro bit the head off the fish and offered it to Ellendrii again. He thought the smell of the blood might spark the hunter instinct but Ellendrii ignored it completely.

Aro ate the head of the fish and then rested his own head down next to his friend's. He continued to offer the fish but to no avail. Aro felt his eyelids getting heavy now.

"Please…please…eat…"

It felt good to close his eyes. He sighed. It felt good to lie down as well. So good.

Soon, Aro had drifted off to sleep next to his unconscious friend.

***

Aro's eyes slowly opened. There was a curious light, maybe it was the sun? He focused on Ellendrii and saw someone else moving around over his friend.

"Ellendrii?" said Aro sleepily. Whatever was moving around near Ellendrii came towards Aro. Aro's eyes tried to focus on it but he was still weak from not eating.

He blinked and stared. What he saw was a strange transparent canine-like skull with dark eye sockets and white glowing orbs in them for eyes. It cocked its head to one side and twitched one of its black fuzzy, pointed ears.

Aro stared and then jumped up and backed off in fear and a sudden surge of energy brought on by that all too familiar sense of panic. What was this creature? Was it another Narg'tok? They had black pointy ears too. But this had a dog-like face, not the horror that was the Narg'tok's visage.

Aro snarled all the same and brought everything into perspective finally. He felt so drained. But the skull was not a mirage. It was real and it was attached to a transparent canine body with a black mane running from the back of its head all the way down to the base of its tail. The tail was tipped with black fur as well.

But the skull, the transparent body, those weren't the strangest thing about this odd newcomer. Aro couldn't believe what he was seeing or that this was a real creature and he still thought that he was imagining things. It couldn't be! It must be markings, surely?

Because something like that couldn't possibly exist…

Chapter 19
Respite

What stood before Aro was surely nothing that could possibly exist or even make sense in nature. Aro rubbed his eyes a few times thinking even now that it must be his fatigue and not his vision. His eyes were lying to him.

Along with the transparent canine body and skull with the black fuzzy pointed ears and fluffy mane and tail tip, he could see what was inside the creature's body. It appeared to be a tiny ecosystem.

There was a pond in its belly with fish swimming in it. Tropical orchids were somehow latched onto the inside of its shoulder and a small twiggy tree was growing inside its upper hind leg. Hanging down from the inside of its spine and nearly dangling into the water of the pond was a weeping willow style plant and in each of its paws were small, smooth, oval pebbles that gently rattled as it moved them. But most extraordinary of all was a small, yellow bird sat in the branches of the tiny tree in the creature's hind leg. The bird looked perfectly happy in there and was sat watching Aro. The creature was around the size of the two friends. It didn't make a move to attack him; it just looked at him and waited for him to calm down.

After a while, Aro did indeed calm down a little, curiosity getting the better of him and he couldn't resist going for a closer look. Cautiously, and watching for any hostile behaviour, he approached it. He walked all around it, looking at it. It seemed just as curious about him and the two circled each other, observing the other one.

Finally, Aro decided to see if he could communicate with the creature.

"My name is Aro" said Aro, "What is yours?"

The creature made a sound like the chink and crackle of glass. It was the sound its teeth made as they came together when it moved its jaws in response.

"Rivniann" it replied. Aro could only just understand it. It was such an odd, foreign sound.

Aro still stared at it, momentarily forgetting his friend in trouble. Rivniann didn't seem to mind the fact he was being stared at. Presumably he was used to it.

Then Aro spied Ellendrii's form out of the corner of his eye and suddenly remembered why they were there. He rushed over to his unconscious friend. Ellendrii was still breathing but it was still also very shallow.

"Ellendrii!" Aro cried, gently rocking his friend's body back and forth a little to see if he could get a reaction. Rivniann came over and put a glass paw on Ellendrii's body, looking at Aro pointedly.

"He's nearly dead and I don't know what to do" said Aro, plonking himself down in utter defeat next to his prone friend.

"Lives" said Rivniann and patted Ellendrii's mane gently. The pebbles in his paw rattled and chinked softly. Aro looked at him.

"Yes he's alive but he won't be for longer unless I can find a way to fix him and save him."

"Lives" repeated Rivniann.

"You're not very good with words are you" Aro said, his natural rudeness once again coming through despite himself.

Rivniann ignored the rudeness and put his other paw on Ellendrii's mane. His paws glowed, the glow travelling through his transparent body and filling it. The fish in his tummy came to the surface of their little pond and looked out and the small bird became alert. Rivniann put his head back and opened his skeletal jaws. From somewhere underneath the weeping willow branches that ran the length of his spine, a flood of butterflies spilled out, flying along his body and through his neck, erupting out of his jaws and filling the sky with their bold colours. Aro could only sit and stare dumbfounded at what was happening. He really had no idea what was happening but whatever it was couldn't be worse than what had already happened so he decided to just go with it.

The butterflies filled the sky and then swooped back down, enveloping the unconscious Gryphie completely. Rivniann had stepped back and was watching them. Aro was staring even harder and feeling his stomach churn with worry. Where was Ellendrii? He couldn't see him anymore. He had

351

been completely engulfed with magnificent colours and patterns. He had a feeling that Rivniann was trying to help. He felt no threat from the strange creature and butterflies were nice things, surely they wouldn't be doing something dreadful like devouring his friend.

Aro's mind raced. What if they flew off him and all that was left was bones?? Aro shook his head. No, it wouldn't be like that.

Finally the butterflies dispersed and flew back into Rivniann's jaws. They disappeared where they had come from. Everything was silent. Aro stared at Ellendrii, who was still there of course, unharmed. And he was breathing properly now!

Slowly, Ellendrii opened his eyes and lifted his head a little, blinking.

"ELLENDRII!!" roared Aro in glee, bounding up to him. Rivniann put a paw on Aro's shoulder and shook his head.

"Gently" he said. Aro calmed down and sat quietly next to his friend.

"Are you ok?" he asked Ellendrii. Ellendrii looked at him but didn't speak. He did however, smile and nod softly.

"Can you talk?" asked Aro. Before Ellendrii could do anything, Rivniann spoke.

"Tired" he said. Aro nodded, understanding.

"I thought you were dead Ellendrii. I carried you, wanting to get you out of the Forest of Foreboding and we ended up here. I didn't know what to do or how to save you. So I went to sleep. I'm so tired and hungry. I couldn't get you to eat or do anything and I thought you would die. When I woke up, Rivniann was here." Aro pointed to Rivniann, who sat down with them and nodded. It's helped you, I think…"

Rivniann cut in.

"He" he said.

"Sorry, *he* helped you, I think" said Aro. Aro glanced at Rivniann and now noticed he was indeed male since it's not usually hard to tell the gender of canine creatures. Aro just hadn't noticed before.

Ellendrii nodded at all this and tried to sit up. He managed to get his forelegs underneath him but he wasn't strong enough to push up with them yet so he remained where he was.

Rivniann turned from them; he turned to the stream and dipped a pebbled paw into it. His paw caused ripples and suddenly several fish jumped out onto the shore where they were.

"Eat" said Rivniann. The others obliged without complaint. But they both secretly wished that they found it as easy to catch fish as Rivniann!

After they had finished, Ellendrii felt stronger and found his voice.

"Thank you, Rivniann. I am very grateful for you saving my life. I am indebted to you." He bowed his head in respect. Rivniann twitched an ear and looked at him quirkily.

"Nothing" he said and shrugged, his glowing eyes going black briefly as though he had blinked.

"But may I ask why?" asked Ellendrii, "Why did you save my life?"

"Life. Sacred" replied Rivniann. Clearly his funny voice was either not well used or he had trouble with speech. They suspected it was the latter since he had no skin or lips to properly enunciate with. Ellendrii thought wildly that maybe he had saved his life because he was meant to fulfil his quest! And now was the time to ask if Rivniann had heard of the SilvaGryphie, so Ellendrii asked.

To their surprise, Rivniann answered that he had!

Ellendrii tried to sit up with excitement but his strength was just not there yet.

"Do you know where to find her?" he asked, his heart leaping for joy. His heart soon sank again though because Rivniann answered "No".

"How do you know about her then?" asked Ellendrii.

"Saw" said Rivniann.

"You saw her?"

"Yes"

"When?"

Rivniann looked to the sky to indicate the past and a past memory.

"Time. Ago." He said. Ellendrii sighed.

353

"A long time ago?" asked Ellendrii.

"Yes" was the reply. This clearly wasn't getting any easier. Aro butted in.

"What *are* you?" he asked.

"Shardog" replied Rivniann.

"Are there any more Shardogs?" asked Aro.

"Yes" came the reply.

"Where are they?" asked Aro. Ellendrii was looking at him now with the feeling that he was asking too many questions.

"Away" said Rivniann. Whether that meant they had gone away or that they were just away somewhere else, it was unsure. Neither of them asked. The fact was that there was one here and he had helped them. And they were grateful beyond words.

Ellendrii had been watching Rivniann's body all the time that they had been talking. He couldn't help himself. If Rivniann had noticed, he wasn't saying. Ellendrii really wanted to know how Rivniann lived with a mini ecosystem inside him. Instead he turned his attention to Aro, who was trying to talk to him.

"Do you remember anything that happened?" asked Aro.

"I remember the Narg'tok attacking us. I remember feeling nothing but fear and foreboding looking at its hideous face. If you could call it that. It kept changing and transitioning into horrid images. I can't even describe them."

"Neither can I" said Aro.

"I remember it stared at me and I couldn't move. I was paralysed with fear. I saw it approaching me but I don't remember anything past that. Just fear and pain. I don't know what was going on."

"It had latched onto you with its horrible mouth. It was sucking onto your chest. I don't know what it was doing exactly, I can only think that it was sucking your life out because you were getting weaker. All the colour was being drained from your fur. It was awful to see. Your eyes went white. I was sure it had blinded you. I managed to break free of its horrible spell for a while, long enough to make my way over to you and get it off you. Luckily we were stood fairly close together. You just collapsed when it let go of you though. I had no idea what to do except try and find help or get us out of the forest. So I put you on my back because my needles hadn't grown back at that point so I could safely carry you. If they had grown back or if I'd had any on my back, I would have fired them off anyway so I could carry you. I didn't want to drag you cos I thought I might hurt you and I certainly didn't want to do that. Plus you'd get muddy and I know how you Gryphies hate to be muddy." Aro winked at him and grinned cheekily. Ellendrii smiled good naturedly. It was nice to have a light hearted moment for once in this horrible forest.

"And so you brought me here" said Ellendrii.

"Yeah. I was so relieved to see the sun again. I felt really good. Being in the dark all the time with no sun for so many sun cycles really got me down, more than I thought actually. I only realized the extent of it when I had reached this sunny dell. And the rest is history I guess. I just looked around, tried and failed to get you to eat and then fell asleep, exhausted."

"Thank you, Aro. Thank you for saving me."

"I didn't save you, he did" Aro gestured to Rivniann.

"You both did" replied Ellendrii, "If you hadn't brought me here, I would have died back there anyway. It took both of you to rescue me and I am grateful to you for it. I owe both of you my life and this quest. Speaking of which, Rivniann, did you say you'd actually *met* the SilvaGryphie?"

"Yes" was the one word reply.

"Wow!" replied Ellendrii. Actually, Rivniann had only said that he'd *seen* her, not met her but Ellendrii had taken it the wrong way. It turned out though that he had met her anyway.

"What was she like?" asked Ellendrii.

"Nice" said Rivniann.

Great, the one creature they'd met so far who had actually met the SilvaGryphie and it had to be the one who spoke the fewest words. Ellendrii sighed. He really wanted to know more but he would have to word himself carefully in order to get decent replies out of their new friend. He figured questions with yes/no answers would be the best bet.

"Was she big?"

"Yes"

"Bigger than me?"

"Yes"
"Much bigger?"
"Yes"
"Was she pretty?"
"Yes"
"Was she white?"
"Yes"
"Was she fluffy like a cloud?"
"Yes"
"Was she polite to you"
"Yes"
"Did she speak much of the Gryphies?"
"No"
"Did she say where she was going?"
"No"
"Where she had come from?"
"No"
"So she didn't say where she lived?"
"No"
"Did she say why she was passing through?"
"No"
"Was she here long?"
"No"
"She didn't stay?"
"No"
Ellendrii was running out of questions now.
"Did she look magical?" asked Aro.
"Yes" said Rivniann.
"Cool!" replied Aro.
"So she was just passing through, she didn't stay long, she was pretty, she was nice, she was bigger than me and she was white and fluffy like a cloud."
"Yes" said Rivniann.
Ellendrii looked around, then had an idea.
"Which way did she go when she left?" he asked. To their relief, Rivniann pointed the way they were headed; out of the Forest of Foreboding. He only wished that she had said more to Rivniann. Still, maybe she had just greeted him in passing

or something. No one would want to spend long in this awful forest. He wondered why Rivniann did.

"Rivniann, I'm sorry this can't be a yes or no question, but why have you made your home in the middle of this awful forest? Was this part nicer than the rest when you got here or did you make it this way?"

Rivniann replied with some difficulty. He didn't seem to mind the difficulty but he struggled with his wording.

"Shardog. Create. Life. Forest. Needed. Life. I. Create. This." He motioned to the area around them with one rattling paw.

Ellendrii wondered if more Shardogs came to the forest, would they be able to transform it into something beautiful instead of what it was already. So he asked this too.

"No. If. We. Changed. This. Forest. Creatures. Live. Nowhere. Else." Rivniann replied.

So if they changed the whole forest to look like this lovely part they were currently in, the creatures of the forest, no matter how horrible they were would have nowhere to live because their habitat would be changed. It would upset the balance of the forest even if it was a horrible place full of fear and loathing. Ellendrii could understand that. Rivniann appeared to be the sort of creature who respected all life.

"When you came here, did the forest creatures attack you?" asked Ellendrii.

"Little" said Rivniann, lifting a paw and tilting it to the left and right to show a midway gesture.

"Do they leave you alone now?" asked Ellendrii.

"Yes" said Rivniann.

"What do you eat? Cos there are fish in you but they're still alive" Aro asked him.

Rivniann perked up.

"Don't. Eat." He said. He seemed happy to describe this to them.

"Water. Out. I. Drink. Refresh."

He went over to the stream and to their mutual horror and embarrassment, he started to pee in it! The water of the little pond in his tummy started to go down lower and lower until there was barely any water left and the fish flopped about.

Then he dipped his jaws into the stream and drank for a long time, refilling the pond in his belly. Afterwards he stood up.

"See" he said. The others nodded.

So it seemed Rivniann didn't eat. He peed out the old water and drank in fresh water to refresh the pond inside him that provided water for the fish and the other creatures inside. The butterflies and probably the little bird too.

"Refresh. Life." He said and opened his jaws. The bird flew out.

"Others. Come." He said.

Ellendrii and Aro gathered that creatures didn't actually live in him for long; they merely took a vacation inside him. Maybe to be safe from predators. They respected him and came and went. Some bees flew into his jaws and pollinated the flowers inside him, then flew back out again since he kept his mouth open. The pair marvelled at this. He was certainly an unusual creature.

Rivniann sighed and rolled on the ground. The water sloshed inside him. He didn't roll upside down or who knows what would happen to the poor fish inside him, but he rolled from side to side. He opened his jaws, chin rested on the ground and a couple of fluffy dust mice ran into him, down his throat and into his chest cavity where they sat, looking out with apparent glee. Rivniann sat up, the dust mice staring out of his chest at the pair of onlookers. It was certainly different.

"That's really neat" said Aro.

"Thanks" replied Rivniann and nodded his head.

Ellendrii was trying to sit up. He'd managed to push himself up a little more and soon got himself into a sitting position.

"Is it ok if we stay here a while and rest?" he asked Rivniann.

"Yes" replied the Shardog and the pair thanked him.

So they stayed with Rivniann for a while and rested. Aro and Rivniann caught fish in the stream and the water was safe for them to drink their fill. Ellendrii was eager to carry on but his weakness prevented that. He also wanted to fly up and out of the trees and have a look to see how much more of the forest was left for them to go through before they left Rivniann's dell.

Rivniann hung around with them. He seemed to enjoy the company and he was never far away. He even slept beside them. He said it was safe to sleep in the open here. Nothing would harm them. In truth, it was only safe because he was with them. There were a lot of nasty creatures in the forest and they would come into his dell from time to time but Rivniann was a nature nurturer and the creatures who relied on him for food and protection would chase away anything nasty. They would warn things away as well. Most creatures in the forest knew that Rivniann was not to be messed with. Only those who didn't know or were young and reckless would attempt to hunt Rivniann or those he protected. And that wasn't often.

Ellendrii and Aro enjoyed the company. Knowing someone who was native (and not angry with them for whatever reason) was nice and reassuring as well. It made them both feel safer because Rivniann knew the forest and its ways and he told them a lot about the creatures that resided there. A surprising amount, given that he spoke in one word sentences and they were few and far between. But with Ellendrii carefully asking him questions about the things around them, easy questions that he could answer mostly with a simple yes or no, they learned things much faster about the forest.

They also found out that they were nearly out of the forest as well. Rivniann had come there of course to nurture a part of it and offer a safe haven for creatures that were badly hunted. In return he himself wouldn't be hunted either. His body was delicate and if broken, it didn't heal. He had cracks and scratches on him from past battles but luckily nothing so serious that it badly damaged him. Because he protected and defended creatures, they would fight for him if he was attacked. He relied on this help; this ecosystem. He told the pair that most Shardogs could be found in places where creatures needed to be protected. So the forest was one ideal place. Other Shardogs wandered and took creatures with them from place to place, helping to move things around and settle creatures in new places if they were required there to help the balance of the ecosystem in that place.

It was all so fascinating to Ellendrii and Aro to meet a creature like this. Aro couldn't help asking how Shardogs were born though or even how they reproduced. Rivniann told him that they form in ice and come to life. The ice becomes hard and turns to the glass-like substance that their bodies are made of. Shardog young are empty of course when they are born and their particular coming of age makes sense to be when they get their first inhabitant inside them. It may be just moss or some grass but that means the Shardog has its first responsibility and it must work to protect and grow these things. As they get more things inside them, they grow a little. And a little more and more again and they never stop growing so long as they get more inside them. Most of them stop growing because they accept that only so many things fit inside them though. A Shardog that is too large is more prone to damage. Shardogs die when they are smashed. The lights in their eye sockets go out and they die, returning to ice and soaking into the ground once more.

Rivniann told them that there are only a few very large Shardogs. One of them has a whole forest ecosystem inside her! She is known as the mother of nature and has countless creatures living within her safe glassy body. She is the largest Shardog known to exist and is naturally very old and wise, as these things should be when they take on the responsibility of so much life. Her body has grown hard and tough with time. The transparency of her body is covered with green, fresh life. This is why she has lived for so long. She is harder to break! Not that many things attack Shardogs but some creatures like to try their luck of course. And the Shardog will get injured in the process. Things attack them not because they want to eat them but because they want to eat what is inside them. Some creatures don't have the sort of brain that can process the fact the thing they want to eat is inside something else. They don't see the Shardog's body in the way since it is transparent and so they rush in and smash the Shardog accidentally in an attempt to attack what they can see inside. Sometimes a small hunter will get inside a Shardog and create chaos with its ecosystem. Shardogs only allow certain things to enter their jaws but if they aren't paying attention and something slips in, it can destroy everything inside them. This means the Shardog must remove everything inside it and start fresh. They don't shrink back down to something that can only hold few things. Shardogs will only grow, not shrink. If their ecosystems get messed up, they will vomit out everything within them and start again. They will start by collecting moss, plants, water, things to help encourage creatures to go inside and start a new little world there. Unlike young Shardogs, the adult Shardog's responsibility is to recreate anew what was lost.

Shardogs can live indefinitely if they haven't been smashed or badly injured. No one knows the age of the mother of nature because she has been around as long as anyone can remember. Ellendrii did ask where she resided but Rivniann didn't know. He had seen her though, on his travels before he reached the Forest of Foreboding.

They also asked how old Rivniann was. He told them he was several seasons old. He wasn't an adult yet which was why he wasn't as big as he hoped to be. That would take time and trust from little creatures seeking his safety. The dust mice had decided to stay inside him for now and they ran and played. Aro couldn't help watching them. He was hungry.

Shardogs will travel a long way to find the right things to live inside them. It's like finding the ingredients for a cake or a meal. It has to all be just right and work with each other or the ecosystem inside them will fall apart and they will have to start again. All Shardogs are "born" with the instincts they need to start the ecosystem off right but they do make mistakes. Mostly introducing the wrong creature or plant into their bodies that messes up the rest of it. It is the most embarrassing thing for a Shardog to make that mistake and mess it up badly enough that they have to start again. Rivniann said that had never happened to him but the pair suspected he wasn't quite telling the truth. He'd never admit it if he wasn't anyway. His little pride was on the line!

With Rivniann and Aro's care, Ellendrii was soon strong enough to stand and then he became strong enough to walk.

He spent time exploring his surroundings and lounging in the sun because he had missed it and he was fully aware that there may be another few sun cycles ahead of them in the Forest of Foreboding.

Several sun cycles went past. The pair could count them now since they could actually *see* the sun. Ellendrii stretched his wings early one sun and looked to the sky.

"Sure you're ready?" asked Aro as he and Rivniann looked on.

"I'm ready" replied Ellendrii. He was not going to pass up the chance to fly and plus he wanted to know how much more of this place they needed to get through before they reached the other side. Taking off straight upward was always a problem for a creature as big as a Gryphie. Most large birds need a run up before they take to the sky and Gryphies are no different. But they do have strong wing muscles so if they need to, they can take off vertically.

He lifted his wings and beat them down fast, lifting himself off the ground and kicking up with his feet. He rose into the air and took off, his large wings creating dust clouds and shaking the grass and plants all around. The pair sat watching him get higher and higher and eventually leave the canopy of the trees. He was airborne!

Flying up higher, Ellendrii looked down at the terrible forest. He looked back the way they had come and he looked forward to the way they were going and he was very happy to note that they didn't have far to go until they left. He flew along to the edge of the forest to see if the trees Kraarz had told him about were there, so they knew they were going the right way. They should come across the creatures who spoke a foreign language, the ones that forced the Wind Hounds back. He was too high to see anything in the trees but he could certainly see the trees and the land beyond. He felt refreshed beyond words. For the two of them to travel and not have to risk starvation on the sea or lost in the forest would be a wonderful thing!

Looking back the way they had come, Ellendrii saw the Forest of Foreboding as far as the eye could see; it was vast! To think they had come all that way! The Wind Hounds and their city was in the past now and the coast was far behind them. Ellendrii spent a little time up there flying around. He didn't want to go back down now. It would be so easy to just carry on. Leave Aro with Rivniann. He knew the Lizariaous would be safe with the Shardog and Ellendrii could carry on much faster by flight than by walking. He could find the SilvaGryphie and bring her back with him. She was this way! Rivniann had said she was!

But then again what if he got injured along the way? Aro had saved him. If it wasn't for Aro taking him to Rivniann's dell, Ellendrii would be dead. Sure it would be easier to carry on by flight but without someone to look out for him and he to look out for them, it was far more risky. He had to go back whether he liked it or not. He liked it though. Aro was good company. Ellendrii flew back and landed with the others.

"Well?" asked Aro, eagerly.

"I saw the edge of the forest. I flew to it. It's not far at all now, we're nearly out! And I saw the trees those rude little creatures live in too. So we're on the right track. Plus as Rivniann said, it's the way the SilvaGryphie went."

Aro jumped for joy and made Rivniann jump in surprise.

"Careful, Aro!" said Ellendrii smiling.

"Sorry" Aro apologized to Rivniann.

"Fine" Rivniann said. He would have smiled if he could create an expression. His ears and body language spoke far better than his smiling face ever could.

It was however, Rivniann's turn to ask a question.

"Why look?" he asked. Two words in one sentence was a big thing for him it seemed.

"Why look for what?" asked Ellendrii.

"SilvaGryphie" replied Rivniann.

"To prove some idiots wrong" grinned Ellendrii and Aro sniggered. Things were looking up for once and they would soon be on their way out of this awful place. When Ellendrii had been up there, he had seen how much nicer this part of the forest was than the rest. The blackened trees that went as far as the eye could see were interrupted by the greenness of Rivniann's trees and it was like an oasis in the desert. If the two of them knew what that was of course.

363

Rivniann nodded and twitched his ears, his tail wagging, the black fluffy tip swishing to and fro.

Ellendrii and Aro spent time refilling their gourds and getting fish for the bag to take with them. The rest had done them a lot of good and had been much needed; now they could carry on without collapsing from starvation. Rivniann helped them get the food and pack it into Ellendrii's bag. They planned to leave at sunrise the next sun cycle.

As Aro slept, Ellendrii talked to Rivniann.

"How can I ever repay you for what you have done for us" he said.

"No" said Rivniann shaking his head.

"Help. Good. Enough. For. Me." He put a pebbled paw on Ellendrii's shoulder and wagged his tail. Being able to help someone in need was repayment for him. Now the pair could go safely and well and the satisfaction of that was all Rivniann wanted. Ellendrii still wanted to give him something to remember them by though. He rifled through his bag and found a healing herb. It was dried but he thought Rivniann could make use of it. He gave it to his new friend and Rivniann examined it. Then he swallowed it.

Ellendrii would normally have been shocked and puzzled but of course this was a Shardog doing this; not just any creature!

The herb went down Rivniann's throat and settled near the edge of the pond. One of the dust mice picked it up and carried it to the little tree that grew in his back leg. The herb attached itself to the tree and came back to life again, growing on the side of the tree. The little dust mouse jumped up and down and squeaked happily. Rivniann wagged his tail.

"Now. Others. Can. Heal." He said with a nod. So now, creatures who were injured could come to him, go inside and use the herb to heal themselves. Even though Rivniann could heal them, some creatures were too proud to accept help and this was a good way they could help themselves.

Despite himself, Ellendrii felt the urge to hug Rivniann and did before he'd even thought about it.

"Thank you" he said, embracing his friend. Rivniann put a foreleg around Ellendrii, the pebbles running down from his paw to his leg and then back into his paw again as he lowered it.

"Welcome" he said.

Ellendrii curled up next to Aro and fell asleep as the caring Rivniann watched over them both.

***

The next sun cycle, Ellendrii and Aro were up bright and early at sunrise and Rivniann walked with them to the edge of his little territory.

"Thank you for all you've done" said Ellendrii.

"Yeah thanks! Hope to see you again somecycle!" put in Aro.

"Welcome. Safe. Journey." Crackled and chinked Rivniann, tail wagging. As they left, they could hear him waving to them. Somehow going back into the dark forest didn't seem so bad now. They felt refreshed and hopeful since Ellendrii knew that they didn't have further to go until they got out of there. And Aro hadn't upset a new friend, which made a nice change!

Ellendrii wondered if they would see more Shardogs or even the mother of nature on their travels. Rivniann hadn't specified where the Shardogs mostly resided. He thought he would keep an eye out for more of them on their travels.

The two of them forced their way through the undergrowth when it got to that familiar thickness. They took it in turns as usual. It got darker again the deeper they went but they didn't have to worry because it wasn't long before they were coming back into the sparser stuff again. They were nearly out!

The sun was high in the sky when they finally made it out of the Forest of Foreboding. They reached a fresh, grassy area and sat down for a rest and some food. They hadn't eaten since being in the dell and they had only stopped once for a drink. Ahead of them in the distance stretched the area of trees and whatever lived in them. The air was fresh and clear and the two of them shifted around in the grass, enjoying the nice feel of it under their feet instead of the awful grey soil of the forest. They also enjoyed the sun shining

365

down on them. Even though it had been sunny in the dell, they felt more of the sun out in the open here. They had wandered a little way away from the forest now and down the slight incline of a hill. The trees were in a shallow valley. It stretched as far as Aro could see and he breathed in deeply. The trees were very very tall and had branches full of fresh, green leaves at intervals up their narrow trunks.

"This place doesn't smell of death and foreboding!" he exclaimed and lay down, rolling onto his side and smiling up at Ellendrii.

"I'm so glad to be out of there" murmured Ellendrii. "I swear if I had flown up and not been able to see the other side of that wretched place, I would have gone mad."

"Good thing you could see the other side then!" said Aro happily.

"Tell me about it" muttered Ellendrii. He stretched and lay on the grass next to Aro.

"It's so refreshing to be out here and in the sort of environment we're used to! Now we just have to sneak through those woods down there and hope that none of the natives spot us. We'll try going round them. If we go around and not through, we shouldn't be trespassing too badly on their territory and we should be able to pass through without trouble.

A while later, they headed down to the trees. They quietly made their way to the outskirts of them and walked, keeping a low profile and hoping nothing would spot them. They heard rustling in the trees but didn't look or do anything to acknowledge it. They wanted to put through with their body language that they were harmless and not interested in contact or conflict with anyone; they just wanted to be left alone.

However, they didn't take into account that maybe some of the creatures on the ground in their dens under rocks and in burrows might notice them pass. Especially when Aro stepped in one by accident. It had been a sweet little wooden house, a little small one, a simple one that resembled the float shack the pair had traversed the vast water in. But after Aro's great paw had come down upon it, it was in pieces and a smashed mess.

"Aro!! Watch where you're walking!" snapped Ellendrii. "You'll get us into trouble again!"

"Sorry" replied Aro, hanging his head, "I thought it was only things in the trees we had to watch out for, I wasn't thinking about where I was walking."

"Where were you looking then?"

"Straight ahead."

"Not down, keeping a low profile and body language?"

"Err no, Lizariaouses don't do that. When we keep a low body language, we hang our heads low and looked fixedly straight ahead of us. I was looking at you."

"Well you *should* be looking *down!*" snapped Ellendrii, cuffing him across the ears.

"Ow, hey!" protested Aro.

"If we get into trouble again because of you, I think I'll explode!" snapped Ellendrii.

"I said I was sorry!" whined Aro. "It's not my fault whatever lives here can't decide if it wants to live in the trees or on the ground!"

"You should know by now that things are different in these lands from what we're used to. You should always..." Ellendrii trailed off.

"I should always what?" asked Aro. He was looking at Ellendrii pointedly.

"Don't move..." said Ellendrii.

"Oh and why's that?" replied Aro with a disbelieving tone. "Is my foot in one of their nests or something?"

"No. But they are...all around us..." muttered Ellendrii. Aro looked up and saw that they were indeed surrounded by small creatures. They resembled what we would think of as a cross between a squirrel and a rabbit. They had long ears like a rabbit, paws like a squirrel or rat and long, bushy tails. Some of them didn't have bushy tails though; they were more like the tail of a chinchilla or gerbil and they were shorter. All of them had glowing insects circling their tails though. And they all wore white masks with patterns on them and glowing eye holes. The pair couldn't see their faces at all.

What they *could* see was that these creatures were chirring angrily and advancing on them.

Chapter 20
Language Barrier

Ellendrii and Aro had backed into each other and were both facing out at the threat. The creatures were mostly black and grey in colouration but a few were more brown and grey. They noticed that each mask had different markings on it, making each creature an individual. Most of them had two glowing bugs circling their tail but a few had more and one had them circling the whole of the tail; there must have been eight or nine of them. Most of these glowing bugs glowed yellow but some glowed orange and pink. A few of the creatures also wore accessories such as armlets, necklets and bracelets, which were all made from natural materials.

These creatures are called Kanniths. Since they don't speak an understandable language, the two friends can't find out their name so for simplicity, that is how we will refer to them throughout this encounter.

One came forward, it had six bugs circling its tail and they glowed orange. It chuffed at them with a voice like an angry squirrel. Some of them had sticks and they waved them at the pair, threateningly.

Aro growled at them and Ellendrii stood his ground.

"We just want to pass through" he said, speaking slowly.

The Kanniths advanced on them and tried to herd them back towards the forest. When they found the pair wouldn't move, they started to prod them with their sticks. They were noisy little creatures who appeared to believe that the noisier they were; the more threatening they would be. Aro growled more loudly.

"Aro, we have to be non-threatening to them or they will just keep on doing what they are doing. I think they think we came from the forest and they want us to go back to where we belong."

"We *did* come from the forest though" said Aro.

"No, I think they think we live in the forest and are creatures of the forest which is why they are scared of us."

"They don't look scared" muttered Aro in annoyance as one poked a stick at his rump. He spun his head round and growled loudly at it but it only persisted.

"Try a little submissive body language. We want to show them that we won't harm them."

"I will harm them if they keep smacking me with sticks! Can't we just roar and flame them and scare them away?"

"It won't work. The trees are alive with them, we're far outnumbered. They only have sticks at the moment but how long before they physically attack or kill us? They could, considering their numbers."

"You Gryphies are all about peace aren't you? When will you learn that peace doesn't always work?"

"Peace is always a good option. Then you live to fight another sun cycle. When will *you* learn that it's not always about barging in with ferocity and anger? Just *try* it, Aro."

Aro grumbled and grunted.

"FINE, but when they just attack us anyway while our guards are down, I will tear them all to pieces and drown them in their own blood!" he spat.

"Charming" muttered Ellendrii and adopted a peaceful stance with his ears and body low and his head bowed. Surely even though their language was different, they would recognize a universal body language. Aro did the same, flattening his needles to show that he wasn't hostile and wouldn't shoot them. He grunted and bowed his head low.

The Kanniths still tried to herd them back to the forest but they wouldn't budge and eventually the creatures stopped prodding them. A noble looking Kannith with a huge bushy tail and ten purple glowing bugs circling the length of it came forward. They hadn't seen one with bugs of this colour circling its tail yet so they figured that judging by the size and stance of this one, it was probably their leader. He sat before the pair of them and gestured with his paws.

Of course, neither of them understood but they did sit down in a similar manner to how this leader was sat, just in case that was what they should do. It seemed ok. Ellendrii wasn't sure how to act or what to say to tell him that they were passing through and meant no harm. He didn't understand the

370

gestures of the Kannith but he supposed their leader wanted to know why the two strangers were there.

"We are…" said Ellendrii and made a walking motion with his fingers, "Passing through…" He made the motion as though it was walking a long way. He pointed at the forest and then pointed to beyond the Kannith territory and then he pointed to himself and Aro and then pointed beyond the Kannith territory again.

The leader seemed more interested in Ellendrii's dextrous hands than what he was actually pointing at or motioning. The little creature came right up to him and grabbed his arm, pulling it down to a more suitable height and examining Ellendrii's hand with interest, then comparing it with his own. Ellendrii had longer fingers than the Kannith leader. The Kanniths had three fingers and a thumb on their front feet but only three toes on the back ones. So they both had a similar setup in the way of fingers and toes. Ellendrii was glad the leader was curious about him; it meant that maybe the pair could pass through unharmed. The hostility had gone from the others when they saw their leader examining Ellendrii. Some of them came closer once they saw the two weren't attacking the leader.

One of these was an old Kannith who, like the leader, had a lot of glowing bugs going along his tail. He had twelve orange bugs and Ellendrii was surprised that he had more than the leader. Maybe they had more depending on age or wisdom. This Elder had a long gnarled stick and walked carefully. His fur was silver and looked aged yet in perfect, shiny condition. They could only assume that maybe his fur had been black when he was younger.

The Elder examined the two of them as well but then he smelled the herbs in Ellendrii's bag and without even asking, he had opened it and was foraging inside.

"Hey!" began Aro but Ellendrii motioned for him to shut up.

"If he wants to take something, let him. We need to be on their good side if we want to go through here. It really doesn't matter."

371

Aro shut up and watched the Elder pull out some leaves that were used for binding wounds. They were large leaves, nearly as big as he was! The Elder took the leaves away and returned with a large mushroom and placed it in the bag. He nodded to Ellendrii and twitched his ears. It was bizarre for the pair of them not being able to see the faces of the Kanniths. This was, they assumed, why body language was so important.

After that, the other Kanniths backed off. It appeared that a fair trade was all that was needed in order to pass through here. Ellendrii figured that others who had tried to pass through had been offended by the Kanniths' initial hostility and attacked them or been forced back to the forest. It was quite difficult to let your guard down and be submissive when faced with hostile creatures who looked like they might attack at any moment.

The Leader nodded to Ellendrii and Aro and then motioned for them to follow him. It appeared that the leaves they had taken were of great use to the Kanniths, which was why they were more hospitable now. Ellendrii warned Aro to let him do all the communicating though. It was more important now more than ever that they didn't mess this up.

They wanted to get moving but they knew it would be rude not to follow the Leader and do as he wished. They had already spent long enough in the forest.

The Leader took them to his tree. As they walked, they noticed the Kanniths' small wooden hut homes on the ground and up in the trees too. They had made little tree houses with wooden walkways leading to them. It was a whole little city up in the trees.

At the base of the Leader's tree, there was a little sitting area, they assumed this was where he held meetings with others or did leaderly things. He sat down and they followed suit.

The Leader chirred and chiffed and made a leaf shape with his hands. He nodded and his eyes glowed brightly. He wagged his tail and chirped.

Ellendrii and Aro bowed their heads and wagged their tails in a similar fashion. The Leader motioned to the territory by making large circular movements with his hands. He pointed to Ellendrii and Aro. They weren't sure what he meant though. Could they explore? Was he telling them this all belonged to him? Was he asking them to feel at home? Ellendrii sighed. This was one scenario he had never even dreamed of being in. Normally creatures that couldn't talk their own language were meal creatures and although the pair of them could quite comfortably eat the Kanniths, they had intelligence and they could communicate despite not speaking the same language. Also they showed a curiosity about the pair that they hadn't noticed with other creatures. At least not in this way.

While they were sat there with the Leader, other Kanniths, mostly young ones, came and looked at them. A few were even bold enough to climb all over Aro. He sat patiently but Ellendrii could see that he didn't appreciate it. One young Kannith clambered up one of Aro's needles and was about to touch the poisonous tip of it when Aro rattled them quickly in warning and the Kanniths, startled, fled.

The Leader didn't like this and he chirred in anger at Aro.

Aro made a sign for a needle, pointed to them and then motioned dying, to try and show that they were dangerous and not to go near them. He did this a couple of times in various ways, just to make sure the Kanniths understood. They nodded. This was the general show of understanding, the pair learned. They would nod to show they had understood what they had been shown. And the Kanniths didn't go near his needles again.

Now the Leader wished to talk to them. He pointed to the forest and then made a motion for a creature coming out of the forest. He accompanied these signs with chirrs and chirps even though the pair couldn't understand. They assumed the other Kanniths could understand what these noises meant.

Then he motioned claws with his hands, scratching at the air. He pointed to the Kanniths in the trees and made pushing motions, then made the same motions in the direction of the forest. Ellendrii and Aro watched carefully and nodded once they had understood.

Basically, nasty creatures came out of the forest so the Kanniths would herd them back in again, to protect themselves and to stop the bad from the forest escaping.

He presented his hand to the pair, out flat and palm up, then the other hand he motioned in the same way. And then he shrugged and looked at them.

He was asking where they came from.

Ellendrii pointed to the forest and then shook his head. He pointed to his wings and then to the sky and nodded. He pointed to Aro and himself and then pointed in the direction of the forest but slightly higher, to try and show that they had come from beyond the forest. He wasn't sure what knowledge these creatures had of the world beyond that vast forest but he didn't want to confuse matters by trying to sign for the water or coming over it on the float. He guessed that the Kanniths knew their territory and the bad things that came from the forest.

The Leader, thankfully, nodded. His glowing eyes blinked every so often. So now he knew that they had come from beyond the forest and not *from* the forest. A few other Kanniths had once again gathered round out of curiosity in the newcomers.

Ellendrii wanted to ask the Leader if he had seen the SilvaGryphie but he had no idea how to sign for that. So he decided to try and show him in a different way. He wanted to draw a picture of her on the ground. The ground underneath the tree was bare and there was no grass there, as there was in other places, probably because the tree was used so much. He needed a stick though. Instead of getting up and finding one, for fear of offending the Leader if it looked like he was going to leave before the conversation was over, he pointed to a branch of the tree. Then he motioned breaking the branch and then he pointed at himself.

The Leader looked at what he was doing and his glowing eyes became dull. He shook his head and then motioned with both his hands, palms up, for Ellendrii to try and explain again.

Ellendrii pointed at the branch and then pointed at himself.

The Leader ran up the tree and motioned for Ellendrii to follow him. He thought that Ellendrii wanted to see his home. Ellendrii followed and Aro watched, unable to climb of course. The tree was smaller than the ones Ellendrii was used to from the Forest back home. It didn't entirely hold his weight that well. He felt the branches bending a little under his weight and this made him feel very unsure as he climbed higher.

Annoyingly, the Leader's little home was high up in the branches of the tree and Ellendrii found that despite his fairly light weight and hollow skeleton, he still couldn't reach it. He could however, reach a branch. He wasn't going to purposefully pull one off though in case that offended the Kannith. This was *his* tree after all, and Ellendrii himself would have been annoyed if someone had broken a branch of his own tree simply to draw a picture in the dirt.

So Ellendrii put a foot on one of the branches and pressed down hard, in the pretence that the branch had merely broken under his weight. Then he pretended to fall a little and slid back down to the ground. The branch was lying on the ground next to him. He hung his head sadly and looked up at the tree, and then he pointed to the tree, pointed to himself and then shook his head. The Leader followed him back down and patted him on the leg in understanding.

Ellendrii picked up the branch and pointed one finger in the air as though he had had an idea and then he began to draw on the ground with the branch. It was a small, twiggy branch and fine for doing a scrawly drawing with. The Leader watched with interest.

Ellendrii drew a Gryphie with fluffy fur and big wings. He pointed to himself and Aro and then to the drawing and shrugged in the manner of asking a question, then cocked his head to one side and pointed to the picture again.

The Leader looked at the picture and then at Ellendrii and then at the picture again. Then he clapped his hands. He had thought Ellendrii was asking what he thought of the picture. Ellendrii shook his head, pointed to the picture and then to him and Aro and then out beyond the Kannith territory. Then he shrugged.

375

The Leader pointed to him and Aro and pointed out of the Kannith territory and nodded. Ellendrii wasn't sure what he meant. He assumed that the Leader thought he was being asked if the pair of them could carry on their journey and the Leader was saying that they could. The Leader thought the drawing was of Ellendrii.

Ellendrii shook his head and pointed to the picture, then to himself and then shook his head again. He waved his hands in the air from side to side in a "no" motion. The Leader watched carefully. Ellendrii really had no idea how to ask this question. He sat down and sighed.

"He can't understand me" he said to Aro.

"Have you seen the SilvaGryphie?" asked Aro to the Leader. The Leader looked puzzled.

"That wouldn't work" said Ellendrii.

"It was worth a try" replied Aro, "Just in case."

"I guess. But it's a hard question to ask. I'm not used to communicating like this" said Ellendrii sadly.

"Maybe we should just go. I understood that much. That we're allowed to go" replied Aro.

"Yeah you're right. We're behind time now anyway. Not that it's a race or anything but getting lost in that awful forest didn't help"

The Leader chittered and chuffed and hopped around. He wasn't keen on the pair talking to each other because he couldn't understand what they were saying.

Ellendrii bowed his head in apology. Then he pointed to himself and Aro and pointed out beyond the Kannith territory in the direction they were headed.

The Leader nodded and stood up. He motioned for them to go and patted Ellendrii on the arm in a "safe journey" kind of manner.

Ellendrii smiled and nodded. The Leader's mask was very intricate up close. The white material it was made of looked a lot like bone and it was carefully carved with patterns. Ellendrii assumed higher ranking or older Kanniths would have more intricate patterns on their masks and he was right. The baby Kanniths' masks were nearly bare. He wondered what they needed to do to get more details on their masks. Some coming of age stuff similar to the Wind Hounds he assumed; only the masks were made by the Kanniths and not naturally formed like the Wind Hounds' markings. He wondered if they really were bone. Maybe the bones of larger creatures that the Kanniths found dead or something.

He and Aro headed through their territory. It was vast for such small creatures and there were many of them.

"I'm guessing they defend themselves by sheer numbers" said Ellendrii, "Cos they certainly don't seem like the sort of creatures that could do much harm to other things by themselves."

"They eat bugs. I've seen some of them eat" said Aro. "I wonder if they get hungry and eat the ones on their tails" he smirked.

"Doubtful. That seems to be some sort of relationship. I'm assuming those bugs hang around the Kanniths' tails so other bugs won't eat them. The Kanniths eat bugs, after all. Any bug that tries to eat the ones around their tails would get eaten itself."

"You're more observant than I am" laughed Aro.

Ellendrii was going to reply that "It was a Gryphie thing" but he decided against it. Aro tended to get irritable if he thought there was any contest of that kind between the two of them.

As they walked, Kanniths came to see them and run alongside them. Some jumped onto their backs and came along for the ride a little way. Youngsters in particular and then their parents would usually arrive and tell them off. And yes, they did talk to each other in chirps and vocals and not sign language.

There were no larger predators here that hunted the Kanniths because the Kanniths would scare them away. It was a haven for the little squirrelish creatures. Some of the tree trunks had symbols on them, painted in plant juice or bug juice or something that had been found, maybe berry juice Ellendrii pondered. He had also noticed that the males had the big bushy tails and the females had the smaller, lesser furred tails, as Kraarz had mentioned. Males seemed to use their tail in courtship rituals. The bigger and bushier, the more impressive it was. Mothers had litters by the look of it too. There was usually one mother ordering a few of the smaller ones around and they didn't seem to babysit other mothers' youngsters either.

"I wish we could understand them better. I really want to know if they have seen the SilvaGryphie" said Ellendrii.

"Yeah it would be useful but we have no way of showing them what she looks like" replied Aro.

"I'm not very good at making her on the ground" said Ellendrii, "He just thought it was a picture of myself."

"Can't blame him. You're the only Gryphie he's probably seen" replied Aro.

"Yeah. Good thing I never used my wings or I'd be giving them all rides" chuckled Ellendrii. Aro smirked.

"Hey, there's that Elder one" said Ellendrii, pointing. "I wonder what he did with those leaves. And what that mushroom is that he gave us."

"Those leaves seemed important to him" said Aro.

"I'm gunna ask him!" said Ellendrii and went over to the Elder.

"I thought we were in a hurry though…" muttered Aro but followed.

Ellendrii went up to the Elder, who bowed his head in greeting, glowing eyes blinking. Ellendrii pointed to his bag and then made the shape of the leaf in the air and then shrugged.

The Elder nodded and motioned for them to follow him. They did and he took them to a little wooden hut nearby. The Elder pointed to the small hole in the side that served as a window and then pointed to one of his glowing eyes, then to Ellendrii and then to the hole again. He wanted Ellendrii to look inside and Ellendrii obliged.

Inside was a Kannith sleeping soundly and wrapped up in one of the large leaves.

"It's bedding?" asked Ellendrii and made a sign for sleeping, then shrugged.

The Elder shook his head. He coughed and then made a motion for wrapping himself up and sleeping.

"Ah, it's for healing the sick" said Ellendrii. Wrapping yourself up in one of the leaves when you're sick is apparently a cure if you're a Kannith.

Ellendrii coughed and motioned wrapping himself up and then pointed to the window hole and nodded. The Elder nodded too. Ellendrii took out the mushroom and pointed to it, then put his head on one side in puzzlement.

The Elder nodded and made an eating motion. Then he motioned sleeping. The mushroom put you to sleep. Why this was a useful thing, Ellendrii wasn't sure. Maybe it was for insomnia? Ellendrii nodded anyway and bowed his head in thanks. He assumed it was a fair trade. The mushroom would put the sick to sleep but not heal them, whereas the leaves would heal them as well. So he thought anyway.

Ellendrii pointed to himself and Aro and then pointed to the way they were headed, bowing his head afterwards. The Elder nodded and patted Ellendrii's arm, which seemed to be the customary goodbye sign.

They headed onwards through the territory.

"I like the little things they've built in the trees" said Ellendrii, "They will keep them dry when it rains. I guess it's a bit easier when you're small. I couldn't imagine us building shelters like that in our trees. We're just too big."

"Yeah, although looking at them *does* make me feel kinda hungry…" muttered Aro, trailing off.

"Don't even *think* about it! You can't eat these, they're intelligent like us! They might speak a different language but they make sense."

"Pfft says you. You eat sea vultures and forest deer and they probably talk to each other like these things do. At least Lizariaouses don't care."

"Yeah but sea vultures and forest deer have never tried to talk to us or anything. These things do. So it's different. Besides, we have to eat something."

"You guys can eat meat and plants though. We can only eat meat! So there's an excuse for you. Eat bugs or berries."

"Ergh, bugs, like the Sky Gryphies eat. The very thought makes my stomach churn. I couldn't stop eating meat anyway. Gryphies NEED meat. It's part of our balanced diet."

"Bugs *are* meat" said Aro, with a smirk.

"*You* eat them then" said Ellendrii.

"I'd eat them happily!" replied Aro. "It doesn't bother me in the least."

Ellendrii pulled up a nearby rock and showed Aro the squirming grubs underneath it. He looked around. The Kanniths hadn't noticed and if they had, they didn't care. He wasn't damaging anything important.

"Eat those then" said Ellendrii, pointing at the grubs.

"I will if you will" grinned Aro.

"I hate you sometimes" said Ellendrii.

"Well, will you?" asked Aro.

"These are worse than bugs. Look at them squirm!" Ellendrii felt sick looking at them. They looked rather slimy.

"Well then I won't eat them. Remember, it doesn't bother me. Even these ones."

"Have you ever had one before?" asked Ellendrii.

"Yes" lied Aro.

"Are they tasty?" asked Ellendrii.

"They're good and meaty" lied Aro. "Trust me!"

Ellendrii's stomach was grumbling but that didn't make the grubs look any more appetizing.

"Ok, we'll try together then" said Ellendrii. They picked a grub each and Ellendrii put the rock back down.

Aro held his up to his muzzle.

"Together" said Ellendrii and Aro nodded.

After a short pause, they both popped the grubs into their mouths. Aro chewed his up and swallowed it.

"No worse than a rockrat" he said, "And no fur to choke on either!"

Ellendrii was struggling with his.

"Just swallow it if you can't chew it" said Aro. Ellendrii looked rather green. Some Kanniths had gathered round to watch them.

Ellendrii swallowed it down but then retched and puked it back up again. The Kanniths chittered and sniggered all around them. Grubs were one of their favourite foods! Aro laughed too, rolling around in the grass.

"Oh wow, it was really *that* bad? You Gryphies have weak constitutions" he roared, laughing.

"Shut up" spat Ellendrii, ears back and frowning.

"I hadn't actually had one before" admitted Aro, "And even *I* didn't find it *that* bad."

"You lied? You grikker!" snapped Ellendrii.

"Well I had to get you to eat it somehow" smirked Aro.

"But I didn't eat it, it made me throw up! Now I'm hungrier than ever!" Ellendrii snapped.

"Let's eat something then. We have some fish in that bag of yours. I'm assuming that Elder creature didn't take that too"

"No, he didn't" replied Ellendrii and they sat down to eat. The fish felt odd in Ellendrii's mouth. After that awful grub, everything felt weird and slimy. Fish were kind of slimy anyway but these had dried out a little at least. They had a drink and then headed on. The shallow valley was very long and it deepened as they carried on. The trees kept on going though and were alive with Kanniths.

"Hey, why don't you fly up and see how much further we have to go before we get to the end of their territory" suggested Aro.

"I'd rather fly after we've left their territory. I'm not sure if they would be freaked out when they learn I can fly. And then there is that giving them rides thing which I'm afraid they will want to do. They already keep coming up and riding on us every so often" replied Ellendrii.

"*You* not use your wings? I'm shocked" said Aro, with an expression of mock surprise on his face.

"I just think it's safer" said Ellendrii.

"They're used to us; I really don't think that you'll freak them out. I've seen birds fly overhead, I'm sure that they'll think nothing of you taking flight" persuaded Aro.

"Ok fine but if it freaks them out, I'm blaming you" said Ellendrii and spread his wings.

Aro rolled his eyes as his friend took flight into the air and flew up past the trees. The Kanniths in the trees nearly fell out of them in surprise and they all stared at Ellendrii.

Going up higher, Ellendrii saw that the trees didn't go on much longer. They were nearly past the territory of these creatures. He saw that beyond their territory, the valley was deeper with the sides going up much more steeply either side. The valley seemed to narrow too, so Ellendrii figured it might be a good idea to climb up one of the sides and gain a higher perspective on where they had to go. In the distance, a silvery lake stretched out, wide and sparkling in the sunlight. He thought they should head for that lake and maybe go around it for a while. He knew that lakes had fresh water in them similar to the one in Shernaron, so they wouldn't need to struggle with drinking and there would probably be things to hunt around the lake as well. Anything to make their journey easier.

Ellendrii flew back down carefully into the trees and alighted next to Aro. The Kanniths all immediately rushed up to him and clambered on top of him. They made flapping motions with their forelegs and pointed upward.

"What did I tell you!" snarled Ellendrii at Aro who was trying his best to look innocent.

"Aww just give them a little ride!" said Aro. "You don't want to upset them!" He smiled innocently as the little white masked creatures waited patiently for Ellendrii to take off. They held his mane fur in their hands and clung to the five long black backwards pointing spikes that ran the length of Ellendrii's spine. One even sat on his head and held onto his mane there too.

Ellendrii sighed and took to the sky again. Aro watched him go. Next to him, the Leader of the Kanniths sat and nodded his head in approval. Aro had actually told them that Ellendrii would give them a ride if they wanted. He had pointed at the Kanniths and then at Ellendrii and then made a flapping motion and pointed upwards. This had made them really excited. Well Ellendrii had gone on and on about not wanting to fly in case this happened, Aro just *had* to make it happen! Besides it was harmless enough. Unless a Kannith fell to its death of course. Then *Ellendrii* would be pissing off another culture for once! That wasn't Aro's plan though. He wasn't *that* mean not even in joking and he had hoped that wouldn't happen. Because after all, if that had happened, it would be *his* fault, although indirectly.

Ellendrii did have to admit it was fun impressing another culture like this. The Kanniths all squeaked with joy as he flew along and he had to resist doing a loop the loop. After a while he came back down again but he had to go back up again because the Leader, Elder and another load of youngsters wanted to go flying.

This went on for a while. In the end he felt like he'd taken the whole tribe of them up in the air. He hadn't of course, because that would probably have taken several sun cycles but it was beginning to get dark by the time he had finished showing them all what flying was like. He was also rather tired. The Leader had stuck around to watch or maybe supervise and make sure everything happened safely, not to mention having several more goes on Ellendrii's back in the sky.

As the sun started to set, Ellendrii pointed to himself and Aro and then closed his eyes, making a sleeping motion and pointed to the area around, asking if they could stay for the moon.

The Leader nodded and motioned for them to follow him, which they did. He had no sheltered place for them to sleep but he showed them a nice spot under some trees and not too far away from their current position so they could easily carry on come sunrise. They thanked him and settled down.

"Well, thanks to your wonderful suggestion of me giving them all rides, we're still here instead of actually making it out of here and being able to carry on before sunrise" said Ellendrii, frowning at Aro.

Aro shrugged.

"Hey, at least we're among friends. At least it's not that horrible Forest of Foreboding. We can carry on fresh come sunrise" he said, laying his head down on his paws.

"I guess you're right. We've no idea how further we need to go before we find the SilvaGryphie anyway. While I was up in the sky I saw we had nearly left this territory and there is a deep valley beyond. I thought we could climb up one of the sides and head towards a lake out in the distance."

"Isn't that going in a curve and not a straight line though?" asked Aro.

"It doesn't matter. That only mattered in the forest because we were following the path that the Wind Hounds went. Now the land is free for us to explore. We only wanted to get out of the forest and not get lost and the best way to find our way out was to take the path of the Wind Hounds and get to where we are now" explained Ellendrii.

"Ah I see. So long as we don't head in exactly the wrong direction. The lake is off to the left or the right?" asked Aro.

"The right" replied Ellendrii.

"Well let's hope the right is the right direction for the SilvaGryphie" said Aro.

"We could carry on straight but we would have a better view of the land by getting out of this valley" said Ellendrii.

"Yeah true" replied Aro.

Some young Kanniths played around nearby and moved closer to the pair once they saw they had settled down. Chirping and squeaking happily, the little Kanniths settled with them.

"Guess they feel safe with us" said Ellendrii as one cuddled up next to him.

Aro just frowned with a couple curled up on his head.

"So long as they don't move around too much while I'm trying to sleep" he said, "Or wake me up. Cos if they do…"

"You'll put up with it" said Ellendrii, with a small snarl. Aro sighed.

"Yes, I'll put up with it" he repeated through gritted teeth. Ellendrii nodded.

The two settled down as the moon rose higher in the sky, chatting and listening to the world around them. It made a delightful change to sleeping in the forest even though the last couple of moon cycles they had slept in the dell with Rivniann. At least here they knew they were safe and they could get a good sleep instead of having to be on the alert. The moon cycles they had slept in the dell were the best sleep they'd had for a long while. Travelling through the forest had been so tiring!

The sun rose the next morning and they were surrounded by the Kanniths running around and playing. The little creatures soon went off to look for bugs, leaving Ellendrii and Aro alone.

"Well they didn't wake me up" yawned Aro.

"Me neither although one did step on my eye just before I fell asleep and their glows disturbed my sleep a little" muttered Ellendrii.

The young Kanniths had only one glowing bug circling their tails. Ones who had two, the bugs flew in opposite directions to each other around their tails. Ones with two or more had every other bug on their tail flying in one direction and vice versa.

"I'm surprised they woke you. You're used to sleeping in a tree and seeing the sun rise whenever it rises. I would have thought they'dve disturbed me more since I sleep in a cave" observed Aro.

"Have you SEEN how you sleep? Like a snoring log. I wouldn't think even a storm would wake you up" said Ellendrii.

"Storms *do* wake me up" said Aro.

"If they hit your cave" muttered Ellendrii.

"What?"

"Nothing."

The two got up, stretched and carried on walking. They hadn't bothered with breakfast, figuring they would hunt once they had left this territory. There was nothing to eat here except Kanniths and bugs and they wouldn't eat the former for obvious reasons. Ellendrii had had enough of bugs already. And grubs!

They had found that each abode of the Kanniths was different and unique according to those who inhabited it. At first glance they appeared to look all the same but they didn't. Ellendrii guessed that they were hand made by those that they belonged to. Most of the ground houses were small but the ones in the trees were much larger and more ornate as most of the little creatures lived in the trees. They put more effort into them and Ellendrii hazarded a guess that the ones in the trees were higher ranking than the ones that had to live on the ground. Even though there appeared to be nothing that hunted them, the ones on the ground were still more at risk than the ones in the trees. Ellendrii had also noticed that there were sentries in the trees, watching their every move and also watching the movements of the Kanniths too. They themselves never appeared to move. They had pink glowing bugs circling their tails. Ellendrii hadn't seen anything yet that would cause them to, even if it was something such as a Kannith misbehaving, so he wasn't sure what would cause them to move. A predator in the area he supposed. He wondered if anything nasty had come out of the forest and damaged the Kanniths' population. He assumed it had happened or they wouldn't be so protective of their territory. He really wished he could ask them but he knew it was too complicated a question to sign properly. At least Rivniann could do yes or no and understand their speech. These creatures couldn't understand them at all.

The sentries watching Aro made him a bit nervous but he never let on. He didn't want Ellendrii to know that he didn't like being watched. Lizariaouses were meant to be brave. But even they got unnerved at times.

The trees looked nothing like the ones in Shernaron. The Shernaron evergreen trees had thick trunks and sturdy branches. These had narrow trunks and spindly branches, which was why they had had trouble holding Ellendrii when he'd tried to climb one. Nevertheless, he could see Kanniths even at the very tops of these trees and they were completely unbothered by the height. He supposed that their trees were the same to them as his were to him; strong and able to support a climber.

In the distance, he and Aro could see an end to the trees. They had nearly left the relative safety of this territory and were ready to go wherever the journey took them. The younger Kanniths were still following them but they all trailed off the closer the pair got to the edge of this sparse forest. It was dangerous near the edge. If there were any predators around, they could pick off unwary youngsters with relative ease near the edge of it. Ellendrii wondered if anything bad had tried to come in from this side of the territory. He wished he'd asked but it was just too much of an effort to try and communicate. Besides, they would find out soon enough.

"I'm gunna miss these little things" said Aro as the last one left them and went back to its parents.

"I'm surprised you haven't sneakily eaten one" said Ellendrii.

"I was tempted a few times" grinned Aro.

"I could see they annoyed you a few times as well" observed Ellendrii.

"Well, yeah but now they're gone, I kinda miss them" replied Aro.

"Well I'm sure we'll find something else you can hang around with" Ellendrii told him.

"I hope we've passed the worst of this though. I don't want to have to go through anything else like the Forest of Foreboding or the Repulsators or Narg'tok."

"I can't promise we won't come up against anything like that again but so long as we're together looking out for each other, I think we'll be ok" replied Ellendrii.

The white masked sentries nodded to the pair as they made their way to the edge of the territory and they nodded back in a sign of respect.

"I wish I could thank them for helping us out and being nice" said Ellendrii.

"Their Elder took those leaves; that was what won them over. I'm sure they saw that as thanks" replied Aro. "Besides, think how stupid those Wind Hounds are for not sussing out how to be friends with these creatures and having to go back through the Forest of Foreboding again, the grikking idiots! And having the scars to prove it! We did better than that. Not only did we make it out ok but we also made friends with those little creatures."

"You're right! It all went well; we're getting better at meeting other creatures! Them and Rivniann and…Midnyte Comet…" Ellendrii looked wistful. Aro shoved him.

"Grow up, it's just a kitten crush" snorted Aro, laughing.

"I am NOT a kitten!!" spat Ellendrii, his nostrils flaring blue.

"Hey I was only joking. Your reaction shows how immature you are!" laughed Aro.

"Since when did you suddenly grow up?" snapped Ellendrii.

Aro shrugged.

"Since we're still alive and have passed all the obstacles we've encountered so far" he grinned. Ellendrii grinned too. He'd never actually expected them to have got this far.

But there was still a long way to go.

Chapter 21
Moving Again

Ellendrii and Aro left the Kannith tree territory and headed into the valley. As they walked, the sides of the valley started to steepen.

"I think we should find a path up to the top. There must be one somewhere or something we can use as a path" suggested Ellendrii, thinking it would be easier for Aro.

Aro nodded. It was probably for the best that Ellendrii hadn't told him why he had thought of a path as it would have made Aro feel like a burden. Ellendrii was kind that way. When he thought to be at least.

There were still trees around the place although they were few and far between now the Kannith territory was behind them.

"I wonder what other creatures we will meet" pondered Ellendrii.

"I don't care so long as they're friendly and we can understand them and they don't get their feelings hurt so easily" muttered Aro.

Ellendrii sighed.

"You're not still sore about that are you?" he asked his friend, looking at him pointedly as they walked.

"Ergh a bit. On the one claw, I feel bad about what happened but on the other, Scerniss shouldn't have been such a sensitive idiot. He should have accepted that we were from a different place and might not understand and so question their ideas and rituals."

"Well at least you feel bad about it. You don't often feel bad about much" said Ellendrii.

"I do only cos I hang around with you so much and you have er…that thing…you know…" he trailed off.

"Compassion? Understanding? A conscience?" suggested Ellendrii, helpfully.

"Hey I wouldn't go *that* far" smirked Aro.

"I know *you* wouldn't. But *I* would!" smiled Ellendrii, "I have *all* those things! That's what being a Gryphie is all about.

I know we get along now but no offence, I can see why our two species have fallen out in the past."

"Yeah, me too" frowned Aro. Although he liked the Gryphies and they were humble, he still kinda loathed the pride they had about their temperament and what they "stood" for. As far as that was concerned and even though they were friends, he often thought that Ellendrii was a bit of a fool in some respects. What's wrong with rushing in needles rattling instead of trying to "talk things through" with an enemy?

At least the weather was nice anyway, it wasn't raining or anything. He looked up at the sky. Oh, wait, there it was. A dark cloud annoyingly floating around.

Soon enough, the rest of the sky became dark too and it started to rain. They continued in the rain for a while before Ellendrii started to complain that his fur was too wet. His soaked mane clung to his face and neck. The hair on his head was pretty long, so when it rained, it tended to stick to his face and get in his eyes. He brushed it back but whenever he shook himself it would flop back onto his face again. So they decided to seek shelter. The trees were not of the type to give good shelter unless there were a few trees together. So the few trees they passed now were no good. Since they wanted to make their way up the side of the valley anyway, they turned to the steep rocky places either side of them. The valley was fairly wide but the sides were still getting steeper.

They figured they might find a cave or something around there since it was pretty rocky. They didn't find a cave but they did find a sheltered part where some rocks had fallen on top of one another and so provided a place for them to get in under and out of the rain.

The rain was falling more heavily now.

The pair looked out at it from their cramped shelter. Even though Ellendrii had gathered his wings around him, Aro still moaned that they were taking up all the space. Ellendrii sighed and tried to gather them in more tightly. His leather bag was also soaked and the things inside had got a bit wet too. He would need to dry out the herbs if he didn't want them to go mouldy or rotten. The gourds were still pretty full. He had assumed the Kanniths didn't need a water source because they were so small that they could comfortably live on dew and rain.

Aro didn't mind the rain. There were very few things that Lizariaouses minded. He was happy in the wet or the dry and his scaly skin dried much faster than the fur of a Gryphie. The only thing that bothered him was too much sun because his skin was mostly black and he would overheat easily. Being thick skinned though, he could still take quite a bit of sun before he started to feel sick from heat stroke.

They waited for the rain to stop.

And waited.

And waited.

By the time it let up, it was nearly dark so the pair of them decided to sleep under the shelter. The size of the rocky shelter though made it uncomfortable to sleep and Aro ended up sleeping outside because he was sick of Ellendrii moving so much and hitting him with his wings.

"Stupid wings" muttered Aro as he left the shelter and went to lie a little way away outside of it. He looked up at the sky. It was a little less cloudy and there were a few stars to be seen in the gaps in the clouds. It looked strange and illuminated in the moonlight with the dark shapes of the clouds and then the brighter, starry sky above.

Laying down, he listened to the life around him. He could hear nameless creatures going about their moonly business and small rustles in the bushes all around. It was a nice valley, full of green grass and a range of different plants. Aro still missed his barren home of Dyarkroeen though. But this was oddly relaxing. The only thing it was missing was the loud cries of the cave cats every so often as they spoke to each other in the dark. The moon was a natural light source in this valley and the clouds were clearing up. The next sun cycle should hold good weather if Aro's experience had taught him anything at all about it.

He glanced over at the sleeping form of Ellendrii. The Gryphie was partly curled up with one wing sticking out of the shelter and snoring softly. Aro was glad he had gone to lie outside. Even though he wouldn't admit it, Aro still had a jealousy thing going on with Ellendrii's wings. He probably always would. He would just try not to moan too much or mention it because he knew it made his friend feel bad. After all; Ellendrii couldn't help having wings, it was just the way he was. Neither could Aro help having needles along his back. The flying thing was the one thing that kept Aro from being completely accepting of Ellendrii as his friend. It was true he would do anything for the Gryphie or to defend or help him. But the flying thing was still somewhat of an unspoken wedge between them.

Aro rested his head on his paws and closed his eyes. It was then he heard something that made him start and sit bolt upright. His heart raced. It had sounded very much like a Repulsator; the one thing that had terrified him beyond all reason and made him deeply ashamed of his lack of Lizariaous bravery. In truth, most Lizariaouses were brave simply because they didn't have the brains to feel fear. Aro, having hung around with Ellendrii and channelled a little of his emotions and also because Aro was young, did have the capacity for fear.

Aro breathed silently, eyes wide and looking around. He listened for the sound again and sat up listening for quite some time. His heart was racing and he felt a rush of chill flowing through him. His needles were tensed just in case he needed to defend himself; not that that would have helped much against a Repulsator.

After a while, he calmed down somewhat as he heard nothing else. He relaxed a little and finally lay down again. He stayed awake for quite some time before his eyes slowly began to close and he sighed, getting tired now. As he was drifting off to sleep, he heard the noise again. It had the same effect on him; he jumped awake and sat up, listening and watching. His eyes were of some use in the dark and the moonlight did help but he could still see nothing. The shuddering gasp that he had heard didn't occur again and he could see nothing floating around, nor smell the putrid stench of rot and blood.

He shook his head. Maybe he was imagining it. He had been drifting off to sleep after all. He was wide awake now and it took him quite a while to settle again. He got up and turned around, adjusted his position and lay back down again, resting his head on his paws once more. However, he did try and curl up as small as he could though; not that it would help him should something attack him; he just felt more protected, as most of us do when we're scared. Curling his tail around himself and adjusting his needles so he could fire them off with ease if he needed to, he prepared to go to sleep for the third time that moon cycle.

Then he heard the sound again. He nearly jumped but had been sort of ready to hear it and more awake as well so he just lay quietly and listened to see if he could hear in what direction it was coming from and go to investigate. IF he had the courage that is! Nothing had attacked him so far so he was prepared to go and check out what the source of the sound was if necessary.

All was quiet and he wanted so badly to go to sleep but he knew he wouldn't be able to if he kept hearing this sound and it kept waking him. After a while, he heard the shuddering, gasping sound again and turned his head quickly as he listened to it, to determine from what direction it was coming from. It appeared to be coming from around the area of the rocks, so, standing up; Aro headed over to the rocks and listened closely. In the dim light, he could see Ellendrii's tail flicking nearby as he slept and dreamed. Aro was worried that whatever it was would attack Ellendrii while he slept, since whatever it was was around here.

Aro stood, in front of Ellendrii defensively, looking out into the valley silently listening. After a while, he heard the sound again, from behind him. He spun round. That was where Ellendrii was sleeping! His heart racing, Aro stood staring at Ellendrii and trying to see if there was something in the shelter with him. The horrible rasping, shudder had come from around there. Aro put his head under the rocks, a small snarl crossing his lips and still listening hard. He looked as hard as he could but in the darkness of the rocky shelter it was even harder to see anything. He didn't want to wake or worry Ellendrii because he knew the Gryphie needed sleep as much as Aro did.

He stared into the shelter for what seemed like ages when suddenly he heard the awful sound again only this time it was deathly close!

Aro jumped out of his skin and leaped back, only to discover that the sound was in fact coming from Ellendrii himself! The Gryphie was dreaming, Aro could only assume. Though why he was making such an odd noise required closer investigation.

It turned out that Ellendrii was sleeping with his hand close to his nose and every so often his hand was blocking his own breathing somewhat, so it came out as a horrible Repulsator style shudder. Aro breathed a huge sigh of relief and gently moved Ellendrii's hand so it was no longer so close to his nose and he wouldn't make the terrible sound anymore.

Aro shook his head and went back to where he had been laying. He was relieved that the sound was nothing to be scared of but at the same time, he felt like an idiot being scared of something that was harmless. He decided not to tell Ellendrii what had happened that moon cycle. He curled up and was soon in a deep and peaceful sleep.

The next morning, Aro was awoken by Ellendrii. The sun was high in the sky and the two of them had overslept.

"Come on or we'll never get there" said Ellendrii, preparing to leave.

"We don't even know where "there" is" replied Aro, "And besides, I'm hungry, can we eat first?"

"We can eat on the way! I can't believe it's this late! Why didn't you wake up sooner? I was in a dark shelter but you're outside in the light, surely you could have woken up at sunrise?"

"Well we obviously needed the rest or we wouldn't have slept for so long" said Aro. He of course didn't mention the real reason he had overslept despite the bright light of the sun.

Ellendrii shared out the last of the food from the leather bag. They figured there would be something to eat at the lake they were heading towards so they took the chance of finishing the fish that was in the bag. Aro was sick of fish by this time. And they would probably have more at the lake he supposed. Or maybe they would get lucky and there would be something else to eat at the lake. It was most likely a good spot for other meal creatures to live too.

They headed along the valley looking for a path up the ever steepening sides. After a while, Ellendrii sighed and stopped.

"I don't think we'll find a path and if we carry on much longer, the sides will be too steep to climb. We'll have to try and make our way up here. The lake is off to the right so that's where we'll start. Over there." Ellendrii pointed and they headed in that direction.

"If it's too steep we'll head back the way we've come" he said. Aro nodded, knowing full well that Ellendrii could easily fly up; it was *him* who needed a place to climb.

At the foot of the incline, they stopped and looked up, seeing if they could figure a way to ascend safely. They walked along a little way until they had found a spot that offered places for paws that could be stood on or gripped.

Then they headed up. Ellendrii let Aro go first. He followed. He wasn't about to take the easy route and fly because he knew it would make his friend feel inadequate.

As they climbed, Aro sparked up a conversation much to Ellendrii's surprise. He figured they would climb in silence so they could preserve their energy and concentrate on the job at hand.

"Did you have any moonmares last moon?" asked Aro. He really wanted to know if Ellendrii's weird noises were caused by bad dreams.

"Hmm now you mention it, I did. I haven't had a moon cycle's sleep where my dreams haven't been bad. I keep having moonmares about that awful forest and the things in it. Mostly about when the Narg'tok attacked me. I dream I feel the same way as I did back then and I'm reliving it. It's horrible. I can't breathe or fight because I'm paralysed by the fear I see in its face. If you can call it a face that is. I see a swirling mass that strikes fear into my very core. I hate it. I can't seem to have a good moon cycle's rest. What about you? Do you have bad dreams too?" Ellendrii asked.

"Yeah I do" replied Aro. He didn't elaborate. Ellendrii wanted to know why and Aro didn't want to admit that his own moonmares had been caused by the fear of the Repulsators. It was turning into a phobia, as it had affected Aro in a very negative way. Most of the time he didn't think much about it but whenever he saw or heard, as he had done the previous moon, anything that reminded him of those awful mutant rat creatures, his mind would race and the fear would come tumbling back. For him it wasn't like the Narg'tok. With the Narg'tok, he was forced into fear. But the Repulsators just brought it out in him naturally. Still without his consent though but still, naturally.

The last thing he wanted to do was admit this fear to his friend though. He didn't want Ellendrii to think he was a wuss. That was frowned upon in Lizariaous society and even if Ellendrii understood, Aro would still feel ashamed.

"I don't know which was more frightening; the Narg'tok or those awful Repulsators" said Ellendrii. Aro knew which scared *him* more.

"I dunno either" he said, blankly. "They were both scary."

"I agree. Anyway, let's not talk about that anymore. I wonder how close we are to the top. It looks closer than it is" said Ellendrii, looking up.

"A bit like being on the vast water really. The shore looks closer than it is" replied Aro. Ellendrii nodded.

Presently, they came to a part of the valley side that was harder to climb than what they had yet encountered. There wasn't a place to comfortably put their feet. The valley side was rocky with sparse strands of longish grass sticking up here and there. Normally it was easy to find a foothold but at this particular part, they couldn't find a place to ascend safely.

Looking around, they saw that there was a place slightly higher up that they could grab hold of. Aro grabbed onto the rock above them with his claws and a hard shove from Ellendrii got him up there. He then pulled Ellendrii up with his paws. Ellendrii *could* have flown up but again, he didn't want to take the easy way. He wanted to show Aro that he was willing to do things *his* way, as a sign of friendship and respect. Sometimes we need to sacrifice small luxuries for the benefit of others and this was one of those times.

They carried on climbing and were soon nearly at the top. They were both very tired though. The top steepened considerably and now they were starting to struggle. Mostly because they were tired and partly because it was that much steeper.

Suddenly, Aro slipped and slid into Ellendrii. Ellendrii couldn't hold them both from the precarious perch he was on and they both slid down, struggling to get ahold of somewhere before they got hurt or fell down too far. They didn't much like the idea of starting this all over again. Luckily they didn't slide too far. It was only about a couple of metres or so. Ellendrii had originally thought that it might not be a good idea having the heavier of the two of them going up ahead but out of respect he had let Aro go first.

Now they decided to change around a little and ascended the valley side next to each other so if one of them lost their footing or slipped, the other could grab hold of them and pull them back up again. This was a far easier way of making it up the valley side and they had soon reached the top. They climbed over and out with some difficulty and rested at the top.

"Wow, that was some climb!" said Ellendrii.

"Ergh, never again. I'm glad the land all looks pretty flat now" replied Aro, laying out flat on the ground and catching his breath.

They both looked out in the direction they were headed and they could see the silver sheen of a vast lake in the far distance stretching out and sparkling in the sunlight.

"Ah, fresh water! We can fill the gourds up again for the next part of our journey" said Ellendrii.

"Speaking of water…" began Aro and put a paw out.

"Yeah I could do with a drink too" agreed Ellendrii and got out the gourds so they could have a drink together. At least now they didn't have the worry of not being able to find food and water. For a while at least.

They set off again for the lake.

"Hey El, have you thought about what we're gunna do when we get there? Walk around it? Try to cross it?" asked Aro.

"I dunno, we'll try to walk around it for a while I think. At least then we can make use of the water and possible food we'll be able to find there. All creatures need water so there will be a lot living around the lake or visiting it to drink and I would think they would be easy pickings for us."

"I'm gunna be starving by the time we get there though" said Aro, "I'm already hungry."

"Me too but we gotta hold out till we get there, well, unless we find anything on the way that we can eat. It's a pity you won't eat berries like I do."

"Hey we've been through this before" warned Aro, "Lizariaouses live for meat, end of discussion!"

Ellendrii wisely didn't push it any more.

The ground up there was fairly flat and again, rich in grass. The grass was fairly tall as well and came up to their tummies as they walked. Ellendrii thought it tickled somewhat. Aro just charged through it without thought.

They were walking for a while before Ellendrii felt uncomfortable. His leg hurt for some reason. He looked at it but could see nothing wrong so he carried on walking. As they carried on, it felt worse and worse and in the end he sat down on a lone rock to inspect it more closely.

"What's up?" asked Aro, backtracking because he had been walking ahead and hadn't realized Ellendrii had sat down.

"My leg hurts" replied Ellendrii and looked at it. It was one of his back legs, the right one. Looking down at his soft, short and dense fur; he saw two small stones. They were red and smooth and seemed to be stuck on him. He touched them with a finger and they seemed to squirm, which hurt him more.

"Ow, what are these? They seem to be living." He poked them but again they squirmed and hurt him. They were about the size of the smaller scales on Aro's face.

"I want to pull them off but every time I touch them they move and hurt me" he winced.

"Hmm…" Aro looked at them closely. "I think they're attached to you which is why they hurt you."

"Oh, no grik!" snapped Ellendrii, sarcastically.

"I was only making an observation" replied Aro. "But if you want to get them off yourself then do so! You clearly don't need *my* help cos you're a smart Gryphie!" He sat down nearby with his back to Ellendrii.

Ellendrii looked at him and shook his head. That was overly harsh. Aro's short temperedness often got on his nerves.

"Well sorry but they hurt!" he said. Aro ignored him. Ellendrii's pain, frustration and puzzlement at the couple of things on his leg was making him snappy.

He placed a thumb and forefinger either side of one of the pebble things and tugged on it gently. It hurt him badly but he carried on, pulling a bit harder, which of course hurt more. He growled in frustration and snarled at his leg.

Aro was watching him over his shoulder by this time and smirked mentally since he thought the Gryphie looked stupid growling at his own leg.

Ellendrii thought to maybe flame the pebble things so he let out a small flame from one of his nostrils. The blue fire brushed over the red pebble it had been aimed at but it only made the thing tighten its grip, which was excruciating for the poor Gryphie and he yelped. Aro wanted to ask him if he needed help but he also wanted Ellendrii to be taught a lesson and he was secretly pleased that Ellendrii was struggling to get them off. Serves him right! Gryphies *aren't* all that smart after all!

Ellendrii then proceeded to roar at his leg, as loud as he could in the hopes of deafening these creatures into falling off him. But that didn't work either and they were completely unphased by it. Then he had another idea.

"Aro, can you help please? I'm sorry I yelled at you" he pleaded. Aro snorted.

"Oh yeah you're only sorry cos you're struggling so much to get them off" he said, "Cos YOU can't do it!"

"Look, I really am sorry. These things really hurt. I wish you'd get one so you could understand how much they hurt."

"Yeah well it's useful to have thick skin" spat Aro.

Ellendrii hung his head and gritted his teeth. Aro was trying his patience and the things were really hurting him. There was a burning sensation all up his leg by this time. He sighed in annoyance and tried to calm himself down.

"Please can you come over and help?" he said through gritted teeth. This was because of the pain but Aro wrongly assumed it was because Ellendrii was forcing his plea.

"Really, does it give you *that* much trouble to ask for help from a species who isn't as smart as you?" snarled Aro, his short temper showing through.

"LOOK. I am in PAIN. Just come over and help me will you?? I don't mean to be this snappy or presumptuous but I'm losing my temper because these things are hurting me and I can't get them off. If I move them they hurt me. If I flame them they cling on more tightly. If I roar at them it does nothing!" Ellendrii sighed. "I am panicking because I don't know what to do and it's making me grumpy. So now you know, can you help me figure out a way to get them off?"

"Ok, ok" replied Aro, walking over to him. "Sorry I lost my temper. I need to stop assuming things I guess but it's hard."

"I understand" replied Ellendrii.

Aro looked closely at the things on Ellendrii's leg.

"Can you drip some poison on them?" asked Ellendrii.

"I can try" replied Aro and reached back, gripping one of his needles and firing it off into his paw. He brought it round and held it over the pebble thing in question.

"Please try not to get any on me if you can" said Ellendrii meekly, afraid that he would upset the short tempered Lizariaous again and he wouldn't help.

"I'll try not to but in truth it will only kill you if it gets into an open wound" said Aro.

Carefully he dripped the tiniest amount of poison onto the red pebble. But it squirmed and latched on even more firmly, burying itself into Ellendrii's flesh and making him cry out in pain.

"I think these things ARE wounding me. Don't use the poison again" said Ellendrii through gritted teeth from the effort of talking while in so much pain.

"Ok, ok" said Aro and threw the needle to one side. "We need to make them let go of you somehow" he said.

"Yeah but everything we do makes them latch on harder" said Ellendrii sadly.

"True, but everything we've done so far has hurt or annoyed them. Maybe if we try something that *doesn't* hurt them?" suggested Aro.

"What can we do that doesn't hurt them? Right now I want to tear them off me but it's too painful to do so so I'm at a loss."

"Maybe we can...gross them out..." Aro said slowly, staring at the things on Ellendrii's leg.

"What, like spit on them or something?" asked Ellendrii.

"No, I was thinking of peeing on them" replied Aro.

"ARO!! That's horrible! Besides, if you pee on them, you'll pee on me and I'm NOT having you pee on my leg. I'd rather put up with the grikking things."

"I don't see any other way I can pee on them and not pee on you" said Aro.

"You're doing this to get me back for snapping at you earlier" said Ellendrii.

"No I'm not! Besides, what if it works? Surely it would be worth it?"

"Yeah but if it doesn't work then it wouldn't be worth it and I'd be covered in pee!"

"You can wash it off at the lake!"

"Wait; the lake! I can go swimming in there and drown these things!" Ellendrii said, elated.

"Yeah but then they'd die and they might not let go of you. They'd be dead and still clinging to you. With MY method, they will drop off and run away!" said Aro.

"What if they LIKE Lizariaous urine?" asked Ellendrii.

"Trust me, NOTHING likes Lizariaous urine!" replied Aro.

"I really don't think peeing on them is the answer" said Ellendrii, "There must be some other way."

"Well if it's not, what have you lost? You can wash it off at the lake. You can even fly there and I'll catch up if it makes you feel any better."

"I'd still have to wash it off even if it DID work" said Ellendrii.

"Yeah but you wouldn't fly there in that case because you'd be so grateful to me for helping get rid of them that you would be *proud* to walk to the lake with me!"

"I wouldn't go *that* far…" muttered Ellendrii.

"Just look away when I do it and pretend it's warm rain" suggested Aro helpfully.

"I haven't said you could do it yet" replied Ellendrii.

"Well if you can think of another option then go ahead" said Aro.

Ellendrii wordlessly grabbed hold of one of the pebbles and yanked on it. He was in so much pain that his eyes were watering but anything was better than being peed on by a Lizariaous. Or any other creature for that matter.

The thing didn't come off though and the pain spread to the rest of Ellendrii's leg so he felt he might not even be able to walk again. After a long silent pause, he finally relented.

"Ok fine. You can pee on them. But I really don't think it will work. It's a stupid idea." Ellendrii offered his leg to Aro and looked away, shutting his eyes tightly and preparing himself for the worst.

Aro sighed, rolled his eyes and took aim at his friend's leg.

Ellendrii nearly threw up when he felt the warm wetness running down his leg. The smell didn't make him feel any better either.

"Ok, done" said Aro. "And oh look…" He pointed to Ellendrii's soggy leg.

"I'm gunna be sick I just know it" muttered Ellendrii but he glanced down at his leg and saw the red pebbles had indeed fallen off.

Aro looked very proud of himself. Ellendrii felt his stomach churn but at least the pain was subsiding. Where the things had been were large red puncture wounds, the same size as the red pebbles. Tiny trickles of blood oozed out of them.

Ellendrii rifled through his leather bag for some healing herbs. The rain from the previous sun cycle had thankfully not made them too wet and Ellendrii had taken them out and laid them to dry while the pair had been asleep so the herbs were dry again now. He placed some healing herbs on the wounds and wrapped his leg in a flat leaf wrapping.

Meanwhile, Aro was looking for the pebbles because he wanted to squish them. He soon found them scurrying through the grass, not far from where they had fallen and he stepped on them both, squashing them into flat bloody messes on the ground. He wanted to make sure Ellendrii wouldn't pick any more up and he also wanted to kill them for what they had done to his friend.

By the time he had finished and gone back to Ellendrii, the Gryphie was ready to continue. However, he realized now that there would probably be more of these red pebble creatures in the tall grass to bite him and his leg was throbbing from where they had been latched onto him. So he had decided to fly despite his reservations about doing it and making Aro feel bad. Aro said nothing when he explained about the reason for his sudden flight, only nodded and smiled. Aro understood. Ellendrii wanted to keep weight off his leg too. The red pebble things didn't bother with Aro because they couldn't get a grip on his tough skin.

So they carried on like that for a while, with Aro walking and Ellendrii flying. Although Ellendrii had trouble flying so slowly. It was more effort from him and required more lift in order to fly at a walking pace. So he decided to challenge Aro to a race to the lake.

"Hey Aro! Are you up for a race?" he called to his friend. Aro, never one to back down from such a challenge nodded and agreed and together they raced to the lake.

Ellendrii could fly faster than Aro could run, easily, but he kept his pace within a fair speed so as not to completely outpace the Lizariaous. The sun shone down on the two friends as they raced. Aro running through the tall grass and Ellendrii flying happily over him.

It felt great to stretch their legs and make a good effort on their journey. They had been slowed down by other creatures, rain and other obstacles but they were finally making a good pace to get to where they were going, wherever that was.

Wherever the SilvaGryphie was! They wouldn't stop until they had found her!

It wasn't really a race in the end; it was more just running and flying for the fun of it. Ellendrii's leg didn't hurt at all when there was no weight on it and he found flying to be much easier. He knew he could wash it off in the lake. And the Lizariaous pee as well. That smelled a little too strong for the comfort of Ellendrii's nostrils. At least the motion of his wings was sweeping the smell of the pee away from him and the breeze gave his nostrils some respite.

Aro was galloping happily along down below. He had got tired of walking anyway. He enjoyed stretching his legs. He could remember the last time he had run and it hadn't been a pleasant one. But this was running for fun and not for his life.

The lake got closer and closer and finally they reached it. Ellendrii didn't let up his speed but dived headfirst into the water. He wanted the stink of pee to be off now and he wanted to refresh and clean the wounds on his leg.

Since they had reached the lake at the same time, neither of them really won but by that time they had forgotten it was a race and just enjoyed the progress of their journey.

Seeing Ellendrii dive in, Aro didn't let up either and leaped into the lake, plopping in with a huge wave from his sturdy body and flailing legs. He sank like a rock but with swimming motions he made his way back to the surface again and bobbed about in the water, waiting for Ellendrii to emerge.

Ellendrii was enjoying his underwater diving and stayed under for as long as his breath would hold before breaking through the surface of the water a little way away from Aro.

The pair of them had got quite hot with their race and it was refreshing to cool off in the water. The water was clear and fresh and not salty at all. Aro was drinking in great gulps of it as he swam around.

Ellendrii swam to the shore and got out, shaking himself dry and sitting down to watch his friend play in the water. He sniffed his leg. Yes, the smell of Lizariaous pee had gone! He was clean again! The dressing he had put on his leg had stayed on. Back in the Forest, Lunara had showed him how to tie a dressing in such a way that it would stay on until the patient wanted to remove it.

Aro clambered out onto the shore next to Ellendrii and collapsed tired and happy from his outburst of energy. Aro could hear the water he had drunk sloshing around inside him and he was vaguely amused by it.

"Well, we made it! Now, let's hunt!" said Ellendrii getting up.

"I will in a minute" replied Aro, who wanted to rest a bit. Ellendrii nodded and went to find himself some food. He could fish fairly easily but he really wanted meat other than fish for a change so he went to see what sort of creatures lived by the riverside and if any of them were good to eat. He also hoped they wouldn't speak the same language as him, since that would of course put him off eating them. He supposed there must be a lot of lesser evolved things around at the side of a large body of water. There were a few back in Shernaron. Mostly small creatures and the Gryphies didn't often hunt them but there was no reason why they couldn't. It just happened that the river back home was not their hunting ground. But this one was Ellendrii's hunting ground now!

He looked around carefully, poking his nose into reeds and other riverside plant life. There were some curious flowers with huge, brightly coloured heads growing nearby and it was in these that he found his next meal. It was a type of bird but it had bat-like wings; similar to a Gryphie in fact. When he went near the large flowers, several of these birds flew into the air, presumably as a decoy if they had nests buried among the bases of the flowering plants. The stalks of them were very tall, like a sunflower but the flower heads looked nothing like sunflowers that you or I would know of.

Ellendrii had encountered creatures like these before and knew of their decoy tricks. So he ignored the ones that took flight and took the easier advantage of catching one that was sitting on a nest and so was more reluctant to move. The bird created a huge noise as Ellendrii approached it, hoping to scare him off catching it. It deafened the Gryphie and he laid his ears back in an effort to block out the awful din somehow. He wasted no time in pouncing on the bird and killing it quickly. This sent ones on nearby nests into a frenzy of fearful screeching and he hurried away as fast as he could with his kill before he was deafened completely.

Meanwhile, Aro had shot down one of the birds that had taken to the sky and was already tucking into his meal happily. Ellendrii joined him with his bird.

"Ah, it feels great to eat proper meat again! I'm not used to eating fish" said Aro with his mouth full, as usual.

"I agree" said Ellendrii, sitting next to him and looking at his own kill.

The bird's wings were black and its body was a dark, navy blue that shone a purplish in the sun. It had a long, straight beak which was green and black feet to match its wings. Its eyes were very odd; the pupil was a flower shape. Each wing had three clawed fingers and a clawed thumb. Ellendrii had noticed some of these birds fishing some way away as he had headed back to join Aro. They were very fast but a fair size, so they made a nice meal and didn't take too much to catch. Again, it made a nice change to have something go easily for once. Ellendrii tucked into his bird.

Aro was gulping his down without even chewing. He would probably have terrible gas later on. Ellendrii ate his delicately, savouring it.

"Yes, I think we will head alongside this lake for a while. Food is plentiful and easy to catch and we have a water source. This lake will end and we can decide where to go from there" said Ellendrii.

"Ok" replied Aro with his mouth full again.

They finished their food, washed it down with a drink and started the walk alongside the lake.

It wasn't long before they came across some other creatures swimming around in the lake. They resembled what we would think of as otters. They had dense, glistening fur and short, catlike ears with muzzles to match. They had long tails and a row of spikes going down their lithe bodies. Here and there, there was a patch of glittering turquoise scales on their bodies and they were mostly either orange, lilac or white. They had webbed paws for swimming and appeared to be able to go underwater with the aid of air bubbles that enveloped them.

As they saw the pair approach, they stopped their underwater antics and watched them. Ellendrii decided to speak to them, since they were all staring so intently at him and Aro and he felt a bit apprehensive in case they thought the two would attack. He wanted them to know that they were just passing through. After all, these creatures might have a similar view of strangers as the Kanniths – and may not speak the same language as the two of them either.

"We're just passing through here peacefully. We mean you no harm." Ellendrii displayed friendly body language with a hint of submission. Aro tried to as well.

One of the creatures sat on a rock nearby and spoke to them.

"You can pass. We won't stop you. We are the Aqwakitts and this is where we live; our territory. So long as you don't attack or hassle us, you are free to travel along here. You will find our kind in many places in this lake. The whole of the lake is ours. You may swim in it if you wish, so long as you don't pose any threat to us. We treat others how they treat us, after all" he said.

"Thank you" said Ellendrii, gratefully.

"I am Ellendrii the Gryphie and this is Aro the Lizariaous, my friend. We are looking for the SilvaGryphie" he explained.

"Hmm, can't say as I've heard of it" said the Aqwakitt, rubbing its chin and pondering. This Aqwakitt was orange.

"What does it look like? We might be able to help!"

"Well it…*she* looks like me, only larger and beautiful with fluffy fur" explained Ellendrii.

The Aqwakitt's eyes widened.

"Oh!! Yes we do know what she is! She lives here!" it said excitedly.

Ellendrii and Aro looked at each other and felt a rush of excitement.

"I'll take you to her!" said the Aqwakitt and motioned for them to follow.

Chapter 22
A Different World

Ellendrii and Aro excitedly followed the Aqwakitt as it lead them to the water's edge some way away.

"She's down there!" it said, pointing.

"Wait, what?" asked Ellendrii.

"Oh yeah, you're like us, you can't breathe under water. Don't worry; I'll take you to her safely. My name is Harrixx by the way" said the Aqwakitt.

"I didn't know she lived underwater" said Aro, peering into the lake.

"Neither did I" said Ellendrii, "Gryphies don't live underwater, or at least none of the ones I've met do."

"But you haven't met her, so you wouldn't know. Besides, she *is* the SilvaGryphie, surely she can live where she likes?" asked Aro.

"I…guess" said Ellendrii, still unsure.

Two other Aqwakitts came rushing over. They were both white and looked identical except for their eyes, which had "complete heterochromia". One's left eye was blue and the right was green and the other's left was green and the right was blue.

"Are they going swimming?" they asked excitedly.

"Yes they are" replied Harrixx.

"Can we take them, pleeeeassse?" they pleaded.

"I guess so" replied Harrixx and then to Ellendrii and Aro, he said; "This is Aira and Airu. They are twins and they love to swim."

"Hi" replied Aro, "I'm Aro"

"Nice to meet you!" they replied enthusiastically. They had a weird way of speaking in unison. Aro guessed it was because they were twins. He'd heard a lot about twins having weird psychic powers. He'd never been sure of the authenticity until now. Of course it could just have been that the pair of them liked to speak in unison.

Ellendrii looked around and sighed.

"Aro" he said quietly and motioned for his friend to follow him a little way away from the three Aqwakitts.

"Just a minute" said Aro to the three of them and he followed Ellendrii.

"Aro, I really think this is a stupid idea" said Ellendrii.

"Why?" asked Aro.

"Gryphies don't live underwater. I think these guys must be mistaken about this."

"They said they've seen her. She might be in an underwater cave or something living in a pocket of air. If she's *that* powerful, she probably has enemies. Maybe she's in hiding? Maybe someone has threatened her?"

"I hardly think so. The creator of all Gryphies? Hiding? Really? That's really stupid, Aro."

"But surely if we're looking for her we need to look everywhere. We don't know where she is or what sort of a place she's living in. Already she's something of fantastical stories and legends. Why couldn't she live underwater? There are Gryphies living up in the sky so high that the Forest ones struggle to breathe up there. Grik, there are even Gryphies living on the seemingly uninhabitable Dark Plains. So why then would one who lives underwater be any different?" argued Aro.

"Because, the ones in the sky fly. We all fly. So it makes sense some would be better flyers than others and live in a place more suited to them. There are the Deamon Gryphies yes and they live on the Dark Plains. I've never been there but the fact they're called "Plains" would suggest that there isn't any water there. From what my father has told me there isn't water there, well there is some but not a lot of it and none of them live *in* it. There are no Gryphies living in the lake back home and even the Gryphers live in the Forest, not underwater. It just seems all a bit ridiculous. And besides, how do you know these creatures aren't trying to trick you? Take you under the water and then drown you?"

"I don't see anything remotely offensive about them. Besides, they have water bubbles. I'm sure they intend to put them around us anyway so we wouldn't drown. You're over thinking all of this." Aro said.

"Oh, says the Lizariaous who has seen as much as me that we need to be wary of" spat Ellendrii.

"Yeah well the Narg'tok didn't look nice when it turned around. Rivniann was nice and helped us. And then there's Midnyte Comet... I've come to realize that the nasty creatures we encounter all look threatening. The nice ones don't. That's how I know which ones to be careful of. These guys look harmless to me and they're friendly and helpful. The little tree creatures were similar. They let us stay with them. Things that are dangerous don't hesitate to show they're dangerous in the first place" Aro explained.

He had a point and Ellendrii could understand that but he was still distrustful of the Aqwakitts, mostly because he couldn't imagine the SilvaGryphie living underwater. Surely her beautiful fur would get soggy? In all the stories he'd heard about her, there was no mention of her swimming or living underwater. In fact most Gryphies assumed she lived in a huge beautiful tree or just the other side of the vast water to look after all the souls who had passed over. Then again, how true had that been? There were no dead souls here and no huge tree and the land beyond the vast water in fact contained a myriad of different species that they were learning about and experiencing the cultures of.

So maybe the whole living underwater thing wasn't that farfetched. Maybe she had scales instead of fur and the whole thing had been mistaken or changed as the stories passed down through the generations. After all, they *had* encountered a creature with a transparent body and an ecosystem inside and the very idea of that was impossible but it had happened and did exist.

Ellendrii sighed.

"Ok ok you've convinced me. But you can go under. If they try anything at least we won't both be in the same helpless situation."

"I really don't think they'll "try" anything but sure I'll go under and then come back up and show you how right I am!" grinned Aro and nudged him. Ellendrii snorted but good naturedly.

"Ok. I'll sit at the edge of the water and watch then" he said to Aro and the two of them returned to the water where the Aqwakitts were waiting for them.

"Everything ok?" asked Harrixx.

"Yeah we're fine" replied Aro, "Just needed to sort something out."

"Ok! Well, are you ready? Aira and Airu can take you to her" explained Harrixx.

"I'll sit out here with you, Harrixx, if you don't mind" said Ellendrii, "I'll go down if Aro says it's actually her."

"Fair enough. But it is her. She's just like you described her to be" Harrixx shrugged, finding Ellendrii's wariness a little puzzling.

Ellendrii nodded and sat down. We'll see, he thought.

Meanwhile, Aro had waded into the water and the two Aqwakitts were swimming in the deeper water just ahead of him. He pushed off with his feet and paddled to them.

"A little further! You need to be in the deeper water, hold your breath and dive down so we can make the bubble" said Aira.

"Ok" replied Aro. This was *so* weird, especially for a creature to whom water was not a natural place to be. It was like the vast water all over again but this time at least had the bonus that he could get back to land when he wished. Ellendrii's fear had struck a chord with him though and now some of his confidence in their new friends had dampened somewhat. No pun intended.

Ellendrii sat watching. At least if they tried anything to hurt Aro, he would be able to threaten Harrixx. That's if they even cared about their own. They didn't appear to have a leader or anyone in charge.

Aira and Airu swam around Aro in circles, waiting for him to dive under the water.

"Won't the bubble make me float more though?" he asked.

"No, it's a special bubble. You can swim anywhere in it and it gives you air. But it does get smaller with the more air you breathe while inside it. We'll make yours nice and big.

Your friend is quite far down in the lake and more towards the middle" explained Aira.

"Surely it would make more sense for me to swim out a little more then?" asked Aro.

"We thought we would give you a tour of the lake as well. It's lovely swimming underwater; it's a whole other world. You feel like you're *flying*."

This got Aro's attention!

"Ok" he said, "bubble me!" And he dived under the water as deep as he could go. Who cares how it worked? He wanted to feel like he was flying! Right now when he opened his eyes, everything was blurry. He could see the two forms of the Aqwakitts surrounding him and then he could suddenly see clearly. They had formed a bubble around his head. He still held his breath though. He knew that he would be able to breathe if he started to but he just couldn't get his body to do so. He tried to clear his mind and override the natural tendency to hold his breath. He ended up breathing fast, eyes wide and mildly panicked. He floundered around in the water and hyperventilated. Then he made his way to the surface and the bubble popped.

"You ok?" Aira had surfaced nearby.

"Yeah, it's just weird to get used to. Can we try again?" asked Aro.

"Of course! If you've never done it before it can be weird. The young Aqwakitts always have trouble the first few times they try."

"Also, is the bubble just going to be around my head?" asked Aro, "I thought it was around the whole body."

"No, for you, just your head. We can swim completely enveloped in the bubbles but you aren't used to it. It's hard to swim when you're in the bubble. We don't expect you to have to deal with that too. We like to keep our fur dry. You don't have fur so you can just have the bubble around your head instead. And about the air getting less and the bubble shrinking while you swim, don't worry, we will top the bubble up with air if it gets too small. We won't let you drown, don't worry" she said brightly.

Aro felt his heart skip a beat when she mentioned drowning. He sincerely hoped she wouldn't let him drown! Especially after Ellendrii's fear of it. He somehow really wanted to be right with this so not drowning was very important, otherwise he would have been wrong about it all and Ellendrii would have been all "I told you so!" and Aro really didn't want that. *He* wanted to be right for once!

Aira flipped around in the water and waited for Aro to dive back down so they could form the bubble around his head again. They tried to do it faster this time so he didn't hold his breath for so long and so wouldn't have the same problem. The longer he held his breath, the more his body got used to the idea.

He saw the bubble form around his head again. It was large enough that the spike on the back of his skull didn't pierce it, although this was a worry for him so he decided to ask the Aqwakitts about it after he had adjusted to breathing with the bubble.

He tried to calm himself again and breathe slowly. His body still couldn't get used to the fast he was underwater and was breathing too. It kept making him think he would suffocate. So he closed his eyes and pretended he was back on the land. He cleared his mind and breathed calmly. After a while, he opened his eyes and carried on the same calm breaths. Now he just had to swim and keep on breathing calmly. Doing all this was a chore and a struggle for him. He dived down deeper but had to surface again because he started to hyperventilate once more.

Aira had followed him.

"It's ok, we'll just keep trying till you get it right. You're just not used to it but that will pass, you'll be ok" she told him.

"I feel stupid" replied Aro, "I should have got it by now."

"We didn't expect you to get the hang of it very soon though. It takes a few tries to get used to. At least you can breathe. Now you just have to keep the same frame of mind while you swim and you'll have it! You're halfway there!" Aira told him, reassuringly.

"Ok, ok, I can do this!" said Aro and dived under again.

On the shore, Ellendrii stared hard. What in Shernaron was he doing? Why did he keep coming back up again?

Harrixx answered Ellendrii's mental question.

"He's having trouble adjusting to breathing underwater. His body naturally thinks he won't be able to breathe under there so he's having to come back up again because he's panicking. It happens to all first time divers, don't worry."

"Oh, ok. I would have thought it would be easy. He's surrounded by a bubble. Where's the problem?" said Ellendrii.

"Yes but his instincts are telling him he won't be able to breathe, so he's panicking. To his eyes, he is underwater and thus can't breathe. It's hard to override natural instincts." Harrixx explained.

Ellendrii nodded. "Ok, I guess so" he said. He thought Aro was struggling for no reason though. It wasn't *that* hard, surely?

On his third try, Aro got the hang of it and began to swim and breathe at the same time. He did have moments where his body was freaking out a little and he breathed too fast but mostly he was ok. He also found to his delight that he could speak and hear in the bubble as well. The two Aqwakitts had bubbles around their heads.

"Hey, I thought you said that the bubble around your entire body was better cos your fur didn't get wet?" he said.

"It's true but we're going to be doing a lot of swimming so this is just easier" replied Airu.

"Oh. Wait, *how* much swimming?" asked Aro, eyes wide. He hadn't realized the SilvaGryphie would be *that* far away!

"More than it would be easy to use the full body bubble" replied Airu. Helpful.

"Hey, what about the spike on my head. Will that pierce the bubble when it gets smaller?" asked Aro.

"No. Sharpness doesn't break bubbles. Dryness breaks them. And don't worry about the water coming in when it reaches your spike. Suction prevents that" explained Airu helpfully.

"Oh" said Aro, thoroughly confused.

They swam out a little way more, so that the ground under them fell away and the bottom of the lake was too dark to see.

"Look down" said Aira.

Aro did and gasped. It *was* like flying! He could see fish swimming around below him and before the lake bottom got too deep and dark, some underwater plants as well! He couldn't help just staring and watching and marvelling at what he saw. It was incredible! It was indeed a whole other world down there. He'd never seen anything like this before. He would have to try something like this at the lake in Shernaron. He would ask them how to make a bubble of his own so he could do this if they made it back home.

"Do you like it?" asked Aira.

"It's amazing!" replied Aro in awe.

"We think so too!" laughed Airu, swimming around and doing loop the loops in the water, playfully.

They swam deeper and Aro was amazed at everything he saw. It took him back to being a kid again, when everything was new. The sun filtered through the clear water and reflected off the shiny scales of the fish. They weren't as bright as the fish from the vast water but they were very nice to look at and Aro loved it. Ellendrii didn't know what he was missing!

Actually, no, he probably did. He swam underwater a lot in the lake in Shernaron but Aro guessed that he wouldn't have such a good view without a bubble to help him.

They reached some underwater plants and swam through them. They felt weird on Aro's skin but he liked it. The fish swam very close to him and if he reached out a paw, he could touch them. He went to grab one but Airu warned him not to.

"No, because you can't eat it and you don't want to hinder yourself carrying it" she said.

"Is it poisonous then?" asked Aro.

"No, but how will you get it to your mouth without popping the bubble?"

"Oh…right." Aro felt silly. Airu giggled.

When they spoke to each other, their voices sounded odd and echoey, Aro presumed because of the bubbles. He was glad they could talk though; he had assumed that they wouldn't be able to once they were in the bubbles.

The two Aqwakitts had sinewy bodies and swam with ease. Aro looked a little clumpy swimming with them, sturdily doggy-paddling alongside them. He couldn't do any of the swift, fluid moves that they could under the water. He did have a much stronger stroke though when he swept his legs out and back to propel himself along. He found though that if he laid his needles flat against his back that he could swim faster, so he did that.

Aira swam up beside him.

"What ARE you?" she asked. "You look so different from us"

"I'm a Lizariaous. I come from a place where there is NO water" said Aro, mysteriously.

"WOW" said Airu, swimming up as well and joining in on the conversation. Of course there was water in Dyarkroeen, just not much.

"How do you live without water? It is the life giver" said Airu.

"I dunno, we've just always lived without it. We're earth creatures and live in caves" replied Aro.

"There is a cave here. We will take you to it so you can see what our caves look like. We can't live in them though because they are underwater and although we love the water, we live outside of it. One of us dared another to spend the moon cycle in the cave and they did do it but only just. Their bubble was tiny by the time the sun rose."

"What did they get in return for spending the moon cycle there?" asked Aro.

"Satisfaction" replied Airu, shortly.

They swam in silence to the cave. It certainly was a very beautiful one. Lots of different water plants grew around it and along the insides and a variety of pretty fish swam around the mouth of it. They all scattered when the three explorers arrived though. Other, stranger life forms grew around the cave too. They looked like plants but moved like animals. They had long, chunky branches that moved and waved and reached towards Aro when he got too close.

"What ARE they?" he marvelled.

"Oh those, we call them touchy plants because when you get too close, they reach out and touch you. It's a hunting thing. They reach out and touch the fish and the fish stick to them and the plant draws the fish in and its tendrils surround it and I think it eats it. But we are bigger so the tendrils just stick to us a bit" explained Aira.

Aro let the plant touch him. It sort of stuck to him and felt weird. He carried on swimming. He didn't really like strange plants touching him.

As they entered the cave, there were larger fish and a myriad of plant life within. The fish still swam away though, even the ones that looked like they might bite or harm the three newcomers to this place.

"So, none of these fish hurt then? They don't attack us?" asked Aro, staring at the huge teeth one fish possessed.

"Oh no, they don't bother us; they all swim away and we never come into conflict with them" said Airu.

Aro sighed with relief.

"Thank grik for that" he muttered.

"Thank what?" asked Airu.

"Huh? Grik?" Aro looked puzzled.

"What does that mean?" asked Airu.

"It's an insult word. We say it when we're angry or to insult someone" said Aro.

"Oh" said Airu. "We don't have words like that. We just bite someone when we're angry with them. Does "grik" mean anything in particular?"

"Yeah, you know when something dies and it decays and goes all gooey and stinky? It smells so foul that it burns your nostrils and you can smell it for sun cycles or even lunars afterwards? The gooey decayed mess is grik. That's why we use it as an insult. Because there is nothing that is grosser or more horrible."

"So it's gooey rotten flesh then?" asked Airu.

"Yeah" said Aro.

"Then why were you thanking it?" asked Airu.

"Err…I dunno, it's just a saying I guess. Thank grik for that. Like when you want to be snarky about something or just…I dunno. Why do words mean anything? We just use

417

them in the order we were taught as kids, as our parents were taught and their parents before them. It just happens that way. That's the reason I suppose. I got that phrase from my Dad. Ellendrii says it too and Gryphies swear far less than Lizariaouses do. Then again he *may* have got it off me because he hangs around with me so much, or maybe it's because we're both young…" he swam off talking and not paying attention to where he was going. Before he knew what was happening, he was in a mass of the touchy plants.

"Aaah!! Get them off me!!" he screamed, flailing around.

"Don't move around so much, you'll break your bubble and drown" yelled Aira. "Let me help you!"

She swam over to him and helped untangle him from the invasive plants.

"Ergh, that was horrible" he said, disgustedly.

"They're harmless…well, we think so anyway. We haven't ever found any that dragged us in on mass and we weren't strong enough to get away from. And the young Aqwakitts aren't allowed down here where the plants are." Aira said.

"Shall we leave this cave now? I think I prefer my own cave, back home. The most that comes into that are cave cats and I can eat them" said Aro.

"What's a cave cat?" asked Airu.

" A meal creature" replied Aro, "Do you eat meat?"

"Sometimes. But mostly we eat water plants" replied Airu.

They left the cave and carried on swimming. Aro made the most of every step of their journey because he felt it was the closest to flying that he would ever get again. For a while, they swam in silence. The two Aqwakitts had shown other creatures around their lake before and they knew that to many of them it was a new and fascinating experience so they let him enjoy it.

"How much further?" asked Aro, after a while. Although he was enjoying the view, he was also getting tired.

"It's not far now. The middle of the lake" said Airu. "We will have to swim deeper because it's right at the bottom."

"Ok" replied Aro.

As they swam, there were more and more plants and they soon came to an underwater passageway.

"You get to it through here" explained Aira. "It's quite well hidden. It's not a case of just swimming to the middle of the lake and then diving under, or like your friend, flying to the middle and diving. You won't find it that way."

"Ok" said Aro again, as they reached the entrance to the passageway and swam into it. He assumed the "it" they referred to was the SilvaGryphie's secret hideout. He himself did find it a little unusual about her current abode but unlike Ellendrii, who had clear ideas on where she lived due to the stories he had heard, Aro was more open to interpretation regarding her home. And maybe she was in fact hiding. Maybe they could help her! Maybe they could fight off what was coming after her and save her! And she would be eternally grateful and take them back to Shernaron and give them both a special gift as a token of her appreciation! Ellendrii would be the fastest and most respected Gryphie in the sky kingdom and he, Aro, would be given wings so he would be able to fly as well! His mind became deeply lost in the fantastical and farfetched.

Aira was swimming in front, with Aro following and then Airu coming last. Aro was just glad nothing would attack them. It made a nice change from the territories they had come through so far. Well, some of them at least. It was just refreshing.

Aira suddenly turned to Aro and blew into his air bubble, making it a little larger.

"We don't want to make it too big or it won't fit through the passage and it will pop. But at the same time you were getting low on air." Aira told him.

"How did you know? You weren't even looking at me" said Aro.

"I noticed as we came in here" replied Aira, simply.

"Oh" said Aro, dumbly. He had been quite impressed with how easily she had been able to turn around in such a narrow space. She could quite literally fold her body in half if she wanted to. Aro couldn't turn at all. His body nearly filled the passageway. The Aqwakitts were quite a bit smaller than he was. He was a little worried also that the passageway would get narrower and he would get stuck.

"How many others have you brought through here, of my size?" he asked.

"None, why?" asked Aira.

"I won't get stuck, will I?" asked Aro.

"I hope not! If you do, we will have to go back and you won't find your silver Gryphie" said Aira.

"Ellendrii would probably kill me then" muttered Aro.

Ellendrii was now laying down at the water's edge. He had got bored sitting up and uncomfortable and so he lay down to wait for his friend. After a while he turned to Harrixx and asked how much longer they would be.

"They're probably showing him around" replied Harrixx.

"He doesn't even like swimming a lot" said Ellendrii. He wondered why his friend was so determined with this thing. He also wondered why he himself wasn't. It wasn't THAT unusual for their legendary creator to live underwater, surely? But Ellendrii had his doubts. There was just something that didn't click with all this.

"Do you get a lot of visitors?" he asked Harrixx.

"Yes, a lot pass by here and we try to be accommodating to them. The lake is large and they stay in this area for a while before moving on. We don't get many who are hostile to us, luckily. We are not good at defending ourselves. We tend to get into the water if we're attacked and either hide or swim away from the attacker. We've never encountered any hostile creatures that outnumbered us or could surround the lake so we've always been safe. We can live in the lake for quite a while before needing to come back to land. We can't live under the water but we have food and water at our disposal there and so can live quite comfortably until the threat is gone. The only downside is that treading water for a long time obviously tires us out. So we have to make it to a side of the lake that there is no threat. We come out of the lake to sleep but we can go a fair while without sleep. We have no predators here. The lake fish and other creatures are harmless and we live in peace with them. While we do eat fish sometimes, we much prefer to stick to eating the plants and underwater grasses. While your friend is out with the

Aqwakitts, would you like me to show you around and show you what life is like here?" asked Harrixx.

"No thanks. I'm happy waiting for him" replied Ellendrii. He didn't want to stray too far from keeping the lake in sight, especially the part that Aro had dived into. Of course he had no idea what he would do if the Aqwakitts he was with chose to kill him underwater. That much of their trust was in these creatures' hands at least. He just had to have faith that they wouldn't do that to his friend. However, if they harmed a scale on Aro's body, Ellendrii would not hesitate to flame down their little community and the difference between him and other attackers is that he could fly and he would catch and kill those who took to the water to escape.

Ellendrii had become extremely defensive due to the other threats they had encountered. He had been ok with the Kanniths and Rivniann but he still couldn't get himself to trust the fact that the SilvaGryphie lived with the Aqwakitts. He spent most of his time waiting for Aro and watching the lake. He got hungry and wanted to go hunting but he refused to leave his place of guarding and keeping an eye out for Aro. At one point he wanted to take to the sky but at the same time he didn't want the Aqwakitts to think that he was overly suspicious of them because they might take offence and as he had learned, it was very precarious what creatures took offence to.

Harrixx got bored and left him. He was a little conversational but seemed to have no interest whatsoever in their community so Harrixx felt his time was better spent elsewhere.

Ellendrii watched other Aqwakitts playing in the water. They certainly seemed a happy species. He had no real idea why he didn't altogether trust them. There was just something off about all this. He decided to focus his thoughts on the next stage of their journey if they didn't find the SilvaGryphie here, while he waited for Aro to return and he tried not to worry too much. He wanted to be prepared.

He figured as they had talked about, they would follow the lake around and then decide where to go from there. From his position at the lakeside he could see some mountains in the distance. They rose up very high, up to the clouds in fact and were capped with snow. If she was anywhere; that looked very much like a place where a white creature with long fluffy fur would live. He looked around some more. There was a lot of flat land off to the east of the lake and to the west it seemed like there was another valley. The mountains would be difficult to climb but he was sure they would make it ok. So long as they started at sunrise and hoped that there wouldn't be more than a sun cycle's travel up them. He wondered if there would be any food and decided they would catch some and take it with them just in case. Only they would catch birds this time, not fish for once!

Ellendrii was happy enough despite his worry for Aro, to rest and relax in the nice weather. There was a slight breeze but the sun was high in the sky and he sighed, glad of the rest. He needed to make the most of it; the next stage of the journey, if they had to do it, would be more difficult. Ellendrii checked the dressing on his leg. It was still secured. He wondered how it was healing. It didn't hurt as much to move. He hoped it would be healed by the next sun cycle at least. He figured it wouldn't take that long to finish the trip around the lake and his leg should be ok to climb. Otherwise he would have to fly no matter what Aro thought of it!

His thoughts returned to Aro. He was still worried about him. He was such a faithful friend. Even though they had their differences and fell out at times, nothing could break their friendship. And this journey had so far been the most trying thing for their friendship that he had encountered. He remembered the time on the float when Aro had had too much salt water and gone mad. That had been scary. He hoped that wouldn't happen again. But he also remembered when Aro had saved him and took him to Rivniann, even though he hadn't known that Rivniann lived in that dell and could help. Aro was loyal. He wondered if the other Lizariaouses had the same loyalty for their friends. He assumed so. Mordred was friends with Ellendrii's parents, after all and had been for many seasons now. His father and Mordred often hung out together and chatted about grown up boring things like the state of their territories and how they were approaching and solving certain problems and issues in them. Ellendrii had never found any of that very interesting. But come to think of it, he and Aro were grown up now. They certainly had to be, to overcome all they had been through till now. He really wished his parents knew how they were doing and that they were safe. Diabloss and Leida would have no idea if their son was even alive. He wondered how long he and Aro had been gone as well. He had lost count. He'd kept count at the beginning but the Forest of Foreboding had completely thrown him off. They hadn't been gone a season yet but he suspected they had been gone at least one lunar.

Ellendrii's heart ached at the thought of his mother crying because she thought he was dead. After all, they had all assumed that the SilvaGryphie was just the other side of the vast water and the pair wouldn't be gone that long. Or they had hoped that at least. They certainly had hoped that. And they had of course known that it may not be true but they all just had faith in the legends and stories and that was what they believed. How wrong they had been! The whole thing with the souls of the dead and the SilvaGryphie owning the whole of the world beyond Shernaron. Ellendrii didn't want to have to go back and tell everyone that their whole belief system was wrong. He decided that he would tell his parents the whole story and no one else. After all, it would be a shame to lose the magic idea of the souls drifting across the vast water from the funeral pyre. What would they do with their dead if they knew? Probably just burn them anywhere. Faith gave them hope and uplifted their hearts so they knew they would meet their loved ones again when they took their own journey across the vast water.

Ellendrii assumed not many Gryphies knew about his and Aro's journey to find the SilvaGryphie. Apart from Lunara and his parents and Aro's parents. Did Jadariol know? He couldn't remember but he now sincerely hoped that everyone who knew wouldn't say much. Or else everyone would ask him what had been going on and what he had seen when and if he got back and he felt bad lying to them. Besides, look how exciting their adventure had been so far! He couldn't hide that from curious Gryphies. Didn't they deserve to know what wonders (and horrors!) lay beyond that vast stretch of disgusting salty water? Ellendrii suddenly felt torn between telling the truth or just not saying anything. He felt that maybe if he told the truth to his parents and those close to him and told them not to tell and just didn't tell anyone anything else then he would have the best of both worlds. He would get to tell the truth and the full adventure while still keeping it a secret from others and maintaining their beliefs about Gryphie life.

And what about the SilvaGryphie? Well that would only reinforce their belief system. Although maybe she would tell them a few different things and change how they viewed the world anyway. Maybe she would say they had it all wrong all these seasons and in fact there was another life and another world beyond the vast water and that wasn't where the souls went. BUT then again if the souls didn't cross the water, where did they go? He assumed they didn't go up to the sky because that was where the Sky Gryphies were. So did they maybe sink into the water instead? Maybe she WAS living under the water and the souls went down to her and she looked after them? After all, that was the current belief; that they joined her after they died.

Of course he and Aro would not be returning unless they found her, so imagining what would happen if they returned alone was not even an option or a subconscious thought in Ellendrii's head. He KNEW that they would return WITH her or not at all. Maybe he could ask her advice. Or maybe once the other Gryphies saw her, they would be so awed that they wouldn't need or want to ask Ellendrii anything about his journey. He would have found the legendary SilvaGryphie and that would be that.

He assumed also that upon their journey home, she would know the way. Ellendrii had no idea what way was the right way to get to where she was but he was pretty sure their journey home would be shorter because she would know the best path or direction to take in order to get back to Shernaron. He still had no idea really how to get their float back from the Wind Hounds but maybe once they saw how amazing the SilvaGryphie was, they would just give it back and ask no more questions. She may even scare them into respecting himself and Aro. And be all "How DARE you take offence to someone who knows so little about your culture and says the wrong thing by accident; how DARE you be so unforgiving!" Ellendrii chuckled at this.

Meanwhile, Aro and the two Aqwakitts had reached the end of the passageway and were back out in the water again. He had assumed they would end up in a cave or something since this part of the lake couldn't be got to by air or swimming on the surface. But when he looked up, he saw nothing of the sort.

"Hey, Aira, how come you can't get to this part by flying or swimming on the surface? I thought we would end up in another underwater cave or something but I can see the sunlight above me." He motioned upwards where the sun shone in although very far away and very dimly. They were very very deep in the water.

"We take certain paths to get to certain places" explained Aira, "And if we had swum along the surface and dived down, we would have had trouble finding the correct place to find your silver Gryphie. Whereas if we take a path or direction we are familiar with, we can go straight to it. Sure it might take longer than diving straight down from the surface but since we've never dived down to come to this place, we don't know where to dive from and we would have had to find it first. The lake is so big that it would have been a lot of trial and error."

"That's stupid" replied Aro, "You could just find where she is and then swim up to the surface from there and see where you are."

"Yeah that would work in principle but you would still not be able to remember the exact spot you surfaced when you next came here so we just prefer to take our paths to the different places we're looking for." Aira shrugged it off. Well, if it worked for them. Aro shut up and just let them lead him after that.

"We're nearly there now" said Aira. Aro was glad.

Swimming down lower, they came to a large outcrop of rock. There was something stood on it, at an angle as though

it had been knocked or nudged over a little. At first, Aro
thought it was just a strangely shaped rock and ignored it.

They carried on swimming in the direction of the outcrop
and the odd rock that sat upon it. The dim sunlight that has
reached all the way down here hits the rock and shines off it
beautifully. Shafts of sunlight surround the outcrop as well and
Aro can't help but pay it closer attention as they reach it. It's
an interesting place, unlike anything else they've swum past
so far.

"Ok, here we are" said Aira.

"Huh?" Aro looked at her, puzzled. "She lives around
here?" he asked.

"Yeah, you mean you can't see her? She's big enough"
Aira looked irritated.

Aro gave her a sceptical look and nearly snorted into his
bubble, but didn't, because he didn't want the inside to get
wet.

Grumpily, he turned around and suddenly his eyes
became wide and he gasped.

There she was!

Chapter 23
Clues

Aro stared. She was there alright, but she wasn't alive. She had been immortalized in the strangely angled rock. She was a statue! Life-size and acutely detailed. The rock was silver and glowed dully. He suddenly realized why the Aqwakitts had called her the "silver Gryphie" that was all they thought she was. The statue that rested at the bottom of their lake. They had mistaken the pronunciation of her name!

Aira and Airu swam around the statue happily.

"She's lovely, isn't she?" they said in unison.

"Erm…yes, she is. But we were looking for the *real* SilvaGryphie; not a statue of her" explained Aro.

"There's a *real* one? We've never seen a *real* one" said the two Aqwakitts.

Aro grunted.

"So all this time I thought she lived in a cave at the bottom of your lake or something and in reality she was just a carved statue. Well I feel like an idiot."

"Well you never asked if she was alive or not; all you wanted was a silver Gryphie. And this is a silver Gryphie" said Aira.

"No, SILVAGryphie, SILVA; not silver. Geez. Talk about crossed vines. Well this is indeed a silver Gryphie but it isn't what we are looking for. However, it *is* a carving of her. I wonder who carved it?"

"I dunno, it's been down here forever; we can't remember a time when it wasn't here. Maybe it was made before we got here or maybe we made it but so long ago that no one can remember." Aira shrugged.

Aro swam up to the statue and had a close look. It was so intricate, almost as if it actually was the real SilvaGryphie but someone had turned her to stone. Every hair, every muscle in her beautiful wings, every detail of her face was so real. He reached out and gently ran a paw over the stone. It was so smooth too. It must have been carved by a master; to get rough stone that smooth. Or maybe the water had made it that way but there was barely any current here so that couldn't possibly have happened. The other thing was that the stone had no moss; it was not greened like a lot of the other rock under the water. This was immaculate. And around her neck was a necklace that held a beautiful deep blue stone. It shone in the faint rays of light that made it down to this depth. Aro examined it closely, then he touched it and pressed on it to see if anything happened. Nothing happened. He was a little disappointed.

"Ellendrii has to see this. I wonder if we can take it to him." Aro pondered.

"Are you kidding? It's huge, how will we get it out?" said Airu.

"Yeah good point" admitted Aro, "We'll bring him here to see it instead."

The others mutually agreed and they swam back to get Ellendrii. This time with no detours or explorations.

Ellendrii was still patiently waiting but he was getting a bit fidgety by now. He was still worried they may have drowned his friend. Then he saw them approaching him from afar and he perked up.

"Aro!! Did you find her?" he yelled, excitedly from the shore.

Aro didn't want to admit he had been wrong and she wasn't actually living under the water but he didn't want to lie either so he said;

"Sort of, but you need to see for yourself, come out here!" he motioned to the water that they floated in and Ellendrii flew out and dived in.

"What do you mean "sort of"? That makes no sense."

Aro sighed in annoyance.

"Ergh, we didn't find her; she's not down there. We found a statue carved to look like her. I want you to see it. It's very very detailed and looks incredibly lifelike. And there is a weird blue stone set into it as though she's wearing a necklace or something. You need to come and see it. It's not far and we'll take you straight there."

The Aqwakitts swam around and splashed about waiting to give Ellendrii his breathing bubble so he could go and see for himself.

"Ok, well at least I was right about a Gryphie living under the water. But all the same, I really wanted to be proved wrong about this particular thing" said Ellendrii.

"Yeah no kidding, if you'd been wrong not only could I have gloated about it but also we would have finally found her. Something told me this wouldn't be that easy" said Aro.

"So, what do I have to do for the bubble then?" asked Ellendrii and the Aqwakitts explained in unison. The pair dived under with them and they each formed the bubbles around their heads.

Ellendrii freaked out in a similar way to how Aro had done. He burst through the water's surface, breathing rapidly.

"Sorry, sorry, I just…I thought I would be able to do it."

"It's ok" said Aira, "Try again!" She smiled and lead Ellendrii back into the water and they tried again with the bubble.

It was four tries before the Gryphie's body could adjust to breathing under the water and doing something completely against all his instincts. Aro was amused at this because it took Ellendrii longer to adjust to it than it did him. But he was polite enough for once not to say.

Once they were both comfortable, they headed to the statue. As Aro had done, Ellendrii marvelled at all the wonderful things he saw under the water. Things he wouldn't normally be able to see even if he swam under the water since if you open your eyes in the water, everything is blurry.

Aro secretly pretended he was flying over the fish and plants down below. He pretended he was a great sky hunter. Quietly though; so as not to embarrass himself in front of the others. He suspected they might laugh at him.

They swam through the tunnel. Ellendrii had some trouble getting his wings through but once he had learned how to hold them in order to keep them against him, he was ok.

They followed the two Aqwakitts out the other side and to the deepest part of the lake where the statue was.

"Wow…everything is so different down here. It's such an experience" marvelled Ellendrii as they approached the statue. He hadn't noticed it yet; all he saw was rocks and he was far more interested in the marine life all around him.

There the statue stood, majestic in the dim light. The SilvaGryphie was in a standing pose with her wings pointing straight upwards and her gaze across the vastness of the water before her.

Ellendrii was filled with awe. The rest of what he had seen had kept him quiet with awe but he was even more silenced by this spectacle.

"She's…beautiful" he breathed, swimming up to the statue and looking more closely.

"I could imagine her moving at any moment! So this is what she really looks like? Just like in the stories!"

She was more the size of a Deamon Gryphie than a regular one but she was much larger than Diabloss. Ellendrii had never ever seen a Gryphie of this size. And he could only presume she was the size of a Deamon Gryphie; not having seen one before. Diabloss was bigger than any other Gryphie he knew and he was aware that his mother had been far larger than his non-Deamon father. She was truly a marvel not to be messed with. And yet she looked gentle. Beautiful, majestic and gentle. Not threatening at all. Her stone muzzle was carved with a soft, motherly expression. Her eyes were open and the details of those were incredible too; right down to the iris and pupils. Even the eyelashes had been carved. She had a huge, soft looking mane about her shoulders that went down her back too. She looked like she was more suited to a colder climate. Her tail was long and graceful; her limbs were graceful but sturdy at the same time. They were strong looking and she had an unusual tailspade that was narrow, ornate and meshed. Her wings were partly feathered and partly like the Forest Gryphies and she had four fingers and a thumb claw. And of course, poking out from under her mane fur was the blue stone which seemed to be part of an intricate, wide necklace. The stone was in the shape of a Gryphie's head in front profile. Ellendrii swam to it and inspected it very closely. It had a sheen to it and a strange shape within, that was a paler, shimmering colour. The shape seemed to move and transform when he looked at it from different angles. Like Aro had done, he felt the urge to touch the stone and see if anything happened. The moving shape in it rippled and gathered around the finger that rested on the stone. It was very bizarre.

"Aro, come here" he said to his friend, who obliged.

"What?" asked Aro.

"Dig out this stone if you can" said Ellendrii.

"But that's part of the statue, surely it would break it if I took it out?" asked Aro.

"Just have a go. I feel we have to take it with us" replied Ellendrii.

"Ok, whatever you say" shrugged Aro and dug at the stone with his powerful black claws. The two Aqwakitts were sat on top of the statue, resting on her back. Being so large, the statue easily accommodated both the little water creatures. They watched Aro work with interest.

The stone was hard and difficult to dig into but Aro tried his best to hook out the stone in her necklace.

"Are you sure you have no idea who made this?" asked Ellendrii.

"We're sure. We've just always known it was here. Our parents showed us and probably theirs before them. We know every inch of this lake" said Aira.

"We dunno where it came from" said Airu. "But it's very nice, isn't it? What does it mean to you? Your friend said you're looking for the real version of this statue. So you mean that the creature carved from this rock is actually real and alive somewhere?"

"Yes, she is the founder of all my species. But not his." Ellendrii was quick to point this out and motion to Aro who was still hard at work. "We tell stories about her and I decided to come and find her."

He saw Aro looking at him.

"Ok well I didn't decide; I came looking for her to prove someone else wrong and prove that she does exist. We just never knew that she was so far away."

431

"Why would you tell stories about something that didn't exist?" asked Airu. "That doesn't make sense."

"Sometimes stories are made up to help others. So they tell of things that aren't real. But then again we weren't sure, I suppose, if she existed or not. We thought she did at one time but then she may have died by now, if she isn't immortal that is." Ellendrii explained. "We like to think she is immortal. She is the one who brought the Gryphie species to Shernaron. She made us and she wanted a good home for us so she took us to our home. She would have kept on living with us but some Gryphies started to worship her like a god and she didn't want that so she left. She wanted to be seen as equal, so anyone could go to her for advice or hang out with her. But since she created all of us, it's easy to imagine how some of us may have wanted to worship her."

"Gryphies are weird" muttered Aro. Thankfully, Ellendrii didn't hear.

"I dunno who created us" said Airu.

"Our parents of course" said Aira.

"Oh yeah! Of course!" replied Airu and the pair burst out laughing.

Even though swimming is enjoyed by Gryphies, getting wet and thus losing fire power is not a favoured thing by them. But with the bubble, Ellendrii didn't even feel like he was getting that wet despite that his body was. His face was dry. He swam around a little as he waited for Aro to get the stone out of the SilvaGryphie statue's chest. Ellendrii hadn't had a proper look around anyway so he felt inclined to now. He didn't intend to go back in the water to explore, so he made the most of it now. He hadn't had the chance to really on the way there.

He had a similar curiosity to Aro and swam up to plants and fish for closer looks, touching the plants. He found something a little like what we would call an anemone except that this was bright purple with yellow spots and it was as big as his hand. He poked it with his tail and it shrank back uncomfortably.

He also encountered some of the touchy plants. He didn't like those much. He had got his tail stuck in them and they

432

were holding onto him. It felt weird and he took fright and swam away from them as fast as he could. It was then that he had the idea to race the two Aqwakitts. He thought they would probably win but since he had enjoyed racing the Wind Hound and he liked sky races back home, racing in the water would be different and fun.

"Hey you two, want to race?" he challenged the Aqwakitts.

"Yes!" they said in unison, "But you must be aware we will beat you! This is our domain here."

"I know, I only wanted to for the fun of it" said Ellendrii.

"Fair enough" said the Aqwakitts as one. "We'll race from the statue to that sun beam over there." They pointed to the place they had decided upon. "And back!" they put in before Ellendrii could reply.

"Of course!" Ellendrii grinned. This would be a nice challenge!

Aro was just getting his claws in under the top of the blue Gryphie shaped stone when the race began. He looked around at them, rolled his eyes and continued with his work.

The three lined up to start the race and the Aqwakitts counted down.

"3…2…1…GO!" they yelled together and the three of them raced off. Ellendrii was struggling. Swimming through water offered far more resistance than flying did. The Aqwakitts sailed through the water easily because they had smooth bodies with fur specially adapted for swimming. They also had webbed feet too, which helped a lot and they were a streamlined shape.

Ellendrii was none of these things. He used his wings to push himself along. He had done this before; it was pretty much flying under water and he was pretty fast doing it but he was still not as swift as the Aqwakitts. They had reached the shaft of light before he did and he was still swimming for it when they had turned around and passed him.

They got back to the finish line way before he did. He felt sort of pathetic swimming back when they had finished and were floating, waiting for him to get there.

Aro had seen this and yelled to him.

"Not so fast now, are you!" he called. Even though he supported his friend, it was good somehow to see him lose for once. It would mean he couldn't get too bigheaded.

"Oh yeah? That stone out yet?" yelled Ellendrii.

"No" grumbled Aro and carried on with his job.

They waited around a little more and finally Aro got the stone out. They half expected the statue to do something when the stone was removed from it but it did nothing except stand there, slightly tilted on the outcrop of rock just as they had found it.

Ellendrii took to the surface and flew back to shore with the stone because he was eager to examine it and although it had been fun swimming underwater and he had enjoyed exploring, he wasn't that comfortable with being in the water for a long period of time, being pyrokinetic and all.

Aro swam back with the Aqwakitts and got there quite a while later than Ellendrii. Mostly because he wanted to make the most of it and explore on his way back.

Ellendrii alighted on the shore and sat down to examine the blue stone. The shaft of light or shine or whatever it was inside it fascinated him. He tested out different things with it for a while. Shining it in the sun, touching it, tilting the stone so the shine changed. He finally realized that the strange shine in it was actually a form of pointer. He had discovered this by sitting and aiming the stone all around him. Whenever it went east; it formed into the shape of a pointer or arrow. To the east was the flat land and beyond that, the snow topped mountain range. Just like he had thought. He wanted to head for those mountains and this stone seemed to think that was the direction to take. So, was it a stone that would take them to the SilvaGryphie? What would they have to lose? After all, assuming it would lead them to her was just as good as making their own way there. Either way they might get lost and never find her so it was a good enough gamble to take. He fiddled with the stone some more, just to make sure that it was indeed a pointer. Some of the Aqwakitts showed a little interest but not much. They certainly weren't as curious as the Kanniths. Ellendrii presumed that they were more used to creatures passing through their territory.

Finally, Aro came back. The sun was lower in the sky and evening was quickly drawing in when the Lizariaous and the two Aqwakitts returned. Aro clambered out and shook himself. His needles rattled violently. He headed over to where Ellendrii was now lying on his back holding the stone in his hands and tilting and turning it. It was so fascinating and so fun to play with as well. He turned it like a compass but no matter how he did it, it always formed the shape of an arrow when pointed east.

"Whatcha doing?" asked Aro, plonking himself down next to his friend.

"Looking at this stone. It forms an arrow shape when I point it in the direction of that mountain range over there in the distance, look..." Ellendrii showed him. Aro looked with some interest.

"So, what...you think it will lead us to her?" he asked.

"Possibly. What have we got to lose?" said Ellendrii.

"Yeah says he who was afraid of traps and the Aqwakitts drowning us. What makes this more trustworthy?" asked Aro.

"It was on a statue of the SilvaGryphie" replied Ellendrii, very sure of himself. "And I trust her."

"We don't even know who carved that" said Aro. Well at least it hadn't been as scary as those horrid statues in the ruins of the Repulsators.

"Sometimes you need to trust a sign" replied Ellendrii, "And this was a sign. Like I said, we have nothing to lose and we can afford to just go with it. It'll be ok. Besides, I feel better with a guide."

"I guess so. I wonder why someone would build a statue under the water though."

"I think it was the Aqwakitts, except they made it so long ago that none of them remember. I think the SilvaGryphie used to live around here, maybe when the Aqwakitts first settled. They love the water so that's probably why they made it under there." Ellendrii said.

"Maybe" Aro shrugged, "So, we're following where that blue Gryphie stone thing points now then?"

"Yes." Ellendrii replied, very sure of himself.

"Are we gunna wait till next sun or set off now?" asked Aro.

"We may as well set off now" said Ellendrii, "I don't want to waste any more time. Besides, we'll travel by the lake for a while and before we break off from it, we can catch some food to take with us on the next part of our journey."

Aro nodded and they set off, saying farewell to the two helpful Aqwakitts, Aira and Airu.

The two friends followed the lake around, laughing and joking and happy to be in the sun and by a good water and food source and not in a horrible dark forest. This felt more normal to them. They caught some dinner and then carried on. As the moon came out, they reached the place where they would leave the lake and head out over the grass to the mountain range far in the distance.

They decided to sleep here so they could have breakfast, stock up the bag with food and water and head out with good supplies the next sun cycle.

They found a place to sleep at the lakeside, curled up next to each other and settled down to sleep. They heard moon time bird calls, insects chirping and the splashes and occasional voices of the Aqwakitts in the water and around the lake. Despite these sounds, it was very peaceful and they both slept deeply and well this moon cycle.

The sun rose and Aro slept in. Ellendrii caught some breakfast for them and went about catching some of the lake birds as their food for the next part of the journey. He had packed them into the bag and he was just filling the gourds with water when Aro finally decided to wake up and join him.

"Sleep well?" Ellendrii asked, with a hint of sarcasm.

"Yeah, very" replied Aro with a yawn, completely missing it. Ellendrii rolled his eyes.

"Your breakfast bird is over there" he pointed and Aro all but pounced on the dead bird and devoured it hungrily.

"It's a good thing Aqwakitts don't eat those or you wouldn't have had any breakfast this sun cycle or at least none that I had caught" said Ellendrii.

"Ok I get it, I slept late. But I've had moonmares for moon cycles since we left that stupid forest as I know you have too, so cut me some slack here. It's not my fault. Besides, you want to make it to those mountains before moon rises then I need to be well rested." Aro pointed out.

"Yes but at the same time, the later we start, the less ground we'll get behind us and we may not reach the mountains by moonrise" replied Ellendrii, packing the last of the gourds into his bag.

"Ok, ok have it your way, you win" Aro said, because he was sick of arguing and also because he felt a little guilty for oversleeping. But at the same time he felt that Ellendrii could have woken him if he really wanted him to get up so they could get going. Waking a sleeping Lizariaous is never a safe thing to do but there was the option of throwing water at him from a distance and avoid being shot by a needle. At least avoid it a little, anyway.

"Come on then" said Ellendrii and they headed away from the lake. Ellendrii was sad to see it go. It had been very useful. Now they were back out into new and uncertain ground. The grass was just as long as before and Ellendrii chose to fly, so he could avoid the bugs latching on to him again. From the sky though, as they made their way through the grass, he could see what was beyond it and it made his heart quicken with anxiety. It was not a terrain that excited him. Quite the opposite in fact.

Because the grass had been tall, neither of them could see over it and see that there was another terrain past the grass but before the mountains. They had both just assumed that the grass had gone right to the base of the mountains.

Sometimes Ellendrii regretted that he could fly. Not always, but occasionally. Aro noticed the drop of his friend's face and queried him over it.

"Nothing, it's nothing. Just…I just umm…need to pee!" Ellendrii flew off and pretended to relieve himself. He didn't need to land in order to relieve himself but he pretended that he did and the fact that the little bug things might bite him again was the reason his face had fallen. He really didn't want to tell Aro just yet about what they were approaching. He was sure that Aro would suggest they went a different direction and question the stone's wisdom and although yes it was only a blue stone; it was a blue stone in the shape of a Gryphie's head that had been found on a statue of the SilvaGryphie and Ellendrii wanted it to guide them. It just felt right to him. It didn't feel right to Aro though and he would surely have said to ignore it and go another way.

Lizariaouses didn't believe in such things.

So they went on and finally neared the edge of the grassland. And the grass started to get shorter. Ellendrii fretted because they would see it soon and he really didn't want Aro to suggest they went a different way. Despite how it looked, Ellendrii knew they must cross it.

And it looked foul.

Aro's ears perked up. He had seen it.

"Oh wow…what the grik…" he breathed as they approached the new terrain. The grass had got shorter towards the edge, as though it had trouble growing so close to something so horrible and had eventually died away altogether, giving way for the new, barren landscape. There was nothing growing there. No creatures crossing their path. No birds flying in the sky. Nothing. The ground was a flesh colour and blotchy in places. Here and there were pits and craters on the landscape that looked like sores. They oozed a foul smelling fluid. It was just like walking on something that was dead and rotting, except it was indeed hard ground and didn't give way when Aro put a foot on it. A few rivers of red flowed in the distance and the heat rose from the ground in a putrid mist. Looking beyond the land, the mountains rose up in the distance. This horrible terrain stretched right to them. They had a lot of ground to cover and already the stench was burning Ellendrii's delicate nostrils. He looked down.

Aro was making his way onto this new land with interest. Ellendrii had been sure it would gross his friend out but apparently it didn't seem to.

"It's just like back home in Dyarkroeen except…fouler" Aro exclaimed.

"And you're ok walking on it?" asked Ellendrii, his own faith in flying completely restored.

"Yeah it's fine" replied Aro.

"Even the stink?" asked Ellendrii.

"Ah it only smells like my cave if I leave meat in there too long" said Aro, oddly reassuringly.

Ellendrii shrugged. Fair enough. He should have told Aro sooner. Then maybe he would have run to it and they would have made their way faster.

Aro couldn't resist staring into one of the craters when he reached one. It exploded and covered his head in the horrible putrid white liquid. Ellendrii shuddered. Even Aro wasn't cool with this though and he sputtered and shook it off.

"Blegh! Some went in my mouth!" he spat and decided to avoid the craters after that. The gas and things that came out of them seemed to indicate some sort of sulphuric chemicals deep underground. It just appeared on the outside to resemble rotting meat. Ellendrii knew there was probably a reasonable explanation for all this but his imagination couldn't help trying to tell him what his eyes thought they were seeing.

Aro meanwhile had decided to lick the red water that flowed in the small streams here and there on this odd terrain. The streams flowed in small trenches in the rocky land. He leaned down into one and tried some of the water. And then he spat it out.

"Nice?" chided Ellendrii with a smirk. Aro should really stop tasting or trying or looking at everything.

"Blegh no! I thought it would taste like blood but it's bitter and horrible!"

"Even if it tasted like blood, drinking it would be stupid. Besides, I have water here. Why not just ask me for some?" suggested Ellendrii.

"Because I wanted to try this" replied Aro stubbornly.

"Ok, ok" said Ellendrii smiling and got out a gourd. He flew down low and handed it to Aro. Aro drank thirstily.

"Be careful not to drink too much, we don't know when we'll find water again" warned Ellendrii.

"Up there" replied Aro, pointing to the snowy tops of the mountains.

"And how many sun cycles I wonder, will it take for us to get up there" pondered Ellendrii a little mockingly.

Aro just grunted and handed the gourd back to Ellendrii. Then he noticed something.

"Hey, Ellendrii, why didn't you land and give that to me?" he asked with a small smile.

"I don't need to land when I can hover low and give it to you" said Ellendrii.

"Ah well something tells me you didn't land cos you're too scared to set foot on this ground" Aro said, quite correctly.

"No I'm not. I told you, hovering is just easier. Why should I land when I just need to go back into the air again" replied Ellendrii, defensively.

"Come to think of it, you never landed after we got out of that grassy area and arrived here. I expected you to land since there are no bugs here that can bite you. So, why did you keep in the sky?" asked Aro.

"I dunno, I just felt like it" lied Ellendrii.

"Well you're making me feel bad" said Aro, "Walk with me so I can chat to you. It's harder to chat to you up there. My neck hurts from having to look up so much."

"My legs are tired from walking, ok? So that's the real reason I decided to fly. I'm saving my energy for when we climb the mountain so I can climb with you instead of flying up."

"No, the *real* reason you decided to fly is because you don't want to touch this ground. It grosses you out and you don't want to touch it cos Gryphies are so vain!"

"We are not!" snapped Ellendrii.

"Then walk down here with me" replied Aro without missing a beat.

"I'm happy up here" replied Ellendrii.

"Ok, fine, then at least fly a little closer" replied Aro.

"Ok" replied Ellendrii, happy that his friend had dropped the subject and he flew down lower. No sooner had he done that than Aro jumped into the air, grabbed Ellendrii's tailspade and pulled him down so he hit the ground with a thud.

"OWW! ARO!! Why did you do that?" Ellendrii demanded, standing up angrily.

"To get you to touch the ground" smirked Aro.

Ellendrii looked down, then at Aro, then down again and leaped back into the sky like he had been shot.

"I was right!! You DO hate the idea of walking on this ground!" laughed Aro. The fact he had been proved right far outweighed the fact that Ellendrii was in the sky again.

"Ok fine, you're right. Happy? I don't want to touch it cos it's icky. And it's NOT because Gryphies are vain, we just have standards. I don't like the idea of walking on something that looks like a rotten corpse. I don't know how you can walk on it either but then I guess it's more in your nature than mine. Am I not allowed to do as I wish? If I don't want to walk on it, can't I fly? If you didn't want to do something, I wouldn't force you to."

"Na, it's fine. I got you to stand on it, that's good enough for me. If you wanna fly then fly." Aro said.

"Thank you" said Ellendrii, now a little embarrassed about the whole thing and having to admit his distain at the horrible fleshy ground.

Ellendrii didn't have to feel satisfied at being able to fly for long though because it started to rain. They didn't notice at first what the rain looked like. They only noticed that it was getting wet.

Neither of them put two and two together, mostly because they couldn't do maths but also the idea that the colour of the rain must somehow dictate the colour of the streams of red water that were here and there. Aro only noticed when Ellendrii flew ahead a little way and he got a better look at the Gryphie in some way other than from underneath.

Ellendrii was a bit red. Aro looked at himself, puzzled. His skin was black so it was hard to tell but on the scales he had that were turquoise, he noticed those were a bit pinkish too. Then he realized, very slowly because Lizariaouses aren't fast thinkers, that the rain was in fact red like blood.

"Hey Ellendrii!" he called.

Ellendrii looked down and fell back to him.

"This rain is bloody" observed Aro. Ellendrii held out a hand and let some rain fall on it.

"GRIK!!" he swore loudly. "What the…" He looked up into the sky as though for some confirmation of his recent find. Nothing happened except more rain fell.

He looked down at Aro, who had a big grin on his face.

"What's up with you?" asked Ellendrii.

"Well, you didn't want to touch the land but it seems this territory has touched you anyway" Aro sniggered.

"Oh ha ha" spat Ellendrii sarcastically. Aro just laughed more.

"Let's get a move on. There's nowhere to shelter out here but I don't fancy being soaked in red so we'd better try to move faster for the mountains" said Ellendrii.

"Oh you're just saying that cos you're getting all wet and bloody. It doesn't affect me, so I don't need to hurry" said Aro.

"Yes you do or I'll leave you behind" said Ellendrii.

"I don't care. It's a flat stretch between here and there so we're not likely to lose each other. And don't even think about challenging me to a race. I know you're faster than me cos you can fly."

Ellendrii hadn't been thinking that but he may have done if he'd wanted something to make Aro hurry.

"Oh, well in that case I'll fly to the mountains and wait for you. On the top. And then if you get hungry or thirsty along the way it will be your own fault for not hurrying!"

"That's not fair!" whined Aro.

"Yes it is. We need to hurry and find the SilvaGryphie anyway. Just cos you like it here, I don't and I will get out of here as fast as I can. If you don't want to come with me, that's fine, but I have the food and water and you don't."

"Then can't you leave me a gourd and a bird for my journey?" asked Aro.

"Nope, if you want those, you need to move" replied Ellendrii stubbornly.

"FINE. You convinced me, ok??" Aro said and started to run.

"That's better!" smiled Ellendrii. This will get him back for his smart idea of peeing on my leg thought Ellendrii, who was still sure that Aro had done that because he wanted to do something gross and territorial more so than having the bright idea that those bugs would fall off his friend.

So the pair ran and flew across the land. Aro dodged the craters and whatever shot out of them and Ellendrii kept pace with him because he didn't want to fly too far ahead. He had been difficult enough as it was with Aro, he didn't want to annoy him any more by leaving him behind after he had agreed to run. Aro bounded and leaped over the streams in their little valleys and inlets and the rain pounded down on the pair of them. It appeared to be getting heavier, much to Ellendrii's dismay and was oddly starting to weigh down on his wings. Normal rain didn't do this so why would this rain do it? It seemed thicker too; more bloodlike and less like the watery kind he was used to. So it wasn't just red water, it did indeed look like blood. It smelled like it too and Ellendrii wrinkled his nose up. It was overwhelming by now and his fur was soaked through with it. As he flew, he looked down into the liquid streams below and saw what a state he was in. Of course the red liquid in the streams showed him as red anyway but he could see how wet he was. He had hoped this rain would ease off. And why exactly, was it blood? This was nearly as disturbing as the Forest of Foreboding had been even if it was less dangerous.

Aro ran relentlessly, hardly tiring, which was unusual for him. But he was leaner and hungrier than he had been before they started this journey; they both were. They found they could run much faster when they needed to and their muscles had grown strong from all the travelling they had done.

Aro had always been pretty lean but he also had the chunky, sturdiness of a Lizariaous. Now he was lean and muscular and determined. Ellendrii's thoughts drifted to what their parents would say the next time they saw them. Ellendrii looked up at his own wing muscles as he flew. The muscles were sinewy and well used. The fact they had spent so long in the Forest of Foreboding where he hadn't flown, didn't seem to have affected the muscle that he had built up from crossing the vast water.

They both tired less easily now as well. Having spent sun cycles just on the move, they had far greater stamina than they had when they started out. They also found that they were less hungry the more they travelled. Their bodies were adjusting to the fact that they couldn't always eat whenever they were hungry like they could back home and all the food

443

they did eat went straight back into energy again for the next stage of their journey. Truly they had grown up.

The terrain stretched for miles ahead of them but they made progress and the mountains soon loomed overhead. They were huge, vast and tall. Ellendrii presumed there must be a whole other world on top of them. He had the stone on a piece of twine around his neck so he could check it regularly. They were still following the direction of the shining arrow so he hoped they were on the right track.

Down below, Aro had slowed to a trot because finally he was getting tired. He had run several miles and was doing very well so Ellendrii slowed too and allowed the pair of them to just take the rest slowly. The rain had ironically, stopped.

Ellendrii felt the rain dripping off him and shook as best he could while in the air. He felt filthy and bloody. He could see it on his arms as he looked down. All his fur was "blood" soaked. Still, being in the air dried it fairly fast and it didn't dry like blood; crusty and uncomfortable. It dried like a dye and just left his fur with a reddish tinge.

He was glad the crater marked ground and the rising heat and stench would soon be behind them though. He figured that they would try and find a different way back altogether. What with this awful terrain and the Forest of Foreboding, it really was not worth heading back past this way. Then again if they took a different route how could they know that it wouldn't be worse? Ellendrii pondered all this over as they approached the mountain range.

The horrible terrain was easing off a little and becoming browner and less fleshy. The craters were now few and far between as well. Ellendrii's wings were tired so he decided to land and walk with Aro.

"Finally came down did we?" asked Aro but he was only playing.

"Yeah, well my wings were tired" replied Ellendrii.

"You're lucky. You have either legs or wings to fall back on when one or other gets tired. I only have my legs" pointed out Aro. He wasn't doing it maliciously, but he wanted to make Ellendrii aware that he shouldn't complain when he had advantages over the Lizariaous.

444

"I didn't in the Forest of Foreboding" said Ellendrii. "I *had* to walk then."

"Ok fair enough" agreed Aro.

"Are you tired? We'll have a rest anyway when we reach the mountains. I think we should rest this moon cycle and try and make it up there in a whole sun cycle instead of now. We've no idea if there's anywhere we can sleep on the way up and it looks pretty hard going. I checked as we approached and I can't see any paths or anything so we'll just have to do our best. It might take more than one sun cycle to climb it but that's the risk we'll have to take."

"I'm a bit tired, yeah. I'm catching up my strength because we're walking but yeah I think we should try and make it in one sun cycle. We can start at sunrise and I promise not to oversleep this time!" Aro grinned.

"Ok! We could just start and keep climbing through next moon cycle if need be. It's not like we're not used to staying up all moon till the following sun" said Ellendrii.

"Yeah we could do that if it's not too dark. The moon seems to be good and bright here though." Aro said.

As they reached the foot of the mountains though and looked up, the sheer height and hugeness of what they had to ascend hit them and they suddenly felt very small.

Chapter 24
Upward

They stood and stared up at the vastness before them, taking it in before they proceeded any further. They breathed in awe. From where they stood, they couldn't even see the top, only rocks upon rocks upon rocky mountain face.

Aro swallowed.

"You sure we can do this?" he asked Ellendrii, "Maybe I should stay here and you fly up and see what's up there and I...I go around."

"That wouldn't work. These mountains stretch who knows where. Besides, look at the Gryphie stone. It's pointing upward, not around." Ellendrii showed his friend the blue stone. When he aimed it at the mountain, it pointed straight up. But when he aimed it to one side in the direction of following the mountain's base, it pointed to the left instead of straight ahead, indicating up the mountain and not around.

"Grik" muttered Aro. More climbing. Still, needs must and at least they would get some rest before climbing up. The sun was low in the sky now and they sat down and ate and drank.

They wandered around a little and tried to see if there was a way up, to help get them off to a good start. But no, there wasn't. While Ellendrii searched around and flew up a little way to become more accustomed to what they were about to ascend, Aro lay down and looked out at the land they had just crossed. He could see the tall grass way in the distance and nothing much beyond it. It was obviously similar to the view they had had from the other side and it appeared to be the land they had just travelled across and grass and nothing else. But he knew the lake was there and the funny little Aqwakitts. Still, here it was peaceful. Actually, a bit *too* peaceful. He was used to hearing other creatures even if the calls were few and far between. But nothing lived in that barren landscape and they were too far away to hear what lived in the grass.

Presently, Ellendrii returned and sat down with him. Now for a proper rest!

"Did you find anything? Like a path or an easier way up?" asked Aro.

"Not really. There are no paths anyway. We'll just have to be careful. The face of the mountainside is rocky so it won't be hard to get up, we'll have to hold on to the rocks and use them to our advantage. I haven't flown that far up but I noticed that the further up I went, up above I think I saw some snow here and there. I've no doubt there is more at the top. It'll be fun since we don't see snow that often, well except in the cold season. It will be weird seeing it at this time of the seasons. This is the warm season. I suppose the snow is up there because it's colder. So weird though when the sun is shining and things are so warm down here for there to be freezing snow up there."

"No weirder than where we've come from" said Aro, gesturing to the barren terrain before them.

"Yeah I guess. Hopefully there won't be anything horrid up there either" said Ellendrii.

"We can hope but I bet there will be. Like some huge predatory creature that freezes us to death by breathing on us or something" said Aro.

"Really?" said Ellendrii with a sigh.

"Well, maybe not. But it's not too farfetched since we've encountered things that sucked out our life force, tried to steal our eyes, bitten us, scared us, whispered to us, chased us...want me to go on?"

"Ok you have a point. We'll have to hope there's nothing dangerous up there. If there is, well, we've got this far and we'll be ready. Anyway I found a likely place we can at least start climbing. It's over there. So we'll start from there when the sun rises. And you'd better not make me wake you. I value my body and don't want it damaged by sunrise grumpiness."

"It'll be fine, I'll be awake. If not, then throw a lake bird at me. That'll wake me and get me in the mood for hunting too! Then you'll see what happens to someone who wakes me and *you* won't need to get hurt!" said Aro with a grin.

"I'll do that" replied Ellendrii, his face pale.

447

Soon the moon was up and the pair of them settled down for the moon cycle. Aro fell asleep right away but Ellendrii found the ground too hard to sleep comfortably on. He'd slept in worse places, sure but at the moment he wanted something softer. He wished he'd brought some grass along with him for a bed but he knew that it would probably contain those awful bugs so it was probably better that he hadn't thought to do it.

After a while of not being able to sleep and being really uncomfortable as well, Ellendrii rifled through his bag and looked for something that might help. He had some delicately scented herbs to relax and a lot of healing herbs but nothing that might help. As he looked deeper in the bag, he found the mushroom the Kanniths had given him in exchange for the leaf they had taken. He turned it over in his hand, examining it closely. Didn't they say that this was for sleeping? That it didn't heal but if you ate it, it would put you to sleep? He thought back and remembered that they did in fact say that; or gestured it anyway. So he thought he would give it a try.

He sniffed the mushroom and licked it. It seemed to taste ok so he popped it in his mouth, chewed it up and swallowed it. Nothing seemed to happen. He wasn't sure what was supposed to happen anyway.

It came on suddenly, the drowsiness. Everything went blurry as though he had gone a long time without sleep. Ellendrii was lying down and he found that he couldn't even sit up; his whole body was tired. Suddenly his drooping head fell forward, plonk! And he was asleep.

The next sun cycle, Aro was awake first, bright and early at sunrise. He stretched, yawned, got up, stretched again and went over to Ellendrii to get some food from the bag. Only to find that the Gryphie was still asleep.

"After *all* you said" muttered Aro. He wanted to eat his lake bird first but decided it would be a better idea to wake Ellendrii because they could eat together. If he ate first and then woke him, he would have to wait for him to eat and that would take longer.

So he jabbed his friend, hard, in the ribs and Ellendrii woke up with a jump and a growl.

"HEY!! What did you do that for?" he demanded.

"Err, you were still asleep, after all you said about ME being over sleeping, you did it instead! Why weren't you up?" asked Aro.

"I…I couldn't get to sleep so I ate that mushroom that those white faced creatures gave us. It was for sleeping." Ellendrii explained.

"But you were shattered, why would you need to eat that?" asked Aro.

"I was shattered, yes, but this ground is hard and uncomfortable. I normally have trouble sleeping on ground like this but last moon cycle was the worst. Not to mention that unwholesome smell that's wafting in from the place we just crossed."

"Ah you're just fussy, this ground is fine!" argued Aro, rolling on the ground for effect.

"For you maybe, cave sleeper. Don't forget I'm used to sleeping on a tree branch or in the hollow of a tree with a warm, grassy bed."

"I have a bed. It's grassy" said Aro.

"Yeah but you replace the grass so little that it soon wears away and you end up sleeping on the rock anyway" said Ellendrii.

"Fussy!" said Aro and laughed.

Ellendrii grunted and threw one of the dead birds at Aro.

"Eat. Let's go." He said sternly. Aro nodded in a submissive pretence and they ate their food together. They drank and then they prepared to climb the mountain.

"I tell you what, it will be good to get up and away from that horrible place" said Ellendrii, pointing to the barren land.

"I don't really smell it anymore. Your nose is too sensitive" said Aro.

"Unlike your brain" muttered Ellendrii. Aro, thankfully, didn't hear.

Ellendrii lead them to the place he had found the previous moon.

"Here, we can start this way and make our way up. We have to be careful as we climb though because if we get to a part we can no longer carry on our ascent, we will have to backtrack and find another way and it will take longer. We

449

want to get up there fast, before the sun sets ideally so I will sometimes fly up and check our journey to make sure it is easy to move on ahead and we don't get stuck. Is that ok with you?" asked Ellendrii.

"If you have to then you have to. But do some climbing sometimes. If you just hover around while I climb, I'm gunna feel like grik." Aro said, earnestly.

Ellendrii told him not to worry and that he would climb too. He just wanted to make sure they could get up in one go without getting stuck and having to go back a little way to get to a part where they could continue.

Aro reluctantly agreed and they headed up the mountain. The first few steps seemed the hardest because of the whole moving off the flat ground and moving onto something more vertical. But soon he was making his way with relative ease. Because he wasn't as heavy as he had been when they started out, he found it a lot easier to get from rock to rock.

However, in no way did he jump from rock to rock with the deftest of ease, unlike Ellendrii whose wings once again came in handy, this time for balance. Wings and a tail offered great balance as he climbed. Aro on the other hand only had his tail. But he did have the opposable thumb claws on both his front and back feet unlike Ellendrii who only had them on his front, so Aro could grip the rock better.

Aro tried to ignore the fact that Ellendrii was much better at this and continued on his way. They had been going for a while, so that when Aro looked down, the ground was slowly getting further away. He also had a good view now of the crater land and the tall grass and the lake sparkling in the distance. And beyond that, the valley. He could see nearly as far as they had come since leaving the Forest of Foreboding. He couldn't see the Kannith territory or the forest though; both were buried in the valley and far away. He was a bit glad he couldn't see that awful forest. Nothing to remind him of the Repulsators that still haunted his moonmares. He sincerely hoped they wouldn't encounter anything else like that on their journey.

Ellendrii, who was plotting the course up the mountain went first, which meant that Aro kept getting a really good view of how easy the Gryphie was finding the climb. He was also used to climbing trees, which again made it easy for him. Aro decided to concentrate more on what he was doing and look down instead of straight ahead instead. Besides, then he could pay attention to where he was actually putting his feet and that was the important thing.

They climbed till mid-sun and instead of stopping, carried on. The most they had was a quick drink to refresh themselves and then it was back to climbing again. The heat of the climb was slowly dying down the higher they got. And they soon realized that they would certainly not be able to make this climb all in one go either. The mountain was just too tall and it would take two sun cycles at least.

Ellendrii had not accounted for this. He had no idea that they might have to rest somewhere that it would be freezing cold. Also he did not account for Aro's lungs and the thinner air. It only occurred to him as he looked out and down at the land below as the sun was beginning to set on the first sun cycle. They couldn't rest even if they wanted to. It was too cold to sleep.

Ellendrii took off from his current position and flew around to try and find a cave or something they might be able to shelter in for the moon cycle. He couldn't find anything though, so they had to keep going. He didn't know if they could make it for the whole moon cycle and the next sun cycle without sleep but he figured if they came across anything that they might be able to shelter in, they would and then they would carry on, regardless of what time it was.

So they carried on into the moon cycle. Luckily for them, the moon was big and round in the sky and shone down its pale blue light, helping them to see as they climbed.

"This is kinda cool" said Aro. They hadn't spoken much since they had been saving their energy for climbing and talking only uses energy.

"Yeah it is. It's a nice atmosphere" replied Ellendrii, pausing for a while and looking out at the land down below. The lake shimmered like crystal in the moonlight and he smiled, enjoying the magic of the moment.

They carried on, their movement and the effort keeping them warm as they continued. They only struggled if the moon decided to disappear behind a wandering cloud. In which case they paused in case they put a foot wrong and stumbled or worse, slipped.

Ellendrii had told Aro that he was looking for a cave and for Aro to keep his eyes out for one too or anything they could shelter together under that might keep them warm as they slept. Ellendrii mentally kicked himself for not having the large leaves anymore. They weren't big enough to completely cover the pair of them but they would have offered some protection against the elements for sure. Never mind, it was too late now. The pair travelled by moonlight which seemed to get ever brighter the higher they went, because they were closer to the moon.

The light shone over the rock and highlighted a darker spot, which Ellendrii rushed to investigate and sure enough it was a small cave, just big enough that they could both fit in it.

"In all honesty I'm pretty tired" admitted Aro when Ellendrii showed him.

"Let's sleep then. We'll be warmer in there and we can cuddle together for heat" said Ellendrii.

"So long as you don't snore or wave your wings about" Aro remembered the last time they had tried to share a shelter this small and the almost funny scare he'd had when Ellendrii had been snoring and he'd thought it was a Repulsator.

"I won't. There's nowhere to move in there anyway. You go in first and get comfy. Make sure your needles are out of the way and I'll follow and put my wing over you to keep you warm. I have fur, so I keep my body heat better than you do."

Yeah, rub it in thought Aro, but at the same time he was very grateful for Ellendrii's friendship and caring nature. If it came to a real contest of brute strength anyway, where Gryphies excelled in so many ways, in a fight to the death; a Lizariaous would usually win. Their skin could stand quite a bit of flaming before it hurt them badly and their needles were poisonous. But of course since these two were friends, Aro didn't compare those kinds of things between the two species.

So, Aro got into the shelter and Ellendrii followed and they cuddled together for warmth. Gryphies use their wings also like a blanket to keep themselves warm. Soon the pair of them were fast asleep. Their bodies were already warm because of the physical excursions they'd put them through climbing up the mountain.

But when they awoke, it was a different story. They were both cold and there was a thin layer of frost on their bodies from where they had sweated and it had frozen on them. They crickled and cracked as they clambered out of the shelter and shook themselves off.

"Ergh, I'm freezing!" shivered Aro. "I don't like this. Couldn't that stupid stone have told us to go somewhere similar to the lake, that was warm and nice and plentiful in food?"

"I wish it could have" replied Ellendrii solemnly.

They had a quick breakfast; one bird which they shared, in order to ration the food, and carried on quickly so they could warm up again. They were soon warm from climbing and felt a bit better.

Being up so high, Aro soon felt a little vertigo. Ellendrii was used to these heights and even though Aro had wanted to fly and Ellendrii had carried him, it hadn't been *this* high. Nor had he ever lingered this high. But he didn't want to admit that he was afraid so he said nothing and tried not to look down. Ellendrii, thankfully, didn't notice. He was too busy plotting their course.

Aro started to feel a bit wobbly on his feet. The air was now quite thin and he wasn't used to it. He was struggling to breathe.

"Ellendrii…can…can we…go a…bit…slower…please?" he asked. Ellendrii obliged and they moved upward more slowly than they had been going. Ellendrii didn't mind though. He understood perfectly that not everyone could handle this thin air, as someone who came from a race of Forest Gryphies most of which couldn't handle the domain of the Sky Gryphies. He wondered why the SilvaGryphie had made the two species in many ways so different to each other. He wondered too, if she had made the mysterious Deamon

Gryphies. He thought of all these things as they slowly continued. When they had awoken, it was mid-sun and he wanted to clear a lot more of the mountain before the next moon. Trying to find another place to sleep was probably going to be a problem. And with Aro going more slowly now, not that it was his fault, they were not making very good time now.

He was also keeping an eye on the stone as well, to make sure that they were still going in the right direction but it was still pointing determinedly upwards, to his slight dismay. Why couldn't she live in a cave on the side of this mountain or something? Still, no one said this journey would be easy! And he never expected it to be.

He went at Aro's pace. Still leading but not going too fast. He had to lead to work out the next part but at the same time he kept looking back and making sure he wasn't too far in front of Aro.

Aro had to sit and rest a lot more now. He was fatigued and struggling to breathe but Ellendrii was patient with him. As they sat, barely talking, Ellendrii's mind went back to the statue of the SilvaGryphie under the lake. It was a big mystery and still bugged him. Why, when, what, who made it? How did they make it? If it was the Aqwakitts did they make it on land and drag it under the water or did they make it under the water? And why? And *was* it them? Because they didn't remember. Or was it another creature.

OR! Was it Gryphies on their way to Shernaron with the SilvaGryphie, what could be eons ago? Was that the sculpture the ones who wanted to worship her had made? He had endless questions. He wanted to ask her when they finally met her. If she even knew about the statue. And the stone. How did it know where she was? DID it actually know where she was? Where in fact was it leading them? To her or to something else? Maybe she was no longer alive. Maybe it was taking them to her grave? He held the stone in his hand and lightly ran his finger over it. The shine followed his finger and formed around it but whenever he took his finger away, it went back to a pointing sign again, pointing up the mountain.

454

But Rivniann had seen her. And *that* hadn't been that long ago, had it? So she must still be alive. Surely she was immortal? He sighed. He really hoped that when they met her, she would answer all these questions.

Aro was feeling better and able to continue, so they did for a while. Then they came to a wide ledge that they could rest properly on and lay down.

"I'm sorry Ellendrii, I'm sorry I can't breathe up here" said Aro sadly.

"It's not your fault" Ellendrii told him.

"Yes it is, now we're slower than ever. I was really getting on so well climbing and now I'm struggling" Aro sighed with annoyance.

"I'm going to fly out and see how much further we have to go" said Ellendrii and took off from the edge, into the sky and out so he could see the mountain more clearly. He returned soon after.

"Well, I can't see much. There is a layer of cloud there and the peak of the mountain is above it. But we're close to the cloud now and the peak can't be that much higher. You wanted to see what it was like above here, then now you will see! You can find out what it's like to be up here in the clouds where I go often and above them is where the Sky Gryphies live, so above these clouds would be a similar place!" Ellendrii explained. Aro brightened a little.

"You just need to adjust to the air here and that will take time but you can do it! I know you can! I don't mind going more slowly, cos let's face it if we don't, you won't get used to it and you'll get sick. At least we're making better progress than we were in that awful forest. We're nearly at the top!" Ellendrii said, reassuringly.

"Thanks El. I dunno what I'd do without you. Oh, wait, without you I'd be back home in my cave with my Mum and Dad and bratty sisters and Dyarkroeen and those tasty cave cats." Aro said. It was only a joke but it made Ellendrii think he was trying to make him feel bad.

"Hey, you insisted on coming with me here. You didn't *have* to, you know" he said, a little put out.

"Yeah and what would you do without me? You'd have died in the Forest of Foreboding and your life force would belong to a Narg'tok. So isn't it just as well I *did* insist on coming along? Besides, I'd rather be here saving your tail than being bored exploring at home. What we're doing, well it's the ultimate in an exploring adventure!! I've still got no regrets" Aro grinned.

"Well thank grik for that" sighed Ellendrii, realizing the joke. Aro laughed. Because if you couldn't laugh, you would cry. If you stopped to think how far away you were from home, how young you were, how much danger you had faced and would still face, you would cry. It was only determination and solid belief that Ellendrii was still determined to find the SilvaGryphie. And with the stone to help him, he was more certain than he had ever been that it was all worth it and that they were on the right track.

It was nice to be able to sit and stretch and relax on this ledge up high on the mountain and look down, in Aro's case, without fear on the land below. Neither of them could quite believe how high they had climbed. It was nothing for Ellendrii when he was flying but to climb it was a different matter and he actually felt more achievement because he had climbed instead of taking the easy way out and flying.

After a while, they continued again. They were starting to get to the slightly more snowy parts of the mountain now. Some of the rocks were crumbling here and there too, they weren't sure why but Ellendrii asserted that it was because of the cold.

As Aro reached for a rock near his head to climb up a little further, his paw grabbed hold of it and he was hoisting himself up when the whole thing gave way and he lost his footing, sliding backward.

"Ellendrii! Help me!" he cried in fear as he fell backwards.

Ellendrii spun round and reached out a hand to grab him but he was too late and missed. He saw his friend fall back and crash on some of the rocky mountainside below. Aro was unmoving and unconscious, his needles smashed since he had landed on his back. Ellendrii flew down, shaking and panicky.

"Aro! ARO!! Aro are you ok? Oh, Aro, speak to me…" he nudged the prone form of his friend but Aro didn't move or respond. He was breathing but he was hurt. Some of his needles had splintered and cut into him and he was bleeding. Ellendrii carefully pulled the splinters out. He wasn't sure what to do. Should he move him? Should he wait till he woke up? He would get cold, he couldn't leave him there. He felt he needed to get him to some sort of shelter but he didn't want to leave him to go look and what if he regained consciousness while Ellendrii was away looking? He decided to stay and keep him warm as best he could until he woke up.

Luckily he didn't have to wait long. Just as he had clambered onto the rock beside Aro and placed a wing over him and settled down as comfortably as he could, Aro started to come round. He groaned and winced and tried to move.

"Aro, you fell on your back. Be careful, I don't know how badly injured you are" said Ellendrii, trying to keep Aro still so that he didn't move too fast and injure himself more.

"I lost my footing…" groaned Aro, "Arghh my back!"

"Slowly roll over if you can so I can see the damage" Ellendrii told him. It was hard for Aro to roll over on rocks but he managed to do it as best he could and got onto his side. Ellendrii took a close look at his back and shattered needles. His back was covered in bleeding red cuts and gashed from where he'd landed on the rocks. The smallest needle at the end of his spine was still intact but the whole needle was leaning at a right angle and looked very painful. Ellendrii wasn't sure how the needles connected to Aro's spine but he hoped that no spinal damage had been done due to this needle pointing at such an angle as that.

"Is it bad?" asked Aro.

"Not as bad as I thought. I think your needles cushioned your fall to an extent but they are all broken and shattered and the smallest one is pointing to one side."

With discomfort and a few grunts and groans, Aro got himself onto his front with his legs under him so he could push up with them when he wanted to get up. He tensed up and shot out all his busted needles at once. All but the smallest one shot out and left the usual holes along his spine where the new ones would grow out.

Lizariaouses can shoot whatever needle they wish. They can shoot out one at a time or several or all of them and they can control which ones they want to fire. So Aro knew that the smallest one hadn't been released. Ellendrii saw him tense up and try to fire the needle out but nothing happened. It didn't even move.

"Great" muttered Aro, "Nerve damage. I can't shoot that one out because I've damaged the nerves attached to it so even if I try, I can't get it to release. That'll take some time to heal."

"So it's not that it's at a weird angle?" asked Ellendrii, who didn't know much about how Lizariaouses let loose their needles.

"No, that doesn't matter. If it was at a weird angle and I hadn't damaged the nerves, I'd still be able to fire it and the next one would grow straight. I need to get rid of it to help it heal properly. The next one that grows will grow straight but I won't be able to fire it for a while until the nerves have healed. Since I'm hurt, I can't reach round and take it out. Ellendrii, you'll have to pull it out for me. Just take hold of it and give it a good yank and it will pop out. Think you can do that?" Aro asked him.

"I dunno, will it hurt or poison me?" asked Ellendrii.

"Not unless you touch the tip of it" said Aro. "It's better to grab it at the base anyway and pull. You can't put as much power behind it if you grab it by the end."

"Ok I'll give it a try" said Ellendrii, very unsure. He'd only ever touched a Lizariaous needle once and that was an old one he'd found buried in the Forest left over from the war that had happened before he was born. He was told it was one of Zephirak's needles. He never found out if that was true or not.

Ellendrii grabbed hold of the needle and pulled on it but it wouldn't budge.

"Just yank on it. It won't hurt me, the nerves aren't in that part of it. It will come away easier because it's broken" Aro advised.

458

"Ok, I'll pull harder" said Ellendrii and this time held it in both hands and pulled. With a lot of effort, the needle finally popped off and Ellendrii fell backwards.

"Thanks" said Aro, "Now it will grow back properly and when the nerves repair, I will be able to use it again. Now I just gotta get up. Somehow."

With great effort, he got all his legs underneath himself and pushed up with them. Finally he was on his feet, after wobbling a lot. It hurt to walk and he limped because his back was hurt but he was ok other than that.

However, it would make climbing a lot harder.

Ellendrii threw the needle to one side and went to make sure his friend was ok.

"It's not much further now" he said, "We can make it!"

They had pretty much reached the cloudy area so really all they had to do was climb through the clouds and out to the peak above. However, neither of them really took into account that the clouds would prevent them seeing anything very well. They would have to be even more careful now.

Aro was in pain now as he climbed but he was determined to carry on. He could rest when he reached the top, he insisted and wouldn't have Ellendrii tell him any different. Sitting around would mean that not only would he still hurt; he would get cold as well, so it was better to keep moving. Ellendrii tried desperately to find places and ways that would make it easier for Aro. He wished he could carry him but even a slightly malnourished Aro was too heavy to carry up the side of a mountain.

They reached the clouds and the air got colder and moister as they ascended into them. Aro reached out a paw and ran it through the clouds with awe. He had never touched a cloud before! So *this* was what it was like when Ellendrii went cloud dodging!

Ellendrii spoke more now than he had done during their climb. Before, Aro had just been following him; walking where he walked but now Ellendrii had to call out to Aro so he would be able to follow him without being able to see him properly. He had to describe where Aro needed to put his feet so he could move on without the same accident happening. It was only lucky that it hadn't been worse.

Ellendrii had been terrified that Aro had broken a bone or something or was dead or they would be stranded there somehow or he would have to leave him to go find help. He was glad that Lizariaouses were sturdy creatures that could take a battering before they got badly injured.

"We're nearly there, Aro, are you doing ok?" Ellendrii called down.

"Yeah I'm ok. It hurts but I'm trying to ignore that. I think my back is bruised but it could be worse. At least I landed on my back and didn't break a leg or something" called back Aro, voicing Ellendrii's fears.

"It's not far now" said Ellendrii reassuringly, "There won't be that much mountain beyond the clouds I wouldn't imagine. And once we get through the clouds, just wait and see how peaceful and beautiful it will be! We'll be able to see what being above the clouds is like here. And you will finally be able to see it too. Aren't you glad you came now? That you insisted? You're getting to see things you could only dream of and never would have been able to see back home."

Aro had to admit that Ellendrii was right. He had "flown" in the water and he had seen a bird's eye, or Gryphie's eye view of the land they had travelled to get to the mountain and now he was going to see a whole other world above the clouds in the quiet, snowy realm of the mountains. Surely the SilvaGryphie would be here! It seemed just the place where she would live. Cold, high up in the clouds; a perfect place!

Ellendrii thought the same thing and for once the two of them were connected on something; their idea of where the SilvaGryphie might be!

They carried on through the misty clouds and finally broke through the other side. Aro had to stop and take it all in. It was like nothing he had ever seen before; just like being under the water had been.

The peaks of the mountains stuck through the clouds and everything was covered in a pink haze as the sun was going down further in the sky. The sun was bright up here and it was chilly but the heat of the sun could also be felt as well. The snow shone in the sunlight, pretty and cold. And it was so quiet! No birds sang; nothing. The snow always makes things quiet of course but this was beyond anything that Aro had ever experienced and close to beyond anything that Ellendrii had experienced. He wondered if the Skylands were like this in the cold season as well. The chilly air made them shiver but they also shivered with high adrenaline and excitement as well.

They continued on their way. The outcrops up here came along more often than lower down for some reason and it was less of a steep climb as well. Finally the pair of them reached the top. It was oddly flat and not as rocky as they thought it would be. The mountain was huge and the range stretched as far as they could see. They felt safe up here though. There weren't many plants or trees this high up however and nowhere that they could see to shelter. Ellendrii figured he would have to work out a way to build something to keep them warm. From what though, he didn't know.

Aro just stood looking around dumbfounded at everything. He didn't care about the cold; he was more excited to see the white – pink world around him and marvel at it since he would probably never see it again. He walked to the edge of the mountain top they were on and peered down through to the ground between some small gaps in the clouds. It was hard to believe they had climbed all the way up here from down there. He felt a rush of excitement about it all.

Ellendrii flew into the air. He couldn't help himself. He wanted to do some cloud dodging! Plus he *was* feeling a little chilly and needed to warm up somehow. He dived in and out of the clouds. Aro stood watching him and for once didn't feel jealous. He felt like a part of Ellendrii's world in the sky.

Ellendrii flew down into the clouds and up high into the sky, trailing cloud behind him. He let out a few short blue flame bursts as well from inside the clouds. They illuminated the cloud all around and died out before he flew out of them again. The clouds, being moist, hindered his firepower somewhat, but it was powerful enough that he could still use quite a lot of it despite it being weaker than usual. However, he couldn't keep flaming for long. After the short blasts of flame, he stopped and just flew around.

Aro ran around through any cloud that had settled on the lower parts of the mountain top where it went down into tiny valleys all around. To him this felt like Ellendrii's cloud dodging and he could finally experience it for himself.

They both felt free up here. Aro's pains were numbed by the cold and his back and haunches felt better as he ran around, getting proper movement into them.

At last Ellendrii joined Aro on the ground and they ate together and had a drink. The sun was getting ever lower in the sky and the pink of the snow became deeper, finally turning to a hue of purple as the moon came out. The stars were all so clear up here, above the clouds. But the air was getting much colder and Ellendrii could still find nothing to cover them as they slept. They both looked around for some kind of shelter but could find nothing at all to sleep under.

"What will we do if we freeze?" asked Aro.

"Not wake up I guess" replied Ellendrii.

"Wow, that's helpful" murmured Aro, rolling his eyes.

"Well I don't know. I've no idea how to make a shelter when we have nothing to make it from and there's no caves we can get into either. I haven't seen any other creatures up here to ask for help and we have nothing in the bag to help cover or warm us. If I could find some wood or something to burn, I could light that but there is nothing here. That's the only reason I didn't burn something coming up here. I expected something to be available as we went but there are less and less plants the higher we go."

"Isn't there something we can burn inside your bag?" asked Aro.

"Not that will burn for long enough or that we don't need for some other reason. Most of what's in my bag are healing herbs and I need them in case we get injured. I can't afford to use those for firewood." Ellendrii explained. "And we're NOT using the decoration that Midnyte gave me!" He added.

"But you could fly out and look for something? Maybe fly back down the mountain a little way and find some wood?" asked Aro.

"Yeah I can try. I'll have to get it from somewhere where it is dry and not damp or it won't light, even with my fire power. Or it might light but it won't stay lit for very long. While I'm out, dig a hole in the snow, see if you can get down to ground under it. If we try and burn the wood on the snow, it will melt and put out the fire. That is why this is so difficult. Ergh it would be so much easier in Shernaron where I have my tree to hide in."

"Yeah and it doesn't snow in Dyarkroeen so I'd have no trouble; I could just hide in my cave. It's chilly and damp in there but in the cold season it's much warmer than being outside! I'll find a place and dig down to the ground then" said Aro. Ellendrii nodded and flew off to find some firewood.

Aro searched around for a place that didn't look too deeply covered in snow. Everywhere was in the open out here which he wasn't keen on, being used to sleeping in the shelter of his cave. He found a suitable spot and dug with his powerful claws. His back hurt a little as he worked but he ignored it. It would probably be stiff by the time he awoke the next sun cycle. The snow was deep and he dug and dug, only pausing to look up at the moon that lighted his work so well.

Finally he got down to the ground and then enlarged the hole he'd started so it would be big enough that they could both lie on the ground instead of the cold snow and so it wouldn't put the fire out. The thin air didn't affect Gryphie fire, after all. All that would affect it would be the damp of the snow.

Meanwhile Ellendrii had had to fly down pretty far to find something that he could burn for the fire. He found a few small straggly trees and figured that if he pulled up a couple of them, they could break them up and carry what they didn't use for the fire to use the next moon cycle.

He returned with the two trees and Aro helped him snap their thin trunks. They would do for a few moon cycles at least and by that time the pair hoped to either have found the SilvaGryphie in this arctic wilderness or have gone down the other side of the mountain following the Gryphie stone's directions.

They arranged the logs on the bare ground and Ellendrii lit them. The blue flames leapt into the air and burned happily on the thin dry logs. This would do for now! The pair of them settled down around the fire, glad of its warmth. They would lay and chat and then eventually fall asleep and the fire would be out by sunrise.

"It's a good thing we're so resourceful" observed Aro sleepily.

"Yeah I think we survive very well" replied Ellendrii, "I just wish our parents could see how well we're doing." He sighed and rested his chin on his forelegs, gazing into the fire with nostalgic eyes.

"Yeah me too" said Aro and did similar.

The pair of them gazed into the hot blue flames for a long, silent while, just thinking about what everyone else was up to back home. It was so far away from them now; a distant memory.

Aro broke the silence.

"I really hope we find her up here" he muttered.

"Me too, I'm tired in all honesty but I will keep my word and we will find her wherever she is!" replied Ellendrii. "Because if I don't find her and go back empty handed, then it will be humiliating and they will all tease me for the rest of my life."

"It won't be for me though" smirked Aro. Ellendrii gave him a look.

"Besides," continued Aro, "It won't be humiliating so long as you don't go back up to the Sky Gryphies again. They never have to see you ever again and you'll never know what they think or even if they remember you. I'm sure once they found out you'd gone on this quest or even just after you left, they probably put you right out of their minds and just wrote it off that you would fail, not attempt it or even that it just discouraged you and they'll forget about you and the SilvaGryphie."

"I doubt that. I knocked them all down with my flying abilities. I think I will be in their minds for a long time to come" said Ellendrii. When Aro looked at him with one eyeridge cocked in mocking accusation of his "vanity", Ellendrii hurriedly added;

"Er for a while at least of course!" He looked awkward. Aro just rested his head back on his paws again.

I wonder if they *do* remember me though, thought Ellendrii. Or if they even care.

Chapter 25
Snow Cycle

They awoke when the sun rose, both feeling the cold and the fire long since died. Aro shivered and curled into a smaller ball, not yet remembering where he was. Ellendrii lifted his head and looked around, sleepy and with icy fur.

The sun was shining warm and yellow on the snow. But not warm enough to comfort the pair of them as they lay on the frozen ground. The wood had all burned up and was reduced to a pile of ashes.

Ellendrii got up and nudged Aro.

"Come on, let's get moving. We mustn't dawdle too much up here or we'll die of the cold. Plus we'll have to find food at some point as well but we'll carry on for as long as we can. Just keep your eyes out for something we can eat. I don't want to resort to eating the bark of these logs!" Ellendrii tried to joke but Aro just shot him an unimpressed look and stood up slowly and painfully because, as he had suspected would happen, his back had become stiff while he slept. He moved all his limbs around and stretched his back and legs. He moved his tail from side to side to get all the joints working again. His needles had all grown back except the smallest, damaged one which was taking longer. The nerves still needed time to heal.

Ellendrii carried the logs on his back, tethered with vines. He had wanted Aro to carry them because he already had the leather bag but of course Aro's back was bad at the moment so he wasn't of much help.

They continued for a while, till the sun was high in the sky. When they sat down for a rest, Aro marvelled at the amount of snow around them.

"You know, we could build some great snow statues here. So others will know we've been here" suggested Ellendrii, seeing his friend's expression as he viewed the white everywhere. "I doubt they would melt too fast."

"That's a great idea! Let's build statues of ourselves!" said Aro.

466

"Ok! We'll try to make them as realistic as that stone carving of the SilvaGryphie" replied Ellendrii. Aro nodded and they both set to work. They had walked for long enough and this journey didn't have to be all travelling and no fun, after all! So they wanted to be through this snowy world faster; they were still young and needed to play and entertain themselves along the way.

Aro had gathered a big pile of snow, remarkably a similar size to himself but that was where the resemblance ended. It just looked like a shapeless mass and Ellendrii pointed that fact out to him but Aro insisted that he had barely started and still had a lot to do with it. Ellendrii was more tactful with his and decided to do a sculpture of himself lying down. Aro was still trying to make his sculpture stand – in vain. The legs kept collapsing when he tried to add the body on to them. He really had no idea of how snow worked.

Ellendrii packed his snow in hard and solid so he hoped his sculpture would last longer. The harder he packed it in, the more icy it became and he felt he could use this to his advantage when it came to doing his wings, which would be folded of course.

"You know, trying to make a standing snow sculpture of yourself is silly. It won't work" observed Ellendrii. He was just putting the finishing touches to the wings on his one. The head and legs were fairly shapeless at this point, as was the tail.

"It will! I'm very good at this! I'm even going to fire my needles out and put them on the sculpture for added detail!" replied Aro.

"Yeah and that's fine but the legs won't hold up the heavy body. It's collapsing in on itself" said Ellendrii.

"It will! I just need to dig underneath where the legs will go, to make my belly" replied Aro, digging and disappearing under his snow sculpture. Which then promptly collapsed on him once he had managed to dig out the snow and tried to pull himself back out again.

"Grik" he muttered from somewhere underneath the snow.

Ellendrii grabbed his tail and pulled him out. He couldn't help but laugh and that only annoyed Aro more.

467

"Well yours isn't so amazing" snorted Aro. Secretly he was impressed by Ellendrii's sculpture but he would never let on. It was all because Gryphies had more dextrous fingers and Lizariaouses only had clumpy paws and claws.

"Why don't you try and make yours lying down" suggested Ellendrii. "It might work better?"

"I guess" sighed Aro.

"Look, you can make him lying down with his head raised looking across the snow like a leader!" said Ellendrii, trying to warm his friend to the idea.

"Yeah, I can!!" Aro was getting into it now.

At least he had persuaded Aro to try and make his sculpture more sensibly.

They carried on for a while until Ellendrii felt something hard smack him in the back of the head.

"Ow!" he snapped, spinning round.

What he saw was Aro giggling and rolling around in the snow because he'd just got Ellendrii with a snowball.

"Oh so that's your game!" roared Ellendrii and swiftly moulded his own snowball, lobbing it at his laughing friend and hitting him square on the rump. Aro stopped laughing and solemnly got to his feet.

Silently, he rolled a large hefty snowball and threw it at Ellendrii with force that was maybe a little too much. Ellendrii only just managed to dodge it. Lizariaous snowballs are not to be taken lightly. They are large and solid and really hurt if they happen to catch you or worse, hit you straight on and wind you.

"That was close" yelled Ellendrii. He already had another snowball waiting and he pelted Aro with it. Aro was a bit slower than Ellendrii was and he kept getting caught. However, it was better that Ellendrii got Aro than the other way around because Aro didn't know what was a sensible size to make the snowballs and what was a sensible strength to throw them without hurting his friend. Lizariaouses played much more roughly than Gryphies.

Ellendrii thought he would play Aro at his game and made a snowball as big as he could, rose up on two legs and threw it with force at Aro.

This'll get him thought Ellendrii.

Aro, by some bizarre miracle actually ducked the snowball and it flew off behind him.

"Well I didn't hit you but I got your snow sculpture!" laughed Ellendrii. Aro looked round at his sculpture.

"Err, Ellendrii, that's not my snow sculpture; mine is over there" and he pointed behind and just left of Ellendrii.

"It's not? Well it's not mine…" Ellendrii trailed off and his eyes grew wide and he went a bit pale. Aro's "sculpture" was moving.

"A…Aro…behind you…" muttered Ellendrii, unable to yell the words.

Aro cocked his head on one side.

"What??" he yelled.

Ellendrii pointed, waving his finger franticly at his friend. Aro glanced over his shoulder and then yelped as the creature behind him lunged at him with huge blood stained claws.

The creature was large, stocky and bear-like. It was covered in thick, white fur and had a bear-like face and limbs too. But its tail was more like that of a giant anteater and it had the claws to match. It had larger ears than a bear but of a similar shape and they curled back a little, with fluffy fringes on them. The creature's eyes were bizarre; the pupils were a star shape and upon closer inspection (as close as Aro had observed before he legged it), the fur was faintly coloured like an aurora. So faint though that the creature appeared to be white and tinged with only a very slight pastel colour. Along its spine there were several bony spikes, connected by a membrane similar to a Gryphie's wing.

The bear-thing chased after Aro and Ellendrii could only morbidly marvel at something actually hunting a Lizariaous. He had never ever seen anything like this, well apart from the Wind Hounds who may or may not have been out for Aro's blood. But this creature was running him down with the intent to kill him. Hunting him as Aro would hunt a cave cat. Ellendrii flew into the air and shot fire bolts at the bear-thing, aiming for any part of it that might slow it down. He couldn't get to its legs very well because they were sturdy and underneath the creature; they were also not long enough for him to get a proper aim at. He had been aiming for its head but the head was such a small part of it, he decided to aim at the fin along its back that opened and closed slightly as it ran.

Aro was firing off his needles at the creature in panic. He was aiming of course behind him so he could shoot them off as he ran but he had no idea where he was aiming since he couldn't see over his shoulder and daren't possibly trip up or slow down by looking. So he shot them all off and used them all up. And they all missed. One bounced off the creature's thick fur.

Ellendrii flew in closer and shot a large and well aimed fireball at the creature's fin as it opened slightly. He got it on the second try and it burned a hole in the fin. The creature roared in pain and stopped in its tracks to inspect itself. It rolled in the snow to get rid of the burning sensation and make sure that there wasn't further damage.

Ellendrii hovered in the air and roared threateningly.

"GO! NOW! OR I'LL KILL YOU!" he boomed at the creature. It raised up on its hind legs and swiped at the air.

"NO!" it called to him, "I WILL RUN YOU DOWN AND DEVOUR YOU BOTH!" It turned its attention to Aro again, who had stopped to catch his breath. Ellendrii swooped down between the creature and his friend. He roared and rumbled at the creature, spreading his wings wide in an attempt to look larger and more threatening. The creature got back on its hind legs again and slashed at the air between them.

The two of them faced off, glaring at each other, trying to stare the other down.

Suddenly there was a flash of black and Aro had flown at the creature, knocking it to the ground and digging his claws into its thick fur. The creature, completely taken by surprise, fell to the snow and paused briefly before fighting back.

It tried to grab Aro with its claws, knock him off, slash at him, hoping to damage him. Aro couldn't penetrate past its thick fur with his claws no matter how hard he tried. The fur had the same effect as armour plating. He bit and clawed for all he was worth and tried going for its face before it managed to throw him off.

Before it could get to its feet though, Ellendrii was upon it and he had managed to get near its neck, his mouth and nostrils flaring with blue as he prepared to flame it right in the face. The logs he carried on his back were light, luckily and didn't hinder his movement too much.

To his surprise, the creature winced and closed its eyes. It turned its face away once it found out that it couldn't budge the Gryphie. He was using his wings to help him as well and kept batting its large paws and claws away no matter how they tried to hurt him.

Ellendrii suspected the creature was pretending in order for him to let his guard down. He didn't play into the possible pretence.

"Leave us!" he roared at its face.

The creature didn't look at him, but whimpered with its eyes still closed.

"I'm so hungry, I need to eat and you're the only creatures I've seen for sun cycles up here. Normally there is plenty of food but lately it's become scarcer. Please don't hurt me. I was only doing what was natural."

Ellendrii could feel her large bulk shivering beneath him and he felt sorry for her.

"I have food with me. I will give you it but you must promise not to hunt me or my friend" he told her.

The creature nodded, still with tightly closed eyes and looking away from him.

Ellendrii got off her and opened his leather bag. There were two more lake birds in the bag and he placed them near her.

"These in exchange for our lives" he said to her.

The creature opened her eyes slowly and cautiously got to her feet. With one huge paw, she scooped up the lake birds towards herself and lifted them to her mouth, eating them both at once. He could see the nerves in her back twitching with pain where he had damaged her back fin and the fur around the area was pink with blood.

Ellendrii sighed. He decided to make another bargain with her.

"What's your name?" he asked.

"A'urealiz" she replied, not looking at him.

"I am Ellendrii, a Gryphie from a far away land called Shernaron. My friend is called Aro and he is a Lizariaous from a land near to Shernaron, called Dyarkroeen" Ellendrii said quietly.

"I am an Ursquach" said A'urealiz, "I live here in the mountains."

"Do you live by yourself?" asked Ellendrii. He wanted to be sure that no more Ursquaches would find and attack them upon hearing that he had harmed their friend.

"Yes. Unless it's time to breed. We all live as solitaries" said A'urealiz.

"So you know the mountains well?" asked Ellendrii.

"Yes" came the short reply.

"Can you escort us over the mountains in return for me healing your wounds?" asked Ellendrii, not really sure what her reply would be.

"I can" she said, "I need my fin. If I don't have the use of it, I will freeze and die. So I have no other choice."

"You use it to warm you?" asked Ellendrii.

"Yes, it soaks up the sun and the warmth is stored in my fur. I have thick fur but sometimes it is too cold even for me up here." She was starting to look at him now for brief intervals.

Ellendrii figured that she would make a good bodyguard and she had knowledge of the mountains and would be of use to them as well. Plus she was a hunter and even though she had had trouble finding food lately, if there were large meal creatures to be had up here, she would be able to bring them down with relative ease, being that much bigger than him and Aro.

"I will heal you then. In return for your company, knowledge and protection. I will help you find food as well." Ellendrii said, looking through his bag for the right herb.

A'urealiz just nodded. She had been brought right down to ground level in fear of his fire and how it would kill her in the long run. He had damaged the middle section of her fin and the fire had burned away much of the skin there so there was a gaping hole. Ellendrii didn't want to tell her that if she didn't help them, he would burn the whole thing up but he didn't need to; she was already aware of the consequences that would happen if she dared to attack either of them again. She could have refused his offer of course if she had felt she didn't want to help them because of how he had injured her but the fact that he was offering to heal her in return for her help and fix the damage he had done had brought her round. Plus the fact he had given his last two lake birds to her made her feel in a weird way indebted to him, albeit in a sort of morbid way. He had injured her but at the same time he had saved her. She felt her body warming a little now due to digesting the food.

Aro came creeping up.

"Ellendrii, what are you doing?" he asked through gritted teeth and keeping a heavy eye on A'urealiz.

"This is A'urealiz the Ursquach and she will be guiding us through the rest of the mountain range, protecting us, helping us hunt and imparting her knowledge to us.

"I am sorry I attacked you" muttered A'urealiz in the general direction of Aro. She would not look at him. She was a giant brought down to mouse size before two smarter creatures. Or at least one smarter creature; Ellendrii. She had fear of his fire and would remain submissive to him because she was in his debt.

"Well, I wasn't even knocked out and I've lost the plot like I was but fair enough" said Aro with a shrug. "She isn't going to attack us again though, right?"

"No. Like I said, she will be protecting us" said Ellendrii, applying the last bit of herb mixture to her damaged fin and then scrambling down off her.

"It will heal up faster now" said Ellendrii to A'urealiz, who looked grateful. She stood up. Then, looking down at him from her full bipedal height, she asked him gruffly;

"So, what brings you to my territory then?"

"We are looking for the SilvaGryphie" said Ellendrii. He could tell by the look on her face that she had never seen the SilvaGryphie before and it made his heart sink somewhat. The SilvaGryphie was so mysterious. But A'urealiz spoke up.

"I have heard of this creature. They say it has flown over these mountains before and its wingspan is so vast that it covers the whole range in shadow as it passes. I have not seen it though; it is just a rumour."

"Who did you hear it from?" asked Ellendrii.

"Other Ursquaches" replied A'urealiz.

"And of course since you all live as solitaries, they've seen it and not you."

"Yes."

Aro muttered something along the lines of this sort of stuff always happening and A'urealiz lowered her head to him and quietly spoke.

"I am only not eating you because your friend wills it and I am in his debt. That doesn't mean that I might not get hungry one moon cycle, kill you and drag you off where your friend won't see or find me again."

Aro shivered and moved quickly away from her. Whether she was joking or not remained to be seen. Or hopefully not seen, in the case of Aro!

"What do you normally eat?" asked Ellendrii, puzzled that there would be a sudden shortage of food.

"There are small creatures that live in the snow. They tunnel under the ground where it is warmer, under the snow and I normally eat those. They are about your size, maybe a little smaller."

They sounded large to Ellendrii, more like forest deer than "small creatures that live in the snow"

"But I haven't seen any lately and I am worried that they may have left or something" continued A'urealiz.

"Well, how do you hunt them? Do you dig them out or just find them and chase them down?" asked Ellendrii.

"I find them and chase them down" replied A'urealiz. "They are white like the snow but my eyes can see them stand out against the snow when they would normally be camouflaged to another's eyes. Because they are camouflaged to hunters, it makes them more confident than something that knows it can be seen, so I can sneak up on them with ease and kill them."

"So you've never thought about digging them out then? Your claws are big and powerful enough to dig surely?"

"That is not how I hunt though" replied A'urealiz.

"Sometimes we have to change how we hunt to adapt" explained Ellendrii.

"But I don't know whereabouts they live under the ground" replied A'urealiz.

"Can you sniff them out?"

"No. The snow prevents me from smelling things under it. It's the moisture."

"Hmm, then you have to look for other clues to where they live or have been, like droppings or paw marks in the snow."

"You know, I never thought of that…"

"So you would've, no offence, starved because you didn't think?" said Ellendrii and the Ursquach nodded sadly and stupidly. She felt like a fool now.

"Well then, shall we see if we can find some of these creatures to hunt?" suggested Ellendrii.

"Yes! I call them burrowing birds. You need to know that they look like birds but without wings and with four legs. Each of their feet has digging claws and they have broad beaks for shovelling earth. They have short stumpy tails as well. Their tracks look like this…" and she used a single large claw to draw a shape in the snow.

"That is about life-size" she told him and he measured it up against his own hand. It was slightly smaller but the claws were longer than his fingers. He was happily thinking that these creatures would make a great meal for them and fill them up nicely. If they caught two of them, A'urealiz would have one for herself and he and Aro could share the other. Aro had been watching them at length but not saying anything. He dared not, after A'urealiz' threat.

"So then, let's look for tracks and droppings and see if we can find some. I will help you to begin with and then you will know how to hunt them after we have left you" said Ellendrii.

"Why though?" asked A'urealiz.

"Why what?"

"Why are you helping me? After I hunted your friend and was going to kill him. Why do you care if I live or die?" she asked.

"Because I have morals" replied Ellendrii, "You are helping us and I am helping you. We had no quarrel with you

475

in the first place and you only attacked him because you were driven by hunger. It must also be lonely out here by yourself with no friends and no one to keep you company."

"Not really. I am alone with my thoughts. We are solitaries and like to be alone" said A'urealiz. "Of course, I am happy to accompany you to the end of the mountains and aid you on your journey here" she added quickly, afraid that she would offend the Gryphie. It was unusual that a creature so big and powerful would be in fear of someone smaller but smarter than her. She could easily have caved his skull in with one swipe of her paw, after all.

"Ah that's fair enough" said Ellendrii, "Each to his own." He shrugged as they continued on their way, keeping an eye out for droppings or tracks. Tracks were the more likely candidate because they would last longer. Droppings, being warm, would sink into the snow and be lost. Provided that they were solid of course. There was no hope of finding them if they were watery like a regular bird's.

"How big is this mountain range?" asked Ellendrii, looking ahead of them and into the distance as the peaks seemed to go on forever.

"Vast" replied A'urealiz. "It is the whole of the Ursquach territory and since we all live by ourselves, it needs to be big to accommodate us all!"

Ellendrii nodded in agreement. He got out the Gryphie stone and checked it every so often and A'urealiz questioned him over it.

"It's leading us to the SilvaGryphie. We found it embedded into a statue of her and Aro dug it off. It points our way and we need to keep an eye on it as we travel."

A'urealiz nodded. Far be it for her to question the reasons behind this or why he trusted that it would lead the way without knowing that for sure.

It was Aro who found the tracks first. He called to Ellendrii as he had been trailing behind a little, due to not really seeing eye to eye with A'urealiz. And not just because of her height!

The three of them inspected the tracks and A'urealiz confirmed that they did indeed belong to the burrowing birds.

Now they just had to follow them and hope that the tracks lead to the home of these meal creatures.

They seemed to disappear into the snow and the three could only assume that this was where the bird had dug in and under it to its subterranean home.

"A'urealiz, you need to dig. After all, this is how you'll be hunting them after we've gone" said Ellendrii. The large bear creature nodded and began to dig, scooping up large quantities of snow and creating quite a pile of it behind her as she worked. Because she was the one digging, there was becoming a large and gaping hole in the snow and it took nearly nothing for her to get to ground level. Now they just had to dig around and find the entrance to the burrowing bird's home. Then she would be able to dig them out where they lived. They had to be careful though because the birds would probably try to retreat deeper into the ground to escape, so speed was of the essence.

Ellendrii found the hole and A'urealiz started to dig.

"You need to dig fast and you have to be able to grab the burrowing bird before it can escape. I suggest scooping it up and out of the ground with your claws so it's out in the snow and killing it before it has a chance to get back underground again" advised Ellendrii.

A'urealiz nodded and Aro silently snorted that such a large and dangerous creature was taking the advice of a stranger, who was weaker than she. Not that he had a problem at all with Ellendrii being the smart one and helping out but A'urealiz *had* tried to kill him and he was still annoyed about that.

A'urealiz was now using her nose, since there was no snow to hinder her sense of smell and she was sniffing out the earthy birdlike creatures. She suddenly started to dig quite franticly in one place and soon threw out a muddy, earthy creature with a barrel shaped body and stubby legs. The creature grunted in terror and flailed in the snow where it landed, trying, in a panic, to get back to its feet so it could retreat back underground.

But A'urealiz was upon it in seconds; surprisingly fast for something of her size and bulk and the creature didn't stand a chance. She killed it in one blow and it lay in the snow, lifeless now.

"Good job!" smiled Ellendrii and bounded over to inspect her kill more closely.

The burrowing bird was actually pure white; it was just the earth where it resided that had muddied it and it had a wide, grey beak. The tail was indeed stubby and a little pointed at the end. Ellendrii could only assume it may use the tail to feel its way. The beaked face was covered in thin, sensitive whiskers, just behind the beak and over the top of the head and it had small eyes and no visible ears. These things weren't needed underground where it was too dark to see and touch was the most important sense. He assumed the hearing must be pretty acute though.

A'urealiz nudged the dead burrowing bird towards Ellendrii with her paw.

"It's yours. I will catch another for myself" she said.

"Are you sure?" asked Ellendrii.

"Yes, you gave me your meat and you must be hungry now. I have eaten more recently than you have. I want you to eat this."

"Thank you, A'urealiz" replied Ellendrii gratefully. He beckoned Aro to come over and they shared the burrowing bird together while A'urealiz went looking for another. She couldn't try at the same burrow because the others in that area would all have retreated upon hearing the alarm cries of the one she caught.

They were most of the way through their meal when they heard a scream and she had caught another one for herself. This way of hunting was certainly working out better for her than the old method.

The three of them ate happily and soon felt warmer. They had gathered a little body heat from hunting but the food really got them feeling warmer in the core.

Ellendrii looked over at the hungry A'urealiz tucking into her meal and noticed how the light shone on her fur. It sparkled many colours and was pretty in the late sunlight. Even though she was a large, hulking creature who wasn't as smart as him, she still had her charm, he supposed. He was glad of her company on this part of the journey.

She and Aro had sort of come to terms with each other now. She only really looked at him hungrily in mock but he was still a bit worried that she might turn around and devour him at some point. Still, with her more effective method of hunting, this was less likely to happen. The burrowing bird was fat and delicious and Ellendrii and Aro soon found themselves feeling pretty full. Ellendrii stashed the remaining meat in his leather bag for later. They didn't need to hunt another of these creatures until the next sun cycle and only one a sun cycle would easily suffice to keep the pair of them full. If that.

"You said before that the burrowing birds are hard to spot in the snow because they are white, but these we pulled out of the ground are muddy and earthy, surely that is hard to remove from their fur so they would appear brown and not white?" asked Ellendrii.

"They dig around under the snow to clean themselves before they come up to the surface. The water in the snow washes the mud off them" explained A'urealiz.

"Ah" muttered Ellendrii, "Smart."

They all returned to the journey after their meal, feeling full and warmer and more satisfied.

They walked and walked and chatted and walked some more and soon the sun set and the moon was out once again. Ellendrii untied some of the logs from his back and set about arranging them in order to make a fire.

"What are you doing?" asked A'urealiz.

"I'm going to make a fire to keep us warm as we fall asleep" said Ellendrii.

"You don't dig a sleeping den?" asked A'urealiz, genuinely surprised.

"I don't know what that is" replied Ellendrii with a shrug.

"I will show you" said A'urealiz and she started to dig into a snow drift. Soon she had dug out a sizeable snow cave and she settled inside it.

"Being in the snow will keep you fairly warm and protect you from the wind" she explained.

Ellendrii marvelled at it and went for a closer look.

"I never knew this! Last moon cycle Aro and I just made a fire and then hoped for the best when we woke at sunrise."

A'urealiz looked proud.

"Well now I have shown you something!" she beamed.

"Yes and I can arrange the logs at the mouth of the den and make the fire and it will heat it all!" Ellendrii exclaimed.

"No, it will melt it all" said A'urealiz.

"Oh yeah" said Ellendrii and slumped. "I didn't think of that."

"It's ok. We will keep warm enough in here without the fire" said A'urealiz.

"I guess I don't need all these logs I've lugged around this whole sun cycle then" sighed Ellendrii. Aro chuckled. Then he paled at the thought of sleeping in the same den as A'urealiz.

For a while, the three of them sat and star gazed.

"My ancestors are up there" said A'urealiz quietly.

"That's weird cos mine are down there" said Aro, pointing at the ground.

"They don't take their place in the stars?" asked A'urealiz, genuinely surprised.

"Nope, they melt into the earth to go to their death caves" said Aro.

"Oh, how odd. What about you, Ellendrii…?"

"Err well…I used to think that the dead flew high across the vast water where I live and ended up over here but I found out that's not true. We've encountered another land with more territories than I can count and no resting place for our departed souls. So I'm not sure where they go anymore." Ellendrii looked a bit sad.

"That's no reason to stop believing" said A'urealiz. "The rest of your kind still believe that they come over here, you only don't because you *are* over here and you see it's not true. But that makes no difference in the scale of things."

"Yeah I probably won't tell the rest of the gathering the truth about where their relatives end up. Which even I can't tell now."

"At least I will always know where mine go" said Aro, happily.

Ah to be a simple minded Lizariaous thought Ellendrii.

"So, why do you think that your kind goes to the stars?" Ellendrii asked A'urealiz.

"Because their bodies disappear and that is how I know. They disperse into the sky and become the stars. That is why the stars are there. Each one is my kind, watching over me and looking down at me from above. They come out at moon cycle because that is when the world is at rest, when it is peaceful and quiet and I can hear them speaking" she explained.

"It's quiet up here during the sun cycles though" said Aro.

"Ah, but not the quiet of moon cycles. That is a different kind of quiet; the peaceful kind. The kind you can sleep in."

Aro said nothing. It was all a bit weird and confusing to him. The sun and moon cycles up here were all the same level of quiet to him.

Ellendrii understood though and he smiled.

"Yes, and there is nothing more peaceful than looking up at the moon sky. And up here, we are so close to the stars! I could almost reach out and touch them!" He lifted himself slowly into the sky with his wings and flew up high with one arm stretched above his head, reaching for the stars.

"Yes!" cried A'urealiz, standing up and rising onto her back legs, claws extended to the stars.

Aro just sat watching them and thinking they were both mad.

Ellendrii landed a few moments later and smiled.

"Yeah, I understand how you feel, A'urealiz" he said.

She nodded, for once glad that she wasn't being solitary and alone.

A while later, the three of them retired to the sleeping den. A'urealiz first since she was the biggest. Aro had to be careful to lay with his back to the wall of the den so he didn't poke anyone else with his regenerating needles. Ellendrii curled up next to A'urealiz, who put a heavy paw on him in an awkward embrace. It pretty much squished him but he was too polite to tell her to move it.

Aro and Ellendrii were much warmer in this sleeping den, and also of course because they were sleeping next to a large fluffy Ursquach.

The sun shone in on them and warmed Ellendrii's face with its rays the next sun cycle. He yawned a little and covered his head with a hand, curling around and burying his face in A'urealiz' fur. She shifted in her sleep but didn't wake. Aro was pressed up against the wall of the sleeping den and only woke because he was uncomfortable.

After a while, they were all awake and exiting the den to greet the sun.

They travelled straight away, without eating breakfast. Ellendrii had the leftover meat in his bag and they ate snow for water. The gourds were still fairly full from the lake, so Ellendrii intended to keep them that way if there was plenty of snow to get water from.

The Gryphie stone was pointing to the north east now, so that is the way they headed. They didn't meet many other creatures but sometimes they would see an Ursquach at a distance. Ellendrii would glance up at A'urealiz when this happened but she never even registered the presence of another of her kind. She knew they were there but it was clearly not the breeding time so she ignored them and they her.

Ellendrii was annoyed that still no one seemed to know where the SilvaGryphie lived. It was just frustrating that other creatures had seen her but still no one knew where she could be found. So close and yet so far away!

As it turned out, they didn't need protection really. There were no other creatures up there aside from the illusive burrowing birds and the occasional Ursquach but the latter was usually so far away that it was impossible to be a threat.

Still, he was glad of her company. If nothing else she had a few stories to tell about her life and she was still a good bodyguard. They didn't try to start another snowball fight though, just in case!

"Have you had kittens?" asked Ellendrii, wondering if she'd ever had a family of any kind or any contact with another Ursquach.

"Kittens?" she asked, puzzled.

"Kids" said Aro, helpfully.

"Kids?" she didn't know what that was either.

"Have you ever given birth to little Ursquaches" said Ellendrii, bluntly.

"Oh yes, I've had two litters before. They are all grown up and gone now. They don't stick around for long. Probably because they always see their mother as being bossy and they think they know better. I found one of them dead a while back. He was the one who most thought that he knew best."

"You weren't sad that your son was dead?" asked Ellendrii, shocked.

"Well, yes but at the same time, that is life and we can't all survive. Everyone dies. Some are just younger than others when they do." A'urealiz replied.

Ellendrii didn't argue; she had a point. At least it was...looking on the bright side?

Suddenly, Aro took a step and ended up buried in the snow.

"Yes, it is deep there" warned A'urealiz, just a little too late.

"Gee thanks" said the Aro shaped hole in the snow. Ellendrii had wisely chosen this moment to fly.

They continued on. Ellendrii carried on flying because, to be honest, he couldn't feel his feet. A'urealiz had large, fluffy feet and it didn't bother her at all. The snow didn't seem to clump in her fur either, unlike Ellendrii. And Aro who was always complaining that he didn't have as many advantages as Gryphies was lucky for once because he didn't have fur to get covered in snow.

"It must be nice to fly" said A'urealiz, looking up at Ellendrii.

"I really enjoy it, it is my passion" replied Ellendrii.

"As it would be mine if I could do it" smiled A'urealiz.

They travelled for another sun cycle, slept in another sleeping den and then carried on. They let A'urealiz catch the food when she was hungry and Ellendrii saved any that they didn't eat. So they didn't need to hunt every time they were hungry.

The Gryphie stone had soon guided them to the edge of the mountains and the next step of their journey would soon be underway.

They stood for a while, looking out over the clouds and whatever lay beyond. The clouds were especially thick here and some where a greyish colour. Ellendrii assumed that maybe it was raining down below or something. It had been nice also that they hadn't been soaked in blood-rain again. That had been an unpleasant and rather worrying experience.

"Well then, it looks like this is goodbye. Thank you so much for escorting us across your territory, A'urealiz. We are both very grateful for your help." Ellendrii bowed his head in respect to their travelling companion.

"And thank you for healing me and helping me find a better way to hunt. If you pass back this way, please find me and say hi! I would love to travel with you again!" A'urealiz rose up on her hind legs and scooped both Ellendrii and Aro up in a huge fuzzy bear hug.

Ellendrii and Aro gasped for breath as they felt their bodies lovingly crushed.

As they descended down the mountain, A'urealiz stood and looked down at them, watching them as they disappeared from view.

"I think she will really miss us" said Ellendrii quietly.

"Well I won't miss being nearly her meal" said Aro, "But yeah" he added quickly, "I think I'll miss her too."

Chapter 26
Descent

Going down the mountain wasn't quite as tiring but it was still a bit nerve wracking. Aro was afraid that he would fall. Ellendrii was keeping an eye on the Gryphie stone the whole time.

They made it past the clouds and could see the land below them now. But it looked very strange. Everywhere was grey and there wasn't a single tree that wasn't a barren, skeletal and burned structure.

Ellendrii squinted as they went down, trying to work out what all this was. There had been a huge fire, that much he knew. How it had started or what the cause was remained a mystery though.

"It looks horrid down there. Are you sure we're going in the right direction?" asked Aro.

"Well that's the way the Gryphie stone is pointing" replied Ellendrii, also not sure.

"Ergh well I guess if we were travelling without it, we wouldn't have gone this way. What if we go back up and continue on until this part's passed?" Aro asked hopefully.

"That wouldn't work" replied Ellendrii, "Besides you want to find the SilvaGryphie right? We'll have to hope this part doesn't last for long. It looks like there was a huge fire down there. Everything is just ash. Beyond charred. Look at the trees! It looks horrible."

"Yeah make me feel better about it, thanks" replied Aro sarcastically.

"Sorry, I'm not making it much better am I? But at least it will be warmer down there."

"I'd put up with the cold if it meant I could breathe" sputtered Aro. They could both smell the smoke now and it wouldn't be long before the scent and ash that they could see fill the sky like snow would get in their lungs and make them cough. Or at least Aro. Ellendrii, being pyrokinetic, could handle that sort of atmosphere since of course he breathed fire anyway.

"We'll take our time going down and then decide what we'll do when we get there" suggested Ellendrii.

"Ok" replied Aro. He really missed the lake.

They continued on and then rested, ate some burrowing bird and carried on down. On the way they found some crudely carved caves to shelter in for the moon cycle.

Peering out at the dark, Ellendrii worried what the atmosphere at the bottom of the mountain would be like and it occurred to him again that Aro coming was in some ways a bit of a drawback. Yes, he had saved Ellendrii but at the same time there had been so many places that Ellendrii could just fly past and save himself from getting into danger. They would be putting themselves at risk simply because Aro couldn't fly and they would both have to walk to get past the area below.

When it was light and they had got below the clouds, Ellendrii had had a better look at the next stage of their journey. The ashen ground and destroyed trees lead to a mountain the other side. This mountain was not snow capped and was quite a way away from where they were. The sides of it looked blackened and unpleasant and Ellendrii deeply hoped the Gryphie stone wouldn't lead them up there. It looked very foreboding and dark. Ellendrii shuddered at the thought of going near it. It seemed to scream danger to all his instincts.

Aro lay down next to him.

"So, what do you think of it all then?" he asked, which was a rather general question.

"I dunno. We have to go where the stone leads us but I don't like the look of it down there, it doesn't read right, you know? And that weird mountain way in the distance. Something in my head is screaming at me not to go near it. What about you?"

"I'm bummed out we have to go down there and traverse that unpleasant looking land. As for the mountain, I dunno, maybe we'll go around it or something and not near it? I'm just dreading trying to breathe down there. Already my throat feels dry."

"We still have quite a lot of water luckily, so you can take sips of it when you feel really bad. It seems there are positives and negatives to all these lands we travel through" replied Ellendrii.

"I dunno, I don't see any positives for *this* land" muttered Aro.

Ellendrii had to agree there.

"We'll see. You never know, maybe we'll find another helpful creature like A'urealiz and it won't be so bad" suggested Ellendrii.

"True. And we did think she was the enemy at first" said Aro.

"Yeah, I'm glad it all worked out in the end. I think that she was glad of the company, at least for a little while anyway" replied Ellendrii and Aro nodded in agreement.

"I wonder if she misses us" he said.

"I shouldn't think so. We haven't been gone long enough." Ellendrii yawned and rested his chin on his forearms. He looked up at the sky. The clouds obscured the moon. It was nothing like the beautiful clear sky up in the mountains.

"I wonder how long we've been gone from home though" said Aro quietly.

"I was thinking that. We have no way of telling though. But the weather is getting milder so I think that the warmest season is passing and we're going on to the season of the brown leaves. So we've probably been gone a lunar or so, maybe? Or a couple of lunars?"

"It's that grikking Forest of Foreboding that threw us off. I was trying to keep track, you were too right?"

"Yeah Aro, I was trying to keep track too. That forest was awful. I hated not being able to tell what time of the sun or moon it was. And not being able to sleep."

"Yeah" replied Aro. He still didn't want to admit he had moonmares about the Repulsators.

"We stayed a while with the Wind Hounds" said Ellendrii.

"And Midnyte" smirked Aro and Ellendrii's ears indicated his bashful response. He assumed wrongly that Aro hadn't noticed.

"Still wanna see her again?" asked Aro.

"We will I'm sure, on our way home" replied Ellendrii.

"IF we go back the same way. I wonder if that Gryphie stone works both ways or if it will just fade out and become a normal stone once we find her."

"She will be with us so we can always ask her if she can take us back a different way" replied Ellendrii, "I'm sure she wouldn't mind. We can ask her to show us a different way. I'm sure she would be only too happy to oblige!"

"If she's as nice as you think she is" muttered Aro.

"She will be. If she wasn't there wouldn't be so many good stories about her. I've not heard a bad thing about her."

"Like the good stories about where the dead go across the vast water" Aro said, pointedly.

"Well we'll just have to hope she's nice" snapped Ellendrii, tired of Aro's negativity.

"Sorry" muttered Aro half-heartedly and only really doing it because Ellendrii snapped and not because he really meant it. He thought the Gryphies were too ritualistic in their ways. Lizariaouses weren't really at all.

They were quiet for a while. Ellendrii was stewing and Aro was slightly grumpy and put out. Neither of them were willing to break the silence and Ellendrii eventually went to sleep. Aro got up and left him and went to wander around outside and look inside the other roughly hewn caves nearby. He gathered that something had made them in a hurry to shelter from something.

Peering into one, he squinted in the darkness and sniffed. He could smell smoke and dust and the faint smell that something living had once been in there. And the smell that the living thing had never left. He entered a little way, still sniffing and smelled something charred. Burnt meat.

Going in a little further, he found the creature that had seeked shelter from the fire. Its charred corpse laying at the back of the cave. Aro sniffed it. It smelled like ash but he couldn't resist trying a little. He had never had cooked meat this black before. The closest he had to something flame grilled was if Ellendrii used his fire to kill it. But this ashen black corpse was different. He started to eat it. He was hungry and besides, it would save some of the food they had in the bag if he ate this.

The taste was charred but nice enough. He still liked his meat raw and bloody best but this was an interesting change and the meat itself was firmer and without the wobbliness of raw meat. Whatever it was that had unwittingly cooked itself was well worth a meal for a hungry Lizariaous. He ate everything. Even the bones. They tasted different cooked too and they seemed brittle but he enjoyed it enough.

After the meal he sat in the mouth of the cave and decided to sleep there. He knew Ellendrii had probably snapped at him because he was tired but they were both tired so that wasn't much of an excuse really. He felt Ellendrii could be a bit proud at times but he was still a great friend and Aro cared deeply about him despite the aspects where he didn't see eye to eye with the Gryphie or understand his point of view.

Aro settled down and fell asleep quickly with a full tummy and feeling warmer and happier now.

The next sun cycle, Ellendrii awoke with a yawn and a stretch and looked around for Aro. He couldn't find him and didn't know of course that the Lizariaous had gone and slept elsewhere.

"Aro?" he called. Nothing.

"ARO!!" he roared but still nothing.

"Ergh, he's playing a prank on me cos I snapped at him last moon" muttered Ellendrii in annoyance and stalked out of the cave and went to look for his wayward friend. He shouldn't take things so seriously thought Ellendrii. I had just been annoyed at his attitude and the fact that he rarely even tries to understand my culture. Where is he?

Ellendrii peered into the first of the caves he came to. Since it was light now, he could clearly see to the back and the cave was empty save for a mound of burnt looking stuff at the back.

He went to the next one but that was empty too. Again there was a mound of something that was black and charred. It smelled like it had been alive at some point but Ellendrii didn't care about possible food right now. The more caves he looked in, the more frightened he became for Aro's safety and the worse he felt for snapping at him. Some were entirely empty but most had a burned corpse or something inside at the back of some poor creature that had cowered from the fire but died anyway.

Finally Ellendrii came to the cave that contained a snoring Aro.

"ARO!" he roared and the Lizariaous jumped awake.

"I thought you'd gone missing!" cried Ellendrii, relieved now that he had found him.

"Na, I'm fine, I just went exploring and I found these caves" Aro replied, sitting up.

"Sorry I snapped at you last moon" said Ellendrii quietly.

"It's alright" replied Aro with a shrug. He'd forgiven him by this point.

"These cave things are odd" said Ellendrii, examining the one that Aro resided in.

"They were dug out in a hurry. Creatures tried to escape the fire but ended up getting cooked instead. I ate one last moon cycle" said Aro.

"But it could be poisonous or something!" said Ellendrii with concern.

"Ah my stomach can take it. Besides, it was tasty! Different from eating raw meat. Dunno if I could live on it though. I like my meat raw. Have you ever cooked *your* food?" asked Aro.

"Yeah sometimes we do. Especially in the colder seasons. Eating something hot warms us up too. I know a fresh kill is warm but at the same time, if something is cooked up with fire, it's much hotter and more warming."

"You gunna eat before we move on?" asked Aro, "You may as well so we can save the food in the bag. I doubt there is anything down there worth chewing on. It looked completely destroyed judging by the trees we've seen. Any creatures would be a pile of ash by now. I'm guessing the smoke killed these. They weren't destroyed completely because they're up higher."

"Wow, you're knowledgeable all of a sudden!" laughed Ellendrii and Aro looked proud of himself.

"Yeah well I got thinking when I was eating that last moon cycle and I guess I put it all together in my head" replied Aro.

"I will have something to eat though before we go" said Ellendrii in agreement.

"And I will too. May as well not let the food go to waste" said Aro and they both found a corpse each and devoured them before they moved on.

On the way down, Aro slipped a few times but he was ok. It was nothing as bad as when they had been climbing. His smallest needle still hadn't grown back fully like the others but he had ignored this. He never really thought about his needles much except when he was using them and he knew time would heal the nerves in it and it would work again. He was just glad it was the smallest one and not a more useful one; the longer needles.

Finally they made it back down. It took less time and they used less energy of course than climbing. But when they reached the ground, the air was thick with floating ash and the atmosphere was stuffy and dry. They could hear crackling nearby as wood burned off.

"The fire happened recently" said Ellendrii, stating the obvious.

"Yeah, I just hope it's all gone and we won't get stuck in it or something. What direction does the Gryphie stone say we should go from here?" asked Aro.

Ellendrii stood on his hind legs and examined the stone around his neck. He would have sat but he didn't want an ashy bottom.

"Ok, it's pointing in that direction" he said, pointing the way with a finger.

"Great. That's towards that horrible looking mountain" replied Aro.

"Well maybe it will change direction before we get there" said Ellendrii with hope.

They set out, the ash felt weird under their feet and the air made Aro cough like crazy. He stopped for a sip of water often. Ellendrii felt sorry for him but he had no other idea of how to curb it at least a little than constantly having a sip of water. In the end, he had to tie a gourd around Aro's neck so that he could have a sip more easily than keep getting it out of Ellendrii's bag and stopping all the time. Because the longer they took, the more he would cough and the worse it would get.

The world around them was as silent as it had been at the top of the mountain, but this time it was a deathly silence instead of a peaceful one. Not a bird flew in the sky and nothing living crossed their path. Instead, there were blackened corpses. It was a harrowing sight. They could see the corpses of creatures that had curled up and hoped for the best and been burned to death. Creatures that had done the opposite thing and tried unsuccessfully to run. Some had climbed trees to get out of the way of the fire but the trees had either been burnt up as well or fallen and the corpses lay scattered around them. As they got closer to the horrible mountain, the destruction of the fire was greater. The corpses on the outlying area for example, were charred and damaged but were still recognizable that they had once been living. After a while of walking, everything was just ash. Only the largest and strongest trees had taken longer to burn and their remains still stood.

"This is horrible" said Ellendrii quietly, "What could have caused such destruction? Pyrokinetics couldn't do this. Our fire is powerful, yes, but it wouldn't do this damage. There would have to be millions of us and we would use our fire up even after a short while of flaming full pelt at the landscape. It would take a full pelt flaming anyway, to do this…"

"I…don't…know" was all Aro could say between his small coughs and hacks. He wondered if he would ever breathe properly again.

"Maybe it was a large creature…" pondered Ellendrii.

"Maybe…the SilvaGryphie" joked Aro despite his condition.

"Actually, I think she *would* be able to do this kind of damage so that would actually be possible" replied Ellendrii, "Although I hope it wasn't!"

"Probably…not…" muttered Aro and coughed again.

"All these poor creatures…and the amount of trees still standing suggests this place was once thriving. Maybe even a wood or forest of some kind…" Ellendrii looked around more as they walked.

"The...ground is...warm" was all Aro could say.

The ground was warm; sometimes a little *too* warm in places. Ellendrii hopped about a couple of times, having more sensitive feet than Aro. He walked upright because his hands were more sensitive even than his feet for some reason so he decided to get less parts of him on the ground just as a precaution. But then again if his feet got burned, he could always fly. He had decided not to fly at this precise moment though because it would blow the ash around everywhere and make Aro's cough worse.

They came up to a nearby tree and Ellendrii casually poked it as they passed. It crumbled to dust on the ground. Ellendrii's eyes grew wide and he decided not to touch anything again. They didn't see many corpses now. The larger creatures were the only ones that were still somewhat recognizable as things that had once lived. The smaller, fragile ones had been burned down to nothing.

They didn't stop to eat but continued on their journey, eating some of the food from Ellendrii's bag. By this time the sun was lower in the sky but they were determined to get through this part swiftly. They couldn't afford to sleep there with Aro's chest and cough like it was. They ate quickly because the ash in the air kept threatening to contaminate their food before they had put it in their mouths. Ellendrii couldn't let the food touch the ground and had to hand feed it to Aro. Aro gulped it down quickly and ended up with indigestion but the moist food helped soothe his scratchy throat.

They continued on their way, following the direction of the Gryphie stone, getting ever closer to the mountain.

As they approached it, still quite a way off but close enough that they could hear it. It rumbled angrily and they could feel the vibrations in the ground.

"I don't like this. I feel like the mountain is going to attack us" blurted out Aro and went into fits of coughing afterwards.

"I hear you" replied Ellendrii, "It's screaming danger at me. It's like it's growling at us and warning us to keep away. But why?"

"In case whatever made the fire comes back?" asked Aro, amidst coughs.

"It's warmer here" observed Ellendrii, "The ground is warmer and so is the air and there is more ash in the sky. The trees are no longer around either. We seem to be close to where the fire started. But why is it worse here than it was back there at the foot of that other mountain?"

"It's…like…it…came from…here" Aro managed before he started to cough violently again.

Ellendrii looked around thoughtfully.

"Yes, it's like it started here and came from here which is why the land and creatures back there aren't as badly burnt."

"Who…cares…let's just…keep…going" sputtered Aro.

They hadn't actually stopped but the thoughtful Ellendrii was walking a little more slowly than the choking Aro.

"I care because if the fire came from here, there could still be danger here. What if whatever made it comes back or lives here? What if whatever made it was aiming at intruders and we're next?"

"It's…all…quiet…now…so let's…just keep…on…" said Aro. He felt like he would collapse, his breathing felt so tight in his throat now. It was alright for Ellendrii. He wished his friend would pay more attention to the current plight he was in right now.

"Just keep your eyes open" said Ellendrii, looking up into the sky and then across at the forbidding mountain before them. It was not as tall as the snow capped mountains but Ellendrii sincerely hoped that the Gryphie stone wouldn't make them climb it. They were getting closer and closer to it now.

The mountain continued to growl and rumble deeply at them as they approached and Aro started to walk faster.

"Don't' go too fast" warned Ellendrii, "If you do, you will breathe faster to keep up with your pace and that will make you cough more."

"I'll try…not to…" replied Aro, slowing down again. It was a vicious circle. If he walked faster, he would need to breathe faster, but if he went more slowly, it would take longer and he would spend longer in that horrible suffocating atmosphere.

They carried on as the moon came out and still carried on.

"I…hope…there will be…water…nearby" said Aro.

"I hardly think so" replied Ellendrii, "The fire will have made it disappear. It dries up in heat, so the nearest water is probably quite a way away."

"Yeah…that's it…destroy…my hope" coughed Aro.

"I wasn't. But I wanted to make you aware of the situation. I'm not going to lie to you, Aro. We are both survivors now and we do things the nitty gritty way, not smooth it over with false hope. I wouldn't have said there was water nearby because that creates false hope and you get even more disappointed when you find no water. By telling you the truth, if we *do* find water unexpectedly nearby, then it will be a pleasant surprise!"

"Yeah but the…truth…hurts" muttered Aro.

"Of course. But at least it prepares you" replied Ellendrii. Aro snorted and coughed. Ellendrii wasn't sure if it was because of what he had just said or if the Lizariaous was merely uncomfortable with the atmosphere.

The mountain loomed up ahead. Ellendrii suddenly noticed something about it that he hadn't before, because of the ash in the air and the cloudy sky. There was actually a billowing cloud of smoke coming out of the top of the mountain! That must be causing the ash, he assumed.

And that was also why the air was harder to breathe here. The top of the mountain appeared to be open and the smoke was coming out of it.

Ellendrii and Aro had never seen a volcano before and had no idea that the earth could make fire and smoke of its own. All this area had been damaged in the wake of a recent volcanic eruption, which was why there was so much destruction and why their senses and instincts screamed at them to keep away from the dangerous mountain. And it had been one hell of an eruption as well, to do all *that* damage!

"The mountain is making smoke, how odd" observed Ellendrii.

"Let's…just…get away…from it…" said Aro.

The Gryphie stone still resolutely pointed to the mountain. Ellendrii could see at the foot of it, a path that lead between the mountain and some rock the other side. He predicted that it would lead them along that path. He was grateful for the stone in that it lead them by foot as opposed to by air, which is how Gryphies normally travel. He assumed the stone had been made either by Gryphies or for Gryphies or maybe both and he wondered how or if the stone knew they were on foot.

"If it's any help, we're going that way" said Ellendrii, pointing.

"THAT…way? But its…near the mountain…" complained Aro, "We need to…head…away from…the mountain…"

"Sorry but that's the way we have to go. The sky is cloudy so when it gets dark we won't be able to see much at all. We need to get to that path and carry on beyond it. The rock goes up high there and it's probably more sheltered from all this ash."

Ellendrii looked. Yes, they would be right next to the mountain but they would pass it fairly fast he thought and be out of the way of it. They must get to the path before the moon rose fully or they wouldn't be able to find it and they would really struggle then. They couldn't afford to spend the moon cycle in that atmosphere.

So they carried on, more swiftly now but not so much so that Aro struggled to breathe more so than he did currently.

The silence was nearly as stifling as the atmosphere. It just screamed death and destruction and the fear that the pair of them would be next.

Suddenly the mountain rumbled loudly, more loudly than it had previously and a huge cloud of smoke came out of it. Ellendrii looked up at it and there seemed to be something orange and glowing at the top where the smoke was coming from. It looked like liquid of some kind but it was too hard to see since it was so far away. Nevertheless, he could see the liquid starting to trickle down from the top of the mountain. The rumblings made his heart beat faster in a panic. He had no idea why he felt like this but it was pure fear and the need to flee that started to overwhelm him now. It was similar for Aro. They had both sped up their pace.

The ash they were tramping through was kicking up with the motion of their faster footsteps.

"El, we need to move…" coughed Aro.

"I know, but you can't run because you'll take in more air with breathing faster" pointed out Ellendrii.

"I…know…but I would…rather have…a…cough than…die…" Aro blurted and started to gallop.

"Ok, then head for the path!" roared Ellendrii and followed him. All bets were off now as the two raced for their lives. The mountain started to roar and oozing, burning liquid shot out of the top of it.

This was what had destroyed the land.

Ellendrii and Aro looked back at the mountain and saw the deadly searing liquid bursting out of it. They didn't need another look. They ran for it, faster and faster, reaching the path like they'd been shot out of a cannon and running through the rocky path that followed the entrance.

They ran for a long time. Finally they collapsed, unable to carry on. Aro was the first to tire and then Ellendrii. Ellendrii had always had a lot of stamina although the stamina of the air for him far outmatched that of his land travel.

Aro was coughing his guts up but the air was cleaner and fresher here and for some reason the fire and heat had not reached here; only the other side of the burning mountain. Ellendrii figured that it was because the rocks had formed a natural detour for the liquid heat from the mountain so it had been sent off elsewhere instead of reaching this part of the land.

"Drink!" yelled Ellendrii as Aro flailed on the ground, his body shuddering violently with each cough.

"For grik sake, DRINK!" roared Ellendrii and grabbed the gourd from around Aro's neck, opening it and tipping the contents into his mouth.

Aro drank gratefully and it eased his cough. Finally, he spoke.

"My…throat…feels like…it's on…fire…" he panted. He was sore and tired from coughing so much.

"It's ok" Ellendrii comforted him, standing with the gourd ready in case he needed any more.

He declined to joke about having a burning throat would mean Aro would know how *he* felt! Being able to breathe fire and all. Aro probably wouldn't have found it funny at this precise moment.

They rested and slept where they were. Too tired to carry on or find a place to sleep. They pretty much ended up falling asleep without even giving their bodies permission to do so. At this point, none of it mattered.

The next sun cycle, the pair of them woke up late, when the sun was higher in the sky. They felt groggy and Aro had a sore throat. When he spoke, his voice was hoarse and Ellendrii gave him some more water and something to eat.

"I had no idea that mountains could create fire" said Ellendrii quietly, "I was so scared. I've never been scared of what we as Gryphies create. Fire has never scared me." He sat staring at the ground, his eyes wide in a startling and unpleasant revelation.

"And the colour of it…it wasn't fire like mine. It was a strange orange colour. I don't like this. I don't like what we are discovering in these lands."

If Aro had known, he would have said that Ellendrii's blue fire was far hotter than the usual orange/yellow fire. But of course all this was new to him too and he did not know, because he hadn't encountered this type of fire before or even heard of it. As far as Ellendrii was concerned though, it had destroyed what looked like it had been a wood of some sort and countless frightened creatures and it was powerful and dangerous. But the fact that he was actually scared of fire, that terrified him.

"But we can't go back, can we? It's too far…" he trailed off. Aro had never seen his friend like this and that in itself frightened him.

"Look, there's nothing like that back at home. It's not native to us so there's no reason to fear it. We don't live near it so it doesn't affect us. So don't be scared, it's ok…" he put a calming paw on Ellendrii's shoulder but he could feel the Gryphie shaking slightly under his paw.

"It's not that. We will have to go back though here when we go home, or at least there is a possibility we will. I don't think I can handle being frightened of something that has always comforted me. It's like everything is turning on its head."

"Hey, I've been scared of stuff too. Some of it gave me moonmares..." Aro tried to comfort him, hoarsely.

"Yeah we both had moonmares but this is different. Not even in the great war did Gryphie fire cause damage like that..."

"Yeah but most of the fighting happened in the Outlands. So there's nothing out there to destroy. If it had happened in the Forest, I'm sure there would have been far more damage done." Aro didn't realize how right he was. Only a little of the fighting had happened in the Forest. The Gryphie fire would have burned it quickly to the ground if they hadn't held back and fought with their teeth and claws instead.

"But...this..." Ellendrii trailed off again. It would be harder than that to get him out of this state of panic he had got himself into.

Aro sighed and grunted.

"Ok fine, do you know how hard it has been for me to sleep since the Forest of Foreboding?? How every single moon cycle I have moonmares about what we saw in there? Not just like the ones we've "both" been having. These are about the Repulsators. I was so deathly afraid of them and I can't let them go. And the Narg'tok. Seeing it do that to you...THAT terrified me. But the Repulsators, for some reason I can't get them out of my head. I want you to know that there have been many things that I too never wanted to see on this journey. I knew it wouldn't be safe at times but I could never have imagined that some of the things we've encountered would be so terrifying.

I wanted to come on this journey cos I thought it would be fun. And yeah, to a point it has been. I wanted to come because I wanted to explore but I didn't expect it to be more dangerous than back home. Not in the ways we've seen anyway. You might hate that burning mountain and feel that now not even the safety of your fire is guaranteed but I want you to know that we've encountered things that have scared me beyond belief and I never thought that was possible, being as I'm a Lizariaous and we fear nothing. Fear is not in our nature. I know I'm young and the younger members of our species get scared more easily but I never thought that I would feel this kind of fear. The fear that's kept me up during the moon cycles after we left the Forest of Foreboding and the fear that still gives me moonmares every single moon cycle without fail even now. We've seen and done so much since then but I can't get those stupid rat things out of my head. I didn't want to tell you because it makes me seem cowardly. I'm not *supposed* to be scared of *anything*. Do you realize how grikking stupid that makes me feel? Well I'm just putting it out there that you're not alone in your fear. So don't for a second think that I don't understand simply because it's *fire* you fear." He erupted into a barrage of coughing as soon as he'd finished this long winded but very true and heartfelt speech.

Ellendrii looked up.

"I'm sorry I freaked out like that, Aro. I didn't know you were so frightened too."

"Don't get all sympathizing on me. I don't need that. And I'm not trying to shift the problem so it's mine and not yours. But I wanted you to understand that we're in this together and if you're going through something because we've seen or encountered something, it's likely I'm going through the same thing so there's no need to feel like you can't cope or that it will stop you. Together we're strong and we'll see this through. But I do admit that at times I've regretted coming along. However, ultimately I don't. Ultimately I'm glad I came along because I've seen things I couldn't even have dreamed of."

"Yeah. I admit that I've regretted going on this journey. And yes…I…I regretted letting you come along as well at times…" Ellendrii hung his head in shame.

"It's ok" replied Aro, "I thought you probably might. I know you've found me annoying before."

"All friends find each other annoying at times though. And families do too. And you're like my brother, Aro. I mean that." Ellendrii smiled.

Aro was rendered speechless for once. His brother! He had always wanted a brother. He was sick of his two stuck up sisters.

"That really means a lot" said Aro, still hoarse. "Thank you. I would be proud to be called your brother."

Ellendrii nodded and smiled.

"Thank you, Aro. I know it took a lot for you to tell me about your fears" he said.

"Yeah and you admitting that you wish at times I hadn't come along. But hey, how could I not? Even though we've been through grik at times, I wouldn't swap these memories for the world. I mean, all the experiences we've had so far. The Wind Hounds, yeah I know it ended badly, Rivniann was nice and those creatures with the masks. The Aqwakitts and your distrust of them…" Aro sniggered.

"Yeah well, after being in the Forest of Foreboding, how could I trust something I thought seemed friendly on the outside but was still capable of drowning us. Besides, the fact that they knew where the SilvaGryphie was seemed all too good to be true. And it was."

"Yeah but at the same time they had just got it wrong. It *was* the SilvaGryphie but just not as we know her" replied Aro. "And even though it all ended badly with the Wind Hounds, I really enjoyed staying with them and learning all their quirky weird culture."

"It wasn't weird" laughed Ellendrii. Aro laughed too, then started to cough and had to have another drink.

"We need to save the water as best we can" said Ellendrii. "Try to only take small sips. We don't know where there will be water next."

"I know" replied Aro.

"Shall we continue?" asked Ellendrii.

"So long as you're feeling better" replied Aro.

"Yeah I'm fine. I need to remember that the burning mountain is just there and we have passed it and I don't have to live with it so it can't affect me. I really can't wait to go back home though, where everything is normal and Gryphies are the only creatures that breathe fire."

"Thinking about it, you thought that yellow orange fire was weird but do you remember Midnyte Comet's acidfire? It was bright green!" Aro said pointedly.

"Oh yeah, I'd completely forgotten…"

"How could you forget the love of your life?" grinned Aro, prodding Ellendrii playfully in the side.

"Oh shut up! Don't start that again! Yeah she was cute but she wanted to live alone so it wouldn't have worked out anyway."

"So that's the only reason you never stayed with her then? Nothing about the search for the SilvaGryphie?"

"Well yeah and that…" Ellendrii was blushing.

"So *would* you have stayed with her if she had wanted you to?" asked Aro.

"I would have completed my quest first and then gone back to her" said Ellendrii with a proud stance.

Aro burst out laughing and rolled around on the ground, erupting into coughs as well.

"Oh shut up!" snapped Ellendrii, "Let's get going."

He stood up and started to walk away, looking at the Gryphie stone at the same time.

Aro quickly followed.

"You know what?" sniggered Aro.

"What" said Ellendrii, not really a question and he had an unimpressed look on his face.

"I love winding you up about Midnyte!" laughed Aro.

"AAAAAGGHHHH!!" screamed Ellendrii and took to the sky.

"If you're going to wind me up, then I'm flying the rest of the way and you can walk!" he called down to his friend.

"Then you'll have more peace and quiet to think about her" called up Aro.

Ellendrii, not to be outdone, landed and changed the subject.

"I thought actually that it would be useful to fly up and see where the journey will take us next" he said.

"Ha, yeah right!" snorted Aro.

"Yes." Ellendrii said.

"Whatever" shrugged Aro.

At least the subject of the burning mountain was now out of Ellendrii's mind. That was also part of Aro's plan. And since they had started talking about the experiences and the other creatures they had met, why not mention Midnyte?

"You know," said Ellendrii, "If you *dare* to wind me up when I get a life partner back home, we will both flame your butt!"

"I would never do such a thing!" said Aro, feigning innocence, which didn't work at all. It is impossible for a Lizariaous to look innocent.

"You bet you wouldn't or you would have a singed butt!" said Ellendrii. Aro supposed he wasn't actually joking and that he and whoever female he took to be his life partner would actually follow through with this insinuated promise.

"Ok ok, maybe I won't. Maybe." Aro said. Ellendrii suspected that may or may not happen depending on Aro's mood at the time.

"Anyway, where are we off to next? I hope it will be somewhere nice" said Aro. Ellendrii flew up for a look. When he came back down, he told Aro what he had seen.

"The rocks here carry on for a while. Beyond these it just looks barren." Ellendrii told him.

"Ah, then I should feel right at home then!" said Aro.

"You better hope it has food" replied Ellendrii.

"And caves!" said Aro.

"Food is more important. Anyway, it's quite a way off yet."

"Well then, let's go!" said Aro and the two friends continued on their journey in high spirits and ready for whatever they would encounter next.

Chapter 27
Fresh Air

Ellendrii and Aro made their way through the rocky land, glad of the fresher air here. Aro's cough got a little better the longer they travelled and Ellendrii was glad of that also. It was weird hearing his friend's voice so changed from what he was used to.

They journeyed for about a sun cycle, constantly following the direction the Gryphie stone lead them and eventually the barren land gave way to sand. It appeared to be a desert land they had entered into now.

The only problem was that they hadn't found anything to eat yet. There were no meal creatures in the barren territory and not even another friendly creature to guide them or at least give them advice as to where they might find food or water.

They were heavily rationing the water from the gourds and there wasn't much left. They had about four pieces of burrowing bird left in the bag. Even though they were eating less, due to now being used to it, they still needed something to keep their energy up or they would get weak again as they had in the Forest of Foreboding. And not being able to find a living thing in this desert did not bode well for catching more food to replenish what they had.

At first, they were happy enough to travel in this desert land. The sand felt funny against their feet and it was pleasant to walk on. But of course it was also dry and hot and didn't help Aro's throat, which was still recovering from the burning mountain. He couldn't take the sips he had been from the gourd because now they needed to ration the water.

"How far do you think this desert will go on?" he asked Ellendrii.

"Dunno. I flew up to see but it's all desert as far as my eyes can see. Still, at least there's no danger here. No burning mountains or hunters. So far at least."

"I wonder how much longer the food will last" pondered Aro.

"We have two pieces each. I would wait till you *have* to eat before you have one. I don't like that it's all out in the open here. We're both used to sleeping under cover and there is no cover out here. I haven't even seen a plant or tree yet. Maybe we should have found a way around or something…" Ellendrii wondered.

"That would've been hard though even with flying. I really hope that stone knows where it's going. If we carry on travelling as much as we can, we should clear this desert faster" said Aro.

"Less sleep, more travel!" declared Ellendrii and they both laughed. But they were both getting ever more fatigued.

Ellendrii chose to fly after about half a sun cycle in the desert because the sand was too hot for his feet. Aro's feet were tougher and it didn't bother him much. He just loped along, a lean wiry Lizariaous youngster whose legs were strong from walking and whose bones showed a little through his thick skin. Ellendrii observed this. Aro had always been so chunky and sturdy. It was odd to see him like this. The change hadn't really hit Ellendrii until he was flying and watching his friend as they travelled. Up close, and seeing Aro every sun cycle, he hadn't really noticed the change in either of them. He assumed his body must be the same. It never occurred to Ellendrii that they would change like this.

Aro's head was down now as he normally walked these sun cycles. His head low, just trudging along to their destination wherever it may be. He never held it high really. They were both tired. At times they were travelling by sheer determination through this desert, just going where the stone told them to out of habit now and the blind faith that it would lead them to the SilvaGryphie.

The sand made their bodies dusty. Aro's skin looked paler now since the black of his scales was obscured by the dust. Ellendrii never bothered to try and dust himself off; there wasn't any point as the sand would only cling to him again as they travelled.

Two sun cycles passed in this desert and the food had all gone now. They had just finished their second pieces. The gourds were only half full each. They slept when they were too tired to walk, as they had done in the Forest of Foreboding and travelled by moon as well as sun because the sky was clear here and the moonlight guided them. It was only easy going in as much as the terrain was easy enough to travel over.

The fact they still could find no food or water became an increasing concern for them. They tried not to think about it but their starving stomachs and dry mouths made this difficult.

Finally, they also ran out of water.

"I dunno how much longer I can carry on. My throat is killing me" said Aro hoarsely.

"Yeah join the club" muttered Ellendrii, who was still keeping to the air. Flying took up far more energy than walking though, but he couldn't keep to the sand for long because it burned his feet. Aro had suggested firing off his needles and letting Ellendrii sit on his back to travel, which was very kind of him but Ellendrii politely refused. By flying, he was also keeping an eye out on how much longer the desert went on.

However, disappointingly, it was still sand as far as the eye could see.

They continued on their way for another sun cycle and at moon they stopped for a rest. Ellendrii could walk on the sand in the moonlight since it was colder and easier to stand on. And it saved his wings.

Most of their travelling was now at moon when it was cooler. Ellendrii was too weak to fly for long periods. Aro was nearly ready to give up.

"This was a stupid mission anyway" he muttered early one moon cycle, "I don't know what the grik possessed El to even go on such a dead end journey. SilvaGryphie. Yeah others have seen her but it's no indication as to where she lives. Total grikking rubbish. We'll never find her. I dunno why we're still doing this. We should've turned back at the burning mountain and given up. Nothing is worth this. Nothing. We'll just die out here and no one will know where we are or what happened to us. Our bodies will be buried in the sand."

Ellendrii, thankfully, didn't hear his muttering. He was travelling up ahead. Aro had dropped back because he was so tired. Ellendrii was flying and walking and taking it in turns when either his legs or wings got too tired, he would switch to the other.

He was also muttering.

"If we don't find food soon, I've sentenced us both to death out here. We'll both die of hunger and thirst and this is all my fault. We should have turned back ages ago and tried to find another way across this desert. I dunno how much longer I can carry on. I'm so weak. Aro is worse. What have I done?? Too late to turn back now. We must keep going and hope that the desert will end soon. We must travel by moon. Yes…"

For most of the moon cycle they wandered like this until finally, Aro fell down. And stayed down. His feet and legs were just too tired.

"Aro! Are you ok??" cried Ellendrii, rushing to his friend's side.

Aro didn't speak; he just blinked up at Ellendrii and coughed a little. He was too weak to even speak.

"Aro, I'm so sorry. I had no idea this desert would be so big. I should have flown over it and seen how far it went on before we approached it properly. What have I done??" Ellendrii rested his head on Aro and sobbed. His wet tears ran down Aro's body in little streams, parting the dust that covered his scales.

"It's ok…" Aro's voice quietly spoke.

"It's not" replied Ellendrii.

A soft wind was rising around and blowing the sand about. Ellendrii covered Aro with his wings as the wind picked up more. They hadn't seen it because, despite the moon to light their way, it was still really dark but there was a huge sand storm coming. It was whipping up the sand in the distance and the breeze was a prelude to what was about to come.

Lying on the ground felt good and the pair of them were quietly resting and dozing off by this time. But the sand storm was getting closer. Ellendrii heard it but never registered anything because he was in that state of between consciousness and unconsciousness when you don't really register what a sound is or what something will do and he was lulled off into a slumber when the sand storm hit fully.

They both were.

There was a rush of wind and it whipped up all around them, waking them both with a jump and making them sit up and pay attention. Not for long though because the wind had caught in Ellendrii's wings and was dragging him off Aro and into the sky.

"AROOOO!!!" roared Ellendrii as the wind took him off. He couldn't see for the sand and dust and it stung his eyes. He couldn't open them or control his wings and movements and he had no choice but to let it take him. If he fought it, it would hurt him and there was no point because he just wasn't strong enough in his current state. He probably wouldn't have been had he been in peak condition. Not even a Gryphie's mighty wings could stop the winds of nature.

Swirling round and round, Ellendrii was caught up and pushed from here to there in the wind. It blew in his ears, deafening him with its roar; louder than the roar of any Gryphie alive, he was sure. He tried to hold his wings close to himself but the wind buffeted him and blew him around, pulling out his wings a little and once it had its grip, he could no longer keep them in. He tried to pull his wing back against his body but at that moment a huge gust of wind pulled at it, ripping its arm and yanking it out of its socket. Ellendrii roared in pain. He couldn't move it anymore. It was useless. And the fact that he had no way to pull it back in meant that it was at the mercy of the sand storm. He had managed to get the other wing back in against his body again and held it there with his last remaining strength. He just needed to wait this out until it died down. If he could only do that, then he could get back on the ground and try and find Aro. Right now though, the only thought on his mind was trying to lessen the damage that was being caused to his body. He tried to hold his tail in as well. Round and round the wind swirled him. He felt sick but there was nothing much inside him to throw up, so he just continued to feel sick as the wind toyed with him.

His eyes were still tightly closed. This was like the storm on the vast water only more painful and frightening and there was no island here with a kind dragon on who would help him and Aro recover. Nothing. No one and nothing. Not even Aro. Where was Aro? Where was anyone? No one was here to help him. He was certain he would die out here in the desert. If the wind didn't get him, the lack of food and water would.

He felt dizzy now as the wind tossed him around like a feather. Again he regretted this fool's mission. But what else was there? To Ellendrii, flying was his life. He felt he had no choice other than to do this.

All through the moon cycle the wind played with him. Blowing him here and there and weakening him even more. By the time the sand storm died down and dropped him, Ellendrii was nearly unconscious with fatigue and the pain of his damaged wing.

He found himself at sunrise, buried under a pile of sand. Thankfully his head was stuck out enough that he had been able to breathe. He pulled himself out of the sand drift with a lot of effort and fell face first into the sand a little way away, from the effort of it all.

He managed to sit up and test his wings. One of them hurt but still folded fine and he could move it normally. But the other one he couldn't move at all. It had been pulled out of its socket where the arm of his wing met his body. Moving it hurt and it just hung limply at his side. Thankfully he hadn't lost his important leather bag with its healing herbs and gourds (although empty) and Midnyte's decoration in. He couldn't travel with his wing dragging in the sand so he would have to bind it up to his body.

Ellendrii reached into the bag and pulled out some of the twine that was used for binding healing leaves to wounds. The twine was strong and it would be perfect for binding his wing. He rifled around in the bag and got out some herbs as well that he thought he could bind into the wing with the twine. After all, something was better than nothing. He didn't realize that this wasn't actually the sort of wound that could be healed by herbs. He would have to have the wing popped back into its socket.

He sat on his haunches and nimbly used his hands to bind his wing. It was a bit difficult though because he couldn't hold the wing to his body without using one hand. So he had to hold his wing in place with one hand and try to get the twine around his body and the wing with the other. And it was hard. He gave up on that and instead tried to wrap the twine around his body first and then deal with the wing. That made it a bit easier. But he still had to hold the wing in place before he could wrap the twine around it.

The sun was starting to heat things up and he was getting a little agitated at his wing not behaving how he wanted it to. In the end he wrapped his other wing round the front of his body to try and lift the damaged wing up a little closer so he could pull it in the rest of the way with the twine. This, although it looked a little ridiculous, worked.

He pulled the twine tighter around him and in doing so, pulled his wing up and in place against his body. He tied the binding securely and bit off the excess, which he returned to the bag and fastened the bag back up.

Feeling a bit better about his situation, he stood up. His legs hurt like grik but he knew he must now try to find Aro. And that would be very hard considering he couldn't fly at the moment.

Ellendrii headed out into the desert. He checked the Gryphie stone every so often as always but now he wasn't sure about following it because Aro might be in the opposite direction.

As he walked, he tried roaring for his friend. There was no reply though. How would he ever be able to find Aro? He could be anywhere! Ellendrii felt lost without his travelling companion. And to make matters worse, the sand was hurting his feet again. It burned more with every step he took. If he had even as much use of his wing that he could lift himself even slightly to get off the sand a little, it would be a help. But since he couldn't open his wing out, he had no chance of doing that. He tried hopping but it took too much energy. Finally the sand was just too hot to walk on and he could travel no further.

He would have sat down in defeat but of course then he would have burnt his bottom, so he didn't try that.

"Come on, Ellendrii, think! How will you walk on this sand? What can you do to help yourself?" he said aloud to himself.

Out of desperation, he looked in his leather bag to see if there was anything in there that might help. Some herbs, some twine, vines, small leaves. No big leaves. Big ones might be helpful. If he still had them. He could have used them to cover his feet to stop the hot sand burning them. But maybe…maybe he could use something else to cover them?

Ellendrii thought. And sweated. And thought some more.

Finally, he settled on binding his feet with the twine too. It was the only thing he could think of. The twine was flat, whereas the vines weren't, so it would be comfortable to walk on at least.

So, Ellendrii set about binding his feet as well. He had used nearly all the twine by the time he had finished. It had come in very handy.

Stashing what was left back in the bag, Ellendrii stood and set out once again. This felt much better! Sure, the sand still felt hot, but at least now it didn't burn him. He was proud of his survival skills. Lunara hadn't taught him anything like this because honestly and completely expectedly, she hadn't looked past things that were familiar. So if it wasn't something from Shernaron, she couldn't imagine it or prepare him for it. And nothing much that they had encountered had been even similar to things in Shernaron or the Outlands or Dyarkroeen. Even the Gryphie Mountains weren't much like the mountain they had climbed because the Gryphie Mountains aren't covered in snow most of the time and the only time they are is the cold season and Ellendrii had never climbed them because he could fly. Aro had just never climbed them because it was not something that interested him.

"Ok, better. Now, how the grik do I get ahold of Aro? This desert is who knows how big!" Ellendrii muttered to himself.

His heart suddenly skipped a beat. What if Aro was dead? He couldn't be positive that the Lizariaous was alive, after all. Ellendrii felt his blood run cold, despite the hot sun. Aro had been in a worse state than Ellendrii had been. After all,

Ellendrii had some tolerance of the heat, like he had done in the realm of the burning mountain.

So what do I do? He thought. Carry on without Aro? Go back and look for him? But he might be in front of me...

Ellendrii was lost.

Aro wasn't dead. But he was stuck. He had been buried by the sand and was breathing by some miracle through an air pocket. He was weak and struggled to move to get himself out of his predicament. The sand storm had whipped him up as well and blown him around like a toy. It had been horrible. He had shot out all his needles in case the wind broke any of them off and damaged him again. Those nerves were just beginning to heal, after all and he couldn't of course shoot off the smallest, damaged one until they had.

He had tried calling for Ellendrii at first but then realized that it was useless and stopped. The wind was too loud for one thing and for another, his throat really hurt him. Plus he was pretty much hoarse so how would Ellendrii hear him anyway?

So he had let the wind take him and toss him around until finally he ended up buried in the sand that the wind had also whipped up.

And here he was, breathing through an air pocket and completely buried in the sand. He wasn't that far down but it was far enough to confuse him. He needed to move his body and try and feel for a way out. He didn't know if he was facing up or down but he tried to move his front legs and paws and dig as best he could. There was nowhere really for the sand to go though, which made it all the more difficult.

Then he heard something and sniffed softly. Not too hard or he would get a noseful of sand!

Something brushed alongside him. Another creature! Something that lived under the sand. He didn't know if it would hurt him or not and he didn't want to take that chance. However, he couldn't kill it unless it got near his snout because he couldn't move. But that's exactly the part of him the creature was headed for. It could sense the liquid in his eyes and mouth and was very thirsty, just as Aro was. So it was headed for that because it needed to drink.

Given the chance, the creature would have crawled into his mouth, down his throat and eaten him from the inside out but Aro was not going to let it have that chance. It thought he was dead. Another victim of the sand storm, a rare treat for it to dine upon.

Aro waited for it to crawl into his mouth and then he clamped his jaws down on it, chewing and biting swiftly in case it bit or stung him. He couldn't feel any pain though and the creature was a decent size too. And plump. He gathered that since it lived in the desert, it could probably store water in its body so it didn't dehydrate and he would be correct.

He chewed the creature up and swallowed it hungrily. Its blood tasted so good! And its flesh made him feel even more hungry. He sincerely hoped another one would come along soon.

So he pondered if he should just stay there and wait for more of these creatures to dig their way to him so he could eat them or head on out of the sand and try to find Ellendrii. All his senses and instincts told him to wait and be patient and eat more. So that is what he did.

The creatures soon found him and he ate each one that came to him in search of food. Because food was such a rarity in the desert, these creatures would flock to a corpse to feast upon it. So Aro was in no shortage of food. He ate and drank these creatures until he was full and then he ate and drank more of them. He really wanted to catch some and take them with him so he could give them to Ellendrii when he found him but Aro could think of no way to transport them so, regretfully, he ate his last one and then began trying to work his way out of the sand.

It didn't take him long to find out he was in fact digging downwards. So he had to somehow get his body facing the other way and dig back up. Instead what he did was dig out and round and then upwards so he could get out of the sand.

He emerged from the sand into a late sun cycle. This was perfect! He could easily travel and find Ellendrii then. He knew his friend would be up in the air, flying around and trying to spot him on the ground so Aro thought it would be as simple as walking around looking up at the sky to spy Ellendrii. Then he would roar to him and shoot up any needles that had grown back and they would be reunited.

Also, now, Aro knew how to get food. Bury yourself and pretend to be dead.

Feeling much more himself, the Lizariaous headed into the desert to find his friend.

The moon was high when he began to feel a bit despondent. Why hadn't he seen Ellendrii yet? Surely the Gryphie would be flying all over the place looking for him? It had been ages since he had dug himself out of the sand. He had much more energy now though so he carried on but he was still concerned.

After a while, it occurred to Aro that maybe Ellendrii was injured in some way. Maybe he couldn't fly? Maybe he couldn't even look for him? Maybe he had been knocked unconscious, ended up under the sand and been eaten by those creatures? That was a horrible thought. Aro shook his head and got rid of the idea. Ellendrii was alive; he *had* to be! After all, he needed to find the SilvaGryphie, right?

Aro started to wonder about if Ellendrii hadn't made it. If Aro found him dead somewhere. Would; *could* Aro continue the journey alone? He knew deep down that if Ellendrii had died, he would have to continue on. For the sake of his friend and Ellendrii's memory. It needed to be done. If he gave up and went home, sure, his family would be happy to see him, but what about Ellendrii's family? If Aro came home without his best friend, Ellendrii's family would be heartbroken. And how would Aro live that down? Just abandoning the journey because Ellendrii hadn't made it.

He knew that whatever it took, he would continue looking for the SilvaGryphie in Ellendrii's place. He wouldn't be able to continue knowing that he had never tried. So he continued on and hoped with all his heart that Ellendrii was still alive.

Ellendrii meanwhile, was very much alive although of course still weak, because unlike Aro, he hadn't eaten or drunk anything. And he was running out of ideas of how to find Aro. He thought that maybe he would continue in the direction the Gryphie stone was taking him and he hoped that Aro would be able to continue the same way.

But what if Aro had got turned around during the sand storm? What then? He would be going in the wrong direction. Ellendrii tried to clear his head and think. What did they do back home to alert each other of their position? Not that they got separated to this extent back home but if they did, what would they do? Gryphies travel further apart than Lizariaouses do because they can fly. So how do Gryphies let each other know where they are? Yes, they roar, but also, they flame into the sky!

Of course, that was it! Ellendrii would flame into the sky to let Aro know where he was. Then, Ellendrii would continue going the way he was going and flame every so often and hope that Aro would be able to see and follow him. If he continued heading the way the Gryphie stone was taking him, that would make sense. If he headed back, Aro may already be ahead of him so he would be making them further apart. And if he went forward, Aro would follow if he could see the flame signals and they should both hopefully, end up in the same place.

It was moon cycle now, which made it very much easier to see blue fire in the sky and for that, Ellendrii was thankful.

So he threw his head back and let out a powerful burst of flame into the moonlit sky. He repeated this several times in the hopes that wherever Aro was, he would see it. The terrain was pretty flat, luckily, so Aro should easily be able to see Ellendrii's fire. Ellendrii stopped flaming and listened but heard nothing. He assumed Aro's voice wouldn't be able to roar because he hadn't had anything to drink. Well, Ellendrii was wrong but he was also right in a way because Aro's throat, although more lubricated, was still not strong enough to let out a good, powerful roar like he used to be able to do.

Ellendrii flamed a few more times and listened. Then he continued on his way, flaming every so often until he was too tired to do so and decided to have a little nap. It was moon time after all, and he was tired. He was still weak and he had noticed that his flaming had got weaker much faster than it normally did. So he would have to take it easy on the flaming and either only shoot a powerful flame less regularly or shoot a weaker flame more regularly.

He settled down in the sand and fell quickly asleep.

Aro had seen the flame out in the distance! Sadly though, the sand storm had taken him back quite a way but now at least he knew in which direction to head to get to Ellendrii.

He hadn't noticed the fire at first; he had been too busy doing his customary slow, lean lope along the sand and hoping to find his friend somewhere. He had given up trying to find ways to communicate with Ellendrii, if he was even able to. It was only by chance that he looked up to the sky and saw a jet of blue fire in the distance and his heart soared! There was only one creature with blue fire out here and that was Ellendrii!

But then his heart sank. What if Ellendrii was in a fight? What if that fire was him trying to defend himself from something? Aro picked up his pace. He didn't want to run because he would wear himself out more quickly and then have to rest for longer but his lope became a trot and he headed for where he had seen the fire. As he made his way for it, he noticed that the flames were being shot off further away after a while. Which meant that it was unlikely that Ellendrii was in a fight. It was more likely that he was trying to signal Aro to come and find him. But why was he walking away? Aro couldn't understand that. Surely he would wait for Aro? It couldn't be the sun burning him up and making him want to move because it was moon time.

Or maybe Ellendrii didn't know where Aro was so he was wandering around looking for him and firing the flames up in the hopes Aro would follow? Whatever the reason, Aro now knew that Ellendrii was alive and that was all he needed to know. Now he could find him! He kept going for a long while though and saw no more flames. He wondered what had happened to Ellendrii, who was of course asleep at this point but Aro wasn't to know that.

What if something had attacked Ellendrii?

Why do you always have to jump to bad conclusions, Aro? He asked himself. He mentally gave himself a slap. No. He wasn't in trouble. He was probably tired from flaming so much and having a rest. That would make more sense. Aro still carried on. He was prepared to trot all moon cycle if he had to, because he needed to get to Ellendrii and be reunited so they could continue and get out of here. He kept going.

The sun rose on Ellendrii and he was soon up and moving on. He was desperately hungry and thirsty but he still carried on flaming as best he could as he travelled onward. He still couldn't see an end to the dreaded desert but there was now something in the distance that made him feel a little more excited. It looked like something other than sand for once. He wished he could fly up and investigate. He hadn't tried to move his wing since he bound it to his body but sleeping last moon had been difficult and annoying. He could only lie on one side. So, no rolling about in his sleep! He was making his way much more slowly now though. He was struggling. The bindings on his feet helped the heat but they did not help the fact that his feet and legs ached terribly from walking. It was a small mercy that the sand was soft and it wasn't like walking on rocks at least. He paused, flaming into the sky and carried on. The flames were smaller and more pathetic now though; certainly nothing to be proud of. But it was the best that poor Ellendrii could do right now.

Aro had continued to follow him. Too afraid to sleep in case the travelling Ellendrii got too far away from him and he could no longer see the fire. However, now, the flames were moving more slowly. There was less space between each flame than there had been at first, which meant that Ellendrii was either starting to worry that Aro wasn't seeing them or he was travelling at a slower pace. Aro was very glad when the flames started back up again after Ellendrii had woken up. He had actually started to wander off course so it was good that he had been able to see the flames again and keep going. And what was better was that the flames were now getting closer! What's more was that Aro could now see something in

517

the distance; different terrain maybe? Anything would be better than the desert. Well, maybe not *anything*. Not a Forest of Foreboding or rocky mountains that are hard to climb. Anything within reason. Ok, maybe Aro was hoping for another lake. Anything with water. He was starting to get hungry and thirsty again but didn't have time to bury himself and pretend to be dead. He kept going.

Ellendrii carried on flaming but it was getting too much for him now. He was trying so hard. Would Aro find him? Had he even seen Ellendrii's signals? Ellendrii only had hope to hold onto now. He was starting to fail again and fell down in the hot sand. He managed to sit up but could walk no further. He figured the best thing he could do was to stay in one place and flame every so often and just hope that Aro would find him. If Aro was still alive.

Aro was getting ever closer to the weakened Ellendrii. In fact he could see something in the distance that looked very much like his friend!

"ELLENDRIII!" he yelled but his voice was still weak and wouldn't carry, so Aro had to run instead. He galloped with glee, the closer he got, the clearer he could see the form of the Gryphie sitting in the hot sand in the distance. He had never felt happier in his life than he did now. He had found Ellendrii!

Aro galloped up to his friend, wanting to pounce on him and greet him but knowing that he mustn't. And for the first time as he approached, he saw, as Ellendrii had done with him, how changed his friend was. Ellendrii's spine was showing and his bones clearly showed in his haunches and legs. Also, his wing was bound. Aro slowed down to a trot and came around Ellendrii from the side, not wanting to take him by surprise. As he came around him, Ellendrii raised his head to the sky in preparation to flame again.

"Ellendrii!" Aro said quickly and the Gryphie looked round.

"Aro?" he said weakly.

"Yes!! It's me! I've found you!" laughed Aro.

"You've found me!" Ellendrii smiled, "I'm so glad! I'm so weak. I flamed as much as I could."

"It's ok, I'm here now. I travelled as fast as I could when I saw your flame signals. I was way back the way we had come and it all looked the same to me. I thought you were dead..."

"I thought you were dead too" replied Ellendrii. Aro sat next to him, still smiling. Then he cast his gaze over Ellendrii's wing.

"What happened?" he asked the Gryphie, motioning a paw towards Ellendrii's bound wing.

"The sand storm, it took me up into the air and pulled my wing. I can't move it now. It's useless. So I tied it to my body so it wouldn't get in the way" Ellendrii looked downtrodden. His flying and his freedom was gone.

"It will heal though" said Aro, "I'm sure. Did you put herbs on it?"

"Yeah I did, when I bound it up. Hopefully they will work on it but I still can't move it in the joint. I think it's broken" replied Ellendrii.

"We'll fix it, somehow. Either the herbs will or we will find someone who can help" said Aro, reassuringly.

"You sound strong, how?" asked Ellendrii.

"I got buried in the sand during the storm and there are creatures down there. They thought I was dead and crawled into my mouth to drink but I ate them. You can eat too! We just need to bury ourselves in the sand and pretend to be dead and they all come running to us...or uhh...crawling. Slithering?"

"I'm too weak to do that" said Ellendrii. "Aro, I'm not sure that I can continue."

"No, you must continue! We have to keep going! Besides, there is something in the distance that might be the end of the desert. I saw it too. We need to get to there."

"But what if it's not, Aro? What if it's just a rocky ridge or something and there is more desert beyond it? I'm not strong enough to take that risk."

Aro growled in frustration.

"Look, you are NOT giving up! I'LL go and hunt. You sit there and don't die." He stalked off a little way away and started to dig.

Ellendrii was a bit taken aback. He did as he was told and stayed in position, sitting in the hot sun and feeling on his last legs.

Aro dug down deeply and covered himself over with sand afterwards. It was quiet for a long time. The sand shifted every so often as Aro fought to breathe or killed anything that came up to him. Ellendrii felt his eyes closing and he lay down in the sand and rested his head on his hands. He sighed. He was so tired. He had found Aro. That was it now. Aro must continue. He would give him the Gryphie stone when he returned.

Ellendrii had given up.

After a while, Aro returned with four of the plump hunters from under the sand in his mouth, all dead. He dropped them in front of his unconscious friend and nudged him awake.

Ellendrii looked up.

"Eat" growled Aro.

Ellendrii looked at the food but made no move to eat it.

"EAT!!" roared Aro, sick of this now. He would NOT let Ellendrii just give up when food was there in front of him. All was not lost yet!

Ellendrii winced but still made no move to eat the food.

Aro growled in frustration, picked up one of the burrowing creatures and shoved it at Ellendrii's snout, all the while demanding that he ate it. If Ellendrii wouldn't eat by himself, Aro would have to make him eat.

"What, you want me to chew it for you too? Because I will!" growled Aro.

Finally, Ellendrii sat up and put a hand out.

"Give it to me, I'll eat. Stop nagging me. But if we find nothing but desert out there then I will give up and you won't stop me. I've had enough. I'm too tired, Aro. I wanted to find you, at first to carry on but after a while I realized I needed to give you the Gryphie stone so you can carry on for me."

"Shut up and eat, grikhead!" snapped Aro rudely.

Ellendrii did as he was told. Aro sat there and watched him eat all four of the meal creatures. They were odd, plump, wormlike things but neither of the friends cared that they were probably eating bugs at this point, nor did it really occur to them. It was food and drink and it was helping them to live.

In Aro's eyes, the only way to make Ellendrii carry on and restore his faith in living was to bully him into it the Lizariaous way. In reality, Aro was very scared for his friend and lashing out like this was the only way he could think of to react. He *needed* Ellendrii to eat and carry on. And the state of Ellendrii's body; that scared Aro even more. He had no idea if he looked the same, not having something that would show his reflection.

Aro sat and watched over Ellendrii as his strength slowly came back to him. Aro went out and hunted more for them both and made Ellendrii eat again.

The sun set.

Aro hunted.

Ellendrii ate.

Aro ate.

Aro hunted more.

They ate.

They slept.

The sun rose.

They awoke.

Ellendrii sat up and stretched and winced because it hurt his wing. Aro was already awake.

"Ready to travel again, El?" asked Aro, all trace of the bullying from previously, gone.

"Yes" was the one word reply and Ellendrii stood. He checked the Gryphie stone and they headed towards the things in the distance. Ellendrii didn't say much. He was grateful to Aro but at the same time felt extremely guilty about the fact he had been perfectly willing to give up. After all this. After all they'd been through. And Aro had pulled him out of it. He didn't know what to say to his friend to thank him. Would anything even be enough to show his gratitude? That was the second time Aro had saved him now.

Ellendrii felt bad. This whole thing had been his idea but without the strength and stubbornness of the Lizariaous, he would never have been able to complete this journey; he would have died back in the Forest of Foreboding at the teeth of a Narg'tok. And he had been *so* sure of himself before he set out, trying to dissuade Aro from accompanying him.

He would never, ever do that again.

Aro didn't need thanks; he knew Ellendrii was grateful. The fact that Ellendrii had got back up and they were headed on their way was good enough for Aro. He had got him going again and that was all that mattered.

They didn't speak as they headed on their way. Both of them felt stronger now. They were used to their stomachs being empty or near empty and having that familiar pang of hunger but now they both felt satisfied and able to continue.

With the guidance of the Gryphie stone, the pair made their way to the shapes in the distance, which unfortunately turned out to be more mountains.

"Oh no" moaned Aro, sitting down, "Not this again!" He stared up at them as they stretched far above his head.

"No Aro, I don't think so" replied Ellendrii. Aro looked round.

"The Gryphie stone doesn't want us to go over them. It wants us to go *through* them" he said. Aro walked around a piece of rock that jutted out and joined Ellendrii at the entrance to a cave that had previously been obscured by said piece of rock and there the Gryphie stone pointed the way; into a cave.

The pair of them stared into the darkness.

"Well?" said Ellendrii. "Let's go then!"

They headed inside. It all seemed dark. There was a long passage before them that seemed to go nowhere else but straight ahead so that is the direction they headed in now. They had to duck in places but they continued on, not knowing where this would lead. Aro felt at home. It was good to be in the dark, dampness of a cave and out of the heat and dryness of the desert. No more dust and sand for them! Chances are, this cave would also contain another much needed thing; water!

Chapter 28
The Cavern

They headed along the tunnel. The roof of it soon got higher and they could walk without ducking their heads. Now that they were out of the sun, they felt more alive and seemed to find more energy within themselves so neither of them loped along with their heads down. This place was a much needed and much welcomed change to the desert.

The roof got higher and higher and the tunnel opened out into a vast cavern full of glowing crystals. The ceiling reached high up into the darkness. Some of the dark was obliterated by the crystals and the rest reached up higher than the glow could fill.

The pair of them just stood and marvelled at this new place.

"Wow…it's beautiful!" breathed Ellendrii, "I wish I could fly up and investigate" he added, mournfully.

"Yeah but there might be something horrible up there that attacks you. Just cos it looks nice doesn't mean it's all good" said Aro.

"True, but we could do with a break from the bad, surely? I mean, this sort of environment is a much easier thing to travel through than the snow, desert or much of the rest of the things we've seen over the last lunar. Cos I'm pretty sure we were in that desert for the best part of a lunar."

"Na, you think time goes so fast. I bet we weren't. Maybe half a lunar but no more than that" argued Aro.

"So you have a better concept of time than a Gryphie?" asked Ellendrii, half joking.

"I'm just saying" replied Aro. The subject was dropped and they headed into this great cavern.

It was a beautiful and mysterious place, full of things they could never have imagined existed. The glowing crystals were one thing, although they had seen similar to these in other places. But the huge mushrooms and other fungi that grew from floor to ceiling in the cave were magnificent! They also glowed in colours and there were whites, purples, blues and pinks. Aro stood under one and just stared at it, with his mouth hanging open in awe.

The walls of this cavern were full of life. Green plants grew here and there and little bugs and creatures clambered around and hopped nimbly from leaf to leaf. There was a strange blue-green moss, which also gave off a faint glow and the floor was smooth with a few pointed rocks here and there at the edges of the paths. Small creatures flitted about near the ceiling and sat on the tops of the mushrooms, looking at the pair of travellers curiously and there was a fresh smell of life and water.

Ellendrii and Aro continued on their way, being lead by the Gryphie stone. These caverns were vast and they suspected they must have covered the entire range of rocky mountains that the pair of them had approached outside.

Aro breathed in deeply.

"This is more like it!" he said. The moistness of the air had cleared his throat somewhat and he no longer felt or sounded as hoarse as he had outside.

"I think this will do us both good. We need to feed and rest here; a proper rest and proper sleep" said Ellendrii. Aro nodded.

They soon came to an underground river and stopped beside it to rest. Ellendrii unbound his hands and feet and washed them in the water. Aro took a dunk right in to get all the dust off him. Normally he didn't mind being dirty, but his scales felt dry and uncomfortable so he wanted to wash in the water himself. The river was deep enough that his feet didn't touch the bottom but not so deep that he would drown. It flowed gently.

Ellendrii soon joined him but he had not unbound his wing. It still hurt too much to move and he figured if it was bound, it would restrict his movement and hopefully heal faster. The pair of them swam around in the water, enjoying the freshness of it and laughing together. Ellendrii floated on his back and stared up at the ceiling. Little crystals in the ceiling glowed here and there and lit up the whole place. It was like looking at stars in the sky and Ellendrii loved it.

Aro didn't pay that much attention to it; he was too busy chasing some fish or something under the water. He bumped into Ellendrii and Ellendrii splashed him in retaliation.

"Hey!" yelled Aro and splashed Ellendrii back. Which of course turned into a water war!

After a while, they were tired again and they both climbed out to sit down and rest.

"Well this makes a nice change. It's about time we found somewhere, you know, NICE for a change" said Aro. Ellendrii nodded.

"We should be able to find things to eat here and this water is fresh and good to drink" he replied.

"It's so nice in here. I hope there's nothing dangerous around" said Aro.

"Well I wouldn't try eating those glowing mushrooms, just in case" warned Ellendrii.

"As if I would!" retorted Aro. Ellendrii just laughed.

"All the little creatures around here though" observed Ellendrii, pointing. "It's full of life."

"Of course it is, because they can't live outside" said Aro.

"True; they would never survive out there. We nearly didn't." Ellendrii paused. "Aro, I want to thank you...for... you know, back in the desert? I would never have made it if it wasn't for you" said Ellendrii quietly. Even though he felt awkward and guilty, he couldn't *not* thank Aro for saving his life yet again.

"It's ok" replied Aro, casually brushing it off. He knew how Ellendrii felt. He also knew Ellendrii would do the same for him.

Ellendrii nodded and felt better about the whole thing. He just wanted to let his friend know his gratitude.

The pair of them felt much safer in the cavern and fished about in the water for something to eat. Ellendrii saved some fish to one side for later.

"Do we *have* to stockpile fish? I'm really bored with it. There must be something not quite as...moist that we can put in the bag instead. It's starting to smell of fish" said Aro.

"I would've thought you would be the last to complain about how something smelled" replied Ellendrii, but he had to agree that he was a bit sick of fish as well.

"I'm only stockpiling it in case we don't find anything else that's good to eat. If we do, then we can store that in the bag instead and eat the fish" Ellendrii explained. Aro thought this was a good enough idea and went with it.

After a while, they moved away from the river and carried on. They had about six fish in the bag to keep them going on their journey and they had refilled the last remaining gourd. Most of all, they were happy to have found water again. They had drank more than their fill of water at the river, afraid that they would end up short. After drinking as much as they could, they filled the gourd and placed it back in the bag.

Of course, having drunk so much water, they made their way more slowly than they had been, feeling full of water and fish. This didn't bother either of them that much though; they were just grateful for the nourishment.

Leaving the river, they headed through another tunnel. This one was narrow but not as narrow as the one they had come in by. It was lined again with glowing crystals and the pair of them felt happy and cosy in here, even though it was damp and cool. Ellendrii was glad of the crystals, otherwise he would've had to use his fire to light the way and he doubted keeping it alight in this moist air would really work. Also, they had nothing to burn as a torch.

"I really like this place" said Aro, looking around as they walked.

"Yeah, it's nice. I've never seen a cave like this before. The mushrooms are huge! I've never seen such interesting plant life. I wonder if any of it could be used for healing. I'm sure Lunara would be interested in the properties of some of these plants. Do you think it would be a good idea to take some of them back to Shernaron, like samples or something? That could maybe be seeded and then we could grow them as well?" asked Ellendrii.

Aro wasn't that interested in plants but he pretended to show interest anyway, for the sake of his friend.

"Well yeah we could take some back. But what if they grow and we can't control them and they take up all of Shernaron or run wild or kill your native plants?" he pointed out.

"Why do you always have to make things have a nasty edge?" asked Ellendrii.

"I'm a Lizariaous" replied Aro, rolling his eyes. Honestly.

But Ellendrii decided to take some samples anyway. They may not even be alive when the pair of them made it back home; *if* the pair of them made it back home. At the very least, they would be dried samples and could be used for something.

So, Ellendrii picked a few of the smaller mushrooms that grew around and took some of the moss as well. This tunnel they were in now was full of tiny, glowing mushrooms. It appeared that the larger the space was, the larger the mushrooms grew. This tunnel had a fairly low ceiling, although not so low that they had to duck. But the cavern they had been in previously had been huge and vast and the mushrooms were as well.

They entered into another cavern. This wasn't quite as tall and it was smaller too. The whole thing was lit by the glowing crystals and mushrooms and they could see right up to the ceiling, not a single spot was hidden in shadow. Tiny lizards clambered around on the ceiling, looking curiously down at the pair of newcomers.

Aro looked up at them.

"I wonder if they would be good to eat" he pondered.

"We've just eaten" said Ellendrii.

"Yeah but I mean, we could fit lots of those into the bag because they are small" suggested Aro.

"True, but how will we get them? They appear to only be up higher than we can reach." He neglected to mention the obvious; that he could no longer fly.

"We can bait them" said Aro. "Get a fish out of your bag and we'll see if we can lure them down with it."

"What, and wait right by it? They won't come down with us here." Ellendrii pointed out.

"Well in that case we'll have to set a trap for them. Or throw something over them when they come and get the fish" said Aro.

"We've got nothing we can throw on them though. In case you forgot, I traded those large leaves we had" said Ellendrii.

Aro pondered. What could they throw on the lizards if they came down to get the fish?

Then he had another idea.

"I know! I could dig a hole in the floor and then cover it with something, put the fish on top and then when the lizards come down, they will fall through it and be trapped!" Aro said, grinning.

Ellendrii sighed.

"Ok, for one, I don't think destroying a part of this cavern for our own means is a good idea. For another, the lizards are light, they wouldn't fall through the covering. And for a third, they can climb up walls and they would just climb out of the hole, probably before we got there. So your plan wouldn't work. Let's just keep going, shall we? We have some food. We might find something more reachable as we travel."

Aro grunted.

"Fine. Ok then. I really wish you could fly up and get them."

"Well I can't, so let's just drop the subject, shall we?" Ellendrii replied, maybe a little too snappily. Aro quietened down and they carried on.

After some time of wandering, they came to a huge, vast cavern that seemed to go on for ages. It was full of the huge mushrooms, they sprang up like a forest. Ellendrii stood, looking up at them, longing to fly up and investigate what was on top of them. He could see small creatures running around up there and desperately wanted to see what they were.

As they wandered among the mushroom forest in one part of the cavern, Aro yawned a little.

"Hey, El, maybe this would be a good place to rest? We haven't rested properly and slept since we got here so maybe this would be a good spot?" he suggested.

Ellendrii agreed and they sat down. Neither of them were hungry or thirsty, having stuffed themselves earlier, so they just sat and chatted.

"How's your wing?" ventured Aro.

"It's ok. It doesn't hurt but that's only because I can't move it. I might take the bindings off it next sun and see how it's doing. The bindings have been on it for a while now. It might have healed but I wanted to give it a while longer. One more moon cycle. Rest heals."

"Yeah I'm sure it'll be fine when you unbind it" said Aro. He really hoped his friend's wing would be ok. And not just so Ellendrii could fly up and catch some of those lizards.

Honest.

"I wonder what's beyond here. I wish that stone of yours would tell us how far we have to go still before we get there" said Aro.

"Weirdly enough, the stone's glow has been getting brighter as we've been travelling. When we first found it, the glow was not as bright as it is now. So maybe that's an indication to how close we are to the SilvaGryphie. Who knows, maybe she is the other side of these caverns?"

"We can always hope" replied Aro.

They sat, looking up at the glowing undersides of the mushrooms. It all seemed so relaxing. It also smelled musty but not in a bad way. In a nostalgic way that made them think of seasons past and when they were growing up.

It made Ellendrii think back to when he met Aro.

Ellendrii was just a young kitten and although his parents and Aro's parents were friends, the two youngsters had not yet met. In fact they didn't meet until they were some seasons old. Diabloss would go and visit Mordred and Schaarl regularly, to check up on how things were going in Dyarkroeen and it had been quite a while after the war before either pair had their own young. They wanted to be sure the war and troublemakers regarding the war that were left over as supporters of Zephirak had all been sorted out and there was no fear of it all starting back up again due to whatever support still remained of him. Luckily there weren't many anyway. The few supporters he had were dissolved into the rest of the pack and there were too few of them to start anything. The rest of the pack had only followed Zephirak because he had been the leader. Now Mordred was the leader, they did, by law, follow him without question.

Diabloss and Mordred decided to let Aro and Ellendrii meet one sun cycle. Aro's sisters weren't interested in meeting Ellendrii but the parents thought that their sons had the potential to be friends and help strengthen the unity of the two species.

Before they met, Aro and Ellendrii had only seen adults of the opposing species and never someone their own age. The meeting was certainly interesting.

Aro came to the Forest with his father. Ellendrii was small and couldn't even fly yet.

"Ellendrii," said Diabloss, "This is Aro, the son of Mordred and Schaarl; our friends."

Ellendrii crept out from Leida's feet where he had been sat. Leida had brought him down from their tree and he had sat quietly between her feet as she sat and waited for Diabloss and Mordred. Ellendrii was a quiet kitten, he had not yet made any other friends his own age because he was shy and because he was also very young. Gryphies normally made friends in flight school and he had not yet been to flight school since his father would be teaching him at first.

Aro bounded right up to the little Gryphie. He was so young that he only had two needles on his back and they were short.

"Hia!" he said, smiling. "I'm Aro!"

Ellendrii stopped when he saw Aro bounding up so confidently.

"I'm Ellendrii" he replied. He had only come forward because Leida had told him to do so when Aro arrived; because it was polite to be forthcoming and welcoming. Ellendrii hadn't really wanted to but he didn't want his mother to be disappointed with him so he had done as he was told.

"Nice to meet you!" said Aro, bounding round and round Ellendrii, who had plonked himself down on his rump once he found he was unable to keep track with Aro's energy. He had been turning around as Aro bounded round him. Now he just sat, a little overwhelmed.

"Ellendrii" said Leida, "Why don't you show Aro our tree?"

"Umm, ok" replied Ellendrii and lead Aro to their tree.

"This is where we live" said Ellendrii.

"Cool! I live in a cave! Do you sleep up there? How do you get up there?" asked Aro, firing out the questions.

"We climb. There isn't enough room to fly because the trees are close together. I can't fly though, I'm too young but I will learn" said Ellendrii, which was impressive considering how shy he was.

"Do you want to fly?" asked Aro.

"I don't know" said Ellendrii, "Because I don't know what it's like. When I know what it's like, then I will decide."

"Cool!" said Aro, "Show me how to climb up then!" He looked up at the tree.

Ellendrii complied and easily climbed up the tree and onto the lowest branch. He wasn't allowed up too high in case he fell and if he wanted to go higher, he would sit on Leida or Diabloss' back and go up that way. The sleeping chamber was near the top of the tree so when it was time to sleep, they would carry him up.

Aro stood on his back legs with his front legs scrabbling up the tree trunk but of course he couldn't climb up. His anatomy and weight wouldn't allow him to climb nimbly like a Gryphie. He sat down and looked up at Ellendrii.

"Ok, let's go exploring!" He called up. "I love exploring! How far away from your parents can you go?"

"Not far" came Ellendrii's little voice. He climbed down to join Aro.

"Oh, I'm allowed quite far from mine, so long as they can still see me!" said Aro, brightly.

"I like to stay close to mine" said Ellendrii.

"Aww, we can't do anything fun unless we go further away and get out and explore" replied Aro.

"Yes we can, we can play games like Which One?" explained Ellendrii.

"What's that?" asked Aro.

"It's a game where one of you has a small item and they hide it from the other, under one of their hands or feet and the other has to guess which hand or foot it's under. I play it with Mum" said Ellendrii.

"Ohh...I just play fight with Dad. I need to learn how to fight and stay on top of the pack. I might even be leader one sun cycle!" Aro said excitedly. "But we'll play your game, cos I've never played a game like that before."

"Ok, let me find something to hide first" said Ellendrii and ran to the tree to get a small object that they might play with.

The parents looked on. They had been watching.

"Well, I think they will be good friends" said Diabloss.

"I agree" nodded Mordred and they all smiled at the antics of the youngsters.

Ellendrii's memories flashed back to the present. He looked at Aro, who had fallen asleep. Ellendrii smiled. He remembered that Aro had really brought him out of himself; not that it really helped him make any more friends of his own kind and maybe Aro was a bit to blame because he was loud and boisterous and outspoken at times but Ellendrii figured that if the other Gryphies couldn't handle that then it was their loss. He liked Aro, Aro was a good friend and species made no difference. A friend is a friend; it doesn't matter what they look like, only how they act and how good a friend they are.

Ellendrii settled down and closed his eyes. His thoughts drifted to dreams and he dreamed about being back home and exploring Shernaron with Aro.

They awoke some time later. Of course, they didn't know if it was sun cycle or moon cycle but they were well rested and ready to carry on. Aro awoke first and was wandering around, checking things out and as usual, being nosy and exploring. He was also keeping an eye out for danger, because of course you never know what might be lurking around, especially on a journey like this. But other than little creatures here and there and the usual things that this area seemed to contain; there was nothing out of the ordinary.

"Ah, you're awake!" said Aro. "I didn't want to wake you in case you needed more sleep. So I thought I'd look around a bit."

"Yeah that's fine. Find anything?" asked Ellendrii.

"Nope, not really. Just more mushrooms and moss. We'll look for some more water if we can. It'll save the gourd."

"Good idea. You didn't find any while you were exploring?"

"I didn't want to wander too far away in case you woke up and didn't know where I was."

"Thanks. Well, let's head on then. The Gryphie stone says we need to keep going through the mushrooms" said Ellendrii, getting up.

They set off again, following the Gryphie stone. Neither of them ate; they weren't hungry yet so they didn't push it. They wouldn't eat unless they were hungry, there wasn't any point in eating needlessly.

The mushroom forest went on for a long while. They could hear things skittering and scrambling above them and they both dearly wanted to know what it was. Mostly because the last time they had heard anything like this was in the Forest of Foreboding and it unnerved them to not know what it was.

In the end, Ellendrii decided to try and climb up and see. He could shimmy up the stalk of the mushroom easily enough but climbing out and around the cap of it was more difficult. In the end he got himself high enough up the stalk that he could jump onto the top of a shorter mushroom nearby. He found this much harder to do with only one useable wing. He used his wings for balance when he jumped so it was easy to understand that he struggled.

Aro wished he could climb. He called up from below.

"What do you see?" he asked.

"Not much, just the tops of mushrooms. But it is like a whole other world up here. I can see all these little creatures running around across the tops of them."

"See any of those lizards? Can you catch a few?" yelled up Aro.

Ellendrii sighed.

"Yeah I see some. I'll try my best" he called down and went about trying to catch a lizard for Aro.

The lizards were small and they were mostly green with purple extremities. Purple legs and tails and snouts. They were very fast too and Ellendrii struggled to catch one. In the end he lost patience with trying to grab them and just flamed a few. They fell off, charred, into his hands and he chucked them down to Aro.

"Mmm! Crispy!" called up Aro from down below.

Ellendrii tried one himself. They were so small that even a slight flaming cooked them good and proper and it would have been near impossible to kill them and keep them raw by flaming.

Ellendrii climbed back down.

"Ok, let's go. You got your lizards and I put some in the bag too, for if we need them another time. They should keep a bit longer if they are cooked."

"Awesome, thanks!" smiled Aro.

They came to the end of the mushroom forest and out into the vast cavern again. They could technically have gone around the mushrooms but they both wanted to go through them because it just seemed more fun and a different experience.

They could hear creatures here and there making little noises and the noises echoing around the cavern. It was strange to hear all the echoes.

"I wonder if these glowing crystals are worth anything or are useful for anything, other than looking pretty" pondered Ellendrii.

"You could always put some in the bag to take back" suggested Aro.

"Yeah I think I'll do that but only a couple. I don't want the bag getting too heavy."

"I can carry it if it gets too heavy" said Aro.

"Yeah but you might lose it like the gourd you had around your neck."

"Hey, I lost that in the sand storm. Besides, it was empty anyway."

"Yeah but we can't afford to lose any more things. I've kept this bag on me even though we've been through storms and things have attacked us. *I'll* look after it."

"Ok, ok, I was just trying to help" mooched Aro.

"I understand" replied Ellendrii, "And I appreciate it but I want to look after the bag, just in case. If I lose it, it will be my own fault."

"And I can laugh at you and rub it in" replied Aro brightly.

"Yes" replied Ellendrii, frowning. Aro laughed.

Carrying on, they followed their ears and found the river again so they stopped for a drink. Ellendrii sat next to the river and looked at his reflection. Now he could see for himself how thin his own body had become. He looked rather haggard. Still, he matched Aro, he supposed. He spied the binding on his wing and decided that now was the time to remove it. It had been on for quite a while now. He had planned to remove it when they woke up but had forgotten, so he felt now was a good time. He could wash it too and check to see if there was a wound there. He gently untied the binding and unwrapped it from his wing. He kept it round his body just in case he needed to do it up again. It was much easier to do it this way instead of fighting with it again. Loosening it, he tried to move his wing. He winced and saw that the joint was still out of his socket. It confused him. He didn't understand what was wrong or what had happened because he'd never been told about joints and sockets and this was all new to him. He'd only ever been taught what to do with breaks, strains or wounds.

If he had strained it, surely it would be healed by now or feel better but it didn't. The joint felt loose and looking at his shoulder, he saw the shape of where the wing arm met his body looked wrong.

Aro came bounding up through the shallow water and splashed him. Ellendrii didn't join in with the game though; he carried on looking at his wing and trying to work out what was wrong. Aro splashed him again and Ellendrii gave a warning growl that told him to stop without even looking at him. Aro stopped and came to see what was wrong.

"Hey El, you ok?" he asked.

"Not really. I can't work out what's wrong with my wing. It's not strained, sprained or wounded. I can't move it. It might be broken I guess. I really hope not. If it's broken, I won't be able to fly for the rest of this journey. A break takes over a lunar to heal and I don't have enough herbs for that or even a proper dressing. This binding is only temporary. I don't have any more twine, or at least not enough to make a new binding with if this one needs replacing. I don't know what to do, Aro."

"Let me have a look at it" said Aro, moving closer and examining the damage.

"Ah!" he exclaimed.

"What?" asked Ellendrii, worried that something was wrong.

"I know how to fix this. Lizariaouses get this quite a bit when they've been fighting or sometimes if they spend too long digging or have an accident while they work. You've popped the joint out of the socket. If you want it fixed, it won't fix itself. I can fix it but it will hurt you. Do you think you can handle some pain?"

"Well, how much will it hurt?" asked Ellendrii, warily.

"Quite a bit but not for long. If you keep still and don't try to tense up too much. I can pop it back in but you have to be patient and try to be calm about it. If you move while I'm doing it, it will take longer. Stay still and I'll be able to get it back in first time."

"Ok, I can try. I'll do my best" Ellendrii felt nervous. What if it went wrong? What if Aro made it worse? He trusted his friend but his wings were his most prized possession and if Aro managed to make the damage worse, Ellendrii feared he would never fly again.

"You just gotta trust me. You *do* trust me, right?" asked Aro.

"Yes I do" said Ellendrii. "Have you done this before?" he asked.

"Oh yeah, loads of times" Aro lied. He'd never done it before. But he wasn't about to tell Ellendrii that.

"Ok, then I'll let you do it" said Ellendrii and offered Aro the damaged wing.

"Ok, keep still while I do this" said Aro. Ellendrii complied but he looked very worried and nervous all the same.

Aro examined the damage and felt around with his paws to see where the socket and the ball of the joint were.

"Ok, when I push on you, push against me, no matter how much it hurts. I'm going to push the joint back in. If you push against me then it will pop back into place. If you don't, then it will hurt more. Are you ready?"

"Yeah, I'm ready" replied Ellendrii, tensing himself a little.

"Ok" said Aro and put his paw against the affected area. He found the ball of the joint and then quick as a flash, shoved it back in the socket. It made a pop sound and clicked back into place. Ellendrii screamed with surprise and pain at the sensation and then shied away from Aro but luckily Aro had already fixed it. Ellendrii lay on the ground, panting and shivering with his eyes tightly shut and his teeth gritted.

Aro sat and watched him.

"It's ok, it's done now" he said. Ellendrii nodded but he couldn't move just yet. He wanted the burning sensation to go.

After a while, he sat up and tried to move the wing. He could move it again although it hurt but he could now fold it against his body and hold it off the ground, when before he couldn't even move it.

"It'll get better. Now it's back in, the pain will go. But you left it out for a long time so be careful when you fly next and take it slowly" advised Aro. Ellendrii nodded.

"Thank you so much, Aro. I'm indebted to you. Even more so now." Ellendrii felt bad. Aro had saved his life twice and saved his wing too; and thus his flying, which was most important to him and what had he done in return?? According to Ellendrii, nothing. Well, maybe helping Aro escape the Wind Hounds.

"Ah it's nothing" said Aro, brushing it off with a shrug and a dismissive wave of his paw.

"Well, thank you anyway" said Ellendrii. Aro smiled.

"So, which way is that stone telling us to go now?" he asked.

Ellendrii checked it and it was telling them to go just to the left. So that was the way they went. Ellendrii had put the twine back in his bag in case they needed it again for anything.

They finally left the huge cavern and went into another tunnel. This one lead to a very strange place. Again, everything was lit with the glowing crystals. Aro had dug up three small ones to take with them in the bag in case they would come in handy later and as they headed down the tunnel, they heard a strange sound coming from the direction they were headed in. It sounded like a wailing.

"Oh great, there's something down there" said Aro. So long as it wasn't a Repulsator shuddering, it would be fine. Luckily Repulsators only haunt abandoned buildings but Aro and Ellendrii didn't know that. But it didn't sound like a Repulsator. Was it something in pain?

At the end of the tunnel they came to a small courtyard style chamber. The whole thing was surrounded by many different tunnels leading off of it like a catacomb.

"It's a good thing we have the Gryphie stone or we'd get lost in here" said Aro.

"Wait, you were questioning how we could trust it a while ago" said Ellendrii.

"Yeah but it's better than nothing" admitted Aro. Ellendrii nodded confidently.

The moaning sound filled this chamber and echoed all around it. It creeped the two travellers out and they wanted to get out of this area as fast as possible so they followed the direction the Gryphie stone pointed them in and hurried down the tunnel it lead them down. The moaning was louder though and seemed to fill the very air they breathed. It was everywhere; they couldn't even pinpoint one area. It chilled them to the bone and they continued on their way shivering. The tunnel was so pretty and pleasant with its glowing crystals and moss but the atmosphere was clouded with the moaning. The longer it went on though; the more the pair of them got used to it and thought less about it.

"What do you think it is?" asked Aro, calming down after a while of nothing bad happening or attacking them.

"I don't know but whatever it is, it must be in one of the other tunnels. At least our path is lit. We must continue to just head the way of the Gryphie stone and try not to think too much about it."

"But what if we encounter it?"

"Well, it sounds like it's in pain whatever it is, so in that case it's not going to be a threat. Even if it is a threat, if it's in pain it can't hurt us because it would mean that whatever it is is damaged in some way and so can't attack us."

"I hope you're right, El."

"So do I, Aro. So do I."

They carried on, having no choice but to continue and hope that the stone would lead them somewhere else more pleasant instead. But of course it didn't. The moaning just got louder, which indicated that they were probably getting closer to whatever it was, although it was hard to tell because the sound echoed everywhere so much. It echoed down all the tunnels they went in. And they were travelling through quite a few.

After the chamber, they went down one of the tunnels from it but others branched off these and lead to other tunnels, which others branched off. It was like they were in a warren but instead of being underground, it was in caves. The walls were rocky and they were still picked out by the glowing crystals.

Until that is, the crystals got less and less. And less. And soon, there were none.

Ellendrii and Aro stopped in their tracks and looked down the tunnel they were in. They had noticed the crystals getting scarcer and had hoped with all their hearts that this wouldn't happen. Maybe they would have been lead into a tunnel where crystals were plentiful? But, having no other choice than to follow the path of the Gryphie stone lest they get completely lost, they continued on. They had even passed other tunnels that they looked down and were alive with crystals and they had wanted to go down those instead. Aro even suggested that maybe if they went down one of those, maybe the stone would lead them on another path but

Ellendrii said this was too big a risk to take since then they might get completely lost.

Still, nevertheless, Aro had persuaded him to walk down one a little way and see what the stone did. But it merely pointed back the way Ellendrii had come and continued to do so until he had turned around and gone back out of the tunnel.

"What do we do? We can't just wander down there without seeing the way? How will we know where the tunnels are to go down? The Gryphie stone glows and it is pretty bright but it's not bright enough to light our way" said Aro, with a worried look.

"Don't worry" replied Ellendrii. "Remember we picked up some crystals? I'll carry one and it will light our way. This tunnel is plenty high enough for me to stand on two legs and walk and hold the crystal at the same time. And then when we come to tunnels leading off here, we can check the Gryphie stone to see if that's the way we go." He rifled around in the bag and took out the largest of the three small crystals. It had a good glow to it and it would do well enough to light their way as they continued.

They walked for a while more, all the while the moaning haunting them.

"I hope we get out of here soon. I hate this" said Aro.

"Yeah, you and me both" muttered Ellendrii. "At least we have this crystal to light our way." They had already turned down about four different tunnels. Ellendrii wondered who had built this place. Had it been dug out of the rock? Was it put here to confuse those who were looking for the SilvaGryphie? Had she herself made this place so that she wouldn't be found by those who wanted to worship her? Or was it just here for the hell of it, to get on creatures' nerves as they tried to travel through it. Ellendrii didn't know. And was the moaning from a creature or simply a natural sound of wind whistling down the tunnels from outside? He felt that he could feel a very faint breeze down some of the tunnels they travelled through. He wondered if they were getting near to the exit of the caverns.

It was a shame because the caverns themselves had been so beautiful and unusual. These tunnels were getting very frustrating.

"We must be near the end of them soon" said Aro. "I mean, how long are they going to be?"

"I dunno. Maybe they are confusing the Gryphie stone and we're going round in circles? I dunno, some of them must be doubling back on themselves. Does the stone know this? Is it actually just leading us round and round now with no way of getting anywhere?"

"Oh, well that's great" replied Aro sarcastically. "So we'll never get out of here; we'll just go round and round till we go mad or something. Or get tired and can't go on anymore."

"We mustn't rest. I want to get out of here before we do" said Ellendrii.

"Well, so do I" replied Aro. "I don't want to be stuck in here any more than you do. All I hear is that awful moaning. I can't even hear the sounds of the little creatures from the cavern. When we first came into these tunnels, we could still hear them."

"I know. Maybe the moaning has scared them all off. I feel nothing living here anymore. Even the moss, have you noticed? There is no moss growing anymore. No small mushrooms, nothing. Only dark passages and that horrible moaning noise."

"Do you think if we had chosen a different tunnel in that chamber with all those tunnel entrances in that we might have ended up somewhere nicer? I've got a horrible feeling things are going to turn bad again" said Aro with a worried sound to his voice.

"We had no choice. We *had* to take this one, it's the one the Gryphie stone told us to take! I can't help what we find here any more than you can. If we'd chosen a different one and gone against what path the stone gave us, then we would have got lost."

"No we wouldn't. We would probably have found the right path in another place at another time and maybe less of this moaning and a path that's still lit for us. If as you said, the

Gryphie stone is getting confused then it would have made no difference if we'd chosen a different tunnel to begin with."

"Aro, it doesn't matter. We can't go back and rechoose and we would never even have thought of doing something like that at the time so there's no point dwelling on it. We just have to carry on going the way we're going and hope that we're not going round in circles. I don't think we are though. If we were going in circles, we would have met up with a tunnel that had crystals or moss in and so far once they had finished, we've found no more tunnels with them in so we must be going the right way and not in circles. All these tunnels are new. I'd leave a trail if I could but I can't because I don't have enough in the bag to waste" said Ellendrii.

"I could always leave a pee trail" suggested Aro.

"No. Just...no." replied Ellendrii and that was that for Aro's great ideas.

They carried on wandering through the labyrinthine tunnels. After a while, neither of them spoke but then the moaning got too much so they started up an idle conversation again.

It was then that their noses picked up a horrible smell.

Chapter 29
Boneyard

Aro sniffed the air and grimaced. It was a bit too much even for him.

"What *is* that? Do you smell that??" he asked Ellendrii.

"I'm trying not to" replied his friend.

The glowing crystal lit their way as well as the ever strengthening glow from the Gryphie stone but the pair of them didn't feel any better about their current situation. The smell was getting worse as they headed down the tunnel they were in.

"Maybe we'll turn off this tunnel?" suggested Ellendrii.

"I hope we will" muttered Aro. He was secretly worried about that king Repulsator with its conjoined heads and hideous shuddering noise. Still, he hadn't heard shuddering so he felt a little more at ease at least. But that didn't make the smell any better.

"Let's move a bit faster" said Ellendrii, "I want to get out of this stinky area quickly."

Aro agreed this was a good idea and they got a move on.

The smell did get worse but the tunnels started to get wider now. The pair of them seemed to think that this was a sign of the whole thing coming to an end and getting out the other side. Neither of them were that happy to be in the shelter of this place anymore. The cave had been a nice place to rest and drink but these tunnels were horrible and neither of them relished being here.

It was starting to feel a bit airier too, suggesting that there was an opening coming up. Whether the Gryphie stone would guide them out of it or just down another tunnel remained to be seen but they sincerely hoped that it would guide them out of this daunting and strange place with its odd moaning and horrible smell. Although to be fair, the moaning stopped once the smell got really bad. Ellendrii thought that maybe whatever made the moaning wouldn't go near the smell. But the moaning had trailed off into the distance a while back now. The smell was the stench of death and rot. It was the smell of danger and if either of them listened to their senses, they would have fled back the way they came and heeded their senses and noses.

But they kept going.

"I can't decide which is worse; that creepy moaning or the stench that's assaulting our nostrils right now" said Aro.

"You don't normally care about smells like this though" said Ellendrii.

"I do when they're *this* bad" replied Aro, pawing at his nose as they made their way swiftly down the tunnels. "It reminds me of the barren place we found after we left the lake. Only with just a smell and without the horrid red rain and craters."

"This smells like many things have died and been left to rot" said Ellendrii.

"What are we heading into now?" muttered Aro, feeling very worried. Ellendrii said nothing, just shook his head. He didn't know either.

Soon the pair of them saw light up ahead and felt a little brighter about their situation. They could smell fresh air and they were only too happy that the Gryphie stone was telling them to proceed.

"Maybe it won't smell so bad out there" said Aro, again being the first to point out the obvious and also complain about the smell.

"I'm sure it will be fine" replied Ellendrii, "Well, unless it's full of...dead...things..." he trailed off as they reached the mouth of the tunnel and just stopped, standing with his mouth agape and staring at what he saw before them. Aro walked up beside him and stopped as well, staring at what lay ahead.

Bones. Hundreds of them. Maybe even thousands of them. It was a killing ground. All sorts of different bones from all sorts of different creatures in all sorts of different sizes. None of which Ellendrii or Aro recognized as creatures they knew of course, but that was only at first glance.

"What *is* this place?" muttered Aro, both awed and horrified in equal parts.

"I have no idea. I've never seen anything like it. Look at all the bones! And yet I can't smell much. I guess the wind is blowing the smell away from us now. It's not nearly as strong as in that tunnel we just came out of."

"Thank grik" grumbled Aro.

Ellendrii just stared out over it all. The tunnel had opened out on a valley of the dead. The pair of them stood just up a little cliff. They would have to go down and make their way through the boneyard if the Gryphie stone was pointing them true. The cliffs either side were a similar rocky kind to most of them around here. The tops of these though were thinly covered with grass.

"What do you think happened?" asked Aro.

"I dunno. A mass dying? Something wiped out an entire race of…something? But then they wouldn't all be different. Maybe lots of different creatures lived in this valley and something wiped them all out. Maybe another burning mountain? A sickness? I dunno…"

"I don't like it" said Aro. "Is there another way around?"

"Nope, it's pointing down into the valley. We must go through it. Why are you making such a fuss? You should be used to this."

"Not like this. What if something killed all these creatures and it's still there? What then??"

"Then we will be extra careful to keep an eye out for it" replied Ellendrii.

"What if it's already seen us? What if it's watching us right now?"

"You're freaking out too much, I thought you were the brave one."

"I am. But a creature that's able to kill on this scale would put fear into even a Lizariaous."

"We don't know it was a creature that did this. It might have been a natural disaster or an illness. Don't jump to conclusions. We will make our way down there and just be careful and observant and keep an eye out for any signs of life or threat."

"Ok, we'll be extra careful then" agreed Aro.

"I just hope that if it was a sickness, that we won't catch it" Ellendrii said quietly.

"This is insane" muttered Aro; referring to the situation, the bones and pretty much everything else that was going through his mind right now.

The pair of them carefully made their way down the crumbling rocky cliff and towards the boneyard down below. Ellendrii did keep an eye out for the possibility of any paths that went along the valley walls that they could walk along instead of having to go through the bones but he could see nothing. The walls were steep and unclimbable.

They reached the first bones. Aro felt a little hungry; he couldn't deny it. The bones did look quite nice. But these ones also looked old as well. They were paled by the sun and faded. Some of them were cracked and brittle. Whatever happened here happened a long time ago. Possibly even seasons ago. The sun bleached bones were old.

"These are old" said Aro, stating the obvious but it just felt better to say it aloud.

"I noticed. Maybe whatever happened was a long time ago and there is no danger now." Ellendrii picked up one of the bones and snapped it easily. The snap echoed slightly.

"Shhh!! What if something hears us?" asked Aro.

"Good point. Try not to step on any bones" replied Ellendrii. Aro rolled his eyes.

They started out into the tangle of bones all around them. Some were huge rib cages and other large bones littered about. Some were tiny. A small, crushed skeleton lay to the side of the path they were walking along. Bones interrupted their journey every so often and they had to step over them.

And the skulls! Skulls of all shapes and sizes littered the ground around them. It was quite amazing to look at. They tried to see if any of them were recognizable but there didn't appear to be any that were familiar.

Back at home, Aro had tried to collect bones at one point. Each meal he had, he saved the bones and he was trying to accumulate a collection of them in the back of his cave. But every time he got hungry and couldn't be bothered to hunt, he found himself nibbling on the bones. So instead he changed it to a skull collection. That worked a little better but there was the problem of young Lizariaouses coming into his cave and stealing them while he was out.

One sun cycle he returned home and saw an unnatural amount of young Lizariaouses wearing cave cat skull helmets. And his skull collection was gone. He was not happy and ran around trying to get the wayward skulls back. The sneaky little kids wouldn't give them back, even going so far as to lie to him about where they found them. He pointed out to them that he knew they were his because he recognized them by smell. So then fights would break out. In Lizariaous society, you don't need proof that someone has stolen something; if you know it's yours, you can fight for it and take it back. The fact that these kids were younger than him made no difference. An adult would fight a kid to get something that he or she wanted. Such was Lizariaous way. Anyway, the long and the short of it was that Aro's skull collection didn't work out. He only managed to get back three skulls, which he fought for.

Any others; the thieves had been sneaky and snuck off with them.

Aro was reminded of his skull collection now. He wanted to take some back home and show them off but they would probably only end up getting stolen by those sneaky kids again. The only time a kid or another Lizariaous wouldn't steal from someone was if they feared them or of course if it was the leader of the pack. No one stole from Mordred! Kids tended to take liberties of course but even they drew the line at stealing from the leader. And things were only stolen if they were left in caves unattended. So mostly, the only things Lizariaouses kept in their caves were worthless things like bedding materials, if they used them. No one would steal that. Even if they were cold; because no one would admit to being cold. Admitting things like that was a sign of weakness.

Aro stepped on a bone and it cracked under his weight.

"Aro!!" snapped Ellendrii, as quietly as he could.

"Sorry! I didn't see it!" Aro was clumsy like that.

"Well be more careful, we don't know what's out there or around here for that matter.

Something could be hiding out in the skulls. We might get swarmed or something. What if it's a plague of little creatures that eat our flesh from our bones? Just be careful!"

"I really don't think it's that. Besides, you said yourself that these are old."

"No, you said that Aro."

"Oh yeah. Sorry. Everything is blurred."

"Have a drink then. Better yet, let's stop for a rest and something to eat and drink."

Ellendrii sat down in a bare patch on the ground and got out the gourd and a couple of cave lizards for them. The sun was high in the sky. Ellendrii was pretty sure they would get to the next stage of their journey before sunset and they wouldn't have to sleep here. He hadn't flown up to take a look ahead because his wing still hurt from popping it out of its socket and he didn't want to strain it just in case it wasn't properly healed yet.

Aro was glad of the food.

They sat in silence, eating and looking at their surroundings. Ellendrii noticed some birds sitting on the bones here and there and looking at them. He assumed it was for anything that might be left over. These were strange birds. They resembled a cross between a bird, a bat and a rat. Their faces had beaks and raven-like qualities. They had bat-like wings, bird bodies and rat tails and feet. They were covered in fur like a rat as well.

"Interesting. I've never seen these birds before but I've heard of them in stories. I think they have them around the Metal Mountains or out in that direction. They're called Dravens and they eat mostly carrion." Ellendrii observed.

"Well so long as they don't eat us, I'm all good with it" replied Aro with his mouth full of lizard.

"No, they only eat dead things and they don't hunt. We're safe."

"Good" was Aro's one word reply.

The Dravens wheeled lazily in the sky, flying down if they saw anything that might be worth eating on the ground. Ellendrii noticed that a lot of them headed off in the direction he and Aro were headed. There weren't so many sitting on these old bones but there were a fair amount of them heading elsewhere. Ellendrii wondered why; if there were fresher bones further along. He hoped not. These old bones weren't that scary but fresh, bloody ones, possibly with meat still on them would certainly be something to be worried about.

A Draven flew a little too close to Aro and he snapped at it. His jaws closed with a click and the bird squawked and flew away. It had been after his lizard.

Ellendrii had finished his lizard and drank his fill of water, again not drinking too much now they were unsure of where they would next find water. He stood on a large skull and looked out ahead of them. It was hard to see how long this boneyard went on for. He flexed his wing and felt the joint bending. It was ok, not too painful. He flexed his other wing and then flexed both of them. He pondered about flying. Suddenly there was a crunch and he found he had fallen through the brittle skull he was stood on. Aro laughed. Ellendrii shushed him and winced as he pulled his leg out of the skull.

"I KNEW that was going to happen!" laughed Aro. Ellendrii pulled a face.

"And you told *me* to be quiet!" Aro sniggered.

"Oh shut up!" replied Ellendrii and decided not to stand on any of the bones again.

They headed onward now.

"It's not too bad. At least we have the Dravens for company. It means that it might not have been a contagious sickness that wiped out these creatures" said Aro.

"Yeah and there are far too many different kinds of them for them to all be local to this area. So it wasn't a sickness. But if it was a hunter, that makes it even worse! We'll just have to hope the hunter isn't still around."

"It's probably not around. It's probably long gone. These are old bones. I don't think there's anything to worry about" replied Aro.

"You're confident suddenly" observed Ellendrii.

"Yeah, well, I don't smell danger. I think we'll be just fine." Aro smiled.

"I hope you're right" said Ellendrii.

They followed the path of the Gryphie stone while the Dravens squawked around them. The bird creatures didn't care much about the two travellers. They were only interested in anything that might be left on the bones. It did bother Ellendrii though. If these were old bones, surely the birds would know that. They wouldn't bother about bones that had been there a long time surely? So, had the bones been placed there for another reason? Had old bones been put there recently for some purpose? Maybe to lull the traveller into thinking that the bones were old when in fact it was a trap? Ellendrii was thinking nineteen to the dozen about all this.

The birds were too curious about the bones for them to have been there a long time. And yet from the look of them, they looked like they had been there for seasons. But everything else didn't quite add up.

Looking around, Ellendrii noticed the bones around them now were newer. They were clearly newer. Less brittle and bleached by the sun and more in order as well. The older bones had been strewn around in a disorderly fashion and very few were complete skeletons. These bones they walked past now were still clean of meat but they looked and smelled fresher. They didn't have the musty smell of the old ones.

"Aro, these bones are newer" said Ellendrii quietly as they walked.

"What? Newer? They look old to me" replied Aro.

"They look newer to me. I don't know why. The others were pale and cracked. These ones haven't been here as long I swear."

"Does it make much difference?" asked Aro.

"Yes. Because it doesn't make sense. Why would the bones be getting newer? Fresher?"

"That's going a bit far. Fresher? I wouldn't say that. Wait till we find some with meat on them" Aro grinned, "Then I'll believe you. And I'll eat some!"

"Think what you like. I know I'm right" said Ellendrii firmly. Aro shrugged.

"That's fair enough. Think what you like. I was just saying I would like more defined proof. These are white and clean

550

like the other ones are. I see no real difference."

Ellendrii said nothing in reply. His mind was racing a mile a minute now. *Why* were these bones seemingly newer?

As they continued on, Ellendrii's theory was to be proved right. Now they were finding far more intact bodies and ones with remnants of flesh on them. Here, the Dravens flocked.

"HA! I told you! The further we go, the fresher the bones are. Look, all these skeletons have meat hanging off them."

"Ok, so you were right. Big deal. I wonder if any of these are good to eat though…" Aro looked at the skeletons hungrily.

Ellendrii had no idea. There were a mix of different creatures here, of all sizes as before. Some were huge and looked like they would be a real task to take down, much less kill. He wondered how all these creatures ended up here, poor unfortunate things. Some were very small and resembled what we would call rodents. Others were huge and bulky.

Although with the small amounts of flesh, it was hard to tell what, exactly any of these were. But from the skulls and body shapes, there was a large variety there. What could have killed them all? How did they get here?

All these questions raced through Ellendrii's mind as they carried on their way. They kept on going and came across even fresher kills. Hundreds of them. Some even had skin on them in places but they were still largely eaten.

"Do you think someone is feeding the Dravens?" asked Ellendrii.

"Why would anyone do that?" said Aro, answering with a question. "They can find food for themselves and I doubt there is a shortage of these birds so why would anyone hunt for food for them?"

"Well, when Gryphies are sick, their friends hunt for them." Ellendrii explained.

"But Dravens don't hunt and you wouldn't hunt for a creature that wasn't your own species. Even if it was a friend, like me, you would only hunt for that one friend. The idea of someone leaving this food here for Dravens would be pointless."

"Yeah, you're right. I'm thinking up bigger and weirder ideas because I really don't know what's going on" said Ellendrii.

"Who cares. We're just passing through. It doesn't matter. Let's just pass through and get this all over with. We can think about it at the next stage of our journey. Or at least you can. It's all irrelevant to me. You think too much."

"And you don't think at all" said Ellendrii, which was a bit mean.

"I know. It's safer that way" said Aro, not taking offence in the slightest. "Bite first, ask questions later."

"Yeah I suppose in some ways not thinking about these things is a bit less worrying."

"It's not *over* thinking them. It's fine to think about stuff but nothing is worth *over* thinking for."

Ellendrii was again surprised at his friend's unlikely wisdom. Aro had a point. Ellendrii *was* over thinking all this. He decided to try and not do that as much. But to a creature as curious as a Gryphie; that was pretty hard to do.

In time, they came across pretty fresh looking dead creatures. All of them were partially eaten in some way but the Dravens were here in flocks. The creatures' skins were covered in all sorts of different types of fur, scales, feathers, even just skin by itself. Ellendrii and Aro walked slowly through this part, marvelling at all the different creatures they could see. Most of them were alien to the two travellers.

Some though, stood out. There was a Kannith, some Aqwakitts and an Ursquach, much to Ellendrii's dismay. It looked just like A'urealiz. Luckily though, it didn't smell like her and he knew it wasn't her. Where did all these creatures come from? Were they passing through here, had they lived here? Unlikely he thought, on both accounts. None of these creatures seemed like the kind that travelled beyond their own territories. Were they hunted and gathered from their respective territories and then brought here? Maybe when they thought they were dying, they would come here in a ceremony like the Wind Hounds or something. Ellendrii knew he shouldn't over think but he just couldn't help himself.

He was getting a little nervous now as well. There's only so much one can take of death, especially when one is wandering through a mass boneyard. Ellendrii stopped suddenly. Aro, who was behind him, bumped into him and asked why he had stopped.

"I don't feel safe. The bones were ok but this is different. I don't like walking through all these bodies. It's weird and unnerving. I feel like we'll be next. Regardless of why they are here, I don't like it."

"And you think I do? Seriously, this is too much death for even me!" said Aro. "But we gotta keep going. After all, the dead can't hurt you. It's the living you gotta worry about!" Aro tried to smile but he found that deep down even he wasn't happy about this situation.

"So what do you wanna do? We can't go back. I can't see a way up either." Aro looked around.

"No," Ellendrii replied, "We won't go back, we need to keep going. But we must hurry now. Since there are no bones and these are all bodies, we don't have to worry about stepping on anything or alerting anyone. We can just hurry past all this and hope we come to the end of it soon." Aro agreed that this was a good idea and they hurried on.

They made it past the bodies and the land in front of them was bare and dusty. Both of them felt better about this.

There were bones here and there but no complete skeletons; just a scattering of bones occasionally around the place.

"I'm glad that's over. Hope we don't encounter anything like that again" said Ellendrii. Aro felt the same way. Yeah they had only been dead bodies but all the same, it's never good to walk through an open boneyard like that.

"So, where to next?" asked Aro.

"Straight ahead" said Ellendrii, looking at the stone around his neck. They walked on in silence, only now, Aro walked next to Ellendrii instead of behind him.

Ellendrii's mind was racing. What was with the dead things? He still really wanted to know. He figured that maybe there had been a rush stampede or something and they had fallen in from the top of the valley cliffs around. Why some were that much older than others remained a mystery though. Maybe some fell in a long time ago due to something happening to them and then the same thing happened again seasons later. Maybe something had scared them?

Ellendrii glanced at Aro. He was eating something. It was a leg.

"Aro, where did you get that?"

"What? This? I swiped it off one of those bodies. May as well save what food we have and eat what we find along the way" said Aro, correctly so.

Ellendrii agreed this was a good idea and so they went back and gathered food from some of the bodies. They sat and ate and stored some in the bag from the smaller corpses. Ellendrii went looking for small animals to put in the bag and keep them going when they needed it.

While he did that, Aro sat and ate pretty much everything in his sights. He wanted to try one of everything and he was soon stuffed full and felt a bit sick.

"Well that serves you right" scolded Ellendrii.

"But there is so much that I hadn't tried! This was the perfect opportunity! All I eat back home is cave cats, sea vultures and the occasional rock hog. I wanted something different."

"You've been *having* different things though! This whole journey neither of us have eaten the things that we normally eat."

"Yeah and so why not take this opportunity to broaden the range of food even more? Come on Ellendrii, tuck in! Eat what you like! If it tastes bad then just spit it out!"

"And what if it's poisoned? We don't know what of these creatures is good to eat! You can't just eat one of everything!"

"Well, I can't now because I'm full." Aro belched loudly. Ellendrii rolled his eyes.

"Eat for me!" said Aro, "All the things I haven't tried but wanted to, you try them and tell me what they're like!"

"What if it's something I don't want to eat though?" asked Ellendrii.

"Then have a little nibble and let me know. You don't have to eat it all. Either that or just eat what you want and tell me if

554

it's nice. Might I recommend though, that thing over there and that other thing there. Both are delicious!" Aro pointed to some of the dead creatures and Ellendrii took his advice. He agreed on one of them but he found the other to have a bitter under taste and he didn't like it.

So he stashed away some of the first creature because they both liked that one.

It was actually pretty fun, he had to admit, trying all this new food. He had to be careful not to over eat though. His stomach wasn't used to it and he would be very sick if he did that. He tried to try just a little of each thing. Just a mouthful; or two if he liked it.

Aro watched him, amused.

"See? I told you it was fun! There are so many different things to try!"

"Well at least it's better than getting worried about it all. I'd rather do this than be creeped out by why these bodies are here."

"Looking for the light in the dark always helps" said Aro. He knew this to be the case. Look for the positives in the negatives, although it wasn't easy to do that at times. Ellendrii knew this too but sometimes forgot it. Right now even though they were a bit weirded out by the bodies, the advantage was that there was food there and plenty of it.

They tried not to eat anything that looked too different to what they were used to eating though. For example, some of the scaled creatures. They looked nauseating colours and not appetizing at all.

Finally, Ellendrii sat down with Aro and looked satisfied.

"You have some good ideas at times" he grinned at his friend. Aro nodded.

"Of course I do!" he replied.

"You ready to carry on?" asked Ellendrii.

"Yeah I think so. But now we're past the bodies, can we walk more slowly? I'm too full to walk fast."

"Yeah. To be honest, I'm too full to walk fast too!"

They both laughed and carried on, leaving the bodies behind but with plenty of meat stocked in their bag to feel nicely prepared for anything else they might encounter. They left the Dravens behind too. The birds were far more interested in the meat and bones than anything else.

Walking along, Ellendrii looked up at the top of the surrounding cliffs.

"I wonder where we'll go from here" he said quietly.

"I dunno. Somewhere nice and not dangerous" replied Aro.

"Here's a question for you. If you could go anywhere, where would it be?" asked Ellendrii curiously.

"Hmm, probably somewhere with plenty of food. A flat hunting ground, with short grass that's easy on my feet. A large pool or lake. A bit like the lake we saw. Caves with some sort of paths leading to them but not too far off the ground. And a way to cover the cave to keep out intruders! That would be my ideal place to visit."

"But would it also be your ideal place to live?" asked Ellendrii.

"No, that's Dyarkroeen. Well, maybe with the cave covers."

"You could always make one you know."

"I don't have a big enough rock for it though."

"Well, what about digging a rock out from somewhere? You can dig through rock, just make your own."

"That never occurred to me before. Thanks, El! I'll do that when we get back home. Ok, you, same question."

"Hmm, a place to visit. I think something with a varied ecosystem with something of everything. Nice things of course. But somewhere with plenty of high spots where I can fly and sit so I can look out over everything."

"So, like Shernaron then really…" Aro laughed.

"Yeah to be honest the Forest is my home and the Skylands are my ideal home. I just hope I can live there one sun cycle."

"If you lived up there, how would you and I hang out?"

"I'd come and visit you every sun cycle! Don't worry" Ellendrii smiled.

"Ok, so long as you do!"

"Don't worry, I will" Ellendrii nodded. He wouldn't desert his best friend even if he went to live with the Sky Gryphies.

Aro was confident that Ellendrii would keep his word.

"Hey El, you Gryphies call each other right? Using fire or roars?"

"Yes we do."

"Well did you ever think of calling the SilvaGryphie?"

"If I knew that would work, I wouldn't have us go on this journey. I did try it back in Shernaron but of course as I suspected, nothing happened. So yeah, it doesn't work with her. Only Gryphies that are nearby. And I can't guarantee where she is so that would be a pointless thing to do. And I'm certainly not calling her here. I don't feel it's safe enough. Actually, on this journey I haven't felt like many places were safe enough so I never did. If we reach the end of the journey or at least where the Gryphie stone has told us to go and if she isn't there, I will call her then. I don't know when the end will be or when the stone will stop giving us directions but whenever that happens, I will call for her. Maybe that is how we summon her at the end."

"And what if she doesn't listen?"

"Then I will be very disappointed in her. I have respect for the SilvaGryphie and all she has done. She is a legend among my species; she is our creator. I really don't think she would let a call from one of her creations go unanswered."

"You have a lot of faith in her."

"You tend to have a lot of faith in someone you have heard about since you were a kitten. I've heard about her all my life and I've heard all the things she's done for my species and how she looks after us when we pass over." Aro made to make a comment on that but Ellendrii raised a hand and stopped him. "Yes, I know that everything we thought about that was false but there's still no reason why she wouldn't look after the dead after they have gone wherever they go after they die. We don't have any proof that *that* doesn't happen!"

Aro nodded.

"Yeah that's true I guess. Hey wait, it never occurred to me. What if she only likes Gryphies? What if she doesn't like me or something? How will we get her back to Shernaron that way? What if she won't travel with us because I'm there?"

"That's silly. Of course she won't mind you being there. You've helped me so much and when I tell her that, she will understand. Besides, I've no doubt she'll be really impressed with how far we've come just to find her. Who wouldn't be impressed?"

"I wonder what our parents will think." Aro thought about his family again and this sparked Ellendrii to think about his also.

"They'll be impressed too" said Ellendrii, "Why wouldn't they be? Wait till they hear all we have to tell them! I'm really looking forward to it. It will take all sun cycle, that's for sure! We'll gather both our families together and tell them at the same time. After all, if we tell them together then you and I can remind each other of things the other might have forgotten."

"I'm looking forward to that" said Aro, the excitement apparent in his voice.

"But first, I will take her to see the Sky Gryphies. That is what I am really looking forward to. The looks on their faces when we show them that we found her!"

"Yeah but El, we haven't found her yet."

"I know, I know. But it's good to be prepared, right?"

"Yeah, true. Just don't get too excited, ok?" Aro warned him.

"I won't, don't worry. I'm used to disappointment. Like, I really thought I would get into the Elite Flyers since I did better than them all when we did that challenge. But no, they sent me off to find the SilvaGryphie. Knowing I would probably fail." Ellendrii muttered the last part in annoyance.

"I wonder what they're thinking now" pondered Aro.

"Probably nothing. They've probably forgotten all about me. After all, it's been at least a season since we left. They think I either didn't bother or did and then died, I'm sure. Idiots."

"If they're such idiots and tried to lead you astray, why did you give into them? Why would you want to live with them?"

"I wanted to prove them wrong. As for living with them, well, it's really more for the flying that I want to live up there. It's more the sort of territory that suits me. Besides, I bet a

558

load of them will be impressed that I've brought back the SilvaGryphie with me and they wouldn't dare question me after that." Ellendrii looked thoughtful. "Come to think of it, it's not the first time a Sky Gryphie and a Forest Gryphie have come together. I think my great cousin Iseera is a Skybrid. That's a Sky Gryphie hybrid. She comes from far away. I don't know if the other parent of hers is from the Forest though but I know one is a Sky Gryphie. We don't have much to do with her. She is my Dad's cousin. We rarely see her. I think I've seen her once in my whole life. It's possible that Sky and Forest united to create her between them."

"Did you see her up there when you went?" asked Aro.

"No. I'm not sure if she lives up there. Or that she would know me. She would know my Dad though but he can't go up that high."

"Ok, so it might be possible then that you would be accepted among them."

"Of course it's possible! They're not all bad or prejudiced."

"Just...most of them." Aro wasn't so sure.

"No. In fact one of their leaders was ok. She showed me around anyway. Whether or not she was being genuinely kind, I don't know. But anyway, they will all eat their words when we bring back the SilvaGryphie!"

"I admire your confidence" replied Aro. "We haven't found her yet."

"I know. But I'm not giving up."

"Wouldn't it be funny if when we returned, we were adults?" Aro sniggered.

"Haha yeah that would be pretty neat. I don't care how old we are when we go back, so long as we go back with the SilvaGryphie."

"What if we're really old and when we go back, our parents are dead. And you're too old to live in the Skylands?"

"Wow Aro, that's a morbid thought. I don't think it will take *that* long."

"But you won't stop until you find her. Eventually we will have gone so far that we won't be able to find our way home."

"That doesn't matter. I'm sure she will know how to get us home."

"But what if we give up before then? It means we can never go home unless we find her."

"We're not giving up, Aro. We WILL find her!"

"I'm just wondering how long the confidence will last is all."

"As long as it takes" replied Ellendrii.

"Well, I hope so. Because one sun cycle it will be too late to go back. I just hope that sun cycle never comes."

"What's got into you? You were fine earlier. Or maybe that was because you had food."

"It's not that El, it's that I wanted to think about all the options is all. But we will keep on going and see where we end up. I'm happy to travel with you. There is so much to explore, after all!" Aro smiled. Ellendrii smiled too.

"That's more like it! Lots of places to explore and new things to discover and we will discover them all. We'll go back wiser than Lunara!"

They both laughed. Maybe they would!

As they made their way through the valley, they passed a cave. It was enormous. They could hear a sound coming from it and it made them both curious and nervous at the same time.

"That's the biggest cave I've ever seen. It makes Zephirak's old cave back home look tiny" observed Aro.

"It is pretty big" said Ellendrii as they both paused to stare in awe at the size of the cave. It seemed to go over halfway up the valley wall, nearly up to the top in fact and it was nearly as wide as it was tall. But there wasn't much to see inside. It was very dark. It daunted the two travellers.

"It's incredible" breathed Aro.

"Yeah it is. But we're supposed to go this way, so come on" Ellendrii started to head past the cave but Aro stayed.

"We don't want distractions, Aro. Let's just keep going shall we?" Ellendrii said firmly.

"I just want to go up for a closer look" mumbled Aro, taking a step towards the cave.

"I'm sorry, where was your mind earlier? Have you forgotten? There might be something in there that killed all those creatures?" Ellendrii warned.

Aro looked back at him.

"Yeah…sorry. Ok, let's go then" he turned away from the enormous cave and joined Ellendrii.

"That was a bit dumb headed" snapped Ellendrii. "Besides, we need to be heading on."

"I kinda miss staying with creatures or resting for a while" said Aro.

"We need to find creatures to stay with though. We haven't seen much of anything since the cave and they were only meal creatures, not those we could actually communicate with. Maybe we can if we find another civilized species like the Wind Hounds."

"Yeah another species that doesn't try to kill me or whatever they were trying to do to me" replied Aro.

"Well you just need to be careful what you say to them. You've done ok since then. You were with Rivniann for longer than I was and didn't grik it up. So you're ok."

"Thanks El, you're right! I've got better than I was" Aro smiled cheekily.

It was then that the pair of them jumped because they heard a rumbling behind them. The two of them spun around in shock as they saw something starting to move in the cave…

Chapter 30
Attack

Ellendrii and Aro tensed themselves as they saw something moving in the vast cavern that Aro had wanted to explore only moments ago.

Ellendrii nudged Aro and made to run. Aro got the message and they both quickly fled and hid behind a rock a little way away.

Something came out of the cave. The creature was massive and it emerged slowly. They watched in fear as they saw more of it with every step it took.

It was covered from head to toe in armour plating. Literally; all of it. There didn't seem to be a place on its body that wasn't armoured. On its shoulders and upper legs the armour rose into sharp points at the top, as well as on its elbow and hock joints. Even the knuckles on its paws were curved into sharp points and it had short, thick, powerful claws.

Either side of its short, thick tail there were three curved spikes. They were like blades and graduated to a smaller size near the end of its tail. Along its back there were six short dumpy spikes and it had two longer, curved spikes on the back of its neck. On the underside of its neck there was armour plating and its chest had two similar curved spikes. It had great curved horns upon its head that twisted forward, perfect to cause a great deal of damage should it charge at its victim. Along its jawline were yet more curved spikes; three long ones either side of its jaws. Its chin had two more shorter spikes; the front one slightly longer than the one behind it. There were three small curved spikes travelling the length of its head.

It had a snarling muzzle, the mouth of which was filled with multiple rows of razor sharp sickle-like teeth. Finally, its eyes were yellow and had slitted main pupils with smaller, dot-like pupils around the eyeball itself.

Its colouration was reds, oranges and browns. They suspected the red parts on its body were probably blood stains.

They couldn't help shivering as the mass of living armour looked at its surroundings.

That must be what killed all those other creatures thought Ellendrii. He wanted to say this to Aro but it was pretty obvious and he figured Aro was probably thinking the same thing. Aro was crouched down next to him, barely daring to breathe.

Ellendrii nudged his friend to try and get him to peek over the rock. His colouration was better for disguise than the blue and purple of Ellendrii's face. Aro got the hint and peered over at the creature. The creature hadn't seen him luckily but unfortunately it was sniffing the air and it would probably be able to smell them both before too long. It sniffed the ground as well and snarled. It had picked up their scent! It looked up and sniffed the air again.

They both wanted to bolt but they knew better than to make a run for it in the open. The creature looked sturdy and slow but they knew they shouldn't judge on appearances. It also looked incredibly dangerous. And if it had indeed killed all those other creatures, then it definitely *was* incredibly dangerous!

Neither of them knew what to do and neither of them dared say a word. It would be down to their natural instincts as to what they did next. If the creature did find them, *then* would be the time to panic and communicate. For now they just watched it.

It frowned and snarled deeply, sniffing more. Then it started to follow the scent trail! The pair of them tensed ready to run.

Ellendrii was looking around from his place behind the rock. He would of course take to the sky but Aro would have to go on foot and that would be trickier. If he could make it to the end of the creature's territory before it caught him, he would be ok. They needed to make it to the end of the valley and try to get somewhere else from there. Climbing up the sides of the valley they already knew would be too hard.

There were no paths and in panic, Aro would probably slip back down and that would be too big a risk to take. Ellendrii wished he was able to carry his friend over longer distances but wasn't willing to take the risk and drop Aro if he tried to carry him away.

The creature had its nose to the ground. Even though they couldn't see its ears, they suspected it would be able to hear them if it wasn't looking at them. Its freakish, multiple pupilled eyes looked around as it sniffed. Every so often it raised its head and sniffed the air, keeping on with the scent trail.

Aro watched as it came closer and Ellendrii saw his haunches tense more. They would have to just make a run for it before this creature got too close. It was a few metres away now and would definitely find them if it got much closer. Aro looked at Ellendrii and Ellendrii nodded.

The pair of them bolted. Ellendrii took to the sky. His wing was a bit tender and stiff from not using it and he struggled to gain height at first but he got there. As for Aro, he just ran out from behind the rock and carried on, not looking back.

The creature raised its head, roared angrily and gave chase.

"It's behind you! RUN!!" yelled Ellendrii, hovering in the sky. He knew it probably wouldn't work but he flamed the creature, flying over it and slightly behind so that it wouldn't think to jump up and snap him. He thought it would be too heavy to jump in the air anyway but its speed certainly wasn't hindered by its armour. It was gaining on Aro pretty swiftly. It ignored Ellendrii's flames and the fire did absolutely nothing to it. Not a mark was left on its brownish armour. It didn't even get madder or acknowledge Ellendrii's blue fire.

Aro was too scared to even scream; he concentrated all his energy on running for his life. He didn't know for sure if this thing was going to kill him but he was pretty confident that would be the case. Both of them had wondered why there were SO many dead creatures. Maybe this thing killed everything that came into this valley. It didn't look like it ate everything that came into this valley though.

Aro's legs hurt from the sheer power he was putting into the run. This was far worse than the run in with the Wind Hounds. This thing was alien and terrifying to them both. Its look signified its temperament, as well as its angry face.

Aro could hear its heavy breathing as he ran; and it was getting louder as the creature gained on him. Ellendrii flew slightly ahead of the creature, checking out its face. Then he flew ahead, up into the sky, doubled back on himself and flew past the creature, flaming it in the face as he did so. Maybe he could blind it. There didn't seem to be any other way to hurt it so it would give up the chase even for a moment so Aro could gain a bit of ground between them. But the creature paid him no attention; merely closed its eyes and the fire did nothing to harm it. It did however, make it angrier. The creature roared at Ellendrii, warding him off with threatening noise. Ellendrii decided to take a different approach and check out the armour on this thing. He was looking for a weak spot.

He flew around the creature and examined it from a safe distance. There seemed to be not a single part of its body that didn't have armour plating. But, upon closer inspection, he spied a weakness in the protection. There was a part of its body, just behind its front legs that only had a scattering of armour plates. Ellendrii could probably attack it there and at least hurt it. A well shot needle into that part may even be enough to poison the creature.

"Aro!! Shoot one of your needles into the air!" called Ellendrii to his terrified friend. Aro, confused, did as he was told and Ellendrii flew down and caught the needle in his hand, near the base so there was less risk of being poisoned. As the pair of them continued running, Ellendrii veered away from them and once again doubled back on himself, a little way up ahead so that he hoped his path would cross the creature's as it passed him and he would be able to stick the needle in its side. He had to time it incredibly accurately but with his flying prowess, that was the least difficult part of the task.

He timed himself and then charged at the creature, swooping at it in the sky, down and catching it at just the right moment to run it through with the needle. The creature roared at Ellendrii in pain and anger, pausing the chase for now and allowing Aro some time to escape or at least gain some space between them, which he was only too glad to do.

Meanwhile, Ellendrii faced off against the creature. He was back in the sky now and hovering out of reach. The creature was furious. The needle stuck out of its side and it didn't attempt to remove it. Instead, it aimed all its rage at Ellendrii, looking up at him and roaring furiously. Then suddenly it shot something out of its mouth at the Gryphie. It was a gooey liquid of some sort and caught Ellendrii on his foot. Ellendrii screamed and flapped around in panic. A searing pain shot up his entire leg and he was horrified to see when he looked down, that the flesh from his foot had melted away down to the bone. This made him panic even more and he didn't see when the creature shot another glob of acid at him. This one hit him in the wing and burned a hole through it. The burn spread and the hole was a considerable size before it stopped burning. Ellendrii screamed again, struggling to fly now and losing altitude. The creature paced angrily below, looking up at him and waited for the inevitable fall into its vicious claws.

By this time, Ellendrii was in shock as he flapped and flailed in the air. His foot felt like it was on fire. It had come completely unexpectedly to him and he was panicking badly. The skin on his wing stung as the air blew through it. Ellendrii didn't think to attack any more, now he was frightened and the only thought in his mind was to get away from this attacker and try and find Aro. With considerable trouble, he flew in the direction Aro had gone but his flight was slow and painful and he struggled to keep high enough in the sky that the creature couldn't reach him. The creature followed him down below, waiting for him to fall.

The acid it had shot out at him was very very high in concentration and as a result, if the creature wanted to use it in as concentrated a form, it would use a lot of it at once and thus not have as much for future use. So it used it sparingly. Ellendrii of course didn't know this and now he was terrified he might get hit with it again. As he fled, the creature galloped along below. Ellendrii was panting; the effort with flying he had to make now was almost too much and it was total fear and the need to survive that was driving him to keep going despite the pain. He looked up ahead and his heart sank. The valley had a dead end! Aro was trying to make his way up the side of it and having little luck since he kept stumbling and sliding back down every time he made any sort of progress at all. He wasn't even halfway up yet.

"Aro!" Ellendrii screamed. "Get away fast! The creature will spit acid at you!"

Aro looked up, panicked and saw Ellendrii's wing immediately. His heart pretty much leaped to his mouth and he scrambled up the slope faster. But of course without properly checking the places to stand or go up, he started to slip back down much faster.

Ellendrii looked around for a way for them to escape. He was finding it increasingly difficult to stay in the sky and he knew he would have to land soon. His wing muscles burned in protest as well as the horrible feeling of his injured wing and foot.

"Aro!! Turn back! We need to get back to the cave! This is a dead end!" he called to his friend.

"How??" called back Aro. "I'll have to run past that thing in order to get there and I don't know how much longer I can run for. I was nearly caught running here."

"You have to or it will reach you and you will die. I'll fly at it as you pass and hope that you can get by while I distract it!"

"You'll die! It will spit more acid at you and kill you!" roared back Aro.

"It's the only way!" called Ellendrii. "Do as I say, NOW!!" As he spoke the last word, he flamed the ground in front of Aro, causing him to leap back in fright and slide the rest of the way down the slope.

When he reached the bottom, Aro turned and fled back the way they had come. The creature was nearly there though and Ellendrii had to be fast to fly at it and distract it so Aro could get past. He swooped down at the creature, which roared and snapped at him in surprise. Aro fled past them and back towards the cave and boneyard.

Ellendrii swiped at the creature's face with his tail but the thing shot out some more acid and caught his other wing, rendering it useless and Ellendrii crashed to the ground, skidding to a halt nearby. This time the acidic goop had hit him near one of his wing fingers and burned through it completely.

Ellendrii roared in agony as the creature advanced on him.

"Thresh will kill you!" it roared, "Devour your flesh!"

"GRIK OFF AND LEAVE US ALONE!!!" roared Ellendrii, flaming Thresh in the face as he approached. Thresh just growled at him and the fire, again, did nothing. Ellendrii stumbled to his feet and limped as fast as he could, with Thresh in pursuit. It was difficult with only three legs but it was just too painful to put his injured foot on the ground. The only small mercy was that in being a back leg that was injured, it didn't impede his movements as much as a front leg would have if that had been injured. He could still put his weight on his front legs as the motion of his body carried him forward.

He had no idea why this creature was so angry and attacking them. He figured Thresh must be very territorial or something. His foot hurt but he tried to ignore it as he limped as fast as he could to reach his friend. When he finally reached him, neither spoke, but they made it back to the cave and past it. Thresh was still chasing and now gaining ground on them. Ellendrii had no idea how he could be so fast or so relentless and he deeply wished Thresh would tire soon.

He and Aro had to rest. They figured they could lose Thresh in the boneyard so they made for large bodies to hide behind. They also split apart, forcing Thresh to just pursue one of them. He chose Aro because Ellendrii was injured and less of a threat.

Ellendrii found a large dead creature and ducked down behind it. Aro wasn't as fortunate. Thresh could see where he was going and this made it far more difficult for him to successfully hide. Ellendrii desperately wanted to help Aro but he was frightened. His foot and wing burned and throbbed and he had to rest; the effort of limping had used up more energy than if he hadn't been injured. He hid; a natural instinct that overrode all others. He needed to survive.

Thresh didn't shoot acid at Aro. He just chased him round and round and Aro got even more tired. Thresh knew that Aro would be coming to the end of his stamina and he was basically just running him out now.

Suddenly, Aro tripped and fell. He tried to pull himself upright and get up but Thresh was upon him before he even knew what was happening. Thresh held the unfortunate Lizariaous down with one heavy paw. He was considerably larger than Aro. The paw that held him was between his needles, where the one Aro had shot out had been. Thresh swiped his other paw right through the row of needles on Aro's back, smashing them all to pieces and causing Aro to roar out in panic, feeling his main defence being destroyed. Not that the poison from his needles seemed to affect Thresh but having the needles on his back reassured him all the same. He struggled, though he was tired and tried to get out of Thresh's grip. It was a small mercy he was on his belly and not on his back where Thresh could tear open his stomach. But now his needles were gone, he was easy enough to flip over onto his back, which was what Thresh was currently trying to do. Aro dug his claws into the ground and refused to budge.

Thresh roared angrily at his stubbornness and roughly dug his claws deeply into Aro's back. The few thicker scales Aro had on his back did near to nothing to protect him from this attack. Aro screamed in fear and also anger at being knocked down so easily by his attacker and flipped his tail around, trying to find a place to get Thresh so that he would let him go. But the tail blade just hit armour and there was nothing Aro could do.

Until his tail blade got caught on the needle that was still stuck in Thresh's side and the creature roared in pain and fell back a little, giving Aro just enough time to scramble out from under him and get away. Thresh was trying to get to the needle to pull it out but his bulky armour prevented him from reaching it and, annoyed, he had to abandon the task. He switched his sights to Aro but Aro had gone.

Thresh got even angrier and charged around at the dead bodies, using his horns to get under them and flip them into the air and away from him. He was tired of playing hide and seek!

Aro had dived behind a nearby body of what looked like an Ursquach, though it was so covered in blood that it was hard to tell. Thresh soon found him though, as he flipped the body into the air and exposed Aro behind it. Aro fled again. There was no point trying to fight this creature. This time he tried to head for the cave but Thresh knew this and charged full pelt at Aro. Aro was still tired from running all the time and he had no chance in escaping. Thresh got his horns under him and threw him into the air. One of them stuck Aro in the leg and he roared in pain as he flew through the air and landed, thankfully, on a dead body. However, he also landed awkwardly and found he had hurt a front leg. He couldn't move it and he assumed it was broken.

Ellendrii was angry now and he had charged out at Thresh and thrown himself onto Thresh's back. He wasn't entirely sure what to do when he was there though, since even the back of Thresh's neck was armour plated and there was no way to get through it. Flaming him in the back of the head just made him angrier. Ellendrii was in a lot of pain already and any more just added to the feeling which had now become a constant throb. Thresh bucked and reared, then finally fell onto his side and rolled Ellendrii off. Ellendrii had to move before he was squashed under the bulk of his enemy and he retreated.

Thresh got up and turned on Ellendrii.

"Why are…you…fighting us?" Ellendrii found the voice to ask.

"Thresh will kill you!" roared Thresh. Speaking in third person seemed to be his thing.

"But why? We are just passing through…please…let us…pass…peace…" but Ellendrii was cut off as Thresh charged him and flipped him with his horns too. Ellendrii tried instinctively to open his wings as he sailed into the air but he was descending before he knew it and only succeeded in landing on his wing badly. Now he was permanently grounded.

Ellendrii and Aro quivered as Thresh approached them. It was just like Flynn had said way back in the Furmine necropolis. Gryphies and Lizariaouses had nothing that hunted them; they didn't know how terrifying it was to be hunted; to be sniffed out like a meal creature. Now as they lay injured before Thresh, they both realized that this was how the Furmines must feel. The ones that Mettalika had tortured; the ones who are hunted and toyed with, who beg for mercy when none is given. Now they were at the other end of the food chain.

And they were terrified.

Ellendrii knew the only way was to try again to reason with Thresh and distract him while the pair of them regained their stamina. With Aro's injured front leg though, they were considerably slowed down. It wouldn't have been quite as bad if it had been a back leg; it was easier to hold a back leg up than try to run on one front leg that would take the brunt of the weight as his body shifted forwards to run.

"Please let us pass! You have food here, you don't need to kill us! Please don't hurt us anymore!" pleaded Ellendrii.

"Thresh will KILL you" said Thresh. Clearly he wasn't that communicable.

"Why? Why do you want to kill us?"

"Thresh kills ALL!"

"Why do you kill all though? Can't you just spare us?"

"Thresh like to kill!"

"We can g…give you something in return for sparing us though!" Ellendrii fumbled with his bag and offered the glowing crystals. Thresh merely knocked them out of Ellendrii's shaking hands.

"Ok, maybe not that…what about these?" asked Ellendrii, offering the gourd. "This is full of water, surely you get thirsty?"

"Thresh drinks the blood of his enemies!" roared Thresh.

"Er…ok, maybe these then? They are healing herbs for your wounds…" Ellendrii offered but got a similar response to the crystals.

Then Thresh swiped with one large paw and ripped the bag off Ellendrii's shoulder, throwing it to one side. Ellendrii drew back in fear.

"P...please don't kill us...please..." he whimpered. Thresh just continued to look bad tempered and growl at them.

"It won't work" said Aro, "He won't listen. He just wants to kill everyone who passes through here. He doesn't even eat them. What a waste." Aro narrowed his eyes at Thresh.

"Yeah you grikking heard me you stupid grikker. You don't even eat all you hunt. What a stupid excuse for a hunter you are! Or can't you manage all this meat?"

"What are you doing" muttered Ellendrii. "We don't want to grik him off more than he is already..."

"Trust me" muttered back Aro. Then to Thresh he said; "I bet you can't eat all this meat. Look, you just let it rot and leave it to the Dravens. Draven food. That's all you're doing. Feeding this flock of birds. Or are they your pets? Thresh's precious little pets that eat all his food! Look at them, Thresh! Invading YOUR territory, eating YOUR meat! Stealing from YOU!" Aro gestured with his good paw at all the carcasses that were crawling with the rat-ravens and Thresh's anger grew.

"NO!!" he roared. "THRESH'S MEAT!!" and he charged blindly at all the Dravens nearby, getting beside himself with rage now that Aro had put this thought into his mindless head.

Thresh ran about, flipping some corpses, charging at others, doing all he could to scare the birds off. They flew into the air and hovered, some of them landing again on corpses further away from the irate hunter.

"Quick!" muttered Aro to Ellendrii. He didn't need to be told twice. The two of them snuck off and made their way quickly back in the direction of the cave.

"I...don't...get it...why did the...Gryphie stone...try to get us...to go...this way?" asked Ellendrii. It had lead them not only into danger but also to a dead end.

"Maybe...it's broken..." replied Aro as they fled, both of them limping from their injuries.

"He...will...see we've gone..." said Ellendrii. It was true, Thresh would notice their absence and come after them before they had the chance to get to the cave. There was no way they would make it that far before Thresh got bored of chasing the Dravens.

"Let's...get as...far as...we can..." replied Aro.

And they ran. But of course Ellendrii was right and Thresh soon noticed they had gone. He tired of chasing the Dravens and he had got even madder when they flew up and landed again. He had wasted the rest of his acid in his rage and shot down three of them. The birds lay on the ground, dead, with the acid eating through their flesh. It bubbled and popped as the bird melted into the ground.

Thresh looked around with a grunt. The intruders had gone; they were no longer in the place they had been lying. He looked around him and saw them galloping off into the distance. With a huge, mighty roar, he gave chase. It appeared that his anger was what was giving him stamina.

Ellendrii and Aro didn't even need to look back to know that he was following them again. They could hear him; his grunting and breathing gave him away. They both wished they had found a place to hide. Aro's mind raced as he tried to think of another way to distract the idiotic but extremely dangerous predator so they could get closer to the cave. Maybe he could trick him.

Aro skidded to a halt and spun around to face the approaching danger of Thresh.

"What are you doing??" demanded Ellendrii, pausing and turning to his friend.

"Do me a favour and run" replied Aro, "I have another plan."

"I won't leave you here! We're in this together!" roared Ellendrii in fear.

"I said GO! Grik off! Find the SilvaGryphie. This is YOUR quest, NOT mine. I'll keep him busy and you get back to the cave."

"No, Aro!" cried Ellendrii. But Aro's head snapped round and his jaws clipped Ellendrii on the wing painfully.

"GET OUT OF HERE NOW!!" he snapped at his friend and Ellendrii, shocked and hurt ran for it.

Working together to get rid of Thresh wasn't working. So, if even one of them made it, it would be worth it in Aro's eyes. And if Ellendrii was who made it, then it would be even more worth it. The time had come for Aro to prove his worth and defend his friend. He had come on this journey not only as a friend and travelling companion but also in his mind, to protect Ellendrii. And if sacrificing himself in order for Ellendrii to make it was the way it had to be done then so be it.

Aro set his body and faced Thresh, who was closing the distance between them. Aro's injured front leg was lifted uselessly but there was enough of him that was uninjured that he could definitely give this guy a run for his money and let Ellendrii get away safely.

All Ellendrii had to do was get to the cave. He highly doubted Thresh would follow him in. He was too big and bulky for one thing.

As Thresh approached, he lowered his head and prepared to charge at Aro and slice him asunder.

Aro knew this would happen though and managed to dodge at the last minute. He skidded out of the way as Thresh charged through. But Thresh kept on going. He was after Ellendrii!

"Hey! Grikker! FIGHT ME YOU WIMP!!" roared Aro.

Thresh spun round and roared back at him, charging again.

Aro again, skidded to one side. He mockingly swiped his tail at Thresh, which only angered him more.

"You're too slow, you stupid grikker. I've travelled a long way, I am leaner and faster AND smarter than you. You probably live in that musty cave of yours all the time and only come out to provide your little Draven friends with food" Aro mocked.

"THRESH DOES NOT!" roared Thresh and chased after Aro now. Aro turned and dodged around the corpses with his last remaining strength. He was leading Thresh away from Ellendrii.

Thresh didn't dodge around them; he careened through them. He threw them to one side and charged after Aro.

Aro managed to run around one corpse and round to the other side, leaving Thresh to carry on going the other way. Aro laughed at this and headed in the direction Ellendrii had gone. Ellendrii had had enough of a head start that he would be well on his way to the bones and the cave beyond them. He looked back and Thresh was still headed away from him.

HA! Idiot! He laughed to himself and carried on. He sincerely hoped Thresh wouldn't turn and come back for him because he was getting very tired now and he knew he wouldn't be able to outrun him anymore.

He panted, carrying on. Suddenly he felt a shooting pain at his haunch and fell, skidding to a halt in the dust. What had happened?

Thresh had a small amount of acid left and shot it at Aro as he ran. The creature had realized that Aro had gone, turned and saw him running in the opposite direction. He had run after him and in order to catch Aro while he was quite a way away, Thresh had used the last tiny drop of acid, knowing it would at least be enough to hurt Aro and make him fall.

Thresh was upon the unfortunate Lizariaous before he knew what was happening.

Aro screamed in sheer fear as Thresh pinned him to the ground. There was no escape now.

"Thresh won't let you escape again" he growled. Aro tried to get his tail blade under the needle again but couldn't get near it since the two of them weren't quite in the right position for him to do so.

"Don't try anything stupid" growled Thresh. Aro whimpered now. He wanted to mouth off at his attacker but the pain was too much and he couldn't even speak. Thresh adjusted his weight on Aro and pain shot through him.

Now he wanted to plead with Thresh but he couldn't. He didn't have the will anymore. They had come all this way. He only hoped Ellendrii would escape. He rested his head on the ground. Thresh wouldn't be able to bite his neck though because of the blade that grew out of the back of Aro's skull. It covered his neck in this position and protected it. It was his last line of defence.

Suddenly he felt a searing pain shoot up his skull. Thresh had grabbed the blade between his teeth and ripped it off.

"That's better. Now Thresh can get to your neck" snarled Thresh. So he wasn't as stupid as Aro had thought. Then again this was a calmer Thresh, a more dangerous Thresh. One that wasn't charging around blindly. One that knew he could make a nice kill and his victim couldn't get away.

Now Aro's final will to survive kicked in. He scrabbled about in the dust with his one good front leg and tried to move his back legs without much success because of Thresh's weight.

Thresh lowered his head and gently, softly, took hold of Aro's neck in his teeth. Aro yelped and whimpered, struggling more. This was it. This was the end for him. He made one last desperate attempt to escape. He needed to, he must! Ellendrii!

Thresh slowly sank his teeth into Aro's neck. Then, quick as a flash, Thresh snapped his teeth together, breaking through Aro's neck like a twig, killing him instantly.

Thresh let go of Aro, letting him fall limply on the ground. He lifted his weight off Aro and stood up, looking in the direction Ellendrii had taken.

He snarled.

Ellendrii was still making his way to the cave. It was the only thing he could do. He wanted so badly to turn back and help Aro but he knew that it wasn't what Aro had wanted. It would damage Aro's pride and put them both at risk. He only hoped Aro could hold Thresh off or find some smart way of killing him. He limped more slowly now because of his damaged foot. But he was making good distance and had reached the bleached bones in the earlier part of the boneyard.

The Gryphie stone around his neck was constantly pointing behind him now. He had lost the precious leather bag with all the bits and pieces from their trip as well as Midnyte's hand made decoration and the food. He knew they would be able to find more food in the cave though so it wasn't so much of a problem but the gourd and healing herbs were gone and he was gutted about losing the decoration Midnyte had given to him. He hoped that the poison would get to Thresh and maybe kill him off. The poison would be in his body, working its way through him now and maybe it would weaken him. That's if of course, he didn't have immunity to it. Ellendrii sincerely hoped he didn't.

He figured he would get back to the cave and wait for Aro to return and they would figure it out from there. That's if Aro made it of course. Ellendrii was terrified that Thresh would kill him. But Aro was a Lizariaous and Ellendrii couldn't think of a braver or stronger travelling companion than him to help them both along. Even though Aro wasn't smart, he was good at fighting and that's what they both needed right now.

The cave entrance was now in Ellendrii's view in the distance. He breathed a sigh of relief and felt extra strength upon seeing it. Then he heard something coming up behind him.

Ah, Aro! He must have made it! I wonder how he tricked Thresh into losing us. Or maybe he found Thresh's weakness and defeated him in the end! Ellendrii thought as he ran.

But as the other approached, he found it didn't sound like Aro's breathing. It was too heavy.

Ellendrii risked it and glanced behind him. His heart skipped a beat and he felt sick and panicked. It was Thresh! Where was Aro?

Ellendrii carried on, trying to run faster but failing. He was too tired and injured. There was no way he would outrun Thresh now. He was too far away from the cave to reach it before Thresh reached him. He couldn't understand how Thresh had reached him so quickly.

Thresh was fuelled by adrenaline and anger and it made him able to just keep going. He was on Ellendrii's tail now and trying to snap at it as the Gryphie ran. Ellendrii curved his tail and tried to keep it away from Thresh's jaws but it was hard to do that and run at the same time. His tail naturally swayed from side to side as he ran. So he decided to sway it more strongly in the hopes that he could hit Thresh in the face with it.

Thresh was trying to catch it between his teeth though and Ellendrii swayed it harder, to try and stop him. It was difficult to pay attention to what Thresh was doing while also trying not to trip over the scattered bones he was running through. In the end, Ellendrii needed to concentrate on where he was going instead of trying to smack Thresh in the face.

He felt a shooting pain go up his tail and yelped. Looking back, he saw Thresh had bitten half of his tail clean off and was now trying to snap at the remainder of it.

Ellendrii couldn't make it. He was too slow with his damaged foot, too much in pain from his wings and tail and Thresh was soon upon him. Thresh leaped forwards and his claws tackled Ellendrii's haunches like a lioness hunting down a gazelle and Ellendrii fell to the ground as his back legs gave out. Already limping with one, it was already half useless when Thresh tackled him.

Thresh went to pounce on Ellendrii as he had with Aro but Ellendrii even now was trying to crawl away. He knew it was useless but he wanted to do his very best to escape. It couldn't all come to this! To him being killed. He had no idea if Aro was still alive. Maybe he was injured somewhere. He hoped that if he died, Aro would find him and carry on. Blind hope.

He saw the slope that lead to the cave exit and the tunnels beyond up ahead. He tried to drag himself towards it. Thresh watched him, amused.

"Did you honestly think you could escape Thresh? No one escapes Thresh! Your friend didn't escape Thresh."

Ellendrii stopped.

"Yes, Thresh tore your friend's neck out. He is dead. Soon, so you will be too."

Ellendrii looked around. Aro was dead? Ellendrii's heart sank. It couldn't be! Thresh was messing with his head, putting these thoughts into his mind to make him think Aro was dead and so destroy his hope and ability to carry on.

"Thresh drowned him in his own blood!" roared Thresh, throwing back his head and laughing.

"NO!" roared Ellendrii and gathered his last remaining strength to turn and lunge at Thresh with all his power and might.

Thresh simply raised a paw and batted the Gryphie away like an annoying fly.

"YES!" grinned Thresh, showing off his terrible teeth. Row upon row of them. A mouth full of killing tools soaked in Aro's blood, which ran down his chin.

Ellendrii sat up where he had landed and snarled at Thresh.

"You grikking MONSTER!!" he roared. "We were looking for the SilvaGryphie, we were travelling together! He was my FRIEND!!!"

"Thresh doesn't care. Thresh just likes to kill. You were a nice challenge. Now you will die like your friend" said the appalling creature that stood before him.

Ellendrii tried to get to his feet. His whole body hurt from when he had landed on the ground and his wings and foot still stung. The pain in his tail was so much that it was a dull, constant throb now.

He wanted so badly to fight Thresh but he knew he would meet the same fate as his friend. Thresh was just too strong and too well protected. There was no way he could win. And apparently the poison had no effect on Thresh at all. The needle still stuck out of his side.

Ellendrii had one final idea. If he could push that needle in Thresh's side deeper, maybe he would pierce an important organ inside the creature's body and manage to kill him from internal bleeding or something. Anything. Anything to try and escape. He didn't want Aro to have died in vain. He *had* to keep going and find the SilvaGryphie. Even if the Gryphie stone was broken.

At least if he killed Thresh he would be able to pass through this valley and try to climb out the other side without being hindered by a creature who wanted to kill him. He was also incredibly angry and heartbroken that Thresh had killed his best friend. Ellendrii would avenge Aro's death! He couldn't let Thresh live.

"So, you think you can kill me, do you, Thresh?" Ellendrii asked him, very slowly starting to limp forward and around Thresh.

"Thresh doesn't think, Thresh *knows* he can kill you" replied the creature.

"You're right, Thresh, you DON'T think!" roared Ellendrii, suddenly rushing around Thresh and charging at the needle in his side.

However, he was not fast enough and Thresh turned as Ellendrii got closer. He whipped his spiked tail around, right into Ellendrii, catching him in the side and knocking him down painfully. Even though Thresh's tail was fairly short, he could whip it around quite fast if he moved his body with it. Ellendrii lay there, panting and quivering in pain.

"Thresh is not stupid. Thresh cannot get the needle out of his side but he knows you wanted to push it further in and kill Thresh. That won't happen. Now you will die and join your friend. Dead. On the ground in your own blood with the other corpses." Thresh advanced on Ellendrii and he found he couldn't even move let alone stand. It was far too painful. He couldn't drag himself away. He was completely at Thresh's mercy.

Still, Ellendrii's instincts were to flee and he thrashed helplessly on the ground, only stopping because he was so fatigued by this time. He looked at himself. Maybe he was looking at someone else's body? He knew it was attached to him but he suddenly felt disconnected from it. He was so thin and tired now, even though they had eaten in the cave and the boneyard and that had given them the energy required to keep up this pointless fight for so long. They hadn't really stood a chance.

He wondered if he was dying. He felt faint and his breathing was shallower than before.

"You will be easier to kill" said Thresh, standing over him. "You do not have the neck protection Thresh had to remove from your friend before Thresh killed him."

"I…hate…you" replied Ellendrii. He spat on the ground in front of Thresh and snarled up at him.

"Be careful not to insult Thresh any more or Thresh will torture you before Thresh kills you. Your friend's death was too quick for someone like him, who insulted Thresh like he did. Thresh killed him fast though because Thresh needed to catch up with you. But now Thresh can take his time. There is no hurry." Thresh placed a claw under Ellendrii's chin and lifted his head to look at him. Ellendrii growled at him, nostrils flaring with blue but without the energy to flame his enemy in the face.

"Insolent fool!" snapped Thresh. Ellendrii snarled. He would *not* let this monster get the better of him.

"Thresh will crush your skull!" snapped Thresh and placed a heavy paw on Ellendrii's skull, which was delicate in comparison. He pushed Ellendrii's head to the ground and kept on pushing down.

"Thresh will pop your head like a bubble" growled Thresh. Ellendrii's vision started to go red and blurry. And the pain. He couldn't move. He closed his eyes.

So this is how it ended.

He had failed.

Chapter 31
Revelation

Darkness.
Red – black.
Nothingness.
Then, light.
A bright, white light.
A bright, silver light.

Ellendrii opened his eyes slowly. Everything was pale colours, pastels, pale light. It had a softness to it that was calming.

He knew he was dead. So this was what it was like. He looked at himself and saw there wasn't a scratch or mark on his body. His foot had returned to normal as well; it was no longer melted by acid. He checked his wings and they were immaculate, with no holes in and the burned finger bones on them were also healed. As he moved, he felt no pain. Everything felt refreshed and calm. He looked around carefully.

He couldn't see much of anything really. It was all just soft colours and shapes merging and separating. Clouds almost. It smelled like fresh dew. He looked down. He was lying on something smooth and velvety. It felt pleasant under his touch. He wanted to stand up but he was afraid of finding out more. What the afterlife was really like. Now he would see for himself and this scared him but awed him at the same time. He spent a while longer looking around and watching the colours around him in their soft pastel hues.

It was then that he saw a face. It was looking at him but was almost merged with the scenery and pastels around. Two beautiful eyes gazed at him. They were a violet blue like the moonlit sky. They reminded him of Midnyte Comet's wings in that it seemed like he could see into the galaxies as he looked into them. A delicate muzzle formed below them and two long, elegant ears with curled tips formed above them. The fur was a pearlescent white, it shone a rainbow of pastel colours as the light and shade moved over it, ever changing like when light and shade hit a bubble. At the base of the neck there was a thick, fluffy mane or ruff with longer, soft fur. The mane extended along the spine down to the tail, which was also fluffy. The thicker fur at the base of the tail tapered out to shorter fur and an elaborate meshed tailspade at the end. The tailspade shone silver in the light, shiny and almost crystal-like.

The legs were similar to his own in structure; Forest Gryphie style legs. The only real difference was that the legs of this creature had longer fur at the elbows and hocks. The bottom of the mane extended down between the front legs and tapered towards the belly. The claws were like glass in appearance; elegant but powerful and crystal clear. Finally, the wings of this creature were almost indescribable. The backs of them had slightly longer fur that got shorter towards the fingertips. The thumb claws were similar to the ones on the feet and the other wing fingers didn't have claws, as with most Gryphies but just tapered to points. Only these were slightly curved, adding to the elegant look of this creature. There were four wing fingers and a thumb claw on each wing. But the underside of the wings was the thing that really blew Ellendrii away. He thought looking into Midnyte's wings was incredible; but looking into the wings of this creature was truly like seeing into eternity and could not possibly be described in words in a way that would even be close to doing them justice. It's the sort of thing that can't be described; you need to see it for yourself.

This beautiful creature had slowly appeared before him and he just lay there and stared. He had no idea what it was and didn't even start to possibly think that he was in the presence of the one he had been searching for for so long. The SilvaGryphie.

Then, she spoke. It was an odd feeling. Her voice seemed to be all around him and in his own head at the same time. Also, her mouth didn't move with the words; it merely opened at times or she made an expression according to what she was talking about.

"You have been searching for me" she stated.

"Y…you're her? The one in the stories? The SilvaGryphie? I…I wasn't even sure since I didn't really know what you looked like but…but you're so beautiful…"

"Did you think I wouldn't be?"

"It's not that. I just…I've heard descriptions of you, like you have white fur and a mane and such but…to see you for real…"

"You were so blown away by my appearance that you almost forgot what you were doing here in the first place?" she asked with a smile.

"Yes. I'm guessing you knew that because you know everything since you're the creator of my species?" Ellendrii felt dumb talking to her. He felt his order of wording was stupid and that she would judge him. After all, he was just a mere Forest Gryphie. She was…well the SilvaGryphie!

"I know that because I have been watching you. I still watch over my gathering in Shernaron you know. I know what you all do. But I saw how determined you were to find me against all the odds and so I helped you."

"Helped us? How did you help us?? We both died!" Ellendrii got to his feet now as it suddenly dawned on him and he remembered. He was bold enough and felt it well within his rights to be angry at her for not helping them more.

"I put the Gryphie stone in that statue. I made it show you the way because I knew you would get lost. I wanted you to find me so your journey and determination wouldn't be in vain."

"But it lead us to Thresh…and death…Aro…" Ellendrii plonked down on his rump and a tear rolled down his cheek.

"But you found me. That was what you wanted. No matter what the consequences."

"I didn't want to die though. And Aro. I should never have let him come along."

"You know you wouldn't have made it without him."

"But why didn't you help us? Like in the Forest of Foreboding, when we nearly died in the desert, the Narg'tok, Thresh?"

"Because I could see you were doing well by yourselves. You were learning and growing. You've changed a lot since you left Shernaron. You've grown up. You are adults now."

"No we're not, we're dead! Aro is dead! Thresh killed us. This is the afterlife."

"Why do you keep saying that? Jumping to conclusions. Why do you think this is the afterlife?"

"Because Thresh killed us. Unless he was joking about Aro but I highly doubt that."

"Look at you. Arguing with me like this. Aro is alive and this isn't the afterlife. This is my domain. The dimension I made for myself. I will take you to Aro." She was chuckling at his outburst and confidence.

"What? How can he be alive? He killed both of us. I felt what it was like to die. He crushed my skull."

"And why would two little deaths stop me from reversing it? I created an entire species plus sub-species and found a place for them all to live. Now, do you want to see your friend or not? Because I could just put you back in Thresh's territory and he can kill you all over again. There is a fine line between being argumentative and just plain disrespect."

"Sorry. I...I was just angry..." Ellendrii stood and prepared to follow her.

"That is fine. But you need to know when to be quiet and listen and learn the patience to wait for things to be explained to you."

She started to walk and he walked alongside her. She was huge, much larger than even his father. Probably larger than a full blooded Deamon Gryphie (I can tell you now that she most definitely was larger than any Gryphie) and he was awed all over again when he walked beside her. His head only came up to her elbow. Her gait was unusual too. It was half walking, half floating. Everything was so misty and airy here, wherever they were. There were no objects anywhere; everything was just the same floating pastels and the ground looked much like the area above it. The ground was the same velvety type of ground that he had been lying on.

Soon, he saw a black shape in the distance. It was the curled up form of Aro. He nearly ran to him but remembered he was in the presence of the creator and he restrained himself. He didn't want her to be angry or annoyed with him considering she could apparently quite easily do what she wished with him and his life.

They reached Aro. He was curled up asleep and uninjured. The SilvaGryphie put her hand on his body and he slowly woke up, lifting his head.

"Aro?" asked Ellendrii, going up to him timidly.

"El? Where am I? What's going on?" Aro sat up and then the SilvaGryphie spoke.

"Now, before the questions start coming, I will answer them. Sit, Ellendrii and listen, Aro.

I was watching you as I watch everyone in Shernaron. I saw the great war and everything that came before and after it. The downfall of Mettalika and Zephirak and the rise of peace between your two species. I didn't intervene because you need to learn and grow by yourselves and if I had done something then they would probably have started worshipping me again and I didn't want that. Really, I am as humble as the next Gryphie. Which is as you know, why I left." She paused as Aro shook his head, the sound of her voice being new to him.

"So, I saw your birth, Ellendrii, your kittenhood, your passion for flying, as I have watched all the other little kittens grow and learn. Your friendship with Aro and then your determination to do something with your wings and flying abilities. I knew the Sky Gryphies were telling you to find me because they thought you couldn't do it and I really hoped that you would at least attempt to come and look for me. Because I happen to frown upon how full of themselves they are. So I watched you set out over the vast water, meeting other creatures along the way and getting into and out of trouble. I let you do it all yourselves because I wanted to see the lengths to which my own species would go to in order to do something like this. I didn't butt in or help until I saw you both get killed. I don't really interfere because I think it's wrong but I saw how far you both came and to just allow you to die like that was such a waste after how far you had come to find me.

It needed to all be worth it. So I saved your lives and brought you here to my home."

"So you just watched us out of curiosity?" asked Ellendrii.

"I let the same things happen that would happen had I not existed. I let you get on with it and grow and learn and travel because if I kept interfering with the affairs of my creations, it would get complicated very fast and it wouldn't be fair on other species that do not have a creator such as myself. Can you understand that?"

"Yes…" Ellendrii was cut off as Aro spoke.

"So, do you watch over Dyarkroeen too? Or just Shernaron?"

"Isn't that obvious? Were you not listening to me? What did I say?"

"Just…Shernaron?"

"Yes, well done." Aro looked sheepish.

"So, where *is* your home?" asked Ellendrii. "Where are we now?"

"My home is a different dimension. Like I said I made it myself and it is calm, peaceful and restful."

"So, would we have found it if we'd got past Thresh?"

"Yes, in fact you were nearly there. You had to climb out of that valley with Thresh in and I thought you would get past him without waking him. He sleeps a lot. It was unfortunate that he awoke and saw you. Past the valley, there was a misty territory and that would be where you would have been able to step into my domain. Sadly you never made it that far."

"How did you bring us back to life though? I was terrified and it hurt so much…" Aro said.

"It's easy, when you know how. I just took your bodies back to my domain and healed you. It didn't take long."

"Well, that sounds simple enough" said Ellendrii before Aro could open his mouth and possibly mess things up.

"I really need to know though. Going to find you, meeting you, going where no other Gryphie has gone before, it destroyed our beliefs in what happens after you die. You weren't past the vast water at all. Do you even care for the dead souls?" Ellendrii asked.

"Ah, I knew this would be coming. The answer is no. I am not dead myself, this isn't some sort of afterlife and I have nothing to do with the souls of the dead. All that about the vast water and me being beyond it to take care of those who pass over is just a story to give strength to the belief. It makes Gryphies feel better about dying, that's all. I put it in the minds of the original Forest Gryphies when I first brought them to Shernaron. And that is how it has been ever since. And I strongly advise that you don't say anything to the other Gryphies about the truth of this matter." She looked at Ellendrii sternly and he nodded.

"Along the way, we met others who had seen you…" said Ellendrii.

"Oh, quite probably. I don't stay here all the time. I like to go out and fly around, as we all do. None of us stay at home. I have flown over the Forest of Foreboding before and those little Aqwakitts have seen me as well. Most creatures ignore me since I fly high up. But as you can see, I am a large creature so it's hard not to at least notice me in some way."

"That reminds me, the Gryphie stone and all the things I found. My leather bag is gone and I lost all the things inside it like the mushrooms, moss, glowing crystals and…and a very important gift from a friend. It's a shame I can't take those things back to Shernaron to show the others."

"Ah, these" said the SilvaGryphie and Ellendrii's bag and the Gryphie stone slowly materialized in the pale shifting colours. They floated gently to the ground like feathers and Ellendrii hesitated for a few moments before picking them up.

"What will the Gryphie stone do now we've found you?" he asked.

"It will no longer point to me. It will just shine in the sun. You cannot come back here" she replied.

"After that adventure, we won't be coming back for a long time! …No offence of course…" said Aro and the SilvaGryphie smiled.

"I would not expect you to come back but I would not want you to either. This is a once in a lifetime journey."

"Er…speaking of coming back, could you come back home with us and prove those Sky Gryphies wrong? We would be really grateful" said Ellendrii, carefully. He really hoped she would say yes. He was afraid she would say no and that they had found her, met her and that was surely enough? But of course they didn't have proof and that was what they needed. Ideally the SilvaGryphie coming back with them.

"Well after all the trouble you went through to get here, I suppose I could show my face in Shernaron again. It will be the first time I've been back physically since I left at the dawn of your settling there."

"Thank you SO much!" Ellendrii said gratefully, with a respectful bow of his head. He knew they would be much safer on the journey back with her travelling alongside them.

"I have a question" said Aro and Ellendrii cringed.

"Go ahead" replied the SilvaGryphie.

"How come you made all the Gryphies so much smaller than you?" he asked.

"You know, I really have no idea. I guess it was just how I felt at the time. I didn't want them to be so big that they would struggle to fit in in this world. If they were too big, they wouldn't be able to climb the trees or sit in them."

"But then you could just make the trees bigger?" asked Aro.

"I wanted to create something that would fit in with the current environment without me messing with things. Besides, though I created the Gryphies, I cannot interfere with the balance of nature. That is why my sub-species of Gryphies fit in with the different lands of Shernaron. The mountains, the valley, the Forest, the Skylands. It all works with the balance of nature and that is how they all survive. I am proud of my work. Sure, you all got into a fight with the native creatures but it was sorted out and you did it by yourselves and I am proud of your species for that."

"Wait, does that mean the Lizariaouses were around before the Gryphies?" asked Ellendrii.

"Yes, the Lizariaous is an old species, very old. Much older than the Gryphies. They lived in Dyarkroeen for many, many seasons before I brought the Gryphies to Shernaron. Not that anyone can remember of course. I had hoped that

the Outlands would serve to keep both species apart and they did for a while. But of course, both species were curious and the Lizariaouses found out about the Gryphies when they saw them in the sky and obviously, they got curious and followed them back to the Forest and were then aware of them. So, the two species met. It's nice to see that there was good that came of the war. Before it, your two species just tolerated each other. But now a union has been formed between you and you all live in peace. I mean, I never thought in a million seasons that a Gryphie AND a Lizariaous together would seek me out. And yet here you are."

"What about the...Deamon Gryphies though? My Dad is half Deamon and he is bigger than the rest of us. You've only mentioned the territories of Shernaron; what about the Dark Plains? Did you create the Deamon Gryphies and place them there?" asked Ellendrii, curiously. He was puzzled as to why she never seemed to mention the Deamons. The SilvaGryphie looked slightly awkward at hearing his question.

"Well...yes I did create the Deamon Gryphies as well. Only they were uh...an early work that didn't really turn out as I had hoped. That is why I placed them in an environment that would mean cutting them off from most of the other creatures around the area. I experimented a little when I created them but soon learned it was best to stick with what was natural instead of using "artistic licence" shall we say."

Ellendrii and Aro exchanged quick glances. It seemed the SilvaGryphie had created something she didn't particularly want to acknowledge or was a little ashamed of, which was why she had tried to put it somewhere where it wouldn't be too noticeable. Ellendrii felt even more curious now about them but decided not to probe any further regarding the Deamons. He turned his attention elsewhere instead.

"While we were travelling here, we met a creature that looked like a Gryphie. Her name was Midnyte Comet. D...Did you create her too?" Ellendrii felt he had to ask.

"There are a lot of things that happen with the passage of time. Certain things spring up with the changing tides. Certain things are unique" she answered mysteriously.

Ellendrii frowned. Well that didn't help. Except maybe Midnyte was unique? But he knew that.

"El only asked because he has a crush on her" blurted out Aro, "I reckon he would like to pick her up on the way back home and take her back to Shernaron to be his life partner.

"Shut UP Aro!!" growled Ellendrii but the SilvaGryphie merely chuckled.

"You will find someone but it won't be her" she told him.

"How do you know that? Can you see into the future?" asked Ellendrii, very curious now.

"I can only see certain things. But I can definitely see that you won't end up with Midnyte Comet, unless you move to her island and stick around, annoy her and try to become her life partner that way. But she would be difficult to persuade. It is better to just part on good terms as friends than leave a bad taste in both your mouths over it. I can assure you she is the sort who would not appreciate you going back there for her."

"Do you know her then?" asked Ellendrii.

"I know a lot of things and I know when is a good time to leave things."

Ellendrii looked sad.

"Ok, I'll leave it. I don't want to annoy her."

"Very good" replied the SilvaGryphie.

"Does all your domain look like this?" asked Aro.

"Yes, unless I will something into existence. Such as where I sleep. There is a raised section I sleep on."

"Do you eat the same as the rest of us?" asked Aro.

"Yes, I need to hunt as well. I can't just create food to eat. I would end up getting no nourishment from it and becoming ill. I need to hunt like you do."

"Do you breathe blue fire like Ellendrii?" asked Aro.

"Yes, and I am a Fire Master as well."

"Could you…"

"Make something with my fire for your amusement?" The SilvaGryphie asked with a small eye roll.

"If it's not too much trouble" said Aro meekly.

"It's never trouble" she replied and proceeded to blow out a large trail of blue fire which slowly formed the shape of Aro and Ellendrii. The two fire friends walked along and met the

SilvaGryphie and then they all flew into the air and disappeared.

"That's SO amazing" garbled Aro in awe.

"I'm surprised Ellendrii hasn't tried something like this, he is multi-talented"

"I…I am?"

"You would be able to do it with practice. You have the ability. But maybe save that for another sun cycle, one after you come back to Shernaron triumphant with the SilvaGryphie by your side."

Ellendrii blushed deep red. Aro had never seen him blush as much as he did now. He giggled and Ellendrii coughed and turned with his back to the pair of them and pretended to be checking out something behind him.

"How big is your err…domain?" asked Ellendrii.

"As big as I need it to be" replied the SilvaGryphie.

"Well, we should be safe going back with you. I bet you're not scared of Repulsators or the Narg'tok are you? Or Thresh for that matter" said Aro.

"Who said we would be walking? That would take far too long. We can get back to Shernaron in less than a sun cycle if we fly."

"So, you mean to say that if I had flown here, I would have made it in less than a sun cycle?" asked Ellendrii, "That doesn't make sense. We spent like, six or more sun cycles crossing the vast water by flight. I know I was pulling the float but I was still flying."

"I mean to say that I will be flying back with you and I can fly much faster than you can, Ellendrii. We will fly back the way you came and you will be able to see all you passed on the way here. Weather does not affect me but I'm sure there won't be stormy weather when we fly across the vast water. I don't often run into bad weather." She was of course referring to her abilities as a creator and even though she didn't mess with nature, it wasn't unknown for her to make the weather more manageable when she was passing through places.

"What about me though?" asked Aro.

"And how will I keep up with you?" asked Ellendrii.

"You will both ride on my back. I will do the flying. Aro, if you get cold, you can curl up in my long fur and keep warm."

"Thank you so much!" said Aro, gratefully while thinking FINALLY I WILL GET TO FLY PROPERLY!!!

"Will we be able to talk or wave to those we've met, who were actually nice to us?" asked Ellendrii.

"You can but I won't be stopping to land. I want to get you both back to where you belong and so I will not be dawdling."

"Thanks anyway. I just wanted to let our friends know that we made it and to say goodbye and wish them well" said Ellendrii.

"He means that he wants to see Midnyte Comet one last time" giggled Aro.

"Not just her! What about A'urealiz and the Aqwakitts, Rivniann and those funny little creatures that lived in the trees? And the Wind Hounds!"

"Don't speak to me about the Wind Hounds" replied Aro with a snort.

"Hey, it was *you* who insulted *them*! It was *your* fault, not theirs. You can't be mad at them for something that you brought upon yourself and that wouldn't have happened had you not waited at least until we were completely out of earshot or back in the structure we were staying in."

"Well they shouldn't have been so difficult and just accepted that other creatures might not understand their ways and so question them" growled Aro.

"And you need to learn more respect. Those who are different are there to be learned from. Do not question to their faces the things that are important to them. You can question in your mind or to your friend but not in front of that creature. How would you like it if your ways were mocked? If they mocked how you hunt, what you eat, how you bury your dead?"

"I guess I'd be annoyed..."

"And now do you understand better?"

"Yeah I guess. I didn't mess up again though. I kept my mouth shut! Even when we were around those tree creatures who we needed to sign to in order to get them to understand us."

"Those were called Kanniths. I enjoyed watching your patience with them."

"We didn't have much of a choice really" said Ellendrii, "We either learned how they communicated or they would've killed us or forced us back into that wretched forest."

"Ah yes that forest. I don't like that place either. Except as you found, Rivniann is the nicest creature there. The only nice creature there. But the Kanniths taught you both to be careful and respect others. I knew Aro especially struggled with things like that. So it was good you met them."

"You didn't uhh…kind of arrange that we should meet them, did you?" asked Ellendrii.

"No. I didn't "arrange" that you met any of the things you encountered along your way. That was just up to life and fate and things that are meant to be. If you were not meant to meet me then there would have been nothing I could have done about it. That is all down to fate and I can't control that. None of us can."

So, Ellendrii thought, she isn't all powerful after all. But she is powerful enough and he knew that she would definitely be able to hold her own.

"What happened to Thresh?" asked Ellendrii.

"I flamed him. It didn't do much, but it did give him a fright. Charred his armour quite badly too. He fled and hid in his cave. He's still in there as far as I'm aware. My fire is more powerful than any Gryphie's but his armour is a great protection for him even so. I carried your bodies back here and healed you. It didn't take long but it would have been quicker of course if you hadn't been dead."

"You should've killed him" muttered Aro.

"And that would have made me just as bad as him. I kept him alive; spared him. But I did give him the fright of his life and it will be a while before he will have the confidence to show his face again. Plus he has pretty bad scarring all over his body from my fire and I broke his pride."

"I suppose that's ok" said Ellendrii.

"Should've killed him" muttered Aro.

"Ah, Lizariaouses" smiled the SilvaGryphie.

"If you have the power to do all these things and can fly fast and stuff and want to get us back home, then why are you giving us a ride? Surely you could just use whatever powers you have to get us there immediately? Not that I'm complaining of course, I want to see all the places we've been and those we met along the way." Ellendrii said.

"I could indeed get you back instantly. But I thought it would be more fulfilling for all of us if I gave you a ride home. You would get to spend longer with me that way and since you came all this way to meet me, it would be mean of me to take you back instantly and forgo the pleasure of spending time with me after all you've been through. Plus I know Aro really wanted to fly properly."

"Yes, I really do" said Aro excitedly.

"There you go" said the SilvaGryphie.

"Makes sense" smiled Ellendrii. "I wonder where the sun is?"

"In the sky" replied the SilvaGryphie.

"I mean what time of sun cycle it is" said Ellendrii. She had known what he meant.

"It's early enough that we can start soon."

"Ok. How long were we resting?" asked Ellendrii.

"About three sun cycles. I had healed you fast enough but your bodies still needed to rest. Your spirits were weak and tired and in need of proper sleep, which has been few and far between during the moon cycles of your travels."

"No wonder I felt so refreshed" said Aro, grinning. The SilvaGryphie smiled and nodded.

"I can't tell you how happy we are to have found you though" said Ellendrii.

"You don't need to, I already know" she replied.

"Of course. As well as watching us, did you know how we were feeling at the time? Could you read our thoughts as well?" asked Ellendrii.

"I could have but I didn't. There was no need to. I could see what you were going through."

Probably just as well thought Aro. Even though she would probably know he was terrified of Repulsators, he really didn't need her reading his thoughts and finding out the full extent of it.

Ellendrii was thinking up more things to ask her.

"Why didn't you just move in the other side of the vast water so that the beliefs of our species would be true?"

"Because that is where the Wind Hounds live" replied the SilvaGryphie.

"But you could make your…err…this place there, surely?" asked Ellendrii.

"Yes but I still need space for my dimension and it was too close to their territory. The other side of the valley where Thresh lives is uninhabited so I have chosen to live here. It is quiet, pleasant country and I like it. Also, given the location, very few find me here. I can close the entrance to my dimension but I like to keep it open when I leave, so I can come back in easily. Very few get past Thresh, so no one comes up here. They either die by Thresh or see the boneyard and turn back. If the moaning tunnels don't put them off first that is. Those caves in that mountain are so nice that as soon as travellers hear the awful moaning, they turn back and just enjoy exploring the tunnels instead. I chose this location very carefully. And of course I wanted to be nowhere near Shernaron in case my species found me and got some stupid ideas in their heads like they did last time. I would have stayed with you if they hadn't started to elevate me to the title of god and worship me. I lived in the valley back when I was living in Shernaron. We reached Shernaron and I set everyone out where they were supposed to live. Then I stayed but as time went by, more and more of them either worshipped me or tried to rely on me to solve their problems. So I left and I put into all their minds that I lived the other side of the vast water and that it was too far to fly. I managed to make them forget about the fact that I had until recently back then been living with them and left it at that. But then there were the few idiots who decided to try and fly across the vast water and come and find me. None of them made it though. And you wouldn't have either, if you hadn't had the float for Aro and the chance to rest. They would set out but flying all the time and not resting soon took its toll on them and they

would fall in the water and drown. They never reached the island. They weren't strong enough to fly that far without stopping. So my legend would live on in the stories that they told about me. The memories that they did have. Because I'd only just left, I simply let them remember when I had been there and think nothing more about it. When I left them, I did it without warning because I didn't want to be followed. I let them all think I had lived there in the past and left seasons ago. So the stories have remained the same over the seasons."

"Do you know how long we've been gone?" asked Ellendrii.

"Just over two seasons. So, a long time. It doesn't seem like it because the weather is different depending on what place you're in."

"I wonder if our parents think we're dead" pondered Ellendrii.

"I know what they think but it is not my place to say. Some things I cannot tell you and you need to find out for yourselves."

"I sort of thought you'd say that" said Ellendrii.

"And yet you still asked."

"Well, just in case!" Ellendrii smiled sheepishly. The SilvaGryphie smiled too.

It occurred to both Ellendrii and Aro that neither of them felt hungry. They couldn't remember the last time they ate but they still didn't feel hungry. Ellendrii questioned the SilvaGryphie over this.

"When I healed you, it healed your appetites too. You will get hungry again of course but you won't need to eat until we get to Shernaron. It's just easier that way than bothering to go out hunting. Even though I hunt, I will often catch something large and bring it back here and live off it for a long time. Even though I am bigger, my appetite is the same as yours."

"Did you model our appetites on your own then?" asked Ellendrii.

"No, because I am a higher being. I simply don't need to eat as often as a creature of my size would normally. So the smaller Gryphies that I created have an appetite that is right

for their size. I guess my appetite is also right for their size."
She chuckled, amused at her own ideas.

"Well I'm glad. I've felt hungry almost non-stop while we were travelling and it was annoying. We were less hungry later in the journey though, which was refreshing" said Ellendrii.

"Your stomachs have shrunk because you aren't eating as often. It happens as a defence against starvation" explained the SilvaGryphie.

"Hmm, useful" said Ellendrii.

Aro hadn't said much. He was just happy and relaxed and glad they were going home. He had no idea how horrified Ellendrii must have been to learn of his death. He also felt mad at himself for not defeating Thresh. Even though Thresh had been larger and more powerful but all the same, a Lizariaous should be able to put up a good fight and he felt that he hadn't put up any sort of fight at all really. He felt the ground under his paws. The velvet might be nice for Gryphies but for him, it didn't feel right. He was used to rock! He idly wondered if there was a creature that had created the Lizariaouses too and wanted to ask the SilvaGryphie but he figured she probably wouldn't know anyway since she had arrived after Lizariaouses had started to exist in Dyarkroeen. Aro's mind was deep in thought.

"Well you two, are you ready to go back to Shernaron?" she asked them.

"Definitely!" yelled Aro, speaking now.

"Yes, I'm ready to go back. I can't wait to see their faces when they see you!" Ellendrii grinned. The SilvaGryphie smiled good naturedly.

"I have to say it will be pleasant to actually go back to Shernaron physically and seeing how it's all looking. It's not really the same when you astral project yourself to a place."

"When you what?" asked Ellendrii.

"It doesn't matter" replied the SilvaGryphie. *"Now, follow me."*

They both followed her, I would describe where but since the whole of her domain looked alike, that would be hard to do. So they followed her until she stopped, which they assumed to be the edge of her domain. Ellendrii had walked along looking at her beautiful white fur with its pearly colours shining when the light and shade changed on it as she walked. Aro wasn't paying much attention to anything because he was just eager to get out and get back home. He had enjoyed this trip but really, he wanted things to go back to normal now. He was tired of encountering new dangers around every corner, creatures that were easily insulted, strange glowing plants, terrain that he didn't like and other stuff that they had encountered that he had had enough of.

"Ok, climb up onto my back" she told them, lying down and dropping her wings so they could climb up.

Ellendrii did so easily but Aro struggled a little. He didn't want to dig his claws in and hurt her so he was being even more careful than Ellendrii. In the end she had to lift one of her wings to help him up. Finally they were both sat on her fluffy back. Ellendrii was at the front and Aro sat behind him. They didn't hinder the movement of her wings because she was so much larger than they were.

Ellendrii peered over her head.

"This is gunna be awesome!" he roared happily.

"Umm…El…could I maybe sit at the front?" asked Aro. "I really want to get the full flying experience…"

"Ok, you can" said Ellendrii and they swapped places.

"Are you ready now?" asked the SilvaGryphie and they both said that they were.

"Excellent" she said, spreading her wings.

"Then let's go!" And she took off, leaving her domain and emerging from the mist into the sky over the valley where Thresh lived.

They were on their way home!

Chapter 32
Flight

For the benefit of her passengers, the SilvaGryphie didn't fly too high. This way, Ellendrii and Aro could see down below pretty clearly. They passed over the horrible boneyard and Thresh's domain. There was no sign of the cruel creature.

"He is cowering in his cavern" laughed the SilvaGryphie. *"He will come out again though. Given time. I didn't kill him also because I need him to be around and scare creatures away so they don't find my domain."*

"I am so glad we don't have to walk back through there" said Aro, looking down from his perch just behind her head. Ellendrii didn't have such a good view but he didn't really care much. Aro was enjoying it and he deserved to after all he'd been through.

"You won't see the cavern, obviously we will fly over the mountain range instead. But you will see that at least. It looks much like the mountain tops you crossed."

"Are there more Ursquaches up there?" asked Ellendrii.

"Most likely. That is one of my hunting grounds. They are among the creatures I eat. There are plenty of them if you know where to look and I certainly haven't hunted it dry. That means eaten all the food up there."

"You eat them? Oh well, I guess we all have to eat something. But I really liked A'urealiz" said Ellendrii.

"She was an exception. Most of them aren't nice like she was. They would hunt and kill you and the males are even worse than the females. So don't think that just because you meet one nice creature, that the entire species is like that."

They flew over the mountain range and did see a couple of Ursquaches down below. Obviously, none of them were A'urealiz because she didn't live on those mountains. They also weren't quite as snowy as the others had been either. The snow was very patchy and only a little on the very peaks. The SilvaGryphie explained that these mountains weren't as high as the others the pair of them had climbed.

"I wish we'd climbed up these instead then" said Aro.

"Wasn't it easier and more pleasant to go through the caves though?" asked the SilvaGryphie.

"Well yes but…"

"I could have got the Gryphie stone to take you over these mountains too but I thought it would be quicker and easier to let you go through and see the pretty caves."

"Yeah I can understand that" replied Aro.

"Have you been in the caves then?" asked Ellendrii, "I would have thought you were too big?"

"I can get into them but it is a tight squeeze, annoyingly" she replied.

Aro looked down as they flew and breathed the air in deeply.

"I LOVE this!! I'm so happy I finally get to fly and see what all the fuss is about. Seeing the clouds from the top of a mountain and swimming under a lake don't even come close to this!"

"I'm glad you enjoy it. It is your reward for keeping Ellendrii safe. Thank you, Aro."

"Hey no worries, he's my best friend. I'll always be here for him!"

The SilvaGryphie smiled.

"My creation finally fits in. It is all complete" she sighed as they flew. It was all working out.

"It all looks so small from up here. Kinda like when you look down at the ground and all the bugs are crawling about. I bet you've been so high that you could imagine my species as bugs, eh El?" Aro asked, looking back at him.

"Well, yeah. But I wouldn't call you bugs. That's kinda insulting. I don't think about it much. When I first learned to fly, yeah, it was a novelty but because we fly to live, to survive and we all do it, it's just a part of life and we don't really think anything more of it than that."

"Ha, you're being modest. Flying is your LIFE and you think about it all the time" retorted Aro.

"Well, yeah, I guess you're right there" replied Ellendrii. He did think about flying all the time but he still rarely marvelled at it apart from when he was cloud dodging or when he visited the Skylands.

Looking down, the pair of them now saw they were passing over the barren desert land where they had nearly dehydrated and died and Ellendrii's wing had been damaged in the sand storm. He was reminded of the SilvaGryphie saying that there would be no storms as they flew through these dangerous areas and he sincerely hoped she was right. He clutched his leather bag to him. It no longer had the gourd in but it did have the items they had found.

"I would've liked the desert if it hadn't been so hot and dusty and stretched on for AGES" sighed Aro.

"At least we found food to eat, though it was in an unlikely place" replied Ellendrii.

"I was surprised you both survived so well when you were separated. I thought then that you would die and I would have to come and save you. But you were very resourceful."

"Thank you" said Ellendrii. "The heat and dryness was difficult."

"I was just glad that the next place we had to go was that cave or I don't think we could have survived without resting and drinking again. Look how the sand makes shapes. You can only see them from above." Aro observed.

"Yes, the wind blows it like that. Whenever there is a sand storm, the desert is reshaped and changes. It is ever changing and ever shifting. I think it is an interesting place so long as you can visit and then get away in one sun cycle."

"I'm surprised anything lives there actually. Those creatures under the sand were a pleasant surprise" said Aro.

"I didn't think you would find those. It was one good thing that came from the sand storm at least. If the storm hadn't happened, you wouldn't have had anything to eat or drink and I don't know how you would have survived. See, always find the positive in the negative. Something bad happens? Try to find the positive in it."

"I try but when I thought Aro had died, there was no positive side to it" said Ellendrii sadly.

"But there was. He died fighting for his best friend; you! He died trying to save you and that was for a good cause. So there was a positive in it. You just need to look harder. Even

when it looks like there is no hope. There were plenty of times on your journey when you felt like giving up hope."

"That's true. But all the same if something really bad happens, then it's very hard to find something good about it."

"I know."

They continued over the desert and Aro could now see the burning mountain rising up in the distance. Ellendrii shrank back. He didn't want to see this thing again. It was evil to him. Something with that much strangely coloured fire that could destroy so much of the land. He pretended to examine the SilvaGryphie's long back fur as they flew, admiring the beauty of it and holding strands of it into the light. It even smelled nice. Her smell was reassuring like the smell of his own mother and he liked that. He felt safe with her.

He felt safe. So why was he frightened of this burning mountain? It couldn't harm him. After all, he was with the SilvaGryphie. She had brought him back from the dead and surely she would stop any fire mountain from destroying him.

He kept his wings folded close so he didn't impede her own wing movements. Looking around him, he saw the full scale of her wings and the powerful muscles she was using to fly with. The gentle ripple of them and the way the sheen of her fur shone in the sun as they flew.

He still couldn't really believe it. Now, given time to think because Aro and the SilvaGryphie were chatting to each other, he was finally "alone" with his thoughts, which were starting to wander and desperately try to keep themselves occupied because of the burning mountain that was approaching down below. He was here, with her, the answer to seemingly all his problems with getting into the Elite Flyers. And yet he had never found her. She had found him. She had saved them both in the end because they wouldn't give up. It was ironic really. He had been hoping to find her and had been right with the idea of the Gryphie stone leading them to her and yet after all that, he hadn't actually found her. He had died trying to find her. They both had.

His thoughts were interrupted by Aro suddenly exclaiming.

"Wow, that's amazing!" and Ellendrii couldn't help but look. And when he looked he nearly screamed.

They were flying over the top of the burning mountain and the top of it looked like it had been cut off, to reveal what was inside it. And it was full of hot, red, angry molten fire. Ellendrii could feel the heat of it as they flew overhead.

"Do not worry, it won't erupt. We are safe" said the SilvaGryphie as they flew over the top.

"It's horrible" muttered Ellendrii.

"He doesn't like it" said Aro, "He's scared of the damage it does."

"It won't damage you now but yes, it does damage the land around it when it erupts. They don't erupt that often though. This one hadn't erupted for many seasons, which is why the trees had all grown up around it and why there is so much carnage and ash. It will be a long time before any of them grow back again. Look how white and pale the ground is. From here, it is almost like looking at snow."

"I don't like it. I thought Gryphies had the most powerful fire but we could never do that much damage" said Ellendrii.

"Then you should be glad that this is not a living creature and can only damage what's around it. And there are none of these in Shernaron, not even dormant ones so there is no worry of anything like that destroying your territory" she reassured him.

Ellendrii felt a little better but it was still such an eerie, quiet and terrifying place to walk through. It spoke of death without smelling of death, unlike the boneyard.

At least they were high up enough that the ash didn't get down Aro's throat. He was looking all around him as excited as what we might understand to be when you take your dog out in the car and he sticks his head out of the window.

The flight was also very smooth. Being so large, the SilvaGryphie flapped her wings only every so often and glided on wind currents as well, which made the journey more comfortable for her passengers.

"Well, at least there are none of these things in or near Shernaron" remarked Ellendrii with relief.

"Yes, I chose a good place for you to live that was safe" the SilvaGryphie replied. Ellendrii agreed there and was glad of it.

Aro couldn't believe that fire somehow grew out of mountains. He'd always been lead to believe it was just something Gryphies breathed. As Ellendrii did too.

The SilvaGryphie didn't elaborate on what the burning mountain was or why it was there as they flew over it. Ellendrii was glad when they had reached the other side of it and were flying over the ashen ground. It just looked white from where they were. The trees looked like twigs; what was left of them.

"I'm glad we're high enough up that it doesn't affect our lungs" said Aro. "I hated that. It was ok for a creature who breathes fire but what with everything else I was hoarse when we got out and arrived in the cave. Good thing there was lots of water in there that I could recover with."

"And now you know why I guided you through the cave and not over the top of it. I wanted you both to actually survive your ordeal and in order for that to happen, I had to guide you through a place where you could replenish your bodies. If you'd gone over the top, you would have died."

"But we did die" replied Ellendrii.

"That was a technicality. I thought you wouldn't actually wake Thresh up. And if Aro hadn't dawdled around his cavern then you wouldn't have woken him. I thought you both would have learned enough by that time to know a dangerous place when you were in it and just keep moving."

"Sorry, I couldn't help myself. I miss my cave. And this was the biggest cave I'd ever seen. Surely you can understand my fascination with it?" said Aro.

"I can understand but your common sense needed to rule at that moment, not your head or your curiosity."

"I know, I know" grumbled Aro.

They had reached the mountain range where A'urealiz lived. Ellendrii kept an eye out for her.

"I will fly lower so you can greet your friend. I know where she is right now" said the SilvaGryphie and flew lower.

Sure enough, A'urealiz was trudging through the snow. The fin on her back was healing well now and as they flew overhead, Ellendrii let out a blue fireball into the air and she looked up.

"Hey! A'urealiz! We found her! We found the SilvaGryphie!" roared Ellendrii.

"Well done!" yelled back the Ursquach happily.

The SilvaGryphie flew around A'urealiz so she could get a good look at her beauty and the pair of adventurers sat on her back.

"We're going home now! She's taking us back to where we came from and I am going to show her to those disbelievers in the sky!" roared Ellendrii.

"Good luck my friends!" roared A'urealiz from down below. The SilvaGryphie flew overhead and she sat back and watched them as they passed her.

"Goodbye A'urealiz and thank you for helping us across the mountains!" yelled Aro.

"Good luck in your lives, my friends!" she called after them. "If you ever come back, you know where to find me!"

"Take care, A'urealiz!" Ellendrii and Aro called out together and waved to her as they flew off. They knew they wouldn't be back and so probably did A'urealiz but it was nice to leave an open invitation there.

The SilvaGryphie flew down low, kicking up snow in huge flurries as she passed, her wings flapping powerfully and whipping up a frosty wind. The sun sparkled through the snow flurries and it was beautiful. Her fur glistened and sparkled against the snow and Ellendrii kept getting glimpses of the mythical underside of her wings as she moved them up and then down again.

Aro snuggled into her fluffy mane, feeling warm despite that they were in the air in a cold climate. It was like snuggling into soft down and it was wonderfully warm. It made for a very comfortable flying position.

Over the snow they went and it looked similar to the white of the ash, only this was pure and untouched, aside from where they saw Ursquach tracks or a few wandering individuals of the bear-like species. Ellendrii tried to follow the tracks with his eyes but they flew up higher and he found it harder to follow them then.

It was so weird flying as a passenger for him. He remembered vaguely when he was a kitten and riding on Diabloss or Leida's backs but those were distant and dull memories, soon covered by the memories of him learning to fly himself and then flying by himself. And of course the memories of all the awesome things he had done while flying, including of course, visiting the Skylands.

They saw the clouds around the edge of the mountain range coming up and remembered scaling the side of the hugely high mountain and arriving above those clouds. Aro could never even have dreamed that they would be flying back this way.

It had never occurred to Ellendrii that the SilvaGryphie would actually give them a lift back, nor did it occur to him that it would take so little time. They were already clearing the snowy mountains and the sun was high in the sky.

Peering over her head, Aro could see the lake sparkling in the distance, as he had when they were ascending the mountain. He saw it through the clouds. The SilvaGryphie cut through the clouds and then dodged high above them where the sun shone down warmly on her and her passengers.

"This is how I cloud dodge" she smiled and started to show off, dodging up and down, through, inside and out of the clouds. They felt cold when she flew through them and there was some turbulence, which surprised Aro. When he looked to the sky, the clouds always looked so soft. Ellendrii on the other hand knew what this was like.

Suddenly she did a loop-the-loop and flew upside down briefly as she made the circle of the loop. Aro screamed in terror, clinging on for dear life. Ellendrii screamed in joy, loving this and making the most of the ride.

"Please don't do that again" whimpered Aro, still clinging on to her mane.

"Don't worry, you won't fall off. Not even if I do this!" and she started to fly upside down, which terrified Aro even more.

"AAARRGHHHH! I'm starting to lose interest in flyingggggg!!!!" roared Aro, clinging on tighter.

"You won't fall though"

"Try telling that to my instincts!"

"Ok, I'll fly properly" she replied and righted herself.

"Spoilsport" muttered Ellendrii.

"I don't want to scare your friend" said the SilvaGryphie and that was the end of her acrobatics.

"I thought you wanted to fly, Aro. Don't tell me that if you could fly, you wouldn't want to do any tricks?" snapped Ellendrii.

"I would…but if I was flying myself, then I would be in charge and not holding on to someone else. I know she said I wouldn't fall but I still felt like I would and that scared me." Ellendrii said nothing. Aro was right in a way but he still wondered that if the Lizariaous could fly, would he do all the tricks and acrobatics that Ellendrii did?

The pair of them were silenced as they flew over the horrible landscape that looked like rotting flesh. Aro hoped it wouldn't rain again. It looked even worse from up here somehow. At least when they were close to it, they couldn't see as much of it. As it was from up here they saw the barren reddish ground with its cracks and lesions and the red rivers and streams flowing through it. They looked like veins, like it was a whole nervous system or something. And there was that awful smell again.

"We never understood this land. It's so different to all the others we've travelled through" said Ellendrii.

"It is cursed. The land itself is organic and the red rain that falls from the sky is because the water that flows through this land is red as well. You didn't drink any, did you?"

"Surely you would know that? But no, we didn't. Well, I don't think we did…Aro?" Ellendrii looked at his friend.

"No I didn't drink it" he replied, remembering he had in fact had a taste but didn't actually swallow it; he had spat it out.

"I don't know all that you did because I wasn't watching you all the time. I had other things to do as well, you know. Like hunt and sleep and enjoy life." The SilvaGryphie smiled.

"I only kept an eye on you. I didn't watch you intently."

"I guess you would've got bored then huh?" asked Aro.

"Or wanted to intervene when we were in real trouble?" asked Ellendrii.

"Oh I know that you were capable of getting yourselves out of most trouble" she replied.

"So, you only intervened when we died?" asked Ellendrii.

"I would have intervened at any point if you had died. And I would have revealed myself to you as well, as I have done."

"We should've died sooner" said Aro.

"But I would not have been so impressed if you had died sooner and you would not have learned all you have if you had died sooner, either." She had a point.

"Argh, Aro, why did you have to go looking in that cave? If Thresh hadn't woken up then we could have climbed up the side of the valley, no matter how difficult and made it out and found her! And we wouldn't have had to go through all that trauma either." Ellendrii glared at his friend.

"The trauma. Come to think of it, all those things that happened with Thresh and the injuries we got and dying as well, I'm trying to picture it but it all seems fuzzy somehow and blurred. I can't remember it that well." Aro pointed out. Ellendrii thought about it and found his mind was the same way regarding those particular events.

"I did that so you wouldn't have it preying on your minds. Dying is very traumatic and so were the injuries that Thresh gave you and what he did to you. So you can remember what he did but not in any great detail and in time that will fade as well. I didn't want it affecting your minds. There are other things you've gone through in this journey that will stay with you but I felt there was a limit as to how much of the really bad stuff should stay in your minds so I blurred the memories with Thresh."

"I can remember what he looked like and I know he spat acid and damaged my foot and my wing but I can't remember exactly what that looked like" pondered Ellendrii.

"Because you were too traumatized about it" replied the SilvaGryphie.

"Well then thanks! We both appreciate it, if it helps us not to have moonmares" said Ellendrii.

"Worse than we have been having anyway" muttered Aro. "Could you blur other memories for us I wonder?" he asked her.

"You mean the Repulsators. No, sadly not. You need to remember the other stuff in order to learn and grow. I can't just blur out all the bad things from this journey. That would be unfair. Life needs a balance and you will remember things like that too. But with time and as with many memories, those too will fade and blur. But it will take time."

"Grik" muttered Aro.

They were now approaching the lake. They could see the tiny forms of the Aqwakitts down below splashing about in the water.

"Ah, the Aqwakitts. A simple yet sweet species and very helpful. I lived here for a while before I went and made my own dimension to live in because I believed it would be safer. They were the ones who made that statue of me, the one in the middle of the lake that I placed the Gryphie stone into. They too started to worship me because of my beauty. So I threw their statue into the lake, wiped their minds of me and left. They never remembered who made that statue or why. All they know is that it is a silver coloured statue of a Gryphie."

"Yeeeah tell me about it. What a mix up that was" said Aro, rolling his eyes. "I believed them too!"

"Technically they weren't lying though" replied Ellendrii.

"I guess" mooched Aro.

"I will show myself to them as we pass, but just this once because when I return, I will be flying too high for them to see me."

"They won't admire you or something, will they?" asked Ellendrii. It seemed creatures rather liked trying to make a deity out of the SilvaGryphie.

"Doubtful. Just smile and wave, boys!" She flew down lower, near the surface of the lake, trailing the tip of one wing in it. A spray of pretty rainbow sunlit sparkles kicked up behind her wing as they flew.

The Aqwakitts stopped their frolicking and playing and either stood or floated in the water watching her.

Ellendrii and Aro waved to them as they passed.

"You found her!" yelled Aira and Airu in unison, jumping up and down and waving too.

"Yes! This is the *real* SilvaGryphie!" yelled back Ellendrii.

"She's much prettier than that old statue" the two Aqwakitts agreed, again in unison, which was of course a thing of theirs.

The SilvaGryphie flew lower, letting her legs kick up a huge spray of water. She flew in a circle in the middle of the lake, flying under the spray she was kicking up. The water sparkled beautifully, little droplets landing on her white fur like dew. Her ornate tailspade drew patterns in the water's surface as they flew and then she was up, into the sky leaving the Aqwakitts far below. Some had swum out to where she had been, the water droplets still landing on them from the spray she had created. They dived and danced and back flipped with glee, happy that the two adventurers had found what they were searching for and marvelling at the beauty of what they had found as well.

"It's a lovely lake. We enjoyed our time there" said Ellendrii.

"After El got over his distrust of the Aqwakitts" sniggered Aro.

"It's not my fault if I thought they were gunna drown you" remarked Ellendrii.

"Yeah but not everything was bad. You were right about the statue not being the SilvaGryphie but you were also wrong because it was her, in a way. And there was the Gryphie stone inside. Without which, we would've got lost along the way" replied Aro.

"That's not what you said while we were travelling. You questioned the stone and wondered why we should be following it and what if it wasn't a way to her."

"Yeah but you rightly said it was better than nothing and we had nothing to lose" shrugged Aro.

Ellendrii agreed.

"Hey look! There's the tall grass where I peed on you to get rid of those blood sucking things!" yelled Aro suddenly, pointing to the grass below.

"Gee, thanks for reminding me of that" murmured Ellendrii, rolling his eyes.

"I have to say that was rather funny though" smiled the SilvaGryphie.

"Don't you start too!" grumbled Ellendrii and the other two laughed.

"You'll never let me forget that, will you?" said Ellendrii to Aro.

"Course not. It was funny! I'm telling the others when we get back you know."

"Which others?"

"ALL the others!"

"ARO!!"

Aro laughed so much that he nearly fell off. Then Ellendrii laughed.

"Yeah, you can probably guess that the lake was a welcome break after that" said Ellendrii and the SilvaGryphie nodded.

"Hey, there's the valley we came out of over there" said Ellendrii, pointing.

"There were quite a few valleys actually, on the way to find you" said Aro to the SilvaGryphie.

"Yes, there are a lot of them in this part of the land. But they aren't too troublesome. Some of them have worse things in than others though, as you discovered."

"Yeeeah" was Aro's only reply to that. He was glad that there hadn't been more things like Thresh to encounter.

Ellendrii looked behind them to get one last look at the sparkling lake. There was long grass at this point in their journey almost as far as the eye could see. The other side of the valley that they came out of was also long grass but in the distance was what looked like a dark, foreboding and pointed mountain range.

"What's over there then? If we'd decided to go that way?" he asked.

"Well I knew you wouldn't decide to go that way, even if you had come out of the valley that side. The look of it is enough to put anyone off. Those mountains are the domain of a race of nasty and dangerous creatures called Draxals. They wouldn't have spoken to you, let you pass or reasoned with you. They kill on sight because they eat everything. They are not fussy. They tear every creature apart that they encounter.

They are vicious and formidable and attack en masse and you would not have had a chance against them."

"Ooookay well I'm glad we never went that way" said Ellendrii. In truth, neither of them had really noticed what was that way. They were too interested in the lake because it meant being able to drink and refill their gourds.

They flew over the valley of the Kanniths and could see them all in their trees. Always alert, the little creatures saw the SilvaGryphie fly overhead and sent up alarm calls to each other. The trees bristled with them.

Ellendrii wanted to wave but wasn't sure if they would understand or just get scared.

"I can fly lower but not too low, they will jump onto me and possibly attack. I'll fly low enough that they will be able to see you if they remember who you are." She flew lower, a few metres off the tops of the trees and the little creatures with their strange white masks and lack of faces hopped around, looking up and readying themselves for possible attack.

Aro and Ellendrii waved to them but none of them seemed to recognize them. But then why would they? Did they have short memories? And they didn't really know what the pair of them were in search of anyway or really why they passed through the Kannith territory. The little creatures just watched and prepared but none of them remembered or recognized the pair of them.

"They don't remember you. I doubt even the leader would remember you. Sorry. They are more primitive than we are and don't have a mind that works like ours does. They remember only their own kind, that which they can understand and things like where to find food, where they live and other general survival skills. You were just a possible threat that turned into two friendly and harmless passersby and they probably forgot about you within a few sun cycles, not seeing you around after that."

"I understand" said Ellendrii. He was still a bit sad though.

Passing the trees now, they saw ahead of them the dreaded Forest of Foreboding. Aro shrank back into the SilvaGryphie's mane and Ellendrii swallowed.

"Don't worry you two, we won't be going into it. Not even to wave to your Shardog friend."

"Rivniann? I really wanted to see that other Shardog he spoke of. The mother of all nature or something. Pity we never saw her." Aro sighed.

"It was lucky you found him though. Even though his part of the forest looks different, he is not easy to find in there. The forest is huge and easy to get lost in."

"Yeah, we guessed that" said Ellendrii, having feared they would never leave it. It took them long enough to get through the wretched forest.

Looking down as they flew over it, the darkened leaves and trees looked just as ominous from above as they did from between. Some of the tops of these trees bubbled with strange, squirming things that looked like leeches.

"What's the story on that forest anyway? Is that cursed too?" asked Ellendrii.

"No, it's just not a pleasant place to be. The inhabitants as you saw were not pleasant, none of them. Except Rivniann of course."

"But we found the remains of a temple or something in there" said Ellendrii. Aro visibly cringed.

"That temple belonged to an ancient species that died out. You probably saw statues of them in there. They were equally as terrible as the forest they had their abode in. If they had still been alive, you would have been caught by them and sacrificed. They loved to torture and sacrifice creatures like you. Or any creatures for that matter."

"Like the Repulsators?" asked Ellendrii. Aro glared at him for mentioning them.

"No, they came afterwards. They only haunt derelict structures. Things that have lain empty for a long time. They never haunt inhabited places. So there is no need to worry, Aro." She looked back as him and smiled.

"Well I'll have to make sure all our caves are lived in, in that case" said Aro.

"They don't live in caves. Only built structures. For example, the Wind Hounds' homes. They would haunt those if they laid empty for a long time. Luckily the Wind Hounds *never leave their homes to go like that. They are too clean and careful. Repulsators love things that are going to ruin. They like the larger structures better."*

"That would serve those vain Wind Hounds right if they got Repulsators haunting them" muttered Aro. He felt the dog-like creatures needed a good scare or something to put the fear of death into them.

"We've been through this, Aro. You just need to be more respectful" said Ellendrii.

"And equally *they* need to be less easily insulted" said Aro.

"Well, we will be reaching Kazétos soon and Lord Scerniss will probably see you. Would you like to fly higher and avoid being seen by him and the others?" asked the SilvaGryphie.

"No, I want to see them and I want to make Aro apologize" said Ellendrii. Aro glared at him.

"Very well" she replied

Neither of them really wanted to look down at the Forest of Foreboding. They were happy to just look straight ahead and get this part of the journey over as fast as possible. Sensing this, the SilvaGryphie picked up the pace and they were soon nearing the end of the blackened horror that was the Forest of Foreboding.

Leaving it now, Ellendrii could see Kazétos approaching. The white city looked beautiful in the sunlight as they approached it. They could see the Wind Hounds down below, going about their business. Some were even racing around the city square as they had raced against Ellendrii when the pair were there.

Ellendrii idly wondered if their float was still there. They passed Lord Scerniss' temple and the regal Lord of the Wind Hounds could be seen soaking up the sun just outside of the temple, on the steps leading in to it.

Ellendrii shot out a blue fireball as he had to alert A'urealiz to their presence. The SilvaGryphie warned him to be careful; they didn't want Lord Scerniss to think that they were attacking him. They saw him look up and then get to his feet.

The SilvaGryphie took this moment to fly lower and hover in the air.

"Lord Scerniss! We found the SilvaGryphie!" called down Ellendrii. He nudged Aro so hard that it made the Lizariaous yelp and wince.

"And…I'm sorry for insulting you, your highness" he called down humbly, knowing that this was what Ellendrii wanted him to say.

"I have to say I'm impressed that you made it through the forest" called back the Lord of the Wind Hounds.

"We all thought you would surely die when we chased you away. The creature you have brought back is truly beautiful." Even he was in awe of her.

"I am the SilvaGryphie and I am taking these two safely home to where they come from" she told him. He shook his head, not used to her voice, as Aro had been the first time he had heard her.

"Very good" he said, "Make sure they make it back safely. And Aro…" Aro sank back a little as Lord Scerniss' piercing eyes bored into him.

"You are forgiven this time because you were ignorant but if we ever meet again, be sure to be more respectful."

He didn't even *need* to issue a verbal warning; Aro had been warned.

"Yes sir!" said Aro, saluting him in the way of the Lizariaous. Lord Scerniss understood this and nodded.

"See? And everything's fine" said Ellendrii. Aro just sighed. It was good that he had made peace with Lord Scerniss and thus, the rest of the Wind Hounds but at the same time, apologizing was not something he was used to or liked doing.

"Goodbye!" roared Ellendrii and Aro waved to him. Lord Scerniss smiled up at them.

"Goodbye and good luck!" he called. The SilvaGryphie flew up into the sky, the sunlight shining off her fur and leaving the Wind Hound king in awe.

"Well, if she was what they were searching for, she was certainly worth finding" he said to himself as he watched them fly away.

They reached the white cliffs and the beautiful bathing pools, flying over the breeze of Wind Hounds and houndlets that bathed and swam in them. Ellendrii and Aro spied their friends, Addis, Kaisey and Sarris and called to them. The houndlets looked up, eyes wide as they saw the SilvaGryphie and her two passengers. They jumped about excitedly and waved back to them.

"They were nice to stay with despite the wrong stuff that happened" admitted Aro.

"And because I got you to apologize, now they will always welcome us back" said Ellendrii.

"We won't be coming back though, will we? It was hard enough getting across the vast water to even get this far."

"Well, yeah. But they don't know that. Leaving it so that we're always welcome back here means leaving on good terms with them and that's important. I really enjoyed our time with them. They were so interesting. They taught me a lot anyway." Ellendrii told him.

"Yeah, true" said Aro. They were heading for the vast water now. Not long till they would be back in Shernaron and how surprised their parents would be!

Aro was grinning now. His grin only widened as they spied the island in the middle of the sea and as it grew when they approached it. Luckily Ellendrii didn't see or even notice his friend's expression.

As they neared the island, Ellendrii had a funny feeling inside him. His heart felt airy like butterflies. He hoped so badly that they would see Midnyte, at least see her even if he didn't have the chance to speak to her.

"Don't worry, you will see her" the SilvaGryphie said and with that, she shot out a huge fireball that lit up the entire sky with bright blue flames. They painted a whole canvas of different images of Ellendrii and Aro and their journey to find her. The images swirled and changed above the island itself. Midnyte Comet wouldn't be able to miss or ignore it.

Then, they saw her. She had flown out of the trees to see what the fuss was about.

Ellendrii's eyes grew wide and his heart did that funny fluttering thing again when he saw her. He couldn't stop himself, he dived off the SilvaGryphie's back and into the air, somersaulting with joy at seeing Midnyte again and flying towards her. She recognized him instantly and went to greet him.

"We did it, Midnyte! We found her!" he cried, flying up to her and all around her excitedly. She laughed.

"I can see that!" she said, "And she is beautiful! I thought you two would surely have died by now. It's been so long since I saw you." Aro waved to her from where he was perched on the SilvaGryphie and Midnyte waved back to him.

"Well actually, we *did* die but the SilvaGryphie saved us" Ellendrii explained.

"Really? That must've been scary" she said with concern.

"I can't remember much of it" replied Ellendrii truthfully.

"That's good" she replied. The SilvaGryphie approached with Aro and the three of them hovered in the sky for a while, catching up. Ellendrii ran briefly over what had happened since they last saw her. Her face was a mixture of awe, interest and concern as he told her what had happened.

"So we're off back home now" he said finally.

"Sounds like you've been on quite the adventure" she replied with a smile.

"Yes and now…I guess…it's time for…goodbye" said Ellendrii sadly.

"It is" replied Midnyte, putting a paw gently on his shoulder, "But I will always remember you" she told him with a smile.

The SilvaGryphie hung back a little, to allow the pair of them room and privacy to talk, much to Aro's annoyance because then he couldn't hear what they were saying.

"And I will never forget you; I still have your decoration to remind me of you" smiled Ellendrii with moist eyes and a smile.

Suddenly she embraced him in a warm hug. Ellendrii's surprise was evident but he quickly overcame it and hugged her too. Drawing back, she smiled softly at him.

"May you always have good fortune and good health in life and peace in death" she said with a respectful nod of her head.

"And you too" he replied, doing the same. She smiled.

"Goodbye both of you!" she said flying back a little.

"Goodbye Midnyte!" the two of them roared back to her. Ellendrii flew back onto the SilvaGryphie and took his place on her back again. But as they flew away, he saw Midnyte Comet shoot up a beautiful green flame into the sky that lit up the whole island. He smiled.

He would certainly never forget her.

Facing forward now they were homebound for Shernaron. Aro was excited to be back at home and to see his parents and yes, even his sisters again. Ellendrii was now focusing his mind on visiting the Skylands and proving himself to Sierra and Reo.

Haha, what a shock they would have!

Chapter 33
Proof

The coast of Shernaron was now in sight but the SilvaGryphie was ascending in the sky a little.

"I will fly to Dyarkroeen first and let Aro down. He cannot come with us, as he probably realizes."

"Yeah yeah, I know. If you can bring me back from the dead, couldn't you make it so that I can breathe at high altitudes?" he asked, hopefully.

"Sadly not" she replied, *"This is Ellendrii's moment now. He must do this alone."*

Aro nodded. He knew this was none of his concern but at the same time he *so* wanted to see the Skylands.

"I will fly higher though, so as not to spoil the surprise. Ellendrii wanted to visit the Skylands first and then see his family. So I mustn't let any of them see me and to do that I will fly at cloud level. It will be slightly lower than those mountains you went up so Aro will be able to handle it."

"Thank you" said Ellendrii. Aro felt a bit like a burden but said nothing.

They flew over Shernaron, Ellendrii and Aro could see the Forest down below and they took a turn to the left and headed across the Outlands. Ellendrii could see the welcome sight of other Gryphies flying around down below and his heart ached to see his parents again but he knew that he would see them in time, just not now. It wouldn't be too long though.

"Look on the bright side, Aro. At least you get to see your parents now. I have to wait until we've been to the Skylands. I just hope I don't see Mum or Dad down there because I know I will want to fly down and see them."

"Yeah I guess" replied Aro but he was ever the adventurer and although he wanted to see his own family just as badly, he also wanted to see the looks on the faces of the disbelievers when they saw Ellendrii come back with the SilvaGryphie.

Still, he paid attention to what was passing down below because this was interesting; seeing what he was so familiar with; his own home only from above. He wanted to take it all in and enjoy it all before the ride ended.

Then he saw Dyarkroeen by air and his eyes widened at this new view of the place he knew so well.

"Wow, look at them all!" he said, amazed, referring to the Lizariaouses that wandered around down below. He tried to spot his sisters but he couldn't see them.

The aerial view of the caves was something he was particularly enjoying. He hardly dared blink for fear that he might miss something. Ellendrii was used to this view of Aro's home and hardly paid any attention to it; he was too busy concentrating on what he would say to Sierra and Reo when he came to them with the SilvaGryphie. After getting over his amusement at the look on their faces first of course! He swore to himself that he would take it seriously and not laugh at them.

The SilvaGryphie had flown to the far side of Dyarkroeen and was descending now.

"Don't you wanna come and meet my parents?" asked Aro, who had been sure that she would have dropped him off at his cave even though of course she probably had no idea where he lived. He just assumed she knew.

"I would but I really want to get Ellendrii up to the Skylands and show myself. I want to remain a surprise for the Gryphies and if I spend too long here, some might spot me. But, if you go to Ellendrii's home in the Forest, we will be coming back there and you can bring your parents and they can meet me that way. I will drop you here for now. It won't take long in the Skylands anyway."

Aro nodded, feeling a little better at this. His parents would get to see her after all! She landed on the dusty ground and lowered herself so Aro could climb down.

"I hope flying has been all that you dreamed it would be, Aro" she said to him with a smile and the young Lizariaous nodded excitedly.

"All that and more!" he yelled in glee. Ellendrii smiled. He was glad that his friend finally got to experience flying after all this time and all that wishing and wanting to get into the air. It can't have been easy for him wanting something so impossible. He was glad that the fabled SilvaGryphie was the one to finally show him how fun flying was.

Ellendrii stayed where he was and the SilvaGryphie rose up on all fours again, taking to the air with a single sweep of her mighty wings.

From the ground, Aro watched them go.

"Good luck! You show 'em, El!!" he roared.

"I will!" called back Ellendrii and waved to his friend. He watched Aro get smaller and smaller as the SilvaGryphie took to the higher sky and headed for the floating islands of the Sky Gryphies up beyond the clouds.

"One thing I never liked about the Sky Gryphies was the vanity they developed with their heads both literally and metaphorically in the clouds. Just because you are higher up in your environment doesn't mean that you are higher than those below you."

"Why didn't you intervene then?" asked Ellendrii.

"I wanted them to grow and learn by themselves like the Forest Gryphies and Mountain Gryphies have done. Mistakes become lessons if you learn from them. Yes they kept to themselves but for all the wrong reasons. But despite their flaws, they have built much beauty on the floating islands and I am still proud of them in a way. I just hope that getting to meet me will set them back on track again. They stopped believing in me a long time ago, whereas the other sub-species still tell stories about me even now. The Sky Gryphies don't. They sent you on a mission to find something that not even they themselves believed existed. And that is low; even for them."

Ellendrii mulled all this over as they flew, breaking through the clouds and finally seeing the floating Skylands in the distance. A couple of passing Sky Gryphies saw the SilvaGryphie and simply didn't know what she was. They stared at her. After all, a species that no longer believes in something soon forgets what it has been told it looks like. A few others however, did recognize her and they nearly fell out of the sky in shock. They started flying haphazardly towards the Sky Temple where Sierra and Reo no doubt were. The largest and most beautiful one.

"Have you been watching over these guys as you have with us in the Forest?" asked Ellendrii.

"Yes, I watch over all of you. I know of their temples and their daily lives. It's nice to actually see them for real though instead of simply travelling here in my mind" the SilvaGryphie was heading towards Sierra and Reo's Sky Temple now. Ellendrii clambered up higher on her neck so he could see over her head and watch where they were going. He saw the temple now.

"Have you decided what you will say?" she asked.

"Yes I have" he replied with confidence and sat himself higher on her. She smiled.

"Well then, let's go greet the non-believers!" and with a mighty roar and a blast into the sky of wild blue flames, she let everyone know they had arrived.

Ellendrii saw Sierra and Reo come out of the temple and walk out onto their flight ledge and stare up at them. Ellendrii could see Sierra's look of annoyance and Reo's look of utter shock and he grinned.

"SKY GRYPHIES! I HAVE BROUGHT THE SILVAGRYPHIE TO YOU, AS YOU REQUESTED!" he roared.

All the Sky Gryphies in the area stopped what they were doing and either stood or hovered to look in awe at the beauty of the creature that they were now in the presence of. Ellendrii could see gatherings of them whispering to each other or pairs of them hovering in the air, talking and pointing in stunned surprise. Younger Sky Gryphies who hadn't been told of the SilvaGryphie were confused and the older ones who remembered the stories were in shock.

The SilvaGryphie landed squarely on Sierra and Reo's island, towering over them and glowering at them.

"My friend Ellendrii tells me you don't believe in me anymore. That you sent him on a quest you knew he would fail. I am your creator and I am disappointed in you. I did not create this sub-species to be close minded, intolerant, distrustful, vain or prejudiced." Her eyes burned through Sierra and Reo's very souls and they shrank back. Her size alone was enough to frighten them into complete submission.

"Have you no respect for anyone except your own? Bow your heads and wings in my presence!" the SilvaGryphie's voice boomed out in their minds and they did as they were told.

"W…we're sorry…" muttered Reo, with his eyes tightly shut.

"Time will tell if you are sorry. Actions speak louder than words, Reo." She looked around at the other Sky Gryphies. *"ALL of you need to heed these words and become more accepting of those who you assume are lower than you are. I did not create any Gryphies to be higher than any others. Each sub-species is a complimentary edge on a many faceted territory. You need to get your heads out of the clouds."*

She nudged Ellendrii with her shoulder as a suggestion and he took to the sky and flew down, alighting on the ground beside her.

"Sierra, Reo, I bring you the SilvaGryphie. Now you must keep your side of the bargain." Ellendrii said solemnly.

Sierra raised her head and spoke.

"It seems you have and we will keep our side of the deal. You are now a member of the Sky Gryphie Elite Flyers. You may also come and go as you please as well and we will prepare a Skyland and temple of your own so that you may live or visit when you wish." She did not look happy about having to admit she and her brother had been wrong or that they now needed to accept a Forest Gryphie into their midst. In fact she spoke through slightly gritted teeth, which amused Ellendrii.

"Good. And when I leave, I want both of you Sky Gryphie leaders to maintain the same tolerance and respect of Forest and other Gryphies as I would want you to. If I hear that you have gone against your word and hurt or betrayed Ellendrii, I will raze these Skylands to ashes, do you understand me?"

Sierra and Reo nodded.

That was kinda harsh thought Ellendrii and then he heard the SilvaGryphie's voice in his mind.

"No harsher than they deserved. Sadly with these Gryphies, you need to speak to them in this way or they just won't listen. There is no escaping. They need to know how

angry and disappointed I am with them. They will be ok then if
they are afraid of the consequences of not treating you fairly."

"Thank you for accepting me" said Ellendrii and the two
leaders nodded humbly.

"One thing though; *why* did you send me on a quest that
you knew I would fail? That was a nasty thing to do when all I
wanted to do was join the ranks of your Elite Flyers. Was that
so bad?"

Reo spoke.

"We did it because…well because we didn't want to, I
know it sounds harsh, be tainted by another type of Gryphie.
We've always held ourselves in high regard because of where
we are and I guess…I guess it *did* go to our heads and we
made a mistake. We went too far."

"You didn't *have* to go though" Sierra butted in. "We didn't
expect you to actually go and risk your life finding the
SilvaGryphie. We thought that since you were young, you
would just give up. That was also why we set you a hard task.
We thought you would fly back down to the Forest and just
give up on that idea and do something else."

"But I looked up to you guys. I looked up to the Elite
Flyers. Surely even the fact that a Forest Gryphie even
wanted to push himself to go up against the best of the best
was a task in itself. And also the fact I did so well in that flying
contest. You *knew* I was right for the flyers but you still
refused to let me in on the principal of vanity. That's the worst
thing I think here. I am of the quality that you were looking for,
even a bit better than that but you wouldn't let me in because I
was from the *Forest*. That's just kinda…sad." Ellendrii shook
his head and looked at the leaders. He was still a Gryphie
after all, what difference did it make where he was from if he
could do the job as well as the Sky Gryphies?

"In fact," he continued, "by that very reasoning I honestly
don't know why I came back to a gathering of Gryphies who
see my kind as lower and not as good as themselves. Except
that maybe my passion for flying outweighs all that. It
outweighs the fact you never wanted me and that I was never
really welcome up here. And the thing is I want you to want
me up here because I am an asset to the flyers. Not simply

627

out of fear that the SilvaGryphie will hurt you if you don't take me into the squad. Do you understand this?"

"Yes" was the one word reply from Sierra. She looked at Ellendrii harshly and a little down her snout. The SilvaGryphie looked disapproving at this.

"And you know what? I don't regret going on that journey. My friend Aro the Lizariaous came with me and we learned and grew so much. It was an experience that I don't regret at all even though I nearly died several times and then I…" he trailed off as the SilvaGryphie slowly shook her head, looking at him. She didn't want him to say he had actually been killed.

"…and then I felt indebted to Aro because he saved my life. We saw so many new things and met so many new creatures. Not all of them were nice. But ultimately, if it wasn't for your selfish desire to get rid of me, I would never have gone on such an amazing journey or met such an amazing Gryphie" he gestured to the SilvaGryphie and she smiled.

"Well you certainly look different to the Ellendrii we sent out some seasons ago to find her" Sierra said.

"Look, I really love flying. I really, really want to be part of the Elite Flyers. That doesn't mean that the whole Forest gathering is going to come up here with me you know. Most of the others can't breathe at this altitude. It would only be me. Is that so hard and difficult to accept? I don't want to be a part of the flyers if the leaders don't want me here, or any of the rest of the gathering for that matter. So, journey, quests, contests aside, do YOU want me to be in the flyers? Answer truthfully. If you want me to go then I will. Yes I will be disappointed and yes my life goals are pretty much shattered but think what an asset I would be if you let me stay?" Ellendrii looked at the leaders for their answer. The SilvaGryphie kept out of it for now. She could easily subdue them and make them take Ellendrii on but she didn't want to, because it was not what *he* wanted.

Sierra sighed.

"I do admit that we were prejudiced against your kind and I am fully aware that we are all Gryphies even though some of us look different. Also, when you flew in the contest, you blew both me and Reo away. You were amazing. We just didn't want to admit that because our pride wouldn't allow it. We thought you would fly and then fail but when you succeeded, we panicked. So that was the idea we pulled out. To go and find a creature too amazing to even exist; one that we had given up believing in long ago because we couldn't see past our own stupid noses to accept that there are different things out there. At one point we had a story going that the Sky Gryphies had created the Forest and Mountain Gryphies. Yes yes I know it's incredibly self-centred. Our mother started that one but it sort of dwindled, which was good. We're not that big on telling stories anyway and they need to be kept to continuity and all that and we just can't be bothered. But Ellendrii, you did so much and tried so hard even though we didn't make you feel welcome. You did amazingly in the contest and then to actually go out and find the creator of all Gryphies, that is truly incredible. How can we turn you away when you've done all that? And no that's not my fear speaking. It's the truth. We can't. The Sky Gryphies welcome you to our Skylands. You are welcome to live and fly with us. And we say this from the bottom of our hearts and souls. You are welcome, Ellendrii." She bowed her head to him in respect and Reo did the same.

Ellendrii was speechless. He never thought that the leaders of the Sky Gryphies would actually be so sincere. Finally he found his voice.

"Well then, thank you. I do appreciate it and I accept your humble offer to live and fly with you." He bowed his head as well.

"Well done, Sky Gryphies. Maybe there is hope for you yet. Showing humbleness and humility and acceptance of someone different than you." She smiled at the two leaders and they smiled back.

"We're sorry our greeting wasn't more pleasant" said Reo, "We welcome you to our lands also, for as long as you wish to stay with us."

"I don't plan to stay for long. I need to greet Ellendrii's parents but I will stay a while and take advantage of your hospitality. It seems you've come a long way from your beginnings on these floating islands. I am impressed by your

Sky Temples. It's nice how you have each put a part of yourselves in them with the scales. Very creative!" She looked around.

"We can give you a tour if you like" suggested Reo.

"I have seen it all but it would be nice to see it in front of my actual face" she answered,

"Yes, I will come on a tour with you. So long as you don't take long, I still need to greet Ellendrii's family and Aro's too."

"It won't take long. We will show you only the most special places" said Sierra, taking to the sky.

"Can I come too?" asked Ellendrii.

"Yes of course! After all, you need to choose a Skyland to live on" replied Sierra.

The four of them took to the sky and traversed the territory of the Sky Gryphies. Flying next to the SilvaGryphie felt a lot different to riding on her back. She was so large that he had to fly a way away from her or she might accidentally smack him with her mighty wings. So he flew beside and just under her. He stared up at the inside of her wings every so often to marvel at the undersides of them. He couldn't work out really what he was seeing in them but it was beautiful and went on for eternity. He half thought he could fly into her wings and enter a new world within them. Of course he wasn't willing to take that risk. She might get annoyed for one thing and for another it would put them both at risk him flying into her wings.

As they proceeded, many other Sky Gryphies flew around, following them, watching them, all awed at the visitor. All knowing that this was probably the first and last time they would see her so they wanted to get a good look so that she would live on forever in their minds.

I wonder why the SilvaGryphie didn't just change the opinions of the leaders and make them all accept me pondered Ellendrii in his own mind. If she can change the minds of the Aqwakitts then surely it wouldn't be that hard...

"I wanted you all to work it out for yourselves and come to a decision without my interference of course" she told him in his mind.

Oh yeah, that makes more sense he agreed.

"As I've said before, I never like to interfere even though I have the power to."

They flew over a group of the floating islands and Sierra spoke up.

"These are the Skylands belonging to the Sky Gryphie Elite Flyers. You may choose one here. We like to keep things organized and together, which is why these are all together."

Ellendrii looked down at the Skylands. Each one had a temple but a couple of them had bare, scale-less temples which indicated that they were unoccupied. It seemed the flyers got temples of their own, unlike the rest of the Sky Gryphies although they were all small and none of them were as big as the grand temple that Sierra and Reo lived in. He chose a central one with others near to it. He couldn't believe it though. His parents didn't even know if he was still alive and yet here he was choosing a new home!

"You can move into it whenever you like. It has been marked for you now and no one else will set foot in it. It is your property" said Sierra.

"Thank you!" said Ellendrii, gratefully. He hoped that Aro would have got to the Forest with his parents by now and told Diabloss and Leida that their son was still alive, had made it back and was on his way.

"You can decorate it how you wish" continued Sierra, "Although you might have some trouble with placing scales on it. You can choose something else to use instead I'm sure."

Ellendrii looked at the Sky Temple that was his own and pondered what he would put on it. He had no scales of course and the Sky Gryphies never wasted a scale. If one was shed, they would use it on their own temple. So he would have to improvise. He thought he would use the glowing crystals he had found. But they might be better inside than out. He needed to think about this more carefully. He was only sad that Aro couldn't visit and would never be able to see the temple himself. Even if the SilvaGryphie brought Aro up here, he would have trouble with the thin air.

The SilvaGryphie flew down to Ellendrii's temple and alighted on the top. She didn't seem to have any trouble perching on a place so precarious. She looked down at the temple and her claws gripped the top tightly. Suddenly the temple started to glow and Ellendrii stared. What was she doing??

Before his very eyes, the surface of the cave-like structure became patterned with swirls, wings and feathers. It chinked and changed and reformed in such a way that the surface sparkled even more as the sun hit it. Even though it was small, it was now a thing of beauty and stood out as something special. She hadn't made it grand or resplendent but just special in its own way, without having the need for scales to decorate it with.

All the gathered Sky Gryphies stared in awe, Sierra and Reo included! It was nowhere near as beautiful as their temple but it was still magnificent and eye-catching. The SilvaGryphie didn't want to put their noses out of joint but at the same time she wanted to give something to Ellendrii that he would enjoy.

"Thank you, SilvaGryphie!" called Ellendrii to her as she sat atop the temple.

"It was no trouble at all" she smiled. As for the Sky Gryphies, they knew that Ellendrii was to be respected.

After a short tour, Sierra, Reo, the SilvaGryphie and Ellendrii returned to Sierra and Reo's Sky Temple and they treated their guests to some fresh fruit and bugs. Ellendrii politely declined the bugs but he did enjoy the juicy fruit.

"I'm sorry we were so hostile before. I guess that's how we always are when newcomers arrive here. Ellendrii was the first we had seen in a long time. Obviously with the air problems, we don't get many visitors from down in the Forest or the Mountains. Since we don't see much of anyone other than ourselves it's easy to get carried away and think that we are the only ones who matter" said Sierra, enjoying a large orange fruit similar to a mango.

"Well I hope you learned some humility and respect" said the SilvaGryphie.

"Oh yes, we won't be so proud again. Though we do have a lot to be proud of, there is also a lot we can learn about the rest of the world. Ellendrii, what did you see out there? Across the vast water?" Sierra asked.

"Many things. There was a race of creatures called Wind Hounds and we made friends with their leader, Lord Scerniss. He was certainly not to be messed with. We also met Kanniths, Aqwakitts, an Ursquach and a monster called Thresh who attacked us. Not all the creatures we met were nice. A lot of them were though and we learned a lot about their cultures." Ellendrii explained.

"Was the SilvaGryphie's home very far?" asked Reo.

"Far enough" replied Ellendrii mysteriously. Reo nodded.

"Luckily she gave us a lift back" continued Ellendrii, "Or the trip would have taken twice as long."

Thinking about it, they had got back in less than a sun cycle. It was just past mid-sun as they sat there now. He wondered if the SilvaGryphie could fly faster because of her size or something. She must be just faster at flying. And stronger too. Or maybe she used her mind to get them home faster. Or maybe this was a dream and they were actually dead? He shook his head. All these thoughts were confusing him now.

"So the trip was really hard then?" asked Reo.

"Yeah it was pretty hard. We went through so many different kinds of elements both on land and in water and saw many things. There was desert, rain, a lake, a cave, a boneyard, snowy mountains, valleys, so many things. And a horrible black forest."

"Well one thing's for sure. *We* couldn't have done anything like that" Reo said. His sister gave him a look.

"What? We couldn't!" he retorted.

"Nor would we have wanted to" she said, "So if we ever need anything difficult done again, *you* can do it!"

"That is not the point of this" said the SilvaGryphie, *"You need to do more than you do now. All you do is frolic and fly and you wouldn't even get involved in the war of the Gryphies and Lizariaouses."*

"That was because it didn't concern us. Surely it's better not to stick your nose in where it's not wanted?" Sierra said.

"But it was wanted. And who better to add fire and flight power than the Gryphies of the skies? The Lizariaouses

633

would never have suspected you swooping in and helping the Gryphies of the Forest and Mountains."

"But they won. The good won. We weren't needed. They did it without us. Besides, you know as well as I that we have...problems with the ground. That is if you are really the one who created us." Sierra was ever the sceptic.

"I believe you refer to the ground walkers as "ground bound" which is completely wrong since they are not bound to the ground at all, in fact most of them still fly. Just not as high as you."

Sierra and Reo looked decidedly awkward at this comment.

"Well, we just don't like to get involved in things that don't concern us, so that's really why we didn't fight with them. None of it was anything to do with us, the Lizariaouses can't fly or even shoot their needles as high as our homes so why would we swoop in to help?"

"Yes you say that and that would really be a good enough reason but the thing is that the real reason that you never got involved was because of fear and the fact that you didn't want anything to do with the Gryphies from down below. Don't try to lie to me. Diabloss came and asked for your help and you refused, being too stuck up to lend a hand."

Sierra and Reo looked decidedly uncomfortable now.

"Ok, ok, yes we didn't fight because we couldn't be bothered and didn't want to help. But they still won so it's in the past now, no harm done, yes?" said Reo while Sierra looked on.

"Yes it is but just remember for next time that your help might be needed and to be open with helping others. You never know, one sun cycle you might be in trouble and who would help you if all you are to them is stuck up and unfriendly? Just think about that and keep it in your mind."

"We will" replied Sierra, knowing that the SilvaGryphie was right but still being too proud to admit that once again they were in the wrong. "It won't happen again, we guarantee that and we will help if any help is needed."

"Good. Because you never know." The SilvaGryphie looked them both in the eyes sternly and they laid their ears back submissively.

Ellendrii just watched all this. Since the war was before his time, he had no idea about these things, but it annoyed him that his own father had asked them and they refused to help.

"Don't worry, SilvaGryphie, if their help is needed again, I am here and I will ensure that they help." He too looked at the two leaders but they were less than submissive towards him; the young adventurer. He wasn't the SilvaGryphie, after all. They just gave him a look that said "Don't push your luck, newcomer. We are still the leaders and your authority here."

Ellendrii wisely changed his expression. He wondered in seasons to come what would happen if the Sky Gryphies got new leaders and if they would be as difficult as Sierra and Reo despite that the pair had admitted their errors. He knew that he had more guts than they did though, after what he had been through and he could take quiet satisfaction in this fact all the same.

The SilvaGryphie had said nothing to Ellendrii's remark, letting nature take its course and the Gryphie learn by himself what not to say.

As they sat there, chatting, the sky was full with Sky Gryphies who were curious about the SilvaGryphie. They hovered around and some dared to land on the Skyland itself.

Mothers brought their kittens to see the fabled creature and youngsters tried to get in for a closer look.

You're popular thought Ellendrii, hoping the SilvaGryphie would hear him and respond in his own mind where no one else could hear.

"They will always be curious about things they've never seen. It's healthy to be curious in this way. They want to see me. Many know that they will never see me again. I don't mind. They are welcome to come and look at me."

Sierra and Reo mind though thought Ellendrii. He could see the pair of leaders were clearly unhappy about Sky Gryphies landing on their piece of floating land.

"They feel like their personal space is being invaded. Unlike the other Sky Gryphies, the leaders are not used to sharing their temple as the others do. This is why. I think I will move to a more neutral space and greet them there. Then we will go to the Forest and I will meet your parents! Follow me."

To the leaders, she said; *"It seems there are too many crowding round here wishing to meet me, so I will fly to the neutral meeting island where you greet newcomers and I will chat to them there and answer their questions. Ellendrii is coming with me. It was nice to meet you two and remember what I said."* She looked at them sternly, her beautiful galactic violet eyes shimmering.

"Yes, it was nice to meet you too and prove your existence. And Ellendrii, thank you for bringing her back to see us. You deserve your place in the Sky Gryphie Elite Flyers and on our Skylands." Reo said. He said it genuinely as well, which was nice Ellendrii thought.

Sierra bowed her head respectfully to the SilvaGryphie and Ellendrii. Ellendrii did the same to his new leaders. It would be interesting living in a society that had leaders. No one really lead the Forest Gryphies. Diabloss was the strongest but that was only because he was half Deamon.

The SilvaGryphie and Ellendrii took to the sky, jumping off the edge of the leaders' Skyland and into the wild blue yonder and they flew to the meeting island.

She landed and Ellendrii landed next to her. They were naturally followed by the rest of the Sky Gryphies who had been so eager to meet her. As soon as they landed and the Sky Gryphies knew that was where they would be resting for a bit, they all hovered around or gathered on the island. It wasn't big enough for all of them but they did their best to squeeze on. At the expense of touching the SilvaGryphie and possibly invading her personal space too. She didn't seem to mind though. Ellendrii wondered what she was like when she was angry. A force to be reckoned with no doubt. He suspected she would be able to do more damage than that burning mountain they had passed.

"Now I can take your questions!" she said to the surrounding gathering. *"I will point and then if I point to you,*

you can ask and I will answer. This will make it easier for all of us and so I'm not bombarded with questions all at once."

She pointed to the first onlooker.

"Where do you come from?" he asked.

"I come from across the vast water, from the land of Forever" was the reply and she pointed to someone else.

"Do you breathe fire like us?"

"Yes I do"

"Are you a Fire Master?"

"Yes, I am."

"Oooh, oooh, can you show us?"

The SilvaGryphie obliged and showed them a scene of their Elite Flyers with Ellendrii at the head doing all sorts of acrobatical things in the air. Her fire manipulation was so advanced that you could easily see who the fire depicted. It was incredibly detailed, unlike any other fire manipulation Ellendrii had seen. Yes, Tranzoss was good but even her fire magic didn't come close to this!

"Do you have any tips for fire manipulation?"

"It needs to come from within. You need to live the fire and be the fire and direct your thoughts into the fire. If you can't do it, don't worry, very few can. But if you have the ability then make your thoughts become the flames."

"What colour is your fur?" this was a young Gryphie who was confused.

"It is mostly white but shines every colour in the sky spectrum depending on what light it is in" she explained. Sky spectrum is the Gryphie word for rainbow.

"Are there others like you?"

"No, it is only me."

"Are you as good a flyer as the Elite?" this was another young Gryphie.

"I am better. Everything they can do, I can do tenfold." The young Gryphie looked awed at this.

"Do you ever get too hot with all that fur?"

"Not at all!"

"How old are you?"

"Older than all Gryphies that have come before you."

"I can see something in your wings, what sort of patterning is that?"

"It is the patterning of everything; of eternity and all that has been and will be. A window to the very soul."

"Wow, that's amazing! How did you get that to happen?"

"Only one question per Gryphie please or we'll be here until the moon rises!"

"Aww" the young Gryphie waffled off.

"Do you eat the same things as us? Do you eat more?"

"Yes to both those questions. Remember what I said about question numbers!"

"Does anything scare you?"

"Yes; we all have fears."

"How long did it take to create all our species?"

"Quite a while. And a lot of imagination" the SilvaGryphie smiled.

"Where did you create us?"

"Ah, an interesting one. It was a land far from here, before you reach this place. This was where I decided to put you all so that you could grow and learn. It needed to be a perfect place for all of you. In fact it is a place I still visit often. But you can never go there sadly."

She continued on for a while answering questions until finally she deemed it time to stop since it was getting later. She wanted to leave Shernaron at moonrise.

"It was great to meet you" was the general reaction to her visit and she and the Sky Gryphies parted on good terms. Sierra and Reo had even been humbled by her presence in the end and all was good.

As Ellendrii and the SilvaGryphie left the sky kingdom, Ellendrii turned to her as they flew.

"I think it was good you visited them. It's changed them for the better and I think that the visit enlightened them all. Especially Sierra and Reo."

"I think it will take a while for them to fully get over their vanity and attitude but they can do it. I expect them to anyway. That is the nice thing about my creations. You all have the ability to learn and correct yourselves when you take

a wrong step and that is the asset that I think I take the most pride in.”

"I really hope that this is the start of a great new alliance with them" said Ellendrii.

"I think it will be. Everything happens for a reason and there are always good sides to things even when it looks bad. The good that came of this was that you succeeded. The good that came of you going on your journey in the first place was that in the end the fact you succeeded will bring the Sky and Forest Gryphies closer together. So the lands are more united. Just like the good that came of the war was that Gryphies and Lizariaouses now live in total peace. Even before Zephirak started his nonsense, peace was only just holding on. Sometimes you need to go through the bad as your parents did, to find the good the other side. And even though bad things happen, if something good comes of it then it is worth it in the end. And it helps us learn and grow as individuals. The things you learned on your journey you couldn't possibly have learned without risking yourself or by going to other lands.”

"That's a good way of looking at things. It makes me feel more positive" said Ellendrii.

"Yes, I always think it makes me feel more positive too" smiled the SilvaGryphie.

They had left the cloud covering now and were headed towards the Forest from the cliffs. Now was the time for the Gryphies to see their great creator and the young Gryphie who had brought her back to them!

As with the Sky Gryphies, everyone looked up in awe or flew nearby to get a closer look.

Aren't you tired of all the attention? Ellendrii asked her in his mind.

"I don't mind it. After all, I am alone most of the time. Since I rarely get this kind of attention I can be patient. However, I wouldn't like it all the time. I would soon grow bored of it.”

I'm getting a bit bored of it now actually Ellendrii laughed privately. No offence, he added.

"None taken; it is perfectly understandable. I can't blame you really" she replied as they swooped in lower to the Forest while the trees got thicker.

"We will land and walk from here" she said and the pair of them landed.

"I want to walk into your Forest's clearing to meet your parents. Hopefully Aro will have brought his parents along too."

"It's easier to walk through the Forest anyway. We never fly and land in it unless we land in the trees and climb down. Our wings would break the tree branches and we would lose the shelter the trees offer from the weather. We look after our Forest; it's our home" said Ellendrii.

"I understand that and I'm glad you take care of the land that I put you in. It is your job to care about where you live and keep it nice. Keep it a place you are proud to live in."

The pair of them made their way to the clearing and the tree that Ellendrii shared with his parents. He could see Lunara's ancient tree in the distance even now and his heart leaped.

He would finally get to see his parents again!

Chapter 34
Back Again

Ellendrii got more and more excited as they walked and could barely contain himself. He couldn't wait to show his parents the things he had found and tell them of his and Aro's adventures. He had really wanted to be the one to tell them that he and Aro had survived too but he had no doubt that Aro would have told them by now.

Due to her size, the SilvaGryphie had to bow her head as she walked under some of the trees. All the other Gryphies were stopping and staring. They *all* knew who she was.

There were whispered exclamations of "It's her! It's the SilvaGryphie!" and "She's come back to us!" As well as gasps of surprise and awe, similar to the Sky Gryphies except of course the Forest Gryphies all believed in her and knew her from their stories.

Some of them talked amongst themselves about Ellendrii being with her as well. Word had got out about him leaving to find her.

"Is that Leida's kitten? Ellendrii?"

"I thought he was dead!"

"He's been gone so long…"

"He's brought her back to us!"

"He found her! I thought he had surely perished…"

Ellendrii heard his own name floating among the words that they were speaking and he felt both awkward and proud in equal measure. Would they herald him a hero for what he had done? Or be jealous? A small part of him would have liked the fame but most of him just wanted to slink away and be the same Gryphie he had been before he left. Which of course he would never be. He had matured now.

The SilvaGryphie smiled and nodded to the Gryphies who were closest. Some of them bowed to her and she bowed her head back to them in response. They were elated whenever she paid them any attention. Most of them would acknowledge her and then go back into the Forest so they didn't annoy her. Some of them walked alongside her and

Ellendrii for a little, looking at her but they would soon leave them. It was difficult to have a lot of Gryphies walking along the Forest trails together or side by side. Ellendrii walked ahead of her, as though leading her although she knew where they were going. But this way it would be as though he was bringing her back. If she lead the way, it would defeat the look they wanted to go for; and the truth.

Coming into the clearing, Ellendrii first saw his father since Diabloss was the largest of them waiting. There was also his mother of course, as well as Aro, Mordred and Schaarl. Lunara and Jadariol were there too. Jadariol had been visiting his friend at the time. Hiryasis was with her and he peered out of the tree, his eyes going wide when he saw the SilvaGryphie.

Ellendrii wanted to rush up and hug his mother but instead he did a mature thing and announced their arrival.

"Mother, Father, I have travelled far and brought back the SilvaGryphie, as I said I would!" He stood before his approaching parents; the SilvaGryphie stood behind him smiling.

"Oh Ellendrii!" smiled his mother, coming up and being the one to first embrace him tightly.

"We thought you were dead, son" said Diabloss, coming up and ruffling Ellendrii's hair.

"Aro! Did you tell them I hadn't made it?" demanded Ellendrii from somewhere in his mother's hug.

"No! No not at all…I was going to but Dad said that it would upset them too much and put them through unneeded grief. I thought it would be more dramatic personally…" Aro looked sheepishly at Mordred, who frowned.

"Aro came and told us that you would be returning after you had met with the Sky Gryphies and proved them wrong" said Diabloss, "So, did you?"

Leida let her son go so he could speak.

"Yes I did! They weren't happy about it but that was just tough. They also admitted they had thought I wouldn't return or not even bother to go and why they sent me in the first place. But now it's all sorted. They accepted me into the Elite Flyers and even gave me a Sky Temple of my own so I can go and stay there or when I move out, I can move there and live on a Skyland myself. I don't think that they will cause me any trouble now."

"Moving out? But you've only just got home..." Leida looked sad.

"I won't move out instantly. And I'll just go and stay every so often so I can get used to life there before I actually move in anyway. Besides, when I go to live there I will visit here often, don't worry." Ellendrii smiled at his mother warmly. There was no way he'd rush off to live somewhere different immediately. He needed to spend time with his parents, tell them of his and Aro's adventures and catch up with all that had happened since they had left.

"So, you're the SilvaGryphie then" said Diabloss, looking up at a Gryphie that was actually larger than him for once.

"Yes I am. And I am very pleased to meet the parents who raised such a courageous and determined Gryphie." She bowed down to Leida and Diabloss respectfully.

"I am also very pleased to meet two of the strongest and most resourceful Gryphies from the great war. I was watching over you, Leida when you learned and grew and didn't give up despite being shy and quiet. You've come so far." She turned to Lunara; *"And you, who were so young and so brave. It's nice to see that you have taken over Mystik's work. You are an asset to the Forest and I am proud of your achievements."*

Lunara blushed.

"Thank you very much. I do try. But I have so much more to learn."

"And I know you will" she smiled at Lunara, who blushed more.

The SilvaGryphie smiled and nodded to Aro's parents.

"You, too have raised a fine kid. Aro risked his life for his friend and the pair of them would never have made it without the help of each other. You should be proud of Aro and his love of adventure."

"We are, very much so" replied Schaarl, "And we are so glad they both made it. We had given up hope as well that Aro and Ellendrii would return."

"We thought they would turn back halfway through the vast water or something. We never expected them to actually travel far enough to find you. Not that we had no faith in them you understand, but it was just that it was so far and we thought they would probably give up and turn back and find a different way to do it." Mordred said.

Diabloss chuckled.

"We did actually think that they would come back having decided to get someone to disguise themselves as the SilvaGryphie and pretend that that was her. After all, I don't think the Sky Gryphies really know what she looks like so we all figured it wouldn't matter. But when the moon came out and then the sun rose the next cycle, and as the sun cycles wore on we started to realize the serious truth and that was that they had gone" he explained.

"We didn't mean to worry you but we knew that the longer we were gone, the more worried you would be" Ellendrii looked around and there were Gryphies sat all about nearby or sitting in the trees watching and listening. He really wanted to tell his parents how and where they had found her but with all these others listening, it would mean ruining the whole thing of her living across the vast water and looking after the souls of the dead and thus ruin their beliefs. He didn't know what to do. He looked up at the SilvaGryphie, who was now sat next to him and hoped she would read his thoughts on the matter.

"Yes, I know" he heard her voice in his head. *"You will have to describe it carefully. I think everyone pretty much knows that you took too long for me to be just the other side of the vast water. We will hold on to the beliefs but you'll need to tell them though I look after the souls, I am just further away. I am not just the other side of the vast water; but further than that. It will spoil a little of the magic and mystery but it will help keep the belief solid for the most part."*

Ellendrii nodded and continued.

"We travelled over the vast water and made it to the other side. Or what we thought was the other side. We were caught in a storm and our float was destroyed. We washed up on a large island, which was why we thought it was the other side of the vast water. We met a helpful Gryphie-like creature called Midnyte Comet, who…"

"Who Ellendrii has a crush on!" interrupted Aro cheekily.

"ARO!!" snapped Ellendrii and death glared his friend, who grinned at him.

"Ah, his first love" said Leida softly. "You didn't bring her back then?" she asked.

"No, because she was happy living by herself on her island so that is where we left her" explained Ellendrii.

"You could always visit her" suggested his mother.

"No, because she lives several sun cycles away and I wouldn't want to risk the storms again. It was a love not meant to be, sadly." Ellendrii looked wistful.

"But she knew your feelings?" asked Diabloss.

"Yes she did. But she was too old for me anyway. Now, can I carry on without Aro interrupting??" Ellendrii mock glared at Aro. Aro looked innocent and nodded.

"So, after we rebuilt the float with Midnyte's help, we carried on and reached the other side of the vast water, where we found the domain of the Wind Hounds. They are an advanced race of creatures who live in these structure things they built out of the white rock there. They had a lot of rituals and things they considered to be important and we stayed with them for a couple of sun cycles while we rested. We left the float with them too. But unfortunately (he glared at Aro again at this point) *someone* accidentally insulted their customs and they chased us away."

Aro looked sheepish.

"For the record, I *did* actually apologize to them on the way home…just so you know…" he spoke up.

"Anyway, we had been trying to decide how to make the next stage of the journey which was through the Forest of Foreboding; a horrible black forest. Since the Wind Hounds chased us into the forest, we couldn't plan. All we could do was try and get through there as fast as possible. They didn't follow us. We had gained some knowledge about the forest when we were staying with the Wind Hounds since a couple of them had been in there but others who had gone in had died."

At this point Leida looked horrified.

"So, you were going into a place where you might possibly die?" she asked.

"Yeah, well we made it didn't we? But yes, we did. There was no way around it and the only way to get past it was to walk since we couldn't fly. It was too big to carry Aro over it. Anyway, we spent many sun cycles in it. We lost track of time because it was dark and everything looked the same. And the creatures we encountered in there were the stuff of moonmares; they were terrifying!"

"I still get moonmares about the Repulsators" muttered Aro.

"What are those?" asked Diabloss.

"We'll tell you more in detail at another time" said Ellendrii, "We're just going over a rough outline of the journey so you all will know where and how we found her. In my words of course."

The others nodded and he continued.

"When we finally got through the forest, and I nearly died but Aro and another friend called Rivniann saved me…"

"From a Narg'tok!" put in Aro quickly, to which Mordred looked shocked.

"…we ended up in a valley full of these little creatures that spoke a different language. We sort of worked out a way of communication with them and they didn't trouble us at all. We stayed there for a sun cycle and the next sun we left and headed towards a huge lake…" Ellendrii gave Aro a warning look since he looked very much like he was about to mention the embarrassing pee incident. He coughed and looked away.

"…the lake was beautiful and rich in meal creatures. We stayed there a while and made friends with the local creatures called Aqwakitts. They let us swim underwater using these air bubbles they put around our heads so we could breathe and they thought they had found the SilvaGryphie! I didn't believe she lived under water for some reason, but Aro believed them. It turned out that the SilvaGryphie in question was not real; but a statue of her with a glowing stone embedded in her chest. Aro dug the stone out and we dubbed it the Gryphie stone, well, I called it that, because of its shape. Here it is…"

He got the Gryphie stone out of his bag and showed them all. It no longer glowed but it did shine in the light of the early evening sun that streamed in through the trees.

The others looked at it with interest and commented on its shape; that of a Gryphie's head.

"So I thought that maybe, since there was a sort of arrow shape in it that changed direction when I changed position, that it was something that might lead us to her. It was the only thing we had to go on, after all, so we went with it. I may have been completely wrong in my assumption but what did we have to lose?"

"Except going in completely the wrong direction of course" muttered Aro.

"Yeah but we didn't, so there's no need to even think about that possibility" chuckled Ellendrii with a sweatdrop.

The SilvaGryphie smiled.

"Anyway, so we followed it and it lead us into this horrible area that looked like flesh and rained blood. Then we climbed a mountain and had some fun in the snow as well. It was so high! We met a creature called A'urealiz. She's an Ursquach and she attacked us at first but then ended up helping us. Once we had gone back down again, we came into an area with a huge horrifying burning mountain. It had destroyed the whole landscape with its fire and it freaked me out a bit."

"More than a bit" murmured Aro but thankfully no one heard him.

"We crossed a desert and again we nearly died because of the terrain and lack of water. Then we went through a cave where we were able to rest and recover and eat and drink some. We left that through these weird tunnels that smelled odd and we could hear moaning through. We ended up in another valley and a boneyard which we had to go through. Unfortunately there was a creature living in this boneyard called Thresh and he attacked us." Ellendrii stopped and looked up at the SilvaGryphie, unsure if he should tell them that he and Aro died or not. She helpfully continued.

"Thresh attacked them but I stepped in and saved them. I lived the other side of that valley in my own special home I had created for myself and I heard their cries of panic. I

healed them and brought them back here. And the rest as they say, is history."

"Wow, what an incredible adventure! I half wish I had joined you" said Leida.

"You wouldn't have liked it, Mum. It was dangerous and most of the time we were scared for our lives whether we were in trouble or just worrying about what we might encounter next. We spent most of our time like that. It sounds nice but I will fill you both in on the rest of the details later." Ellendrii glanced around them, hoping his Mum and Dad would understand that it was because of the extra company that he didn't want to tell too much. His parents, thankfully, got the message and nodded.

The SilvaGryphie didn't mind Ellendrii telling his parents but that was pretty much where it ended for giving out details that would destroy the beliefs of the Gryphies.

"Well it still sounds like quite the adventure and I think after that you fully deserve to get into the Elite Flyers. Grik, even if you hadn't managed to find her and came back without her I think you still would have deserved to get into them. You went through a lot, I can tell even with as little as you've said. I can see both of you have changed physically. You're both lean and well travelled and even have the marks to show it…" Diabloss said.

"You stand differently; more confident. Even your eyes and expression are different. They are well travelled now and older" Leida said, smiling. "We are proud of you, son."

"Thank you, both of you. I know you didn't want me to go and there were times when I really wish I had listened to you. But in the end I found the SilvaGryphie; I reached my goal. I have no regrets."

"Neither do I" spoke up Aro, "Even though at times Ellendrii got sick of me and sometimes I too wondered why I went. I was scared and I missed my parents; we both did."

Ellendrii nodded.

"We missed you too. It was hard to go a sun cycle without worrying about you. After the first lunar passed, we got more worried. When the second lunar passed, we started to think that maybe you'd got lost or died. We couldn't help thinking these things. Obviously we also hoped that you were just travelling a long way but due to all of us thinking that she was only the other side of the vast water, we thought it wouldn't take as long. We were obviously wrong about that." Leida looked at the SilvaGryphie.

"I do live the other side of the vast water, just as you believe. And I do look after all those who have passed away. I watch over them in my own dimension of my own creation. But I just live further away than you believed. It would be strange if I was the other side of the vast water since that is where the Wind Hounds live. My own dimension is on the Plain of Mists, otherwise known as the Land of Forever and that has to be very far away. For spiritual reasons."

The assembled gathering all nodded because she was their creator and whatever she said they took as gospel anyway. She wasn't really lying though; she really did live in another dimension and that was where it was.

"I couldn't imagine going on such a huge journey though. I mean, it seemed easy enough which is probably why they went on it; because they thought it was only across the vast water, but they could have ended up anywhere" said Lunara.

"I guess we may not have gone if we'd known there was so much room for error. We could easily have gone the wrong way and got lost and never found our way home. And it was lucky that the SilvaGryphie kindly carried us home. It would have taken so much longer, twice as long in fact if we'd walked home the way we had gone there. Sometimes I did see us not making it back and just growing so old that we couldn't make it back home, settling down somewhere and living there the rest of our lives" said Ellendrii.

"So you mean to tell me that if you'd known that it wasn't just across the vast water that we wouldn't have gone?" asked Aro.

"Well I wouldn't have been so confident about it. I dunno. I may have gone but then again I may not have. Feeling as determined as I was was mostly brought on by the fact that I thought all we had to do was cross the water" Ellendrii replied.

"I was watching over them. I watch over you all. I like to know what you are doing. I saw how brave they were and

they had nearly reached where I was anyway, so I stepped in and saved them from Thresh. And I brought them home. I haven't been here since I left. I watch over you via astral projection which is a special ability I have. I don't intervene though and I never will, so there is no point in asking and hoping that I will hear you. That is not the point of watching over you. I want to see how you grow and learn and live by yourselves. I was the one who put the Gryphie stone in that statue. I left it as a clue that I hoped they would find. They were certainly resourceful enough. And it worked and they followed it. Without a little help, they would not have found me. That was the one time I felt I needed to intervene. They were out there in the big wide world with no guidance other than their wits and intrepidation. And I am so proud of them."

"Even me?" asked Aro, "I'm not a Gryphie…"

"Of course you! Like I told you, Ellendrii needed you."

Aro beamed.

"Well, we thought that they would come back empty handed in all honesty" said Diabloss.

"Even though we knew you existed somewhere, the very thought of seeing you was far from our minds. We never thought that they would actually bring you back. I'm sorry Ellendrii and Aro, but we thought, looking at it rationally, that you would just return to us having not found her. We *hoped* that you would find her though." Leida said.

"Oh thanks Mum. So you had no faith in us?" asked Ellendrii, saddened by this.

"No, we did have faith in you. But think about it, none of us has seen our creator. What if she was no longer there? What if it *was* just stories? We believe in her but what if we were wrong? There is room for doubt. And doubt does creep in. We can't help it; no one can."

"Yeah I guess you're right. But guess what? We DID find her! So you were wrong to doubt us!" Ellendrii said cockily.

"Yes we see that now" smiled Diabloss, "And I'm glad we were wrong."

"There will always be doubt. But that is how life is. If you truly believe though, like Ellendrii did, you keep going and you will succeed."

"I believed too!" Aro yelled. "I believed in my friend, Ellendrii. That's why I went with him. And of course adventure" he grinned.

"Thanks Aro" Ellendrii said and hugged him.

"When Aro told us you were back, we were so happy. Well, when we saw him we couldn't believe it. But initially when we saw him and you weren't with him, we feared the worst" said Diabloss.

"See? I didn't even have to say anything anyway" said Aro and Mordred again looked at him sternly.

"They rushed up to us looking panicked and yet hopeful at the same time" said Mordred.

"The first thing we told them was of course that you were still alive and were taking the SilvaGryphie to see the Sky Gryphies" said Schaarl.

"I was elated about this. They are rather up their own and I had hoped that the first thing you did if you found the SilvaGryphie was that you would show her to them and make them eat their words." Diabloss smirked.

Ellendrii was a little puzzled that the Forest Gryphies hadn't showered the SilvaGryphie in questions like the Sky Gryphies had. Obviously they knew enough about her from the stories they told, to not be curious how true the stories were.

There were more Gryphies gathering around though. The clearing was filling up in a similar fashion to how it did when stories were told of a moon cycle.

"I'm glad you brought her to the Forest so we can all meet her" said Leida.

"I needed to come here and see you. I like how you're looking after the Forest. Well done, all of you" she said, smiling.

"Thank you" said Diabloss, speaking for all of them.

"Kinda makes me wish Lizariaouses had a cool creator like you" commented Jadariol.

The SilvaGryphie smiled.

"If it's any consolation; yours is a much, much older species than the Gryphies. You were around long before my creations."

651

"Oh yeah! Well, that *is* kinda cool…" muttered Jadariol, mulling it over.

"Apart from finding the SilvaGryphie, do you have a favourite part of the journey?" asked Lunara to Ellendrii and Aro.

"I did enjoy the lake and swimming with the Aqwakitts. It was like flying underwater and at the time, it was the closest that I'd got to flying…well, until the journey home, which is actually my favourite part! Ellendrii's favourite part was the part with the island and Midnyte Comet" Aro sniggered.

"Thanks Aro, but I can answer things by myself" said Ellendrii. Then he added, "Though for once Aro was right, that was umm…my favourite part…" He coughed.

Aro sniggered.

"You flew underwater?" asked Mordred.

"Well it was swimming but they put air bubbles around our heads so we could breathe. It was amazing. I never knew being underwater could be so interesting. To be honest I never thought there was that much underwater anyway. Wow, was I wrong!" Aro thought back to it and smiled happily.

"Ah yes Ellendrii said about that didn't he. The journey sounds like it was an experience for sure" said Mordred.

The SilvaGryphie found it interesting how they were far more excited about the return of their sons than the fact that their creator was sat right there in the Forest with them. The thought made her proud because it meant that they cared for each other and valued family. And that was important and essential to their survival as a species.

"It's a shame that Midnyte Comet didn't want to come back to the Forest with you though" said Diabloss, "You would have had a mate and at a young age too." He grinned. Ellendrii coughed.

"I prefer the term "Life Partner" to "mate" actually, Dad. I learned it when we were staying in the windy city with the Wind Hounds. It's a much more romantic term and has more meaning."

"Life partner eh? Hmm, yeah it does have a certain ring to it I suppose. It sounds more personal than mate." Diabloss nodded in approval.

"It seems like you have brought back a few lessons and customs with you as well" laughed Leida, "That's no bad thing at all. It will help us grow and learn together. To think that we thought there was nothing across the vast water except the domain of the SilvaGryphie and that there are actually other creatures over there. I think that is the biggest surprise of all. We all thought you would go over and find her easily. You must share with us all the new things you've learned!"

"He will be able to help you all grow and evolve with what he has learned. There are many advantages and good things that will come of their difficult journey together." The SilvaGryphie said.

"It makes even the painful parts worth it" said Ellendrii.

"You didn't get too badly hurt did you?" asked Leida.

"We did, but we survived. I'll tell you more later" said Ellendrii.

It was then that Diabloss, Leida, Mordred and Schaarl heard the SilvaGryphie in their minds speaking only to them.

"I want to tell you now that your sons died when they were trying to find me. I know this is a shock for you but I thought it would be better coming from me so I can explain it properly to you; more properly than they probably would."

The parents all looked shocked. Luckily no one really noticed since Lunara and Jadariol were now talking to Ellendrii and Aro and the other Gryphies were all listening to what they were saying.

"When they encountered Thresh, he killed them both. I intervened and brought them back to life because they had come so far to find me; because their lives were worth saving. I see something special in them and I wanted them to go on. I couldn't let them die because it would all have been for nothing then."

Diabloss was the first to realize that he could reply via his thoughts.

So, why did you let them die in the first place? Couldn't you have intervened before it got that bad? What happened?

Yes, we would all like to know that, thought Mordred firmly.

"It was when they encountered Thresh. I lived up and out of the other side of Thresh's boneyard valley. Unfortunately a curious Aro woke him from his slumber because his cavern is huge and Aro wanted to see inside it. Then they had no hope. Thresh is a vicious, violent and powerful enemy. His body is mostly armour. I assumed that the pair of them would creep past the cave that they should have known quite obviously contained a dangerous hunter and go up the other side of the steep valley and then come to where I resided on the misty plain and find me. Sadly the last part of their journey was cut short because they were killed. I know that you're angry that I didn't intervene sooner but I wanted to see if they could fight their way out of it. I would have healed them afterwards but they had come so far and overcome so much that I thought they would make it. Sadly that was not the case. But there is no mark on them from that battle. Nothing. The only marks and scars they have are from the other parts of the journey where they obtained them."

Yes but surely if you could intervene, you wouldn't have let them travel through such dangerous places in the first place? Leida asked.

"I could have intervened sooner it's true, but if I had, then they wouldn't have learned or seen as much as they did. It was a learning experience. They have brought back much new information to impart to you and they have gained a lot of experience. Can you see that if I had stopped them from doing as much as they did then the journey would have been wasted?"

You could have appeared to them sooner and then showed them around in a manner that would have been safer for them argued Leida.

"I could, but they would never have grown in the way they have. Look at them. Look how lean and strong and well travelled they are! Look how much more confident they are. That doesn't come with being shown things "safely"; it comes with the experience of being in dangerous situations and learning how to get out of them."

But they died thought Leida slowly.

"But they don't remember dying and they don't remember the pain. They only remember it happening as a distant, clouded memory. And they are not changed because that happened. I gave them another chance; I saved them so they could bring me back here and help your species grow more. I saved them because I knew that the Sky Gryphies have to accept Ellendrii into their ranks so that the Forest and Sky Gryphies can become closer. There was a rift between you."

Because the Sky Gryphies are too stuck up to have anything to do with us, thought Diabloss.

"Correction; were." The SilvaGryphie informed him.

"And questioning me and my methods is questioning your own creator. Do not question things you have no clue about. It wasn't what I had planned but I corrected it. They survived and came back to tell you about it. They need to be prepared. You all do. Something big is coming. I can't say what but I will say this; you ALL need to be prepared and you need to know as much as you can in order to survive it. New ways of thinking and new ways to be resourceful. And no, it is not another war. It is something bigger than that. Heed my warning. Unite the sub-species and keep them that way. This will affect ALL of you."

The others thought nothing. They looked at each other and then at the SilvaGryphie in shock and concern.

When will it happen? Diabloss asked her in his mind.

"I can't say. It won't be for a while though but you all need to be ready for anything. Listen and learn from what Ellendrii and Aro tell you about their experiences of what they saw."

We will, thank you for telling us, thought Diabloss.

Will this affect Lizariaouses too? Mordred asked.

"To a lesser extent. It will affect you because it will affect all the creatures in the lands here. It will affect the Gryphies more though. But as I said, not for a while. Just keep alert for anything strange happening. Things that are different or unusual or suspect. Be alert" she warned them.

We will they thought together. Since she wouldn't or couldn't reveal any more information, they couldn't very well freak out about it; which was undoubtedly a good thing. She didn't want them to be paranoid but she did have a feeling something was coming. Even the SilvaGryphie wasn't sure what. It was just a feeling and she wanted to warn at least a couple of members of her creations.

"Don't tell anyone. No one needs to know until something happens. They won't notice but you must. The future of your race relies on it."

The parents all nodded, which caused Ellendrii, Aro and the others to wonder why. Nothing was said though; just a few weird looks directed at them.

"SilvaGryphie, can you give me any tips on healing herbs? I thought I would be ok when Mystik passed. I thought I was prepared. But I'm not as prepared as I thought I was" explained Lunara.

"Her spirit will guide you. You'll know when you have the techniques right. Trust me. And trust in her memory. You know what she taught you, so you have something to go by. Stay on that track and you won't go wrong" said the SilvaGryphie and Lunara thought about it slowly. Then she agreed.

"Thank you, that is what I will do. I will have faith in my knowledge and what she taught me."

"Very good! Keep that attitude!"

The SilvaGryphie turned to everyone now.

"The time has come for me to go now. Ellendrii brought me back to see the Sky Gryphies, which I have done and now I have seen all of you too. The Mountain Gryphies will be jealous, I'm sure." She chuckled and continued; *"Thank you so much for giving me such a warm welcome and not bombarding me with questions like the Sky Gryphies did. I can tell that you are well versed in my exploits. Encourage the stories to be told in the Skylands too, Ellendrii. Teach the Sky Gryphies the ways of the Forest Gryphies' story telling. Help bring you all closer. They have forgotten their origins and it has made them shallow and lost."*

"I do have a question though...how are you projecting your words into our minds like that?" asked Jadariol.

"It is a special gift I have that I can speak to you in your mind without others hearing" she replied, simply. Jadariol shrugged.

"Fair enough" he said.

"Thank you so much for escorting us home" said Ellendrii, bowing low to the SilvaGryphie.

"You are welcome. And thank you for your bravery and skills. Both of you." She looked at Aro too, and he grinned.

"Thanks for showing me what flying's really like" he said happily. "I'll never forget that. And it was well worth waiting for!"

"No problem. I knew that part of the fun of taking you home would be to show you something that previously you could only dream about. I'm glad you found it so enjoyable. Cherish the memory and treasure it, Aro."

"Don't worry, I will! As long as I live!" Aro nodded to her, which was about as close to a respectful bow as a Lizariaous normally got.

"It was also nice to meet the leader of the Lizariaouses and his life partner too" said the SilvaGryphie.

"Same here. It was an honour" replied Mordred, speaking for both of them and Schaarl nodded.

"And to the rest of you, so lovely to see you all. Thank you for your respect" she said, looking around at all the gathered Gryphies in the clearing and those faces she saw peering at her from in the surrounding trees. There was a lot of chattering and Gryphies bowing to her.

"Can we escort you out of the Forest?" asked Ellendrii.

"Thank you, I would be grateful" replied the SilvaGryphie. It was after all, only polite to escort your guest out of where you lived.

So Ellendrii, Aro and the SilvaGryphie walked together for the last time.

Their parents didn't go with them; they felt this was a moment for the three of them and didn't want to impose on that.

At the edge of the Forest, the three stopped.

"So, I guess this is goodbye then" said Ellendrii.

"We probably won't see you again, will we?" asked Aro.

"No, I will be going now. But with a goodbye it means that at least you did meet me. Not many can say that. Only three Lizariaouses and only a handful of the amount of Gryphies

657

that live in the Forest and skies. So you can say you were part of the select few."

"Will you continue to watch over us?" asked Ellendrii.

"Of course! Always know that I am watching over you and wishing you well. Let it bring you confidence."

"But you won't be watching over me..." said Aro, sounding a bit defeated.

"You are not a Gryphie. But I will still see you when I'm keeping an eye on Ellendrii, since the two of you are so close."

Unless Ellendrii goes to live in the Skylands thought Aro.

"Then he will visit you often" the SilvaGryphie told him in his mind.

I forgot you could hear my thoughts, thought Aro. The SilvaGryphie just smiled.

"Both of you, always remember that with determination and hope, you can do anything. And always remember me."

"How could we forget you? You're beautiful!" breathed Ellendrii.

"Someone has another crush" sniggered Aro.

"I do NOT!" snapped Ellendrii.

"He really doesn't; it was just admiration. You need to learn the difference, Aro."

"Ok..." Aro felt silly now.

"Well now I really must go! The sun is going down and the moon will soon rise to replace it. Take care both of you and may good fortune follow both your species until the end of their sun cycles."

She spread her beautiful wings and took to the sky. In a similar fashion to Midnyte Comet's, the SilvaGryphie's wings somehow looked even more beautiful when the sky was darker. Ellendrii and Aro looked up with awe, getting one more glimpse of the fantastical view of eternity in her wings.

"Goodbye and take care!" called Ellendrii and Aro together as the SilvaGryphie rose into the air.

"And you! Always remember me and never forget all that you have learned on your journey to find me!" she called back to them and flew high into the sky, her fur reflecting the beautiful colours of the setting sun.

They watched her go, keeping watch until she was a mere speck in the sky and then nothing. They just stood there, enjoying the gentle breeze and fragrance of the early evening air and the wonderful feeling of finally being back home. Worry free, with their families and those that they knew. Able to do as they wished and no longer with the worry of what might be hiding around the next corner to attack them. It was a great feeling.

"Ahh, it's good to be home" breathed Ellendrii.

"I can hardly believe what we've been through" said Aro; "It weirdly feels so much like a dream or that it never happened."

"It's somehow like we never left? I agree. But we did. And now we're back! And I'm finally in the Elite Flyers where I belong! Thank you, Aro. Thank you so much for being there and helping me and well, everything!"

"Ah, no worries. I did what any good friend would. I'm just glad I could be a part of something so important in your life. It's a good feeling, you know?"

"Yes I do know! Although I'm kinda sad the SilvaGryphie has gone now and that we'll never see her again. It was so great spending time with her. I felt nostalgic, like I was going back to my roots or my birth or something when I was with her." Ellendrii looked up at the sky thoughtfully.

"Yeah and flying with her was cool. But we're back now and we have other stuff to do. I can't wait to tell my parents in more detail about our adventures as well. Some of it was too wild to be true." Aro laughed.

"I agree! Let's go tell them!" said Ellendrii.

"Yes! I'm letting my parents stay in my cave this moon. I bet we'll be up till sunrise with all the stuff I have to tell them haha!"

"Yeah I think me and my parents will be too" laughed Ellendrii.

They walked back through the Forest.

Yes, it was good to be home again.

Chapter 35
Flying High

A lunar had passed since the pair of travellers had returned with the SilvaGryphie and things were going very well.

Aro had made a useful cover for his cave from a large rock he found the other side of Dyarkroeen that he had dug into the perfect shape to cover the front of his cave and it had gone down so well with the other Lizariaouses that some of them had made their own covers for their caves as well. There would certainly be less thieving of valuables from the covered caves!

Ellendrii had got back into his regular routines around the Forest but he had also started new ones getting adjusted to the Skylands as well and been fully inducted into the Sky Gryphie Elite Flyers. Raediaxx had given him a little more training as to how an Elite Flyer properly behaved and even Verniy was actually being nice to him. She had seen him return with the SilvaGryphie and any spite and doubt she had had about him had been lost when she saw the beauty of the creator of the Gryphies in the flesh.

Ellendrii had decided to make his Sky Temple his own by taking up some of the Forest bedding and other bits and pieces from his own tree to help him make the temple more personal. No one really noticed him taking things from the Forest to put in it and he was relieved at that. He had been worried they would insist that he wasn't allowed to bring "tainted" items from the Forest down below into the Skylands but oddly enough their attitude had changed a lot since he came up with the SilvaGryphie and over the next lunar would continue to do so. Ellendrii was pleased by this, even if at first he didn't altogether trust it. He was worried it was just a ruse but he was wrong in that assumption, thankfully.

He became quite good friends with Reo, who he had gone to for advice. He found it hard to get ahold of Sierra and later discovered it was because out of the pair of leaders, she did the most work so she was always off helping or using other leadership skills with the other Sky Gryphies.

Reo introduced Ellendrii to a lot of new things and was a little puzzled as to why he still refused to eat bugs.

"They're very tasty" he explained; "You shouldn't knock them till you've tried them!"

"I have and I just…don't really want to eat any more" replied Ellendrii, "I am happy with berries."

Which was all well and good until Reo tried to sneak a bug into Ellendrii's food one sun cycle. Ellendrii only found out about it because it was a particularly wriggly one and he could feel it in his mouth. He screamed and spat it out.

Reo laughed.

"You scream like a female!" he sniggered. Ellendrii glared at him. This was how their friendship was developing now. Reo couldn't spend all his time messing around with Ellendrii but he did enjoy that it helped him to take a break from his imposing sister and the responsibilities of being a leader. He had tried to make friends with others before but found it difficult because all they saw him as was one of their leaders and so were afraid of being relaxed around him in case he told them off.

With Ellendrii, the laid back and pretty learned Forest Gryphie, he didn't have this trouble.

Another bonus Ellendrii found was that female Sky Gryphies were starting to show an interest in him. Young ones, about his age. He had seen a few admiring his flying skills; which of course only caused him to show off more!

Which of course he did to his full potential. He really was the best flyer in all of Shernaron and he knew it but he never ever let it go to his head. It was his passion and as such, he felt no need to boast about it. It was simply something he enjoyed and planned to make his life goal about.

So far none of them had approached him and he was a little worried about meeting them. He had no idea how to talk to females. He had only really hung out with Aro and wasn't entirely sure how to act around females; especially those of the Sky Gryphies.

He wanted to ask Reo for advice but didn't think he would know enough, since Reo had no life partner of his own and since Reo was always more busy with leader things. So he went to ask his father about it.

Ellendrii tended to spend the moon cycle at his old home and during the sun he would stay in the Skylands as he was getting accustomed to being up there. He wanted to make the transition slowly, not only to get used to it but also so he didn't suddenly run off and leave his parents. He was their only son after all and he had no idea if they would have any more kittens as Gryphies often did. They would have a kitten and then when it was old enough to care for itself, they would have another and so on.

The lack of having a sibling was mostly down to the fact that Leida didn't want any more. She had been reluctant to have one in the first place but Diabloss had gently talked her round to it. Having another would be pushing it, so Diabloss was grateful that she had given him Ellendrii. Having kittens is down to the female Gryphie. If she doesn't want kittens, she is capable of dulling down how receptive she is. So no matter how many times her life partner mates with her; she won't catch. Most females want kittens but as with humans; there are always exceptions. Bringing up kittens is a big responsibility and some female Gryphies just don't feel they are up to the task or simply don't want to.

Most have several kittens though in their lifetime.

So Ellendrii sought out his father to ask his advice. He found him scouting around near the valley and they alighted on a craggy rock together.

"How are you finding it in the Sky Gryphie territory?" asked Diabloss.

"It's great, I'm really enjoying it. I feel that I finally fit in. Flying is such a big part of life up there. I mean, if you can't or don't fly; you are stranded on one Skyland. There are some older Gryphies who can't fly anymore and their families have to visit them and take them food and things. But I've noticed lately that female Sky Gryphies are noticing me. I don't know what to do or how to approach any of them and I don't want to look an idiot in front of them. That would be embarrassing and it might put them all off me" Ellendrii explained.

"Wow, how many of them are looking at you?" asked Diabloss with interest and pride in his son.

"About three or four. I show my flying skills to them but I don't know what to say to them."

"Just be yourself. You'll know when the right time comes. Always be true to yourself though. Don't pretend to be someone you're not or show off too much either. You want them to see the true you and to know who they are falling in love with. And you will probably end up being with several in turn before you find one who is right for you, who you click with and get along well with. You don't want one to fall for you for the wrong reasons; because they think it will make them popular or to only love you for your flying skills. You want someone who loves you for who you are. Do you understand?" Diabloss said.

"Yeah, I think I do. But what about going up and talking to one? How do I do that? Or do I wait for them to come to me?" Ellendrii was puzzled.

"Basically do what your instincts tell you to. But if you see one you like and want to get to know her better, just go up to her and say "Hi!" and then comment on something like the weather or something. Make small talk. If you see something you like about her, like her wings or the colour of her fur, mention that you like it. Females like compliments. See where it goes from there. And don't rush it! You want to become friends with her before you start a relationship with her. She should become your best friend as well as your mate."

"Life partner, Dad."

"Yes, sorry, it's getting used to using the term. But yes, you need a life partner who is a good friend as well. Relationships like this are based on friendship too" explained Diabloss. Ellendrii nodded.

"If you try and make friends with her and find that it is not working out for whatever reason, then just distance yourself from her a little but try not to be rude."

"That'll be hard…I hope that won't happen. I don't want to end up with someone who really likes me but I don't like her.

That will be awkward. How will I tell her to go away?" Ellendrii asked.

"Body language. Use your body and tail and your wings and you don't need to say anything. And don't ask me what to do; it will come naturally to you. That is all I can say." Diabloss looked away from Ellendrii and out at the valley with a faraway look in his eyes. He was reminded of how he got together with Leida; such a shy and quiet Gryphie back then and how patient he had been with her and helped her with training and learning. Because he was so much in love with her. A Gryphie will move mountains for the one they love.

"So, that's it?" asked Ellendrii, who had really been hoping for a blow by blow account of exactly what he should do in every situation and he found himself still nearly as lost as he had been before he asked.

"Yes. You will learn more the more experience you have. I know you will choose a life partner wisely though." Diabloss smiled at his son.

"I am very proud of you, Ellendrii. I never really told you just how proud I am. My own son, going out into the world beyond the vast water and doing and seeing all that you did. I couldn't have dreamed of having a better son than you. I will miss you when you move up to the Skylands."

"Thank you Dad. I will miss you too; and Mum. But I will visit often, I promise and I'm not going up there fully yet. I want to give it a couple of seasons. It feels weird just rushing off and moving somewhere new when all I know is our tree and the Forest and you and Mum and everyone else there. I will miss that. But this is what I want and need to do."

"I understand that," his father replied, "And I fully support it too. I want you to do what makes you happy. I can hardly prevent you from going after all you've done and the journey you made. You are an adult now." Diabloss bowed his head in respect to his son. Ellendrii smiled and blushed a little.

"Yeah but I'm still Ellendrii" he said, trying to break his own awkwardness. In his mind he had simply done what he believed in in order to accomplish his goal.

"I know you are" smiled his Dad.

With the little knowledge he had learned of females, he felt a bit more ready for anything that might crop up regarding his admirers and decided to take it in his stride and see what happened. He was after all, in no hurry to find a life partner. He may have grown but he was still young and preferred to focus on his flying skills for now at least.

Over in Dyarkroeen, Aro had spent the past lunar telling anyone he could about all the amazing adventures they had had and all the things they had seen. Obviously he left out the part where they died and was hazy with the part where they had actually met the SilvaGryphie and her whereabouts and neglected to mention his fear of the Repulsators. He didn't want anyone to tease him and he wanted to appear to be brave and bold like Lizariaouses were supposed to be. Which for the most part he had been. And they were all very impressed to hear about his adventures and especially how he had saved Ellendrii from certain death at the jaws of the Narg'tok.

Some of the younger Lizariaouses didn't believe certain parts of the journey though; such as Rivniann the Shardog. It is hard to comprehend a creature with an ecosystem inside its body without actually seeing it for yourself. It doesn't make sense and to many, it defies the laws of logic and reality.

Others were totally enthralled every time he told the story of their journey though and he was often asked to retell certain parts of it too; especially the most exciting parts.

The journey was told and retold. Aro told it and then other members of the pack would retell it; often to exaggerated falseness and Aro would have to correct them on it once he heard how badly it had come out. He wanted everyone to be fully educated on the truth of what had happened and not to make up ridiculous things. After all, a lot of what had happened had been fantastical enough without being drawn up to something it never was. The funny thing was that Aro's sisters; Zixiniss and Scit had been two of the most interested and amazed at their brother's adventures; even coming to give him the respect that they had always neglected to previously.

"You didn't even come to greet me when we got back though. And you never came to Shernaron to meet the fabled SilvaGryphie we spent so long finding. So how come you're so interested and full of amazement now?" Aro asked them.

"Simple" replied Zixiniss, "We always thought you were a loser with his head in the clouds. Who was only interested in exploring places where he wasn't welcome. Remember when we were little kids and you were always grikking off old Yonn because you kept sneaking into his cave when he was out or asleep? We stopped hanging out with you because you kept getting into trouble and we didn't want to get the blame for it too since it was never our idea in the first place. Always yours. Always because you were so nosy. I'm surprised someone didn't bite your snout off like Muzzl. Besides, Scit got into enough trouble for her attitude back then anyway."

Scit narrowed her eyes at Zixiniss and snarled.

"I had every right to answer back. It was the only way I could get any respect. I knew more. I'm very intelligent actually but no one ever gives me any credit. Was it any wonder I rebelled?"

"Just because you were the first to hatch doesn't make you a know it all" Zixiniss warned her.

"Yeah well, I know that now..." Scit trailed off as Aro spoke up.

"I thought this was about me and the reason why you never involved me and stopped hanging out with me?" he said.

"It was. Sorry, we're not used to hanging out with anyone but each other" said Zixiniss.

"Yeah well I'm not used to hanging out with other Lizariaouses so that makes three of us" remarked Aro.

Scit laughed.

"I guess we're all a bit weird then" she said and the others nodded in amusement. It seemed all Mordred and Schaarl's kids preferred certain company.

"What was your favourite part of the journey though?" asked Scit.

"Well obviously where I rescued El from the Narg'tok. It nearly had me too! It was only my bravery and Lizariaous

666

stubbornness that enabled me to get around its mind tricks and get to him in time." Aro said; it wasn't entirely a lie since of course his favourite part had been the flying at the end but he wanted to focus on a part where he had been particularly brave and looking back, even though he had been very scared, saving the life of his best friend made him feel very brave indeed.

"It must've been freaky seeing one up close like that" said Zixiniss.

"It was. It looked so soft and helpless from behind. I never knew I could feel such fear as I did looking into its horrific face. If you could call it a face that is. It was horrible. Beyond description. I was so scared I wanted to kill myself just to make it stop. Just to get away…" Aro trailed off and stared at the ground. His sisters didn't laugh; they looked concerned.

"You ok?" asked Scit.

Aro tried to cover it over.

"Yeah I'm fine. No worries! Just some of the stuff that happened was pretty scary, that's all. Even for a brave Lizariaous such as myself."

His sisters laughed.

"Well if it helps, we were worried about you and we're glad you're back. Sorry we were such grikheads towards you growing up. We honestly thought you were an idiot" said Scit.

"Gee thanks" said Aro but he was smiling. "Yeah I can understand that. I guess I just lost myself in wanting to explore and adventure with Ellendrii and forgot that maybe I was a bit annoying to everyone else. I didn't know that you missed me though."

"I wouldn't go *that* far. We were just glad you got back safely is all" replied Scit.

"Err, thanks then" said Aro. That was better than nothing, he supposed.

"So, does that mean you'll hang out more with me? El's gunna be in the Sky Gryphie territory a lot more now and I'll have no one to hang out with."

"Hmm, maybe. If you're not too much of an idiot" grinned Scit. They all laughed. Aro felt this was fair enough.

It did make him think though. Even though Ellendrii had said that living with the Sky Gryphies wouldn't affect their friendship, Aro knew it would. After all, Ellendrii would have a new life with the Sky Gryphies and he would be with them all the time after a while, making a new life for himself. Aro feared that he wouldn't have time to hang out anymore, despite what Ellendrii said to the contrary. After seasons had gone by, Aro was scared the pair of them would drift apart and their friendship would dissolve. After all they had been through both here and away.

Aro was struggling to cope with the realization that his friend might disappear from his life in time.

Likewise Ellendrii had thought of this too. The excitement of his current life had died down a little and he was free to think about things for the long term. He worried that he and Aro would drift apart. He didn't really want to spend a lot of time down on the ground and he knew that would put a real strain on their friendship. He needed to work something out to get around this problem and ensure that their friendship would last.

His sunrises mostly revolved around going up to the Skylands to train in the Elite and learn more about the ways that they did things. He would do this until mid-sun and then work some more on his temple. By the time he had finished all this, it was late sun and he didn't have much time to spend with Aro before the moon rose.

So their time together was becoming shorter and shorter.

After a while, Ellendrii's excitement and the temple work slowed down and he was able to spend more time with Aro, which made them both happier. But Ellendrii was still at times more excited about spending time in his new home and occasionally cancelled his meetups with Aro because he wanted to spend time in the new place. Other times Ellendrii secretly didn't want to meet up just to explore the same places over and over and the novelty of the Skylands was drawing him in once more.

He wished that Aro could somehow visit the Skylands but he knew that could never happen. Of course this naturally put more strain on them because he was going to a place that Aro could never see. Even though Aro's thirst for flight was sated; he would still have loved to see the Skylands.

In the end, Ellendrii decided to get it out in the open and talk about it with Aro to see if they could work out something together. So he arranged to meet Aro at Aro's cave at mid-sun.

The pair met and went to sit inside Aro's cave since the sun was very hot and they needed some shade.

"Look, we have to work out about meeting up. I don't want our friendship to drift. I'm worried that the longer time goes on, the more involved I will be in matters in the Sky Gryphie territory and I really don't want to lose you as my friend." Ellendrii explained.

"I was worried about that too, I'm glad you've brought it up" said Aro, "So, what do we do?" he asked.

Ellendrii looked thoughtful for a long time. So long in fact that Aro thought his friend's mind had drifted off topic. In the end, Aro spoke.

"I had an idea," he said; "How about once you've moved up there, cos that is when we'll really struggle to meet up, I go to the cliffs at sunrise and greet you? Surely you still cloud dodge right?" he asked.

"Yeah I do. But I don't know if I'll be doing that then. I guess I will be still."

"How can you not? You love cloud dodging!" Aro exclaimed.

"That's true. Yeah we can greet each other to start the sun cycle" said Ellendrii.

"And if we can't manage to meet up that sun cycle, we will at least have seen each other" replied Aro.

"Sounds good but what will you do on sun cycles that we don't meet up? I mean, have you made any more friends since we got back?" asked Ellendrii. He didn't mean this in an unkind way but he knew how most of the other Lizariaouses didn't share Aro's love of exploring.

"Actually, it's a funny story. My sisters want to hang out more" said Aro and waited for that to sink in.

"Your sisters? But they don't like you" replied Ellendrii.

"I know. But since I got back, they gained a new level of respect for me and they would like to hang out with me more now. Provided that is, that I don't constantly run off and explore or get into trouble. They told me why they stopped hanging out with me when we were little kids and I suppose I can't blame them. I used to do some pretty dumb stuff."
Ellendrii laughed. In his mind, Aro *still* did dumb stuff at times.

"But the fact is, even if we don't meet up every sun cycle, I'll still have others to hang around with and I'm sure I'll make more friends anyway. I seem to have a lot more admirers now I'm a brave adventurer beyond the vast water."

"Yeah, I have too. Of the female kind. It's weird having other Gryphies look at me the way they do" Ellendrii said.

"Oh wow, you should be happy they are!" Aro replied. "No one has with me yet but it will happen, I'm sure" he grinned. "They all think I'm pretty brave in Dyarkroeen."

"Yeah well having this sort of attention makes me feel awkward but I asked my Dad about it and he gave me a bit of advice so I should be ok" replied Ellendrii.

"That's good" said Aro.

"Look, it's all very well greeting each other at sunrise but I want to make time to see you each sun cycle. At least while we can. So I say we'll keep meeting, at mid-sun or just after at least till I move into the Skylands. Then we'll see how it goes from there. I want you to know though Aro, that we'll always be friends, even if we can't see each other every sun cycle. Just cos we might not be able to doesn't mean that we're not friends anymore" said Ellendrii.

"I gotta say that I was worried a bit about coming back because I was scared we'd drift apart. I'm glad I helped you so much on your journey but I thought even though we'd been together through all these times that in seasons to come we would drift away as friends and wouldn't hear from each other anymore." Aro looked sad and his needles drooped.

"Of course that won't happen. Besides, even if we can't see each other every single sun cycle, we will still make time for each other. I guess we've grown up now and we have different responsibilities."

"No, *you* have different responsibilities. I don't even know what I want to do with my life" replied Aro. "Before we left, I never even thought about what I would do with my life. You've always had your life goal pretty much sorted; to do something involving flying. What can *I* do? There are no Lizariaous explorers. Only diggers and protectors and there aren't as many of them as there used to be because we have no need for them anymore. So, what can I do?"

"When your father...excuse me for saying...passes away, won't you be the new leader of the pack?" asked Ellendrii.

"Not unless I fight him for it. That's how it works. It's not passed down. Someone has to challenge the leader. They either kill the old leader, which is what usually happens, or maim him so badly that he will never challenge to get his leadership back. Or just maim him so badly that he will die from it. That's usually the idea if they can't outright kill the old leader." Aro explained.

"Yeah I guess you wouldn't want to kill your own father" said Ellendrii.

"Zephirak killed his own father for the place of leadership but I hate that idea. Mordred is my Dad, why would I kill him? Then again, Lizariaouses will do anything to get where they want to be; even kill their own family but I'm not like that. I guess I've hung around with Gryphies for too long" he chuckled; "Your ways are rubbing off on me."

"Well, do you hear anyone complaining?" asked Ellendrii.

"My Dad is proud of me. He's proud that I helped you. He firmly believes in changing our old ways and forging useful bonds with other species. But we don't all believe that. Still, it is useful to make friends and it expands your knowledge I guess too. I've learned a lot from you, Ellendrii."

"Thank you, Aro. I've learned a lot from you too. You're braver than me." Ellendrii bowed his head to his friend and Aro smiled.

"Well, I *am* a Lizariaous and no matter what others think of us, we're still bold and stupid enough to be called brave" he grinned.

"So, do you have any ideas what you want your life goals to be?" asked Ellendrii, getting back on topic again.

"Something to do with exploring?" said Aro without much confidence, due to the fact that he knew he couldn't really use it as a life goal because it had no real purpose in Lizariaous culture or life.

"How well does your species know Dyarkroeen?" asked Ellendrii.

"Very well. Well, I say that; most of us know the area of Dyarkroeen where the caves we live in very well. And the path, whatever way it might be, to the reservoir."

"And are any of you interested in learning more about parts of Dyarkroeen where they aren't so familiar with?" asked Ellendrii.

"Not really" replied Aro, "We have no reason to learn much about parts we don't live in or travel through and so no interest in learning about it either. It's just how things are. Except for me of course. I know the whole of Dyarkroeen inside out, obviously!"

"Hmm, I do have one idea" said Ellendrii, pondering it all.

"What's that?" asked Aro, interested now and hoping the answer wouldn't be too difficult or ridiculous.

"Well, you could show kids around? So that they learn more about where they live and where they can move into caves when they are older?" Ellendrii suggested.

"It's a good idea. The only problem is that kids are very...well they don't behave like Gryphie kittens. They're rebels and tearaways and constantly rebel and reject rules. I dunno if I could handle showing a pack of them around."

"Really? After all you've been through? After being able to tell them stories of how brave and amazing you've been? Stories that would make any Lizariaous instantly respect you and think twice about questioning you? Stories that you told me many of the kids around here ask you to retell to them? Who wouldn't want to grow up to be as brave and bold and fearless as you? You've got a head start already. Surely if you were offering up adventure tours of Dyarkroeen, most kids would jump at the chance to learn more from the master?"

Aro's face immediately brightened.

"Yes! I *could* do that!" he roared in excitement.

"See? There is something out there for everyone that is perfect for their own individual talent. You just have to find it" smiled Ellendrii.

"I didn't think exploring was much of a talent though" replied Aro.

"Of course it is! And what's better is that you can bring it out in others by showing them how fun it is to explore. The kids will look up to you and want to be like you and exploring is a great way to discover more about the world around them and become better at surviving. You'll do great!"

"Thanks so much, El! I never thought anyone would want to go exploring with me. I never thought there would be any interest in it. And it never occurred to me that I could do this and others would want to do it too."

"Start next sun cycle. If you ask around about who would be interested and then arrange a time you can all meet and then you can show the others all your little tips and tricks for exploring around Dyarkroeen. And the possibilities are endless because even if you've explored all of this territory, there is always the Outlands and you could even bring a pack to Shernaron and show them how we live too. Or alternatively, show a different pack around Dyarkroeen. If there are lots of Lizariaous kids who want to join, you could show a pack around both before and after mid-sun. And you can't possibly explore it all in one go so there's plenty of reason to meet up again with those who enjoyed it the first time. See? There is a place in your life for your own talent. Always believe in yourself. I always have. In both myself and you too." Ellendrii said.

"You're a genius!" roared Aro. "I dunno why I never thought of this before. But then again, Gryphies *are* better at thinking than we are. Thank you so much for suggesting this to me!"

"You're welcome" smiled Ellendrii.

The next sun cycle, they met and Aro told Ellendrii all that had gone on since the previous one.

"Well, I asked around about who would be interested in learning to be an explorer and survivor like me and a surprising amount of others said they would. Even adults; not just kids. So next sun we will meet up and I will show them around. They want to learn survival skills too, though I'm not sure why because we have all the food and drink we need here. Jadariol and his life partner, Lexaron want to tag along too. I was even more surprised about that. Jadariol is really respected around here. He wants to learn more about where to find certain healing plants, though I was sure that Lunara had shown him where most of them were but he feels that by knowing Dyarkroeen better, he might find some here too and won't need to travel so far to collect them."

"See? Even better things are coming of this than you thought!" smiled Ellendrii, "Told you you would be able to use your favourite pastime as a life goal!"

"I suppose I needed more faith in myself. I guess when you're repeatedly told not to be so silly and that you're wasting your time and why are you going gallivanting off to who knows where when you could be training as a digger, you start to doubt yourself. I know I was doubting myself. In fact I had even thought I would give up the whole exploring thing once you'd moved in up there and just try and find something else to do" said Aro.

"Yeah but you'd be miserable in the same way that I would have if I hadn't gone on that journey and made the effort to get to where I wanted to be. Sure I would still have had my flying abilities but I would still feel that they weren't being tested to their limits even in my Dad's squadron. Now we can both be happy knowing that we have the ability to do what we love for the rest of our lives." Ellendrii said.

"You're right. I feel much happier now about the whole thing" replied Aro. Ellendrii nodded.

"I knew you would" he said.

A few sun cycles later, they met again and Aro told Ellendrii how well the tours were going. He had called the whole thing an "Explore Tour" and was proud that he had chosen a name that so cleverly rhymed.

The best thing was that this gave Aro something to do that he enjoyed and that helped take his mind off the fact that

Ellendrii was also busy with his own things. He did two "Explore Tours" a sun cycle and they were a hit. Jadariol insisted on being in both of them each sun cycle since the afternoon one was different to the one at sunrise.

Aro had customized the tours to match the Lizariaouses that were going on them. In time he would customize them even more according to more experienced explorers and ones who had only just joined.

And he knew that if he hadn't been on the journey with Ellendrii, this wouldn't even be happening. It was only because of his experience and the stories he could tell of their adventures that now other Lizariaouses wanted to be like him, when before none of them had wanted to hang around with him because of how different he was.

It seemed that their great journey had helped them both find their place in the world and the territories they lived in.

Ellendrii was sleeping in his Sky Temple for the first time ever since he had been accepted into the Elite Flyers. This moon cycle was a special one but it was also a rather lonely one. He was used to having his parents there just below him in the tree in case he woke up after a moonmare or any other reason he might feel safe in their presence and the thought of sleeping by himself was a daunting one. However, he needed to get used to it.

He was starting out by only sleeping there every so often to get used to it. Right now he was sat outside his temple, admiring the bright moonlight that shone down on the cloud layers below. It was all so beautiful. He felt so close to the stars that he could count them.

He wondered how the other friends they had met were doing. Probably doing their own things. Midnyte would be on her island and the Wind Hounds would be relaxing by the moonlight in their pools or maybe watching the beautiful lights in the sky.

Rivniann would be caring for his little creatures and his patch of the Forest of Foreboding and Ellendrii assumed that A'urealiz's wounds would be healed by now. And the Kanniths and the Aqwakitts. And the SilvaGryphie.

He wondered if she was watching him right now and what she was thinking. He was happy that he had helped Aro find his place; he deserved it after all. He was the best friend Ellendrii could ever ask or hope for. Ellendrii felt blessed to have such a good and loyal friend by his side.

It was true that when Ellendrii was by himself, he would speak aloud to the SilvaGryphie, despite that she could probably hear his thoughts. It somehow comforted him to know that she might be there looking out for him. Of course she would not interfere; that was not her way, but he did at least want her to know that he was thinking of her and that he would forever be grateful that she had shown herself to them and brought them back home safely. He wondered if he would ever hear her voice in his mind again. He hoped he would but somehow he knew he wouldn't. He had kept the Gryphie stone tied around his neck with a strong piece of twine similar to how he had worn it when they were travelling.

He sighed and looked around him. The Sky Temples had little stones embedded into the walls in some places that a Gryphie could light with its fire and it would stay lit until the Gryphie blew the fire out. It was very useful for dark moon cycles to light up inside the temples. However, this was not a dark moon cycle. The moon was full and round. He had also used the three glowing crystals to decorate the darker parts inside his Sky Temple; to great effect.

Ellendrii breathed in deeply. The air was mild and smelled sweet and fresh. He was finally here. He had achieved his goal and here he was in his very own Sky Temple in the Skylands on his own little floating Skyland which he could do with as he wished.

He had tried to bring some seeds up from some plants he liked from the Forest and planted them in the ground next to his temple but they hadn't grown. Lunara told him when he asked her for advice that it was probably too high for plants like that to grow. She told him much to his surprise that plants needed to breathe too and the air would affect them differently, which was why different plants grew at different heights and in different areas. This was all new to Ellendrii. He was only disappointed that he couldn't have some of his favourite types of plants with him. Lunara told him it was probably a good thing; it would encourage him to come back to the Forest to see them as well as his parents and Aro.

Ellendrii had agreed. Maybe it was a good thing to keep things where they were. That was where they belonged and it meant that he could enjoy them and feel happily nostalgic when he did see them. The same applied to the mushroom and moss samples he had found. Since the atmosphere was so different to the caves he had found them in, they wouldn't grow and so he ended up giving them to Lunara so she could study them instead.

Now as he looked around at the moonlit sky, he could see Sky Gryphies flying to and from their temples. He could see the Sky Gryphies in the distance taking off and landing from the flight platforms higher up the temples. Closer by though, the Elite Flyers were mostly resting inside their temples. None of them ever slept outside. Ellendrii liked sleeping outside and would in time be contented to sleep on the ground outside his temple or even on top of it. He did have a sleeping quarters inside his temple though; it was high up, akin to where he had slept in his tree and he had hung Midnyte's decoration over where he slept, so it would offer protection for him as he slumbered. He was so happy he hadn't lost it and could now admire it whenever he wished and think of her. For now, he sat on the higher platform outside his sleeping quarters so he could get a good view of the sky around him.

He had met his neighbours already. Thankfully Verniy wasn't one of them as he still didn't really trust her. She was snarky and sly and even though she had changed around him and was nothing like she used to be, he still tried not to engage too much with her. He had two closest neighbours and they were a male Sky Gryphie called Kavik and a female called Zashh. Zashh had shown a little bit of interest in Ellendrii. She was a very powerful flyer and could see potential in him. She was also just a little older than he was. He quite liked her and while he had been working on his temple, he found himself subconsciously keeping an eye out for her.

He was watching for her now without even realizing it. He wondered if she had already gone to sleep or if she was out somewhere. At least this helped him get to sort of know a female Sky Gryphie; by observing her from a distance. Her Sky Temple was dark though; no light inside and no distant figure of her sat on it anywhere. His mind wandered and so did his eyes, forgetting to look out for her for a while and just adjusting once more to the view he would get used to now. Instead of the tops of trees; it was the tops of clouds. Like in dreams he had had so many times before; they were finally a reality. He sighed and lay down, resting his chin on his forelegs.

He and Aro were still lean; they hadn't gained much weight since returning. This didn't bother either of them though; they had far more important things to think about than eating but it was true that they had pigged out a little after they got back; simply because the food was there and they could eat all they wished and that was a wonderful thing to do after going sometimes for so long without anything to eat at all.

Ellendrii, despite how good a flyer he was, had learned a lot of new techniques under Raediaxx's training. He had improved a lot over the last lunar or so that he had been training more. Together with what he had taught himself already, it was pretty clear that Ellendrii was the best flyer in Shernaron. No one could outfly him or beat him or even out manoeuvre him in the air. And yet he still wanted to push himself further. There was only so much Raediaxx could teach him though and eventually he would run out of things to show Ellendrii. Then Ellendrii would have to teach himself some more, until he knew all there was to know about flying. Right now he was thinking deeply about different flying techniques and tricks he knew. When he wasn't doing anything else, when he was just sitting relaxing, his brain was still going all the time thinking deeply about flying and the different things he knew and how to make new things out of the different things he knew. He really did have a one track mind when it came to what he loved. Thinking back to the likes of Zashh, he found he really wanted a life partner who had the same love of flying that he did. He really hoped he could find one, even if it wasn't Zashh after all. Although, given the fact that she was in the Elite Flyers like he was, he supposed that she loved to fly too.

He yawned and stretched a little. He listened to the bugs chirping in the bushes and plants on his island. And he still couldn't understand how the Sky Gryphies could eat them. Squirmy wriggly things. Then again he supposed having to kill a forest deer or a sea vulture was still a challenge. Before it died it was similarly squirmy and wriggly. But not slimy and filled with a questionable goo. The sound of the bugs was relaxing though. There were no glow bugs up here like down in the Forest. Ellendrii wasn't used to not seeing them and back when he had tried to bring seeds up to plant, he had also tried to bring some glow bugs with him too but they had grown lethargic and died because they couldn't breathe properly. This had surprised Ellendrii, who it had never occurred to that bugs need to breathe as well. The air difference which didn't affect him at all, seemed to affect everything else so in the end he gave up trying to bring things from the Forest and contented himself with customizing his island the way he liked it using what he had up there in the clouds.

He rolled onto his back and gazed up at the temple, then onto his side and looked at the wall of the temple. He admired the beauty that the SilvaGryphie had hewn upon its walls. The swirling patterns and intricate designs that he felt he could just get lost in if he stared at them for long enough. It certainly made him feel more like this was truly his home and his place.

His mind drifted to Aro. He was so glad his friend had found a good use for his talent for exploring. It made Ellendrii feel satisfied that through it all, everything that had happened, the bad times and the good, that things had come full circle and they had both found their place in the world.

Before, when they were just a pair of friends who hung out together, Ellendrii had been happy enough. Before that is, he realized that there was more to his talent than just hanging around in the Forest and that there was another outlet that he could use his flying for; the Elite Flyers. So it had circled around from a time that they had been happy doing what they did before Ellendrii found the Sky Gryphies, to a time that once again they were happy doing what they did.

Aro's "Explore Tours" continued to be popular with the Lizariaouses and soon he was doing them every single sun cycle and most of the pack had been on at least one. It helped the pack a lot, just as Ellendrii and Aro knew it would.

Ellendrii continued to live and learn the ways of the Elite Flyers until Raediaxx had taught him all he knew and then Ellendrii continued to learn more. Eventually he moved to his Sky Temple and lived there permanently, but he always made time to go and see Aro, if not every sun cycle, then every other sun cycle.

Ellendrii's little interest in Zashh grew and eventually resulted in him getting to know her better, by, as Diabloss had told him, being himself. They courted and then she moved in with Ellendrii and he didn't feel so alone by himself in his big Sky Temple anymore.

Ellendrii's parents did miss him a lot at first but he had taken so long to move out completely that they didn't miss him terribly and they also knew that he was happy as well, which was the most important thing to them. Leida didn't have any more kittens, as Diabloss suspected she wouldn't. But that just meant they could put more pride and time into their son when he visited.

Mordred and Schaarl were happy to see Aro's skills finally put to good use. Not that they had ever questioned him particularly but Mordred had said in the past that he couldn't waste his time exploring and adventuring forever. Now it was Aro's turn to tell his Dad that actually; he could!

Zixiniss and Scit hung around with Aro when he wasn't doing the tours and helped keep him occupied on the sun cycles when Ellendrii didn't have time to visit. His sisters enjoyed hanging around with him now and often went on the tours themselves, even going as far as to learn more about them and exploring and in time, assist him in taking the tours. This made Aro very happy since he had always been kind of sad that his sisters had lost interest in being around him and alienated him as they had grown older as kids. Now, as adults none of that mattered anymore and they were once again equals, and good friends as well as siblings.

The impossible journey that Ellendrii and Aro took to find the fabled SilvaGryphie had helped not only them but those around them as well and broken down the invisible wall between the Sky Gryphies and the other Gryphies. By taking a chance and just going for it out of sheer determination and a will to succeed, many lives were changed by two best friends.

End